A master storyteller, Si... of eighteen novels (which have sold over 300 million copies), over 200 television scripts, twenty-five major motion pictures and six Broadway plays, ranking him as one of the world's most prolific writers. His first book, *The Naked Face*, was acclaimed by the *New York Times* as 'the best first mystery novel of the year' and subsequently each of his highly popular books have hit No. 1 on the *New York Times* bestseller list. His latest bestseller, *Are You Afraid of the Dark?*, cements Sheldon's reputation as the master of the unexpected.

For more about Sidney Sheldon, visit his website at www.sidneysheldon.com.

For automatic updates on Sidney Sheldon visit HarperCollins.co.uk/sidneysheldon and register for AuthorTracker.

SIDNEY SHELDON

Master of the Game

Naked Face

HARPER

HarperCollins*Publishers*
77–85 Fulham Palace Road,
Hammersmith, London W6 8JB

www.harpercollins.co.uk

This omnibus edition published in 2008 by HarperCollins*Publishers*

A catalogue record for this book is available from the British Library

ISBN 978-0-00-783981-0

Set in Sabon by
Palimpsest Book Production Limited, Polmont, Stirlingshire
Printed and bound in Great Britain by Clays Ltd, St Ives plc

Mixed Sources
Product group from well-managed
forests and other controlled sources
www.fsc.org Cert no. SW-COC-1806
© 1996 Forest Stewardship Council

FSC is a non-profit international organisation established to promote the
responsible management of the world's forests. Products carrying the FSC
label are independently certified to assure consumers that they come
from forests that are managed to meet the social, economic and
ecological needs of present and future generations.

Find out more about HarperCollins and the environment at
www.harpercollins.co.uk/green

Master of the Game

For my brother,
Richard
the Lion-Hearted

My appreciation goes to Miss Geraldine Hunter for her endless patience and assistance in preparing this manuscript.

'And hence one master-passion in the breast,
Like Aaron's serpent, swallows up the rest.'
           – ALEXANDER POPE
             Essay on Man, Epistle II

'Diamonds resist blows to such an extent that an iron hammer may be split in two and even the anvil itself may be displaced. This invincible force, which defies Nature's two most violent forces, iron and fire, can be broken by ram's blood. But it must be steeped in blood that is fresh and warm and, even so, many blows are needed.'
           – PLINY THE ELDER

PROLOGUE

Kate

1982

The large ballroom was crowded with familiar ghosts come to help celebrate her birthday. Kate Blackwell watched them mingle with the flesh-and-blood people, and in her mind, the scene was a dreamlike fantasy as the visitors from another time and place glided around the dance floor with the unsuspecting guests in black tie and long, shimmering evening gowns. There were one hundred people at the party at Cedar Hill House, in Dark Harbor, Maine. *Not counting the ghosts*, Kate Blackwell thought wryly.

She was a slim petite woman, with a regal bearing that made her appear taller than she was. She had a face that one remembered. A proud bone structure, dawn-grey eyes and a stubborn chin, a blending of her Scottish and Dutch ancestors. She had fine, white hair that once had been a luxuriant black cascade, and against the gracefolds of her ivory velvet dress, her skin had the soft translucence old age sometimes brings.

3

I don't feel ninety, Kate Blackwell thought. *Where have all the years gone?* She watched the dancing ghosts. *They know. They were there. They were a part of those years, a part of my life.* She saw Banda, his proud black face beaming. And there was her David, dear David, looking tall and young and handsome, the way he looked when she first fell in love with him, and he was smiling at her, and she thought, *Soon, my darling, soon.* And she wished David could have lived to know his great-grandson.

Kate's eyes searched the large room until she saw him. He was standing near the orchestra, watching the musicians. He was a strikingly handsome boy, almost eight years old, fair-haired, dressed in a black velvet jacket and tartan trousers. Robert was a replica of his great-great-grandfather, Jamie McGregor, the man in the painting above the marble fireplace. As though sensing her eyes on him, Robert turned, and Kate beckoned him to her with a wave of her fingers, the perfect twenty-carat diamond her father had scooped up on a sandy beach almost a hundred years ago scintillating in the radiance of the crystal chandelier. Kate watched with pleasure as Robert threaded his way through the dancers.

I am the past, Kate thought. *He is the future. My great-grandson will take over Kruger-Brent, Limited one day.* He reached her side, and she made room for him on the seat beside her.

'Are you having a nice birthday, Gran?'

'Yes. Thank you, Robert.'

'That's a super orchestra. The conductor's really *bad*.'

Kate looked at him in momentary confusion, then her brow cleared. 'Ah. I presume that means he's good.'

Robert grinned at her. 'Right. You sure don't seem ninety.'

Kate Blackwell laughed. 'Just between the two of us, I don't feel it.'

He slipped his hand in hers, and they sat there in a contented silence, the eighty-two-year difference between them giving them a comfortable affinity. Kate turned to watch her granddaughter dancing. She and her husband were without doubt the handsomest couple on the floor.

Robert's mother saw her son and grandmother seated together and she thought, *What an incredible woman. She's ageless. No one would ever guess all she has lived through.*

The music stopped, and the conductor said, 'Ladies and gentlemen, it's my pleasure to present young Master Robert.'

Robert squeezed his great-grandmother's hand, stood up and walked over to the piano. He sat down, his face serious and intent, and then his fingers began to race across the keyboard. He played Scriabin, and it was like the rippling of moonlight on water.

His mother listened and thought, *He's a genius. He'll grow up to be a great musician.* He was no longer her baby. He was going to belong to the world. When Robert finished, the applause was enthusiastic and genuine.

Earlier, dinner had been served outdoors. The large and formal garden had been festively decorated with lanterns and ribbons and balloons. Musicians played from the terrace while butlers and maids hovered over tables, silent and efficient, making sure the Baccarat glasses and Limoges dishes were kept filled. A telegram was read from the President of the United States. A Supreme Court justice toasted Kate.

The governor eulogized her. '. . . One of the most remarkable women in the history of this nation. Kate Blackwell's endowments to hundreds of charitable causes around the world are legendary. The Blackwell Foundation has contributed to the health and well-being of people in more than fifty countries. To paraphrase the late Sir Winston Churchill, "Never have so many owed so much to one person." I have had the privilege of knowing Kate Blackwell . . .'

Bloody hell! Kate thought. No one knows me. He sounds like he's talking about some saint. What would all these people say if they knew the real Kate Blackwell? Sired by a thief and kidnapped before I was a year old. What would they think if I showed them the bullet scars on my body?

She turned her head and looked at the man who had once tried to kill her. Kate's eyes moved past him to linger on a figure in the shadows, wearing a veil to conceal her face. Over a distant clap of thunder, Kate heard the governor finish his speech and introduce her. She rose to her feet and looked out at the assembled guests. When she spoke, her voice was firm and strong. 'I've lived longer than any of you. As youngsters today would say, "That's no big deal." But I'm glad I made it to this age, because otherwise I wouldn't be here with all you dear friends. I know some of you have travelled from distant countries to be with me tonight, and you must be tired from your journey. It wouldn't be fair for me to expect everyone to have my energy.' There was a roar of laughter, and they applauded her.

'Thank you for making this such a memorable evening. I shall never forget it. For those of you who wish to retire, your rooms are ready. For the others, there will be dancing in the ballroom.' There was another clap of thunder. 'I suggest we all move indoors before we get caught in one of our famous Maine storms.'

Now the dinner and dancing were over, the guests had retired and Kate was alone with her ghosts. She sat in the library, drifting back into the past, and she suddenly felt depressed. *There's no one left to call me Kate*, she thought. *They've all gone.* Her world had shrunk. Wasn't it Longfellow who said, 'The leaves of memory make a mournful rustle in the dark'? She would be entering the dark soon, but not yet. *I still have to do the most important thing of my life*, Kate thought. *Be patient, David. I'll be with you soon.*

'Gran . . .'

Kate opened her eyes. The family had come into the room. She looked at them, one by one, her eyes a pitiless camera, missing nothing. *My family*, Kate thought. *My immortality. A murderer, a grotesque and a psychotic. The Blackwell skeletons. Was this what all the years of hope and pain and suffering had finally come to?*

Her granddaughter stood beside her. 'Are you all right, Gran?'

'I'm a little tired, children. I think I'll go to bed.' She rose to her feet and started towards the stairs, and at that moment there was a violent roar of thunder and the storm broke, the rain rattling against the windows like machine-gun fire. Her family watched as the old woman reached the top of the stairway, a proud, erect figure. There was a blaze of lightning and seconds later a loud clap of thunder. Kate Blackwell turned to look down at them and when she spoke, it was with the accent of her ancestors. 'In South Africa, we used to call this a *donderstorm*.'

The past and present began to merge once again, and she walked down the hallway to her bedroom, surrounded by the familiar, comfortable ghosts.

BOOK ONE

Jamie

1883–1906

ONE

'By God, this is a real *donderstorm*!' Jamie
McGregor said. He had grown up amid the wild
storms of the Scottish Highlands, but he had never
witnessed anything as violent as this. The afternoon
sky had been suddenly obliterated by enormous
clouds of sand, instantly turning day into night.
The dusty sky was lit by flashes of lightning –
weerlig, the Afrikaners called it – that scorched
the air, followed by *donderslag* – thunder. Then the
deluge. Sheets of rain that smashed against the army
of tents and tin huts and turned the dirt streets of
Klipdrift into frenzied streams of mud. The sky was
aroar with rolling peals of thunder, one following
the other like artillery in some celestial war.

Jamie McGregor quickly stepped aside as a
house built of raw brick dissolved into mud, and
he wondered whether the town of Klipdrift was
going to survive.

Klipdrift was not really a town. It was a sprawling canvas village, a seething mass of tents and

11

huts and wagons crowding the banks of the Vaal River, populated by wild-eyed dreamers drawn to South Africa from all parts of the world by the same obsession: diamonds.

Jamie McGregor was one of the dreamers. He was barely eighteen, a handsome lad, tall and fair-haired, with startlingly light grey eyes. There was an attractive ingenuousness about him, an eagerness to please that was endearing. He had a lighthearted disposition and a soul filled with optimism.

He had travelled almost eight thousand miles from his father's farm in the Highlands of Scotland to Edinburgh, London, Cape Town and now Klipdrift. He had given up his rights to the share of the farm that he and his brothers tilled with their father, but Jamie McGregor had no regrets. He knew he was going to be rewarded ten thousand times over. He had left the security of the only life he had ever known and had come to this distant, desolate place because he dreamed of being rich. Jamie was not afraid of hard work, but the rewards of tilling the rocky little farm north of Aberdeen were meager. He worked from sunup to sundown, along with his brothers, his sister, Mary, and his mother and father, and they had little to show for it. He had once attended a fair in Edinburgh and had seen the wondrous things of beauty that money could buy. Money was to make your life easy when you were well, and to take care of your needs when you were ailing. Jamie had seen too many friends and neighbours live and die in poverty.

He remembered his excitement when he first heard about the latest diamond strike in South Africa. The biggest diamond in the world had been found there, lying loose in the sand, and the whole area was rumoured to be a great treasure chest waiting to be opened.

He had broken the news to his family after dinner on a Saturday night. They were seated around an uncleared table in the rude, timbered kitchen when Jamie spoke, his voice shy and at the same time proud. 'I'm going to South Africa to find diamonds. I'll be on my way next week.'

Five pairs of eyes stared at him as though he were crazy.

'You're goin' chasing after diamonds?' his father asked. 'You must be daft, lad. That's all a fairy tale – a temptation of the devil to keep men from doin' an honest day's work.'

'Why do you nae tell us where you're gettin' the money to go?' his brother Ian asked. 'It's halfway 'round the world. You hae no money.'

'If I had money,' Jamie retorted, 'I wouldn't have to go looking for diamonds, would I? Nobody there has money. I'll be an equal with all of them. I've got brains and a strong back. I'll not fail.'

His sister, Mary, said, 'Annie Cord will be disappointed. She expects to be your bride one day, Jamie.'

Jamie adored his sister. She was older than he. Twenty-four, and she looked forty. She had never owned a beautiful thing in her life. *I'll change that*, Jamie promised himself.

His mother silently picked up the platter that held the remains of the steaming haggis and walked over to the iron sink.

Late that night she came to Jamie's bedside. She gently placed one hand on Jamie's shoulder, and her strength flooded into him. 'You do what you must, Son. I dinna ken if there be diamonds there, but if there be, you'll find them.' She brought out from behind her a worn leather pouch. 'I've put by a few pounds. You needn't say nothin' to the others. God bless you, Jamie.'

When he left for Edinburgh, he had fifty pounds in the pouch.

It was an arduous journey to South Africa, and it took Jamie McGregor almost a year to make it. He got a job as a waiter in a workingman's restaurant in Edinburgh until he added another fifty pounds to the pouch. Then it was on to London. Jamie was awed by the size of the city, the huge crowds, the noise and the large horse-drawn omnibuses that raced along at five miles an hour. There were hansom cabs everywhere, carrying beautiful women in large hats and swirling skirts and dainty little high-button shoes. He watched in wonder as the ladies alighted from the cabs and carriages to shop at Burlington Arcade, a dazzling cornucopia of silver and dishes and dresses and furs and pottery and apothecary shops crammed with mysterious bottles and jars.

Jamie found lodging at a house at 32 Fitzroy Street. It cost ten shillings a week, but it was the cheapest he could find. He spent his days at the docks, seeking a ship that would take him to South Africa, and his evenings seeing the wondrous sights of London town. One evening he caught a glimpse of Edward, the Prince of Wales, entering a restaurant near Covent Garden by the side door, a beautiful young lady on his arm. She wore a large-flowered hat, and Jamie thought how nice it would look on his sister.

Jamie attended a concert at the Crystal Palace, built for The Great Exhibition in 1851. He visited Drury Lane and at intermission sneaked into the Savoy Theatre, where they had installed the first electric lighting in a British public building. Some streets were lighted by electricity, and Jamie heard that it was possible to talk to someone on the other side of town by means of a wonderful new machine, the telephone. Jamie felt that he was looking at the future.

In spite of all the innovations and activity, England was in the midst of a growing economic crisis that winter. The streets were filled with the unemployed and the hungry, and there were mass demonstrations and street fighting. *I've got to get away from here*, Jamie thought. *I came to escape poverty*. The following day, Jamie signed on as a steward on the *Walmer Castle*, bound for Cape Town, South Africa.

* * *

The sea journey lasted three weeks, with stops at Madeira and St Helena to take on more coal for fuel. It was a rough, turbulent voyage in the dead of winter, and Jamie was seasick from the moment the ship sailed. But he never lost his cheerfulness, for every day brought him nearer to his treasure chest. As the ship moved towards the equator, the climate changed. Miraculously, winter began to thaw into summer, and as they approached the African coast, the days and nights became hot and steamy.

The *Walmer Castle* arrived in Cape Town at early dawn, moving carefully through the narrow channel that divided the great leper settlement of Robben Island from the mainland, and dropped anchor in Table Bay.

Jamie was on deck before sunrise. He watched, mesmerized, as the early-morning fog lifted and revealed the grand spectacle of Table Mountain looming high over the city. He had arrived.

The moment the ship made fast to the wharf, the decks were overrun by a horde of the strangest-looking people Jamie had ever seen. There were touts for all the different hotels – black men, yellow men, brown men and red men frantically offering to bear away luggage – and small boys running back and forth with newspapers and sweets and fruits for sale. Hansom drivers who were half-castes, Parsis or blacks were yelling their eagerness to be hired. Vendors and men pushing drinking carts called attention to their wares. The air was thick with huge black flies. Sailors and porters hustled and halloaed their way through the crowd while passengers vainly tried to keep their luggage together and in sight. It was a babel of voices and noise. People spoke to one another in a language Jamie had never heard.

'Yulle kom van de Kaap, neh?'

'Het julle mine papa zyn wagen gezien?'

'Wat bedui' di?'

'Huistoe!'

He did not understand a word.

Cape Town was utterly unlike anything Jamie had ever seen. No two houses were alike. Next to a large warehouse two or three storeys high, built of bricks or stone, was a small canteen of galvanized iron, then a jeweller's shop with hand-blown plate-glass windows and abutting it a small greengrocer's and next to that a tumble-down tobacconist's.

Jamie was mesmerized by the men, women and children who thronged the streets. He saw a kaffir clad in an old pair of 78th Highland trews and wearing as a coat a sack with slits cut for the arms and head. The kaffir walked behind two Chinese men, hand in hand, who were wearing blue smock frocks, their pigtails carefully coiled up under their conical strat hats. There were stout, red-faced Boer farmers with sun-bleached hair, their wagons loaded with potatoes, corn and leafy vegetables. Men dressed in brown velveteen trousers and coats, with broad-brimmed, soft-felt hats on their heads and long clay pipes in their mouths, strode ahead of their *vraws*, attired in black, with thick black veils and large black-silk poke bonnets. Parsi washer-women with large bundles of soiled clothes on their heads pushed past soldiers in red coats and helmets. It was a fascinating spectacle.

The first thing Jamie did was to seek out an inexpensive boarding-house recommended to him by a sailor aboard ship. The landlady was a dumpy, ample-bosomed, middle-aged widow.

She looked Jamie over and smiled. *'Zoek yulle goud?'*

He blushed. 'I'm sorry – I don't understand.'

'English, yes? You are here to hunt gold? Diamonds?'

'Diamonds. Yes, ma'am.'

She pulled him inside. 'You will like it here. I have all the convenience for young men like you.'

Jamie wondered whether she was one of them. He hoped not.

'I'm Mrs Venster,' she said coyly, 'but my friends call me "Dee-Dee".' She smiled, revealing a gold tooth in front. 'I have a feeling we are going to be very good friends. Ask of me anything.'

'That's very kind of you,' Jamie said. 'Can you tell me where I can get a map of the city?'

With map in hand, Jamie went exploring. On one side of the city were the landward suburbs of Rondebosch, Claremont and Wynberg, stretching along nine miles of thinning plantations and vine-yards. On the other side were the marine suburbs of Sea Point and Green Point. Jamie walked through the rich residential area, down Strand Street and Bree Street, admiring the large, two-storey buildings with their flat roofs and peaked stuccoed fronts – steep terraces rising from the street. He walked until he was finally driven indoors by the flies that seemed to have a personal vendetta against him. They were large and black and attacked in swarms. When Jamie returned to his boardinghouse, he found his room filled with them. They covered the walls and table and bed.

He went to see the landlady. 'Mrs Venster, isn't there anything you can do about the flies in my room? They're –'

She gave a fat, jiggling laugh and pinched Jamie's cheek, '*Myn magtig*. You'll get used to them. You'll see.'

The sanitary arrangements in Cape Town were both primitive and inadequate, and when the sun set, an odoriferous vapour covered the city like a noxious blanket. It was unbearable. But Jamie knew that he would bear it. He needed more money before he could leave. 'You can't survive in the diamond fields without money,' he had been warned. 'They'll charge you just for breathin'.'

On his second day in Cape Town, Jamie found a job driving a team of horses for a delivery firm. On the third day he started working in a restaurant after dinner, washing dishes. He lived on the left-over food that he squirrelled away and took back to the boardinghouse, but it tasted strange to him and he longed for his mother's cock-a-leekie and oatcakes and hot, fresh-made baps. He did not complain, even to himself, as he sacrificed both food and comfort to increase his grubstake. He had made his choice and nothing was going to stop him, not the exhausting labour, nor the foul air he breathed, nor the flies that kept him awake most of the night. He felt desperately lonely. He knew no one in this strange place, and he missed his friends and family. Jamie enjoyed solitude, but loneliness was a constant ache.

At last, the magic day arrived. His pouch held the magnificent sum of two hundred pounds. He was ready. He would leave Cape Town the following morning for the diamond fields.

Reservations for passenger wagons to the diamond fields at Klipdrift were booked by the Inland Transport Company at a small wooden depot near the docks. When Jamie arrived at seven a.m., the depot was already so crowded that he could not get near it. There were hundreds of fortune seekers fighting for seats on the wagons. They had come from as far away as Russia and America, Australia, Germany and England. They shouted in a dozen different tongues, pleading with the besieged ticket sellers to find spaces for them. Jamie watched as a burly Irishman angrily pushed his way out of the office onto the sidewalk, fighting to get through the mob.

'Excuse me,' Jamie said. 'What's going on in there?'

'Nothin',' the Irishman grunted in disgust. 'The bloody wagons are all booked up for the next six weeks.' He saw the look of dismay on Jamie's face. 'That's not the worst of it, lad. The heathen bastards are chargin' fifty pounds a head.'

It was incredible! 'There must be another way to get to the diamond fields.'

'Two ways. You can go Dutch Express, or you can go by foot.'

'What's Dutch Express?'

'Bullock wagon. They travel two miles an hour. By the time you get there, the damned diamonds will all be gone.'

Jamie McGregor had no intention of being delayed until the diamonds were gone. He spent the rest of the morning looking for another means of transportation. Just before noon, he found it. He was passing a livery stable with a sign in front that said MAIL DEPOT. On an impulse, he went inside, where the thinnest man he had ever seen was loading large mail sacks into a dogcart. Jamie watched him a moment.

'Excuse me,' Jamie said. 'Do you carry mail to Klipdrift?'

'That's right. Loadin' up now.'

Jamie felt a sudden surge of hope. 'Do you take passengers?'

'Sometimes.' He looked up and studied Jamie. 'How old are you?'

An odd question. 'Eighteen. Why?'

'We don't take anyone over twenty-one or twenty-two. You in good health?'

An even odder question. 'Yes, sir.'

The thin man straightened up. 'I guess you're fit. I'm leavin' in an hour. The fare's twenty pounds.'

Jamie could not believe his good fortune. 'That's wonderful! I'll get my suitcase and –'

'No suitcase. All you got room for is one shirt and a toothbrush.'

Jamie took a closer look at the dogcart. It was small and roughly built. The body formed a well in which the mail was stored, and over the well was a narrow, cramped space where a person could sit back to back behind the driver. It was going to be an uncomfortable journey.

'It's a deal,' Jamie said. 'I'll fetch my shirt and toothbrush.'

When Jamie returned, the driver was hitching up a horse to the open cart. There were two large young men standing near the cart: one was short and dark, the other was a tall, blond Swede. The men were handing the driver some money.

'Wait a minute,' Jamie called to the driver. 'You said *I* was going.'

'You're all goin',' the driver said. 'Hop in.'

'The *three* of us?'

'That's right.'

Jamie had no idea how the driver expected them all to fit in the small cart, but he knew he was going to be on it when it pulled out.

Jamie introduced himself to his two fellow passengers. 'I'm Jamie McGregor.'

'Wallach,' the short, dark man said.

'Pederson,' the tall blond replied.

Jamie said, 'We're lucky we discovered this, aren't we? It's a good thing everybody doesn't know about it.'

Pederson said, 'Oh, they know about the post carts, McGregor. There just aren't that many fit enough or desperate enough to travel in them.'

Before Jamie could ask what he meant, the driver said, 'Let's go.'

The three men – Jamie in the middle – squeezed into the seat, crowded against each other, their knees cramped, their backs pressing hard against the wooden back of the driver's seat. There was no room to move or breathe. *It's not bad*, Jamie reassured himself.

'Hold on!' the driver sang out, and a moment later they were racing through the streets of Cape Town on their way to the diamond fields at Klipdrift.

By bullock wagon, the journey was relatively comfortable. The wagons transporting passengers from Cape Town to the diamond fields were large and roomy, with tent covers to ward off the blazing winter sun. Each wagon accommodated a dozen passengers and was drawn by teams of horses or mules. Refreshments were provided at regular stations, and the journey took ten days.

The mail cart was different. It never stopped, except to change horses and drivers. The pace was a full gallop, over rough roads and fields and rutted trails. There were no springs on the cart, and each bounce was like the blow of a horse's hoof. Jamie gritted his teeth and thought, *I can stand it until we stop for the night, I'll eat and get some sleep, and in the morning I'll be fine.* But when nighttime came, there was a ten-minute halt for a change of horse and driver, and they were off again at a full gallop.

'When do we stop to eat?' Jamie asked.

'We don't,' the new driver grunted. 'We go straight through. We're carryin' the mails, mister.'

They raced through the long night, travelling over dusty, bumpy roads by moonlight, the little cart bouncing up the rises, plunging down the valleys, springing over the flats. Every inch of Jamie's body was battered and bruised from the constant jolting. He was exhausted, but it was impossible to sleep. Every time he started to doze off, he was jarred awake. His body was cramped and miserable and there was no room to stretch. He was starving and motion-sick. He had no idea how many days it would be before his next meal. It was a six-hundred-mile journey, and Jamie McGregor was not sure he was going to live through it. Neither was he sure that he wanted to.

By the end of the second day and night, the misery had turned to agony. Jamie's travelling companions were in the same sorry state, no longer even able to complain. Jamie understood now why the company insisted that its passengers be young and strong.

When the next dawn came, they entered the Great Karroo, where the real wilderness began. Stretching to infinity, the monstrous veld lay flat and forbidding under a pitiless sun. The passengers were smothered in heat, dust and flies.

Occasionally, through a miasmic haze, Jamie saw groups of men slogging along on foot. There were solitary riders on horseback, and dozens of bullock wagons drawn by eighteen or twenty oxen, handled by drivers and *voorlopers*, with their *sjamboks*, the whips with long leather thongs, crying, 'Trek! Trek!' The huge wagons were laden with a thousand pounds of produce and goods, tents and digging equipment and wood-burning stoves, flour and coal and oil lamps. They carried coffee and rice, Russian hemp, sugar and wines, whiskey and boots and Belfast candles, and blankets. They were the lifeline to the fortune seekers at Klipdrift.

It was not until the mail cart crossed the Orange River that there was a change from the deadly monotony of the veld. The scrub gradually became taller and tinged with green. The earth was redder, patches of grass rippled in the breeze, and low thorn trees began to appear.

I'm going to make it, Jamie thought dully. *I'm going to make it*.

And he could feel hope begin to creep into his tired body.

They had been on the road for four continuous days and nights when they finally arrived at the outskirts of Klipdrift.

Young Jamie McGregor had not known what to expect, but the scene that met his weary, blood-shot eyes was like nothing he ever could have imagined. Klipdrift was a vast panorama of tents and wagons lined up on the main streets and on the shores of the Vaal River. The dirt roadway swarmed with kaffirs, naked except for brightly coloured jackets, and bearded prospectors, butchers, bakers, thieves, teachers. In the centre of Klipdrift, rows of wooden and iron shacks served as shops, canteens, billiard rooms, eating houses, diamond-buying offices and lawyers' rooms. On a corner stood the ramshackle Royal Arch Hotel, a long chain of rooms without windows.

Jamie stepped out of the cart, and promptly fell to the ground, his cramped legs refusing to hold him up. He lay there, his head spinning, until he had strength enough to rise. He stumbled towards the hotel, pushing through the boisterous crowds that thronged the sidewalks and streets. The room they gave him was small, stifling hot and swarming with flies. But it had a cot. Jamie fell onto it, fully dressed, and was asleep instantly. He slept for eighteen hours.

Jamie awoke, his body unbelievably stiff and sore, but his soul filled with exultation. *I am here! I have made it!* Ravenously hungry, he went in search of food. The hotel served none, but there was a small, crowded restaurant across the street, where he devoured fried snook, a large fish resembling pike; carbonaatje, thinly sliced mutton grilled on a spit over a wood fire; a haunch of bok and, for dessert, *koeksister*, a dough deep-fried and soaked in syrup.

Jamie's stomach, so long without food, began to give off alarming symptoms. He decided to let it rest before he continued eating, and turned his attention to his surroundings. At tables all around him, prospectors were feverishly discussing the subject uppermost in everyone's mind: diamonds.

'. . . There's still a few diamonds left around Hopetown, but the mother lode's at New Rush . . .'

'. . . Kimberley's got a bigger population than Joburg . . .'

'. . . About the find up at Dutoitspan last week? They say there's more diamonds there than a man can carry . . .'

'. . . There's a new strike at Christiana. I'm goin' up there tomorrow.'

So it was true. There were diamonds everywhere! Young Jamie was so excited he could hardly finish his huge mug of coffee. He was staggered by the amount of the bill. Two pounds, three shillings for one meal! *I'll have to be very careful*, he thought, as he walked out onto the crowded, noisy street.

A voice behind him said, 'Still planning to get rich, McGregor?'

Jamie turned. It was Pederson, the Swedish boy who had travelled on the dogcart with him.

'I certainly am,' Jamie said.

'Then let's go where the diamonds are.' He pointed. 'The Vaal River's that way.'

They began to walk.

Klipdrift was in a basin, surrounded by hills, and as far as Jamie could see, everything was barren, without a blade of grass or shrub in sight. Red dust rose thick in the air, making it difficult to breathe. The Vaal River was a quarter of a mile away, and as they got closer to it, the air became cooler. Hundreds of prospectors lined both sides of the riverbank, some of them digging for diamonds, others meshing stones in rocking cradles, still others sorting stones at rickety, makeshift tables. The equipment ranged from scientific earth-washing apparatus to old tub boxes and pails. The men were sunburned, unshaven and roughly dressed in a weird assortment of collarless, coloured and striped flannel shirts, corduroy trousers and rubber boots, riding breeches and laced leggings and wide-brimmed felt hats or pith helmets. They all wore broad leather belts with pockets for diamonds or money.

Jamie and Pederson walked to the edge of the riverbank and watched a young boy and an older man struggling to remove a huge ironstone boulder so they could get at the gravel around it. Their shirts were soaked with sweat. Nearby, another team loaded gravel onto a cart to be sieved in a cradle. One of the diggers rocked the cradle while another poured buckets of water into it to wash away the silt. The large pebbles were then emptied onto an improvised sorting table, where they were excitedly inspected.

'It looks easy,' Jamie grinned.

'Don't count on it, McGregor. I've been talking to some of the diggers who have been here a while. I think we've bought a sack of pups.'

'What do you mean?'

'Do you know how many diggers there are in these parts, all hoping to get rich? Twenty bloody thousand! And there aren't enough diamonds to go around, chum. Even if there were, I'm beginning to wonder if it's worth it. You broil in winter, freeze in summer, get drenched in their damned *donderstormen*, and try to cope with the dust and the flies and the stink. You can't get a bath or a decent bed, and there are no sanitary arrangements in this damned town. There are drownings in the Vaal River every week. Some are accidental, but I was told that for most of them it's a way out, the only escape from this hellhole. I don't know why these people keep hanging on.'

'I do.' Jamie looked at the hopeful young boy with the stained shirt. 'The next shovelful of dirt.'

But as they headed back to town, Jamie had to admit that Pederson had a point. They passed carcasses of slaughtered oxen, sheep and goats left to rot outside the tents, next to wide-open trenches that served as lavatories. The place stank to the heavens. Pederson was watching him. 'What are you going to do now?'

'Get some prospecting equipment.'

In the centre of town was a store with a rusted hanging sign that read: SALOMON VAN DER MERWE, GENERAL STORE. A tall black man about Jamie's age was unloading a wagon in front of the store. He was broad-shouldered and heavily muscled, one of the most handsome men Jamie had ever seen. He had soot-black eyes, an aquiline nose and a proud chin. There was a dignity about him, a quiet aloofness. He lifted a heavy wooden box of rifles to his shoulder and, as he turned, he slipped on a leaf fallen from a crate of cabbage. Jamie instinctively reached out an arm to steady him. The black man did not acknowledge Jamie's presence. He turned and walked into the store. A Boer prospector hitching up a mule spat and said distastefully, 'That's Banda, from the Barolong tribe. Works for Mr van der Merwe. I don't know why he keeps that uppity black. Those fuckin' Bantus think they own the earth.'

The store was cool and dark inside, a welcome relief from the hot, bright street, and it was filled with exotic odours. It seemed to Jamie that every inch of space was crammed with merchandise. He walked through the store, marvelling. There were agricultural implements, beer, cans of milk and crocks of butter, cement, fuses and dynamite and gunpowder, crockery, furniture, guns and haberdashery, oil and paint and varnish, bacon and dried fruit, saddlery and harness, sheep-dip and soap, spirits and stationery and paper, sugar and tea and tobacco and snuff and cigars . . . A dozen shelves were filled from top to bottom with flannel shirts and blankets, shoes, poke bonnets and saddles. *Whoever owns all this*, Jamie thought, *is a rich man*.

A soft voice behind him said, 'Can I help you?'

Jamie turned and found himself facing a young girl. He judged she was about fifteen. She had an interesting face, fineboned and heart-shaped, like a valentine, a pert nose and intense green eyes. Her hair was dark and curling. Jamie, looking at her figure, decided she might be closer to sixteen.

'I'm a prospector,' Jamie announced. 'I'm here to buy some equipment.'

'What is it you need?'

For some reason, Jamie felt he had to impress this girl. 'I – er – you know – the usual.'

She smiled, and there was mischief in her eyes. 'What is the usual, sir?'

'Well . . .' He hesitated. 'A shovel.'

'Will that be all?'

Jamie saw that she was teasing him. He grinned and confessed. 'To tell you the truth, I'm new at this. I don't know what I need.'

She smiled at him, and it was the smile of a woman. 'It depends on where you're planning to prospect, Mr –?'

'McGregor. Jamie McGregor.'

'I'm Margaret van der Merwe.' She glanced nervously towards the rear of the store.

'I'm pleased to meet you, Miss van der Merwe.'

'Did you just arrive?'

'Aye. Yesterday. On the post cart.'

'Someone should have warned you about that. Passengers have died on that trip.' There was anger in her eyes.

Jamie grinned. 'I can't blame them. But I'm very much alive, thank you.'

'And going out to hunt for *mooi klippe*.'

'*Mooi klippe?*'

'That's our Dutch word for diamonds. Pretty pebbles.'

'You're Dutch?'

'My family's from Holland.'

'I'm from Scotland.'

'I could tell that.' Her eyes flicked warily towards the back of the store again. 'There are diamonds around, Mr McGregor, but you must be choosy where you look for them. Most of the diggers are running around chasing their own tails. When someone makes a strike, the rest scavenge off the leavings. If you want to get rich, you have to find a strike of your own.'

'How do I do that?'

'My father might be the one to help you with that. He knows everything. He'll be free in an hour.'

'I'll be back,' Jamie assured her. 'Thank you, Miss van der Merwe.

He went out into the sunshine, filled with a sense of euphoria, his aches and pains forgotten. If

Salomon van der Merwe would advise him where to find diamonds, there was no way Jamie could fail. He would have the jump on all of them. He laughed aloud, with the sheer joy of being young and alive and on his way to riches.

Jamie walked down the main street, passing a blacksmith's, a billiard hall and half a dozen saloons. He came to a sign in front of a decrepit-looking hotel and stopped. The sign read:

R-D MILLER, WARM AND COLD BATHS.
OPEN DAILY FROM 6 A.M. TO 8 P.M.,
WITH THE COMFORTS OF A NEAT
DRESSING ROOM

Jamie thought, *When did I have my last bath? Well, I took a bucket bath on the boat. That was* – He was suddenly aware of how he must smell. He thought of the weekly tub baths in the kitchen at home, and he could hear his mother's voice calling, 'Be sure to wash down below, Jamie.'

He turned and entered the baths. There were two doors inside, one for women and one for men. Jamie entered the men's section and walked up to the aged attendant. 'How much is a bath?'

'Ten shillings for a cold bath, fifteen for a hot.'

Jamie hesitated. The idea of a hot bath after his long journey was almost irresistible. 'Cold,' he said. He could not afford to throw away his money on luxuries. He had mining equipment to buy.

The attendant handed him a small bar of yellow lye soap and a threadbare hand towel and pointed. 'In there, mate.'

Jamie stepped into a small room that contained nothing except a large galvanized-iron bathtub in the centre and a few pegs on the wall. The attendant began filling the tub from a large wooden bucket.

'All ready for you, mister. Just hang your clothes on those pegs.'

Jamie waited until the attendant left and then undressed. He looked down at his grime-covered body and put one foot in the tub. The water was cold, as advertised. He gritted his teeth and plunged in, soaping himself furiously from head to foot. When he finally stepped out of the tub, the water was black. He dried himself as best he could with the worn linen towel and started to get dressed. His pants and shirt were stiff with dirt, and he hated to put them back on. He would have to buy a change of clothes, and this reminded him once more of how little money he had. And he was hungry again.

Jamie left the bathhouse and pushed his way down the crowded street to a saloon called the Sundowner. He ordered a beer and lunch. Lamb cutlets with tomatoes, and sausage and potato salad and pickles. While he ate, he listened to the hopeful conversations around him.

'. . . I hear they found a stone near Colesberg weighin' twenty-one carats. Mark you, if there's *one* diamond up there, there's plenty more . . .'

'. . . There's a new diamond find up in Hebron. I'm thinkin' of goin' there . . .'

'You're a fool. The big diamonds are in the Orange River . . .'

At the bar, a bearded customer in a collarless, striped-flannel shirt and corduroy trousers was nursing a shandygaff in a large glass. 'I got cleaned out in Hebron,' he confided to the bartender. 'I need me a grubstake.'

The bartender was a large, fleshy, bald-headed man with a broken, twisted nose and ferret eyes. He laughed. 'Hell, man, who doesn't? Why do you think I'm tendin' bar? As soon as I have enough money, I'm gonna hightail it up the Orange myself.' He wiped the bar with a dirty rag. 'But I'll tell you what you might do, mister. See Salomon van der Merwe. He owns the general store and half the town.

'What good'll that do me?'

'If he likes you, he might stake you.'

The customer looked at him. 'Yeah? You really think he might?'

'He's done it for a few fellows I know of. You put up your labour, he puts up the money. You split fifty-fifty.'

Jamie McGregor's thoughts leaped ahead. He had been confident that the hundred and twenty pounds he had left would be enough to buy the equipment and food he would need to survive, but the prices in Klipdrift were astonishing. He had noticed in Van der Merwe's store that a hundred-pound sack of Australian flour cost five pounds. One pound of sugar cost a shilling. A bottle of beer cost five shillings. Biscuits were three shillings a pound, and fresh eggs sold for seven shillings a dozen. At that rate, his money would not last long. *My God*, Jamie thought, *at home we could live for a year on what three meals cost here*. But if he could get the backing of someone really wealthy, like Mr van der Merwe . . . Jamie hastily paid for his food and hurried back to the general store.

Salomon van der Merwe was behind the counter, removing the rifles from a wooden crate. He was a small thin man, with a thin, pinched face framed by Dundreary whiskers. He had sandy hair, tiny black eyes, a bulbous nose and pursed lips. *His daughter must take after her mother*, Jamie thought. 'Excuse me, sir . . .'

Van der Merwe looked up. '*Ja?*'

'Mr van der Merwe? My name is Jamie McGregor, sir, I'm from Scotland. I came here to find diamonds.'

'*Ja?* So?'

'I hear you sometimes back prospectors.'

Van der Merwe grumbled, '*Myn magtig!* Who spreads these stories? I help out a few diggers, and everyone thinks I'm Santa Claus.'

'I've saved a hundred and twenty pounds,' Jamie said earnestly. 'But I see that it's not going to buy me much here. I'll go out to the bush with just a shovel if I have to, but I figure my chances would be a lot better if I had a mule and some proper equipment.'

Van der Merwe was studying him with those small, black eyes. '*Wat denk ye?* What makes you think *you* can find diamonds?'

'I've come halfway around the world, Mr van der Merwe, and I'm not going to leave here until I'm rich. If the diamonds are out there, I'll find them. If you help me, I'll make us both rich.'

Van der Merwe grunted, turned his back on Jamie and continued unloading the rifles. Jamie stood there awkwardly, not knowing what more to say. When Van der Merwe spoke again, his question caught Jamie off guard. 'You travel here by bullock wagon, *ja*?'

'No. Post cart.'

The old man turned to study the boy again. He said, finally, 'We talk about it.'

They talked about it at dinner that evening in the room in the back of the store that was the Van der Merwe living quarters. It was a small room that served as a kitchen, dining room and sleeping quarters, with a curtain separating two cots. The lower half of the walls was built of mud and stone, and the upper half was faced with cardboard boxes that had once contained provisions. A square hole, where a piece of the wall had been cut out, served as window. In wet weather it could be closed by placing a board in front of it. The dining table consisted of a long plank stretched across two wooden crates. A large box, turned on its side, served as a cupboard. Jamie guessed that Van der Merwe was not a man who parted easily with his money.

Van der Merwe's daughter moved silently about, preparing dinner. From time to time she cast quick glances at her father, but she never once looked at Jamie. *Why is she so frightened?* Jamie wondered.

When they were seated at the table, Van der Merwe began. 'Let us have a blessing. We Thank Thee, O Lord, for the bounty we receive at Thy hands. We thank Thee for forgiving us our sins and showing us the path of righteousness and delivering us from life's temptations. We thank Thee for a long and fruitful life, and for smiting dead all those who offend Thee. Amen.' And without a breath between, 'Pass me the meat,' he said to his daughter.

The dinner was frugal: a small roast pork, three boiled potatoes and a dish of turnip greens. The portions he served to Jamie were small. The two men talked little during the meal, and Margaret did not speak at all.

When they had finished eating, Van der Merwe said, 'That was fine, Daughter,' and there was pride in his voice. He turned to Jamie. 'We get down to business, *ja?*'

'Yes, sir.'

Van der Merwe picked up a long clay pipe from the top of the wooden cabinet. He filled it with a sweet-smelling tobacco from a small pouch and lighted the pipe. His sharp eyes peered intently at Jamie through the wreaths of smoke.

'The diggers here at Klipdrift are fools. Too few diamonds, too many diggers. A man could break his back here for a year and have nothing to show for it but *schlenters*.'

'I – I'm afraid I'm not familiar with that word, sir.'

'Fool's diamonds. Worthless. Do you follow me?'

'I – Yes, sir. I think so. But what's the answer, sir?'

'The Griquas.'

Jamie looked at him blankly.

'They're an African tribe up north. *They* find diamonds – big ones – and sometimes they bring them to me and I trade them for goods.' The Dutchman lowered his voice to a conspiratorial whisper. 'I know where they find them.'

'But could you nae go after them yourself, Mr van der Merwe?'

Van der Merwe sighed. 'No. I can't leave the store. People would steal me blind. I need someone I can trust to go up there and bring the stones back. When I find the right man, I'll supply him with all the equipment he needs.' He paused to take a long drag on his pipe. 'And I'll tell him where the diamonds are.'

Jamie leaped to his feet, his heart pounding. 'Mr van der Merwe, *I'm* the person you're looking for.

39

Believe me, sir, I'll work night and day.' His voice was charged with excitement. 'I'll bring you back more diamonds than you can count.'

Van der Merwe silently studied him for what seemed to Jamie to be an eternity. When Van der Merwe finally spoke, he said only one word. '*Ja*'

Jamie signed the contract the following morning. It was written in Afrikaans.

'I'll have to explain it to you,' Van der Merwe said. 'It says we're full partners. I put up the capital – you put up the labour. We share everything equally.'

Jamie looked at the contract in Van der Merwe's hand. In the middle of all the incomprehensible foreign words he recognized only a sum: *two pounds*.

Jamie pointed to it. 'What is that for, Mr van der Merwe?'

'It means that in addition to your owning half the diamonds you find, you'll get an extra two pounds for every week you work. Even though I know the diamonds are out there, it's possible you might not find anything, lad. This way you'll at least get something for your labour.'

The man was being more than fair. 'Thank you. Thank you very much, sir.' Jamie could have hugged him.

Van der Merwe said, 'Now let's get you outfitted.'

It took two hours to select the equipment that Jamie would take into the bush with him: a small tent, bedding, cooking utensils, two sieves and a washing cradle, a pick, two shovels, three buckets and one change of socks and underwear. There was an axe and a lantern and paraffin oil, matches and arsenical soap. There were tins of food, biltong, fruit, sugar, coffee and salt. At last everything was in readiness. The black servant, Banda, silently helped Jamie stow everything into backpacks. The huge man never glanced at Jamie and never spoke one word. *He doesn't speak English*, Jamie decided. Margaret was in the store waiting on customers, but if she knew Jamie was there, she gave no indication.

Van der Merwe came over to Jamie. 'Your mule's in front,' he said. 'Banda will help you load up.'

'Thank you, Mr van der Merwe,' Jamie said. 'I –'

Van der Merwe consulted a piece of paper covered with figures 'That will be one hundred and twenty pounds.'

Jamie looked at him blankly. 'W – what? This is part of our deal. We –'

'*Wat bedui'di?*' Van der Merwe's thin face darkened with anger. 'You expect me to *give* you all this, and a fine mule, and make you a partner, and give you two pounds a week on top of *that*? If you're looking for something for nothing, you've come to the wrong place.' He began to unload one of the backpacks.

Jamie said quickly, 'No! Please, Mr van der Merwe. I – I just didn't understand. It's perfectly all right. I have the money right here.' He reached in his pouch and put the last of his savings on the counter.

Van der Merwe hesitated. 'All right,' he said grudgingly. 'Perhaps it was a misunderstanding, neh? This town is full of cheaters. I have to be careful who I do business with.'

'Yes, sir. Of course you do,' Jamie agreed. In his excitement, he had misunderstood the deal. *I'm lucky he's giving me another chance*, Jamie thought.

Van der Merwe reached into his pocket and pulled out a small, wrinkled, hand-drawn map. 'Here is where you'll find the *mooi klippe*. North of here at Magerdam on the northern bank of the Vaal.'

Jamie studied the map, and his heart began to beat faster. 'How many miles is it?'

'Here we measure distance by time. With the mule, you should make the journey in four or five days. Coming back will be slower because of the weight of the diamonds.'

Jamie grinned. '*Ja.*'

When Jamie McGregor stepped back out onto the streets of Klipdrift, he was no longer a tourist. He was a prospector, a digger, on his way to his fortune. Banda had finished loading the supplies onto the back of a frail-looking mule tethered to the hitching post in front of the store.

'Thanks.' Jamie smiled.

Banda turned and looked him in the eye, then

silently walked away. Jamie unhitched the reins and said to the mule, 'Let's go, partner. It's *mooi klippe* time.'

They headed north.

Jamie pitched camp near a stream at nightfall, unloaded and watered and fed the mule, and fixed himself some beef jerky, dried apricots and coffee. The night was filled with strange noises. He heard the grunts and howls and padding of wild animals moving down to the water. He was unprotected, surrounded by the most dangerous beasts in the world, in a strange, primitive country. He jumped at every sound. At any moment he expected to be attacked by fangs and claws leaping at him from out of the darkness. His mind began to drift. He thought of his snug bed at home and the comfort and safety he had always taken for granted. He slept fitfully, his dreams filled with charging lions and elephants, and large, bearded men trying to take an enormous diamond away from him.

At dawn when Jamie awakened, the mule was dead.

TWO

He could not believe it. He looked for a wound of some kind, thinking it must have been attacked by a wild animal during the night, but there was nothing. The beast had died in its sleep. *Mr van der Merwe will hold me responsible for this*, Jamie thought. *But when I bring him diamonds, it won't matter*.

There was no turning back. He would go on to Magerdam without the mule. He heard a sound in the air and looked up. Giant black vultures were beginning to circle high above. Jamie shuddered. Working as quickly as possible, he rearranged his gear, deciding what he had to leave behind, then stowed everything he could carry into a backpack and started off. When he looked back five minutes later, the enormous vultures had covered the body of the dead animal. All that was visible was one long ear. Jamie quickened his step.

It was December, summer in South Africa, and the trek across the veld under the huge orange sun was a horror. Jamie had started out from Klipdrift with a brisk step and a light heart, but as the minutes turned into hours and the hours into days, his steps got slower and his heart became heavier. As far as the eye could see, the monotomous veld shimmered flat and forbidding under the blazing sun and there seemed no end to the grey, stony, desolate plains.

Jamie made camp whenever he came to a watering hole, and he slept with the eerie, nocturnal sounds of the animals all around him. The sounds no longer bothered him. They were proof that there was life in this barren hell, and they made him feel less lonely. One dawn Jamie came across a pride of lions. He watched from a distance as the lioness moved towards her mate and their cubs, carrying a baby impala in her powerful jaws. She dropped the animal in front of the male and moved away while he fed. A reckless cub leaped forwards and dug his teeth into the impala. With one motion, the male raised a paw and swiped the cub across the face, killing it instantly, then went back to his feeding. When he finished, the rest of the family was permitted to move in for the remains of the feast. Jamie slowly backed away from the scene and continued walking.

It took him almost two weeks to cross the Karroo. More than once he was ready to give up. He was not sure he could finish the journey. *I'm a fool. I should have returned to Klipdrift to ask Mr van der Merwe for another mule. But what if*

Van der Merwe had called off the deal? No, I did the right thing.

And so, Jamie kept moving, one step at a time. One day, he saw four figures in the distance, coming towards him. *I'm delirious*, Jamie thought. *It's a mirage.* But the figures came closer, and Jamie's heart began to thud alarmingly. *Men! There is human life here!* He wondered if he had forgotten how to speak. He tried out his voice on the afternoon air, and it sounded as if it belonged to someone long dead. The four men reached him, prospectors returning to Klipdrift, tired and defeated.

'Hello,' Jamie said.

They nodded. One of them said, 'There ain't nothin' ahead, boy. We looked. You're wastin' your time. Go back.'

And they were gone.

Jamie shut his mind to everything but the trackless waste ahead of him. The sun and the black flies were unbearable and there was no place to hide. There were thorn trees, but their branches had been laid to waste by the elephants. Jamie was almost totally blinded by the sun. His fair skin was burned raw, and he was constantly dizzy. Each time he took a breath of air, his lungs seemed to explode. He was no longer walking, he was stumbling, putting one foot in front of the other, mindlessly lurching ahead. One afternoon, with the midday sun beating down on him, he slipped off his backpack and slumped to the ground, too tired to take another step. He closed his eyes and dreamed he was in a giant crucible and the sun was a huge, bright diamond blazing down on him, melting him. He awoke in the middle of the night trembling from the cold. He forced himself to take a few bites of biltong and a drink of tepid water. He knew he must get up and start moving before the sun rose, while the earth and sky were cool. He tried, but the effort was too great. It would be so easy just to lie there forever and never have to take another step. *I'll just sleep for a little while longer*, Jamie thought. But some voice deep within him told him he would never wake up again. They would find his body there as they had found hundreds of others. He remembered the vultures and thought, *No, not my body – my bones*. Slowly and painfully, he forced himself to his feet. His backpack was so heavy he could not lift it. Jamie started walking again, dragging the pack behind him. He had no recollection of how many times he fell onto the sand and staggered to his feet again. Once he screamed into the predawn sky, 'I'm Jamie McGregor, and I'm going to make it. I'm going to live. Do you hear me, God? I'm going to live . . .' Voices were exploding in his head.

You're goin' chasin' diamonds? You must be daft, son. That's a fairy tale – a temptation of the devil to keep men from doin' an honest day's work.

Why do you nae tell us where you're gettin' the

money to go? It's halfway 'round the world. You hae no money.

Mr van der Merwe, I'm the person you're looking for. Believe me, sir, I'll work night and day. I'll bring you back more diamonds than you can count.

And he was finished before he had even started. *You have two choices,* Jamie told himself. *You can go on or you can stay here and die . . . and die . . . and die . . .*

The words echoed endlessly in his head. *You can take one more step,* Jamie thought. Come on, Jamie boy. One more step. One more step . . .

Two days later Jamie McGregor stumbled into the village of Magerdam. The sunburn had long since become infected and his body oozed blood and sera. Both eyes were swollen almost completely shut. He collapsed in the middle of the street, a pile of crumpled clothes holding him together. When sympathetic diggers tried to relieve him of his backpack, Jamie fought them with what little strength he had left, raving deliriously. 'No! Get away from my diamonds. Get away from my diamonds . . .'

He awakened in a small, bare room three days later, naked except for the bandages that covered his body. The first thing he saw when he opened his eyes was a buxom, middle-aged woman seated at the side of his cot.

'Wh – ?' His voice was a croak. He could not get the words out.

'Easy, dear. You've been sick.' She gently lifted

48

his swathed head and gave him a sip of water from a tin cup.

Jamie managed to prop himself up on one elbow. 'Where – ?' He swallowed and tried again. 'Where am I?'

'You're in Magerdam. I'm Alice Jardine. This is my boarding-house. You're going to be fine. You just need a good rest. Now lie back.'

Jamie remembered the strangers who tried to take his backpack away, and he was filled with panic. 'My things, where – ?' He tried to rise from the cot, but the woman's gentle voice stopped him.

'Everything's safe. Not to worry, son.' She pointed to his backpack in a corner of the room.

Jamie lay back on the clean white sheets. *I got here. I made it. Everything is going to be all right now.*

Alice Jardine was a blessing, not only to Jamie McGregor, but to half of Magerdam. In that mining town filled with adventurers, all sharing the same dream, she fed them, nursed them, encouraged them. She was an Englishwoman who had come to South Africa with her husband, when he decided to give up his teaching job in Leeds and join the diamond rush. He had died of fever three weeks after they arrived, but she had decided to stay on. The miners had become the children she never had.

She kept Jamie in bed for four more days, feeding him, changing his bandages and helping him regain his strength. By the fifth day, Jamie was ready to get up.

'I want you to know how grateful I am to you, Mrs Jardine. I can't pay you anything. Not yet. But you'll have a big diamond from me one day soon. That's a promise from Jamie McGregor.'

She smiled at the intensity of the handsome young boy. He was still twenty pounds too thin, and his grey eyes were filled with the horror he had been through, but there was a strength about him, a determination that was awesome. *He's different from the others*, Mrs Jardine thought.

Jamie, dressed in his freshly washed clothes, went out to explore the town. It was Klipdrift on a smaller scale. There were the same tents and wagons and dusty streets, the flimsily built shops and the crowds of prospectors. As Jamie passed a saloon, he heard a roar from inside and entered. A noisy crowd had gathered around a red-shirted Irishman.

'What's going on?' Jamie asked.

'He's going to wet his find.'

'He's what?'

'He struck it rich today, so he stands treat for the whole saloon. He pays me for as much liquor as a saloon-full of thirsty men can swallow.'

Jamie joined in a conversation with several disgruntled diggers sitting at a round table.

'Where you from, McGregor?'

'Scotland.'

'Well, I don't know what horseshit they fed you in Scotland, but there ain't enough diamonds in this fuckin' country to pay expenses.'

They talked of other camps: Gong Gong, Forlorn Hope, Delports, Poormans Kopje, Sixpenny Rush . . .

The diggers all told the same story – of months doing the back-breaking work of moving boulders, digging into the hard soil and squatting over the riverbank sifting the dirt for diamonds. Each day a few diamonds were found; not enough to make a man rich, but enough to keep his dreams alive. The mood of the town was a strange mixture of optimism and pessimism. The optimists were arriving; the pessimists were leaving.

Jamie knew which side he was on.

He approached the red-shirted Irishman, now bleary-eyed with drink, and showed him Van der Merwe's map.

The man glanced at it and tossed it back to Jamie. 'Worthless. That whole area's been picked over. If I was you, I'd try Bad Hope.'

Jamie could not believe it. Van der Merwe's map was what had brought him there, the lodestar that was going to make him rich.

Another digger said, 'Head for Colesberg. That's where they're findin' diamonds, son.'

'Gilfillans Kop – *that's* the place to dig.'

'You'll try Moonlight Rush, if you want my opinion.'

* * *

At supper that night, Alice Jardine said, 'Jamie, one place is as big a gamble as another. Pick your own spot, dig in your pickaxe and pray. That's all these other *experts* are doing.'

After a night of sleepless self-debate, Jamie decided he would forget Van der Merwe's map. Against everyone's advice, he decided to head east, along the Modder River. The following morning Jamie said goodbye to Mrs Jardine and set off.

He walked for three days and two nights, and when he came to a likely-looking spot, he set up his small tent. Huge boulders lay along both sides of the riverbank, and Jamie, using thick branches as levers, laboriously moved them out of the way to get at the gravel that lay beneath.

He dug from dawn until dusk, looking for the yellow clay or the blue diamondiferous soil that would tell him he had found a diamond pipe. But the earth was barren. He dug for a week without finding a single stone. At the end of the week, he moved on.

One day as he walked along, he saw in the distance what looked like a silver house, glowing dazzlingly in the sun. *I'm going blind*, Jamie thought. But as he got closer, he saw that he was approaching a village, and all the houses seemed to be made of silver. Crowds of Indian men, women and children dressed in rags swarmed through the streets. Jamie stared in amazement. The silver houses glistening in the sun were made of tin jam pots, flattened out, fastened together and nailed over the crude shacks. He walked on, and an hour later, when he looked back, he could still see the glow of the village. It was a sight he never forgot.

Jamie kept moving north. He followed the river-bank where the diamonds might be, digging until his arms refused to lift the heavy pick, then sifting the wet gravel through the hand sieve. When it got dark, he slept as though drugged.

At the end of the second week, he moved upstream again, just north of a small settlement called Paardspan. He stopped near a bend in the river and fixed himself a meal of carbonaatje, grilled on a spit over a wood fire, and hot tea, then sat in front of his tent, looking up at the wheeling stars in the vast sky. He had not seen a human being in two weeks, and an eddy of lone-liness washed over him. *What the hell am I doing here?* he wondered. *Sitting in the middle of a blasted wilderness like a bloody fool, killing myself breaking rocks and digging up dirt? I was better off at the farm. Come Saturday, if I don't find a diamond, I'm going home.* He looked up at the uncaring stars and yelled, 'Do you hear me, damn you?' *Oh, Jesus,* he thought, *I'm losing my mind.*

Jamie sat there, idly sifting the sand through his fingers. They closed on a large stone, and he looked at it a moment, then threw it away. He had seen a thousand worthless stones like it in the past weeks. What was it Van der Merwe had called them? *Schlenters*. Yet, there was something about this one that belatedly caught Jamie's attention. He rose, went over to it and picked it up. It was much larger than the other stones and of an odd shape. He rubbed some of the dirt off it against the leg of his trousers and examined it more closely. It *looked* like a diamond. The only thing that made Jamie doubt his senses was the size of it. It was almost as large as a hen's egg. *Oh, God. If it is a diamond* . . . He suddenly had difficulty breathing. He grabbed his lantern and began searching the ground around him. In fifteen minutes he had found four more like it. None of them was as large as the first one, but they were large enough to fill him with a wild excitement.

He was up before dawn, digging like a madman, and by noon he had found half a dozen more diamonds. He spent the next week feverishly digging up diamonds and burying them at night in a safe place where no passers-by could find them. There were fresh diamonds every day, and as Jamie watched his fortune pile up, he was filled with an ineffable joy. Only half of this treasure was his, but it was enough to make him rich beyond anything he had ever dared to dream.

At the end of the week, Jamie made a note on his map and staked out his claim by carefully marking the boundaries with his pick. He dug up his hidden treasure, carefully stored it deep down in his backpack and headed back to Magerdam.

The sign outside the small building read: DIAMANT KOOPER.

Jamie walked into the office, a small, airless room, and he was filled with a sudden sense of trepidation. He had heard dozens of stories of prospectors who had found diamonds that had turned out to be worthless stones. *What if I'm wrong? What if –?*

The assayer was seated at a cluttered desk in the tiny office. 'Somethin' I can do for you?'

Jamie took a deep breath. 'Yes, sir. I would like to have these valued, please.'

Under the watchful eye of the assayer, Jamie started laying the stones on his desk. When he was finished, there was a total of twenty-seven and the assayer was gazing at them in astonishment.

'Where – where did you find these?'

'I'll tell you after you tell me whether they're diamonds.'

The assayer picked up the largest stone and examined it with a jeweller's loupe. 'My God!' he said. 'This is the biggest diamond I've ever seen!' And Jamie realized he had been holding his breath. He could have yelled aloud with joy. 'Where –' the man begged, 'where did these come from?'

'Meet me in the canteen in fifteen minutes,' Jamie grinned, 'and I'll tell you.'

Jamie gathered up the diamonds, put them in his pockets and strode out. He headed for the registration office two doors down the street. 'I want to register a claim,' he said. 'In the names of Salomon van der Merwe and Jamie McGregor.'

He had walked through that door a penniless farm boy and walked out a multimillionaire.

The assayer was in the canteen waiting when Jamie McGregor entered. He had obviously spread the news, because when Jamie walked in there was a sudden, respectful hush. There was a single unspoken question on everyone's mind. Jamie walked up to the bar and said to the bartender, 'I'm here to wet my find.' He turned and faced the crowd. 'Paardspan.'

Alice Jardine was having a cup of tea when Jamie walked into the kitchen. Her face lighted up when she saw him. 'Jamie! Oh, thank God you're back safely!' She took in his dishevelled appearance and flushed face. 'It didn't go well, did it? Never you mind. Have a nice cup of tea with me, dear, and you'll feel better.'

Without a word. Jamie reached into his pocket and pulled out a large diamond. He placed it in Mrs Jardine's hand.

'I've kept my promise,' Jamie said.

She stared at the stone for a long time, and her blue eyes became moist. 'No, Jamie. No.' Her voice was very soft. 'I don't want it. Don't you see, child? It would spoil everything . . .'

When Jamie McGregor returned to Klipdrift, he did it in style. He traded one of his smaller diamonds for a horse and carriage and made a careful note of what he had spent, so that his partner would not be cheated. The trip back to Klipdrift was easy and comfortable, and when Jamie thought of the hell he had gone through on this same journey, he was filled with a sense of wonder. *That's the difference between the rich and the poor*, he thought. *The poor walk; the rich ride in carriages.*

He gave the horse a small flick of the whip and rode on contentedly through the darkening veld.

THREE

Klipdrift had not changed, but Jamie McGregor had. People stared as he rode into town and stopped in front of Van der Merwe's general store. It was not just the expensive horse and carriage that drew the attention of the passers-by; it was the air of jubilation about the young man. They had seen it before in other prospectors who had struck it rich, and it always filled them with a renewed sense of hope for themselves. They stood back and watched as Jamie jumped out of the carriage.

The same large black man was there. Jamie grinned at him. 'Hello! I'm back.'

Banda tied the reins to a hitching post without comment and went inside the store. Jamie followed him.

Salomon van der Merwe was waiting on a customer. The little Dutchman looked up and smiled, and Jamie knew that somehow Van der Merwe had already heard the news. No one could explain it, but news of a diamond strike flashed across the continent with the speed of light.

When Van der Merwe had finished with the customer, he nodded his head towards the back of the store. 'Come, Mr McGregor.'

Jamie followed him. Van der Merwe's daughter was at the stove, preparing lunch. 'Hello, Margaret.'

She flushed and looked away.

'Well! I hear there is good news.' Van der Merwe beamed. He seated himself at the table and pushed the plate and silverware away, clearing a place in front of him.

'That's right, sir.' Proudly, Jamie took a large leather pouch from his jacket pocket and poured the diamonds on the kitchen table. Van der Merwe stared at them, hypnotized, then picked them up slowly, one by one, savoring each one, saving the largest until last. Then he scooped up the diamonds, put them in a chamois bag and put the bag in a large iron safe in the corner and locked it.

When he spoke, there was a note of deep satisfaction in his voice. 'You've done well, Mr McGregor. Very well, indeed.'

'Thank you, sir. This is only the beginning. There are hundreds more there. I don't even dare think about how much they're worth.'

'And you've staked out the claim properly?'

'Yes, sir.' Jamie reached in his pocket and pulled out the registration slip. 'It's registered in both our names.'

Van der Merwe studied the slip, then put it in his pocket. 'You deserve a bonus. Wait here.' He started towards the doorway that led into the shop. 'Come along, Margaret.'

She followed him meekly, and Jamie thought, *She's like a frightened kitten.*

A few minutes later, Van der Merwe returned, alone. 'Here we are.' He opened a purse and carefully counted out fifty pounds.

Jamie looked at him, puzzled. 'What's this for, sir?'

'For you, son. All of it.'

'I – I don't understand.'

'You've been gone twenty-four weeks. At two pounds a week, that's forty-eight pounds, and I'm giving you an extra two pounds as a bonus.'

Jamie laughed. 'I don't need a bonus. I have my share of the diamonds.'

'Your share of the diamonds?'

'Why, yes, sir. My fifty percent. We're partners.'

Van der Merwe was staring at him. 'Partners? Where did you get that idea?'

'Where did I –?' Jamie looked at the Dutchman in bewilderment. 'We have a contract.'

'That is correct. Have you read it?'

'Well, no, sir. It's in Afrikaans, but you said we were fifty-fifty partners.'

The older man shook his head. 'You misunderstood me, Mr McGregor, I don't need any partners. You were working for me. I outfitted you and sent you to find diamonds for me.'

Jamie could feel a slow rage boiling up within him. 'You gave me nothing. I paid you a hundred and twenty pounds for that equipment.'

The old man shrugged. 'I won't waste my valuable time quibbling. Tell you what I'll do. I'll give you an extra five pounds, and we'll call the whole thing quits. I think that's very generous.'

Jamie exploded in a fury. 'We'll nae call the whole thing quits!' In his anger his Scottish burr came back. 'I'm entitled to half that claim. And I'll get it. I registered it in *both* our names.'

Van der Merwe smiled thinly. 'Then you tried to cheat me. I could have you arrested for that.' He shoved the money into Jamie's hand. 'Now take your wages and get out.'

'I'll fight you!'

'Do you have money for a lawyer? I own them all in these parts, boy.'

This isn't happening to me, Jamie thought. *It's a nightmare.* The agony he had gone through, the weeks and months of the burning desert, the punishing physical labour from sunrise to sunset – it all came flooding back. He had nearly died, and now this man was trying to cheat him out of what was his.

He looked Van der Merwe in the eye. 'I'll not let you get away with this. I'm not going to leave Klipdrift. I'll tell everybody here what you've done. I'm going to get my share of those diamonds.'

Van der Merwe started to turn away from the fury in the pale grey eyes. 'You'd better find a doctor, boy,' he muttered. 'I think the sun has addled your wits.'

In a second, Jamie was towering over Van der Merwe. He pulled the thin figure into the air and held him up to eye level. 'I'm going to make you sorry you ever laid eyes on me.' He dropped Van der Merwe to his feet, flung the money on the table and stormed out.

When Jamie McGregor walked into the Sundowner Saloon, it was almost deserted, for most of the prospectors were on their way to Paardspan. Jamie was filled with anger and despair. *It's incredible*, he thought. *One minute I'm as rich as Croesus, and the next minute I'm dead broke. Van der Merwe is a thief, and I'm going to find a way to punish him. But how?* Van der Merwe was right. Jamie could not even afford a lawyer to fight his case. He was a stranger there, and Van der Merwe was a respected member of the community. The only weapon Jamie had was the truth. He would let everyone in South Africa know what Van der Merwe had done.

Smit, the bartender, greeted him. 'Welcome back. Everything's on the house, Mr McGregor. What would you like?'

'A whiskey.'

Smit poured a double and set it in front of Jamie. Jamie downed it in one gulp. He was not used to drinking, and the hard liquor scorched his throat and stomach.

'Another, please.'

'Comin' up. I've always said the Scots could drink anybody under the table.'

The second drink went down easier. Jamie remembered that it was the bartender who had told a digger to go to Van der Merwe for help. 'Did you know Old Man Van der Merwe is a crook? He's trying to cheat me out of my diamonds.'

Smit was sympathetic. 'What? That's terrible. I'm sorry to hear that.'

'He'll nae get away with it.' Jamie's voice was slurred. 'Half those diamonds are mine. He's a thief, and I'm gonna see that everybody knows it.'

'Careful. Van der Merwe's an important man in this town,' the bartender warned. 'If you're goin' up against him, you'll need help. In fact, I know just the person. He hates Van der Merwe as much as you do.' He looked around to make sure no one could overhear him. 'There's an old barn at the end of the street. I'll arrange everything. Be there at ten o'clock tonight.'

'Thanks,' Jamie said gratefully. 'I won't forget you.'

'Ten o'clock. The old barn.'

The barn was a hastily thrown-together structure built of corrugated tin, off the main street at the edge of town. At ten o'clock Jamie arrived there. It was dark, and he felt his way carefully. He could see no one around. He stepped inside. 'Hello . . .'

There was no reply. Jamie went slowly forwards. He could make out the dim shapes of horses moving restlessly in their stalls. Then he heard a sound behind him, and as he started to turn, an iron bar crashed across his shoulder blades, knocking him to the ground. A club thudded against his head, and a giant hand picked him up and held him while fists and boots smashed into his body. The beating seemed to last forever. When the pain became too much to bear and he lost consciousness, cold water was thrown in his face. His eyes fluttered open. He thought he caught a glimpse of Van der Merwe's servant, Banda, and the beating began anew. Jamie could feel his ribs breaking. Something smashed into his leg, and he heard the crunch of bone.

That was when he lost consciousness again.

His body was on fire. Someone was scraping his face with sandpaper, and he vainly tried to lift a hand to protest. He made an effort to open his eyes, but they were swollen shut. Jamie lay there, every fibre of his being screaming with pain, as he tried to remember where he was. He shifted, and the scraping began again. He put out his hand blindly and felt sand. His raw face was lying in hot sand. Slowly, every move an agony, he managed to draw himself up on his knees. He tried to see through his swollen eyes, but he could make out only hazy images. He was somewhere in the middle of the trackless Karroo, naked. It was early morning, but he could feel the sun starting to burn through his body. He felt around blindly for food or a billy can of water. There was nothing. They had left him there for dead. *Salomon van der Merwe. And, of course, Smit, the bartender. Jamie had threatened Van der Merwe, and Van der Merwe had punished him as easily as one punished a small child. But he'll find out I'm no child*, Jamie promised himself. *Not anymore. I'm an avenger*. They'll pay. They will pay. The hatred that coursed through Jamie gave him the strength to sit up. It was a torture for him to breathe. How many ribs had they broken? *I must be careful so they don't puncture my lungs*. Jamie tried to stand up, but fell down with a scream. His right leg was broken and lay at an unnatural angle. He was unable to walk.

But he could crawl.

Jamie McGregor had no idea where he was. They would have taken him to some place off the beaten track, where his body would not be found except by the desert scavengers, the hyenas and secretary birds and vultures. The desert was a vast charnel house. He had seen the bones of men's bodies that had been scavenged, and there had not been a scrap of meat left on the skeleton. Even as Jamie was thinking about it, he heard the rustle of wings above him and the shrill hiss of the vultures. He felt a flood of terror. He was blind. He could not see them. But he could smell them.

He began to crawl.

* * *

He made himself concentrate on the pain. His body was aflame with it, and each small movement brought exquisite rivers of agony. If he moved in a certain way, his broken leg would send out stabbing pains. If he shifted his position slightly to favour his leg, he could feel his ribs grinding against each other. He could not stand the torture of lying still; he could not stand the agony of moving.

He kept crawling.

He could hear them circling above, waiting for him with an ancient, timeless patience. His mind started to wander. He was in the cool kirk at Aberdeen, neatly dressed in his Sunday suit, seated between his two brothers. His sister, Mary, and Annie Cord were wearing beautiful white summer dresses, and Annie Cord was looking at him and smiling. Jamie started to get up and go to her, and his brothers held him back and began to pinch him. The pinches became excruciating shafts of pain, and he was crawling through the desert again, naked, his body broken. The cries of the vultures were louder now, impatient.

Jamie tried to force his eyes open, to see how close they were. He could see nothing except vague, shimmering objects that his terrified imagination turned into feral hyenas and jackals. The wind became their hot, fetid breath caressing his face.

He kept crawling, for he knew that the moment he stopped they would be upon him. He was burning with fever and pain and his body was flayed by the hot sand. And still, he could not give up, not as long as Van der Merwe was unpunished – not as long as Van der Merwe was alive.

He lost all awareness of time. He guessed that he had travelled a mile. In truth, he had moved less than ten yards, crawling in a circle. He could not see where he had been or where he was going. He focused his mind on only one thing: Salomon van der Merwe.

He slipped into unconsciousness and was awakened by a shrieking agony beyond bearing. Someone was stabbing at his leg, and it took Jamie a second to remember where he was and what was happening. He pulled one swollen eye open. An enormous hooded black vulture was attacking his leg, savagely tearing at his flesh, eating him alive with its sharp beak. Jamie saw its beady eyes and the dirty ruff around its neck. He smelled the foul odour of the bird as it sat on his body. Jamie tried to scream, but no sound came out. Frantically he jerked himself forwards, and felt the warm flow of blood pouring from his leg. He could see the shadows of the giant birds all around him, moving in for the kill. He knew that the next time he lost consciousness would be the last time. The instant he stopped, the carrion birds would be at his flesh again. He kept crawling. His mind began to wander into delirium. He heard the loud flapping wings of the birds as they moved closer, forming a circle around him. He was too weak now to fight them off; he had no strength left to resist. He stopped moving and lay still on the burning sand.

The giant birds closed in for their feast.

FOUR

Saturday was market day in Cape Town and the streets were crowded with shoppers looking for bargains, meeting friends and lovers. Boers and Frenchmen, soldiers in colourful uniforms and English ladies in flounced skirts and ruffled blouses mingled in front of the bazaars set up in the town squares at Braameonstein and Park Town and Burgersdorp. Everything was for sale: furniture, horses and carriages and fresh fruit. One could purchase dresses and chessboards, or meat or books in a dozen different languages. On Saturdays, Cape Town was a noisy, bustling fair.

Banda walked along slowly through the crowd, careful not to make eye contact with the whites. It was too dangerous. The streets were filled with blacks, Indians and coloureds, but the white minority ruled. Banda hated them. This was his land, and the whites were the *uitlanders*. There were many tribes in southern Africa: the Basutos, Zulus, Bechuanas, the Matabele – all of them Bantu. The very word *bantu* came from *abantu – the people*. But the Barolongs – Banda's tribe – were the aristocracy. Banda remembered the tales his grandmother told him of the great black kingdom that had once ruled South Africa. *Their* kingdom, *their* country. And now they were enslaved by a handful of white jackals. The whites had pushed them into smaller and smaller territories, until their freedom had been eroded. Now, the only way a black could exist was by *slim*, subservient on the surface, but cunning and clever beneath.

Banda did not know how old he was, for natives had no birth certificates. Their ages were measured by tribal lore: wars and battles, and births and deaths of great chiefs, comets and blizzards and earthquakes, Adam Kok's trek, the death of Chaka and the cattle-killing revolution. But the number of his years made no difference. Banda knew he was the son of a chief, and that he was destined to do something for his people. Once again, the Bantus would rise and rule because of him. The thought of his mission made him walk taller and straighter for a moment, until he felt the eyes of a white man upon him.

Banda hurried east towards the outskirts of town, the district allotted to the blacks. The large homes and attractive shops gradually gave way to tin shacks and lean-tos and huts. He moved down a dirt street, looking over his shoulder to make certain he was not followed. He reached a wooden shack, took one last look around, rapped twice on the door and entered. A thin black woman was seated in a chair in a corner of the room sewing on a dress. Banda nodded to her and then continued on into the bedroom in back.

He looked down at the figure lying on the cot.

Six weeks earlier Jamie McGregor had regained consciousness and found himself on a cot in a strange house. Memory came flooding back. He was in the Karroo again, his body broken, helpless. The vultures . . .

Then Banda had walked into the tiny bedroom, and Jamie knew he had come to kill him. Van der Merwe had somehow learned Jamie was still alive and had sent his servant to finish him off.

'Why didn't your master come himself?' Jamie croaked.

'I have no master.'

'Van der Merwe. He didn't send you?'

'No. He would kill us both if he knew.'

None of this made any sense. 'Where am I? I want to know where I am.'

'Cape Town.'

'That's impossible. How did I get here?'

'I brought you.'

Jamie stared into the black eyes for a long moment before he spoke. 'Why?'

'I need you. I want vengeance.'

'What do you –?'

Banda moved closer. 'Not for me. I do not care about me. Van der Merwe raped my sister. She died giving birth to his baby. My sister was eleven years old.'

Jamie lay back, stunned. 'My God!'

'Since the day she died I have been looking for a white man to help me. I found him that night in the barn where I helped beat you up, Mr McGregor. We dumped you in the Karroo. I was ordered to kill you. I told the others you were dead, and I returned to get you as soon as I could. I was almost too late.'

Jamie could not repress a shudder. He could feel again the foul-smelling carrion birds digging into his flesh.

'The birds were already starting to feast. I carried you to the wagon and hid you at the house of my people. One of our doctors taped your ribs and set your leg and tended to your wounds.'

'And after that?'

'A wagonful of my relatives was leaving for Cape Town. We took you with us. You were out of your head most of the time. Each time you fell asleep, I was afraid you were not going to wake up again.'

Jamie looked into the eyes of the man who had almost murdered him. He had to think. He did not trust this man – and yet he had saved his life. Banda wanted to get at Van der Merwe through him. *That can work both ways*, Jamie decided. More than anything in the world, Jamie wanted to make Van der Merwe pay for what he had done to him.

'All right,' Jamie told Banda. 'I'll find a way to pay Van der Merwe back for both of us.'

For the first time, a thin smile appeared on Banda's face. 'Is he going to die?'

'No,' Jamie told him. 'He's going to live.'

Jamie got out of bed that afternoon for the first time, dizzy and weak. His leg still had not completely healed, and he walked with a slight limp. Banda tried to assist him.

'Let go of me. I can make it on my own.'

Banda watched as Jamie carefully moved across the room.

'I'd like a mirror,' Jamie said. *I must look terrible*, he thought. *How long has it been since I've had a shave?*

Banda returned with a hand mirror, and Jamie held it up to his face. He was looking at a total stranger. His hair had turned snow-white. He had a full, unkempt white beard. His nose had been broken and a ridge of bone pushed it to one side. His face had aged twenty years. There were deep ridges along his sunken cheeks and a livid scar across his chin. But the biggest change was in his eyes. They were eyes that had seen too much pain, felt too much, hated too much. He slowly put down the mirror.

'I'm going out for a walk,' Jamie said.

'Sorry, Mr McGregor. That's not possible.'

'Why not?'

'White men do not come to this part of town, just as blacks never go into the white places. My neighbours do not know you are here. We brought you in at night.'

'How do I leave?'

'I will move you out tonight.'

For the first time, Jamie realized how much Banda had risked for him. Embarrassed, Jamie said, 'I have no money, I need a job.'

'I took a job at the shipyard. They are always looking for men.' He took some money from his pocket. 'Here.'

Jamie took the money. 'I'll pay it back.'

'You will pay my sister back,' Banda told him.

It was midnight when Banda led Jamie out of the shack. Jamie looked around. He was in the middle of a shantytown, a jungle of rusty, corrugated iron shacks and lean-tos, made from rotting planks and torn sacking. The ground, muddy from a recent rain, gave off a rank odour. Jamie wondered how people as proud as Banda could bear spending their lives in a place such as this. 'Isn't there some –?'

'Don't talk, please,' Banda whispered. 'My neighbours are inquisitive.' He led Jamie outside the compound and pointed. 'The centre of town is in that direction. I will see you at the shipyard.'

Jamie checked into the same boardinghouse where he had stayed on his arrival from England. Mrs Venster was behind the desk.

'I'd like a room,' Jamie said.

'Certainly, sir.' She smiled, revealing her gold tooth. 'I'm Mrs Venster.'

'I know.'

'Now how would you know a thing like that?' she asked coyly. 'Have your men friends been tellin' tales out of school?'

'Mrs Venster, don't you remember me? I stayed here last year.'

She took a close look at his scarred face, his broken nose and his white beard, and there was not the slightest sign of recognition. 'I never forget a face, dearie. And I've never seen yours before. But that don't mean we're not going to be good friends, does it? My friends call me "Dee-Dee". What's your name, love?'

And Jamie heard himself saying, 'Travis. Ian Travis.'

The following morning Jamie went to see about work at the shipyard.

The busy foreman said, 'We need strong backs. The problem is you might be a bit old for this kind of work.'

'I'm only nineteen –' Jamie started to say and stopped himself. He remembered that face in the mirror. 'Try me,' he said.

He went to work as a stevedore at nine shillings a day, loading and unloading the ships that came into the harbour. He learned that Banda and the other black stevedores received six shillings a day.

At the first opportunity, Jamie pulled Banda aside and said, 'We have to talk.'

'Not here, Mr McGregor. There's an abandoned

warehouse at the end of the docks. I'll meet you there when the shift is over.'

Banda was waiting when Jamie arrived at the deserted warehouse.

'Tell me about Salomon van der Merwe,' Jamie said.

'What to you want to know?'

'Everything.'

Banda spat. 'He came to South Africa from Holland. From stories I heard, his wife was ugly, but wealthy. She died of some sickness and Van der Merwe took her money and went up to Klipdrift and opened his general store. He got rich cheating diggers.'

'The way he cheated me?'

'That's only one of his ways. Diggers who strike it lucky go to him for money to help them work their claim, and before they know it Van der Merwe owns them.'

'Hasn't anyone ever tried to fight back?'

'How can they? The town clerk's on his payroll. The law says that if forty-five days go by without working a claim, it's open. The town clerk tips off Van der Merwe and he grabs it. There's another trick he uses. Claims have to be staked out at each boundary line with pegs pointing straight up in the air. If the pegs fall down, a jumper can claim the property. Well, when Van der Merwe sees a claim he likes, he sends someone around at night, and in the morning the stakes are on the ground.'

'Jesus!'

'He's made a deal with the bartender, Smit. Smit sends likely-looking prospectors to Van der Merwe, and they sign partnership contracts and if they find diamonds, Van der Merwe takes everything for himself. If they become troublesome, he's got a lot of men on his payroll who follow his orders.'

'I know about that,' Jamie said grimly. 'What else?'

'He's a religious fanatic. He's always praying for the souls of sinners.'

'What about his daughter?' She had to be involved in this.

'Miss Margaret? She's frightened to death of her father. If she even looked at a man, Van der Merwe would kill them both.'

Jamie turned his back and walked over to the door, where he stood looking out at the harbour. He had a lot to think about. 'We'll talk again tomorrow.'

It was in Cape Town that Jamie became aware of the enormous schism between the blacks and whites. The blacks had no rights except the few they were given by those in power. They were herded into conclaves that were ghettos and were allowed to leave only to work for the white man.

'How do you stand it?' Jamie asked Banda one day.

'The hungry lion hides its claws. We will change all this someday. The white man accepts the black man because his muscles are needed, but he must also learn to accept his brain. The more he drives us into a corner, the more he fears us because he knows that one day there may be discrimination and humiliation in reverse. He cannot bear the thought of that. But we will survive because of *isiko*.'

'Who is *isiko*?'

Banda shook his head. 'Not a *who*. A *what*. It is difficult to explain, Mr McGregor. *Isiko* is our roots. It is the feeling of belonging to a nation that has given its name to the Great Zambezi River. Generations ago my ancestors entered the waters of the Zambezi naked, driving their herds before them. Their weakest members were lost, the prey of the swirling waters or hungry crocodiles, but the survivors emerged from the waters stronger and more virile. When a Bantu dies, *isiko* demands that the members of his family retire to the forest so that the rest of the community will not have to share their distress. *Isiko* is the scorn felt for a slave who cringes, the belief that a man can look anyone in the face, that he is worth no more and no less than any other man. Have you heard of John Tengo Jabavu?' He pronounced the name with reverence.

'No.'

'You will, Mr McGregor,' Banda promised. 'You will.' And Banda changed the subject.

Jamie began to feel a growing admiration for Banda. In the beginning there was a wariness between the two men. Jamie had to learn to trust a man who had almost killed him. And Banda had to learn to trust an age-old enemy – a white man. Unlike most of the blacks Jamie had met, Banda was educated.

'Where did you go to school?' Jamie asked.

'Nowhere. I've worked since I was a small boy. My grandmother educated me. She worked for a Boer school-teacher. She learned to read and write so she could teach me to read and write. I owe her everything.'

It was on a late Saturday afternoon after work that Jamie first heard of the Namib Desert in Great Namaqualand. He and Banda were in the deserted warehouse on the docks, sharing an impala stew Banda's mother had cooked. It was good – a little gamey for Jamie's taste, but his bowl was soon empty, and he lay back on some old sacks to question Banda.

'When did you first meet Van der Merwe?'

'When I was working at the diamond beach on the Namib Desert. He owns the beach with two partners. He had just stolen his share from some poor prospector, and he was down there visiting it.'

'If Van der Merwe is so rich, why does he still work at his store?'

'The store is his bait. That's how he gets new prospectors to come to him. And he grows richer.'

Jamie thought of how easily he himself had been

cheated. How trusting that naive young boy had been! He could see Margaret's oval-shaped face as she said, *My father might be the one to help you.* He had thought she was a child until he had noticed her breasts and – Jamie suddenly jumped to his feet, a smile on his face, and the up-turning of his lips made the livid scar across his chin ripple.

'Tell me how you happened to go to work for Van der Merwe.'

'On the day he came to the beach with his daughter – she was about eleven then – I suppose she got bored sitting around and she went into the water and the tide grabbed her. I jumped in and pulled her out. I was a young boy, but I thought Van der Merwe was going to kill me.'

Jamie stared at him. 'Why?'

'Because I had my arms around her. Not because I was black, but because I was a *male*. He can't stand the thought of any man touching his daughter. Someone finally calmed him down and reminded him that I had saved her life. He brought me back to Klipdrift as his servant.' Banda hesitated a moment, then continued. 'Two months later, my sister came to visit me.' His voice was very quiet. 'She was the same age as Van der Merwe's daughter.'

There was nothing Jamie could say.

Finally Banda broke the silence. 'I should have stayed in the Namib Desert. That was an easy job. We'd crawl along the beach picking up diamonds and putting them in little jam tins.'

'Wait a minute. Are you saying that the diamonds are just lying there, on top of the sand?'

'That's what I'm saying, Mr McGregor. But forget what you're thinking. Nobody can get near that field. It's on the ocean, and the waves are up to thirty feet high. They don't even bother guarding the shore. A lot of people have tried to sneak in by sea. They've all been killed by the waves or the reefs.'

'There must be some other way to get in.'

'No. The Namib Desert runs right down to the ocean's shore.'

'What about the entrance to the diamond field?'

'There's a guard tower and a barbed-wire fence. Inside the fence are guards with guns and dogs that'll tear a man to pieces. And they have a new kind of explosive called a land mine. They're buried all over the field. If you don't have a map of the land mines, you'll get blown to bits.'

'How large is the diamond field?'

'It runs for about thirty-five miles.'

Thirty-five miles of diamonds just lying on the sand . . . 'My God!'

'You aren't the first one to get excited about the diamond fields at the Namib, and you won't be the last. I've picked up what was left of people who tried to come in by boat and got torn apart by the reefs. I've seen what those land mines do if a man takes one wrong step, and I've watched those dogs rip out a man's throat. Forget it, Mr

McGregor. I've been there. There's no way in and there's no way out – not alive, that is.'

Jamie was unable to sleep that night. He kept visualizing thirty-five miles of sand sprinkled with enormous diamonds belonging to Van der Merwe. He thought of the sea and the jagged reefs, the dogs hungry to kill, the guards and the land mines. He was not afraid of the danger; he was not afraid of dying. He was only afraid of dying before he repaid Salomon van der Merwe.

On the following Monday Jamie went into a cartographer's shop and bought a map of Great Namaqualand. There was the beach, off the South Atlantic Ocean between Lüderitz to the north and the Orange River Estuary to the south. The area was marked in red: SPERRGEBIET – Forbidden.

Jamie examined every detail of the area on the map, going over it again and again. There were three thousand miles of ocean flowing from South America to South Africa, with nothing to impede the waves, so that their full fury was spent on the deadly reefs of the South Atlantic shore. Forty miles south, down the coastline, was an open beach. *That must be where the poor bastards launched their boats to sail into the forbidden area*, Jamie decided. Looking at the map, he could understand why the shore was not guarded. The reefs would make a landing impossible.

Jamie turned his attention to the land entrance

to the diamond field. According to Banda, the area was fenced in with barbed wire and patrolled twenty-four hours a day by armed guards. At the entrance itself was a manned watch-tower. And even if one did somehow manage to slip past the watchtower into the diamond area, there would be the land mines and guard dogs.

The following day when Jamie met Banda, he asked, 'You said there was a land-mine map of the field?'

'In the Namib Desert? The supervisors have the maps, and they lead the diggers to work. Everybody walks in a single file so no one gets blown up.' His eyes filled with a memory. 'One day my uncle was walking in front of me and he stumbled on a rock and fell on top of a land mine. There wasn't enough left of him to take home to his family.'

Jamie shuddered.

'And then there's the sea *mis*, Mr McGregor. You've never seen a *mis* until you've been in one in the Namib. It rolls in from the ocean and blows all the way across the desert to the mountains and it blots out everything. If you're caught in one of them, you don't dare move. The land-mine maps are not good then because you can't see where you're going. Everybody just sits quietly until the *mis* lifts.'

'How long do they last?'

Banda shrugged. 'Sometimes a few hours, sometimes a few days.'

'Banda, have you ever *seen* a map of those land mines?'

'They're closely guarded.' A worried look crossed his face. 'I'm telling you again, no one can get away with what you're thinking. Once in a while workers will try to smuggle out a diamond. There is a special tree for hanging them. It's a lesson to everybody not to try to steal from the company.'

The whole thing looked impossible. Even if he could manage to get into Van der Merwe's diamond field, there was no way out. Banda was right. He would have to forget about it.

The next day he asked Banda, 'How does Van der Merwe keep the workers from stealing diamonds when they come off their shifts?'

'They're searched. They strip them down mother-naked and then they look up and down every hole they've got. I've seen workers cut gashes in their legs and try to smuggle diamonds out in them. Some drill out their back teeth and stick diamonds up there. They've tried every trick you can think of.' He looked at Jamie and said, 'If you want to live, you'll get that diamond field off your mind.'

Jamie tried. But the idea kept coming back to him, taunting him. Van der Merwe's diamonds just lying on the sand waiting. *Waiting for him*.

The solution came to Jamie that night. He could hardly contain his impatience until he saw Banda.

Without preamble, Jamie said, 'Tell me about the boats that have tried to land on the beach.'

'What about them?'

'What kind of boats were they?'

'Every kind you can think of. A schooner. A tugboat. A big motorboat. Sailboat. Four men even tried it in a rowboat. While I worked the field, there were half a dozen tries. The reefs just chewed the boats to pieces. Everybody drowned.'

Jamie took a deep breath. 'Did anyone ever try to get in by raft?'

Banda was staring at him. *'Raft?'*

'Yes.' Jamie's excitement was growing. 'Think about it. No one ever made it to the shore because the bottoms of their boats were torn out by the reefs. But a *raft* will glide right over those reefs and onto the shore. And it can get out the same way.'

Banda looked at him for a long time. When he spoke, there was a different note in his voice. 'You know, Mr McGregor, you might just have an idea there . . .'

It started as a game, a possible solution to an unsolvable puzzle. But the more Jamie and Banda discussed it, the more excited they became. What had started as idle conversation began to take concrete shape as a plan of action. Because the diamonds were lying on top of the sand, no equipment would be required. They could build their raft, with a sail, on the free beach forty miles south of the *Sperrgebiet* and sail it in at night, unobserved. There were no land mines along the unguarded shore, and the guards and patrols only operated inland. The two men could roam the beach freely, gathering up all the diamonds they could carry.

'We can be on our way out before dawn,' Jamie said, 'with our pockets full of Van der Merwe's diamonds.'

'How do we get out?'

'The same way we got in. We'll paddle the raft over the reefs to the open sea, put up the sail and we're home free.'

Under Jamie's persuasive arguments, Banda's doubts began to melt. He tried to poke holes in the plan and every time he came up with an objection, Jamie answered it. The plan *could* work. The beautiful part of it was its simplicity, and the fact that it would require no money. Only a great deal of nerve.

'All we need is a big bag to put the diamonds in,' Jamie said. His enthusiasm was infectious.

Banda grinned. 'Let's make that *two* big bags.'

The following week they quit their jobs and boarded a bullock wagon to Port Nolloth, the coastal village forty miles south of the forbidden area where they were headed.

At Port Nolloth, they disembarked and looked around. The village was small and primitive, with shanties and tin huts and a few stores, and a pristine white beach that seemed to stretch on forever. There were no reefs here, and the waves lapped gently at the shore. It was a perfect place to launch their raft.

There was no hotel, but the little market rented a room in back to Jamie. Banda found himself a bed in the black quarter of the village.

'We have to find a place to build our raft in secret,' Jamie told Banda. 'We don't want anyone reporting us to the authorities.'

That afternoon they came across an old, abandoned warehouse.

'This will be perfect,' Jamie decided. 'Let's get to work on the raft.'

'Not yet,' Banda told him. 'We'll wait. Buy a bottle of whiskey.'

'What for?'

'You'll see.'

The following morning, Jamie was visited by the district constable, a florid heavy-set man with a large nose covered with the telltale broken veins of a tippler.

'Mornin',' he greeted Jamie. 'I heard we had a visitor. Thought I'd stop by and say hello. I'm Constable Mundy.'

'Ian Travis,' Jamie replied.

'Headin' north, Mr Travis?'

'South. My servant and I are on our way to Cape Town.'

'Ah. I was in Cape Town once. Too bloody big, too bloody noisy.'

'I agree. Can I offer you a drink, Constable?'

'I never drink on duty.' Constable Mundy paused, making a decision. 'However, just this once, I might make an exception, I suppose.'

'Fine.' Jamie brought out the bottle of whiskey, wondering how Banda could have known. He poured out two fingers into a dirty tooth glass and handed it to the constable.

'Thank you, Mr Travis. Where's yours?'

'I can't drink,' Jamie said ruefully. 'Malaria. That's why I'm going to Cape Town. To get medical attention. I'm stopping off here a few days to rest. Travelling's very hard on me.'

Constable Munda was studying him. 'You look pretty healthy.'

'You should see me when the chills start.'

The constable's glass was empty. Jamie filled it.

'Thank you. Don't mind if I do.' He finished the second drink in one swallow and stood up. 'I'd best be gettin' along. You said you and your man will be movin' on in a day or two?'

'As soon as I'm feeling stronger.'

'I'll come back and check on you Friday,' Constable Mundy said.

That night, Jamie and Banda went to work on the raft in the deserted warehouse.

'Banda, have you ever built a raft?'

'Well, to tell you the truth, Mr McGregor, no.'

'Neither have I.' The two men stared at each other. 'How difficult can it be?'

They stole four empty, fifty-gallon wooden oil barrels from behind the market and carried them to the warehouse. When they had them assembled, they spaced them out in a square. Next they gathered four empty crates and placed one over each oil barrel.

Banda looked dubious. 'It doesn't look like a raft to me.'

'We're not finished yet,' Jamie assured him.

There was no planking available so they covered the top layer with whatever was at hand: branches from the stinkwood tree, limbs from the Cape beech, large leaves from the marula. They lashed everything down with thick hemp rope, tying each knot with careful precision.

When they were finished, Banda looked it over. 'It still doesn't look like a raft.'

'It will look better when we get the sail up,' Jamie promised.

They made a mast from a fallen yellowwood tree, and picked up two flat branches for paddles.

'Now all we need is a sail. We need it fast. I'd like to get out of here tonight. Constable Mundy's coming back tomorrow.'

It was Banda who found the sail. He came back late that evening with an enormous piece of blue cloth. 'How's this, Mr McGregor?'

'Perfect. Where did you get it?'

Banda grinned. 'Don't ask. We're in enough trouble.'

They rigged up a square sail with a boom below and a yard on top, and at last it was ready.

'We'll take off at two in the morning when the village is asleep.' Jamie told Banda. 'Better get some rest until then.'

But neither man was able to sleep. Each was filled with the excitement of the adventure that lay ahead.

At two a.m. they met at the warehouse. There was an eagerness in both of them, and an unspoken fear. They were embarking on a journey that would either make them rich or bring them death. There was no middle way.

'It's time,' Jamie announced.

They stepped outside. Nothing was stirring. The night was still and peaceful, with a vast canopy of blue overhead. A sliver of moon appeared high in the sky. *Good*, Jamie thought. *There won't be much light to see us by*. Their timetable was complicated by the fact that they had to leave the village at night so no one would be aware of their departure, and arrive at the diamond beach the next night so they could slip into the field and be safely back at sea before dawn.

'The Benguela current should carry us to the diamond fields sometime in the late afternoon,' Jamie said. 'But we can't go in by daylight. We'll have to stay out of sight at sea until dark.'

Banda nodded. 'We can hide out at one of the little islands off the coast.'

'What islands?'

'There are dozens of them – Mercury, Ichabod, Plum Pudding . . .'

Jamie gave him a strange look. *Plum Pudding?*

'There's also a Roast Beef Island.'

Jamie took out his creased map and consulted it. 'This doesn't show any of those.'

'They're guano islands. The British harvest the bird droppings for fertilizer.'

'Anyone live on those islands?'

'Can't. The smell's too bad. In places the guano is a hundred feet thick. The government uses gangs of deserters and prisoners to pick it up. Some of them die on the island and they just leave the bodies there.'

'That's where we'll hide out,' Jamie decided.

Working quietly, the two men slid open the door to the warehouse and started to lift the raft. It was too heavy to move. They sweated and tugged, but in vain.

'Wait here,' Banda said.

He hurried out. Half an hour later, he returned with a large round log. 'We'll use this. I'll pick up one end and you slide the log underneath.'

Jamie marvelled at Banda's strength as the black man picked up one end of the raft. Quickly, Jamie shoved the log under it. Together they lifted the back end of the raft and it moved easily down the log. When the log had rolled out from under the back end, they repeated the procedure. It was strenuous work, and by the time they got to the beach they were both soaked in perspiration. The operation had taken much longer than Jamie had anticipated. It was almost dawn now. They had to be away before the villagers discovered them and reported what they were doing. Quickly, Jamie attached the sail and checked to make sure everything was working properly. He had a nagging feeling he was forgetting something. He suddenly realized what was bothering him and laughed aloud.

Banda watched him, puzzled. 'Something funny?'

'Before, when I went looking for diamonds I had a ton of equipment. Now all I'm carrying is a compass. It seems too easy.'

Banda said quietly, 'I don't think that's going to be our problem, Mr McGregor.'

'It's time you called me Jamie.'

Banda shook his head in wonder. 'You *really* come from a faraway country.' He grinned, showing even white teeth. 'What the hell – they can hang me only once.' He tasted the name on his lips, then said it aloud. 'Jamie.'

'Let's go get those diamonds.'

They pushed the raft off the sand into the shallow water and both men leaped aboard and started paddling. It took them a few minutes to get adjusted to the pitching and yawing of their strange craft. It was like riding a bobbing cork, but it was going to work. The raft was responding perfectly, moving north with the swift current. Jamie raised the sail and headed out to sea. By the time the villagers awoke, the raft was well over the horizon.

'We've done it!' Jamie said.

Banda shook his head. 'It's not over yet.' He trailed a hand in the cold Benguela current. 'It's just beginning.'

They sailed on, due north past Alexander Bay and the mouth of the Orange River, seeing no signs of life except for flocks of Cape cormorants heading home, and a flight of colourful greater flamingos. Although there were tins of beef and cold rice, and fruit and two canteens of water aboard, they were too nervous to eat. Jamie refused to let his imagination linger on the dangers that lay ahead, but Banda could not help it. He had been there. He was remembering the brutal guards with guns and the dogs and the terrible flesh-tearing land mines, and he wondered how he had ever allowed himself to be talked into this insane venture. He looked over at the Scotsman and thought, *He is the bigger fool. If I die, I die for my baby sister. What does he die for?*

At noon the sharks came. There were half a dozen of them, their fins cutting through the water as they sped towards the raft.

'Black-fin sharks,' Banda announced. 'They're man-eaters.'

Jamie watched the fins skimming closer to the raft. 'What do we do?'

Banda swallowed nervously. 'Truthfully, Jamie, this is my very first experience of this nature.'

The back of a shark nudged the raft, and it almost capsized. The two men grabbed the mast for support. Jamie picked up a paddle and shoved it at a shark, and an instant later the paddle was bitten in two. The sharks surrounded the raft now, swimming in lazy circles, their enormous bodies rubbing up close against the small craft. Each nudge tilted the raft at a precarious angle. It was going to capsize at any moment.

'We've got to get rid of them before they sink us.'

'Get rid of them with what?' Banda asked.

'Hand me a tin of beef.'

'You must be joking. A tin of beef won't satisfy them. They want *us*!'

There was another jolt, and the raft heeled over.

'The beef!' Jamie yelled. 'Get it!'

A second later Banda placed a tin in Jamie's hand. The raft lurched sickeningly.

'Open it halfway. Hurry!'

Banda pulled out his pocketknife and pried the top of the can half open. Jamie took it from him. He felt the sharp, broken edges of the metal with his finger.

'Hold tight!' Jamie warned.

He knelt down at the edge of the raft and waited. Almost immediately, a shark approached the raft, its hugh mouth wide open, revealing long rows of evil, grinning teeth. Jamie went for the eyes. With all his strength, he reached out with both hands and scraped the edge of the broken metal against the eye of the shark, ripping it open. The shark lifted its great body, and for an instant the raft stood on end. The water around them was suddenly stained red. There was a giant thrashing as the sharks moved in on the wounded member of the school. The raft was forgotten. Jamie and Banda watched the great sharks tearing at their helpless victim as the raft sailed further and further away until finally the sharks were out of sight.

Banda took a deep breath and said softly, 'One day I'm going to tell my grandchildren about this. Do you think they'll believe me?'

And they laughed until the tears streamed down their faces.

Late that afternoon, Jamie checked his pocket watch. 'We should be off the diamond beach around midnight. Sunrise is at six-fifteen. That means we'll have four hours to pick up the diamonds and two hours to get back to sea and out of sight. Will four hours be enough, Banda?'

'A hundred men couldn't live long enough to spend what you can pick up on that beach in four hours.' *I just hope we live long enough to pick them up* . . .

They sailed steadily north for the rest of that day, carried by the wind and the tide. Towards evening a small island loomed ahead of them. It looked to be no more than two hundred yards in circumference. As they approached the island, the acrid smell of ammonia grew strong, bringing tears to their eyes. Jamie could understand why no one lived here. The stench was overpowering. But it would make a perfect place for them to hide until nightfall. Jamie adjusted the sail, and the small raft bumped against the rocky shore of the low-lying island. Banda made the raft fast, and the two men stepped ashore. The entire island was covered with what appeared to be millions of birds; cormorants, pelicans, gannets, penguins and flamingos. The thick air was so noisome that it was impossible to breathe. They took half a dozen steps and were thigh deep in guano.

'Let's get back to the raft,' Jamie gasped.

Without a word, Banda followed him.

As they turned to retreat, a flock of pelicans took to the air, revealing an open space on the ground. Lying there were three men. There was no telling how long they had been dead. Their corpses had been perfectly preserved by the ammonia in the air, and their hair had turned a bright red.

A minute later Jamie and Banda were back on the raft, headed out to sea.

They lay off the coast, sail lowered, waiting.

'We'll stay out here until midnight. Then we go in.'

They sat together in silence, each in his own way preparing for whatever lay ahead. The sun was low on the western horizon, painting the dying sky with the wild colours of a mad artist. Then suddenly they were blanketed in darkness.

They waited for two more hours, and Jamie hoisted the sail. The raft began to move east towards the unseen shore. Overhead, clouds parted and a thin wash of moonlight paled down. The raft picked up speed. In the distance the two men could begin to see the faint smudge of the coast. The wind blew stronger, snapping at the sail, pushing the raft towards the shore at an ever-increasing speed. Soon, they could make out the outline of the land, a gigantic parapet of rock. Even from that distance it was possible to see and hear the enormous whitecaps that exploded like thunder over the reefs. It was a terrifying sight from afar, and Jamie wondered what it would be like up close.

He found himself whispering. 'You're sure the beach side isn't guarded?'

Banda did not answer. He pointed to the reefs ahead. Jamie knew what he meant. The reefs were more deadly than any trap man could devise. They were the guardians of the sea, and they never relaxed, never slept. They lay there, patiently waiting for their prey to come to them. *Well*, Jamie thought, *we're going to outsmart you. We're going to float over you.*

The raft had carried them that far. It would carry them the rest of the way. The shore was racing towards them now, and they began to feel the heavy swell of the giant combers. Banda was holding tightly to the mast.

'We're moving pretty fast.'

'Don't worry,' Jamie reassured him. 'When we get closer, I'll lower the sail. That will cut our speed. We'll slide over the reefs nice and easy.'

The momentum of the wind and the waves was picking up, hurtling the raft towards the deadly reefs. Jamie quickly estimated the remaining distance and decided the waves would carry them in to shore without the help of the sail. Hurriedly, he lowered it. Their momentum did not even slow. The raft was completely in the grip of the huge waves now, out of control, hurled forwards from one giant crest to the next. The raft was rocking so violently that the men had to cling to it with both hands. Jamie had expected the entrance to be difficult, but he was totally unprepared for the fury of the seething maelstrom they faced. The reefs loomed in front of them with startling clarity. They could see the waves rushing in against the jagged rocks and exploded into huge, angry geysers. The entire success of the plan depended on bringing the raft over the reefs intact so that they could use it for their escape. Without it, they were dead men.

They were bearing down on the reefs now, propelled by the terrifying power of the waves. The roar of the wind was deafening. The raft was suddenly lifted high in the air by an enormous wave and flung towards the rocks.

'Hold on, Banda!' Jamie shouted. 'We're going in!'

The giant breaker picked up the raft like a matchstick and started to carry it towards shore, over the reef. Both men were hanging on for their lives, fighting the violent bucking motion that threatened to sweep them into the water. Jamie glanced down and caught a glimpse of the razor-sharp reefs below them. In another moment they would be sailing over them, safe in the haven of the shore.

At that instant there was a sudden, tearing wrench as a reef caught one of the barrels underneath the raft and ripped it away. The raft gave a sharp lurch, and another barrel was torn away, and then another. The wind and the pounding waves and the hungry reef were playing with the raft like a toy, tossing it backwards and forwards, spinning it wildly in the air. Jamie and Banda felt the thin wood begin to split beneath their feet.

'Jump!' Jamie yelled.

He dived over the side of the raft, and a giant wave picked him up and shot him towards the beach at the speed of a catapult. He was caught in the grip of an element that was powerful beyond belief. He had no control over what was happening. He was a part of the wave. It was over him and under him and inside him. His body was twisting and turning and his lungs were bursting. Lights began to explode in his head. Jamie thought, *I'm drowning*. And his body was thrown up onto the sandy shore. Jamie lay there gasping, fighting for breath, filling his lungs with the cool, fresh sea air. His chest and legs were scraped raw from the sand, and his clothes were in shreds. Slowly, he sat up and looked around for Banda. He was crouching ten yards away, vomiting seawater. Jamie got to his feet and staggered over to him.

'You all right?'

Banda nodded. He took a deep, shuddering breath and looked up at Jamie. 'I can't swim.'

Jamie helped him to his feet. The two men turned to look at the reef. There was not a sign of their raft. It had been torn to pieces in the wild ocean. They had gotten into the diamond field.

There was no way to get out.

FIVE

Behind them was the raging ocean. Ahead was unbroken desert from the sea to the foothills of the distant, rugged, purple mountains of the Richterveld escarpment, a world of kloofs and canyons and twisted peaks, lit by the pale moon. At the foot of the mountains was the Hexenkessel Valley – 'the witch's cauldron' – a bleak wind trap. It was a primeval, desolate landscape that went back to the beginning of time itself. The only clue that man had ever set foot in this place was a crudely printed sign pounded into the sand. By the light of the moon, they read:

VERBODE GEBIED
SPERRGEBIET

Forbidden.

There was no escape towards the sea. The only direction left open to them was the Namib Desert.

'We'll have to try to cross it and take our chances,' Jamie said.

Banda shook his head. 'The guards will shoot us on sight or hang us. Even if we were lucky enough to slip by the guards and dogs, there's no way to get by the land mines. We're dead men.' There was no fear in him, only a resigned acceptance of his fate.

Jamie looked at Banda and felt a sense of deep regret. He had brought the black man into this, and not once had Banda complained. Even now, knowing there was no escape for them, he did not utter one word of reproach.

Jamie turned to look at the wall of angry waves smashing at the shore, and he thought it was a miracle that they had gotten as far as they had. It was two a.m., four hours before dawn and discovery, and they were both still in one piece. *I'll be damned if I'm ready to give up*, Jamie thought.

'Let's go to work, Banda.'

Banda blinked. 'Doing what?'

'We came here to get diamonds, didn't we? Let's get them.'

Banda stared at the wild-eyed man with his white hair plastered to his skull and his sopping trousers hanging in shreds around his legs. 'What are you talking about?'

'You said they're going to kill us on sight, right? Well, they might as well kill us rich as poor. A miracle got us in here. Maybe a miracle will get us out. And if we do get out, I damned well don't plan to leave empty-handed.'

'You're crazy,' Banda said softly.

'Or we wouldn't be here,' Jamie reminded him.

Banda shrugged. 'What the hell. I have nothing else to do until they find us.'

Jamie stripped off his tattered shirt, and Banda understood and did the same.

'Now. Where are all these big diamonds that you've been talking about?'

'They're everywhere,' Banda promised. And he added, 'Like the guards and the dogs.'

'We'll worry about them later. When do they come down to the beach?'

'When it gets light.'

Jamie thought for a moment. 'Is there a part of the beach where they *don't* come? Someplace we could hide?'

'There's no part of this beach they don't come to, and there's no place you could hide a fly.'

Jamie slapped Banda on the shoulder. 'Right, then. Let's go.'

Jamie watched as Banda got down on his hands and knees and began slowly crawling along the beach, his fingers sifting sand as he moved. In less than two minutes, he stopped and held up a stone, 'I found one!'

Jamie lowered himself to the sand and began moving. The first two stones he found were small. The third must have weighed over fifteen carats. He sat there looking at it for a long moment. It was incredible to him that such a fortune could be picked up so easily. And it all belonged to Salomon van der Merwe and his partners. Jamie kept moving.

In the next three hours, the two men collected more than forty diamonds ranging from two carats to thirty carats. The sky in the east was beginning to lighten. It was the time Jamie had planned to leave, to jump back on the raft, sail over the reefs and make their escape. It was useless to think about that now.

'It will be dawn soon,' Jamie said. 'Let's see how many more diamonds we can find.'

'We're not going to live to spend any of *this*. You want to die *very* rich, don't you?'

'I don't want to die at all.'

They resumed their search, mindlessly scooping up diamond after diamond, and it was as though a madness had taken possession of them. Their piles of diamonds increased, until sixty diamonds worth a king's ransom lay in their torn shirts.

'Do you want me to carry these?' Banda asked.

'No. We can both –' And then Jamie realized what was on Banda's mind. The one caught in actual possession of the diamonds would die more slowly and painfully.

'I'll take them,' Jamie said. He dumped the diamonds into the rag that was left of his shirt, and carefully tied it in a knot. The horizon was light grey now, and the east was becoming stained with the colours of the rising sun.

What next? That was the question! What was the answer? They could stand there and die, or they could move inland towards the desert and die.

'Let's move.'

Jamie and Banda slowly began walking away from the sea, side by side.

'Where do the land mines start?'

'About a hundred yards up ahead.' In the far distance, they heard a dog bark. 'I don't think we're going to have to worry about the land mines. The dogs are heading this way. The morning shift is coming to work.'

'How soon before they reach us?'

'Fifteen minutes. Maybe ten.'

It was almost full dawn now. What had been vague, shimmering patterns turned into small sand dunes and distant mountains. There was no place to hide.

'How many guards are on a shift?'

Banda thought for a moment. 'About ten.'

'Ten guards aren't many for a beach this big.'

'*One* guard is plenty. They've got guns and dogs. The guards aren't blind, and we're not invisible.'

The sound of the barking was closer now. Jamie said, 'Banda I'm sorry. I should never have gotten you into this.'

'You didn't'

And Jamie understood what he meant.

They could hear voices calling in the distance.

Jamie and Banda reached a small dune. 'What if we buried ourselves in the sand?'

'That has been tried. The dogs would find us and rip our throats out. I want my death to be quick. I'm going to let them see me, then start running. That way they'll shoot me. I – I don't want the dogs to get me.'

Jamie gripped Banda's arm. 'We may die, but I'll be damned if we're going to *run* to our deaths. Let's make them work for it.'

They could begin to distinguish words in the distance. 'Keep moving, you lazy bastards,' a voice was yelling. 'Follow me . . . stay in line . . . You've all had a good night's sleep . . . Now let's get some work done . . .'

In spite of his brave words, Jamie found he was retreating from the voice. He turned to look at the sea again. *Was drowning an easier way to die?* He watched the reefs tearing viciously at the demon waves breaking over them and he suddenly saw something else, something beyond the waves. He could not understand what it was. 'Banda, look . . .'

Far out at sea an impenetrable grey wall was moving towards them, blown by the powerful westerly winds.

'It's the sea *mis*!' Banda exclaimed. 'It comes in two or three times a week.'

While they were talking, the *mis* moved closer, like a gigantic grey curtain sweeping across the horizon, blotting out the sky.

The voices had moved closer, too. '*Den dousant!* Damn this *mis*! Another slowdown. The bosses ain't gonna like this . . .'

'We've got a chance!' Jamie said. He was whispering now.

'What chance?'

'The *mis*! They won't be able to see us.'

'That's no help. It's going to lift sometime, and when it does we're still going to be right here. If the guards can't move through the land mines, neither can we. You try to cross this desert in the *mis* and you won't go ten yards before you're blown to pieces. You're looking for one of your miracles.'

'You're damned right I am,' Jamie said.

The sky was darkening overhead. The *mis* was closer, covering the sea, ready to swallow up the shore. It had an eerie, menacing look about it as it rolled towards them, but Jamie thought exultantly. *It's going to save us!*

A voice suddenly called out, 'Hey! You two! What the hell are you doin' there?'

Jamie and Banda turned. At the top of a dune about a hundred yards away was a uniformed guard carrying a rifle. Jamie looked back at the shore. The *mis* was closing in fast.

'You! You two! Come here,' the guard yelled. He lifted his rifle.

Jamie raised his hands. 'I twisted my foot,' he called out. 'I can't walk.'

'Stay where you are,' the guard ordered. 'I'm comin' to get you.' He lowered his rifle and started moving towards them. A quick look back showed that the *mis* had reached the edge of the shore, and was coming in swiftly.

'Run!' Jamie whispered. He turned and raced towards the beach. Banda running close behind him.

'Stop!'

A second later they heard the sharp crack of a rifle, and the sand ahead of them exploded. They kept running, racing to meet the great dark wall of the fog. There was another rifle shot, closer this time, and another, and the next moment the two men were in total darkness. The sea *mis* licked at them, chilling them, smothering them. It was like being buried in cotton. It was impossible to see anything.

The voices were muffled now and distant, bouncing off the *mis* and coming from all directions. They could hear other voices calling to one another.

'Kruger! . . . It's Brent . . . Can you hear me?'

'I hear you, Kruger . . .'

'There're two of them,' the first voice yelled. 'A white man and a black. They're on the beach. Spread your men out. *Skiet hom!* Shoot to kill.'

'Hang on to me,' Jamie whispered.

Banda gripped his arm. 'Where are you going?'

'We're getting out of here.'

Jamie brought his compass up to his face. He could barely see it. He turned until the compass was pointing east. 'This way . . .'

'Wait! We can't walk. Even if we don't bump

into a guard or a dog, we're going to set off a land mine.'

'You said there are a hundred yards before the mines start. Let's get away from the beach.'

They started moving towards the desert, slowly and unsteadily, blind men in an unknown land. Jamie paced off the yards. Whenever they stumbled in the soft sand, they picked themselves up and kept moving. Jamie stopped to check the compass every few feet. When he estimated they had travelled almost a hundred yards, he stopped.

'This should be about where the land mines start. Is there any pattern to the way they're placed? Anything you can think of that could help us?'

'Prayer,' Banda answered. 'Nobody's ever gotten past those land mines, Jamie. They're scattered all over the field, buried about six inches down. We're going to have to stay here until the *mis* lifts and give ourselves up.'

Jamie listened to the cotton-wrapped voices ricocheting around them.

'Kruger! Keep in voice contact . . .'

'Right, Brent . . .'

'Kruger . . .'

'Brent . . .'

Disembodied voices calling to each other in the blinding fog. Jamie's mind was racing, desperately exploring every possible avenue of escape. If they stayed where they were, they would be killed the instant the *mis* lifted. If they tried moving through the field of mines, they would be blown to bits.

'Have you ever seen the land mines?' Jamie whispered.

'I helped bury some of them.'

'What sets them off?'

'A man's weight. Anything over eighty pounds will explode them. That way they don't kill the dogs.'

Jamie took a deep breath. 'Banda, I may have a way for us to get out of here. It might not work. Do you want to gamble with me?'

'What have you got in mind?'

'We're going to cross the mine fields on our bellies. That way we'll distribute our weight across the sand.'

'Oh, Jesus!'

'What do you think?'

'I think I was crazy for ever leaving Cape Town.'

'Are you with me?' He could barely make out Banda's face next to him.

'You don't leave a man a lot of choice, do you?'

'Come on then.'

Jamie carefully stretched himself out flat on the sand. Banda looked at him a moment, took a deep breath and joined him. Slowly the two men began crawling across the sand, towards the minefield.

'When you move,' Jamie whispered, 'don't press down with your hands or your legs. Use your whole body.'

There was no reply. Banda was busy concentrating on staying alive.

*　　*　　*

They were in a smothering, grey vacuum that made it impossible to see anything. At any instant they could bump into a guard, a dog or one of the land mines. Jamie forced all this out of his mind. Their progress was painfully slow. Both men were shirtless, and the sand scraped against their stomachs as they inched forwards. Jamie was aware of how overwhelming the odds were against them. Even if by some chance they did succeed in crossing the desert without getting shot or blown up, they would be confronted by the barbed-wire fence and the armed guards at the watchtower at the entrance. And there was no telling how long the *mis* would last. It could lift at any second, exposing them.

They kept crawling, mindlessly sliding forwards until they lost all track of time. The inches became feet, and the feet became yards, and the yards became miles. They had no idea how long they had been travelling. They were forced to keep their heads close to the ground, and their eyes and ears and noses became filled with sand. Breathing was an effort.

In the distance was the constant echo of the guards' voices. '*Kruger . . . Brent . . . Kruger . . . Brent . . .*'

The two men stopped to rest and check the compass every few minutes, then moved on, beginning their endless crawl again. There was an almost overwhelming temptation to move faster, but that would mean pressing down harder, and Jamie could visualize the metal fragments exploding under him and ripping into his belly. He kept the pace slow. From time to time they could hear other voices around them, but the words were muffled by the fog and it was impossible to tell where they were coming from. *It's a big desert.* Jamie thought hopefully. *We're not going to stumble into anyone.*

Out of nowhere, a large, furry shape leaped at him. It happened so swiftly that Jamie was caught off guard. He felt the huge Alsatian's teeth sinking into his arm. He dropped the bundle of diamonds and tried to pry open the dog's jaw, but he had only one free hand and it was impossible. He felt the warm blood running down his arm. The dog was sinking its teeth in harder now, silent and deadly. Jamie felt himself begin to faint. He heard a dull thud, and then another, and the dog's jaw loosened and its eyes glazed over. Through the mist of pain, Jamie saw Banda smashing the sack of diamonds against the dog's skull. The dog whimpered once and lay still.

'You all right?' Banda breathed anxiously.

Jamie could not speak. He lay there, waiting for the waves of pain to recede. Banda ripped off a piece of his trousers and tied a strip tightly around Jamie's arm to stop the bleeding.

'We've got to keep moving,' Banda warned. 'If there's one of them around, there are more.'

Jamie nodded. Slowly he slid his body forwards, fighting against the terrible throbbing in his arm.

He remembered nothing of the rest of the trek.

He was semi-conscious, an automaton. Something outside him directed his movements. *Arms forwards, pull . . . Arms forwards, pull . . . Arms forwards, pull . . .* It was endless, an odyssey of agony. It was Banda who followed the compass now, and when Jamie started to crawl in the wrong direction Banda gently turned him around. They were surrounded by guards and dogs and land mines and only the *mis* kept them safe. They kept moving, crawling for their lives, until the time came when neither man had the strength to move another inch.

They slept.

When Jamie opened his eyes, something had changed. He lay there on the sand, his body stiff and aching, trying to remember where he was. He could see Banda asleep six feet away, and it all came flooding in. The raft crashing on the reefs . . . the sea *mis* . . . But something was wrong. Jamie sat up, trying to figure out what it was. And his stomach lurched. *He could see Banda! That was what was wrong. The mis was lifting.* Jamie heard voices nearby. He peered through the thin mists of the dissipating fog. They had crawled near the entrance to the diamond field. There was the high guard tower and the barbed-wire fence Banda had described. A crowd of about sixty black workers was moving away from the diamond field towards the gate. They had finished their shift and the next shift was coming in. Jamie got on his knees and crawled over to Banda and shook him. Banda sat up, instantly awake. His eyes turned to the watch-tower and the gate.

'Damn!' he said incredulously. 'We almost made it.'

'We *did* make it! Give me those diamonds!'

Banda handed him the folded shirt. 'What do you –?'

'Follow me.'

'Those guards with the guns at the gate,' Banda said in a low voice, 'they'll know we don't belong here.'

'That's what I'm counting on,' Jamie told him.

The two men moved towards the guards, drifting between the line of departing workers and the line of arriving workers who were yelling at one another, exchanging good-natured catcalls.

'You fellas gonna work your asses off, man. We got a nice sleep in the *mis* . . .'

'How did you arrange for the *mis*, you lucky bastards. . . . ?'

'God listens to me. He ain't gonna listen to you. You're bad . . .'

Jamie and Banda reached the gate. Two huge armed guards stood inside, herding the departing workers over to the small tin hut where they would be thoroughly searched. *They strip them down mother-naked and then they look up and down every hole they've got.* Jamie clutched the tattered shirt in his hand more tightly. He pushed through the line of workers and walked up to a guard. 'Excuse me, sir,' Jamie said. 'Who do we see about a job here?'

Banda was staring at him, petrified.

The guard turned to face Jamie. 'What the hell are you doin' inside the fence?'

'We came in to look for work. I heard there was an opening for a guard, and my servant can dig. I thought –'

The guard eyed the two ragged, disreputable-looking figures. 'Get the hell back outside!'

'We don't want to go outside,' Jamie protested. 'We need jobs, and I was told –'

'This is a restricted area, mister. Didn't you see the signs? Now get the hell out. Both of you!' He pointed to a large bullock wagon outside the fence, filling with the workers who had finished their shift. 'That wagon'll take you to Port Nolloth. If you want a job, you have to apply at the company office there.'

'Oh. Thank you, sir,' Jamie said. He beckoned to Banda, and the two men moved out through the gate to freedom.

The guard glared after them. 'Stupid idiots.'

Ten minutes later, Jamie and Banda were on their way to Port Nolloth. They were carrying with them diamonds worth half a million pounds.

SIX

The expensive carriage rolled down the dusty main street of Klipdrift, drawn by two beautiful matched bays. At the reins was a slender, athletic-looking man with snow-white hair, a white beard and moustache. He was dressed in a fashionable tailored grey suit and ruffled shirt, and in his black cravat was a diamond stickpin. He wore a grey top hat, and on his little finger was a large, sparkling diamond ring. He appeared to be a stranger to the town, but he was not.

Klipdrift had changed considerably since Jamie McGregor had left it a year earlier. It was 1884, and it had grown from a camp to a township. The railway had been completed from Cape Town to Hopetown, with a branch running to Klipdrift, and this had created a whole new wave of immigrants. The town was even more crowded than Jamie remembered, but the people seemed different. There were still many prospectors, but there were also men in business suits and well-dressed matrons walking in and out of stores. Klipdrift had acquired a patina of respectability.

Jamie passed three new dance halls and half a dozen new saloons. He drove by a recently built church and barbershop, and a large hotel called the Grand. He stopped in front of a bank and alighted from the carriage, carelessly tossing the reins to a native boy.

'Water them.'

Jamie entered the bank and said to the manager in a loud voice, 'I wish to deposit one hundred thousand pounds in your bank.'

The word spread quickly, as Jamie had known it would, and by the time he left the bank and entered the Sundowner Saloon, he was the centre of interest. The interior of the saloon had not changed. It was crowded, and curious eyes followed Jamie as he walked up to the bar. Smit nodded deferentially. 'What would you like, sir?' There was no recognition on the bartender's face.

'Whiskey. The best you have.'

'Yes, sir.' He poured the drink. 'You're new in town?'

'Yes.'

'Just passin' through, are you?'

'No. I've heard this is a good town for a man looking for investments.'

The bartender's eyes lighted up. 'You couldn't find better! A man with a hundred – A man with money can do real well for hisself. Matter of fact, I might be of some service to you, sir.'

'Really? How is that?'

Smit leaned forwards, his tone conspiratorial. 'I know a man who runs this town. He's chairman of the Borough Council and head of the Citizen's Committee. He's the most important man in this part of the country. Name of Salomon van der Merwe.'

Jamie took a sip of his drink. 'Never heard of him.'

'He owns that big general store across the street. He can put you on to some good deals. It'd be worth your while to meet him.'

Jamie McGregor took another sip of his drink. 'Have him come over here.'

The bartender glanced at the large diamond ring on Jamie's finger, and at his diamond stickpin. 'Yes, sir. Can I tell him your name?'

'Travis. Ian Travis.'

'Right, Mr Travis. I'm sure Mr van der Merwe will want to meet you.' He poured out another drink. 'Have this while you're waitin'. It's on the house.'

Jamie sat at the bar sipping the whiskey, aware that everyone in the saloon was watching him. Men had departed from Klipdrift wealthy, but no one of such obvious wealth had ever arrived there before. It was something new in their experience.

Fifteen minutes later, the bartender was back, accompanied by Salomon van der Merwe.

Van der Merwe walked up to the bearded, white-haired stranger, held out his hand and smiled. 'Mr Travis, I'm Salomon van der Merwe.'

'Ian Travis.'

Jamie waited for a flicker of recognition, a sign that Van der Merwe found something familiar about him. There was nothing. *But then, why should there be?* Jamie thought. There was nothing left of that naïve, idealistic, eighteen-year-old boy he had been. Smit obsequiously led the two men to a corner table.

As soon as they were seated, Van der Merwe said, 'I understand you're looking for some investments in Klipdrift, Mr Travis.'

'Possibly.'

'I might be able to be of some service. One has to be careful. There are many immoral people around.'

Jamie looked at him and said, 'I'm sure there are.'

It was unreal, sitting there carrying on a polite conversation with the man who had cheated him out of a fortune and then tried to murder him. His hatred for Van der Merwe had consumed him for the last year, his thirst for vengeance was all that had sustained him, kept him alive. And now Van der Merwe was about to feel that vengeance.

'If you don't mind my asking, Mr Travis, how much money were you planning on investing?'

'Oh, around a hundred thousand pounds to begin with,' Jamie said carelessly. He watched Van der Merwe wet his lips. 'Then perhaps three or four hundred thousand more.'

'Er – you should be able to do very well with

that, very well, indeed. With the right guidance, of course,' he added quickly. 'Do you have any idea what you might want to invest in?'

'I thought I'd look around and see what opportunities there were.'

'That's very wise of you.' Van der Merwe nodded sagely. 'Perhaps you would like to come to dinner tonight and we can discuss it? My daughter's an excellent cook. It would be an honour to have you.'

Jamie smiled. 'I'd enjoy that, Mr van der Merwe.' *You have no idea how much I'd enjoy that*, he thought.

It had started.

The journey from the diamond fields of Namib to Cape Town had been uneventful. Jamie and Banda had hiked inland to a small village where a doctor treated Jamie's arm, and they had gotten a lift on a wagon bound for Cape Town. It was a long, difficult ride, but they were oblivious to the discomfort. At Cape Town, Jamie checked into the ornate Royal Hotel on Plein Street – 'Patronized by HRH, the Duke of Edinburgh' – and was escorted to the Royal Suite.

'I want you to send up the best barber in town,' Jamie told the manager. 'Then I want a tailor and a bootmaker up here.'

'At once, sir,' the manager said.

It's wonderful what money can do, Jamie thought.

* * *

The bath in the Royal Suite was heaven. Jamie lay back in the hot water, soaking the tiredness out of his body, thinking back over the past incredible weeks. Had it been only weeks since he and Banda had built that raft? It seemed like years. Jamie thought about the raft sailing them to the *Sperrgebiet*, and the sharks, and the demon waves and the reefs tearing the raft to pieces. The sea *mis* and the crawling over the land mines, and the huge dog on top of him . . . The eerie, muffled cries that would ring in his ears forever: *Kruger . . . Brent . . . Kruger . . . Brent . . .*

But most of all, he thought of Banda. His friend.

When they had reached Cape Town, Jamie had urged, 'Stay with me.'

Banda smiled, showing his beautiful white teeth. 'Life's too dull with you, Jamie. I have to go somewhere and find a little excitement.'

'What will you do now?'

'Well, thanks to you and your wonderful plan about how easy it is to float a raft over the reef, I'm going to buy a farm, find a wife and have a lot of children.'

'All right. Let's go to the *diamant kooper* so I can give you your share of the diamonds.'

'No,' Banda said. 'I don't want it.'

Jamie frowned. 'What are you talking about? Half the diamonds are yours. You're a millionaire.'

'No. Look at my skin, Jamie. If I became a millionaire, my life would not be worth a tickey.'

'You can hide some of the diamonds away. You can –'

'All I need is enough to buy a morgen of farm-land and two oxen to trade for a wife. Two or three little diamonds will get me everything I'll ever want. The rest are yours.'

'That's impossible. You can't give me your share.'

'Yes, I can, Jamie. Because you're going to give me Salomon van der Merwe.'

Jamie looked at Banda for a long moment. 'I promise.'

'Then I'll say good-bye, my friend.'

The two men clasped hands.

'We'll meet again,' Banda said. 'Next time think of something *really* exciting for us to do.'

Banda walked away with three small diamonds carefully tucked in his pocket.

Jamie sent off a bank draught amounting to twenty thousand pounds to his parents, bought the finest carriage and team he could find and headed back to Klipdrift.

The time had come for revenge.

That evening when Jamie McGregor entered Van der Merwe's store, he was gripped by a sensation so unpleasant and so violent that he had to pause to regain control of himself.

Van der Merwe hurried out of the back of the shop, and when he saw who it was, his face lighted up in a big smile. 'Mr Travis!' he said. 'Welcome.'

'Thank you, mister – er – sorry, I don't remember your name . . .'

'Van der Merwe. Salomon van der Merwe. Don't apologize. Dutch names are difficult to remember. Dinner is ready. Margaret!' he called as he led Jamie into the back room. Nothing had changed. Margaret was standing at the stove over a frying pan, her back to them.

'Margaret, this is our guest I spoke of – Mr Travis.'

Margaret turned. 'How do you do?'

There was not a flicker of recognition.

'I'm pleased to meet you,' Jamie nodded.

The customer bell rang and Van der Merwe said, 'Excuse me, I'll be right back. Please make yourself at home, Mr Travis.' He hurried out.

Margaret carried a steaming bowl of vegetables and meat over to the table, and as she hurried to take the bread from the oven Jamie stood there, silently looking at her. She had blossomed in the year since he had seen her. She had become a woman, with a smouldering sexuality that had been lacking before.

'Your father tells me you're an excellent cook.'

Margaret blushed. 'I – I hope so, sir.'

'It's been a long time since I've tasted home cooking. I'm looking forward to this.' Jamie took a large butter dish from Margaret and placed it on the table for her. Margaret was so surprised she almost dropped the plate in her hands. She had never heard of a man who helped in woman's work. She lifted her startled eyes to his face. A broken nose and a scar spoiled what would otherwise have been a too-handsome face. His eyes were light grey and shone with intelligence and a burning intensity. His white hair told her that he was not a young man, and yet there was something very youthful about him. He was tall and strong and – Margaret turned away, embarrassed by his gaze.

Van der Merwe hurried back into the room, rubbing his hands. 'I've closed the shop,' he said. 'Let's sit down and have a fine dinner.'

Jamie was given the place of honour at the table. 'We'll say grace,' Van der Merwe said.

They closed their eyes. Margaret slyly opened hers again, so that she could continue her scrutiny of the elegant stranger while her father's voice droned on. 'We are all sinners in your eyes, O Lord, and must be punished. Give us the strength to bear our hardships on this earth, so that we may enjoy the fruits of heaven when we are called. Thank you, Lord, for helping those of us who deserve to prosper. Amen.'

Salomon van der Merwe began serving. This time the portions he served Jamie were more than generous. They talked as they ate. 'Is this your first time out this way, Mr Travis?'

'Yes,' Jamie said. 'First time.'

'You didn't bring Mrs Travis along, I understand.'

'There is no Mrs Travis. I haven't found anyone who'd have me.' Jamie smiled.

What fool of a woman would refuse him? Margaret wondered. She lowered her eyes, afraid the stranger might read her wicked thoughts.

'Klipdrift is a town of great opportunity, Mr Travis. *Great* opportunity.'

'I'm willing to be shown.' He looked at Margaret, and she blushed.

'If it isn't too personal, Mr Travis, may I ask how you acquired your fortune?'

Margaret was embarrassed by her father's blunt questions, but the stranger did not seem to mind.

'I inherited it from my father,' James said easily.

'Ah, but I'm sure you've had a lot of business experience.'

'Very little, I'm afraid. I need a lot of guidance.'

Van der Merwe brightened. 'It's fate that we met, Mr Travis. I have some very profitable connections. Very profitable, indeed. I can almost guarantee that I can double your money for you in just a few months.' He leaned over and patted Jamie's arm. 'I have a feeling this is a big day for both of us.'

Jamie just smiled.

'I suppose you're staying at the Grand Hotel?'

'That's right.'

'It's criminally expensive. But I suppose to a man of your means.' He beamed at Jamie.

Jamie said, 'I'm told the countryside around here is interesting. Would it be an imposition to ask you to let your daughter show me around a bit tomorrow?'

Margaret felt her heart stop for a second.

Van der Merwe frowned. 'I don't know. She –'

It was an iron-clad rule of Salomon van der Merwe's never to permit any man to be alone with his daughter. In the case of Mr Travis, however, he decided there would be no harm in making an exception. With so much at stake, he did not want to appear inhospitable. 'I can spare Margaret from the store for a short time. You will show our guest around, Margaret?'

'If you wish, Father,' she said quietly.

'That's settled then.' Jamie smiled. 'Shall we say ten o'clock in the morning?'

After the tall, elegantly dressed guest left, Margaret cleared away the table and washed the dishes, in a complete daze. *He must think I'm an idiot.* She went over and over in her mind everything she had contributed to the conversation. Nothing. She had been completely tongue-tied. Why was that? Hadn't she waited on hundreds of men in the store without becoming a stupid fool? Of course they had not looked at her the way Ian Travis had. *Men all have the devil in them, Margaret. I'll not let them corrupt your innocence.* Her father's voice echoed in her mind. Could that be it? The weakness and trembling she had felt when the stranger had looked at her? Was he corrupting her innocence? The thought of it sent a delicious thrill

126

through her body. She looked down at the plate she had dried three times and sat down at the table. She wished her mother were still alive.

Her mother would have understood. Margaret loved her father, but sometimes she had the oppressive feeling that she was his prisoner. It worried her that he never allowed a man to come near her. *I'll never get married*, Margaret thought. *Not until he dies*. Her rebellious thoughts filled her with guilt, and she hurriedly left the room and went into the store, where her father sat behind a desk, working on his accounts.

'Good night, Father.'

Van der Merwe took off his gold-framed spectacles and rubbed his eyes before he raised his arms to embrace his daughter good night. Margaret did not know why she pulled away.

Alone in the curtained-off alcove that served as her bedroom, Margaret studied her face in the small, round mirror that hung on the wall. She had no illusions about her looks. She was not pretty. She was interesting-looking. Nice eyes. High cheekbones. A good figure. She drew nearer to the mirror. What had Ian Travis seen when he looked at her? She began getting undressed. And Ian Travis was in the room with her, watching her, his eyes burning into her. She stepped out of her muslin drawers and camisole and stood naked before him. Her hands slowly caressed the swell of her breasts and felt her hardening nipples. Her fingers slid down across her flat belly and his hands became entwined with hers, moving slowly downward. They were between her legs now, gently touching, stroking, rubbing, harder now, faster and faster until she was caught up in a frantic whirlpool of sensation that finally exploded inside her and she gasped his name and fell to the bed.

They rode out in Jamie's carriage, and he was amazed once more at the changes that had taken place. Where before there had been only a sea of tents, now there were substantial-looking houses, constructed of timber with roofs of corrugated iron or thatch.

'Klipdrift seems very prosperous,' Jamie said as they rode along the main street.

'I suppose it would be interesting for a newcomer,' Margaret said. And she thought, *I've hated it until now*.

They left the town and drove out towards the mining camps along the Vaal River. The seasonal rains had turned the countryside into an enormous, colourful garden, filled with the luxuriant bush Karroo, and the spreading Rhenoster bush and heaths and diosmas plants that could be found nowhere else in the world. As they drove past a group of prospectors, Jamie asked, 'Have there been any big diamond finds lately?'

'Oh, yes, a few. Every time the news gets out, hundreds of new diggers come pouring in. Most of them leave poor and heartbroken. Margaret felt she had to warn him of the danger here. 'Father would not like to hear me say this, but I think it's a terrible business, Mr Travis.'

'For some, probably,' Jamie agreed. 'For some.'

'Do you plan to stay on a while?'

'Yes.'

Margaret felt her heart singing. 'Good.' Then added quickly, 'Father will be pleased.'

They drove around all morning, and from time to time they stopped and Jamie chatted with prospectors. Many of them recognized Margaret and spoke respectfully. There was a warmth to her and an easy friendliness that she did not reveal when she was around her father.

As they drove on, Jamie said, 'Everyone seems to know you.'

She blushed. 'That's because they do business with Father. He supplies most of the diggers.'

Jamie made no comment. He was keenly interested in what he was seeing. The railroad had made an enormous difference. A new combine called De Beers, named after the farmer in whose field the first diamond discovery was made, had bought out its chief rival, a colourful entrepreneur named Barney Barnato, and De Beers was busily consolidating the hundreds of small claims into one organization. Gold had been discovered recently, not far from Kimberley, along with manganese and zinc. Jamie was convinced this was only the beginning, that South Africa was a treasure-house of minerals. There were incredible opportunities here for a man with foresight.

When Jamie and Margaret returned, it was late afternoon. Jamie stopped the carriage in front of Van der Merwe's store and said, 'I would be honoured if you and your father would be my guests at dinner tonight.'

Margaret glowed. 'I'll ask Father. I do so hope he'll say yes. Thank you for a lovely day, Mr Travis.'

And she fled.

The three of them had dinner in the large, square dining room of the new Grand Hotel.

The room was crowded, and Van der Merwe grumbled, 'I don't see how these people can afford to eat here.'

Jamie picked up a menu and glanced at it. A steak cost one pound four shillings, a potato was four shillings and a piece of apple pie ten shillings.

'They're robbers!' Van der Merwe complained. 'A few meals here and a man could eat himself into the poorhouse.'

Jamie wondered what it would take to put Salomon van der Merwe in the poorhouse. He intended to find out. They ordered, and Jamie noticed that Van der Merwe ordered the most expensive items on the menu. Margaret ordered a clear soup. She was too excited to eat. She looked at her hands, remembered what they had done the night before and felt guilty.

'I can afford dinner,' Jamie teased her. 'Order anything you like.'

She blushed. 'Thank you, but I'm – I'm not really very hungry.'

Van der Merwe noticed the blush and looked sharply from Margaret to Jamie. 'My daughter is a rare girl, a rare girl, Mr Travis.'

Jamie nodded. 'I couldn't agree with you more, Mr van der Merwe.'

His words made Margaret so happy that when their dinner was served, she could not even eat the soup. The affect Ian Travis had on her was incredible. She read hidden meanings into his every word and gesture. If he smiled at her, it meant he liked her a lot; if he frowned, it meant he hated her. Margaret's feelings were an emotional thermometer that kept going up and down.

'Did you see anything of interest today?' Van der Merwe asked Jamie.

'No, nothing special,' Jamie said casually.

Van der Merwe leaned forwards. 'Mark my words, sir, this is going to be the fastest-growing area in the world. A man would be smart to invest here now. The new railway's going to turn this place into a second Cape Town.'

'I don't know,' Jamie said dubiously. 'I've heard of too many boomtowns like this going bust. I'm not interested in putting my money into a ghost town.

'Not Klipdrift,' Van der Merwe assured him. 'They're finding more diamonds all the time. And gold.'

Jamie shrugged. 'How long will that last?'

'Well, nobody can be sure of that, of course, but –'

'Exactly.'

'Don't make any hasty decisions,' Van der Merwe urged. 'I wouldn't like to see you lose out on a great opportunity.'

Jamie thought that over, 'Perhaps I am being hasty. Margaret, could you show me around again tomorrow?'

Van der Merwe opened his mouth to object, then closed it. He remembered the words of Mr Thorenson, the banker: *He walked in here and deposited a hundred thousand pounds, cool as you please, Salomon, and he said there'd be a lot more comin'.*

Greed got the better of Van der Merwe. 'Of course she could.'

The following morning, Margaret put on her Sunday dress, ready to meet Jamie. When her father walked in and saw her, his face turned red. 'Do you want the man to think you're some kind of fallen woman – dressin' up to attract him? This is business, girl. Take that off and put on your workin' clothes.'

'But, Papa –'

'Do as I say!'

She did not argue with him. 'Yes, Papa.'

* * *

Van der Merwe watched Margaret and Jamie drive away twenty minutes later. He wondered if he could be making a mistake.

This time Jamie headed the carriage in the opposite direction. There were exciting signs of new developments and building everywhere. *If the mineral discoveries keep up*, Jamie thought – and there was every reason to believe they would – *there is more money to be made here in real estate than in diamonds or gold. Klipdrift will need more banks, hotels, saloons, shops, brothels* . . . The list was endless. So were the opportunities.

Jamie was conscious of Margaret staring at him. 'Is something wrong?' he asked.

'Oh, no,' she said, and quickly looked away.

Jamie studied her now, and noticed the radiance about her. Margaret was aware of his closeness, his maleness. He sensed her feelings. She was a woman without a man.

At noon Jamie drove off the main road down to a wooded area near a stream and stopped under a large baobab tree. He had had the hotel pack a picnic lunch. Margaret put down a tablecloth, unpacked the basket and spread out the food. There was cold roast lamb, fried chicken, yellow saffron rice, quince jam and tangerines and peaches and *soetekoekjes*, almond-topped spice cookies.

'This is a banquet!' Margaret exclaimed. 'I'm afraid I don't deserve all this, Mr Travis.'

'You deserve much more,' Jamie assured her.

Margaret turned away, busying herself with the food.

Jamie took her face between his hands. 'Margaret . . . look at me.'

'Oh! Please. I –' She was trembling.

'Look at me.'

Slowly she lifted her head and looked into his eyes. He pulled her into his arms, and his lips found hers and he held her close, pressing his body against hers.

After a few moments she struggled free, shook her head and said, 'Oh, my God. We mustn't. Oh, we mustn't. We'll go to hell.'

'Heaven.'

'I'm afraid.'

'There's nothing to be afraid of. Do you see my eyes? They can look right inside you. And you know what I see, don't you? You want me to make love to you. And I'm going to. And there's nothing to fear, because you belong to me. You know that, don't you? You belong to me, Margaret. You say it. I belong to Ian. Go on. I – belong – to – Ian.'

'I belong – to Ian.'

His lips were on hers again, and he began to undo the hooks on the back of her bodice. In a moment she stood naked in the soft breeze, and he lowered her gently down to the ground. And the tremulous passage from girlhood to womanhood became an exciting, soaring experience that made Margaret feel more alive than she had ever felt in her life. *I'll remember this moment forever*, she thought. The bed of leaves and the warm caressing breeze on her naked skin, the shadow of the baobab tree that dappled their bodies. They made love again, and it was even more wonderful. She thought, *No woman could ever love anyone as much as I love this man*.

When they were spent, Jamie held her in his strong arms, and she wished she could be there forever. She looked up at him and whispered, 'What are you thinking?'

He grinned and whispered back, 'That I'm bloody starving.'

She laughed, and they rose and had their lunch under the shelter of the trees. Afterwards they swam and lay down to let the hot sun dry them. Jamie took Margaret again, and she thought, *I want this day to go on forever*.

That evening, Jamie and Van der Merwe were seated at a corner table at the Sundowner. 'You were right,' Jamie announced. 'The possibilities here may be greater than I thought.'

Van der Merwe beamed. 'I knew you were too clever a man not to see that, Mr Travis.'

'What exactly would you advise me to do?' Jamie asked.

Van der Merwe glanced around and lowered his voice. 'Just today I got some information on a big new diamond strike north of Pniel. There are ten claims still available. We can divide them up between us. I'll put up fifty thousand pounds for five claims, and you put up fifty thousand pounds for the other five. There are diamonds there by the bushel. We can make millions overnight. What do you think?'

Jamie knew exactly what he thought. Van der Merwe would keep the claims that were profitable and Jamie would end up with the others. In addition, Jamie would have been willing to bet his life that Van der Merwe was not putting up one shilling.

'It sounds interesting,' Jamie said. 'How many prospectors are involved?'

'Only two.'

'Why does it take so much money?' he asked innocently.

'Ah, that's an intelligent question.' He leaned forwards in his chair. 'You see, they know the value of their claim, but they don't have the money to operate it. That's where you and I come in. We give them one hundred thousand pounds and let them keep twenty percent of their fields.

He slipped the twenty percent in so smoothly that it almost went by unnoticed. Jamie was certain the prospectors would be cheated of their diamonds and their money. It would all flow to Van der Merwe.

'We'll have to move fast,' Van der Merwe warned. 'As soon as word of this leaks out –'

'Let's not lose it,' Jamie urged.

Van der Merwe smiled. 'Don't worry, I'll have the contracts drawn up right away.'

In Afrikaans, Jamie thought.

'Now, there are a few other deals I find very interesting, Ian.'

Because it was important to keep his new partner happy, Van der Merwe no longer objected when Jamie asked that Margaret show him around the countryside. Margaret was more in love with Jamie every day. He was the last thing she thought of when she went to bed at night, and the first thing she thought of when she opened her eyes in the morning. Jamie had loosed a sensuality in her that she had not even known existed. It was as though she had suddenly discovered what her body was for, and all the things she had been taught to be ashamed of became glorious gifts to bring pleasure to Jamie. And to herself. Love was a wonderful new country to be explored. A sensual land of hidden valleys and exciting dales and glens and rivers of honey. She could not get enough of it.

In the vast sweep of the countryside, it was easy to find isolated places where they could make love, and each time for Margaret was as exciting as the first time.

The old guilt about her father haunted her. Salomon van der Merwe was an elder of the Dutch Reformed Church, and Margaret knew if he ever found out what she was doing, there would be no forgiveness. Even in the rough frontier community where they lived, where men took their pleasures where they found them, there would be no understanding. There were only two kinds of women in the world – nice girls and whores – and a nice girl did not let a man touch her unless she was married to him. So she would be labelled a whore. *It's so unfair*, she thought. *The giving and taking of love is too beautiful to be evil.* But her growing concern finally made Margaret bring up the subject of marriage.

They were driving along the Vaal River when Margaret spoke. 'Ian, you know how much I –' She did not know how to go on. 'That is, you and I –' In desperation she blurted out, 'How do you feel about marriage?'

Jamie laughed. 'I'm all for it, Margaret. I'm all for it.'

She joined him in his laughter. It was the happiest moment of her life.

On Sunday morning, Salomon van der Merwe invited Jamie to accompany him and Margaret to church. The Nederduits Hervormde Kerk was a large, impressive building done in bastard Gothic, with the pulpit at one end and a huge organ at the other. When they walked in the door, Van der Merwe was greeted with great respect.

'I helped build this church,' he told Jamie proudly. 'I'm a deacon here.'

The service was brimstone and hellfire, and Van

der Merwe sat there, rapt, nodding eagerly, accepting the minister's every word.

He's God's man on Sunday, Jamie thought, *and the rest of the week he belongs to the devil.*

Van der Merwe had placed himself between the two young people, but Margaret was conscious of Jamie's nearness all through the service. *It's a good thing* – she smiled nervously to herself – *that the minister doesn't know what I'm thinking about.*

That evening, Jamie went to visit the Sundowner Saloon. Smit was behind the bar serving drinks. His face brightened when he saw Jamie.

'Good evenin', Mr Travis. What will you have, sir? The usual?'

'Not tonight, Smit. I want to talk to you. In the back room.'

'Certainly, sir.' Smit scented money to be made. He turned to his assistant. 'Mind the bar.'

The back room of the Sundowner was no more than a closet, but it afforded privacy. It contained a round table with four chairs, and in the centre of the table was a lantern. Smit lit it.

'Sit down,' Jamie said.

Smit took a chair. 'Yes, sir. How can I help you?'

'It's you I've come to help, Smit.'

Smit beamed. 'Really, sir?'

'Yes.' Jamie took out a long, thin cigar and lighted it. 'I've decided to let you live.'

An uncertain look flickered over Smit's face. 'I – I don't understand, Mr Travis.'

'Not Travis. The name is McGregor. Jamie McGregor. Remember? A year ago you set me up to be killed. At the barn. For Van der Merwe.'

Smit was frowning now, suddenly wary. 'I don't know what –'

'Shut up and listen to me.' Jamie's voice was like whiplash.

Jamie could see the wheels turning in Smit's mind. He was trying to reconcile the face of the white-haired man in front of him with the eager youth of a year before.

'I'm still alive, and I'm rich – rich enough to hire men to burn this place down and you with it. Are you with me so far, Smit?'

Smit started to protest his ignorance, but he looked into Jamie McGregor's eyes and saw the danger there. Smit said cautiously. 'Yes, sir . . .'

'Van der Merwe pays you to send prospectors to him so he can cheat them out of what they find. That's an interesting little partnership. How much does he pay you?'

There was a silence. Smit was caught between two powerful forces. He did not know which way to jump.

'How much?'

'Two percent,' he said reluctantly.

'I'll give you five. From now on when a likely prospect comes in, you'll send him to me. I'll finance him. The difference is that he'll get his fair share and you'll get yours. Did you really think

Van der Merwe was paying you two percent of what he made? You're a fool.'

Smit nodded. 'Right, Mr Trav – Mr McGregor. I understand.'

Jamie rose to his feet. 'Not completely.' He leaned over the table. 'You're thinking of going to Van der Merwe and telling him about our little conversation. That way, you can collect from both of us. There's only one problem with that, Smit.' His voice dropped to a whisper. 'If you do, you're a dead man.'

SEVEN

Jamie was getting dressed when he heard a tentative knock at the door. He listened, and it was repeated. He walked over to the door and opened it. Margaret stood there.

'Come in, Maggie,' Jamie said. 'Is something wrong?' It was the first time she had come to his hotel room. She stepped inside, but now that she was face to face with him, she found it difficult to speak. She had lain awake all night, wondering how to tell him the news. She was afraid he might never want to see her again.

She looked into his eyes. 'Ian, I'm going to have your baby.'

His face was so still that Margaret was terrified that she had lost him. And suddenly his expression changed to such joy that all her doubts were instantly wiped out. He grabbed her arms and said, 'That's wonderful, Maggie! Wonderful! Have you told your father?'

Margaret pulled back in alarm. 'Oh, no! He –'

She walked over to the Victoria green-plush sofa and sat down. 'You don't know Father. He – he would never understand.'

Jamie was hurriedly putting on his shirt. 'Come on, we're going to tell him together.'

'Are you sure everything will be all right, Ian?'

'I've never been surer of anything in my life.'

Salomon van der Merwe was measuring out strips of biltong for a prospector when Jamie and Margaret strode into the shop. 'Ah, Ian! I'll be with you in a moment.' He hurriedly finished with the customer and walked over to Jamie. 'And how is everything this fine day?' Van der Merwe asked.

'It couldn't be better,' Jamie said happily. 'Your Maggie's going to have a baby.'

There was a sudden stillness in the air. 'I – I don't understand,' Van der Merwe stuttered.

'It's very simple. I've gotten her pregnant.'

The colour drained from Van der Merwe's face. He turned wildly from one to the other. 'This – this isn't true?' A maelstrom of conflicting emotions whirled through Salomon van der Merwe's head. The terrible shock of his precious daughter losing her virginity . . . getting pregnant . . . He would be the laughing stock of the town. But Ian Travis was a very wealthy man. And if they got married quickly . . .

Van der Merwe turned to Jamie. 'You'll get married immediately, of course.'

Jamie looked at him in surprise. '*Married?* You'd

allow Maggie to marry a stupid bairn who let you cheat him out of what belonged to him?'

Van der Merwe's head was spinning. 'What are you talking about, Ian? I never –'

'My name's not Ian,' Jamie said harshly. 'I'm Jamie McGregor. Dinna you recognize me?' He saw the bewildered expression on Van der Merwe's face. 'Nae, a course you don't. That boy is dead. You killed him. But I'm not a man to hold a grudge, Van der Merwe. So I'm giving you a gift. My seed in your daughter's belly.'

And Jamie turned and walked out, leaving the two of them staring after him, stunned.

Margaret had listened in shocked disbelief. He could not mean what he had just said. *He loved her!* He –

Salomon van der Merwe turned on his daughter, in the throes of a terrible rage. 'You whore!' he screamed. *'Whore! Get out! Get out of here!'*

Margaret stood stock-still, unable to grasp the meaning of the awful thing that was happening. Ian blamed her for something her father had done. Ian thought she was part of something bad. *Who was Jamie McGregor? Who –?*

'Go!' Van der Merwe hit her hard across the face. 'I never want to see you again as long as I live.'

Margaret stood there, rooted, her heart pounding, gasping for breath. Her father's face was that of a madman. She turned and fled from the store, not looking back.

* * *

Salomon van der Merwe stood there watching her go, gripped by despair. He had seen what happened to other men's daughters who had disgraced themselves. They had been forced to stand up in church and be publicly pilloried and then exiled from the community. It was proper and fitting punishment, exactly what they deserved. But his Margaret had been given a decent, God-fearing upbringing. *How could she have betrayed him like this?* Van der Merwe visualized his daughter's naked body, coupling with that man, writhing in heat like animals, and he began to have an erection.

He put a Closed sign on the front door of the store and lay on his bed without the strength or the will to move. When word got around town, he would become an object of derision. He would be either pitied or blamed for his daughter's depravity. Either way, it would be unbearable. He had to make certain no one learned about it. He would send the whore out of his sight forever. He knelt and prayed: *O, God! How could you do this to me, your loyal servant? Why have you forsaken me? Let her die, O Lord. Let them both die . . .*

The Sundowners Saloon was crowded with noon trade when Jamie entered. He walked over to the bar and turned to face the room. 'Your attention, please!' The conversation tapered off into silence. 'Drinks on the house for everybody.'

'What is it?' Smit asked. 'A new strike?'

Jamie laughed. 'In a way, my friend. Salomon

van der Merwe's unmarried daughter is pregnant. Mr van der Merwe wants everybody to help him celebrate.'

Smit whispered, 'Oh, Jesus!'

'Jesus had nothing to do with it. Just Jamie McGregor.'

Within an hour, everyone in Klipdrift had heard the news. How Ian Travis was really Jamie McGregor, and how he had gotten Van der Merwe's daughter pregnant. Margaret van der Merwe had fooled the whole town.

'She doesn't look like the kind, does she?'

'Still waters run deep, they say.'

'I wonder how many other men in this town have dipped their wick in that well?'

'She's a shapely girl. I could use a piece of that myself.'

'Why don't you ask her? She's givin' it away.'

And the men laughed.

When Salomon van der Merwe left his store that afternoon, he had come to terms with the dreadful catastrophe that had befallen him. He would send Margaret to Cape Town on the next coach. She could have her bastard there, and there was no need for anyone in Klipdrift to know his shame. Van der Merwe stepped out into the street, hugging his secret, a smile pasted on his lips.

'Afternoon, Mr van der Merwe. I hear you might be stockin' some extra baby clothes.'

'Good day, Salomon. Hear you're gonna get a little helper for your store soon.'

'Hello there, Salomon. I hear a bird watcher just spotted a new species out near the Vaal River. Yes, sir, a stork!'

Salomon van der Merwe turned and blindly stumbled back into his shop, bolting the door behind him.

At the Sundowner Saloon, Jamie was having a whiskey, listening to the flood of gossip around him. It was the biggest scandal Klipdrift had ever had, and the pleasure of the townspeople took in it was intense. *I wish*, Jamie thought, *that Banda were here with me to enjoy this.* This was payment for what Salomon van der Merwe had done to Banda's sister, what he had done to Jamie and to – how many others? But this was only part payment for all the things Salomon van der Merwe had done, just the beginning. Jamie's vengeance would not be complete until Van der Merwe had been totally destroyed. As for Margaret, he had no sympathy for her. She was in on it. What had she said the first day they met? *My father might be the one to help you. He knows everything.* She was a Van der Merwe too, and Jamie would destroy both of them.

Smit walked over to where Jamie was sitting. 'Kin I talk to you a minute, Mr McGregor?'

'What is it?'

Smit cleared his throat self-consciously. 'I know

147

a couple of prospectors who have ten claims up near Pniel. They're producin' diamonds, but these fellas don't have the money to get the proper equipment to work their claim. They're looking' for a partner. I thought you might be interested.'

Jamie studied him. 'These are the men you talked to Van der Merwe about, right?'

Smit nodded, surprised. 'Yes, sir. But I been thinkin' over your proposition. I'd rather do business with you.'

Jamie pulled out a long, thin cigar, and Smit hastened to light it. 'Keep talking.'

Smit did.

In the beginning, prostitution in Klipdrift was on a haphazard basis. The prostitutes were mostly black women, working in sleazy, back-street brothels. The first white prostitutes to arrive in town were part-time barmaids. But as diamond strikes increased and the town prospered, more white prostitutes appeared.

There were now half a dozen sporting houses on the outskirts of Klipdrift, wooden railway huts with tin roofs. The one exception was Madam Agnes's, a respectable-looking two-storey frame structure on Bree Street, off Loop Street, the main thoroughfare, where the wives of the townspeople would not be offended by having to pass in front of it. It was patronized by the husbands of those wives, and by any strangers in town who could afford it. It was expensive, but the women were young and uninhibited, and gave good value for the money. Drinks were served in a reasonably well-decorated drawing room, and it was a rule of Madam Agnes's that no customer was ever rushed or short-changed. Madam Agnes herself was a cheerful, robust redhead in her mid-thirties. She had worked at a brothel in London and been attracted to South Africa by the tales of easy money to be picked up in a mining town like Klipdrift. She had saved enough to open her own establishment, and business had flourished from the beginning.

Madam Agnes prided herself on her understanding of men, but Jamie McGregor was a puzzle to her. He visited often, spent money freely and was always pleasant to the women, but he seemed withdrawn, remote and untouchable. His eyes were what fascinated Agnes. They were pale, bottomless pools, cold. Unlike the other patrons of her house, he never spoke about himself or his past. Madam Agnes had heard hours earlier that Jamie McGregor had deliberately gotten Salomon van der Merwe's daughter pregnant and then refused to marry her. *The bastard!* Madam Agnes thought. But she had to admit that he was an attractive bastard. She watched Jamie now as he walked down the red-carpeted stairs, politely said good night and left.

When Jamie arrived back at his hotel, Margaret was in his room, staring out of the window. She turned as Jamie walked in.

'Hello, Jamie.' Her voice was atremble.

'What are you doing here?'

'I had to talk to you.'

'We have nothing to talk about.'

'I know why you're doing this. You hate my father.' Margaret moved closer to him. 'But you have to know that whatever it was he did to you, I knew nothing about. Please – I beg of you – believe that. Don't hate me. I love you too much.'

Jamie looked at her coldly. 'That's *your* problem, isn't it?'

'Please don't look at me like that. You love me, too . . .'

He was not listening. He was again taking the terrible journey to Paardspan where he had almost died . . . and moving the boulders on the riverbanks until he was ready to drop . . . and finally, miraculously, finding the diamonds . . . Handing them to Van der Merwe and hearing Van der Merwe's voice saying, *You misunderstood me, boy. I don't need any partners. You're working for me. . . . I'm giving you twenty-four hours to get out of town*. And then the savage beating . . . He was smelling the vultures again, feeling their sharp beaks tear into his flesh . . .

As though from a distance, he heard Margaret's voice. 'Don't you remember? I – belong – to – you . . . I love you.'

He shook himself out of his reverie and looked at her. *Love*. He no longer had any idea what the word meant. Van der Merwe had burned every emotion out of him except hate. He lived on that. It was his elixir, his lifeblood. It was what had kept him alive when he fought the sharks and crossed the reef, and crawled over the mines at the diamond fields of the Namib Desert. Poets wrote about love, and singers sang about it, and perhaps it was real, perhaps it existed. But love was for other men. Not for Jamie McGregor.

'You're Salomon van der Merwe's daughter. You're carrying his grandchild in your belly. Get out.'

There was nowhere for Margaret to go. She loved her father, and she needed his forgiveness, but she knew he would never – could never – forgive her. He would make her life a living hell. But she had no choice. She had to go to someone.

Margaret left the hotel and walked towards her father's store. She felt that everyone she passed was staring at her. Some of the men smiled insinuatingly, and she held her head high and walked on. When she reached the store, she hesitated, then stepped inside. The store was deserted. Her father came out from the back.

'Father . . .'

'*You!*' The contempt in his voice was a physical slap. He moved closer, and she could smell the whiskey on his breath. 'I want you to get out of this town. Now. Tonight. You're never to come near here again. Do you hear me? Never!' He pulled some bills from his pocket and threw them on the floor. 'Take them and get out.'

'I'm carrying your grandchild.'

'You're carrying the devil's child!' He moved closer to her, and his hands were knotted into fists. 'Every time people see you strutting around like a whore, they'll think of my shame. When you're gone, they'll forget it.'

She looked at him for a long, lost moment, then turned and blindly stumbled out the door.

'The money, whore!' he yelled. 'You forgot the money!'

There was a cheap boardinghouse at the outskirts of town, and Margaret made her way to it, her mind in a turmoil. When she reached it, she went looking for Mrs Owens, the landlady. Mrs Owens was a plump, pleasant-faced women in her fifties, whose husband had brought her to Klipdrift and abandoned her. A lesser woman would have crumbled, but Mrs Owens was a survivor. She had seen a good many people in trouble in this town, but never anyone in more trouble than the seventeen-year-old girl who stood before her now.

'You wanted to see me?'

'Yes. I was wondering if – if perhaps you had a job for me here.'

'A job? Doing what?'

'Anything. I'm a good cook. I can wait on tables. I'll make the beds. I – I'll –' There was desperation in her voice. 'Oh, please,' she begged. 'Anything!'

Mrs Owens looked at the trembling girl standing

there in front of her, and it broke her heart. 'I suppose I could use an extra hand. How soon can you start?' She could see the relief that lighted Margaret's face.

'Now.'

'I can pay you only –' She thought of a figure and added to it. 'One pound two shilling eleven pence a month, with board and lodging.'

'That will be fine,' Margaret said gratefully.

Salomon van der Merwe seldom appeared now on the streets of Klipdrift. More and more often, his customers found a Closed sign on the front door of his store at all hours of the day. After a while, they took their business elsewhere.

But Salomon van der Merwe still went to church every Sunday. He went not to pray, but to demand of God that He right this terrible iniquity that had been heaped upon the shoulders of his obedient servant. The other parishioners had always looked up to Salomon van der Merwe with the respect due a wealthy and powerful man, but now he could feel the stares and whispers behind his back. The family that occupied the pew next to him moved to another pew. He was a pariah. What broke his spirit completely was the minister's thundering sermon artfully combining Exodus and Ezekiel and Leviticus. 'I, the Lord thy God, am a jealous God, visiting the iniquity of the fathers upon the children. Wherefor, O harlot, hear the word of the Lord. Because thy filthiness was poured out, and thy nakedness discovered through thy whoredomes with thy lovers . . . And the Lord spake unto Moses, saying, 'Do not prostitute thy daughter, to cause her to be a whore; lest the land fall to whoredom and the land become full of wickedness . . .'

Van der Merwe never set foot in church again after that Sunday.

As Salomon van der Merwe's business deteriorated, Jamie McGregor's prospered. The expense of mining for diamonds increased as the digging got deeper, and miners with working claims found they were unable to afford the elaborate equipment needed. The word quickly spread that Jamie McGregor would provide financing in exchange for a share in the mines, and in time Jamie bought out his partners. He invested in real estate and businesses and gold. He was meticulously honest in his dealings, and as his reputation spread, more people came to him to do business.

There were two banks in town, and when one of them failed because of inept management, Jamie bought it, putting in his own people and keeping his name out of the transaction.

Everything Jamie touched seemed to prosper. He was successful and wealthy beyond his boyhood dreams, but it meant little to him. He measured his successes only by Salomon van der Merwe's failures. His revenge had still only begun.

From time to time, Jamie passed Margaret on the street. He took no notice of her.

Jamie had no idea what those chance encounters did to Margaret. The sight of him took her breath away, and she had to stop until she regained control of herself. She still loved him, completely and utterly. Nothing could ever change that. He had used her body to punish her father, but Margaret knew that that could be a double-edged sword. Soon she would have Jamie's baby, and when he saw that baby, his own flesh and blood, he would marry her and give his child a name. Margaret would become Mrs Jamie McGregor, and she asked nothing more from life. At night before Margaret went to sleep, she would touch her swollen belly and whisper, 'Our son.' It was probably foolish to think she could influence its sex, but she did not want to overlook any possibility. Every man wanted a son.

As her womb swelled, Margaret became more frightened. She wished she had someone to talk to. But the women of the town did not speak to her. Their religion taught them punishment, not forgiveness. She was alone, surrounded by strangers, and she wept in the night for herself and for her unborn baby.

Jamie McGregor had bought a two-story building in the heart of Klipdrift, and he used it as headquarters for his growing enterprises. One day, Harry McMillan, Jamie's chief accountant, had a talk with him.

'We're combining your companies,' he told Jamie, 'and we need a corporate name. Do you have any suggestions?'

'I'll think about it.'

Jamie thought about it. In his mind he kept hearing the sound of long-ago echoes piercing the sea *mis* on the diamond field in the Namib Desert, and he knew there was only one name he wanted. He summoned the accountant. 'We're going to call the new company Kruger-Brent. Kruger-Brent Limited.'

Alvin Cory, Jamie's bank manager, stopped in to visit him. 'It's about Mr van der Merwe's loans,' he said. 'He's fallen very far behind. In the past he's been a good risk, but his situation has drastically changed, Mr McGregor. I think we should call in his loans.'

'No.'

Cory looked at Jamie in surprise. 'He came in this morning trying to borrow more money to –'

'Give it to him. Give him everything he wants.'

The manager got to his feet. 'Whatever you say, Mr McGregor. I'll tell him that you –'

'Tell him nothing. Just give him the money.'

Every morning Margaret arose at five o'clock to bake large loaves of wonderful-smelling bread and sourdough biscuits, and when the boarders trooped into the dining room for breakfast, she served them porridge and ham and eggs, buckwheat cakes, sweet rolls and pots of steaming coffee and *naartje*. The majority of the guests at the boardinghouse were prospectors on their way to and from their claims. They would stop off in

156

Klipdrift long enough to have their diamonds appraised, have a bath, get drunk and visit one of the town's brothels – usually in that order. They were for the most part rough, illiterate adventurers.

There was an unwritten law in Klipdrift that nice women were not to be molested. If a man wanted sex, he went to a whore. Margaret van der Merwe, however, was a challenge, for she fitted into neither category. Nice girls who were single did not get pregnant, and the theory went that since Margaret had fallen once, she was probably eager to bed everyone else. All they had to do was ask. They did.

Some of the prospectors were open and blatant; others were leering and furtive. Margaret handled them all with quiet dignity. But one night as Mrs Owens was preparing for bed, she heard screams coming from Margaret's room at the back of the house. The landlady flung the door open and rushed in. One of the guests, a drunken prospector, had ripped off Margaret's nightgown and had her pinned down on the bed.

Mrs Owens was on him like a tiger. She picked up a flatiron and began hitting him with it. She was half the size of the prospector, but it made no difference. Filled with an overpowering rage, she knocked the prospector unconscious and dragged him into the hallway and out to the street. Then she turned and hurried back to Margaret's room, Margaret was wiping the blood off her lips from where the man had bitten her. Her hands were trembling.

'Are you all right, Maggie?'

'Yes. I – thank you, Mrs Owens.'

Unbidden tears sprang into Margaret's eyes. In a town where few people even spoke to her, here was someone who had shown kindness.

Mrs Owens studied Margaret's swollen belly and thought, *The poor dreamer. Jamie McGregor will never marry her.*

The time of confinement was drawing close. Margaret tired easily now, and bending down and getting up again was an effort. Her only joy was when she felt her baby stir inside her. She and her son were completely alone in the world, and she talked to him hour after hour, telling him all the wonderful things that life had in store for him.

Late one evening, shortly after supper, a young black boy appeared at the boardinghouse and handed Margaret a sealed letter.

'I'm to wait for an answer,' the boy told her.

Margaret read the letter, then read it again, very slowly. 'Yes,' she said. 'The answer is yes.'

The following Friday, promptly at noon, Margaret arrived in front of Madam Agnes's bordello. A sign on the front door read Closed. Margaret rapped tentatively on the door, ignoring the startled glances of the passers-by. She wondered if she had made a mistake by coming here. It had been a difficult decision, and she had accepted only out of a terrible loneliness. The letter had read:

Dear Miss van der Merwe:

It's none of my business, but my girls and me have been discussing your unfortunate and unfair situation, and we think it's a damned shame. We would like to help you and your baby. If it would not embarrass you, we would be honoured to have you come to lunch. Would Friday at noon be convenient?

Respectfully yours,
Madam Agnes

P.S. We would be very discreet.

Margaret was debating whether to leave, when the door was opened by Madam Agnes.

She took Margaret's arm and said, 'Come in, dearie. Let's get you out of this damned heat.'

She led her into the parlour, furnished with Victorian red-plush couches and chairs and tables. The room had been decorated with ribbons and streamers and – from God knows where – brightly coloured balloons. Crudely lettered cardboard signs hanging from the ceiling read: WELCOME BABY . . . IT'S GOING TO BE A BOY . . . HAPPY BIRTHDAY.

In the parlour were eight of Madam Agnes's girls, in a variety of sizes, ages and colours. They had all dressed for the occasion under Madam

159

Agnes's tutelage. The wore conservative afternoon gowns and no makeup. *They look,* Margaret thought in wonder, *more respectable than most of the wives in this town.*

Margaret stared at the roomful of prostitutes, not quite knowing what to do. Some of the faces were familiar. Margaret had waited on them when she worked in her father's store. Some of the girls were young and quite beautiful. A few were older and fleshy, with obviously dyed hair. But they all had one thing in common – they *cared*. They were friendly and warm and kind, and they wanted to make her happy.

They hovered around Margaret self-consciously, afraid of saying or doing the wrong thing. No matter what the townspeople said, they knew this was a lady, and they were aware of the difference between Margaret and themselves. They were honoured that she had come to them, and they were determined not to let anything spoil this party for her.

'We fixed you a nice lunch, honey,' Madam Agnes said. 'I hope you're hungry.'

They led her into the dining-room, where a table had been festively set, with a bottle of champagne at Margaret's place. As they walked through the hallway, Margaret glanced towards the stairs that led to the bedrooms on the second floor. She knew Jamie visited here, and she wondered which of the girls he chose. All of them, perhaps. And she studied them again and wondered what it was they had for Jamie that she did not.

The luncheon turned out to be a banquet. It began with a delicious cold soup and salad, followed by fresh carp. After that came mutton and duck with potatoes and vegetables. There was a tipsy cake and cheese and fruit and coffee. Margaret found herself eating heartily and enjoying herself immensely. She was seated at the head of the table, Madam Agnes on her right, and Maggie, a lovely blonde girl who could have been no more than sixteen, on her left. In the beginning the conversation was stilted. The girls had dozens of amusing, bawdy stories to tell, but they were not the kind they felt Margaret should hear. And so they talked about the weather and about how Klipdrift was growing, and about the future of South Africa. They were knowledgeable about politics and the economy and diamonds because they got their information first-hand from experts.

Once, the pretty blonde, Maggie, said, 'Jamie's just found a new diamond field at –' And as the room went suddenly silent and she realized her gaffe, she added nervously. 'That's my *Uncle* Jamie. He's – he's married to my aunt.'

Margaret was surprised by the sudden wave of jealousy that swept through her. Madam Agnes hastily changed the subject.

When the luncheon was finished, Madam Agnes rose and said, 'This way, honey.'

Margaret and the girls followed her into a second parlour which Margaret had not seen before. It was filled with dozens of gifts, all of them beautifully wrapped. Margaret could not believe her eyes.

'I – I don't know what to say.'

'Open them,' Madam Agnes told Margaret.

There was a rocking cradle, handmade bootees, sacques, embroidered bonnets, a long, embroidered cashmere cloak. There were French-kid button shoes, a child's silver cup, gold-lined, and a comb and brush with solid sterling-silver handles. There were solid-gold baby bib pins with beaded edges, a celluloid baby rattle and rubber teething ring and a rocking horse painted dapple grey. There were toy soldiers, brightly coloured wooden blocks and the most beautiful thing of all: a long, white christening dress.

It was like Christmas. It was beyond anything Margaret had ever expected. All the bottled-up loneliness and unhappiness of the past months exploded in her, and she burst into sobs.

Madam Agnes put her arms around her and said to the other girls. 'Get out.'

They quietly left the room. Madam Agnes led Margaret to a couch and sat there holding her until the sobs subsided.

'I – I'm so sorry,' Margaret stammered. 'I – I don't know what came over me.'

'It's all right, honey. This room has seen a lot of problems come and go. And you know what I've learned? Somehow, in the end everything always gets sorted out. You and your baby are gonna be just fine.'

'Thank you,' Margaret whispered. She gestured towards the piles of presents. 'I can never thank you and your friends enough for –'

Madam Agnes squeezed Margaret's hand. 'Don't. You don't have no idea how much fun the girls and me had gettin' all this together. We don't get a chance to do this kind of thing very often. When one of *us* gets pregnant, it's a fuckin' tragedy.' Her hands flew to her mouth and she said. 'Oh! Excuse me!'

Margaret smiled. 'I just want you to know that this has been one of the nicest days of my life.'

'We're real honoured that you came to visit us, honey. As far as I'm concerned, you're worth all the women in this town put together. Those damned bitches! I could kill them for the way they're behavin' to you. And if you don't mind my sayin' so, Jamie McGregor is a damned fool.' She rose to her feet. 'Men! It would be a wonderful world if we could live without the bastards. Or maybe it wouldn't. Who knows?'

Margaret had recovered her composure. She rose to her feet and took Agnes's hand in hers. 'I'll never forget this. Not as long as I live. Someday, when my son is old enough, I'll tell him about this day.'

Madam Agnes frowned. 'You really think you should?'

Margaret smiled. 'I really think I should.'

Madam Agnes saw Margaret to the door. 'I'll have a wagon deliver all the gifts to your boardinghouse, and – good luck to you.'

'Thank you. Oh, thank you.'

And she was gone.

Madam Agnes stood there a moment watching Margaret walk clumsily down the street. Then she turned inside and called loudly. 'All right, ladies. Let's go to work.'

One hour later, Madam Agnes's was open for business as usual.

EIGHT

It was time to spring the trap. Over the previous six months, Jamie McGregor had quietly bought out Van der Merwe's partners in his various enterprises so that Jamie now had control of them. But his obsession was to own Van der Merwe's diamond fields in the Namib. He had paid for those fields a hundred times over with his blood and guts, and very nearly with his life. He had used the diamonds he and Banda had stolen there to build an empire from which to crush Salomon van der Merwe. The task had not yet been completed. Now, Jamie was ready to finish it.

Van der Merwe had gone deeper and deeper into debt. Everyone in town refused to lend him money, except the bank Jamie secretly owned. His standing instruction to his bank manager was, 'Give Salomon van der Merwe everything he wants.'

The general store was almost never open now. Van der Merwe began drinking early in the morning, and in the afternoon he would go to Madam Agnes's and sometimes spend the night there.

One morning Margaret stood at the butcher's counter waiting for the spring chickens Mrs Owens had ordered, when she glanced out the window and saw her father leaving the brothel. She could hardly recognize the unkempt old man shuffling along the street. *I did this to him. Oh, God, forgive me, I did this!*

Salomon van der Merwe had no idea what was happening to him. He knew that somehow through no fault of his own, his life was being destroyed. God had chosen him – as He had once chosen Job – to test the mettle of his faith. Van der Merwe was certain he would triumph over his unseen enemies in the end. All he needed was a little time – time and more money. He had put up his general store as security, the shares he had in six small diamond fields, even his horse and wagon. Finally, there was nothing left but the diamond field in the Namib, and the day he put that up as collateral, Jamie pounced.

'Pull in all his notes,' Jamie ordered his bank manager. 'Give him twenty-four hours to pay up in full, or foreclose.'

'Mr McGregor, he can't possibly come up with that kind of money. He –'

'Twenty-four hours.'

At exactly four o'clock the following afternoon, the assistant manager of the bank appeared at the general store with the marshal and a writ to confiscate all of Salomon van der Merwe's wordly possessions. From his office building across the street, Jamie watched Van der Merwe being evicted from his store. The old man stood outside, blinking helplessly in the sun, not knowing what to do or where to turn. He had been stripped of everything. Jamie's vengeance was complete. *Why is it,* Jamie wondered, *that I feel no sense of triumph?* He was empty inside. The man he destroyed had destroyed him first.

When Jamie walked into Madam Agnes's that night, she said, 'Have you heard the news, Jamie? Salomon van der Merwe blew his brains out an hour ago.'

The funeral was held at the dreary, windswept cemetery outside town. Besides the burying crew, there were only two people in attendance: Margaret and Jamie McGregor. Margaret wore a shapeless black dress to cover her protruding figure. She looked pale and unwell. Jamie stood tall and elegant, withdrawn and remote. The two stood at opposite sides of the grave watching the crude pine-box coffin lowered into the ground. The clods of dirt clattered against the coffin, and to Margaret they seemed to say. *Whore!* . . . *Whore!* . . .

She looked across her father's grave at Jamie, and their eyes met. Jamie's glance was cool and impersonal, as though she were a stranger.

Margaret hated him then. *You stand there feeling nothing, and you're as guilty as I am. We killed him, you and I. In God's eyes, I'm your wife. But we're partners in evil.* She looked down at the open grave and watched the last shovelful of dirt cover the pine box. 'Rest.' she whispered. 'Rest.'

When she looked up, Jamie was gone.

There were two wooden buildings in Klipdrift that served as hospitals, but they were so filthy and unsanitary that more patients died there than lived. Babies were born at home. As Margaret's time for delivery grew closer, Mrs Owens arranged for a black midwife, Hannah. Labour began at three a.m.

'Now you just bear down,' Hannah instructed. 'Nature'll do the rest.'

The first pain brought a smile to Margaret's lips. She was bringing her son into the world, and he would have a name. She would see to it that Jamie McGregor recognized his child. Her son was not going to be punished.

The labour went on, hour after hour, and when some of the boarders stepped into Margaret's bedroom to watch the proceedings, they were sent packing.

'This is personal,' Hannah told Margaret. 'Between you and God and the devil who got you into this trouble.'

'Is it going to be a boy?' Margaret gasped.

Hannah mopped Margaret's brow with a damp

cloth. 'I'll let you know as soon as I check out the plumbin'. Now press down. Real hard! Hard! Harder!'

The contractions began to come closer together and the pain tore through Margaret's body. *Oh, my God, something's wrong*, Margaret thought.

'Bear down!' Hannah said. And suddenly there was a note of alarm in her voice. 'It's twisted around,' she cried. 'I – I can't get it out!'

Through a red mist, Margaret saw Hannah bend down and twist her body, and the room began to fade out, and suddenly there was no more pain. She was floating in space and there was a bright light at the end of a tunnel and someone was beckoning to her, and it was Jamie. *I'm here, Maggie, darling. You're going to give me a fine son.* He had come back to her. She no longer hated him. She knew then she had never hated him. She heard a voice saying, 'It's almost over,' and there was a tearing inside her, and the pain made her scream aloud.

'Now!' Hannah said. 'It's coming.'

And a second later, Margaret felt a wet rush between her legs and there was a triumphant cry from Hannah. She held up a red bundle and said, 'Welcome to Klipdrift. Honey, you got yourself a son.'

She named him Jamie.

Margaret knew the news about the baby would reach Jamie quickly, and she waited for him to call on her or send for her. When several weeks had passed and Margaret had not heard anything, she sent a message to him. The messenger returned thirty minutes later.

Margaret was in a fever of impatience. 'Did you see Mr McGregor?'

'Yes, ma'am.'

'And you gave him the message?'

'Yes, ma'am.'

'What did he *say*?' she demanded.

The boy was embarrassed. 'He – he said he has no son, Miss van der Merwe.'

She locked herself and her baby in her room all that day and all that night and refused to come out. 'Your father's upset just now, Jamie. He thinks your mother did something bad to him. But you're his son, and when he sees you, he's going to take us to live in his house and he's going to love both of us very much. You'll see, darling. Everything is going to be fine.'

In the morning when Mrs Owen knocked on the door, Margaret opened it. She seemed strangely calm.

'Are you all right, Maggie?'

'I'm fine, thank you.' She was dressing Jamie in one of his new outfits. 'I'm going to take Jamie out in his carriage this morning.'

The carriage, from Madam Agnes and her girls, was a thing of beauty. It was made of the finest grade of reed, with a strong cane bottom and solid, bentwood handles. It was upholstered in imported brocade, with piped rolls of silk plush, and it had a parasol hooked on at the back, with a deep ruffle.

Margaret pushed the baby carriage down the narrow sidewalks of Loop Street. An occasional stranger stopped to smile at the baby, but the women of the town averted their eyes or crossed to the other side of the street to avoid Margaret.

Margaret did not even notice. She was looking for one person. Every day that the weather was fine, Margart dressed the baby in one of his beautiful outfits and took him out in the baby carriage. At the end of a week, when Margaret had not once encountered Jamie on the streets, she realized he was deliberately avoiding her. *Well, if he won't come to see his son, his son will go to see him,* Margaret decided.

The following morning, Margaret found Mrs Owens in the parlour. 'I'm taking a little trip, Mrs Owens. I'll be back in a week.'

'The baby's too young to travel, Maggie. He –'

'The baby will be staying in town.'

Mrs Owens frowned. 'You mean *here?*'

'No, Mrs Owens. Not here.'

Jamie McGregor had built his house on a kopje, one of the hills overlooking Klipdrift. It was a low, steep-roofed bungalow with two large wings attached to the main building by wide verandas. The house was surrounded by green lawns studded with trees and a lush rose garden. In the back was the carriage house and separate quarters for the servants. The domestic arrangements were in the charge of Eugenia Talley, a formidable middle-aged widow with six grown children in England.

Margaret arrived at the house with her infant son in her arms at ten in the morning, when she knew Jamie would be at his office. Mrs Talley opened the door and stared in surprise at Margaret and the baby. As did everyone else within a radius of a hundred miles, Mrs Talley knew who they were.

'I'm sorry, but Mr McGregor is not at home,' the housekeeper said, and started to close the door.

Margaret stopped her. 'I didn't come to see Mr McGregor. I brought him his son.'

'I'm afraid I don't know anything about that. You –'

'I'll be gone for one week. I'll return for him then.' She held the baby out. 'His name is Jamie.'

A horrified look came over Mrs Talley's face. 'You can't leave him here! Why, Mr McGregor would –'

'You have a choice,' Margaret informed her. 'You can either take him in the house or have me leave him here on your doorstep. Mr McGregor wouldn't like *that* either.'

Without another word, she thrust the baby into the arms of the housekeeper and walked away.

'Wait! You can't –! Come back here! Miss –!'

Margaret never turned around. Mrs Talley stood there, holding the tiny bundle and thinking. *Oh, my God! Mr McGregor is going to be furious!*

* * *

She had never seen him in such a state. 'How could you have been so *stupid?*' he yelled. 'All you had to do was slam the door in her face!'

'She didn't give me a chance, Mr McGregor. She –'

'I will not have her child in my house!'

In his agitation he paced up and down, pausing to stop in front of the hapless housekeeper from time to time. 'I should fire you for this.'

'She's coming back to pick him up in a week. I –'

'I don't care when she's coming back,' Jamie shouted. 'Get that child out of here. Now! Get rid of it!'

'How do you suggest I do that, Mr McGregor?' she asked stiffly.

'Drop it off in town. There must be someplace you can leave it.'

'Where?'

'How the devil do I know!'

Mrs Talley looked at the tiny bundle she was holding in her arms. The shouting had started the baby crying. 'There are no orphanages in Klipdrift.' She began to rock the baby in her arms, but the screams grew louder. 'Someone has to take care of him.'

Jamie ran his hands through his hair in frustration. 'Damn! All right.' he decided. 'You're the one who so generously took the baby. *You* take care of him.'

'Yes, sir.'

'And stop that unbearable wailing. Understand something, Mrs Talley. I want it kept out of my sight. I don't want to know it's in this house. And when its mother picks it up next week, I don't want to see her. Is that clear?'

The baby started up with renewed vigour.

'Perfectly, Mr McGregor.' And Mrs Talley hurried from the room.

Jamie McGregor sat alone in his den sipping a brandy and smoking a cigar. *That stupid woman. The sight of her baby is supposed to melt my heart, make me go rushing to her and say, 'I love you. I love the baby. I want to marry you.'* Well, he had not even bothered looking at the infant. It had nothing to do with him. He had not sired it out of love, or even lust. It had been sired out of vengeance. He would forever remember the look on Salomon van der Merwe's face when he had told him Margaret was pregnant. That was the beginning. The end was the dirt being thrown onto the wooden coffin. He must find Banda and let him know their mission was finished.

Jamie felt an emptiness. *I need to set new goals*, he thought. He was already wealthy beyond belief. He had acquired hundreds of acres of mineral land. He had bought it for the diamonds that might be found there, and had ended up owning gold, platinum and half a dozen other rare minerals. His bank held mortgages on half the properties in Klipdrift, and his landholdings extended from

Namib to Cape Town. He felt a satisfaction in this, but it was not enough. He had asked his parents to come and join him, but they did not want to leave Scotland. His brothers and sister had married. Jamie sent large sums of money back to his parents, and that gave him pleasure, but his life was at a plateau. A few years earlier it had consisted of exciting highs and lows. He had felt alive. He was alive when he and Banda sailed their raft through the reefs of the *Sperrgebiet*. He was alive crawling over the land mines through the desert sand. It seemed to Jamie that he had not been alive in a long time. He did not admit to himself that he was lonely.

He reached again for the decanter of brandy and saw that it was empty. He had either drunk more than he realized or Mrs Talley was getting careless. Jamie rose from his chair, picked up the brandy snifter and wandered out to the butler's pantry where the liquor was kept. He was opening the bottle when he heard the cooing of an infant. *It! Mrs Talley must have the baby in her quarters, off the kitchen.* She had obeyed his orders to the letter. He had neither seen nor heard the infant in the two days it had been trespassing in his home. Jamie could hear Mrs Talley talking to it in the singsong tone that women used to talk to infants.

'You're a handsome little fellow, aren't you?' She was saying. 'You're just an angel. Yes, you are. An angel.'

The baby cooed again. Jamie walked over to Mrs Talley's open bedroom door and looked inside. From somewhere the housekeeper had obtained a crib and the baby was lying in it. Mrs Talley was leaning over him, and the infant's fist was tightly wrapped around her finger.

'You're a strong little devil, Jamie. You're going to grow up to be a big –' She broke off in surprise as she became aware of her employer standing in the doorway.

'Oh,' she said. 'I – is there something I can get for you, Mr McGregor?'

'No.' He walked over to the crib. 'I was disturbed by the noise in here.' And Jamie took his first look at his son. The baby was bigger than he had expected, and well formed. He seemed to be smiling up at Jamie.

'Oh, I'm sorry, Mr McGregor. He's really such a good baby. And healthy. Just give him your finger and feel how strong he is.'

Without a word, Jamie turned and walked out of the room.

Jamie McGregor had a staff of over fifty employees working on his various enterprises. There was not an employee from the mail boy to the highest executive who did not know how Kruger-Brent, Ltd., got its name, and they all took fierce pride in working for Jamie McGregor. He had recently hired David Blackwell, the sixteen-year-old son of one of his foremen, an American from Oregon who had come to South Africa looking for diamonds. When Blackwell's money ran out, Jamie had hired him to supervise one of the mines. The son went to work for the company one summer, and Jamie found him such a good worker that he offered him a permanent job. Young David Blackwell was intelligent and attractive and had initiative. Jamie knew he could also keep his mouth shut, which is why he chose him to run this particular errand.

'David, I want you to go to Mrs Owen's boardinghouse. There's a woman living there named Margaret van der Merwe.'

If David Blackwell was familiar with the name or her circumstances, he gave no indication of it. 'Yes, sir.'

'You're to speak only to her. She left her baby with my housekeeper. Tell her I want her to pick it up today and get it out of my house.'

'Yes, Mr McGregor.'

Half an hour later, David Blackwell returned. Jamie looked up from his desk.

'Sir. I'm afraid I couldn't do what you asked.'

Jamie rose to his feet. 'Why not?' he demanded. 'It was a simple enough job.'

'Miss van der Merwe wasn't there, sir.'

'Then find her.'

'She left Klipdrift two days ago. She's expected back in five days. If you'd like me to make further inquiries –'

'No.' That was the last thing Jamie wanted. 'Never mind. That's all, David.'

'Yes, sir.' The boy left the office.

Damn that woman! When she returned, she was going to have a surprise coming. She was going to get her baby back!

That evening, Jamie dined at home alone. He was having his brandy in the study when Mrs Talley came in to discuss a household problem. In the middle of a sentence, she suddenly stopped to listen and said, 'Excuse me, Mr McGregor. I hear Jamie crying.' And she hurried out of the room.

Jamie slammed down his brandy snifter, spilling the brandy. *That goddamned baby! And she had the nerve to name him Jamie. He didn't look like a Jamie. He didn't look like anything.*

Ten minutes later, Mrs Talley returned to the study. She saw the spilled drink. 'Shall I get you another brandy?'

'That won't be necessary,' Jamie said coldly. 'What *is* necessary is that you remember who you're working for. I will not be interrupted because of that bastard. Is that quite clear, Mrs Talley?'

'Yes, sir.'

'The sooner that infant you brought into this house is gone, the better it will be for all of us. Do you understand?'

Her lips tightened. 'Yes, sir. Is there anything else?'

'No.'

She turned to leave.

'Mrs Talley . . .'

'Yes, Mr McGregor?'

'You said it was crying. It's not ill, is it?'

'No, sir. Just wet. He needed a change.'

Jamie found the idea revolting. 'That will be all.'

Jamie would have been furious had he been aware that the servants in the house spent hour upon hour discussing him and his son. They all agreed that the master was behaving unreasonably, but they also knew that even to mention the subject would mean instant dismissal. Jamie McGregor was not a man who took kindly to advice from anyone.

The following evening Jamie had a late business meeting. He had made an investment in a new railroad. It was a small one, to be sure, running from his mines in the Namib Desert to De Aar, linking up with the Cape Town-Kimberley line, but it would now be much cheaper to transport his diamonds and gold to the port. The first South Africa Railway had been opened in 1860, running from Dunbar to the Point, and since then new lines had been run from Cape Town to Wellington. Railroads were going to be the steel veins that allowed goods and people to flow freely through the heart of South Africa, and Jamie intended to be a part of them. That was only the beginning of his plan. *After that*, Jamie thought, *ships. My own ships to carry the minerals across the ocean.*

He arrived home after midnight, undressed and

got into bed. He had had a decorator from London design a large, masculine bedroom with a huge bed that had been carved in Cape Town. There was an old Spanish chest in one corner of the room and two enormous wardrobes which held more than fifty suits and thirty pairs of shoes. Jamie cared nothing about clothes, but it was important to him that they be there. He had spent too many days and nights wearing rags.

He was just dozing off when he thought he heard a cry. He sat up and listened. Nothing. Was it the baby? It might have fallen out of its crib. Jamie knew that Mrs Talley was a sound sleeper. It would be dreadful if something happened to the infant while it was in Jamie's house. Then it could become his responsibility. *Damn that woman!* Jamie thought.

He put on a robe and slippers and went through the house to Mrs Talley's room. He listened at her closed door and could hear nothing. Quietly, Jamie pushed open the door. Mrs Talley was sound asleep, huddled under the covers, snoring. Jamie walked over to the crib. The baby lay on its back, its eyes wide open. Jamie moved closer and looked down. There *was* a resemblance, by God! It definitely had Jamie's mouth and chin. Its eyes were blue now, but all babies were born with blue eyes. Jamie could tell by looking at it that it was going to have grey eyes. It moved its little hands in the air and made a cooing sound and smiled up at Jamie. *Now, that's a brave lad*, Jamie thought, *lying there, not making any noise, not screaming like other babies would do.* He peered closer. *Yes, he's a McGregor, all right.*

Tentatively, Jamie reached down and held out a finger. The infant grabbed it with both hands and squeezed tightly. *He's as strong as a bull*, Jamie thought. At that moment, a strained look came over the infant's face, and Jamie could smell a sour odour.

'Mrs Talley!'

She leaped up in bed, filled with alarm. 'What – what is it?'

'The baby needs attention. Do I have to do everything around here?'

And Jamie McGregor stalked out of the room.

'David, do you know anything about babies?'

'In what respect, sir?' David Blackwell asked.

'Well, you know. What they like to play with, things like that.'

The young American said,. 'I think when they're very young they enjoy rattles, Mr McGregor.'

'Pick up a dozen,' Jamie ordered.

'Yes, sir.'

No unnecessary questions. Jamie liked that. David Blackwell was going to go far.

That evening when Jamie arrived home with a small brown package, Mrs Talley said, 'I want to apologize for last night, Mr McGregor. I don't know how I could have slept through it. The baby must have been screaming something terrible for you to have heard it all the way in your room.'

'Don't worry about it,' Jamie said generously. 'As long as one of us heard it.' He handed her the package. 'Give this to it. Some rattles for him to play with. Can't be much fun for him to be a prisoner in that crib all day.'

'Oh, he's not a prisoner, sir. I take him out.'

'Where do you take him?'

'Just in the garden, where I can keep an eye on him.'

Jamie frowned. 'He didn't look well to me last night.'

'He didn't?'

'No. His colour's not good. It wouldn't do for him to get sick before his mother picks him up.'

'Oh, no, sir.'

'Perhaps I'd better have another look at him.'

'Yes, sir. Shall I bring him in here?'

'Do that, Mrs Talley.'

'Right away, Mr McGregor.'

She was back in a few minutes with little Jamie in her arms. The baby was clutching a blue rattle. 'His colour looks fine to me.'

'Well, I could have been wrong. Give him to me.'

Carefully, she held the baby out and Jamie took his son in his arms for the first time. The feeling that swept over him took him completely by surprise. It was as though he had been longing for this moment, living for this moment, without ever knowing it. This was his flesh and blood he was holding in his arms – his son, Jamie McGregor, Jr. What was the point of building an empire, a dynasty, of having diamonds and gold and railroads if you had no one to pass them on to? *What a bloody fool I've been!* Jamie thought. It had never occurred to him until now what was missing. He had been too blinded by his hatred. Looking down into the tiny face, a hardness somewhere deep in the core of him vanished.

'Move Jamie's crib into my bedroom, Mrs Talley.'

Three days later when Margaret appeared at the front door of Jamie's house, Mrs Talley said, 'Mr McGregor is away at his office, Miss van der Merwe, but he asked me to send for him when you came for the baby. He wishes to speak with you.'

Margaret waited in the living room, holding little Jamie in her arms. She had missed him terribly. Several times during the week she had almost lost her resolve and rushed back to Klipdrift, afraid that something might have happened to the baby, that he might have become ill or had an accident. But she had forced herself to stay away, and her plan had worked. Jamie wanted to talk to her! Everything was going to be wonderful. The three of them would be together now.

The moment Jamie walked into the living room, Margaret felt again the familiar rush of emotion. *Oh, God*, she thought, *I love him so much*.

'Hello, Maggie.'

She smiled, a warm, happy smile. 'Hello, Jamie.'

183

'I want my son.'

Margaret's heart sang. 'Of course you want your son, Jamie. I never doubted it.'

'I'll see to it that he's brought up properly. He'll have every advantage I can give him and, naturally, I'll see that you're taken care of.'

Margaret looked at him in confusion. 'I – I don't understand.'

'I said I want my son.'

'I thought – I mean – you and I –'

'No. It's only the boy I want.'

Margaret was filled with a sudden outrage. 'I see. Well, I'll not let you take him away from me.'

Jamie studied her a moment. 'Very well. We'll work out a compromise. You can stay on here with Jamie. You can be his – his governess.' He saw the look on her face. 'What *do* you want?'

'I want my son to have a name,' she said fiercely. 'His father's name.'

'All right. I'll adopt him.'

Margaret looked at him scornfully. 'Adopt my baby? Oh, no. You will not have my son. I feel sorry for you. The great Jamie McGregor. With all your money and power, you have nothing. You're a thing of pity.'

And Jamie stood there watching as Margaret turned and walked out of the house, carrying her son in her arms.

The following morning, Margaret made preparations to leave for America.

* * *

'Running away won't solve anything,' Mrs Owens argued.

'I'm not running away. I'm going someplace where my baby and I can have a new life.'

She could no longer subject herself and her baby to the humiliation Jamie McGregor offered them.

'When will you leave?'

'As soon as possible. We'll take a coach to Worcester and the train from there to Cape Town. I've saved enough to get us to New York.'

'That's a long way to go.'

'It will be worth it. They call America the land of opportunity, don't they? That's all we need.'

Jamie had always prided himself on being a man who remained calm under pressure. Now he went around yelling at everyone in sight. His office was in a constant uproar. Nothing anyone did pleased him. He roared and complained about everything, unable to control himself. He had not slept in three nights. He kept thinking about the conversation with Margaret. *Damn her!* He should have known she would try to push him into marriage. Tricky, just like her father. He had mishandled the negotiations. He had told her he would take care of her, but he had not been specific. Of course. *Money!* He should have offered her money. A thousand pounds – ten thousand pounds – more.

'I have a delicate task for you,' he told David Blackwell.

'Yes, sir.'

'I want you to talk to Miss van der Merwe. Tell her I'm offering her twenty thousand pounds. She'll know what I want in exchange.' Jamie wrote out a cheque. He had long ago learned the lure of money in hand. 'Give this to her.'

'Right, sir.' And David Blackwell was gone.

He returned fifteen minutes later and handed the cheque back to his employer. It had been torn in half. Jamie could feel his face getting red. 'Thank you, David. That will be all.'

So Margaret was holding out for more money. Very well. He would give it to her. But this time he would handle it himself.

Late that afternoon, Jamie McGregor went to Mrs Owen's boardinghouse. 'I want to see Miss van der Merwe,' Jamie said.

'I'm afraid that's not possible,' Mrs Owens informed him. 'She's on her way to America.'

Jamie felt as though he had been hit in the stomach. 'She can't be! When did she leave?'

'She and her son took the noon coach to Worcester.'

The train sitting at the station in Worcester was filled to capacity, the seats and aisles crowded with noisy travellers on their way to Cape Town. There were merchants and their wives, salesmen, prospectors, kaffirs and soldiers and sailors reporting back for duty. Most of them were riding a train for the first time and there was a festive atmosphere among the passengers. Margaret had been able to get a seat near a window, where Jamie would not be crushed by the crowd. She sat there holding her baby close to her, oblivious to those around her, thinking about the new life that lay ahead of them. It would not be easy. Wherever she went, she would be an unmarried woman with a child, an offence to society. But she would find a way to make sure her son had his chance at a decent life. She heard the conductor call, 'All aboard!'

She looked up, and Jamie was standing there. 'Collect your things,' he ordered. 'You're getting off the train.'

He still thinks he can buy me, Margaret thought. 'How much are you offering this time?'

Jamie looked down at his son, peacefully asleep in Margaret's arms. 'I'm offering you marriage.'

NINE

They were married three days later in a brief, private ceremony. The only witness was David Blackwell.

During the wedding ceremony, Jamie McGregor was filled with mixed emotions. He was a man who had grown used to controlling and manipulating others, and this time it was he who had been manipulated. He glanced at Margaret. Standing next to him, she looked almost beautiful. He remembered her passion and abandon, but it was only a memory, nothing more, without heat or emotion. He had used Margaret as an instrument of vengeance, and she had produced his heir.

The minister was saying, 'I now pronounce you man and wife. You may kiss the bride.'

Jamie leaned forwards and briefly touched his lips to Margaret's cheek.

'Let's go home,' Jamie said. His son was waiting for him.

When they returned to the house, Jamie showed Margaret to a bedroom in one of the wings.

'This is your bedroom,' Jamie informed her.

'I see.'

'I'll hire another housekeeper and put Mrs Talley in charge of Jamie. If there's anything you require, tell David Blackwell.'

Margaret felt as though he had struck her. He was treating her like a servant. But that was not important. *My son has a name. That is enough for me.*

Jamie did not return home for dinner. Margaret waited for him, then finally dined alone. That night she lay awake in her bed, aware of every sound in the house. At four o'clock in the morning, she finally fell asleep. Her last thought was to wonder which of the women at Madam Agnes's he had chosen. If Margaret's relationship with Jamie was unchanged since their marriage, her relationship with the townspeople of Klipdrift underwent a miraculous transformation. Overnight, Margaret went from being an outcast to becoming Klipdrift's social arbiter. Most of the people in town depended for their living in one way or another on Jamie McGregor and Kruger-Brent, Ltd. They decided that if Margaret van der Merwe was good enough for Jamie McGregor, she was good enough for them. Now when Margaret took little Jamie for an outing, she was met with smiles and cheery greetings. Invitations poured in. She was invited to teas, charity luncheons and dinners and urged to head civic committees. When she dressed her hair in a different way, dozens of women in town instantly followed suit. She bought a new yellow dress, and yellow dresses were suddenly popular. Margaret handled their fawning in the same manner she had handled their hostility – with quiet dignity.

Jamie came home only to spend time with his son. His attitude towards Margaret remained distant and polite. Each morning at breakfast she played the role of happy wife for the servants' benefit, despite the cool indifference of the man sitting across the table from her. But when Jamie had gone and she could escape to her room, she would be drenched in perspiration. She hated herself. Where was her pride? Because Margaret knew she still loved Jamie. *I'll always love him*, she thought. *God help me.*

Jamie was in Cape Town on a three-day business trip. As he came out of the Royal Hotel, a liveried black driver said, 'Carriage, sir?'

'No,' Jamie said. 'I'll walk.'

'Banda thought you might like to ride.'

Jamie stopped and looked sharply at the man. 'Banda?'

'Yes, Mr McGregor.'

Jamie got into the carriage. The driver flicked his whip and they started off. Jamie sat back in his seat, thinking of Banda, his courage, his friendship. He had tried many times to find him in the last two years, with no success. Now he was on his way to meet his friend.

The driver turned the carriage towards the waterfront, and Jamie knew instantly where they were going. Fifteen minutes later the carriage stopped in front of the deserted warehouse where Jamie and Banda had once planned their adventure into the Namib. *What reckless young fools we were*, Jamie thought. He stepped out of the carriage and approached the warehouse. Banda was waiting for him. He looked exactly the same, except that now he was neatly dressed in a suit and shirt and tie.

They stood there, silently grinning at each other, then they embraced.

'You look prosperous,' Jamie smiled.

Banda nodded. 'I've not done badly. I bought that farm we talked about. I have a wife and two sons, and I raise wheat and ostriches.'

'Ostriches?'

'Their feathers bring in lots of money.'

'Ah. I want to meet your family, Banda.'

Jamie thought of his own family in Scotland, and of how much he missed them. He had been away from home for four years.

'I've been trying to find you.'

'I've been busy, Jamie.' Banda moved closer. 'I had to see you to give you a warning. There's going to be trouble for you.'

Jamie studied him. 'What kind of trouble?'

'The man in charge of the Namib field – Hans Zimmerman – he's bad. The workers hate him. They're talking about walking out. If they do, your guards will try to stop them and there will be a riot.'

Jamie never took his eyes from Banda's face.

'Do you remember I once mentioned a man to you – John Tengo Javabu?'

'Yes. He's a political leader. I've been reading about him. He's been stirring up a *donderstorm*.'

'I'm one of his followers.'

Jamie nodded. 'I see. I'll do what has to be done,' Jamie promised.

'Good. You've become a powerful man, Jamie. I'm glad.'

'Thank you, Banda.'

'And you have a fine-looking son.'

Jamie could not conceal his surprise. 'How do you know that?'

'I like to keep track of my friends.' Banda rose to his feet. 'I have a meeting to go to, Jamie. I'll tell them things will be straightened out at the Namib.'

'Yes. I'll attend to it.' He followed the large black man to the door. 'When will I see you again?'

Banda smiled. 'I'll be around. You can't get rid of me that easily.'

And Banda was gone.

* * *

When Jamie returned to Klipdrift, he sent for young David Blackwell. 'Has there been any trouble at the Namib field, David?'

'No, Mr McGregor.' He hesitated. 'But I have heard rumours that there might be.'

'The supervisor there is Hans Zimmerman. Find out if he's mistreating the workers. If he is, put a stop to it. I want you to go up there yourself.'

'I'll leave in the morning.'

When David arrived at the diamond field at the Namib, he spent two hours quietly talking to the guards and the workers. What he heard filled him with a cold fury. When he had learned what he wanted to know, he went to see Hans Zimmerman.

Hans Zimmerman was a goliath of a man. He weighed three hundred pounds and was six feet, six inches tall. He had a sweaty, porcine face and red-veined eyes, and was one of the most unattractive men David Blackwell had ever seen. He was also one of the most efficient supervisors employed by Kruger-Brent, Ltd. He was seated at a desk in his small office, dwarfing the room, when David walked in.

Zimmerman rose and shook David's hand. 'Pleasure to see you, Mr Blackwell. You should have told me you was comin'.'

David was sure that word of his arrival had already reached Zimmerman.

'Whiskey?'

'No, thank you.'

Zimmerman leaned back in his chair and grinned. 'What can I do for you? Ain't we diggin' up enough diamonds to suit the boss?'

Both men knew that the diamond production at the Namib was excellent. 'I get more work out of my kaffirs than anyone else in the company,' was Zimmerman's boast.

'We've been getting some complaints about conditions here, David said.

The smile faded from Zimmerman's face. 'What kind of complaints?'

'That the men here are being treated badly and –'

Zimmerman leapt to his feet, moving with surprising agility. His face was flushed with anger. 'These ain't men. These are kaffirs. You people sit on your asses at headquarters and –'

'Listen to me,' David said. 'There's no –'

'You listen to *me*! I produce more fuckin' diamonds than anybody else in the company, and you know why? Because I put the fear of God into these bastards.'

'At our other mines,' David said, 'we're paying fifty-nine shillings a month and keep. You're paying your workers only fifty shillings a month.'

'You complainin' 'cause I made a better deal for you? The only thing that counts is profit.'

'Jamie McGregor doesn't agree,' David replied. 'Raise their wages.'

Zimmerman said sullenly, 'Right. It's the boss's money.'

'I hear there's a lot of whipping going on.'

Zimmerman snorted. 'Christ, you can't hurt a native, mister. Their hides are so thick they don't even feel the goddamned whip. It just scares them.'

'Then you've scared three workers to death, Mr Zimmerman.'

Zimmerman shrugged. 'There's plenty more where they came from.'

He's a bloody animal, David thought. *And a dangerous one.* He looked up at the huge supervisor. 'If there's any more trouble here, you're going to be replaced.' He rose to his feet. 'You'll start treating your men like human beings. The punishments are to stop immediately. I've inspected their living quarters. They're pigsties. Clean them up.'

Hans Zimmerman was glaring at him, fighting to control his temper. 'Anything else?' he finally managed to say.

'Yes. I'll be back here in three months. If I don't like what I see, you can find yourself a job with another company. Good day.' David turned and walked out.

Hans Zimmerman stood there for a long time, filled with a simmering rage. *The fools*, he thought. *Uitlanders.* Zimmerman was a Boer, and his father had been a Boer. The land belonged to them and God had put the blacks there to serve them. If God had meant them to be treated like human beings, he would not have made their skins black. Jamie McGregor did not understand that. But what could you expect from an *uitlander*, a native-lover? Hans Zimmerman knew he would have to be a little more careful in the future. But he would show them who was in charge at the Namib.

Kruger-Brent, Ltd., was expanding, and Jamie McGregor was away a good deal of the time. He bought a paper mill in Canada and a shipyard in Australia. When he was home, Jamie spent all his time with his son, who looked more like his father each day. Jamie felt an inordinate pride in the boy. He wanted to take the child with him on his long trips, but Margaret refused to let him.

'He's much too young to travel. When he's older, he can go with you. If you want to be with him, you'll see him here.'

Before Jamie had realized it, his son had had his first birthday, and then his second, and Jamie marvelled at how the time raced by. It was 1887.

To Margaret, the last two years had dragged by. Once a week Jamie would invite guests to dinner and Margaret was his gracious hostess. The other men found her witty and intelligent and enjoyed talking to her. She knew that several of the men found her very attractive indeed, but of course they never made an overt move, for she was the wife of Jamie McGregor.

When the last of the guests had gone, Margaret would ask, 'Did the evening go well for you?'

Jamie would invariably answer, 'Fine. Good night,' and be off to look in on little Jamie. A few minutes later Margaret would hear the front door close as Jamie left the house.

Night after night, Margaret McGregor lay in her bed thinking about her life. She knew how much she was envied by the women in town, and it made her ache, knowing how little there was to envy. She was living out a charade with a husband who treated her worse than a stranger. If only he would notice her! She wondered what he would do if one morning at breakfast she took up the bowl that contained his oatmeal especially imported from Scotland and poured it over his stupid head. She could visualize the expression on his face, and the fantasy tickled her so much that she began to giggle, and the laughter turned into deep, wrenching sobs. *I don't want to love him any more. I won't. I'll stop, somehow, before I'm destroyed . . .*

By 1890, Klipdrift had more than lived up to Jamie's expectations. In the seven years he had been there, it had become a full-fledged boomtown, with prospectors pouring in from every part of the world. It was the same old story. They came by coach and in wagons and on foot. They came with nothing but the rags they wore. They needed food and equipment and shelter and grubstake money, and

Jamie McGregor was there to supply it all. He had shares in dozens of producing diamond and gold mines, and his name and reputation grew. One morning Jamie received a visit from an attorney for De Beers, the giant conglomerate that controlled the huge diamond mines at Kimberley.

'What can I do for you?' Jamie asked.

'I've been sent to make you an offer, Mr McGregor. De Beers would like to buy you out. Name your price.'

It was a heady moment. Jamie grinned and said, 'Name *yours*.'

David Blackwell was becoming more and more important to Jamie. In the young American Jamie McGregor saw himself as he once had been. The boy was honest, intelligent and loyal. Jamie made David his secretary, then his personal assistant and, finally, when the boy was twenty-one, his general manager.

To David Blackwell, Jamie McGregor was a surrogate father. When David's own father suffered a heart attack, it was Jamie who arranged for a hospital and paid for the doctors, and when David's father died, Jamie McGregor took care of the funeral arrangements. In the five years David had worked for Kruger-Brent, Ltd., he had come to admire Jamie more than any man he had ever known. He was aware of the problem between Jamie and Margaret, and deeply regretted it, because he liked them both. *But it's none of my business*, David told himself. *My job is to help Jamie in any way I can.*

Jamie spent more and more time with his son. The boy was five now, and the first time Jamie took him down in the mines, young Jamie talked of nothing else for a week. They went on camping trips, and they slept in a tent under the stars. Jamie was used to the skies of Scotland, where the stars knew their rightful places in the firmament. Here in South Africa, the constellations were confusing. In January Canopus shone brilliantly overhead, while in May it was the Southern Cross that was near the zenith. In June, which was South Africa's winter, Scorpio was the glory of the heavens. It was puzzling. Still, it was a very special feeling for Jamie to lie on the warm earth and look up at the timeless sky with his son at his side and know they were part of the same eternity.

They rose at dawn and shot game for the pot: partridge, guinea fowl, reedbuck and oribi. Little Jamie had his own pony, and father and son rode along the veld carefully avoiding the six-foot holes dug by the ant bear, deep enough to engulf a horse and rider, and the smaller holes dug by the mere-cat.

There was danger on the veld. On one trip Jamie and his son were camped at a riverbed where they were almost killed by a band of migrating springbok. The first sign of trouble was a faint cloud of dust on the horizon. Hares and jackals and mere-cats raced past and large snakes came out of the brush looking for rocks under which to hide. Jamie looked at the horizon again. The dust cloud was coming closer.

'Let's get out of here,' he said.

'Our tent –'

'Leave it!'

The two of them quickly mounted and headed for the top of a high hill. They heard the drumming of hooves and then they could see the front rank of the springbok, racing in a line at least three miles long. There were more than half a million of them, sweeping away everything in their path. Trees were torn down and shrubs were pulverized, and in the wake of the relentless tide were the bodies of hundreds of small animals. Hares, snakes, jackals and guinea fowl were crushed beneath the deadly hooves. The air was filled with dust and thunder, and when it was finally over, Jamie estimated that it had lasted more than three hours.

On Jamie's sixth birthday, his father said, 'I'm going to take you to Cape Town next week and show you what a real city looks like.'

'Can Mother go with us?' Jamie asked. 'She doesn't like shooting, but she likes cities.'

His father ruffled the boy's hair and said, 'She's busy here, Son. Just the two of us men, eh?'

The child was disturbed by the fact that his

mother and father seemed so distant with each other, but then he did not understand it.

They made the journey in Jamie's private railway car. By the year 1891, railways were becoming the pre-eminent means of travel in South Africa, for trains were inexpensive, convenient and fast. The private railway car Jamie ordered built for himself was seventy-one feet long and had four panelled staterooms that could accommodate twelve persons, a salon that could be used as an office, a dining compartment, a barroom and a fully equipped kitchen. The staterooms had brass beds, Pintsch gas lamps and wide picture windows.

'Where are all the passengers?' the young boy asked.

Jamie laughed. 'We're all the passengers. It's your train, Son.'

Young Jamie spent most of the trip staring out the window, marvelling at the endless expanse of land speeding past.

'This is God's land,' his father told him. 'He filled it with precious minerals for us. They're all in the ground, waiting to be discovered. What's been found so far is only the beginning, Jamie.'

When they arrived at Cape Town, young Jamie was awed by the crowds and the huge buildings. Jamie took his son down to the McGregor Shipping Line, and pointed out half a dozen ships loading and unloading in the harbour. 'You see those? They belong to us.'

When they returned to Klipdrift, young Jamie was bursting with the news of all he had seen. 'Papa owns the whole city!' the boy exclaimed. 'You'd love it, Mama. You'll see it next time.'

Margaret hugged her son to her. 'Yes, darling.'

Jamie spent many nights away from home, and Margaret knew he was at Madam Agnes's. She had heard he had bought a house for one of the women so that he could visit her privately. She had no way of knowing whether it was true. Margaret only knew that whoever she was, she wanted to kill her.

To retain her sanity, Margaret forced herself to take an interest in the town. She raised funds to build a new church and started a mission to help the families of prospectors who were in dire need. She demanded that Jamie use one of his railroad cars to transport prospectors free of charge back to Cape Town when they had run out of money and hope.

'You're asking me to throw away good money, woman,' he growled. 'Let 'em walk back the same way they came.'

'They're in no condition to walk,' Margaret argued. 'And if they stay, the town will have to bear the cost of clothing and feeding them.'

'All right,' Jamie finally grumbled. 'But it's a damn fool idea.'

'Thank you, Jamie.'

He watched Margaret march out of his office, and, in spite of himself, he could not help feeling a certain pride in her. *She'd make a fine wife for someone*, Jamie thought.

The name of the woman Jamie set up in a private house was Maggie, the pretty prostitute who had sat next to Margaret at the baby shower. It was ironic, Jamie thought, that she should bear his wife's name. They were nothing alike. This Maggie was a twenty-one-year-old blonde with a pert face and a lush body – a tigress in bed. Jamie had paid Madam Agnes well for letting him take the girl, and he gave Maggie a generous allowance. Jamie was very discreet when he visited the small house. It was almost always at night, and he was certain he was unobserved. In fact, he was observed by many people, but not one of them cared to comment about it. It was Jamie McGregor's town, and he had the right to do anything he pleased.

On this particular evening, Jamie was finding no joy. He had gone to the house anticipating pleasure, but Maggie was in a foul mood. She lay sprawled across the large bed, her rose-coloured dressing gown not quite concealing her ripe breasts or the silky, golden triangle between her thighs. 'I'm sick of stayin' locked up in this damned house,' she said. 'It's like I'm a slave or somethin'! At least at Madam Agnes's there was somethin' goin' on all the time. Why don't you ever take me with you when you travel?'

'I've explained that, Maggie. I can't –'

She leaped out of bed and stood defiantly before him, her dressing gown wide open. 'Horseshit! You take your *son* everywhere. Ain't I as good as your son?'

'No,' Jamie said. His voice was dangerously quiet. 'You're not.' He walked over to the bar and poured himself a brandy. It was his fourth – much more than he usually drank.

'I don't mean a damned thing to you,' Maggie screamed. 'I'm just a piece of arse.' She threw back her head and laughed derisively. 'Big, moral Scotchman!'

'Scot – not Scotchman.'

'For Christ's sake, will you stop criticizin' me? Everythin' I do ain't good enough. Who the hell do you think you are, my bloody father?'

Jamie had had enough. 'You can go back to Madam Agnes's tomorrow. I'll tell her you're coming.' He picked up his hat and headed for the door.

'You can't get rid of me like this, you bastard!' She followed him, wild with anger.

Jamie stopped at the door. 'I just did.' And he disappeared into the night.

To his surprise, he found he was walking unsteadily. His mind seemed fuzzy. Perhaps he had had more than four brandies. He was not sure. He thought about Maggie's naked body in bed that evening, and how she had flaunted it, teasing him, then withdrawing. She had played with him, stroking him and running her soft tongue over his body until he was hard and eager for her. And then she had begun the fight, leaving him inflamed and unsatisfied.

When Jamie reached home, he entered the front hall, and as he started towards his room, he passed the closed door of Margaret's bedroom. There was a light from under the door. She was still awake. Jamie suddenly began to picture Margaret in bed, wearing a thin nightgown. Or perhaps nothing. He remembered how her rich, full body had writhed beneath him under the trees by the Orange River. With the liquor guiding him, he opened Margaret's bedroom door and entered.

She was in bed reading by the light of a kerosene lamp. She looked up in surprise. 'Jamie . . . is something wrong?'

'Cause I decide to pay my wife a l'il visit?' His words were slurred.

She was wearing a sheer nightgown, and Jamie could see her ripe breasts straining against the fabric. *God, she has a lovely body!* He began to take off his clothes.

Margaret leaped out of bed, her eyes very wide. 'What are you doing?'

Jamie kicked the door shut behind him and walked over to her. In a moment, he had thrown her onto the bed and he was next to her, naked. 'God, I want you, Maggie.'

In his drunken confusion, he was not sure which Maggie he wanted. How she fought him! Yes, this was his little wildcat. He laughed as he finally managed to subdue her flailing arms and legs, and she was suddenly open to him and pulling him close and saying, 'Oh, my darling, my darling Jamie. I need you so much,' and he thought, *I shouldn't have been so mean to you. In the morning I'm gonna tell you you don't have to go back to Madam Agnes's . . .*

When Margaret awoke the next morning, she was alone in bed. She could still feel Jamie's strong male body inside hers and she heard him saying, *God, I want you, Maggie,* and she was filled with a wild, complete joy. She had been right all along. He did love her. It had been worth the wait, worth the years of pain and loneliness and humiliation.

Margaret spent the rest of the day in a state of rapture. She bathed and washed her hair and changed her mind a dozen times about which dress would please Jamie most. She sent the cook away so that she herself could prepare Jamie's favourite dishes. She set the dining-room table again and again before she was satisfied with the candles and flowers. She wanted this to be a perfect evening.

Jamie did not come home for dinner. Nor did he come home all night. Margaret sat in the library waiting for him until three o'clock in the morning, and then she went to her bed, alone.

When Jamie returned home the following evening, he nodded politely to Margaret and walked on to his son's room. Margaret stood staring after him in stunned bewilderment, and then slowly turned to look at herself in the mirror. The mirror told her that she had never looked as beautiful, but when she looked closer she could not recognize the eyes. They were the eyes of a stranger.

TEN

'Well, I have some wonderful news for you, Mrs McGregor,' Dr Teeger beamed. 'You're going to have a baby.'

Margaret felt the shock of his words and did not know whether to laugh or cry. *Wonderful news?* To bring another child into a loveless marriage was impossible. Margaret could no longer bear the humiliation. She would have to find a way out, and even as she was thinking it, she felt a sudden wave of nausea that left her drenched in perspiration.

Dr Teeger was saying, 'Morning sickness?'

'A bit.'

He handed her some pills. 'Take these. They'll help. You're in excellent condition, Mrs McGregor. Not a thing to worry about. You run along home and tell the good news to your husband.'

'Yes,' she said dully. 'I'll do that.'

*   *   *

They were at the dinner table when she said, 'I saw the doctor today. I'm going to have a baby.'

Without a word, Jamie threw down his napkin, arose from his chair and stormed out of the room. That was the moment when Margaret learned she could hate Jamie McGregor as deeply as she could love him.

It was a difficult pregnancy, and Margaret spent much of the time in bed, weak and tired. She lay there hour after hour, fantasizing, visualizing Jamie at her feet, begging forgiveness, making wild love to her again. But they were only fantasies. The reality was that she was trapped. She had nowhere to go, and even if she could leave, he would never allow her to take her son with her.

Jamie was seven now, a healthy, handsome boy with a quick mind and a sense of humour. He had drawn closer, to his mother, as though somehow sensing the unhappiness in her. He made little gifts for her in school and brought them home, and Margaret would smile and thank him and try to lift herself out of her depression. When young Jamie asked why his father stayed away nights and never took her out, Margaret would reply, 'Your father is a very important man, Jamie, doing important things, and he's very busy.'

What's between his father and me is my problem, Margaret thought, *and I'll not have Jamie hating his father because of it.*

* * *

Margaret's pregnancy became more and more apparent. When she went out on the street, acquaintances would stop her and say, 'It won't be long now, will it, Mrs McGregor? I'll bet it's going to be a fine boy like little Jamie. Your husband must be a happy man.'

Behind her back, they said, 'Poor thing. She's lookin' peaked – she must have found out about the whore he's taken as his mistress . . .'

Margaret tried to prepare young Jamie for the new arrival. 'You're going to have a new brother or sister, darling. Then you'll have someone to play with all the time. Won't that be nice?'

Jamie hugged her and said, 'It will be more company for you, Mother.'

And Margaret fought to keep back the tears.

The labour pains began at four o'clock in the morning. Mrs Talley sent for Hannah, and the baby was delivered at noon. It was a healthy baby girl, with her mother's mouth and her father's chin, and black hair curling around her little red face. Margaret named her Kate. *It's a good, strong name*, Margaret thought. *And she's going to need her strength. We all are. I've got to take the children away from here. I don't know how yet, but I must find a way.*

David Blackwell burst into Jamie McGregor's office without knocking, and Jamie looked up in surprise. 'What the hell –?'

'They're rioting at the Namib!'

Jamie stood up. '*What?* What happened?'

'One of the black boys was caught trying to steal a diamond. He cut a hole under his armpit and hid the stone inside it. As a lesson, Hans Zimmerman flogged him in front of the other workers. The boy died. He was twelve years old.'

Jamie's face filled with rage. 'Sweet Jesus! I ordered a stop to flogging at all the mines.'

'I warned Zimmerman.'

'Get rid of the bastard.'

'We can't find him.'

'Why not?'

'The blacks have him. The situation's out of control.'

Jamie grabbed his hat. 'Stay here and take care of things until I get back.'

'I don't think it's safe for you to go up there, Mr McGregor. The native that Zimmerman killed was from the Barolong tribe. They don't forgive, and they don't forget. I could –'

But Jamie was gone.

When Jamie McGregor was ten miles away from the diamond field, he could see the smoke. All the huts at the Namib had been set to the torch. *The damned fools!* Jamie thought. *They're burning their own houses.* As his carriage drew closer, he heard the sounds of gunshots and screams. Amid the mass confusion, uniformed constables were shooting at blacks and coloured who were desperately trying to flee. The whites were outnumbered ten to one, but they had the weapons.

When the chief constable, Bernard Sothey, saw Jamie McGregor, he hurried up to him and said, 'Don't worry, Mr McGregor. We'll get every last one of the bastards.'

'The hell you will,' Jamie cried. 'Order your men to stop shooting.'

'*What?* If we –'

'Do as I say!' Jamie watched, sick with rage, as a black woman fell under a hail of bullets. 'Call your men off.'

'As you say, sir.' The chief constable gave orders to an aide, and three minutes later all shooting had stopped.

There were bodies on the ground everywhere. 'If you want my advice,' Sothey said, 'I'd –'

'I don't want your advice. Bring me their leader.'

Two policemen brought a young black up to where Jamie was standing. He was handcuffed and covered with blood, but there was no fear in him. He stood tall and straight, his eyes blazing, and Jamie remembered Banda's word for Bantu pride: *isiko.*

'I'm Jamie McGregor.'

The man spat.

'What happened here was not my doing. I want to make it up to your men.'

'Tell that to their widows.'

Jamie turned to Sothey. 'Where's Hans Zimmerman?'

'We're still looking for him, sir.'

Jamie saw the gleam in the black man's eyes, and he knew that Hans Zimmerman was not going to be found.

He said to the man, 'I'm closing the diamond field down for three days. I want you to talk to your people. Make a list of your complaints, and I'll look at it. I promise you I'll be fair. I'll change everything here that's not right.'

The man studied him, a look of scepticism on his face.

'There will be a new foreman in charge here, and decent working conditions. But I'll expect your men back at work in three days.'

The chief constable said, incredulously, 'You mean you're gonna let him go? He killed some of my men.'

'There will be a full investigation, and –'

There was the sound of a horse galloping towards them, and Jamie turned. It was David Blackwell, and the unexpected sight of him sounded an alarm in Jamie's mind.

David leaped off his horse. 'Mr McGregor, your son has disappeared.'

The world suddenly grew cold.

Half the population of Klipdrift turned out to join in the search. They covered the countryside, looking through gulleys, ravines and klops. There was no trace of the boy.

Jamie was like a man possessed. *He's wandered away somewhere, that's all. He'll be back.*

He went into Margaret's bedroom. She was lying in bed, nursing the baby.

'Is there any news?' she demanded.

'Not yet, but I'll find him.' He looked at his baby daughter for an instant, then turned and walked out without another word.

Mrs Talley came into the room, twisting her hands in her apron. 'Don't you worry, Mrs McGregor. Jamie is a big boy. He knows how to take care of himself.'

Margaret's eyes were blinded by tears. *No one would harm little Jamie, would they? Of course not.*

Mrs Talley reached down and took Kate from Margaret's arms.

'Try to sleep.'

She took the baby into the nursery and laid her down in her crib. Kate was looking up at her, smiling.

'You'd better get some sleep too, little one. You've got a busy life ahead of you.'

Mrs Talley walked out of the room, closing the door behind her.

At midnight, the bedroom window silently slid open and a man climbed into the room. He walked over to the crib, threw a blanket over the infant's head and scooped her up in his arms.

Banda was gone as quickly as he had come.

It was Mrs Talley who discovered that Kate was missing. Her first thought was that Mrs McGregor had come in the night and taken her. She walked into Margaret's bedroom and asked, 'Where's the baby?'

And from the look on Margaret's face, she knew instantly what had happened.

As another day went by with no trace of his son, Jamie was on the verge of collapsing. He approached David Blackwell. 'You don't think anything bad has happened to him?' His voice was barely under control.

David tried to sound convincing. 'I'm sure not, Mr McGregor.'

But he *was* sure. He had warned Jamie McGregor that the Bantus neither forgave nor forgot, and it was a Bantu who had been cruelly murdered. David was certain of one thing: if the Bantus had taken little Jamie, he had died a horrible death, for they would exact their vengeance in kind.

Jamie returned home at dawn, drained. He had led a search party of townspeople, diggers and constables, and they had spent the night looking without success in every conceivable place for the young boy.

David was waiting when Jamie walked into the study. David rose to his feet. 'Mr McGregor, your daughter has been kidnapped.'

Jamie stared at him in silence, his face pale. Then he turned and walked into his bedroom.

Jamie had not been to bed for forty-eight hours, and he fell into bed, utterly exhausted, and slept.

He was under the shade of a large baobab tree and in the distance across the trackless veld a lion was moving towards him. Young Jamie was shaking him. *Wake up, Papa, a lion is coming.* The animal was moving towards them faster now. His son was shaking him harder. *Wake up!* Jamie opened his eyes. Banda was standing over him. Jamie started to speak, but Banda put a hand over Jamie's mouth.

'Quiet!' He allowed Jamie to sit up.

'Where's my son?' Jamie demanded.

'He's dead.'

The room began to spin.

'I'm sorry. I was too late to stop them. Your people spilled Bantu blood. My people demanded vengeance.'

Jamie buried his face in his hands. 'Oh, my God! What did they do to him?'

There was a bottomless sorrow in Banda's voice. 'They left him out in the desert. I – I found his body and buried him.'

'Oh, no! Oh, please, no!'

'I tried to save him, Jamie.'

Jamie slowly nodded, accepting it. Then dully, 'What about my daughter?'

'I took her away before they could get her. She's back in her bedroom, asleep. She'll be all right if you do what you promised.'

Jamie looked up, and his face was a mask of hatred. 'I'll keep my promise. But I want the men who killed my son. They're going to pay.'

Banda said quietly, 'Then you will have to kill my whole tribe, Jamie.'

Banda was gone.

It was only a nightmare, but she kept her eyes tightly closed, because she knew if she opened them the nightmare would become real and her children would be dead. So she played a game. She would keep her eyes squeezed shut until she felt little Jamie's hand on hers saying, 'It's all right, Mother. We're here. We're safe.'

She had been in bed for three days, refusing to talk to anyone or see anyone. Dr Teeger came and went, and Margaret was not even aware of it. In the middle of the night Margaret was lying in bed with her eyes shut when she heard a loud crash from her son's room. She opened her eyes and listened. There was another sound. Little Jamie was back!

Margaret hurriedly got out of bed and ran down the corridor towards the closed door of her son's room. Through the door, she could hear strange animal sounds. Her heart pounding wildly, she pushed the door open.

Her husband lay on the floor, his face and body contorted. One eye was closed and the other stared up at her grotesquely. He was trying to speak, and the words came out as slobbering animal sounds.

Margaret whispered, 'Oh, Jamie – Jamie!'

* * *

Dr Teeger said, 'I'm afraid the news is bad, Mrs McGregor. Your husband has had a severe stroke. There's a fifty-fifty chance he'll live – but if he does, he'll be a vegetable. I'll make arrangements to get him into a private sanitarium where he can get the proper care.'

'No.'

He looked at Margaret in surprise. 'No . . . what?'

'No hospital. I want him here with me.'

The doctor considered for a moment. 'All right. You'll need a nurse. I'll arrange –'

'I don't want a nurse. I'll take care of Jamie myself.'

Dr Teeger shook his head. 'That won't be possible, Mrs McGregor. You don't know what's involved. Your husband is no longer a functioning human being. He's completely paralysed and will be for as long as he lives.'

Margaret said, 'I'll take care of him.'

Now Jamie finally, truly, belonged to her.

ELEVEN

Jamie McGregor lived for exactly one year from the day he was taken ill, and it was the happiest time of Margaret's life. Jamie was totally helpless. He could neither talk nor move. Margaret cared for her husband, tended to all his needs, and kept him at her side day and night. During the day, she propped him up in a wheelchair in the sewing room, and while she knitted sweaters and throwrobes for him, she talked to him. She discussed all the little household problems he had never had time to listen to before, and she told him how well little Kate was getting along. At night she carried Jamie's skeletal body to her bedroom and gently lay him in bed next to her. Margaret tucked him in and they had their one-sided chat until Margaret was ready to go to sleep.

David Blackwell was running Kruger-Brent, Ltd. From time to time, David came to the house with papers for Margaret to sign, and it was painful for

David to see the helpless condition Jamie was in. *I owe this man everything*, David thought.

'You chose well, Jamie,' Margaret told her husband. 'David is a fine man.' She put down her knitting and smiled. 'He reminds me of you a bit. Of course, there was never anyone as clever as you, my darling, and there never will be again. You were so fair to look at, Jamie, and so kind and strong. And you weren't afraid to dream. Now all your dreams have come true. The company is getting bigger every day.' She picked up her knitting again. 'Little Kate is beginning to talk. I'll swear she said "mama" this morning . . .'

Jamie sat there, propped up in his chair, one eye staring ahead.'

'She has your eyes and your mouth. She's going to grow up to be a beauty . . .'

The following morning when Margaret awakened, Jamie McGregor was dead. She took him in her arms and held him close to her.

'Rest, my darling, rest. I've always loved you so much, Jamie. I hope you know that. Good-bye, my own dear love.'

She was alone now. Her husband and her son had left her. There was only herself and her daughter. Margaret walked into the baby's room and looked down at Kate, sleeping in her crib. *Katherine. Kate.* The name came from the Greek, and it meant clear or pure. It was a name given to saints and nuns and queens.

Margaret said aloud, 'Which are you going to be, Kate?'

It was a time of great expansion in South Africa, but was also a time of great strife. There was a long-standing Transvaal dispute between the Boers and the British, and it finally came to a head. On Thursday, October 12, 1899, on Kate' seventh birthday, the British declared war on the Boers, and three days later the Orange Free State was under attack. David tried to persuade Margaret to take Kate and leave South Africa, but Margaret refused to go.

'My husband is here,' she said.

There was nothing David could do to dissuade her. 'I'm going to join with the Boers,' David told her. 'Will you be all right?'

'Yes, of course,' Margaret said. 'I'll try to keep the company going.'

The next morning David was gone.

The British had expected a quick and easy war, no more than a mopping-up operation, and they began with a confident, light-hearted holiday spirit. At the Hyde Park Barracks in London, a send-off supper was given, with a special menu showing a British soldier holding up the head of a boar on a tray. The menu read:

SEND-OFF SUPPER
To the CAPE SQUADRON,
November 27, 1899

MENU
Oysters – Blue Points
Compo Soup
Toady in the Hole
Sandy Sole
Mafeking Mutton
Transvaal Turnips. Cape Sauce
Pretoria Pheasants
White Sauce
Tinker Taters
Peace Pudding. Massa Ices
Dutch Cheese
Dessert

*(You are requested not to throw shells
under the tables)*

Boer Whines – Long Tom
Hollands-in-Skin
Orange Wine

The British were in for a surprise. The Boers were on their own home territory, and they were tough and determined. The first battle of the war took place in Mafeking, hardly more than a village, and for the first time, the British began to realize what they were up against. More troops were quickly sent over from England. They laid siege to Kimberley, and it was only after a fierce and bloody fight that they went on to take Ladysmith. The cannons of the Boers had a longer range than those of the British, so long-range guns were removed from British warships, moved inland and manned by sailors hundreds of miles from their ships.

In Klipdrift, Margaret listened eagerly for news of each battle, and she and those around her lived on rumours, their moods varying from elation to despair, depending on the news. And then one morning one of Margaret's employees came running into her office and said, 'I just heard a report that the British are advancing on Klipdrift. They're going to kill us all!'

'Nonsense. They wouldn't dare touch us.'

Five hours later, Margaret McGregor was a prisoner of war.

Margaret and Kate were taken to Paardeberg, one of the hundreds of prison camps that had sprung up all over South Africa. The prisoners were kept inside an enormous open field, ringed by barbed wire and guarded by armed British soldiers. The conditions were deplorable.

Margaret took Kate in her arms and said, 'Don't worry, darling, nothing's going to happen to you.'

But neither of them believed it. Each day became a calendar of horrors. They watched those around them die by the tens and the hundreds and then by the thousands as fever swept through the camp. There were no doctors or medication for the wounded, and food was scarce. It was a constant nightmare that went on for almost three harrowing years. The worst of it was the feeling of utter helplessness. Margaret and Kate were at the complete mercy of their captors. They were dependent upon them for meals and shelter, for their very lives. Kate lived in terror. She watched the children around her die, and she was afraid that she would be next. She was powerless to protect her mother or herself, and it was a lesson she was never to forget. *Power*. If you had power, you had food. You had medicine. You had freedom. She saw those around her fall ill and die, and she equated power with life. *One day*, Kate thought, *I'll have power. No one will be able to do this to me again.*

The violent battles went on – Belmont and Graspan and Stormberg and Spioenkop – but in the end, the brave Boers were no match for the might of the British Empire. In 1902, after nearly three years of bloody war, the Boers surrendered. Fifty-five thousand Boers fought, and thirty-four thousand of their soldiers, women and children died. But what filled the survivors with a deep savage bitterness was the knowledge that twenty-eight thousand of those died in British concentration camps.

On the day the gates of the camp were flung open, Margaret and Kate returned to Klipdrift. A few weeks later, on a quiet Sunday, David Blackwell arrived. The war had matured him, but he was still the same grave, thoughtful David Margaret had learned to rely upon. David had spent these hellish years fighting and worrying about whether Margaret and Kate were dead or alive. When he found them safe at home, he was filled with joy.

'I wish I could have protected you both,' David told Margaret.

'That's all past, David. We must think only of the future.'

And the future was Kruger-Brent, Ltd.

For the world, the year 1900 was a clean slate on which history was going to be written, a new era that promised peace and limitless hope for everyone. A new century had begun, and it brought with it a series of astonishing inventions that reshaped life around the globe. Steam and electric automobiles were replaced by the combustion engine. There were submarines and airplanes. The world population exploded to a billion and a half people. It was a time to grow and expand, and during the next six years, Margaret and David took full advantage of every opportunity.

During those years, Kate grew up with almost no supervision. Her mother was too busy running the company with David to pay much attention to her. She was a wild child, stubborn and opinionated and intractable. One afternoon when Margaret came home from a business meeting, she saw her fourteen-year-old daughter in the muddy yard in a fistfight with two boys. Margaret stared in horrified disbelief.

'Bloody hell!' she said under her breath. 'That's the girl who one day is going to run Kruger-Brent, Limited! God help us all!'

BOOK TWO

Kate and David

1906–1914

TWELVE

On a hot summer night in 1914, Kate McGregor was working alone in her office at the new Kruger-Brent, Ltd., headquarters building in Johannesburg when she heard the sound of approaching automobiles. She put down the papers she had been studying, walked over to the window and looked out. Two police cars and a paddy wagon had come to a stop in front of the building. Kate watched frowning, as half a dozen uniformed policemen leaped from the cars and hurried to cover the two entrances and exits to the building. It was late, and the streets were deserted. Kate caught a wavy reflection of herself in the window. She was a beautiful woman, with her father's light-grey eyes and her mother's full figure.

There was a knock at the office door and Kate called, 'Come in.'

The door opened and two uniformed men entered. One wore the bars of a superintendent of police.

'What on earth is going on?' Kate demanded.

'I apologise for disturbing you at this late hour, Miss McGregor. I'm Superintendent Cominsky.'

'What's the problem, Superintendent?'

'We've had a report that an escaped killer was seen entering this building a short time ago.'

There was a shocked look on Kate's face. 'Entering *this* building?'

'Yes, ma'am. He's armed and dangerous.'

Kate said nervously, 'Then I would very much appreciate it, Superintendent, if you would find him and get him out of here.'

'That's exactly what we intend to do, Miss McGregor. You haven't seen or heard anything suspicious, have you?'

'No. But I'm alone here, and there are a lot of places a person could hide. I'd like you to have your men search this place thoroughly.

'We'll get started immediately, ma'am.'

The superintendent turned and called to the men in the hallway, 'Spread out. Start at the basement and work your way up to the roof.' He turned to Kate. 'Are any of the offices locked?'

'I don't believe so,' Kate said, 'but if they are, I'll open them for you.'

Superintendent Cominsky could see how nervous she was, and he did not blame her. She would be even more nervous if she knew how desperate the man was for whom they were looking. 'We'll find him,' the superintendent assured Kate.

Kate picked up the report she had been working

on, but she was unable to concentrate. She could hear the police moving through the building, going from office to office. *Would they find him?* She shivered.

The policemen moved slowly, methodically searching every possible hiding place from the basement to the roof. Forty-five minutes later, Superintendent Cominsky returned to Kate's office.

'Not yet, ma'am, but don't worry –'

'I *am* worried, Superintendent. If there is an escaped killer in this building, I want you to find him.'

'We will, Miss McGregor. We have tracking dogs.'

From the corridor came the sound of barking and a moment later a handler came into the office with two large German shepherds on leashes.

'The dogs have been all over the building, sir. They've searched everyplace but this office.'

The superintendent turned to Kate. 'Have you been out of this office anytime in the past hour or so?'

'Yes. I went to look up some records in the file room. Do you think he could have –?' She shuddered. 'I'd like you to check this office, please.'

The superintendent gave a signal and the handler slipped the leashes off the dogs and gave the command. 'Track.'

The dogs went crazy. They raced to a closed door and began barking wildly.

'Oh, my God!' Kate cried. 'He's in there!'

The superintendent pulled out his gun. 'Open it,' he ordered.

The two policemen moved to the closet door with drawn guns and pulled the door open. The closet was empty. One of the dogs raced to another door and pawed excitedly at it.

'Where does that door lead?' Superintendent Cominsky asked.

'To a washroom.'

The two policemen took up places on either side of the door and yanked it open. There was no one inside.

The handler was baffled. 'They've never behaved this way before.' The dogs were racing around the room frantically. 'They've got the scent,' the handler said. 'But where is he?'

Both dogs ran to the drawer of Kate's desk and continued their barking.

'There's your answer,' Kate tried to laugh. 'He's in the drawer.'

Superintendent Cominsky was embarrassed. 'I'm sorry to have troubled you, Miss McGregor.' He turned to the handler and snapped. 'Take these dogs out of here.'

'You're not leaving?' There was concern in Kate's voice.

'Miss McGregor, I can assure you you're perfectly safe. My men have covered every inch of this building. You have my personal guarantee that he's not here. I'm afraid it was a false alarm. My apologies.'

Kate swallowed. 'You certainly know how to bring excitement to a woman's evening.'

Kate stood looking out of the window, watching the last of the police vehicles drive away. When they were out of sight, she opened her desk drawer and pulled out a blood-stained pair of canvas shoes. She carried them down the corridor to a door marked *Private, Authorized Personnel Only*, and entered. The room was bare except for a large, locked, walk-in safe built into the wall, the vault where Kruger-Brent, Ltd. stored its diamonds before shipping. Quickly Kate dialled the combination on the safe and pulled open the giant door. Dozens of metal safe-deposit boxes were built into the sides of the vault, all crammed with diamonds. In the centre of the room, lying on the floor half-conscious, was Banda.

Kate knelt beside him. 'They've gone.'

Banda slowly opened his eyes and managed a weak grin. 'If I had a way out of this vault, do you know how rich I'd be, Kate?'

Kate carefully helped him to his feet. He winced with pain as she touched his arm. She had wrapped a bandage around it, but blood was seeping through.

'Can you put your shoes on?' She had taken them from him earlier, and, to confuse the tracking dogs she knew would be brought in, she had walked around her office in them and then hidden them in her drawer.

Now Kate said, 'Come on. We have to get you out of here.'

Banda shook his head. 'I'll make it on my own. If they catch you helping me, you'll be in more trouble than you can handle.'

'Let me worry about that.'

Banda took a last look around the vault.

'Do you want any samples?' Kate asked. 'You can help yourself.'

Banda looked at her and saw that she was serious. 'Your daddy made me that offer once, a long time ago.'

Kate smiled wryly. 'I know.'

'I don't need money. I just have to leave town for a while.'

'How do you think you're going to get out of Johannesburg?'

'I'll find a way.'

'Listen to me. The police have roadblocks out by now. Every exit from the city will be watched. You won't have a chance by yourself.'

He said stubbornly, 'You've done enough.' He had managed to put his shoes on. He was a forlorn-looking figure, standing there in a torn, bloodied shirt and jacket. His face was seamed and his hair was grey, but when Kate looked at him she saw the tall, handsome figure she had first met as a child.

'Banda, if they catch you, they'll kill you,' Kate said quietly. 'You're coming with me.'

She knew she was right about the roadblocks.

Every exit from Johannesburg would be guarded by police patrols. Banda's capture was a top priority and the authorities had orders to bring him in dead or alive. The railroad stations and roads would be watched.

'I hope you have a better plan than your daddy had,' Banda said. His voice was weak. Kate wondered how much blood he had lost.

'Don't talk. Save your strength. Just leave everything to me.' Kate sounded more confident than she felt. Banda's life was in her hands, and she could not bear it if anything happened to him. She wished again, for the hundredth time, that David was not away. Well, she would simply have to manage without him.

'I'm going to bring my automobile around to the alley,' Kate said. 'Give me ten minutes, then come outside. I'll have the back door of the car open. Get in and lie on the floor. There will be a blanket to cover yourself with.'

'Kate, they're going to search every automobile leaving the city. If –'

'We're not going by automobile. There's a train leaving for Cape Town at eight a.m. I ordered my private car connected to it.'

'You're getting me out of here in your private railroad car?'

'That's right.'

Banda managed a grin. 'You McGregors really like excitement.'

* * *

Thirty minutes later, Kate drove into the railroad yards. Banda was on the floor of the backseat, concealed by a blanket. They had had no trouble passing the roadblocks in the city, but now as Kate's car turned into the train yards, a light suddenly flashed on, and Kate saw that her way was blocked by several policemen. A familiar figure walked towards Kate's car.

'Superintendent Cominsky!'

He registered surprise. 'Miss McGregor, what are you doing here?'

Kate gave him a quick, apprehensive smile. 'You'll think I'm just a silly, weak female, Superintendent, but to tell you the truth, what happened back at the office scared the wits out of me. I decided to leave town until you catch this killer you're looking for. Or have you found him?'

'Not yet, ma'am, but we will. I have a feeling he'll make for these railroad yards. Wherever he runs, we'll catch him.'

'I certainly hope so!'

'Where are you headed?'

'My railway car is on a siding up ahead. I'm taking it to Cape Town.'

'Would you like one of my men to escort you?'

'Oh, thank you, Superintendent, but that won't be necessary. Now that I know where you and your men are, I'll breathe a lot easier, believe me.'

Five minutes later, Kate and Banda were safely inside the private railway car. It was pitch black.

'Sorry about the dark,' Kate said. 'I don't want to light any lamps.'

She helped Banda onto a bed. 'You'll be fine here until morning. When we start to pull out, you'll hide out in the washroom.'

Banda nodded. 'Thank you.'

Kate drew the shades. 'Have you a doctor who will take care of you when we get to Cape Town?'

He looked up into her eyes. '*We?*'

'You didn't think I was going to let you travel alone while I missed all the fun?'

Banda threw back his head and laughed. *She's her father's daughter, all right.*

As dawn was breaking, an engine pulled up to the private railroad car and shunted it onto the main track in back of the train that was leaving for Cape Town. The car rocked back and forth as the connection was made.

At exactly eight o'clock, the train pulled out of the station. Kate had left word that she did not wish to be disturbed. Banda's wound was bleeding again, and Kate attended to it. She had not had a chance to talk to Banda since earlier that evening, when he had stumbled half-dead into her office. Now she said, 'Tell me what happened, Banda.'

Banda looked at her and thought, *Where can I begin?* How could he explain to her the *trekboers* who pushed the Bantus from their ancestral land?

Had it started with them? Or had it started with the giant Oom Paul Kruger, President of the Transvaal, who said in a speech to the South African Parliament, 'We must be the lords over the blacks and let them be a subject race . . .' Or had it begun with the great empire-builder Cecil Rhodes, whose motto was, 'Africa for the whites'? How could he sum up the history of his people in a sentence? He thought of a way. 'The police murdered my son,' Banda said.

The story came pouring out. Banda's older son, Ntombenthle, was attending a political rally when the police charged in to break it up. Some shots were fired, and a riot began. Ntombenthle was arrested, and the next morning he was found hanged in his cell. 'They said it was suicide,' Banda told Kate. 'But I know my son. It was murder.'

'My God, he was so young,' Kate breathed. She thought of all the times they had played together, laughed together. Ntombenthle had been such a handsome boy. 'I'm sorry, Banda. I'm so sorry. But why are they after you?'

'After they killed him I began to rally the blacks. I had to fight back, Kate. I couldn't just sit and do nothing. The police called me an enemy of the state. They arrested me for a robbery I did not commit and sentenced me to prison for twenty years. Four of us made a break. A guard was shot and killed, and they're blaming me. I've never carried a gun in my life.'

'I believe you,' Kate said. 'The first thing we

have to do is get you somewhere where you'll be safe.'

'I'm sorry to involve you in all this.'

'You didn't involve me in anything. You're my friend.'

He smiled. 'You know the first white man I ever heard call me friend? Your daddy.' He sighed. 'How do you think you're going to sneak me off the train at Cape Town?'

'We're not going to Cape Town.'

'But you said –'

'I'm a woman. I have a right to change my mind.'

In the middle of the night when the train stopped at the station at Worcester, Kate arranged to have her private railroad car disconnected and shunted to a siding. When Kate woke up in the morning, she went over to Banda's cot. It was empty. Banda was gone. He had refused to compromise her any further. Kate was sorry, but she was sure he would be safe. He had many friends to take care of him. *David will be proud of me*, Kate thought.

'I can't believe you could be so stupid!' David roared, when Kate returned to Johannesburg and told him the news. 'You not only jeopardized your own safety, but you put the company in danger. If the police had found Banda here, do you know what they would have done?'

Kate said defiantly, 'Yes. They would have killed him.'

David rubbed his forehead in frustration. 'Don't you understand anything?'

'You're bloody right, I do! I understand that you're cold and unfeeling.' Her eyes were ablaze with fury.

'You're still a child.'

She raised her hand to strike him, and David grabbed her arms. 'Kate, you've got to control your temper.'

The words reverberated in Kate's head. *Kate, you've got to learn to control your temper . . .*

It was so long ago. She was four years old, in the middle of a fistfight with a boy who had dared tease her. When David appeared, the boy ran away. Kate started to chase him, and David grabbed her. 'Hold it, Kate. You've got to learn to control your temper. Young ladies don't get into fistfights.'

'I'm not a young lady,' Kate snapped. 'Let go of me.' David released her.

The pink frock she was wearing was muddied and torn, and her cheek was bruised.

'We'd better get you cleaned up before your mother sees you,' David told her.

Kate looked after the retreating boy with regret. 'I could have licked him if you had left me alone.'

David looked down into the passionate little face and laughed. 'You probably could have.'

Mollified, Kate allowed him to pick her up and carry her into her house. She liked being in David's arms. She liked everything about David. He was the only grown-up who understood her. Whenever he was in town, he spent time with her. In relaxed moments, Jamie had told young David about his adventures with Banda, and now David told the stories to Kate. She could not get enough of them.

'Tell me again about the raft they built.'

And David would tell her.

'Tell me about the sharks . . . Tell me about the sea *mis* . . . Tell me about the day . . .'

Kate did not see very much of her mother. Margaret was too involved in running the affairs of Kruger-Brent, Ltd. She did it for Jamie.

Margaret talked to Jamie every night, just as she had during the year before he died. 'David is such a great help, Jamie, and he'll be around when Kate's running the company. I don't want to worry you, but I don't know what to do with that child . . .'

Kate was stubborn and wilful and impossible. She refused to obey her mother or Mrs Talley. If they chose a dress for her to wear, Kate would discard it for another. She would not eat properly. She ate what she wanted to, when she wanted to, and no threat or bribe could sway her. When Kate was forced to go to a birthday party, she found ways to disrupt it. She had no girl friends. She refused to go to dancing class and instead spent her time playing rugby with teenage boys. When Kate finally started school, she set a record for mischief. Margaret found herself going to see the headmistress at least once a month to persuade her to forgive Kate and let her remain in school.

'I don't understand her, Mrs McGregor,' the

headmistress sighed. 'She's extremely bright, but she rebels against simply everything. I don't know what to do with her.'

Neither did Margaret.

The only one who could handle Kate was David. 'I understand you're invited to a birthday party this afternoon,' David said.

'I hate birthday parties.'

David stooped down until he was at her eye level. 'I know you do, Kate. But the father of the little girl who's having the birthday party is a friend of mine. It will make me look bad if you don't attend and behave like a lady.'

Kate stared at him. 'Is he a *good* friend of yours?'

'Yes.'

'I'll go.'

Her manners that afternoon were impeccable.

'I don't know how you do it,' Margaret told David. 'It's magic.'

'She's just high-spirited,' David laughed. 'She'll grow out of it. The important thing is to be careful not to break that spirit.'

'I'll tell you a secret,' Margaret said grimly, 'half the time I'd like to break her neck.'

When Kate was ten, she said to David, 'I want to meet Banda.'

David looked at her in surprise. 'I'm afraid that's not possible, Kate. Banda's farm is a long way from here.'

'Are you going to take me there, David, or do you want me to go by myself?'

The following week David took Kate to Banda's farm. It was a good-sized piece of land, two morgens, and on it Banda raised wheat, sheep and ostriches. The living accommodations were circular huts with walls made of dried mud. Poles supported a cone-shaped roof covered with thatches. Banda stood in front, watching as Kate and David drove up and got out of the carriage. Banda looked at the gangling, serious-faced girl at David's side and said, 'I'd have known you were Jamie McGregor's daughter.'

'And I'd have known you were Banda,' Kate said gravely. 'I came to thank you for saving my father's life.'

Banda laughed. 'Someone's been telling you stories. Come in and meet my family.'

Banda's wife was a beautiful Bantu woman named Ntame. Banda had two sons, Ntombenthle, seven years older than Kate, and Magena, six years older. Ntombenthle was a miniature of his father. He had the same handsome features and proud bearing and an inner dignity.

Kate spent the entire afteroon playing with the two boys. They had dinner in the kitchen of the small, neat farmhouse. David felt uncomfortable eating with a black family. He respected Banda, but it was traditional that there was no socializing between the two races. In addition to that, David was concerned about Banda's political activities. There were reports that he was a disciple of John Tengo Javabu, who was fighting for drastic social changes. Because mine owners could not get enough natives to work for them, the government had imposed a tax of ten shillings on all natives who did not work as mine labourers, and there were riots all over South Africa.

In the late afternoon, David said, 'We'd better get started home, Kate. We have a long ride.'

'Not yet.' Kate turned to Banda. 'Tell me about the sharks . . .'

From that time on, whenever David was in town, Kate made him take her to visit Banda and his family.

David's assurance that Kate would grow out of her high-spiritedness showed no signs of coming to pass. If anything, she grew more wilful every day. She flatly refused to take part in any of the activities that other girls her age participated in. She insisted on going into the mines with David, and he took her hunting and fishing and camping. Kate adored it. One day when Kate and David were fishing the Vaal, and Kate gleefully pulled in a trout larger than anything David had caught, he said, 'You should have been born a boy.'

She turned to him in annoyance. 'Don't be silly, David. Then I couldn't marry you.'

David laughed.

'We *are* going to be married, you know.'

'I'm afraid not, Kate. I'm twenty-two years older

than you. Old enough to be your father. You'll meet a boy one day, a nice young man –'

'I don't want a nice young man,' she said wickedly. 'I want you.'

'If you're really serious,' David said, 'then I'll tell you the secret to a man's heart.'

'Tell me!' Kate said eagerly.

'Through his stomach. Clean that trout and let's have lunch.'

There was not the slightest doubt in Kate's mind that she was going to marry David Blackwell. He was the only man in the world for her.

Once a week Margaret invited David to dinner at the big house. As a rule, Kate preferred to eat dinner in the kitchen with the servants, where she did not have to mind her manners. But on Friday nights when David came, Kate sat in the big dining room. David usually came alone, but occasionally he would bring a female guest and Kate would hate her instantly.

Kate would get David alone for a moment and say, with sweet innocence, 'I've never seen hair that shade of blonde,' or, 'She certainly has peculiar taste in dresses, hasn't she?' or, 'Did she used to be one of Madam Agnes's girls?'

When Kate was fourteen, her headmistress sent for Margaret. 'I run a respectable school, Mrs McGregor. I'm afraid your Kate is a bad influence.'

Margaret sighed. 'What's she done now?'

'She's teaching the other children words they've never heard before.' Her face was grim. 'I might add, Mrs McGregor, that *I've* never heard some of the words before. I can't imagine where the child picked them up.'

Margaret could. Kate picked them up from her street friends. *Well*, Margaret decided, *it is time to end all that.*

The headmistress was saying, 'I do wish you would speak to her. We'll give her another chance, but –'

'No. I have a better idea. I'm going to send Kate away to school.'

When Margaret told David her idea, he grinned. 'She's not going to like that.'

'I can't help it. Now the headmistress is complaining about the language Kate uses. She gets it from those prospectors she's always following around. My daughter's starting to sound like them, look like them and smell like them. Frankly, David, I don't understand her at all. I don't know why she behaves as she does. She's pretty, she's bright, she's –'

'Maybe she's too bright.'

'Well, too bright or not, she's going away to school.'

When Kate arrived home that afternoon, Margaret broke the news to her.

Kate was furious. 'You're trying to get rid of me!'

'Of course I'm not, darling. I just think you'd be better off –'

'I'm better off *here*. All my friends are here. You're trying to separate me from my friends.'

'If you're talking about that riffraff you –'

'They're *not* riffraff. They're as good as anybody.'

'Kate, I'm not going to argue with you. You're going away to a boarding school for young ladies, and that's that.'

'I'll kill myself,' Kate promised.

'All right, darling. There's a razor upstairs, and if you look around, I'm sure you'll find various poisons in the house.'

Kate burst into tears. 'Please don't do this to me, Mother.'

Margaret took her in her arms. 'It's for your own good, Kate. You'll be a young woman soon. You'll be ready for marriage. No man is going to marry a girl who talks and dresses and behaves the way you do.'

'That's not true,' Kate sniffled. 'David doesn't mind.'

'What does David have to do with this?'

'We're going to be married.'

Margaret sighed. 'I'll have Mrs Talley pack your things.'

There were half a dozen good English boarding schools for young girls. Margaret decided that Cheltenham, in Gloucestershire, was best suited for

Kate. It was a school noted for its rigid discipline. It was set on acres of land surrounded by high battlements and, according to its charter, was founded for the daughters of noblemen and gentlemen. David did business with the husband of the headmistress, Mrs Keaton, and he had no trouble arranging for Kate to be enrolled there.

When Kate heard where she was going, she exploded anew. 'I've heard about that school! It's awful. I'll come back like one of those stuffed English dolls. Is that what you'd like?'

'What I would like is for you to learn some manners,' Margaret told her.

'I don't need manners. I've got brains.'

'That's not the first thing a man looks for in a woman,' Margaret said dryly, 'and you're becoming a woman.'

'I don't want to become a woman,' Kate screamed. 'Why the bloody hell can't you just leave me alone?'

'I will not have you using that language.'

And so it went on until the morning arrived when Kate was to leave. Since David was going to London on a business trip, Margaret asked, 'Would you mind seeing that Kate gets to school safely? The Lord only knows where she'll end up if she goes on her own.'

'I'll be happy to,' David said.

'You! You're as bad as my mother! You can't wait to get rid of me.'

David grinned. 'You're wrong. I can wait.'

*　*　*

They travelled by private railway car from Klipdrift to Cape Town and from there by ship to Southampton. The journey took four weeks. Kate's pride would not let her admit it, but she was thrilled to be travelling with David. *It's like a honeymoon*, she thought, *except that we're not married. Not yet.*

Aboard ship, David spent a great deal of time working in his stateroom. Kate curled up on the couch, silently watching him, content to be near him.

Once she asked, 'Don't you get bored working on all those figures, David?'

He put down his pen and looked at her. 'They're not just figures, Kate. They're stories.'

'What kind of stories?'

'If you know how to read them, they're stories about companies we're buying or selling, people who work for us. Thousands of people all over the world earn a living because of the company your father founded.'

'Am I anything like my father?'

'In many ways, yes. He was a stubborn, independent man.'

'Am I a stubborn, independent woman?'

'You're a spoiled brat. The man who marries you is going to have one hell of a life.'

Kate smiled dreamily. *Poor David.*

In the dining room, on their last night at sea, David asked, 'Why are you so difficult, Kate?'

'Am I?'

'You know you are. You drive your poor mother crazy.'

Kate put her hand over his. 'Do I drive you crazy?'

David's face reddened. 'Stop that. I don't understand you.'

'Yes, you do.'

'Why can't you be like other girls your age?'

'I'd rather die first. I don't want to be like anybody else.'

'God knows you're not!'

'You won't marry anyone else until I'm grown up enough for you, will you, David? I'll get older as fast as I can. I promise. Just don't meet anybody you love, please.'

He was touched by her earnestness. He took her hand in his and said, 'Kate, when I get married, I'd like my daughter to be exactly like you.'

Kate rose to her feet and said in a voice that rang through the dining salon, 'You can bloody well go to hell, David Blackwell!' And she stormed out of the room, as everyone stared.

They had three days together in London, and Kate loved every minute of it.

'I have a treat for you,' David told her. 'I got two tickets for *Mrs Wiggs of the Cabbage Patch*.'

'Thank you, David. I want to go to the Gaiety.'

'You can't. That's a – a music-hall revue. That's not for you.'

'I won't know until I see it, will I?' she said stubbornly.

They went to the Gaiety.

Kate loved the look of London. The mixture of motorcars and carriages, the ladies beautifully dressed in lace and tulle and light satins and glittering jewellery, and the men in dinner clothes with piqué waistcoats and white shirtfronts. They had dinner at the Ritz, and a late supper at the Savoy. And when it was time to leave, Kate thought, *We'll come back here. David and I will come back here.*

When they arrived at Cheltenham, they were ushered into the office of Mrs Keaton.

'I want to thank you for enrolling Kate,' David said.

'I'm sure we'll enjoy having her. And it's a pleasure to accommodate a friend of my husband.'

At that moment, Kate knew she had been deceived. It was *David* who had wanted her sent away and had arranged for her to come here.

She was so furious and hurt she refused to say good-bye to him.

THIRTEEN

Cheltenham School was unbearable. There were
rules and regulations for everything. The girls had
to wear identical uniforms, down to their knick-
ers. The school day was ten hours long, and every
minute was rigidly structured. Mrs Keaton ruled
the pupils and her staff with a rod of iron. The
girls were there to learn manners and discipline,
etiquette and decorum, so that they could one day
attract desirable husbands.

Kate wrote her mother, 'It's a bloody prison.
The girls here are awful. All they ever talk about
are bloody clothes and bloody boys. The bloody
teachers are monsters. They'll never keep me here.
I'm going to escape.'

Kate managed to run away from the school three
times, and each time she was caught and brought
back, unrepentant.

At a weekly staff meeting, when Kate's name
was brought up, one of the teachers said, 'The

child is uncontrollable. I think we should send her back to South Africa.'

Mrs Keaton replied, 'I'm inclined to agree with you, but let's look upon it as a challenge. If we can succeed in disciplining Kate McGregor, we can succeed in disciplining anyone.'

Kate remained in school.

To the amazement of her teachers, Kate became interested in the farm that the school maintained. The farm had vegetable gardens, chickens, cows, pigs and horses. Kate spent as much time as possible there, and when Mrs Keaton learned of this, she was immensely pleased.

'You see,' the headmistress told her staff, 'it was simply a question of patience. Kate has finally found her interest in life. One day she will marry a landowner and be of enormous assistance to him.'

The following morning, Oscar Denker, the man in charge of running the farm, came to see the headmistress. 'One of your students,' he said, 'that Kate McGregor – I wish you'd keep her away from my farm.'

'Whatever are you talking about?' Mrs Keaton asked. 'I happen to know she's very interested.'

'Sure she is, but do you know what she's interested in? The animals fornicating, if you'll excuse my language.'

'*What?*'

'That's right. She stands around all day, just watching the animals do it to each other.'

'Bloody hell!' Mrs Keaton said.

Kate still had not forgiven David for sending her into exile, but she missed him terribly. *It's my fate*, she thought gloomily, *to be in love with a man I hate*. She counted the days she was away from him, like a prisoner marking time until the day of release. Kate was afraid he would do something dreadful, like marry another woman while she was trapped in the bloody school. *If he does*, Kate thought, *I'll kill them both. No. I'll just kill her. They'll arrest me and hang me, and when I'm on the gallows, he'll realize that he loves me. But it will be too late. He'll beg me to forgive him. 'Yes, David, my darling, I forgive you. You were too foolish to know when you held a great love in the palm of your hand. You let it fly away like a little bird. Now that little bird is about to be hanged. Good-bye, David.' But at the last minute she would be reprieved and David would take her in his arms and carry her off to some exotic country where the food was better than the bloody slop they served at bloody Cheltenham.*

Kate received a note from David saying he was going to be in London and would come to visit her. Kate's imagination was inflamed. She found a dozen hidden meanings in his note. *Why was he going to be in England? To be near her, of course.*

Why was he coming to visit her? Because he finally knew he loved her and could not bear to be away from her any longer. He was going to sweep her off her feet and take her out of this terrible place. She could scarcely contain her happiness. Kate's fantasy was so real that the day David arrived, Kate went around saying good-bye to her classmates. 'My lover is coming to take me out of here,' she told them.

The girls looked at her in silent disbelief. All except Georgina Christy, who scoffed, 'You're lying again, Kate McGregor.'

'Just wait and see. He's tall and handsome, and he's mad about me.'

When David arrived, he was puzzled by the fact that all the girls in the school seemed to be staring at him. They looked at him and whispered and giggled, and the minute they caught his eye, they blushed and turned away.

'They act as though they've never seen a man before,' David told Kate. He looked at her suspiciously. 'Have you been saying anything about me?'

'Of course not,' Kate said haughtily. 'Why would I do that?'

They ate in the school's large dining room, and David brought Kate up to date on everything that was happening at home. 'Your mother sends her love. She's expecting you home for the summer holiday.'

'How is mother?'

'She's fine. She's working hard.'

'Is the company doing well, David?'

He was surprised by her sudden interest. 'It's doing very well. Why?'

Because, Kate thought, *someday it will belong to me, and you and I will share it*. 'I was just curious.'

He looked at her untouched plate. 'You're not eating.'

Kate was not interested in food. She was waiting for the magic moment, the moment when David would say, '*Come away with me, Kate. You're a woman now, and I want you. We're going to be married*.'

The dessert came and went. Coffee came and went, and still no magic words from David.

It was not until he looked at his watch and said, 'Well, I'd better be going or I'll miss my train,' that Kate realized with a feeling of horror that he had not come to take her away at all. The bastard was going to leave her there to rot!

David had enjoyed his visit with Kate. She was a bright and amusing child, and the waywardness she had once shown was now under control. David patted Kate's hand fondly and asked, 'Is there anything I can do for you before I leave, Kate?'

She looked him in the eye and said sweetly, 'Yes, David, there is. You can do me an enormous favour. *Get out of my bloody life!*' And she walked out of the room with great dignity, her head held high, leaving him sitting there, mouth agape.

* * *

Margaret found that she missed Kate. The girl was unruly and contrary, but Margaret realized that she was the only living person she loved. *She's going to be a great woman*, Margaret thought with pride. *But I want her to have the manners of a lady*.

Kate came home for summer vacation. 'How are you getting along in school?' Margaret asked.

'I hate it! It's like being surrounded by a hundred nannies.'

Margaret studied her daughter. 'Do the other girls feel the same way, Kate?'

'What do *they* know?' she said contemptuously. 'You should *see* the girls at that school! They've been sheltered all their lives. They don't know a damn thing about life.'

'Oh, dear,' Margaret said. 'That must be awful for you.'

'Don't laugh at me, please. They've never even been to South Africa. The only animals they've seen have been in zoos. None of them has ever seen a diamond mine or a gold mine.'

'Underprivileged.'

Kate said, 'All right. But when I turn out like them, you're going to be bloody sorry.'

'Do you think you'll turn out like them?'

Kate grinned wickedly. 'Of course not! Are you mad?'

An hour after Kate arrived home, she was outside playing rugby with the children of the servants.

Margaret watched her through the window and thought, *I'm wasting my money. She's never going to change.*

That evening, at dinner, Kate asked casually, 'Is David in town?'

'He's been in Australia. He'll be back tomorrow, I think.'

'Is he coming to dinner Friday night?'

'Probably.' She studied Kate and said, 'You like David, don't you?'

She shrugged. 'He's all right, I suppose.'

'I see,' Margaret said. She smiled to herself as she remembered Kate's vow to marry David.

'I don't *dislike* him, Mother. I mean, I like him as a human being. I just can't stand him as a *man*.'

When David arrived for dinner Friday night, Kate flew to the door to greet him. She hugged him and whispered in his ear, 'I forgive you. Oh, I've missed you so much, David! Have you missed me?'

Automatically he said, 'Yes.' And then he thought with astonishment, *By God, I have missed her*. He had never known anyone like this child. He had watched her grow up, and each time he encountered her she was a revelation to him. She was almost sixteen years old and she had started to fill out. She had let her black hair grow long, and it fell softly over her shoulders. Her features had matured, and there was a sensuality about her that he had not noticed before. She was a beauty, with a quick intelligence and a strong will. *She's going to be a handful for some man*, David thought.

At dinner David asked, 'How are you getting along in school, Kate?'

'Oh, I just love it,' she gushed. 'I'm really learning a lot. The teachers are wonderful, and I've made a lot of great friends.'

Margaret sat in stunned silence.

'David, will you take me to the mines with you?'

'Is that how you want to waste your vacation?'

'Yes, please.'

A trip down into the mines took a full day, and that meant she would be with David all that time.

'If your mother says it's all right –'

'Please, mother!'

'All right, darling. As long as you're with David, I know you'll be safe.' Margaret hoped David would be safe.

The Kruger-Brent Diamond Mine near Bloemfontein was a gigantic operation, with hundreds of workers engaged in digging, engineering, washing or sorting.

'This is one of the company's most profitable mines,' David told Kate. They were above ground in the manager's office, waiting for an escort to take them down into the mine. Against one wall was a showcase filled with diamonds of all colours and sizes.

'Each diamond has a distinct characteristic,' David explained. 'The original diamonds from the banks of the Vaal are alluvial, and their sides are worn down from the abrasion of centuries.'

He's more handsome than ever, Kate thought. *I love his eyebrows.*

'These stones all come from different mines, but they can be easily identified by their appearance. See this one? You can tell by the size and yellow cast that it comes from Paardspan. De Beer's diamonds have an oily-looking surface and are dodecahedral in shape.'

He's brilliant. He knows everything.

'You can tell this one is from the mine at Kimberley because it's an octahedron. Their diamonds range from smoky-glassy to pure white.'

I wonder if the manager thinks David is my lover. I hope so.

'The colour of a diamond helps determine its value. The colours are named on a scale of one to ten. At the top is the tone blue-white, and at the bottom is the draw, which is a brown colour.'

He smells so wonderful. It's such a – such a male smell. I love his arms and shoulders. I wish –

'Kate!'

She said guiltily, 'Yes, David?'

'Are you listening to me?'

'Of course I am.' There was indignation in her voice. 'I've heard every word.'

They spent the next two hours in the bowels of the mine, and then had lunch. It was Kate's idea of a heavenly day.

* * *

When Kate returned home late in the afternoon, Margaret said, 'Did you enjoy yourself?'

'It was wonderful. Mining is really fascinating.'

Half an hour later, Margaret happened to glance out of the window. Kate was on the ground wrestling with the son of one of the gardeners.

The following year, Kate's letters from school were cautiously optimistic. She had been made captain of the hockey and lacrosse teams, and was at the head of her class scholastically. The school was not really all *that* bad, she wrote, and there were even a few girls in her classes who were reasonably nice. She asked permission to bring two of her friends home for the summer vacation, and Margaret was delighted. The house would be alive again with the sound of youthful laughter. She could not wait for her daughter to come home. Her dreams were all for Kate now. *Jamie and I are the past*, Maggie thought. *Kate is the future. And what a wonderful, bright future it will be!'*

When Kate was home during her vacation, all the eligible young men of Klipdrift flocked around besieging her for dates, but Kate was not interested in any of them. David was in America, and she impatiently awaited his return. When he came to the house, Kate greeted him at the door. She wore a white dress circled in by a black velvet belt that accentuated her lovely bosom. When David embraced her, he was astonished by the warmth of her response. He drew back and looked at her. There was something different about her, something knowing. There was an expression in her eyes he could not define, and it made him vaguely uneasy.

The few times David saw Kate during that vacation she was surrounded by boys, and he found himself wondering which would be the lucky one. David was called back to Australia on business, and when he returned to Klipdrift, Kate was on her way to England.

In Kate's last year of school, David appeared unexpectedly one evening. Usually his visits were preceded by a letter or a telephone call. This time there had been no warning.

'David! What a wonderful surprise!' Kate hugged him. 'You should have told me you were coming. I would have –'

'Kate, I've come to take you home.'

She pulled back and looked up at him. 'Is something wrong?'

'I'm afraid your mother is very ill.'

Kate stood stark still for a moment. 'I'll get ready.'

Kate was shocked by her mother's appearance. She had seen her only a few months earlier, and Margaret had seemed to be in robust health. Now she was pale and emaciated, and the bright spirit had gone out of her eyes. It was as though the cancer that was eating at her flesh had also eaten at her soul.

Kate sat at the side of the bed and held her mother's hand in hers. 'Oh, Mother,' she said. 'I'm so bloody sorry.'

Margaret squeezed her daughter's hand. 'I'm ready, darling. I suppose I've been ready ever since your father died.' She looked up at Kate. 'Do you want to hear something silly? I've never told this to a living soul before.' She hesitated, then went on. 'I've always been worried that there was no one to take proper care of your father. Now I can do it.'

Margaret was buried three days later. Her mother's death shook Kate deeply. She had lost her father and a brother, but she had never known them; they were only storied figments of the past. Her mother's death was real and painful. Kate was eighteen years old and suddenly alone in the world, and the thought of that was frightening.

David watched her standing at her mother's graveside, bravely trying not to cry. But when they returned to the house, Kate broke down, unable to stop sobbing. 'She was always so w-wonderful to me, David, and I was such a r-rotten daughter.'

David tried to console her. 'You've been a wonderful daughter, Kate.'

'I was n-nothing b-but trouble. I'd give any-thing if I could m-make it up to her. I didn't want her to die, David! Why did God do this to her?'

He waited, letting Kate cry herself out. When she was calmer, David said, 'I know it's hard to believe now, but one day this pain will go away. And you know what you'll be left with, Kate? Happy memories. You'll remember all the good things you and your mother had.'

'I suppose so. Only right now it hurts so b-bloody much.'

The following morning they discussed Kate's future.

'You have family in Scotland,' David reminded her.

'No!' Kate replied sharply. 'They're not family. They're relatives.' Her voice was bitter. 'When Father wanted to come to this country, they laughed at him. No one would help him except his mother, and she's dead. No. I won't have anything to do with them.'

David sat there thinking. 'Do you plan to finish out the school term?' Before Kate could answer, David went on. 'I think your mother would have wanted you to.'

'Then I'll do it.' She looked down at the floor, her eyes unseeing. 'Bloody hell,' Kate said.

'I know,' David said gently. 'I know.'

* * *

Kate finished the school term as class valedictorian, and David was there for the graduation.

Riding from Johannesburg to Klipdrift in the private railway car, David said, 'You know, all this will belong to you in a few years. This car, the mines, the company – it's yours. You're a very rich young woman. You can sell the company for many millions of pounds.' He looked at her and added, 'Or you can keep it. You'll have to think about it.'

'I have thought about it,' Kate told him. She looked at him and smiled. 'My father was a pirate, David. A wonderful old pirate. I wish I could have known him. I'm not going to sell this company. Do you know why? Because the pirate named it after two guards who were trying to kill him. Wasn't that a lovely thing to do? Sometimes at night when I can't sleep, I think about my father and Banda crawling through the sea *mis*, and I can hear the voices of the guards: *Kruger . . . Brent . . .*' She looked up at David. 'No, I'll never sell my father's company. Not as long as you'll stay on and run it.'

David said quietly, 'I'll stay as long as you need me.'

'I've decided to enroll in business school.'

'A business school?' There was surprise in his voice.

'This is 1910,' Kate reminded him. 'They have

business schools in Johannesburg where women are allowed to attend.'

'But –'

'You asked me what I wanted to do with my money.' She looked him in the eye and said, 'I want to earn it.'

FOURTEEN

Business school was an exciting new adventure. When Kate had gone to Cheltenham, it had been a chore, a necessary evil. This was different. Every class taught her something useful, something that would help her when she ran the company. The course included accounting, management, international trade and business administration. Once a week David telephoned to see how she was getting along.

'I love it,' Kate told him. 'It's really exciting, David.'

One day she and David would be working together, side by side, late at night, all by themselves. *And one of those nights, David would turn to her and say, 'Kate, darling, I've been such a blind fool. Will you marry me?' And an instant later, she would be in his arms . . .*

But that would have to wait. In the meantime, she had a lot to learn. Resolutely, Kate turned to her homework.

The business course lasted two years, and Kate returned to Klipdrift in time to celebrate her twentieth birthday. David met her at the station. Impulsively, Kate flung her arms around him and hugged him. 'Oh, David, I'm so happy to see you.'

He pulled away and said awkwardly, 'It's nice to see you, Kate.' There was an uncomfortable stiffness in his manner.

'Is something wrong?'

'No. It's – it's just that young ladies don't go around hugging men in public.'

She looked at him a moment. 'I see. I promise not to embarrass you again.'

As they drove to the house, David covertly studied Kate. She was a hauntingly beautiful girl, innocent and vulnerable, and David was determined that he would never take advantage of that.

On Monday morning Kate moved into her new office at Kruger-Brent, Ltd. It was like suddenly being plunged into some exotic and bizarre universe that had its own customs and its own language. There was a bewildering array of divisions, subsidiaries, regional departments, franchises and foreign branches. The products that the company manufactured or owned seemed endless. There were steel mills, cattle ranches, a railroad, a shipping line and, of course, the foundation of the family fortune: diamonds and gold, zinc and platinum and magnesium, mined each hour around the clock, pouring into the coffers of the company.

Power.

It was almost too much to take in. Kate sat in David's office listening to him make decisions that affected thousands of people around the world. The general managers of the various divisions made recommendations, but as often as not, David overruled them.

'Why do you do that? Don't they know their jobs?' Kate asked.

'Of course they do, but that's not the point,' David explained. 'Each manager sees his own division as the centre of the world, and that's as it should be. But someone has to have an overall view and decide what's best for the company. Come on. We're having lunch with someone I want you to meet.'

David took Kate into the large, private dining room adjoining Kate's office. A young, raw-boned man with a lean face and inquisitive brown eyes was waiting for them.

'This is Brad Rogers,' David said. 'Brad, meet your new boss, Kate McGregor.'

Brad Rogers held out his hand. 'I'm pleased to meet you, Miss McGregor.'

'Brad is our secret weapon,' David said. 'He knows as much about Kruger-Brent, Limited, as I do. If I ever leave, you don't have to worry. Brad will be here.'

If I ever leave. The thought of it sent a wave of panic through Kate. *Of course, David would never leave the company.* Kate could think of nothing else through lunch, and when it was over she had no idea what she had eaten.

After lunch, they discussed South Africa.

'We're going to run into trouble soon,' David warned. 'The government has just imposed poll taxes.'

'Exactly what does that mean?' Kate asked.

'It means that blacks, coloureds and Indians have to pay two pounds each for every member of their family. That's more than a month's wages for them.'

Kate thought about Banda and was filled with a sense of apprehension. The discussion moved on to other topics.

Kate enjoyed her new life tremendously. Every decision involved a gamble of millions of pounds. Big business was a matching of wits, the courage to gamble and the instinct to know when to quit and when to press ahead.

'Business is a game,' David told Kate, 'played for fantastic stakes, and you're in competition with experts. If you want to win, you have to learn to be a master of the game.'

And that was what Kate was determined to do. Learn.

Kate lived alone in the big house, except for the servants. She and David continued their ritual Friday-night dinners, but when Kate invited him over on any other night, he invariably found an excuse not to come. During business hours they were together constantly, but even then David seemed to have erected a barrier between them, a wall that Kate was unable to penetrate.

On her twenty-first birthday, all the shares in Kruger-Brent, Ltd., were turned over to Kate. She now officially had control of the company. 'Let's have dinner tonight to celebrate,' she suggested to David.

'I'm sorry, Kate, I have a lot of work to catch up on.'

Kate dined alone that night, wondering why. *Was it she, or was it David?* He would have to be deaf, dumb and blind not to know how she felt about him, how she had always felt about him. She would have to do something about it.

The company was negotiating for a shipping line in the United States.

'Why don't you and Brad go to New York and close the deal?' David suggested to Kate. 'It will be good experience for you.'

Kate would have liked for David to have gone with her, but she was too proud to say so. She would handle this without him. Besides, she had never been to America. She looked forward to the experience.

The closing of the shipping-line deal went smoothly. 'While you're over there,' David had told her, 'you should see something of the country.'

Kate and Brad visited company subsidiaries in Detroit, Chicago, Pittsburgh and New York, and Kate was amazed by the size and energy of the United States. The highlight of Kate's trip was a visit to Dark Harbor, Maine, on an enchanting little island called Islesboro, in Penobscot Bay. She had been invited to dinner at the home of Charles Dana Gibson, the artist. There were twelve people at dinner and, except for Kate, they all had homes on the island.

'This place has an interesting history,' Gibson told Kate. 'Years ago, residents used to get here by small coasting vessels from Boston. When the boat landed, they'd be met by a buggy and taken to their houses.'

'How many people live on this island?' Kate asked.

'About fifty families. Did you see the lighthouse when the ferry docked?'

'Yes.'

'It's run by a lighthouse keeper and his dog. When a boat goes by the dog goes out and rings the bell.'

Kate laughed. 'You're joking.'

'No, ma'am. The funny thing is the dog is deaf as a stone. He puts his ear against the bell to feel if there's any vibration.'

Kate smiled. 'It sounds as if you have a fascinating island here.'

'It might be worth your while staying over and taking a look around in the morning.'

On an impulse, Kate said, 'Why not?'

She spent the night at the island's only hotel, the Islesboro Inn. In the morning she hired a horse and carriage, driven by one of the islanders. They left the centre of Dark Harbor, which consisted of a general store, a hardware store and a small restaurant, and a few minutes later they were driving through a beautiful wooded area. Kate noticed that none of the little winding roads had names, nor were there any names on the mailboxes. She turned to her guide. 'Don't people get lost here without any signs?'

'Nope. The islanders know where everythin' is.'

Kate gave him a sidelong look. 'I see.'

At the lower end of the island, they passed a burial ground.

'Would you stop, please?' Kate asked.

She stepped out of the carriage and walked over to the old cemetery and wandered around looking at the tombstones.

JOB PENDLETON, DIED JANUARY 25, 1794, AGE 47. The epitaph read: *Beneath this stone, I rest my head in slumber sweet; Christ blessed the bed.*

JANE, WIFE OF THOMAS PENDLETON, DIED FEBRUARY 25, 1802, AGE 47.

There were spirits here from another century, from an era long gone. CAPTAIN WILLIAM HATCH, DROWNED IN LONG ISLAND SOUND, OCTOBER 1866, AGE 30 YEARS. The epitaph on his stone read: *Storms all weathered and life's seas crossed.*

Kate stayed there a long time, enjoying the quiet and peace. Finally, she returned to the carriage and they drove on.

'What is it like here in the winter?' Kate asked.

'Cold. The bay used to freeze solid, and they'd come from the mainland by sleigh. Now a' course, we got the ferry.'

They rounded a curve, and there, next to the water below, was a beautiful white-shingled, two-storey house surrounded by delphinium, wild roses and poppies. The shutters on the eight front windows were painted green, and next to the double doors were white benches and six pots of red geraniums. It looked like something out of a fairly tale.

'Who owns that house?'

'That's the old Dreben house. Mrs Dreben died a few months back.'

'Who lives there now?'

'Nobody, I reckon.'

'Do you know if it's for sale?'

The guide looked at Kate and said, 'If it is, it'll probably be bought by the son of one of the families already livin' here. The islanders don't take kindly to strangers.'

It was the wrong thing to say to Kate.

One hour later, she was speaking to a lawyer for the estate. 'It's about the Dreben house,' Kate said. 'Is it for sale?'

The lawyer pursed his lips, 'Well, yes, and no.'

'What does that mean?'

'It's for sale, but a few people are already interested in buying it.'

The old families on the island, Kate thought. 'Have they made an offer?'

'Not yet, but –'

'I'm making one,' Kate said.

He said condescendingly, 'That's an expensive house.'

'Name your price.'

'Fifty thousand dollars.'

'Let's go look at it.'

The inside of the house was even more enchanting than Kate had anticipated. The large, lovely hall faced the sea through a wall of glass. On one side of the hall was a large ballroom, and on the other side, a living room with fruitwood panelling stained by time, and an enormous fireplace. There was a library, and a huge kitchen with an iron stove and a large pine worktable, and off of that was a butler's pantry and laundry room. Downstairs, the house had six bedrooms for the servants and one bathroom. Upstairs was a master bedroom suite and four smaller bedrooms. It was a much larger house than Kate had expected. *But when David and I have our children*, she thought, *we'll need all these rooms*. The grounds ran all the way down to the bay, where there was a private dock.

Kate turned to the lawyer. 'I'll take it.'

She decided to name it Cedar Hill House.

She could not wait to get back to Klipdrift to break the news to David.

On the way back to South Africa, Kate was filled with a wild excitement. The house in Dark Harbor was a sign, a symbol that she and David would be married. She knew he would love the house as much as she did.

On the afternoon Kate and Brad arrived back in Klipdrift, Kate hurried to David's office. He was seated at his desk, working, and the sight of him set Kate's heart pounding. She had not realized how much she had missed him.

David rose to his feet. 'Kate! Welcome home!' And before she could speak, he said, 'I wanted you to be the first to know. I'm getting married.'

FIFTEEN

It had begun casually six weeks earlier. In the middle of a hectic day, David received a message that Tim O'Neil, the friend of an important American diamond buyer, was in Klipdrift and asking if David would be good enough to welcome him and perhaps take him to dinner. David had no time to waste on tourists, but he did not want to offend his customer. He would have asked Kate to entertain the visitor, but she was on a tour of the company's plants in North America with Brad Rogers. *I'm stuck*, David decided. He called the hotel where O'Neil was staying and invited him to dinner that evening.

'My daughter is with me,' O'Neil told him. 'I hope you don't mind if I bring her along?'

David was in no mood to spend the evening with a child. 'Not at all,' he said politely. He would make sure the evening was a short one.

They met at the Grand Hotel, in the dining room. When David arrived, O'Neil and his daughter were already seated at the table. O'Neil was a handsome, grey-haired Irish-American in his early fifties. His daughter, Josephine, was the most beautiful woman David had ever seen. She was in her early thirties, with a stunning figure, soft blond hair and clear blue eyes. The breath went out of David at the sight of her.

'I – I'm sorry I'm late,' he said. 'Some last-minute business.'

Josephine watched his reaction to her with amusement. 'Sometimes that's the most exciting kind,' she said innocently. 'My father tells me you're a very important man, Mr Blackwell.'

'Not really – and it's David.'

She nodded. 'That's a good name. It suggests great strength.'

Before the dinner was over, David decided that Josephine O'Neil was much more than just a beautiful woman. She was intelligent, had a sense of humour and was skilful at making him feel at ease. David felt she was genuinely interested in him. She asked him questions about himself that no one had ever asked before. By the time the evening ended, he was already half in love with her.

'Where's your home?' David asked Tim O'Neil.

'San Francisco.'

'Will you be going back soon?' He made it sound as casual as he could.

'Next week.'

Josephine smiled at David. 'If Klipdrift is as

interesting as it promises to be, I might persuade Father to stay a little longer.'

'I intend to make it as interesting as possible,' David assured her. 'How would you like to go down into a diamond mine?'

'We'd love it,' Josephine answered. 'Thank you.'

At one time David had personally escorted important visitors down into the mines, but he had long since delegated that task to subordinates. Now he heard himself saying, 'Would tomorrow morning be convenient?' He had half a dozen meetings scheduled for the morning, but they suddenly seemed unimportant.

He took the O'Neils down a rockshaft, twelve hundred feet below ground. The shaft was six feet wide and twenty feet long, divided into four compartments, one for pumping, two for hoisting the blue diamondiferous earth and one with a double-decked cage to carry the miners to and from work.

'I've always been curious about something,' Josephine said. 'Why are diamonds measured in carats?'

'The carat was named for the carob seed,' David explained, 'because of its consistency in weight. One carat equals two hundred milligrams, or one one-hundred-forty-second of an ounce.'

Josephine said, 'I'm absolutely fascinated, David.'

And he wondered if she was referring only to

the diamonds. Her nearness was intoxicating. Every time he looked at Josephine, David felt a fresh sense of excitement.

'You really should see something of the countryside,' David told the O'Neils. 'If you're free tomorrow, I'd be happy to take you around.'

Before her father could say anything, Josephine replied, 'That would be lovely.'

David was with Josephine and her father every day after that, and each day David fell more deeply in love. He had never known anyone as bewitching.

When David arrived to pick up the O'Neils for dinner one evening and Tim O'Neil said, 'I'm a bit tired tonight, David. Would you mind if I didn't go along?' David tried to hide his pleasure.

'No, sir. I understand.'

Josephine gave David a mischievous smile. 'I'll try to keep you entertained,' she promised.

David took her to a restaurant in a hotel that had just opened. The room was crowded, but David was recognized and given a table immediately. A three-piece ensemble was playing American music.

David asked, 'Would you like to dance?'

'I'd love to.'

A moment later, Josephine was in his arms on the dance floor, and it was magic. David held her lovely body close to his, and he could feel her respond.

'Josephine, I'm in love with you.'

She put a finger to his lips. 'Please, David . . . don't . . .'

'Why?'

'Because I couldn't marry you.'

'Do you love me?'

She smiled up at him, her blue eyes sparkling. 'I'm crazy about you, my darling. Can't you tell?'

'Then why?'

'Because I could never live in Klipdrift. I'd go mad.'

'You could give it a try.'

'David, I'm tempted, but I know what would happen. If I married you and had to live here, I'd turn into a screaming shrew and we'd end up hating each other. I'd rather we said good-bye this way.'

'I don't want to say good-bye.'

She looked up into his face, and David felt her body melt into his. 'David, is there any chance that you could live in San Francisco?'

It was an impossible idea. 'What would I do there?'

'Let's have breakfast in the morning. I want you to talk to Father.'

Tim O'Neil said, 'Josephine has told me about your conversation last night. Looks like you two have a problem. But I might have a solution, if you're interested.'

'I'm very interested, sir.'

O'Neil picked up a brown-leather briefcase and removed some blueprints. 'Do you know anything about frozen foods?'

'I'm afraid I don't.'

'They first started freezing food in the United States in 1865. The problem was transporting it long distances without the food thawing out. We've got refrigerated railway cars, but no one's been able to come up with a way to refrigerate trucks.' O'Neil tapped the blueprints. 'Until now. I just received a patent on it. This is going to revolutionize the entire food industry, David.'

David glanced at the blueprints. 'I'm afraid these don't mean much to me, Mr O'Neil.'

'That doesn't matter. I'm not looking for a technical expert. I have plenty of those. What I'm looking for is financing and someone to run the business. This isn't some wild pipe dream. I've talked to the top food processors in the business. This is going to be big – bigger than you can imagine. I need someone like you.'

'The company headquarters will be in San Francisco,' Josephine added.

David sat there silent, digesting what he had just heard. 'You say you've been given a patent on this?'

'That's right. I'm all set to move.'

'Would you mind if I borrowed these blueprints and showed them to someone?'

'I have no objection at all.'

* * *

The first thing David did was to check on Tim O'Neil. He learned that O'Neil had a solid reputation in San Francisco. He had been head of the science department at Berkeley College there and was highly regarded. David knew nothing about the freezing of food, but he intended to find out.

'I'll be back in five days, darling. I want you and your father to wait for me.'

'As long as you like. I'll miss you,' Josephine said.

'I'll miss you, too.' And he meant it more than she knew.

David took the train to Johannesburg and made an appointment to see Edward Broderick, the owner of the largest meat-packing plant in South Africa.

'I want your opinion on something.' David handed him the blueprints. 'I need to know if this can work.'

'I don't know a damned thing about frozen foods or trucks, but I know people who do. If you come back this afternoon, I'll have a couple of experts here for you, David.'

At four o'clock that afternoon David returned to the packing plant. He found that he was nervous, in a state of uncertainty, because he was not sure how he wanted the meeting to go. Two weeks earlier, he would have laughed if anyone had even suggested he would ever leave Kruger-Brent, Ltd. It was a part of him. He would have laughed even harder if they had told him he would have considered heading a little food company in San Francisco. It was insane, except for one thing: Josephine O'Neil.

There were two men in the room with Edward Broderick. 'This is Dr Crawford and Mr Kaufman. David Blackwell.'

They exchanged greetings. David asked, 'Have you gentlemen had a chance to look at the blueprints?'

Dr Crawford replied, 'We certainly have, Mr Blackwell. We've been over them thoroughly.'

David took a deep breath. 'And?'

'I understand that the United States Patent Office has granted a patent on this?'

'That's right.'

'Well, Mr Blackwell, whoever got that patent is going to be one very rich man.'

David nodded slowly, filled with conflicting emotions.

'It's like all great inventions – it's so simple you wonder why someone didn't think of it sooner. This one can't miss.'

David did not know how to react. He had half-hoped that the decision would be taken out of his hands. If Tim O'Neil's invention was useless, there was a chance of persuading Josephine to stay in South Africa. But what O'Neil had told him was true. It *did* work. Now David had to make his decision.

He thought of nothing else on the journey back to Klipdrift. If he accepted, it would mean leaving the company, starting up a new, untried business. He was an American, but America was a foreign country to him. He held an important position in one of the most powerful companies in the world. He loved his job. Jamie and Margaret McGregor had been very good to him. And then there was Kate. He had cared for her since she was a baby. He had watched her grow up from a stubborn, dirty-faced tomboy to a lovely young woman. Her life was a photo album in his mind. He turned the pages and there was Kate at four, eight, ten, fourteen, twenty-one – vulnerable, unpredictable . . .

By the time the train arrived at Klipdrift, David had made up his mind. He was going to leave Kruger-Brent, Ltd.

He drove directly to the Grand Hotel and went up to the O'Neils' suite. Josephine opened the door for him.

'David!'

He took her in his arms and kissed her hungrily, feeling her warm body pressing against his.

'Oh, David, I've missed you so much. I don't ever want to be away from you again.'

'You won't have to,' David said slowly. 'I'm going to San Francisco . . .'

David had waited with growing anxiety for Kate to return from the United States. Now that he had made his decision, he was eager to get started on his new life, impatient to marry Josephine.

And now Kate was back, and he was standing in front of her saying, 'I'm getting married.'

Kate heard the words through a roaring in her ears. She felt suddenly faint, and she gripped the edge of the desk for support. *I want to die*, she thought. *Please let me die.*

Somehow, from some deep wellspring of will, she managed a smile. 'Tell me about her, David.' She was proud of how calm her voice sounded. 'Who is she?'

'Her name is Josephine O'Neil. She's been visiting here with her father. I know you two will be good friends, Kate. She's a fine woman.'

'She must be, if you love her, David.'

He hesitated. 'There's one more thing, Kate. I'm going to be leaving the company.'

The world was falling in on her. 'Just because you're getting married, doesn't mean you have to –'

'It isn't that. Josephine's father is starting a new business in San Francisco. They need me.'

'So – so you'll be living in San Francisco.'

'Yes. Brad Rogers can handle my job easily, and we'll pick a top management team to back him up. Kate, I – I can't tell you what a difficult decision this was for me.'

'Of course, David. You – you must love her very much. When do I get to meet the bride?'

David smiled, pleased at how well Kate was

taking the news. 'Tonight, if you're free for dinner.'

'Yes, I'm free.'

She would not let the tears come until she was alone.

The four of them had dinner at the McGregor mansion. The moment Kate saw Josephine, she blanched, *Oh God! No wonder he's in love with her!* She was dazzling. Just being in her presence made Kate feel awkward and ugly. And to make matters worse, Josephine was gracious and charming. And obviously very much in love with David. *Bloody hell!*

During dinner Tim O'Neil told Kate about the new company.

'It sounds very interesting,' Kate said.

'I'm afraid it's no Kruger-Brent, Limited, Miss McGregor. We'll have to start small, but with David running it, we'll do all right.'

'With David running it, you can't miss,' Kate assured him.

The evening was an agony. In the same cataclysmic moment, she had lost the man she loved and the one person who was indispensable to Kruger-Brent, Ltd. She carried on a conversation and managed to get through the evening, but afterwards she had no recollection of what she said or did. She only knew that every time David and Josephine looked at each other or touched, she wanted to kill herself.

On the way back to the hotel, Josephine said, 'She's in love with you, David.'

He smiled. 'Kate? No. We're friends. We have been since she was a baby. She liked you a lot.'

Josephine smiled. *Men are so naïve.*

In David's office the following morning, Tim O'Neil and David sat facing each other. 'I'll need about two months to get my affairs in order here,' David said. 'I've been thinking about the financing we'll need to begin with. If we go to one of the big companies they'll swallow us up and give us a small share. It won't belong to us anymore. I think we should finance it ourselves. I figure it will cost eighty thousand dollars to get started. I've saved the equivalent of about forty thousand dollars. We'll need forty thousand more.'

'I have ten thousand dollars,' Tim O'Neil said. 'And I have a brother who will loan me another five thousand.'

'So, we're twenty-five thousand dollars short,' David said. 'We'll try to borrow that from a bank.'

'We'll leave for San Francisco right away,' O'Neil told David, 'and get everything set up for you.'

Josephine and her father left for the United States two days later. 'Send them to Cape Town in the private railway car, David.' Kate offered.

'That's very generous of you, Kate.'

The morning Josephine left, David felt as though

288

a piece of his life had been taken away. He could not wait to join her in San Francisco.

The next few weeks were taken up with a search for a management team to back up Brad Rogers. A list of possible candidates was carefully drawn up, and Kate and David and Brad spent hours discussing each one.

'. . . Taylor is a good technician, but he's weak on management.'

'What about Simmons?'

'He's good, but he's not ready yet,' Brad decided. 'Give him another five years.'

'Babcock?'

'Not a bad choice. Let's discuss him.'

'What about Peterson?'

'Not enough of a company man,' David said. 'He's too concerned with himself.' And even as he said it, he felt a pang of guilt because he was deserting Kate.

They continued on with the list of names. By the end of the month, they had narrowed the choice to four men to work with Brad Rogers. All of them were working abroad, and they were sent for so that they could be interviewed. The first two interviews went well. 'I'd be satisfied with either one of them,' Kate assured David and Brad.

On the morning the third interview was to take place, David walked into Kate's office, his face pale. 'Is my job still open?'

Kate looked at his expression and stood up in alarm. 'What is it, David?'

'I – I –' He sank into a chair. 'Something has happened.'

Kate was out from behind the desk and by his side in an instant. 'Tell me!'

'I just got a letter from Tim O'Neil. He's sold the business.'

'What do you mean?'

'Exactly what I said. He accepted an offer of two hundred thousand dollars and a royalty for his patent from the Three Star Meat Packing Company in Chicago.' David's voice was filled with bitterness. 'The company would like to hire me to manage it for them. He regrets any inconvenience to me, but he couldn't turn down that kind of money.'

Kate looked at him intently. 'And Josephine? What does she say? She must be furious with her father.'

'There was a letter from her, too. We'll marry as soon as I come to San Francisco.'

'And you're not going?'

'Of course I'm not going!' David exploded. 'Before, I had something to offer. I could have built it into a great company. But they were in too much of a damned hurry for the money.'

'David, you're not being fair when you say "they". Just be –'

'O'Neil would never have made that deal without Josephine's approval.'

'I – I don't know what to say, David.'

'There is nothing to say. Except that I almost made the biggest mistake of my life.'

Kate walked over to the desk and picked up the list of candidates. Slowly, she began to tear it up.

In the weeks that followed, David plunged himself deeply into his work, trying to forget his bitterness and hurt. He received several letters from Josephine O'Neil, and he threw them all away, unread. But he could not get her out of his mind. Kate, deeply aware of David's pain, let him know she was there if he needed her.

Six months had passed since David received the letter from Tim O'Neil. During that time, Kate and David continued to work closely together, travel together and be alone together much of the time. Kate tried to please him in every way she could. She dressed for him, planned things he would enjoy and went out of her way to make his life as happy as possible. As far as she could tell, it was having no effect at all. And finally she lost her patience.

She and David were in Rio de Janeiro, checking on a new mineral find. They had had dinner at their hotel and were in Kate's room going over some figures late at night. Kate had changed to a comfortable kimono and slippers. When they finished, David stretched and said, 'Well, that's it for tonight. I guess I'll go on to bed.'

Kate said quietly, 'Isn't it time you came out of mourning, David?'

He looked at her in surprise. 'Mourning?'

'For Josephine O'Neil.'

'She's out of my life.'

'Then act like it.'

'Just what would you like me to do, Kate,' he asked curtly.

Kate was angry now. Angry at David's blindness, angry about all the wasted time. 'I'll tell you what I'd like you to do – kiss me.'

'What?'

'Bloody hell, David! I'm your boss, damn it!' She moved close to him. 'Kiss me.' And she pressed her lips against his and put her arms around him. She felt him resist and start to draw back. And then slowly his arms circled her body, and he kissed her.

'Kate . . .'

She whispered against his lips. 'I thought you'd never ask . . .'

They were married six weeks later. It was the biggest wedding Klipdrift had ever seen or would see again. It was held in the town's largest church and afterwards there was a reception in the town hall and everyone was invited. There were mountains of food and uncounted cases of beer and whiskey and champagne, and musicians played and the festivities lasted until dawn. When the sun came up, Kate and David slipped away.

'I'll go home and finish packing,' Kate said. 'Pick me up in an hour.'

* * *

In the pale dawn light, Kate entered the huge house alone and went upstairs to her bedroom. She walked over to a painting on the wall and pressed against the frame. The painting flew back, revealing a wall safe. She opened it and brought out a contract. It was for the purchase of the Three Star Meat Packing Company of Chicago by Kate McGregor. Next to it was a contract from the Three Star Meat Packing Company purchasing the rights to Tim O'Neil's freezing process for two hundred thousand dollars. Kate hesitated a moment, then returned the papers to the safe and locked it. David belonged to her now. He had always belonged to her. And to Kruger-Brent, Ltd. Together, they would build it into the biggest, most powerful company in the world.

Just as Jamie and Margaret McGregor would have wanted it.

BOOK THREE

Kruger-Brent, Ltd

1914–1945

SIXTEEN

They were in the library, where Jamie had once liked to sit with his brandy glass in front of him. David was arguing that there was no time for a real honeymoon. 'Someone has to mind the store, Kate.'

'Yes, Mr Blackwell. But who's going to mind me?' She curled up in David's lap, and he felt the warmth of her through her thin dress. The documents he had been reading fell to the floor. Her arms were around him, and he felt her hands sliding down his body. She pressed her hips against him, making slow, small circles, and the papers on the floor were forgotten. She felt him respond and she rose and slipped out of her dress. David watched her, marvelling at her loveliness. How could he have been so blind for so long? She was undressing him now, and there was a sudden urgency in him. They were both naked, and their bodies were pressed together. He stroked her, his fingers lightly touching her face and her neck, down to the swell of her breasts. She was moaning, and his hands moved down until he felt the velvety softness between her legs. His fingers stroked her and she whispered, 'Take me, David,' and they were on the deep, soft rug and she felt the strength of his body on top of her. There was a long sweet thrust and he was inside her, filling her, and she moved to his rhythm. It became a great tidal wave, sweeping her up higher and higher until she thought she could not bear the ecstasy of it. There was a sudden, glorious explosion deep inside her and another and another, and she thought, *I've died and gone to heaven.*

They travelled all over the world, to Paris and Zurich and Sydney and New York, taking care of company business, but wherever they went they carved out moments of time for themselves. They talked late into the night and made love and explored each other's minds and bodies. Kate was an inexhaustible delight to David. She would awaken him in the morning to make wild and pagan love to him, and a few hours later she would be at his side at a business conference, making more sense than anyone else there. She had a natural flair for business that was as rare as it was unexpected. Women were few in the top echelons of the business world. In the beginning Kate was treated with a tolerant condescension, but the attitude quickly changed to a wary respect. Kate took a delight in the manoeuvring and machinations of the game. David watched her outwit men with much greater experience. She had the instincts of a winner. She knew what she wanted and how to get it. *Power.*

They ended their honeymoon with a glorious week in Cedar Hill House at Dark Harbor.

It was on June 28, 1914, that the first talk of war was heard. Kate and David were guests at a country estate in Sussex. It was the age of country-house living and weekend guests were expected to conform to a ritual. Men dressed for breakfast, changed for midmorning lounging, changed for lunch, changed for tea – to a velvet jacket with satin piping – and changed to a formal jacket for dinner.

'For God's sake,' David protested to Kate. 'I feel like a damned peacock.'

'You're a very handsome peacock, my darling,' Kate assured him. 'When you get home, you can walk around naked.'

He took her in his arms. 'I can't wait.'

At dinner, the news came that Francis Ferdinand, heir to the Austrian-Hungarian throne, and his wife, Sophie, had been slain by an assassin.

Their host, Lord Maney, said, 'Nasty business, shooting a woman, what? But no one is going to war over some little Balkan country.'

And the conversation moved on to cricket.

Later in bed, Kate said, 'Do you think there's going to be a war, David?'

'Over some minor archduke being assassinated? No.'

It proved to be a bad guess. Austria-Hungary, suspecting that its neighbour, Serbia, had instigated the plot to assassinate Ferdinand, declared war on Serbia, and by October, most of the world's major powers were at war. It was a new kind of warfare. For the first time, mechanized vehicles were used – airplanes, airships and submarines.

The day Germany declared war, Kate said, 'This can be a wonderful opportunity for us, David.'

David frowned. 'What are you talking about?'

'Nations are going to need guns and ammunition and –'

'They're not getting them from us,' David interrupted firmly. 'We have enough business, Kate. We don't have to make profits from anyone's blood.'

'Aren't you being a bit dramatic? Someone has to make guns.'

'As long as I'm with this company, it won't be us. We won't discuss it again, Kate. The subject is closed.'

And Kate thought, *The bloody hell it is*. For the first time in their marriage, they slept apart. Kate thought, *How can David be such an idealistic ninny?*

And David thought, *How can she be so cold-blooded? The business has changed her*. The days that followed were miserable for both of them. David regretted the emotional chasm between them, but he did not know how to bridge it. Kate was too proud and headstrong to give in to him because she knew she was right.

President Woodrow Wilson had promised to keep the United States out of the war, but as German submarines began torpedoing unarmed passenger ships, and stories of German atrocities spread, pressure began to build up for America to help the Allies. 'Make the world safe for democracy,' was the slogan.

David had learned to fly in the bush country of South Africa, and when the Lafayette Escadrille was formed in France with American pilots, David went to Kate. 'I've got to enlist.'

She was appalled. 'No! It's not your war!'

'It's going to be,' David said quietly. 'The United States can't stay out. I'm an American. I want to help now.'

'You're forty-six years old!'

'I can still fly a plane, Kate. And they need all the help they can get.'

There was no way Kate could dissuade him. They spent the last few days together quietly, their differences forgotten. They loved each other, and that was all that mattered.

The night before David was to leave for France, he said, 'You and Brad Rogers can run the business as well as I can, maybe better.'

'What if something happens to you? I couldn't bear it.'

He held her close. 'Nothing will happen to me, Kate. I'll come back to you with all kinds of medals.'

He left the following morning.

David's absence was death for Kate. It had taken her so long to win him, and now every second of her day there was the ugly, creeping fear of losing him. He was always with her. She found him in the cadence of a stranger's voice, the sudden laughter on a quiet street, a phrase, a scent, a song. He was everywhere. She wrote him long letters every day. Whenever she received a letter from him, she reread it until it was in tatters. He was well, he wrote. The Germans had air superiority, but that would change. There were rumours that America would be helping soon. He would write again when he could. He loved her.

Don't let anything happen to you, my darling. I'll hate you forever if you do.

She tried to forget her loneliness and misery by plunging into work. At the beginning of the war, France and Germany had the best-equipped fighting forces in Europe, but the Allies had far greater manpower, resources and materials. Russia, with the largest army, was badly equipped and poorly commanded.

'They all need help,' Kate told Brad Roger. 'They need tanks and guns and ammunition.'

Brad Rogers was uncomfortable. 'Kate, David doesn't think –'

'David isn't here, Brad. It's up to you and me.'

But Brad Rogers knew that what Kate meant was, *It's up to me.*

Kate could not understand David's attitude about manufacturing armaments. The Allies needed weapons, and Kate felt it was her patriotic duty to supply them. She conferred with the heads of half a dozen friendly nations, and within a year Kruger-Brent, Ltd., was manufacturing guns and tanks, bombs and ammunition. The company supplied trains and tanks and uniforms and guns. Kruger-Brent was rapidly becoming one of the fastest-growing conglomerates in the world. When Kate saw the most recent revenue figures, she said to Brad Rogers, 'Have you seen these? David will have to admit he was mistaken.'

South Africa, meanwhile, was in turmoil. The party leaders had pledged their support to the Allies and accepted responsibility for defending South Africa against Germany, but the majority of Afrikaaners opposed the country's support of Great Britain. They could not forget the past so quickly.

In Europe the war was going badly for the Allies. Fighting on the western front reached a standstill. Both sides dug in, protected by trenches that stretched across France and Belgium, and the soldiers were miserable. Rain filled the dugouts with water and mud, and rats swarmed through the vermin-infested trenches. Kate was grateful that David was fighting his war in the air.

On April 6, 1917, President Wilson declared

war, and David's prediction came true. America began to mobilize.

The first American Expeditionary Force under General John J. Pershing began landing in France on June 26, 1917. New place names became a part of everyone's vocabulary: Saint-Mihiel . . . Château-Thierry . . . the Meuse-Argonne . . . Belleau Wood . . . Verdun . . . The Allies had become an irresistible force, and on November 11, 1918, the war was finally over. The world was safe for democracy.

David was on his way home.

When David disembarked from the troop ship in New York, Kate was there to meet him. They stood staring at each other for one eternal moment, ignoring the noise and the crowds around them, then Kate was in David's arms. He was thinner and tired-looking, and Kate thought, *Oh, God. I've missed him so.* She had a thousand questions to ask him, but they could wait. 'I'm taking you to Cedar Hill House,' Kate told him. 'It's a perfect place for you to rest.'

Kate had done a great deal with the house in anticipation of David's arrival home. The large, airy living room had been furnished with twin sofas covered in old rose-and-green floral chintz. Matching down-filled armchairs were grouped around the fireplace. Over the fireplace was a Vlaminck floral canvas, and, on each side of it, doré sconces. Two sets of French doors opened out onto the veranda, which ran the entire length of the house on three sides, covered with a striped awning. The rooms were bright and airy, and the view of the harbour spectacular.

Kate led David through the house, chattering away happily. He seemed strangely quiet. When they had completed the tour, Kate asked, 'Do you like what I've done with it, darling?'

'It's beautiful, Kate. Now, sit down. I want to talk to you.'

She had a sudden sinking feeling. 'Is anything wrong?'

'We seem to have become a munitions supplier for half the world.'

'Wait until you look at the books,' Kate began. 'Our profit has –'

'I'm talking about something else. As I recall, our profit was pretty good before I left. I thought we agreed we wouldn't get involved in manufacturing war supplies.'

Kate felt an anger rising in her. 'You agreed. I didn't.' She fought to control it. 'Times change, David. We have to change with them.'

He looked at her and asked quietly, 'Have you changed?'

Lying in bed that night, Kate asked herself whether it was she who had changed, or David. Had she become stronger, or had David become weaker? She thought about his argument against manufacturing armaments. It was a weak argument. After all, *someone* was going to supply the merchandise to the Allies, and there was an enormous profit in it. What had happened to David's business sense? She had always looked up to him as one of the cleverest men she knew. But now, she felt that she was more capable of running the business than David. She spent a sleepless night.

In the morning Kate and David had breakfast and walked around the grounds.

'It's really lovely,' David told her. 'I'm glad to be here.'

Kate said, 'About our conversation last night –'

'It's done. I was away, and you did what you thought was right.'

Would I have done the same thing if you had been here? Kate wondered. But she did not say the words aloud. She had done what she had for the sake of the company. *Does the company mean more to me than my marriage?* She was afraid to answer the question.

SEVENTEEN

The next five years witnessed a period of incredible world-wide growth. Kruger-Brent, Ltd., had been founded on diamonds and gold, but it had diversified and expanded all over the world, so that its centre was no longer South Africa. The company recently had acquired a publishing empire, an insurance company and half a million acres of timberland.

One night Kate nudged David awake. 'Darling, let's move the company headquarters.'

David sat up groggily. 'W-what?'

'The business centre of the world today is New York. That's where our headquarters should be. South Africa's too far away from everything. Besides, now that we have the telephone and cable, we can communicate with any of our offices in minutes.'

'Now why didn't I think of that?' David mumbled. And he went back to sleep.

* * *

New York was an exciting new world. On her previous visits there, Kate had felt the quick pulse of the city, but living there was like being caught up at the centre of a matrix. The earth seemed to spin faster, everything moved at a more rapid pace.

Kate and David selected a site for the new company headquarters on Wall Street, and the architects went to work. Kate chose another architect to design a sixteenth-century French Renaissance mansion on Fifth Avenue.

'This city is so damned *noisy*,' David complained.

And it was true. The chatter of riveters filled the air in every part of the city as skyscrapers began to soar into the heavens. New York had become the mecca for trade from all over the world, the headquarters for shipping, insurance, communications and transportation. It was a city bursting with a unique vitality. Kate loved it, but she sensed David's unhappiness.

'David, this is the future. This place is growing, and we'll grow with it.'

'My God, Kate, how much more do you want?'

And without thinking, she replied, 'All there is.'

She could not understand why David had even asked the question. The name of the game was to win, and you won by beating everyone else. It seemed so obvious to her. Why couldn't David see it? David was a good businessman, but there was something missing in him, a hunter, a compulsion to conquer, to be the biggest and the best. Her father had had that spirit, and she had it. Kate was not sure exactly when it had happened, but at some point in her life, the company had become the master, and she the slave. It owned her more than she owned it.

When she tried to explain her feelings to David, he laughed and said, 'You're working too hard.' *She's so much like her father*, David thought. And he was not sure why he found that vaguely disturbing.

How could one work too hard? Kate wondered. There was no greater joy in life. It was when she felt most alive. Each day brought a new set of problems, and each problem was a challenge, a puzzle to be solved, a new game to be won. And she was wonderful at it. She was caught up in something beyond imagination. It had nothing to do with money or achievement; it had to do with *power*. A power that controlled the lives of thousands of people in every corner of the earth. Just as her life had once been controlled. As long as she had power, she would never truly need anyone. It was a weapon that was awesome beyond belief.

Kate was invited to dine with kings and queens and presidents, all seeking her favour, her goodwill. A new Kruger-Brent factory could mean the difference between poverty and riches. *Power*. The company was alive, a growing giant that had to be fed, and sometimes sacrifices were necessary, for the giant could not be shackled. Kate understood that now. It had a rhythm, a pulse, and it had become her own.

* * *

In March, a year after they had moved to New York, Kate felt unwell. David persuaded her to see a doctor.

'His name is John Harley. He's a young doctor with a good reputation.'

Reluctantly, Kate went to see him. John Harley was a thin serious-looking young Bostonian about twenty-six, five years younger than Kate.

'I warn you,' Kate informed him, 'I don't have time to be sick.'

'I'll bear that in mind, Mrs Blackwell. Meanwhile, let's have a look at you.'

Dr Harley examined her, made some tests and said, 'I'm sure it's nothing serious. I'll have the results in a day or two. Give me a call on Wednesday.'

Early Wednesday morning Kate telephoned Dr Harley. 'I have good news for you, Mrs Blackwell,' he said cheerfully. 'You're going to have a baby.'

It was one of the most exciting moments of Kate's life. She could not wait to tell David.

She had never seen David so thrilled. He scooped her up in his strong arms and said, 'It's going to be a girl, and she'll look exactly like you.' He was thinking, *This is exactly what Kate needs. Now she'll stay home more. She'll be more of a wife.*

And Kate was thinking, *It will be a boy. One day he'll take over Kruger-Brent.*

* * *

As the time for the birth of the baby drew nearer, Kate worked shorter hours, but she still went to the office every day.

'Forget about the business and relax,' David advised her.

What he did not understand was that the business *was* Kate's relaxation.

The baby was due in December. 'I'll try for the twenty-fifth,' Kate promised David. 'He'll be our Christmas present.'

It's going to be a perfect Christmas. Kate thought. She was head of a great conglomerate, she was married to the man she loved and she was going to have his baby. If there was irony in the order of her priorities, Kate was not aware of it.

Her body had grown large and clumsy, and it was getting more and more difficult for Kate to go to the office, but whenever David or Brad Rogers suggested she stay home, her answer was, 'My brain is still working.' Two months before the baby was due, David was in South Africa on an inspection tour of the mine at Pniel. He was scheduled to return to New York the following week.

Kate was at her desk when Brad Rogers walked in unannounced. She looked at the grim expression on his face and said, 'We lost the Shannon deal!'

'No. I – Kate, I just got word. There's been an accident. A mine explosion.'

She felt a sharp pang, 'Where? Was it bad? Was anyone killed?'

Brad took a deep breath. 'Half a dozen. Kate – David was with them.'

The words seemed to fill the room and reverberate against the panelled walls, growing louder and louder, until it was a screaming in her ears, a Niagara of sound that was drowning her, and she felt herself being sucked into its centre, deeper and deeper, until she could no longer breathe.

And everything became dark and silent.

The baby was born one hour later, two months premature. Kate named him Anthony James Blackwell, after David's father. *I'll love you, my son, for me, and I'll love you for your father.*

One month later the new Fifth Avenue mansion was ready, and Kate and the baby and a staff of servants moved into it. Two castles in Italy had been stripped to furnish the house. It was a showplace, with elaborately carved sixteenth-century Italian walnut furniture and rose-marble f0loors bordered with sienna-red marble. The panelled library boasted a magnificent eighteenth-century fireplace over which hung a rare Holbein. There was a trophy room with David's gun collection, and an art gallery that Kate filled with Rembrandts and Vermeers and Velázquezes and Bellinis. There was a ballroom and a sun room and a formal dining room and a nursery next to Kate's room, and uncounted bedrooms. In the large formal gardens were statues by Rodin, Augustus Saint-Gaudens and Maillol. It was a palace fit for a king. *And the king is growing up in it*, Kate thought happily.

In 1928, when Tony was four, Kate sent him to nursery school. He was a handsome, solemn little boy, with his mother's grey eyes and stubborn chin. He was given music lessons, and when he was five he attended dancing school. Some of the best times the two of them spent together were at Cedar Hill House in Dark Harbor. Kate bought a yacht, an eighty-foot motor sailer she named the *Corsair*, and she and Tony cruised the waters along the coast of Maine. Tony adored it. But it was the work that gave Kate her greatest pleasure.

There was something mystic about the company Jamie McGregor had founded. It was alive, consuming. It was her lover, and it would never die on a winter day and leave her alone. It would live forever. She would see to it. And one day she would give it to her son.

The only disturbing factor in Kate's life was her homeland. She cared deeply about South Africa. The racial problems there were growing, and Kate was troubled. There were two political camps: the *verkramptes* – the narrow ones, the prosegregationists – and the *verligtes* – the enlightened ones, who wanted to improve the position of blacks. Prime Minister James Hertzog and Jan Smuts had formed a coalition and combined their power to have the New Land Act passed. Blacks were removed from the rolls and were no longer able to vote or own land. Millions of people belonging to different minority groups were disrupted by the new law. The areas that had no minerals, industrial centres or ports were assigned to coloureds, black and Indians.

Kate arranged a meeting in South Africa with several high government officials. 'This is a time bomb,' Kate told them. 'What you're doing is trying to keep eight million people in slavery.'

'It's not slavery, Mrs Blackwell. We're doing this for their own good.'

'Really? How would you explain that?'

'Each race has something to contribute. If the blacks mingle with the whites, they'll lose their individuality. We're trying to protect them.'

'That's bloody nonsense,' Kate retorted. 'South Africa has become a racist hell.'

'That's not true. Blacks from other countries come thousands of miles in order to enter this country. They pay as much as fifty-six pounds for a forged pass. The black is better off here than anywhere else on earth.'

'Then I pity them,' Kate retorted.

'They're primitive children, Mrs Blackwell. It's for their own good.'

Kate left the meeting frustrated and deeply fearful for her country.

Kate was also concerned about Banda. He was in the news a good deal. The South African newspapers were calling him the *scarlet pimpernel*, and there was a grudging admiration in their stories. He escaped the police by disguising himself as a labourer, a chauffeur, a janitor. He had organized a guerrilla army and he headed the police's most-wanted list. One article in the *Cape Times* told of his being carried triumphantly through the streets of a black village on the shoulders of demonstrators. He went from village to village addressing crowds of students, but every time the police got wind of his presence, Banda disappeared. He was said to have a personal bodyguard at a different house every night. Kate knew that nothing would stop him but death.

She had to get in touch with him. She summoned one of her veteran black foremen, a man she trusted. 'William, do you think you can find Banda?'

'Only if he wishes to be found.'

'Try. I want to meet with him.'

'I'll see what I can do.'

The following morning the foreman said, 'If you are free this evening, a car will be waiting to take you out to the country.'

Kate was driven to a small village seventy miles north of Johannesburg. The driver stopped in front of a small frame house, and Kate went inside. Banda was waiting for her. He looked exactly the same as when Kate had last seen him. *And he must be sixty years old*, Kate thought. He had been on the run from the police for years, and yet he appeared serene and calm.

He hugged Kate and said, 'You look more beautiful every time I see you.'

She laughed. 'I'm getting old. I'm going to be forty in a few years.'

'The years sit lightly on you, Kate.'

They went into the kitchen, and while Banda fixed coffee, Kate said, 'I don't like what's happening, Banda. Where is it going to lead?'

'It will get worse,' Banda said simply. 'The government will not allow us to speak with them. The whites have destroyed the bridges between us and them, and one day they will find they need those bridges to reach us. We have our heroes now, Kate. Nehemiah Tile, Mokone, Richard Msimang. The whites goad us and move us around like cattle to pasture.'

'Not all whites think like that,' Kate assured him. 'You have friends who are fighting to change things. It will happen one day, Banda, but it will take time.'

'Time is like sand in an hourglass. It runs out.'

'Banda, what's happened to Ntame and to Magena?'

'My wife and son are in hiding,' Banda said sadly. 'The police are still very busy looking for me.'

'What can I do to help? I can't just sit by and do nothing. Will money help?'

'Money always helps.'

'I will arrange it. What else?'

'Pray. Pray for all of us.'

The following morning, Kate returned to New York.

When Tony was old enough to travel, Kate took him on business trips during his school holidays. He was fond of museums, and he could stand for hours looking at the paintings and statues of the great masters. At home, Tony sketched copies of the paintings on the wall, but he was too self-conscious to let his mother see his work.

He was sweet and bright and fun to be with, and there was a shyness about him that people found appealing. Kate was proud of her son. He was always first in his class. 'You beat all of them, didn't you, darling?' And she would laugh and hold him fiercely in her arms.

And young Tony would try even harder to live up to his mother's expectations.

In 1936, on Tony's twelfth birthday, Kate returned from a trip to the Middle East. She had missed Tony and was eager to see him. He was at home waiting for her. She took him in her arms and hugged him. 'Happy birthday, darling! Has it been a good day?'

'Y-yes, m-ma'am. It's b-b-been wonderful.'

Kate pulled back and looked at him. She had never noticed him stutter before. 'Are you all right, Tony?'

'F-fine, thank you, Mother.'

'You mustn't stammer,' she told him. 'Speak more slowly.'

'Yes, M-mother.'

Over the next few weeks, it got worse. Kate decided to talk to Dr Harley. When he finished the examination, John Harley said, 'Physically, there's nothing wrong with the boy, Kate. Is he under any kind of pressure?'

'My son? Of course not. How can you ask that?'

'Tony's a sensitive boy. Stuttering is very often a physical manifestation of frustration, an inability to cope.'

'You're wrong, John. Tony is at the very top of all the achievement tests in school. Last term he won three awards. Best all-round athlete, best all-round scholar and best student in the arts. I'd hardly call that unable to cope.'

'I see.' He studied her. 'What do you do when Tony stammers, Kate?'

'I correct him, of course.'

'I would suggest that you don't. That will only make him more tense.'

Kate was stung to anger. 'If Tony has any psychological problems, as you seem to think, I can assure you it's not because of his mother. I adore him. And he's aware that I think he's the most fantastic child on earth.'

And that was the core of the problem. No child could live up to that. Dr Harley glanced down at his chart. 'Let's see now. Tony is twelve.'

'Yes.'

'Perhaps it might be good for him if he went away for a while. Maybe a private school somewhere.'

Kate just stared at him.

'Let him be on his own a bit. Just until he finishes high school. They have some excellent schools in Switzerland.'

Switzerland! The idea of Tony being so far away from her was appalling. He was too young, he was not ready yet, he – Dr Harley was watching her. 'I'll think about it,' Kate told him.

That afternoon she cancelled a board meeting and went home early. Tony was in his room, doing homework.

Tony said, 'I g-g-got all A's t-today, M-mother.'

'What would you think of going to school in Switzerland, darling?'

And his eyes lit up and he said, 'M-m-may I?'

Six weeks later, Kate put Tony aboard a ship. He was on his way to the Institute Le Rosey in Rolle, a small town on the shore of Lake Geneva. Kate stood at the New York pier and watched until the huge liner cut loose from the tugboats. *Bloody hell! I'm going to miss him.* Then she turned and walked back to the limousine waiting to take her to the office.

Kate enjoyed working with Brad Rogers. He was forty-six, two years older than Kate. They had become good friends through the years, and she loved him for his devotion to Kruger-Brent. Brad was unmarried and had a variety of attractive girl friends, but gradually Kate became aware that he was half in love with her. More than once he made studiously ambiguous remarks, but she chose to keep their relationship on an impersonal, business level. She broke that pattern only once.

Brad had started seeing someone regularly. He stayed out late every night and came into morning meetings tired and distracted, his mind elsewhere. It was bad for the company. When a month went by and his behaviour was becoming more flagrant, Kate decided that something had to be done. She remembered how close David had come to quitting the company because of a woman. She would not let that happen with Brad.

Kate had planned to travel to Paris alone to acquire an import-export company, but at the last minute she asked Brad to accompany her. They spent the day of their arrival in meetings and that evening had dinner at the Grand Véfour. Afterwards, Kate suggested that Brad join her in her suite at the George V to go over the reports on the new company. When he arrived, Kate was waiting for him in a filmy negligee.

'I brought the revised offer with me,' Brad began, 'so we –'

'That can wait,' Kate said softly. There was an invitation in her voice that made him look at her again. 'I wanted us to be alone Brad.'

'Kate –'

She moved into his arms and held him close.

'My God!' he said, 'I've wanted you for so long.'

'And I you, Brad.'

And they moved into the bedroom.

Kate was a sensual woman, but all of her sexual energy had long since been harnessed into other channels. She was completely fulfilled by her work. She needed Brad for other reasons.

He was on top of her, and she moved her legs apart and felt his hardness in her, and it was neither pleasant nor unpleasant.

'Kate, I've loved you for so long . . .'

He was pressing into her, moving in and out in an ancient, timeless rhythm, and she thought, *They're asking too bloody much for the company. They're going to hold out because they know I really want it.*

Brad was whispering words of endearment in her ear.

I could call off the negotiations and wait for them to come back to me. But what if they don't? Do I dare risk losing the deal?

His rhythm was faster now, and Kate moved her hips, thrusting against his body.

No. They could easily find another buyer. Better to pay them what they want. I'll make up for it by selling off one of their subsidiaries.

Brad was moaning, in a frenzy of delight, and Kate moved faster, bringing him to a climax.

I'll tell them I've decided to meet their terms.

There was a long, shuddering gasp, and Brad

said, 'Oh God, Kate, it was wonderful. Was it good for you, darling?'

'It was heaven.'

She lay in Brad's arms all night, thinking and planning, while he slept. In the morning when he woke up, she said, 'Brad, that woman you've been seeing –'

'My God! You're jealous!' He laughed happily. 'Forget about her. I'll never see her again, I promise.'

Kate never went to bed with Brad again. When he could not understand why she refused him, all she said was, 'You don't know how much I want to, Brad, but I'm afraid we wouldn't be able to work together any longer. We must both make a sacrifice.'

And he was forced to live with that.

As the company kept expanding, Kate set up charitable foundations that contributed to colleges, churches and schools. She kept adding to her art collection. She acquired the great Renaissance and post-Renaissance artists Raphael and Titian, Tintoretto and El Greco; and the baroque painters Rubens, Caravaggio and Van Dyck.

The Blackwell collection was reputed to be the most valuable private collection in the world. *Reputed*, because no one outside the invited guests was permitted to see it. Kate would not allow it to be photographed, nor would she discuss it with the press. She had strict, inflexible rules about the press. The personal life of the Blackwell family was off limits. Neither servants nor employees of the company were permitted to discuss the Blackwell family. It was impossible, of course, to stop rumours and speculation, for Kate Blackwell was an intriguing enigma – one of the richest, most powerful women in the world. There were a thousand questions about her, but few answers.

Kate telephoned the headmistress at Le Rosey. 'I'm calling to find out how Tony is.'

'Ah, he is doing very well, Mrs Blackwsell. Your son is a superb student. He –'

'I wasn't referring to that. I meant –' She hesitated, as though reluctant to admit there could be a weakness in the Blackwell family. 'I meant his stammering.'

'Madame, there is no sign of any stammering. He is perfectly fine.'

Kate heaved an inward sigh of relief. She had known all along that it was only temporary, a passing phase of some kind. So much for doctors!

Tony arrived home four weeks later, and Kate was at the airport to meet him. He looked fit and handsome, and Kate felt a surge of pride. 'Hello, my love, how are you?'

'I'm f-f-fine, M-m-mother. How are y-y-you?'

On his vacations at home. Tony eagerly looked forward to examining the new paintings his mother had acquired while he was away. He was awed by the masters, and enchanted by the French Impressionists: Monet, Renoir, Manet and Morisot. They evoked a magic world for Tony. He bought a set of paints and an easel and went to work. He thought his paintings were terrible, and he still refused to show them to anyone. How could they compare with the exquisite masterpieces?

Kate told him, 'One day all these paintings will belong to you, darling.'

The thought of it filled the thirteen-year-old boy with a sense of unease. His mother did not understand. They could never be truly his, because he had done nothing to earn them. He had a fierce determination somehow to earn his own way. He had ambivalent feelings about being away from his mother, for everything around her was always exciting. She was at the centre of a whirlwind, giving orders, making incredible deals, taking him to exotic places, introducing him to interesting people. She was an awesome figure, and Tony was inordinately proud of her. He thought she was the most fascinating woman in the world. He felt guilty because it was only in her presence that he stuttered.

Kate had no idea how deeply her son was in awe of her until one day when he was home on vacation he asked, 'M-m-mother, do you r-r-run the world?'

And she had laughed and said, 'Of course not. What made you ask such a silly question?'

'All my f-friends at school talk about you. Boy, you're really s-something.'

'I am something,' Kate said. 'I'm your mother.'

Tony wanted more than anything in the world to please Kate. He knew how much the company meant to her, how much she planned on his running it one day, and he was filled with regret, because he knew he could not. That was not what he intended to do with his life.

When he tried to explain this to his mother, she would laugh, 'Nonsense, Tony. You're much too young to know what you want to do with your future.'

And he would begin to stammer.

The idea of being a painter excited Tony. To be able to capture beauty and freeze it for all eternity; that was something worthwhile, he wanted to go abroad and study in Paris, but he knew he would have to broach the subject to his mother very carefully.

They had wonderful times together. Kate was the chatelaine of vast estates. She had acquired homes in Palm Beach and South Carolina, and a stud farm in Kentucky, and she and Tony visited all of them during his vacations. They watched the America's Cup races in Newport, and when they were in New York, they had lunch at Delmonico's and tea at the Plaza and Sunday dinner at Lüchow's. Kate was interested in horse racing, and her stable became one of the finest in the world. When one of Kate's horses was running and Tony was home from school, Kate would take him to the track with her. They would sit in her box and

Tony would watch in wonder as his mother cheered until she was hoarse. He knew her excitement had nothing to do with money.

'It's winning, Tony. Remember that. Winning is what's important.'

They had quiet, lazy times at Dark Harbor. They shopped at Pendleton and Coffin, and had ice-cream sodas at the Dark Harbor Shop. In summer they went sailing and hiking and visited art galleries. In the winter there was skiing and skating and sleigh riding. They would sit in front of a fire in the large fireplace in the library, and Kate would tell her son all the old family stories about his grandfather and Banda, and about the baby shower Madam Agnes and her girls gave for Tony's grandmother. It was a colourful family, a family to be proud of, to cherish.

'Kruger-Brent, Limited, will be yours on one day, Tony. You'll run it and –'

'I d-don't want to r-run it, Mother. I'm not interested in big business or p-power.'

And Kate exploded. 'You bloody fool! What do you know about big business or power? Do you think I go around the world spreading evil? Hurting people? Do you think Kruger-Brent is some kind of ruthless money machine crushing anything that gets in its way? Well, let me tell you something, Son. It's the next best thing to Jesus Christ. We're the resurrection, Tony. We save lives by the hundreds of thousands. When we open a factory in a depressed community or

326

country, those people can afford to build schools and libraries and churches, and give their children decent food and clothing and recreation facilities.' She was breathing hard, carried away by her anger. 'We build factories where people are hungry and out of work, and because of us they're able to live decent lives and hold up their heads. We become their saviours. Don't ever again let me hear you sneer at big business and power.'

All Tony could say was, 'I'm s-s-sorry, M-m-mother.'

And he thought stubbornly: *I'm going to be an artist.*

When Tony was fifteen, Kate suggested he spend his summer vacation in South Africa. He had never been there. 'I can't get away just now, Tony, but you'll find it a fascinating place. I'll make all the arrangements for you.'

'I was s-sort of h-hoping to spend my vacation in Dark Harbor, M-mother.'

'Next summer,' Kate said firmly. 'This summer I would like you to go to Johannesburg.'

Kate carefully briefed the company superintendent in Johannesburg, and together they laid out an itinerary for Tony. Each day was planned with one objective in view: to make this trip as exciting as possible for Tony, to make him realize his future lay with the company.

Kate received a daily report about her son. He had been taken into one of the gold mines. He had spent two days in the diamond fields. He had been on a guided tour of the Kruger-Brent plants and had gone on a safari in Kenya.

A few days before Tony's vacation ended, Kate telephoned the company manager in Johannesburg. 'How is Tony getting along?'

'Oh, he's having a great time, Mrs Blackwell. In fact, this morning he asked if he couldn't stay on a little longer.'

Kate felt a surge of pleasure. 'That's wonderful! Thank you.'

When Tony's vacation was over, he went to Southampton, England, where he boarded a Pan American Airways Systems plane for the United States. Kate flew Pan American whenever possible. It spoiled her for other airlines.

Kate left an important meeting to greet her son when he arrived at the Pan American terminal at the newly built La Guardia Airport in New York. His handsome face was filled with enthusiasm.

'Did you have a good time, darling?'

'South Africa's a f-fantastic country, M-mother. Did you know they f-flew me to the Namib Desert where grandfather s-stole those diamonds from Great-grandfather v-van der Merwe?'

'He didn't steal them, Tony,' Kate corrected him. 'He merely took what was his.'

'Sure,' Tony scoffed. 'Anyway, I was th-there. There was no sea *mis*, but they s-still have the guards and dogs and everything.' He grinned. 'They wouldn't give me any s-samples.'

Kate laughed happily. 'They don't have to give you any samples, darling. One day they will all be yours.'

'*You* t-tell them. They wouldn't l-listen to me.'

She hugged him. 'You *did* enjoy it, didn't you?' She was enormously pleased that at last Tony was excited about his heritage.

'You know what I loved m-most?'

Kate smiled lovingly. 'What?'

'The colours. I p-painted a lot of landscapes th-there. I hated to leave. I want to go back there and p-paint.'

'Paint?' Kate tried to sound enthusiastic. 'That sounds like a wonderful hobby, Tony.'

'No. I don't m-mean as a hobby, Mother. I want to be a p-painter. I've been thinking a lot about it. I'm going to P-Paris to study. I really think I might have some talent.'

Kate felt herself tensing. 'You don't want to spend the rest of your life painting.'

'Yes, I do, M-mother. It's the only thing I really c-care about.'

And Kate knew she had lost.

He has a right to live his own life, Kate thought. *But how can I let him make such a terrible mistake?*

In September, the decision was taken out of both their hands. Europe went to war.

'I want you to enrol in the Wharton School of Finance and Commerce,' Kate informed Tony. 'In two years if you still want to be an artist, you'll have my blessing.' Kate was certain that by then Tony would change his mind. It was inconceivable that her son would choose to spend his life slapping daubs of colour on bits of canvas when he could head the most exciting conglomerate in the world. He was, after all, her son.

To Kate Blackwell, World War II was another great opportunity. There were worldwide shortages of military supplies and materials and Kruger-Brent was able to furnish them. One division of the company provided equipment for the armed forces, while another division took care of civilian needs. The company factories were working twenty-four hours a day.

Kate was certain the United States was not going to be able to remain neutral. President Franklin D. Roosevelt called upon the country to be the great arsenal of democracy, and on March 11, 1941, the Lend-Lease Bill was pushed through Congress. Allied shipping across the Atlantic was menaced by the German blockade. U-boats, the German submarines, attacked and sank scores of Allied ships, fighting in wolf packs of eight.

Germany was a juggernaut that seemingly could not be stopped. In defiance of the Versailles Treaty, Adolf Hitler had built up one of the greatest war machines in history. In a new *Blitzkrieg* technique, Germany attacked Poland, Belgium and the Netherlands, and in rapid succession, the German machine crushed Denmark, Norway, Luxembourg and France.

Kate went into action when she received word that Jews working in the Nazi-confiscated Kruger-Brent, Ltd., factories were being arrested and deported to concentration camps. She made two telephone calls, and the following week she was on her way to Switzerland. When she arrived at the Baur au Lac Hotel in Zurich, there was a message that Colonel Brinkmann wished to see her. Brinkmann had been a manager of the Berlin branch of Kruger-Brent, Ltd. When the factory had been taken over by the Nazi government, Brinkmann was given the rank of colonel and kept in charge.

He came to see Kate at the hotel. He was a thin, precise man with blond hair combed carefully over his balding skull. 'I am delighted to see you, Frau Blackwell. I have a message for you from my government. I am authorized to assure you that as soon as we have won the war, your factories will be returned to you. Germany is going to be the greatest industrial power the world has ever known, and we welcome the collaboration of people such as yourself.'

'What if Germany loses?'

Colonel Brinkmann allowed a small smile to play on his lips. 'We both know that cannot happen, Frau Blackwell. The United States is wise to stay out of Europe's business. I hope it continues to do so.'

'I'm sure you do, Colonel.' She leaned forwards. 'I've heard rumours about Jews being sent to concentration camps and being exterminated. Is that true?'

'British propaganda, I assure you. It is true that *die Juden* are sent to work camps, but I give you my word as an officer that they are being treated as they should be.'

Kate wondered exactly what those words meant. She intended to find out.

The following day Kate made an appointment with a prominent German merchant named Otto Bueller. Bueller was in his fifties, a distinguished-looking man with a compassionate face and eyes that had known deep suffering. They met at a small café near the *Bahnhof*. Herr Bueller selected a table in a deserted corner.

'I've been told,' Kate said softly, 'that you've started an underground to help smuggle Jews into neutral countries. Is that true?'

'It's not true, Mrs Blackwell. Such an act would be treason against the Third Reich.'

'I have also heard that you're in need of funds to run it.'

Herr Bueller shrugged. 'Since there is no underground, I have no need of funds to run it, is that not so?'

His eyes kept nervously darting around the café. This was a man who breathed and slept with danger each day of his life.

'I was hoping I might be of some help,' Kate said carefully. 'Kruger-Brent, Limited, has factories in many neutral and Allied countries. If someone could get the refugees there, I would arrange for them to have employment.'

Herr Bueller sat there sipping a bitter coffee. Finally, he said, 'I know nothing about these things. Politics are dangerous these days. But if you are interested in helping someone in distress, I have an uncle in England who suffers from a terrible, debilitating disease. His doctors bills are very high.'

'How high?'

'Fifty thousand dollars a month. Arrangements would have to be made to deposit the money for his medical expenses in London and transfer the deposits to a Swiss bank.'

'That can be arranged.'

'My uncle would be very pleased.'

Some eight weeks later, a small but steady stream of Jewish refugees began to arrive in Allied countries to go to work in Kruger-Brent factories.

Tony quit school at the end of two years. He went up to Kate's office to tell her the news. 'I t-tried, M-mother. I really d-did. But I've m-made up m-my mind. I want to s-study p-painting. When the w-war is over, I'm g-going to P-paris.'

Each word was like a hammerblow.

'I kn-know you're d-disappointed, but I have to l-live my own life. I think I can be good – *really* good.' He saw the look on Kate's face. 'I've done what you've asked me to do. Now you've got to g-give me my chance. They've accepted me at the Art I-institute in Chicago.'

Kate's mind was in a turmoil. What Tony wanted to do was such a bloody *waste*. All she could say was, 'When do you plan to leave?'

'Enrolment starts on the fifteenth.'

What's the date today?'

'D-december sixth.'

On Sunday, December 7, 1941, squadrons of Nakajima bombers and Zero fighter planes from the Imperial Japanese Navy attacked Pearl Harbor, and the following day, the United States was at war. That afternoon Tony enlisted in the United States Marine Corps. He was sent to Quantico, Virginia, where he was graduated from Officer's Training School, and from there to the South Pacific.

Kate felt as though she were living on the edge of an abyss. Her working day was filled with the pressures of running the company, but every moment at the back of her mind was the fear that she would receive some dreaded news about Tony – that he had been wounded or killed.

The war with Japan was going badly. Japanese bombers struck at American bases on Guam, Midway and Wake islands. They took Singapore in February 1942, and quickly overran New Britain, New Ireland and the Admiralty and Solomon Islands. General Douglas MacArthur was forced to withdraw from the Philippines. The powerful forces of the Axis were slowly conquering the world, and the shadows were darkening everywhere. Kate was afraid that Tony might be taken prisoner of war and tortured. With all her power and influence, there was nothing she could do except pray. Every letter from Tony was a beacon of hope, a sign that, a few short weeks before, he had been alive. 'They keep us in the dark here,' Tony wrote. 'Are the Russians still holding on? The Japanese soldier is brutal, but you have to respect him. He's not afraid to die . . .'

'What's happening in the States? Are factory workers really striking for more money? . . .'

'The PT boats are doing a wonderful job here. Those boys are all heroes . . .'

'You have great connections, Mother. Send us a few hundred F4U's, the new Navy fighters. Miss you . . .'

On August 7, 1942, the Allies began their first offensive action in the Pacific. United States Marines landed on Guadalcanal in the Solomon Islands, and from then on they kept moving to take back the islands the Japanese had conquered.

In Europe, the Allies were enjoying an almost unbroken string of victories. On June 6, 1944, the Allied invasion of Western Europe was launched with landings by American, British and Canadian troops on the Normandy beaches, and a year later, on May 7, 1945, Germany surrendered unconditionally.

In Japan, on August 6, 1945, an atomic bomb

with a destructive force of more than twenty thousand tons of TNT was dropped on Hiroshima. Three days later, another atomic bomb destroyed the city of Nagasaki. On August 14, the Japanese surrendered. The long and bloody war was finally over.

Three months later, Tony returned home. He and Kate were at Dark Harbor, sitting on the terrace looking over the bay dotted with graceful white sails.

The war has changed him, Kate thought. There was a new maturity about Tony. He had grown a small moustache, and looked tanned and fit and handsome. There were lines about his eyes that had not been there before. Kate was sure the years overseas had given him time to reconsider his decision about not going into the company.

'What are your plans now, Son?' Kate asked.

Tony smiled. 'As I was saying before we were so rudely interrupted, Mother – I'm going to P-paris.'

BOOK FOUR

Tony

1946–1950

EIGHTEEN

Tony had been to Paris before, but this time the circumstances were different. The City of Light had been dimmed by the German occupation, but had been saved from destruction when it was declared an open city. The people had suffered a great deal, and though the Nazis had looted the Louvre, Tony found Paris relatively untouched. Besides, this time he was going to live there, to be a part of the city, rather than be a tourist. He could have stayed at Kate's penthouse on Avenue du Maréchal Foch, which had not been damaged during the occupation. Instead, he rented an unfurnished flat in an old converted house behind Grand Montparnasse. The apartment consisted of a living room with a fireplace, a small bedroom and a tiny kitchen that had no refrigerator. Between the bedroom and the kitchen crouched a bathroom with a claw-footed tub and small stained bidet and a temperamental toilet with a broken seat.

When the landlady started to make apologies, Tony stopped her. 'It's perfect.'

He spent all day Saturday at the flea market. Monday and Tuesday he toured the secondhand shops along the Left Bank, and by Wednesday he had the basic furniture he needed. A sofa bed, a scarred table, two overstuffed chairs, an old, ornately carved wardrobe, lamps and a rickety kitchen table and two straight chairs. *Mother would be horrified*, Tony thought. He could have had his apartment crammed with priceless antiques, but that would have been *playing* the part of a young American artist in Paris. He intended to *live* it.

The next step was getting into a good art school. The most prestigious art school in all of France was the Ecole des Beaux-Arts of Paris. Its standards were high, and few Americans were admitted. Tony applied for a place there. *They'll never accept me*, he thought. *But if they do!* Somehow, he had to show his mother he had made the right decision. He submitted three of his paintings and waited four weeks to hear whether he had been accepted. At the end of the fourth week, his concierge handed him a letter from the school. He was to report the following Monday.

The Ecole des Beaux-Arts was a large stone building, two storeys high, with a dozen classrooms filled with students. Tony reported to the head of the school, Maître Gessand, a towering, bitter-looking man with no neck and the thinnest lips Tony had ever seen.

'Your paintings are amateurish,' he told Tony. 'But they show promise. Our committee selected you more for what was *not* in the paintings than for what *was* in them. Do you understand?'

'Not exactly, maître.'

'You will, in time. I am assigning you to Maître Cantal. He will be your teacher for the next five years – if you last that long.'

I'll last that long, Tony promised himself.

Maître Cantal was a very short man, with a totally bald head which he covered with a purple beret. He had dark-brown eyes, a large, bulbous nose and lips like sausages. He greeted Tony with, 'Americans are dilettantes, barbarians. Why are you here?'

'To learn, maître.'

Maître Cantal grunted.

There were twenty-five pupils in the class, most of them French. Easels had been set up around the room, and Tony selected one near the window that overlooked a workingman's bistro. Scattered around the room were plaster casts of various parts of the human anatomy taken from Greek statues. Tony looked around for the model. He could see no one.

'You will begin,' Maître Cantal told the class.

'Excuse me,' Tony said. 'I – I didn't bring my paints with me.'

'You will not need paints. You will spend the first year learning to draw properly.'

The maître pointed to the Greek statuary. 'You

will draw those. If it seems too simple for you, let me warn you: before the year is over, more than half of you will be eliminated.' He warmed to his speech. 'You will spend the first year learning anatomy. The second year – for those of you who pass the course – you will draw from live models, working with oils. The third year – and I assure there will be fewer of you – you will paint with me, in my style, greatly improving on it, naturally. In the fourth and fifth years, you will find your own style, your own voice. Now let us get to work.'

The class went to work.

The maître went around the room, stopping at each easel to make criticisms or comments. When he came to the drawing Tony was working on, he said curtly, 'No! That will not do. What I see is the *outside* of an arm. I want to see the *inside*. Muscles, bones, ligaments. I want to know there is *blood* flowing underneath. Do you know how to do that?'

'Yes, maître. You think it, see it, feel it, and then you draw it.'

When Tony was not in class, he was usually in his apartment sketching. He could have painted from dawn to dawn. Painting gave him a sense of freedom he had never known before. The simple act of sitting in front of an easel with a paintbrush in his hand made him feel godlike. He could create whole worlds with one hand. He could make a tree, a flower, a human, a universe. It was a heady experience. He had been born for this. When he was not painting, he was out on the streets of Paris exploring the fabulous city. Now it was *his* city, the place where his art was being born. There were two Parises, divided by the Seine into the Left Bank and the Right Bank, and they were worlds apart. The Right Bank was for the wealthy, the established. The Left Bank belonged to the students, the artists, the struggling. It was Montparnasse and the Boulevard Raspail and Saint-Germain-de-Prés. It was the Café Flore and Henry Miller and Elliot Paul. For Tony, it was home. He would sit for hours at the Boule Blanche or La Coupole with fellow students, discussing their arcane world.

'I understand the art director of the Guggenheim Museum is in Paris, buying up everything in sight.'

'Tell him to wait for me!'

They all read the same magazines and shared them because they were expensive: *Studio* and *Cahiers d'Art, Formes et Couleurs* and *Gazette des Beaux-Arts*.

Tony had learned French at Le Rosey, and he found it easy to make friends with the other students in his class, for they all shared a common passion. They had no idea who Tony's family was, and they accepted him as one of them. Poor and struggling artists gathered at Café Flore and Les Deux Magots on Boulevard Saint-Germain, and ate at Le Pot d'Etain on the Rue des Canettes or at the Rue de l'Université. None of the others had ever seen the inside of Lasserre or Maxim's.

In 1946, giants were practicing their art in Paris. From time to time, Tony caught glimpses of Pablo Picasso, and one day Tony and a friend saw Marc Chagall, a large, flamboyant man in his fifties, with a wild mop of hair just beginning to turn grey. Chagall was seated at a table across the café, in earnest conversation with a group of people.

'We're lucky to see him,' Tony's friend whispered. 'He comes to Paris very seldom. His home is at Vence, near the Mediterranean coast.'

There was Max Ernst sipping an aperitif at a sidewalk café, and the great Alberto Giacometti walking down the Rue de Rivoli, looking like one of his own sculptures, tall and thin and gnarled. Tony was surprised to note he was clubfooted. Tony met Hans Belmer, who was making a name for himself with erotic paintings of young girls turning into dismembered dolls. But perhaps Tony's most exciting moment came when he was introduced to Braque. The artist was cordial, but Tony was tongue-tied.

The future geniuses haunted the new art galleries, studying their competition. The Drouant-David Gallery was exhibiting an unknown young artist named Bernard Buffet, who had studied at the Ecole des Beaux Arts, and Soutine, Utrillo and Dufy. The students congregated at the Salon d'Automne and the Charpentier

Gallery and Mlle Roussa's Gallery on the Rue de Seine, and spent their spare time gossiping about their successful rivals.

The first time Kate saw Tony's apartment, she was stunned. She wisely made no comment, but she thought, *Bloody hell! How can a son of mine live in this dreary closet?* Aloud she said, 'It has great charm, Tony. I don't see a refrigerator. Where do you keep your food?'

'Out on the w-windowsill.'

Kate walked over to the window, opened it and selected an apple from the sill outside. 'I'm not eating one of your subjects, am I?'

Tony laughed. 'N-no, Mother.'

Kate took a bite. 'Now,' she demanded, 'tell me about your painting.'

'There's n-not much to t-tell yet,' Tony confessed. 'We're just doing d-drawings this year.

'Do you like this Maître Cantal?'

'He's m-marvellous. The important question is whether he l-likes *me*. Only about one-third of the class is going to m-make it to next year.'

Not once did Kate mention Tony's joining the company.

Maître Cantal was not a man to lavish praise. The biggest compliment Tony would get would be a grudging, 'I suppose I've seen worse,' or 'I'm almost beginning to see *underneath*.'

At the end of the school term, Tony was among

the eight advanced to the second-year class. To celebrate, Tony and the other relieved students went to a nightclub in Montmartre, got drunk and spent the night with some young English women who were on a tour of France.

When school started again, Tony began to work with oils and live models. It was like being released from kindergarten. After one year of sketching parts of anatomy, Tony felt he knew every muscle, nerve and gland in the human body. That wasn't drawing – it was *copying*. Now, with a paintbrush in his hand and a live model in front of him, Tony began to create. Even Maître Cantal was impressed.

'You have the *feel*,' he said grudgingly. 'Now we must work on the technique.'

There were about a dozen models who sat for classes at the school. The ones Maître Cantal used most frequently were Carlos, a young man working his way through medical school; Annette, a short, buxom brunette with a clump of red pubic hair and an acne-scarred back; and Dominique Masson, a beautiful young, willowy blonde with delicate cheekbones and deep-green eyes. Dominique also posed for several well-known painters. She was everyone's favourite. Every day after class the male students would gather around her, trying to make a date.

'I never mix pleasure with business,' she told

them. 'Anyway,' she teased, 'it would not be fair. You have all seen what I have to offer. How do I know what you have to offer?'

And the ribald conversation would go on. But Dominique never went out with anyone at the school.

Late one afternoon when all the other students had left and Tony was finishing a painting of Dominique, she came up behind him unexpectedly. 'My nose is too long.'

Tony was flustered. 'Oh. I'm sorry, I'll change it.'

'No, no. The nose in the painting is fine. It is *my* nose that is too long.'

Tony smiled. 'I'm afraid I can't do much about that.'

'A Frenchman would have said, "Your nose is perfect, *chérie*."'

'I like your nose, and I'm not French.'

'Obviously. You have never asked me out. I wonder why.'

Tony was taken aback. 'I – I don't know. I guess it's because everyone else has, and you never go out with anybody.'

Dominique smiled. '*Everybody* goes out with somebody. Good night.'

And she was gone.

Tony noticed that whenever he stayed late, Dominique dressed and then returned to stand behind him and watched him paint.

'You are very good,' she announced one afternoon. 'You are going to be an important painter.'

'Thank you, Dominique. I hope you're right.'

'Painting is very serious to you, *oui*?'

'*Oui.*'

'Would a man who is going to be an important painter like to buy me dinner?' She saw the look of surprise on his face. 'I do not eat much. I must keep my figure.'

Tony laughed. 'Certainly. It would be a pleasure.'

They ate at a bistro near Sacré-Coeur, and they discussed painters and painting. Tony was fascinated with her stories of the well-known artists for whom she posed. As they were having *café au lait*, Dominique said, 'I must tell you, you are as good as any of them.'

Tony was inordinately pleased, but all he said was, 'I have a long way to go.'

Outside the café, Dominique asked, 'Are you going to invite me to see your apartment?'

'If you'd like to. I'm afraid it isn't much.'

When they arrived, Dominique looked around the tiny, messy apartment and shook her head. 'You were right. It is not much. Who takes care of you?'

'A cleaning lady comes in once a week.'

'Fire her. This place is filthy. Don't you have a girl friend?'

'No.'

She studied him a moment. 'You're not a queer?'

'No.'

'Good. It would be a terrible waste. Find me a pail of water and some soap.'

Dominique went to work on the apartment, cleaning and scrubbing and finally tidying up. When she had finished, she said, 'That will have to do for now. My God, I need a bath.'

She went into the tiny bathroom and ran water in the tub. 'How do you fit yourself in this?' she called out.

'I pull up my legs.'

She laughed. 'I would like to see that.'

Fifteen minutes later, she came out of the bathroom with only a towel around her waist, her blonde hair damp and curling. She had a beautiful figure, full breasts, a narrow waist and long, tapering legs. Tony had been unaware of her as a woman before. She had been merely a nude figure to be portrayed on canvas. Oddly enough, the towel changed everything. He felt a sudden rush of blood to his loins.

Dominique was watching him. 'Would you like to make love to me?'

'Very much.'

She slowly removed the towel. 'Show me.'

Tony had never known a woman like Dominique. She gave him everything and asked for nothing. She came over almost every evening to cook for Tony. When they went out to dinner, Dominique insisted on going to inexpensive bistros or sandwich bars. 'You must save your money,' she scolded him. 'It is very difficult even for a good artist to get started. And you are good, *chéri*.'

They went to Les Halles in the small hours of the morning and had onion soup at Pied de Cochon. They went to the Musée Carnavalet and out-of-the-way places where tourists did not go, like Cimetière Père-Lachaise – the final resting place of Oscar Wilde, Frédéric Chopin, Honoré de Balzac and Marcel Proust. They visited the catacombs and spent a lazy holiday week going down the Seine on a barge owned by a friend of Dominique's.

Dominique was a delight to be with. She had a quixotic sense of humour, and whenever Tony was depressed, she would laugh him out of it. She seemed to know everyone in Paris, and she took Tony to interesting parties where he met some of the most prominent figures of the day, like the poet Paul Eluard, and André Breton, in charge of the prestigious Galerie Maeght.

Dominique was a source of constant encouragement. 'You are going to be better than all of them, *chéri*. Believe me. I know.'

If Tony was in the mood to paint at night, Dominique would cheerfully pose for him, even though she had been working all day. *God, I'm lucky*, Tony thought. This was the first time he had been sure someone loved him for what he was, not who he was, and it was a feeling he cherished. Tony was afraid to tell Dominique he was the heir to one of the world's largest fortunes, afraid she would change, afraid they would lose what they had. But for her birthday Tony could not resist buying her a Russian lynx coat.

'It's the most beautiful thing I've ever seen in my life!' Dominique swirled the coat around her and danced around the room. She stopped in the middle of a spin. 'Where did it come from? Tony, where did you get the money to buy this coat?'

He was ready for her. 'It's hot – stolen. I bought it from a little man outside the Rodin Museum. He was anxious to get rid of it. It didn't cost me much more than a good cloth coat would cost at Au Printemps.'

Dominique stared at him a moment, then burst out laughing. 'I'll wear it even if we both go to prison!'

Then she threw her arms around Tony and started to cry. 'Oh, Tony, you idiot. You darling, fantastic idiot.'

It was well worth the lie, Tony decided.

One night Dominique suggested to Tony that he move in with her. Between working at the Ecole des Beaux-Arts and modelling for some of the better-known artists in Paris, Dominique was able to rent a large, modern apartment on Rue Prêtres-Saint Severin. 'You should not be living in a place like this, Tony. It is dreadful. Live with me, and you will not have to pay any rent. I can do your laundry, cook for you and –'

'No, Dominique. Thank you.'

'But why?'

How could he explain? In the beginning he might have told her he was rich, but now it was too late. She would feel he had been making a fool of her. So he said, 'It would be like living off you. You've already given me too much.'

'Then I'm giving up my apartment and moving in here. I want to be with you.'

She moved in the following day.

There was a wonderful, easy intimacy between them. They spent weekends in the country and stopped at little hostels where Tony would set up his easel and paint landscapes, and when they got hungry Dominique would spread out a picnic lunch she had prepared and they would eat in a meadow. Afterwards, they made long, sweet love. Tony had never been so completely happy.

His work was progressing beautifully. One morning Maître Cantal held up one of Tony's paintings and said to the class. 'Look at that body. You can see it *breathing*.'

Tony could hardly wait to tell Dominique that night. 'You know how I got the breathing just right? I hold the model in my arms every night.'

Dominique laughed in excitement and then grew serious. 'Tony, I do not think you need three more years of school. You are ready now. Everyone at the school sees that, even Cantal.'

Tony's fear was that he was not good enough, that he was just another painter, that his work would be lost in the flood of pictures turned out by thousands of artists all over the world every day. He could not bear the thought of it. *Winning is what's important, Tony. Remember that.*

Sometimes when Tony finished a painting he would be filled with a sense of elation and think, *I have talent. I really have talent.* At other times he would look at his work and think, *I'm a bloody amateur.*

With Dominique's encouragement, Tony was gaining more and more confidence in his work. He had finished almost two dozen paintings on his own. Landscapes, still lifes. There was a painting of Dominique lying nude under a tree, the sun dappling her body. A man's jacket and shirt were in the foreground, and the viewer knew the woman awaited her lover.

When Dominique saw the painting, she cried, 'You must have an exhibition!'

'You're mad, Dominique! I'm not ready.'

'You're wrong, *mon cher*.'

Tony arrived home late the next afternoon to find that Dominique was not alone. Anton Goerg, a thin man with an enormous potbelly and protuberant hazel eyes, was with her. He was the owner and proprietor of the Goerg Gallery, a modest gallery on the Rue Dauphine. Tony's paintings were spread around the room.

'What's going on?' Tony asked.

'What's going on, monsieur,' Anton Goerg exclaimed, 'is that I think your work is brilliant.' He clapped Tony on the back. 'I would be honoured to give you a showing in my gallery.'

Tony looked over at Dominique, and she was beaming at him.

'I – I don't know what to say.'

'You have already said it,' Goerg replied. 'On these canvases.'

Tony and Dominique stayed up half the night discussing it.

'I don't feel I'm ready. The critics will crucify me.'

'You're wrong, *chéri*. This is perfect for you. It is a small gallery. Only the local people will come and judge you. There is no way you can get hurt. Monsieur Goerg would never offer to give you an exhibition if he did not believe in you. He agrees with me that you are going to be a very important artist.'

'All right,' Tony finally said. 'Who knows? I might even sell a painting.'

The cable read: ARRIVING PARIS SATURDAY. PLEASE JOIN ME FOR DINNER. LOVE. MOTHER.

Tony's first thought as he watched his mother walk into the studio was, *What a handsome woman she is*. She was in her mid-fifties, hair untinted, with white strands laced through the black. There was a charged vitality about her. Tony had once asked her why she had not remarried. She had answered quietly. 'Only two men were ever important in my life. Your father and you.'

Now, standing in the little apartment in Paris,

facing his mother, Tony said, 'It's g-good to see you, M-mother.'

'Tony, you look absolutely wonderful! The beard is new.' She laughed and ran her fingers through it. 'You look like a young Abe Lincoln.' Her eyes swept the small apartment. 'Thank God you've gotten a good cleaning woman. It looks like a different place.'

Kate walked over to the easel, where Tony had been working on a painting, and she stopped and stared at it for a long time. He stood there, nervously awaiting his mother's reaction.

When Kate spoke, her voice was very soft. 'It's brilliant, Tony. Really brilliant.' There was no effort to conceal the pride she felt. She could not be deceived about art, and there was a fierce exultation in her that her son was so talented.

She turned to face him. 'Let me see more!'

They spent the next two hours going through his stack of paintings. Kate discussed each one in great detail. There was no condescension in her voice. She had failed in her attempt to control his life, and Tony admired her for taking her defeat so gracefully.

Kate said, 'I'll arrange for a showing. I know a few dealers who –'

'Thanks, M-mother, but you d-don't have to. I'm having a showing next F-friday. A g-gallery is giving me an exhibition.'

Kate threw her arms around Tony. 'That's wonderful! Which gallery?'

'The G-goerg Gallery.'

'I don't believe I know it.'

'It's s-small, but I'm not ready for Hammer or W-wildenstein yet.'

She pointed to the painting of Dominique under the tree. 'You're wrong, Tony. I think this –'

There was the sound of the front door opening. 'I'm horny, *chéri*. Take off your –' Dominique saw Kate. 'Oh, *merde!* I'm sorry. I – I didn't know you had company, Tony.'

There was a moment of frozen silence.

'Dominique, this is my m-mother. M-mother, may I present D-dominique Masson.'

The two women stood there, studying each other.

'How do you do, Mrs Blackwell.'

Kate said, 'I've been admiring my son's portrait of you.' The rest was left unspoken.

There was another awkward silence.

'Did Tony tell you he's going to have an exhibition, Mrs Blackwell?'

'Yes, he did. It's wonderful news.'

'Can you s-stay for it, Mother?'

'I'd give anything to be able to be there, but I have a board meeting the day after tomorrow in Johannesburg and there's no way I can miss it. I wish I'd known about it sooner, I'd have rearranged my schedule.'

'It's all r-right,' Tony said. 'I understand.' Tony was nervous that his mother might say more about the company in front of Dominique, but Kate's mind was on the paintings.

'It's important for the right people to see your exhibition.'

'Who are the right people, Mrs Blackwell?'

Kate turned to Dominique. 'Opinion-makers, critics. Someone like Andre d'Usseau – he should be there.'

Andre d'Usseau was the most respected art critic in France. He was a ferocious lion guarding the temple of art, and a single review from him could make or break an artist overnight. D'Usseau was invited to the opening of every exhibition, but he attended only the major ones. Gallery owners and artists trembled, waiting for his reviews to appear. He was a master of the *bon mot*, and his quips flew around Paris on poisoned wings. Andre d'Usseau was the most hated man in Parisian art circles, and the most respected. His mordant wit and savage criticism were tolerated because of his expertise.

Tony turned to Dominique. 'That's a m-mother for you.' Then to Kate, 'Andre d'Usseau doesn't g-go to little galleries.'

'Oh, Tony, he *must* come. He can make you famous overnight.'

'Or b-break me.'

'Don't you believe in yourself?' Kate was watching her son.

'Of course he does,' Dominique said. 'But we couldn't dare hope that Monsier d'Usseau would come.'

'I could probably find some friends who know him.'

Dominique's face lighted up. 'That would be fantastic!' She turned to Tony. '*Chéri*, do you know what it would mean if he came to your opening?'

'Oblivion?'

'Be serious. I know his taste, Tony. I know what he likes. He will adore your paintings.'

Kate said, 'I won't try to arrange for him to come unless you want me to, Tony.'

'Of course he wants it, Mrs Blackwell.'

Tony took a deep breath. 'I'm s-scared, but what the hell! L-let's try.'

'I'll see what I can do.' Kate looked at the painting on the easel for a long, long time, then turned back to Tony. There was a sadness in her eyes. 'Son, I must leave Paris tomorrow. Can we have dinner tonight?'

Tony replied, 'Yes, of course, Mother. *We're* f-free.'

Kate turned to Dominique and said graciously, 'Would you like to have dinner at Maxim's or –'

Tony said quickly, 'Dominique and I know a w-wonderful little café not f-far from here.'

They went to a bistro at the Place Victoire. The food was good and the wine was excellent. The two women seemed to get along well, and Tony was terribly proud of both of them. *It's one of the best nights of my life*, he thought. *I'm with my mother and the woman I'm going to marry*.

The next morning Kate telephoned from the airport. 'I've made a half a dozen phone calls,' she told Tony. 'No one could give me a definite answer about Andrew d'Usseau. But whichever way it goes, darling, I'm proud of you. The paintings are wonderful. Tony, I love you.'

'I l-love you too, M-mother.'

The Goerg Gallery was just large enough to escape being called *intime*. Two dozen of Tony's paintings were being hung on the walls in frantic, last-minute preparation for the opening. On a marble sideboard were slabs of cheese and biscuits and bottles of Chablis. The gallery was empty except for Anton Goerg, Tony, Dominique and a young female assistant who was hanging the last of the paintings.

Anton Goerg looked at his watch. 'The invitations said "seven o'clock." People should start to arrive at any moment now.'

Tony had not expected to be nervous. *And I'm not nervous*, he told himself. *I'm panicky!*

'What if no one shows up?' he asked. 'I mean, what if not one single, bloody person shows up?'

Dominique smiled and stroked his cheek. 'Then we'll have all this cheese and wine for ourselves.'

People began to arrive. Slowly at first, and then in larger numbers. Monsieur Goerg was at the door, effusively greeting them. *They don't look like art buyers to me*, Tony thought grimly. His discerning eye divided them into three categories. There were the artists and art students who attended each exhibition to evaluate the competition; the art dealers who came to every exhibition so they could spread derogatory news about aspiring painters;

and the *arty* crowd, consisting to a large extent of homosexuals and lesbians who seemed to spend their lives around the fringes of the art world. *I'm not going to sell a single, goddamned picture*, Tony decided.

Monsieur Goerg was beckoning to Tony from across the room.

'I don't think I want to meet any of these people,' Tony whispered to Dominique. 'They're here to rip me apart.'

'Nonsense. They came here to meet you. Now be charming, Tony.'

And so, he was charming. He met everybody, smiled a lot and uttered all the appropriate phrases in response to the compliments that were paid him. *But were they really compliments?* Tony wondered. Over the years a vocabulary had developed in art circles to cover exhibitions of unknown painters. Phrases that said everything and nothing.

'You really feel you're there . . .'

'I've never seen a style quite like yours . . .'

'Now, that's a painting!'

'It speaks to me . . .'

'You couldn't have done it any better . . .'

People kept arriving, and Tony wondered whether the attraction was curiosity about his paintings or the free wine and cheese. So far, not one of his paintings had sold, but the wine and cheese were being consumed rapaciously.

'Be patient,' Monsieur Goerg whispered to Tony. 'They are interested. First they must get a smell of the paintings. They see one they like, they keep wandering back to it. Pretty soon they ask the price, and when they nibble, *voilà!* The hook is set!'

'Jesus! I feel like I'm on a fishing cruise,' Tony told Dominique.

Monsieur Goerg bustled up to Tony. 'We've sold one!' he exclaimed. 'The Normandy landscape. Five hundred francs.'

It was a moment that Tony would remember as long as he lived. Someone had bought a painting of his! Someone had thought enough of his work to pay money for it, to hang it in his home or office, to look at it, live with it, show it to friends. It was a small piece of immortality. It was a way of living more than one life, of being in more than one place at the same time. A successful artist was in hundreds of homes and offices and museums all over the world, bringing pleasure to thousands – sometimes millions of people. Tony felt as though he had stepped into the pantheon of Da Vinci and Michelangelo and Rembrandt. He was no longer an amateur painter, he was a professional. Someone had paid money for his work.

Dominique hurried up to him, her eyes bright with excitement. 'You've just sold another one, Tony.'

'Which one?' he asked eagerly.

'The floral.'

The small gallery was filled now with people and loud chatter and the clink of glasses; and suddenly a stillness came over the room. There was an undercurrent of whispers and all eyes turned to the door.

Andre d'Usseau was entering the gallery. He was in his middle fifties, taller than the average Frenchman, with a strong, leonine face and a mane of white hair. He wore a flowing inverness cape and Borsalino hat, and behind him came an entourage of hangers-on. Automatically, everyone in the room began to make way for d'Usseau. There was not one person present who did not know who he was.

Dominique squeezed Tony's hand. 'He's come!' she said. 'He's here!'

Such an honour had never befallen Monsieur Goerg before, and he was beside himself, bowing and scraping before the great man, doing everything but tugging at his forelock.

'Monsieur d'Usseau,' he babbled. 'What a great pleasure this is! What an honour! May I offer you some wine, some cheese?' He cursed himself for not having bought a decent wine.

'Thank you,' the great man replied. 'I have come to feast only my eyes. I would like to meet the artist.'

Tony was too stunned to move. Dominique pushed him forwards.

'Here he is,' Monsieur Goerg said. 'M. Andre d'Usseau, this is Tony Blackwell.'

Tony found his voice. 'How do you do, sir? I – thank you for coming.'

Andre d'Usseau bowed slightly and moved towards the paintings on the walls. Everyone pushed back to give him room. He made his way slowly, looking at each painting long and carefully, then moving on to the next one. Tony tried to read his face, but he could tell nothing. D'Usseau neither frowned nor smiled. He stopped for a long time at one particular painting, a nude of Dominique, then moved on. He made a complete circle of the room, missing nothing. Tony was perspiring profusely.

When Andre d'Usseau had finished, he walked over to Tony. 'I am glad I came,' was all he said.

Within minutes after the famous critic had left, every painting in the gallery was sold. A great new artist was being born, and everyone wanted to be in at the birth.

'I have never seen anything like it,' Monsieur Goerg exclaimed. 'Andre d'Usseau came to my gallery. *My* gallery! All Paris will read about it tomorrow. 'I am glad I came.' Andre d'Usseau is not a man to waste words. This calls for champagne. Let us celebrate.'

Later that night, Tony and Dominique had their own private celebration. Dominique snuggled in his arms. 'I've slept with painters before,' she said, 'but never anyone as famous as you're going to be. Tomorrow everyone in Paris will know who you are.'

And Dominique was right.

* * *

At five o'clock the following morning, Tony and Dominique hurriedly got dressed and went out to get the first edition of the morning paper. It had just arrived at the kiosk. Tony snatched up the paper and turned to the art section. His review was the headline article under the by-line of Andre d'Usseau. Tony read it aloud:

> 'An exhibition by a young American painter, Anthony Blackwell, opened last night at the Goerg Gallery. It was a great learning experience for this critic. I have attended so many exhibitions of talented painters that I had forgotten what truly bad paintings looked like. I was forcibly reminded last night . . .'

Tony's face turned ashen.

'Please don't read any more,' Dominique begged. She tried to take the paper from Tony.

'Let go!' he commanded.

He read on.

> 'At first I thought a joke was being perpetrated. I could not seriously believe that anyone would have the nerve to hang such amateurish paintings and dare to call them art. I searched for the tiniest glimmer of talent. Alas, there was none. They should have hung the painter instead of his paintings. I could earnestly advise that the confused Mr Blackwell return to his real profession,

which I can only assume is that of house painter.'

'I can't believe it,' Dominique whispered. 'I can't believe he couldn't see it. Oh, that bastard!' Dominique began to cry helplessly.

Tony felt as though his chest were filled with lead. He had difficulty breathing. 'He saw it,' he said. 'And he does know, Dominique. He does know.' His voice was filled with pain. 'That's what hurts so much. Christ! What a fool I was!' He started to move away.

'Where are you going. Tony?'

'I don't know.'

He wandered around the cold, dawn streets, unaware of the tears running down his face. Within a few hours, everyone in Paris would have read that review. He would be an object of ridicule. But what hurt more was that he had deluded himself. He had really believed he had a career ahead of him as a painter. At least Andre d'Usseau had saved him from that mistake. *Pieces of posterity*, Tony thought grimly. *Pieces of shit!* He walked into the first open bar and proceeded to get mindlessly drunk.

When Tony finally returned to his apartment, it was five o'clock the following morning.

Dominique was waiting for him, frantic. 'Where have you been, Tony? Your mother has been trying to get in touch with you. She's sick with worry.'

'Did you read it to her?'

'Yes, she insisted. I –'

The telephone rang. Dominique looked at Tony, and picked up the receiver. 'Hello? Yes, Mrs Blackwell. He just walked in.' She held the receiver out to Tony. He hesitated, then took it.'

'Hello, M-mother.'

Kate's voice was filled with distress. 'Tony, darling, listen to me. I can make him print a retraction. I –'

'Mother,' Tony said wearily, 'this isn't a b-business transaction. This is a c-critic expressing an opinion. His opinion is that I should be h-hanged.'

'Darling, I hate to have you hurt like this. I don't think I can stand –' she broke off, unable to continue.

'It's all right, M-mother. I've had my little f-fling. I tried it and it didn't w-work. I don't have what it t-takes. It's as simple as that. I h-hate d'Usseau's guts, but he's the best g-goddamned art critic in the world, I have to g-give him that. He saved me from making a t-terrible mistake.'

'Tony, I wish there was something I could say . . .'

'D'Usseau s-said it all. It's b-better that I f-found it out now instead of t-ten years from now, isn't it? I've got to g-get out of this town.'

'Wait there for me, darling. I'll leave Johannesburg tomorrow and we'll go back to New York together.'

'All right,' Tony said. He replaced the receiver and turned towards Dominique. 'I'm sorry, Dominique. You picked the wrong fellow.'

Dominique said nothing. She just looked at him with eyes filled with an unspeakable sorrow.

The following afternoon at Kruger-Brent's office on Rue Matignon, Kate Blackwell was writing out a cheque. The man seated across the desk from her sighed. 'It is a pity. Your son has talent, Mrs Blackwell. He could have become an important painter.'

Kate stared at him coldly. 'Mr d'Usseau, there are tens of thousands of painters in the world. My son was not meant to be one of the crowd.' She passed the cheque across the desk. 'You fulfiled your part of the bargain, I'm prepared to fulfil mine. Kruger-Brent, Limited, will sponsor art museums in Johannesburg, London and New York. You will be in charge of selecting the paintings – with a handsome commission, of course.'

But long after d'Usseau had gone, Kate sat at her desk, filled with a deep sadness. She loved her son so much. If he ever found out . . . She knew the risk she had taken. But she could not stand by and let Tony throw away his inheritance. No matter what it might cost her, he had to be protected. The company had to be protected. Kate rose, feelng suddenly very tired. It was time to pick up Tony and take him home. She would help him get over this, so he could get on with what he had been born to do.

Run the company.

NINETEEN

For the next two years, Tony Blackwell felt he was on a giant treadmill that was taking him nowhere. He was the heir apparent to an awesome conglomerate. Kruger-Brent's empire had expanded to include paper mills, an airline, banks and a chain of hospitals. Tony learned that a name is a key that opens all doors. There are clubs and organizations and social cliques where the coin of the realm is not money or influence, but the proper name. Tony was accepted for membership in the Union Club, The Brook and The Links Club. He was catered to everywhere he went, but he felt like an imposter. He had done nothing to deserve any of it. He was in the giant shadow of his grandfather, and he felt he was constantly being measured against him. It was unfair, for there were no more mine fields to crawl over, no guards shooting at him, no sharks threatening him. They belonged to a past century, another time, another place, heroic acts committed by a stranger.

Tony worked twice as hard as anyone else at Kruger-Brent, Ltd. He drove himself mercilessly, trying to rid himself of memories too searing to bear. He wrote to Dominique, but his letters were returned unopened. He telephoned Maître Cantal, but Dominique no longer modelled at the school. She had disappeared.

Tony handled his job expertly and methodically, with neither passion nor love, and if he felt a deep emptiness inside himself, no one suspected it. Not even Kate. She received weekly reports on Tony, and she was pleased with them.

'He has a natural aptitude for business,' she told Brad Rogers.

To Kate, the long hours her son worked were proof of how much he loved what he was doing. When Kate thought of how Tony had almost thrown his future away, she shuddered and was grateful she had saved him.

In 1948 the Nationalist Party was in full power in South Africa, with segregation in all public places. Migration was strictly controlled, and families were split up to suit the convenience of the government. Every black man had to carry a *bewyshoek*, and it was more than a pass, it was a lifeline, his birth certificate, his work permit, his tax receipt. It regulated his movements and his life. There were increasing riots in South Africa, and they were ruthlessly put down by the police. From time to time, Kate read newspaper stories about sabotage and unrest, and Banda's name was always prominently mentioned. He was still a leader in the underground, despite his age. *Of course he would fight for his people*, Kate thought. *He's Banda*.

Kate celebrated her fifty-sixth birthday alone with Tony at the house on Fifth Avenue. She thought, *This handsome twenty-four-year-old man across the table can't be my son. I'm too young.* And he was toasting her, 'To m-my f-fantastic m-mother. Happy b-birthday!'

'You should make that to my fantastic *old* mother,' *Soon I'll be retiring*, Kate thought, *but my son will take my place. My son!*

At Kate's insistence, Tony had moved into the mansion on Fifth Avenue.

'The place is too bloody large for me to rattle around in alone,' Kate told him. 'You'll have the whole east wing to yourself and all the privacy you need.' It was easier for Tony to give in than to argue.

Tony and Kate had breakfast together every morning, and the topic of conversation was always Kruger-Brent, Ltd. Tony marvelled that his mother could care so passionately for a faceless, soulless entity, an amorphous collection of buildings and machines and bookkeeping figures. *Where did the magic lie?* With all the myriad mysteries of the world to explore, why would anyone want to waste a lifetime accumulating wealth to pile on more wealth, gathering power that was beyond power?

Tony did not understand his mother. But he loved her. And he tried to live up to what she expected of him.

The Pan American flight from Rome to New York had been uneventful. Tony liked the airline. It was pleasant and efficient. He worked on his overseas acquisitions reports from the time the plane took off, skipping dinner and ignoring the stewardess who kept offering him drinks, pillows or whatever else might appeal to their attractive passenger.

'Thank you, miss. I'm fine.'

'If there's *anything* at all, Mr Blackwell . . .'

'Thank you.'

A middle-aged woman in the seat next to Tony was reading a fashion magazine. As she turned a page, Tony happened to glance over, and he froze. There was a picture of a model wearing a ball gown. It was Dominique. There was no question about it. There were the high, delicate cheekbones and the deep-green eyes, the luxuriant blonde hair. Tony's pulse began to race.

'Excuse me,' Tony said to his seat companion. 'May I borrow that page?'

Early the following morning, Tony called the dress shop and got the name of their advertising agency. He telephoned them. 'I'm trying to locate one of your models,' he told the switchboard operator. 'Could you –'

'One moment, please.'

A man's voice came on. 'May I help you?'

'I saw a photograph in this month's issue of *Vogue*. A model advertising a ball gown for the Rothman stores. Is that your account?'

'Yes.'

'Can you give me the name of your model agency?'

'That would be the Carleton Blessing Agency.' He gave Tony the telephone number.

A minute later, Tony was talking to a woman at the Blessing Agency. 'I'm trying to locate one of your models,' he said. 'Dominique Masson.'

'I'm sorry. It is our policy not to give out personal information.' And the line went dead.

Tony sat there, staring at the receiver. There *had* to be a way to get in touch with Dominique. He went into Brad Roger's office.

'Morning, Tony. Coffee?'

'No, thanks. Brad, have you heard of the Carleton Blessing Model Agency?'

'I should think so. We own it.'

'*What?*'

'It's under the umbrella of one of our subsidiaries.'

'When did we acquire it?'

A couple of years ago. Just about the time you joined the company. What's your interest in it?'

'I'm trying to locate one of their models. She's an old friend.'

'No problem. I'll call and –'

'Never mind. I'll do it. Thanks, Brad.'

A feeling of warm anticipation was building up inside Tony.

*　*　*

Late that afternoon, Tony went uptown to the offices of the Carleton Blessing Agency and gave his name. Sixty seconds later, he was seated in the office of the president, a Mr Tilton.

'This is certainly an honour, Mr Blackwell. I hope there's no problem. Our profits for the last quarter –'

'No problem. I'm interested in one of your models. Dominique Masson.'

Tilton's face lighted up. 'She's turned out to be one of our very best. Your mother has a good eye.'

Tony thought he had misunderstood him. 'I beg your pardon?'

'Your mother personally requested that we engage Dominique. It was part of our deal when Kruger-Brent, Limited, took us over. It's all in our file, if you'd care to –'

'No.' Tony could make no sense of what he was hearing. *Why would his mother –?* 'May I have Dominique's address, please?'

'Certainly, Mr Blackwell. She's doing a layout in Vermont today, but she should be back' – he glanced at a schedule on his desk – 'tomorrow afternoon.'

Tony was waiting outside Dominique's apartment building when a black sedan pulled up and Dominique stepped out. With her was a large, athletic-looking man carrying Dominique's suitcase. Dominique stopped dead when she saw Tony.

'Tony! My God! What – what are you doing here?'

'I need to talk to you.'

'Some other time, buddy,' the athlete said. 'We have a busy afternoon.'

Tony did not even look at him. 'Tell your friend to go away.'

'Hey! Who the hell do you think –?'

Dominique turned to the man. 'Please go, Ben. I'll call you this evening.'

He hesitated a moment, then shrugged. 'Okay.' He glared at Tony, got back in the car and roared off.

Dominique turned to Tony. 'You'd better come inside.'

The apartment was a large duplex with white rugs and drapes and modern furniture. It must have cost a fortune.

'You're doing well,' Tony said.

'Yes. I've been lucky.' Dominique's fingers were picking nervously at her blouse. 'Would you like a drink?'

'No, thanks. I tried to get in touch with you after I left Paris.'

'I moved.'

'To America?'

'Yes.'

'How did you get a job with the Carleton Blessing Agency?'

'I – I answered a newspaper advertisement,' she said lamely.

'When did you first meet my mother, Dominique?'

'I – at your apartment in Paris. Remember? We –'

'No more games,' Tony said. He felt a wild rage building in him. 'It's over. I've never hit a woman in my life, but if you tell me one more lie, I promise you your face won't be fit to photograph.'

Dominique started to speak, but the fury in Tony's eyes stopped her.

'I'll ask you once more. When did you first meet my mother?'

This time there was no hesitation. 'When you were accepted at Ecole des Beaux-Arts. Your mother arranged for me to model there.'

He felt sick to his stomach. He forced himself to go on. 'So I could meet you?'

'Yes, I –'

'And she paid you to become my mistress, to pretend to love me?'

'Yes. It was just after the war – it was terrible. I had no money. Don't you see? But Tony, believe me, I cared. I really cared –'

'Just answer my questions.' The savagery in his voice frightened her. This was a stranger before her, a man capable of untold violence.

'What was the point of it?'

'Your mother wanted me to keep an eye on you.'

He thought of Dominique's tenderness and her love-making – bought and paid for, courtesy of his mother – and he was sick with shame. All along, he had been his mother's puppet, controlled, manipulated. His mother had never given a damn about him. He was not her son. He was her crown prince, her heir apparent. All that mattered to her was the company. He took one last look at Dominique, then turned and stumbled out. She looked after him, her eyes blinded by tears, and she thought, *I didn't lie about loving you, Tony. I didn't lie about that.*

Kate was in the library when Tony walked in, very drunk.

'I t-talked to D-dominique,' he said. 'You t-two m-must have had a w-wonderful time l-laughing at me behind my back.'

Kate felt a quick sense of alarm. 'Tony –'

'From now on I want you to s-stay out of my p-personal l-life. Do you hear me?' And he turned and staggered out of the room.

Kate watched him go, and she was suddenly filled with a terrible sense of foreboding.

TWENTY

The following day, Tony took an apartment in Greenwich Village. There were no more sociable dinners with his mother. He kept his relationship with Kate on an impersonal, business-like basis. From time to time Kate made conciliatory overtures, which Tony ignored.

Kate's heart ached. But she had done what was right for Tony. Just as she had once done what was right for David. She could not have let either of them leave the company. Tony was the one human being in the world Kate loved, and she watched as he became more and more insular, drawing deep within himself, rejecting everyone. He had no friends. Where once he had been warm and outgoing, he was now cool and reserved. He had built a wall around himself that no one was able to breach. *He needs a wife to care for him*, Kate thought. *And a son to carry on. I must help him. I must.*

Brad Rogers came into Kate's office and said,

'I'm afraid we're in for some more trouble, Kate.'

'What's happened?'

He put a cable on her desk. 'The South African Parliament has outlawed the Natives' Representative Council and passed the Communist Act.'

Kate said, 'My God!' The act had nothing to do with communism. It stated that anyone who disagreed with any government policy and tried to change it in any way was guilty under the Communist Act and could be imprisoned.

'It's their way of breaking the black resistance movement,' she said. 'If –' She was interrupted by her secretary.

'There's an overseas call for you. It's Mr Pierce in Johannesburg.'

Jonathan Pierce was the manager of the Johannesburg branch office. Kate picked up the phone. 'Hello, Johnny. How are you?'

'Fine, Kate. I have some news I thought you'd better be aware of.'

'What's that?'

'I've just received a report that the police have captured Banda.'

Kate was on the next flight to Johannesburg. She had alerted the company lawyers to see what could be done for Banda. Even the power and prestige of Kruger-Brent, Ltd., might not be able to help him. He had been designated an enemy of the state, and she dreaded to think what his punishment would be. At least she must see him and talk to him and offer what support she could.

When the plane landed in Johannesburg, Kate went to her office and telephoned the director of prisons.

'He's in an isolation block, Mrs Blackwell, and he's allowed no visitors. However, in your case, I will see what can be done . . .'

The following morning, Kate was at the Johannesburg prison, face to face with Banda. He was manacled and shackled, and there was a glass partition between them. His hair was completely white. Kate had not known what to expect – despair, defiance – but Banda grinned when he saw her and said, 'I knew you'd come. You're just like your daddy. You can't stay away from trouble, can you?'

'Look who's talking,' Kate retorted. 'Bloody hell! How do we get you out of here?'

'In a box. That's the only way they're going to let me go.'

'I have a lot of fancy lawyers who –'

'Forget it, Kate. They caught me fair and square. Now I've got to get away fair and square.'

'What are you talking about?'

'I don't like cages, I never did. And they haven't built one yet that can keep me.'

Kate said, 'Banda, don't try it. Please. They'll kill you.'

'Nothing can kill me,' Banda said. 'You're talking to a man who lived through sharks and land mines and guard dogs.' A soft gleam came into his eyes. 'You know something, Kate? I think maybe that was the best time of my life.'

When Kate went to visit Banda the next day, the superintendent said, 'I'm sorry, Mrs Blackwell. We've had to move him for security reasons.'

'Where is he?'

'I'm not at liberty to say.'

When Kate woke up the following morning, she saw the headline in the newspaper carried in with her breakfast tray. It read: REBEL LEADER KILLED WHILE TRYING TO ESCAPE PRISON. She was at the prison an hour later, in the superintendent's office.

'He was shot during an attempted prison break, Mrs Blackwell. That's all there is to it.'

You're wrong, thought Kate, *there's more. Much more.* Banda was dead, but was his dream of freedom for his people dead?

Two days later, after making the funeral arrangements, Kate was on the plane to New York. She looked out the window to take one last look at her beloved land. The soil was red and rich and fertile, and in the bowels of its earth were treasures beyond man's dreams. This was God's chosen land, and He had been lavish in his generosity. But there was a curse upon the country. *I'll never come back here again*, Kate thought sadly. *Never.*

* * *

One of Brad Rogers's responsibilities was to oversee the Long-Range Planning Department of Kruger-Brent, Ltd. He was brilliant at finding businesses that would make profitable acquisitions.

One day in early May, he walked into Kate Blackwell's office. 'I've come across something interesting, Kate.' He placed two folders on her desk. 'Two companies. If we could pick up either one of them, it would be a coup.'

'Thanks, Brad. I'll look them over tonight.'

That evening, Kate dined alone and studied Brad Rogers's confidential reports on the two companies – Wyatt Oil & Tool and International Technology. The reports were long and detailed, and both ended with the letters NIS, the company code for *Not Interested in Selling*, which meant that if the companies were to be acquired, it would take more than a straightforward business transaction to accomplish it. *And*, Kate thought, *they're well worth taking over*. Each company was privately controlled by a wealthy and strong-minded individual, which eliminated any possibility of a takeover attempt. It was a challenge, and it had been a long time since Kate had faced a challenge. The more she thought about it, the more the possibilities began to excite her. She studied again the confidential balance sheets. Wyatt Oil & Tool was owned by a Texan, Charlie Wyatt, and the company's assets included producing oil wells, a utility company and dozens of potentially profitable oil leases. There was no question about it, Wyatt Oil & Tool would make a handsome acquisition for Kruger-Brent, Ltd.

Kate turned her attention to the second company. International Technology was owned by a German, Count Frederick Hoffman. The company had started with a small steel mill in Essen, and over the years had expanded into a huge conglomerate, with shipyards, petrochemical plants, a fleet of oil tankers and a computer division.

As large as Kruger-Brent, Ltd., was, it could digest only one of these giants. She knew which company she was going after. NIS, the sheet read.

We'll see about that, Kate thought.

Early the following morning, she sent for Brad Rogers. 'I'd love to know how you got hold of those confidential balance sheets,' Kate grinned. 'Tell me about Charlie Wyatt and Frederick Hoffman.'

Brad had done his homework. 'Charlie Wyatt was born in Dallas. Flamboyant, loud, runs his own empire, smart as hell. He started with nothing, got lucky in oil wildcatting, kept expanding and now he owns about half of Texas.'

'How old is he?'

'Forty-seven.'

'Children?'

'One daughter, twenty-five. From what I hear, she's a raving beauty.'

'Is she married?'

'Divorced.'

'Frederick Hoffman.'

'Hoffman's a couple of years younger than Charlie Wyatt. He's a count, comes from a distinguished German family going back to the Middle Ages. He's a widower. His grandfather started with a small steel mill. Frederick Hoffman inherited it from his father and built it into a conglomerate. He was one of the first to get into the computer field. He holds a lot of patents on microprocessors. Every time we use a computer, Count Hoffman gets a royalty.'

'Children?'

'A daughter, twenty-three.'

'What is she like?'

'I couldn't find out,' Brad Rogers apologized. 'It's a very buttoned-up family. They travel in their own little circles.' He hesitated. 'We're probably wasting our time on this, Kate. I had a few drinks with a couple of top executives in both companies. Neither Wyatt nor Hoffman has the slightest interest in a sale, merger or joint venture. As you can see from their financials, they'd be crazy even to think about it.'

That feeling of challenge was there in Kate again, tugging at her.

Ten days later Kate was invited by the President of the United States to a Washington conference of leading international industrialists to discuss assistance to underdeveloped countries. Kate made a telephone call, and shortly afterwards Charlie Wyatt and Count Frederick Hoffman received invitations to attend the conference.

Kate had formed a mental impression of both the Texan and the German, and they fitted her preconceived notions almost precisely. She had never met a shy Texan, and Charlie Wyatt was no exception. He was a huge man – almost six feet four inches – with enormous shoulders and a football player's body that had gone to fat. His face was large and ruddy, and his voice loud and booming. He came off as a good ol' boy – or would have if Kate had not known better. Charlie Wyatt had not built his empire by luck. He was a business genius. Kate had talked to him for less than ten minutes when she knew that there was no way this man could be persuaded to do anything he did not want to do. He was opinionated, and he had a deep stubborn streak. No one was going to cajole him, threaten him or con him out of his company. But Kate had found his Achilles' heel, and that was enough.

Frederick Hoffman was Charlie Wyatt's opposite. He was a handsome man, with an aristocratic face and soft brown hair tinged with grey at the temples. He was punctiliously correct and filled with a sense of old-fashioned courtesy. On the surface, Frederick Hoffman was pleasant and debonair; on the inside Kate sensed a core of steel.

* * *

The conference in Washington lasted three days, and it went well. The meetings were chaired by the Vice-President, and the President made a brief appearance. Everyone there was impressed with Kate Blackwell. She was an attractive, charismatic woman, head of a corporate empire she had helped build, and they were fascinated, as Kate meant them to be.

When Kate got Charlie Wyatt alone for a moment, she asked innocently, 'Is your family with you, Mr Wyatt?'

'I brought my daughter along. She has a little shoppin' to do.'

'Oh, really? How nice.' No one would have suspected that Kate not only knew his daughter was with him, but what kind of dress she had bought at Garfinckel's that morning. 'I'm giving a little dinner party at Dark Harbor, Friday. I'd be pleased if you and your daughter would join us for the weekend.'

Wyatt did not hesitate. 'I've heard a lot about your spread, Mrs Blackwell. I'd sure like to see it.'

Kate smiled. 'Good. I'll make arrangements for you to be flown up there tomorrow night.'

Ten minutes later, Kate was speaking to Frederick Hoffman.

'Are you alone in Washington, Mr Hoffman?' she asked. 'Or is your wife with you?'

'My wife died a few years ago,' Frederick Hoffman told her. 'I'm here with my daughter.'

Kate knew they were staying at the Hay-Adams

Hotel in Suite 418. 'I'm giving a little dinner party at Dark Harbor. I would be delighted if you and your daughter could join us tomorrow for the weekend.'

'I should be getting back to Germany,' Hoffman replied. He studied her a moment, and smiled. 'I suppose another day day or two won't make much difference.'

'Wonderful. I'll arrange transportation for you.'

It was Kate's custom to give a party at the Dark Harbor estate once every two months. Some of the most interesting and powerful people in the world came to these gatherings, and the get-togethers were always fruitful. Kate intended to see to it that this one was a very special party. Her problem was to make sure Tony attended. During the past year, he had seldom bothered to show up, and when he did he had made a perfunctory appearance and left. This time it was imperative that he come and that he stay.

When Kate mentioned the weekend to Tony, he said curtly, 'I c-can't make it. I'm leaving for C-canada Monday and I have a lot of w-work to clean up before I go.'

'This is important,' Kate told him. 'Charlie Wyatt and Count Hoffman are going to be there and they're –'

'I know who they are,' he interrupted. 'I t-talked to Brad Rogers. We haven't got a p-prayer of acquiring either one of those companies.

'I want to give it a try.'

He looked at her and asked, 'W-which one are you after?'

'Wyatt Oil and Tool. It could increase our profits as much as fifteen percent, perhaps more. When the Arab countries realize they have the world by the throat, they're going to form a cartel, and oil prices will skyrocket. Oil is going to turn into liquid gold.'

'What about International T-t-technology?'

Kate shrugged. 'It's a good company, but the plum is Wyatt Oil and Tool. It's a perfect acquisition for us. I need you there, Tony. Canada can wait a few days.'

Tony loathed parties. He hated the endless, boring conversations, the boastful men and the predatory women. But this was business. 'All right.'

All the pieces were in place.

The Wyatts were flown to Maine in a company Cessna, and from the ferry were driven to Cedar Hill House in a limousine. Kate was at the door to greet them. Brad Rogers had been right about Charlie Wyatt's daughter, Lucy. She was strikingly beautiful. She was tall, with black hair and gold-flecked brown eyes, set in almost perfect features. Her sleek Galanos dress outlined a firm, stunning figure. She had, Brad informed Kate, been divorced from a wealthy Italian playboy two years earlier. Kate introduced Lucy to Tony and watched for her son's reaction. There was none. He greeted both the Wyatts with equal courtesy and led them into the bar, where a bartender was waiting to mix drinks.

'What a lovely room,' Lucy exclaimed. Her voice was unexpectedly soft and mellow, with no trace of a Texas accent. 'Do you spend much time here?' she asked Tony.

'No.'

She waited for him to go on. Then, 'Did you grow up here?'

'Partly.'

Kate picked up the conversation, adroitly smoothing over Tony's silence. 'Some of Tony's happiest memories are of this house. The poor man is so busy he doesn't get much chance to come back here and enjoy it, do you, Tony?'

He gave his mother a cool look and said, 'No. As a matter of fact, I should be in C-canada –'

'But he postponed it so he could meet both of you,' Kate finished for him.

'Well, I'm mighty pleased,' Charlie Wyatt said. 'I've heard a lot about you, son.' He grinned. 'You wouldn't want to come to work for me, would you?'

'I don't think that's q-quite what my mother had in mind, Mr Wyatt.'

Charlie Wyatt grinned again. 'I know.' He turned to look at Kate. 'Your mother's quite a lady. You should have seen her rope and hog-tie everybody at that White House meetin'. She –' He stopped as Frederick Hoffman and his daughter,

Marianne, entered the room. Marianne Hoffman was a pale version of her father. She had the same aristocratic features and she had long, blonde hair. She wore an off-white chiffon dress. Next to Lucy Wyatt she looked washed out.

'May I present my daughter, Marianne?' Count Hoffman said. 'I'm sorry we're late,' he apologized. 'The plane was delayed at La Guardia.'

'Oh, what a shame,' Kate said. Tony was aware that Kate had arranged the delay. She had had the Wyatts and the Hoffmans flown up to Maine in separate planes, so that the Wyatts would arrive early and the Hoffman's late. 'We were just having a drink. What would you like?'

'A Scotch, please,' Count Hoffman said.

Kate turned to Marianne. 'And you, my dear?'

'Nothing, thank you.'

A few minutes later, the other guests began to arrive, and Tony circulated among them, playing the part of the gracious host. No one except Kate could have guessed how little the festivities meant to him. It was not, Kate knew, that Tony was bored. It was simply that he was completely removed from what was happening around him. He had lost his pleasure in people. It worried Kate.

Two tables had been set in the large dining room. Kate seated Marianne Hoffman between a Supreme Court justice and a senator at one table, and she seated Lucy Wyatt on Tony's right at the other table. All the men in the room – married and unmarried – were eyeing Lucy. Kate listened to

Lucy trying to draw Tony into conversation. It was obvious that she liked him. Kate smiled to herself. It was a good beginning.

The following morning, Saturday, at breakfast, Charlie Wyatt said to Kate. 'That's a mighty pretty yacht you've got sittin' out there, Mrs Blackwell. How big is it?'

'I'm really not quite sure.' Kate turned to her son. 'Tony, how large is the *Corsair*?'

His mother knew exactly how large it was, but Tony said politely, 'Eighty f-feet.'

'We don't go in much for boats in Texas. We're in too much of a hurry. We do most of our travellin' in planes.' Wyatt gave a booming laugh. 'Guess maybe I'll try it and get my feet wet.'

Kate smiled. 'I was hoping you would let me show you around the island. We could go out on the boat tomorrow.'

Charlie Wyatt looked at her thoughtfully and said, 'That's mighty kind of you, Mrs Blackwell.'

Tony quietly watched the two of them and said nothing. The first move had just been made, and he wondered whether Charlie Wyatt was aware of it. Probably not. He was a clever businessman, but he had never come up against anyone like Kate Blackwell.

Kate turned to Tony and Lucy. 'It's such a beautiful day. Why don't you two go for a sail in the catboat?'

Before Tony could refuse, Lucy said, 'Oh, I'd love that.'

'I'm s-sorry,' Tony said curtly. 'I'm expecting s-some overseas calls.' Tony could feel his mother's disapproving eyes on him.

Kate turned to Marianne Hoffman. 'I haven't seen your father this morning.'

'He's out exploring the island. He's an early riser.'

'I understand you like to ride. We have a fine stable here.'

'Thank you, Mrs Blackwell. I'll just wander around, if you don't mind.'

'Of course not,' Kate turned back to Tony. 'Are you sure you won't change your mind about taking Miss Wyatt for a sail?' There was steel in her voice.

'I'm s-sure.'

It was a small victory, but it was a victory none-theless. The battle was joined, and Tony had no intention of losing it. Not this time. His mother no longer had the power to deceive him. She had used him as a pawn once, and he was fully aware she was planning to try it again; but this time she would fail. She wanted the Wyatt Oil & Tool Company. Charlie Wyatt had no intention of merg-ing or selling his company. But every man has a weakness, and Kate had found his: his daughter. If Lucy were to marry into the Blackwell family, a merger of some kind would become inevitable. Tony looked across the breakfast table at his mother, despising her. She had baited the trap well. Lucy was not only beautiful, she was intelligent and charming. But she was as much of a pawn in this sick game as Tony was, and nothing in the world could induce him to touch her. This was a battle between his mother and himself.

When breakfast was over, Kate rose. 'Tony, before your phone call comes in, why don't you show Miss Wyatt the gardens?'

There was no way Tony could refuse graciously. 'All right.' He would make it short.

Kate turned to Charlie Wyatt. 'Are you interested in rare books? We have quite a collection in the library.'

'I'm interested in anything you want to show me,' the Texan said.

Almost as an afterthought, Kate turned back to Marianne Hoffman. 'Will you be all right, dear?'

'I'll be fine, thank you, Mrs Blackwell. Please don't worry about me.'

'I won't,' Kate said.

And Tony knew she meant it. Miss Hoffman was of no use to Kate, and so she dismissed her. It was done with a light charm and a smile, but beneath it was a single-minded ruthlessness that Tony detested.

Lucy was watching him. 'Are you ready, Tony?'

'Yes.'

Tony and Lucy moved towards the door. They were not quite out of earshot when Tony heard his mother say, 'Don't they make a lovely couple?'

The two of them walked through the large, formal gardens towards the dock where the *Corsair* was tied up. There were acres and acres of wildly coloured flowers staining the summer air with their scent.

'This is a heavenly place,' Lucy said.

'Yes.'

'We don't have flowers like these in Texas.'

'No?'

'It's so quiet and peaceful here.'

'Yes.'

Lucy stopped abruptly and turned to face Tony.

He saw the anger in her face. 'Have I said something to offend you?' he asked.

'You haven't said anything. That's what I find offensive. All I can get out of you is a yes or a no. You make me feel as though I'm – I'm chasing you.'

'Are you?'

She laughed. 'Yes. If I could only teach you to talk, I think we might have something.'

Tony grinned.

'What are you thinking?' Lucy asked.

'Nothing.'

He was thinking of his mother, and how much she hated losing.

Kate was showing Charlie Wyatt the large, oak-panelled library. On the shelves were first editions of Oliver Goldsmith, Laurence Sterne, Tobias Smollett and John Donne, along with a Ben Johnson first folio. There was a Samuel Butler and John Bunyan, and the rare 1813 privately printed edition of *Queen Mab*. Wyatt walked along the shelves of treasures, his eyes gleaming. He paused in front of a beautifully bound edition of John Keats's *Endymion*.

'This is a Roseberg copy,' Charlie Wyatt said.

Kate looked at him in surprise. 'Yes. There are only two known copies.'

'I have the other one,' Wyatt told her.

'I should have known,' Kate laughed. 'That "good ol' Texas boy" act you put on had me fooled.'

Wyatt grinned. 'Did it? It's good camouflage.'

'Where did you go to school?'

'Colorado School of Mining, then Oxford on a Rhodes Scholarship.' He studied Kate a moment. 'I'm told it was you who got me invited to that White House conference.'

She shrugged. 'I merely mentioned your name. They were delighted to have you.'

'That was mighty kind of you, Kate. Now, as long as you and I are alone, why don't you tell me exactly what's on your mind?'

Tony was at work in his private study, a small room off the main downstairs hallway. He was seated in a deep armchair when he heard the door open and someone come in. He turned to look. It was Marianne Hoffman. Before Tony could open his mouth to make his presence known, he heard her gasp.

She was looking at the paintings on the wall. They were Tony's paintings – the few he had brought back from his apartment in Paris, and this was the only room in the house where he would allow them to be hung. He watched her walk around the room, going from painting to painting, and it was too late to say anything.

'I don't believe it,' she murmured.

And Tony felt a sudden anger within him. He knew they were not *that* bad. As he moved, the leather of his chair creaked, and Marianne turned and saw him.

'Oh! I'm sorry,' she apologized. 'I didn't know anyone was in here.'

Tony rose. 'That's quite all right.' His tone was rude. He disliked having his sanctuary invaded. 'Were you looking for something?'

'No. I – I was just wandering around. Your collection of paintings belongs in a museum.'

'Except for these,' Tony heard himself saying.

She was puzzled by the hostility in his voice. She turned to look at the paintings again. She saw the signature. '*You* painted these?'

'I'm sorry if they don't appeal to you.'

'They're fantastic!' She moved towards him. 'I don't understand. If you can do this, why would you ever want to do anything else? You're wonderful. I don't mean you're good. I mean you're *wonderful*.'

Tony stood there, not listening, just wanting her to get out.

'I wanted to be a painter,' Marianne said. 'I studied with Oskar Kokoschka for a year. I finally quit because I knew I never could be as good as I wanted to be. But you!' She turned to the paintings again. 'Did you study in Paris?'

He wished she would leave him alone. 'Yes.'

'And you quit – just like that?'

'Yes.'

'What a pity. You –'

'*There* you are!'

They both turned. Kate was standing in the doorway. She eyed the two of them a moment, then walked over to Marianne. 'I've been looking everywhere for you, Marianne. Your father mentioned that you like orchids. You must see our greenhouse.'

'Thank you,' Marianne murmured. 'I'm really –'

Kate turned to Tony. 'Tony, perhaps you should see to your other guests.' There was a note of sharp displeasure in her voice.

She took Marianne's arm, and they were gone.

There was a fascination to watching his mother manoeuvre people. It was done so smoothly. Not a move was wasted. It had started with the Wyatts arriving early and the Hoffmans arriving late. Lucy being placed next to him at every meal. The private conferences with Charlie Wyatt. It was so damned obvious, and yet Tony had to admit to himself that it was obvious only because he had the key. He knew his mother and the way her mind worked. Lucy Wyatt was a lovely girl. She would make a wonderful wife for someone, but not for him. Not with Kate Blackwell as her sponsor. His mother was a ruthless, calculating bitch, and as long as Tony remembered that, he was safe from her machinations. He wondered what her next move would be.

He did not have to wait long to find out.

They were on the terrace having cocktails. 'Mr Wyatt has been kind enough to invite us to his ranch next weekend,' Kate told Tony. 'Isn't that lovely?' Her face radiated her pleasure. 'I've never seen a Texas ranch.'

Kruger-Brent *owned* a ranch in Texas, and it was probably twice as big as the Wyatt spread.

'You will come, won't you, Tony?' Charlie Wyatt asked.

Lucy said, 'Please do.'

They were ganging up on him. It was a challenge. He decided to accept it. 'I'd be d-delighted.'

'Good.' There was real pleasure on Lucy's face. And on Kate's.

If Lucy is planning to seduce me, Tony thought, *she is wasting her time*. The hurt done to Tony by his mother and Dominique had implanted in him such a deep distrust of females that his only association with them now was with high-priced call girls. Of all the female species, they were the most honest. All they wanted was money and told you how much up front. You paid for what you got, and you got what you paid for. No complications, no tears, no deceit.

Lucy Wyatt was in for a surprise.

* * *

Early Sunday morning. Tony went down to the pool for a swim. Marianne Hoffman was already in the water, wearing a white maillot. She had a lovely figure, tall and slender and graceful. Tony stood there watching her cutting cleanly through the water, her arms flashing up and down in a regular, graceful rhythm. She saw Tony and swam over to him.

'Good morning.'

'Morning. You're good,' Tony said.

Marianne smiled. 'I love sports. I get that from my father.' She pulled herself up to the edge of the pool, and Tony handed her a towel. He watched as she unselfconsciously dried her hair.

'Have you had breakfast?' Tony asked.

'No. I wasn't sure the cook would be up this early.'

'This is a hotel. There's twenty-four-hour service.'

She smiled up at him. 'Nice.'

'Where is your home?'

'Mostly in Munich. We live in an old *Schloss* – a castle – outside the city.'

'Where were you brought up?'

Marianne sighed. 'That's a long story. During the war, I was sent away to school in Switzerland. After that, I went to Oxford, studied at the Sorbonne and lived in London for a few years.' She looked directly into his eyes. 'That's where I've been. Where have you been?'

'Oh, New York, Maine, Switzerland, South Africa, a few years in the South Pacific during the war, Paris . . .' He broke off abruptly, as though he were saying too much.

'Forgive me if I seem to pry, but I can't imagine why you stopped painting.'

'It's not important,' Tony said curtly. 'Let's have breakfast.'

They ate alone on the terrace overlooking the sparkling sweep of the bay. She was easy to talk to. There was a dignity about her, a gentleness that Tony found appealing. She did not flirt, she did not chatter. She seemed genuinely interested in him. Tony found himself attracted to this quiet, sensitive woman. He could not help wondering how much of that attraction was due to the thought that it would spite his mother.

'When do you go back to Germany?'

'Next week,' Marianne replied. 'I'm getting married.'

Her words caught him off guard. 'Oh,' Tony said lamely. 'That's great. Who is he?'

'He's a doctor. I've known him all my life.' *Why had she added that? Did it have some significance?*

On an impulse, Tony asked, 'Will you have dinner with me in New York?'

She studied him, weighing her answer. 'I would enjoy that.'

Tony smiled, pleased. 'It's a date.'

They had dinner at a little seashore restaurant on Long Island. Tony wanted Marianne to himself, away from the eyes of his mother. It was an innocent evening, but Tony knew that if his mother learned about it, she would find some way to poison it. This was a private thing between him and Marianne, and for the brief time it existed, Tony wanted nothing to spoil it. Tony enjoyed Marianne's company even more than he had anticipated. She had a quick, sly sense of humour, and Tony found himself laughing more than he had laughed since he left Paris. She made him feel lighthearted and carefree.

When do you go back to Germany?
Next week . . . I'm getting married.

During the next five days, Tony saw a great deal of Marianne. He cancelled his trip to Canada, and he was not certain why. He had thought it might be a form of rebellion against his mother's plan, a petty vengeance, but if that had been true in the beginning, it was no longer true. He found himself drawn to Marianne more and more strongly. He loved her honesty. It was a quality he had despaired of ever finding.

Since Marianne was a tourist in New York, Tony took her everywhere. They climbed the Statue of Liberty and rode the ferry to Staten Island, went to the top of the Empire State Building, and ate in Chinatown. They spent an entire day at the Metropolitan Museum of Art, and an afternoon at the Frick Collection. They shared the same tastes. They carefully avoided speaking of any personal things, and yet both were conscious of the powerful sexual undercurrent between them. The days spilled into one another, and it was Friday, the day Tony was to leave for the Wyatt Ranch.

'When do you fly back to Germany?'

'Monday morning.' There was no joy in her voice.

Tony left for Houston that afternoon. He could have gone with his mother in one of the company planes, but he preferred to avoid any situation where he and Kate would be alone together. As far as he was concerned, his mother was solely a business partner; brilliant and powerful, devious and dangerous.

There was a Rolls-Royce to pick up Tony at the William P. Hobby Airport in Houston, and he was driven to the ranch by a chauffeur dressed in Levi's and a colourful sport shirt.

'Most folks like to fly direct to the ranch,' the driver told Tony. 'Mr Wyatt's got a big landin' strip there. From here, it's 'bout an hour's drive to the gate, then another half hour before we git to the main house.'

Tony thought he was exaggerating, but he was wrong. The Wyatt Ranch turned out to be more of a town than a ranch. They drove through the main gate onto a private road, and after thirty minutes they began to pass generator buildings and barns and corrals and guest houses and servants' bungalows. The main house was an enormous one-storey ranch house that seemed to go on forever. Tony thought it was depressingly ugly.

Kate had already arrived. She and Charlie Wyatt were seated on the terrace overlooking a swimming pool the size of a small lake. They were in the midst of an intense conversation when Tony appeared. When Wyatt saw him, he broke off abruptly in the middle of a sentence. Tony sensed that he had been the subject of their discussion.

'Here's our boy! Have a good trip, Tony?'

'Yes, th-thank you.'

'Lucy was hoping you'd be able to catch an earlier plane,' Kate said.

Tony turned to look at his mother. 'Was sh-she?'

Charlie Wyatt clapped Tony on the shoulder. 'We're puttin' on a whoppin' barbecue in honour of you and Kate. *Everybody's* flying in for it.'

'That's very k-kind of you,' Tony said. *If they're planning to serve fatted calf*, he thought, *they're going to go hungry.*

Lucy appeared, wearing a white shirt and tight-fitting, well-worn jeans, and Tony had to admit she was breath-takingly lovely.

She went up to him and took his arm. 'Tony! I was wondering if you were coming.'

'S-sorry I'm late,' Tony said. 'I had some b-business to finish up.'

Lucy gave him a warm smile. 'It doesn't matter, as long as you're here. What would you like to do this afternoon?'

'What do you have to offer?'

Lucy looked him in the eye. 'Anything you want,' she said softly.

Kate Blackwell and Charlie Wyatt beamed.

The barbecue was spectacular, even by Texas standards. Approximately two hundred guests had arrived by private plane, Mercedes or Rolls-Royce. Two bands were playing simultaneously in different areas of the grounds. Half a dozen bartenders dispensed champagne, whiskey, soft drinks and beer, while four chefs busily prepared food over outdoor fires. There was barbecued beef, lamb, steaks, chicken and duck. There were bubbling earthen pots of chili, and whole lobsters; crabs and corn on the cob were cooking in the ground. There were baked potatoes and yams and fresh peas in the pod, six kinds of salads, homemade hot biscuits, and corn bread with honey and jam. Four dessert tables were laden with freshly baked pies, cakes and puddings, and a dozen flavours of homemade ice cream. It was the most conspicuous waste Tony had ever seen. It was, he supposed, the difference between new money and old money. Old money's motto was, *If you have it, hide it*. New money's motto was, *If you have it, flaunt it*.

This was flaunting on a scale that was unbelievable. The women were dressed in daring gowns, and the display of jewellery was blinding. Tony stood to one side watching the guests gorging themselves, calling out noisily to old friends. He felt as though he were attending some mindless, decadent rite. Every time he turned around, Tony found himself confronted with a waiter carrying a tray containing large crocks of beluga caviar or pâté or champagne. It seemed to Tony that there were almost as many servants as guests. He listened to conversations around him.

'He came out here from New York to sell me a bill of goods, and I said, "You're wastin' your time, mister. No good oil deal gets east of Houston . . ."'

'You gotta watch out for the smooth talkers. They're all hat and no cattle . . .'

Lucy appeared at Tony's side. 'You're not eating.' She was watching him intently. 'Is anything wrong, Tony?'

'No, everything's fine. It's quite a party.'

She grinned. 'You ain't seen nothin' yet, pardner. Wait until you see the fireworks display.'

'The fireworks display?'

'Uh-huh.' She touched Tony's arm. 'Sorry about the mob scene. It's not always like this. Daddy wanted to impress your mother.' She smiled. 'Tomorrow they'll all be gone.'

So will I, Tony thought grimly. It had been a mistake for him to come here. If his mother wanted the Wyatt Oil & Tool Company so badly, she would have to figure out some other way to get it. His eyes searched the crowd for his mother, and he saw her in the middle of an admiring group. She was beautiful. She was almost sixty years old, but she looked ten years younger. Her face was unlined, and her body was firm and trim, thanks to exercise and daily massage. She was as disciplined with herself as with everyone around her, and in a perverse way, Tony admired her. To a casual onlooker, Kate Blackwell seemed to be having a marvellous time. She was chatting with the guests, beaming, laughing. *She's loathing every moment of this*, Tony thought. *There isn't anything she won't suffer to get what she wants*. He thought of Marianne and of how much she would have hated this kind of senseless orgy. The thought of her was a sudden ache in him.

I'm marrying a doctor. I've known him all my life.

Half an hour later when Lucy came looking for Tony, he was on his way back to New York.

He called Marianne from a telephone booth at the airport. 'I want to see you.'

There was no hesitation. 'Yes.'

Tony had not been able to get Marianne Hoffman out of his thoughts. He had been alone for a long time, but he had not felt lonely. Being away from Marianne was a loneliness, a feeling that a part of him was missing. Being with her was a warmth, a celebration of life, a chasing away of the ugly dark shadows that had been haunting him. He had the terrifying feeling that if he let Marianne go, he would be lost. He needed her as he had never needed anyone in his life.

Marianne met him at his apartment, and as she

walked in the door, there was a hunger in Tony that he had thought forever dead. And he knew the hunger was hers, too, and there were no words for the miracle of it.

She went into his arms, and their emotion was an irresistible riptide that caught them both up and swept them away in a glorious explosion, an eruption, and a contentment beyond words. They were floating together in a velvety softness that knew no time or place, lost in the wondrous glory and magic of each other. Later they lay spent, holding each other, her hair soft against his face.

'I'm going to marry you, Marianne.'

She took his face in her hands and looked searchingly into his eyes. 'Are you sure, Tony?' Her voice was gentle. 'There's a problem, darling.'

'Your engagement?'

'No. I'll break it off. I'm concerned about your mother.'

'She has nothing to do with –'

'No. Let me finish, Tony. She's planning for you to marry Lucy Wyatt.'

'That's *her* plan.' He took her in his arms again. '*My* plans are right here.'

'She'll hate me, Tony. I don't want that.'

'Do you know what I want?' Tony whispered.

And the miracle started all over again.

It was another forty-eight hours before Kate Blackwell heard from Tony. He had disappeared from the Wyatt Ranch without an explanation or good-bye and had flown back to New York. Charlie Wyatt was baffled, and Lucy Wyatt was furious. Kate had made awkward apologies and had taken the company plane back to New York that night. When she reached home, she telephoned Tony at his apartment. There was no answer. Nor was there any answer the following day.

Kate was in her office when the private phone on her desk rang. She knew who it was before she picked it up.

'Tony, are you all right?'

'I'm f-fine, Mother.'

'Where are you?'

'On my h-honeymoon. Marianne Hoffman and I were m-married yesterday.' There was a long, long silence. 'Are you there, M-mother?'

'Yes. I'm here.'

'You might s-say congratulations, or m-much happiness or one of those c-customary phrases.' There was a mocking bitterness in his voice.

Kate said, 'Yes. Yes, of course, I wish you much happiness, Son.'

'Thank you, M-mother.' And the line went dead.

Kate replaced the receiver and pressed down an intercom button. 'Would you please come in, Brad?'

When Brad Rogers walked into the office, Kate said, 'Tony just called.'

Brad took one look at Kate's face and said, 'Jesus! Don't tell me you did it!'

'Tony did it,' Kate smiled. 'We've got the Hoffman empire in our lap.'

Brad Rogers sank into a chair. 'I can't believe it! I know how stubborn Tony can be. How did you ever get him to marry Marianne Hoffman?'

'It was really very simple,' Kate sighed. 'I pushed him in the wrong direction.'

But she knew it was really the right direction. Marianne would be a wonderful wife for Tony. She would dispel the darkness in him.

Lucy had had a hysterectomy.

Marianne would give him a son.

TWENTY-ONE

Six months from the day Tony and Marianne were married, the Hoffman company was absorbed into Kruger-Brent, Ltd. The formal signing of the contracts took place in Munich as a gesture to Frederick Hoffman, who would run the subsidiary from Germany. Tony had been surprised by the meekness with which his mother accepted his marriage. It was not like her to lose gracefully, yet she had been cordial to Marianne when Tony and his bride returned from their honeymoon in the Bahamas, and had told Tony how pleased she was with the marriage. What puzzled Tony was that her sentiments seemed genuine. It was too quick a turn-around, out of character for her. Perhaps, Tony decided, he did not understand his mother as well as he thought he did.

The marriage was a brilliant success from the beginning. Marianne filled a long-felt need in Tony, and everyone around him noticed the change in him – especially Kate.

When Tony took business trips, Marianne accompanied him. They played together, they laughed together, they truly enjoyed each other. Watching them, Kate thought happily, *I have done well for my son.*

It was Marianne who succeeded in healing the breach between Tony and his mother. When they returned from their honeymoon, Marianne said, 'I want to invite your mother to dinner.'

'No. You don't know her, Marianne. She –'

'I want to get to know her. Please, Tony.'

He hated the idea, but in the end he gave in. Tony had been prepared for a grim evening, but he had been surprised. Kate had been touchingly happy to be with them. The following week Kate invited them to the house for dinner, and after that it became a weekly ritual.

Kate and Marianne became friends. They spoke to each other over the telephone several times a week, and lunched together at least once a week.

They were meeting for lunch at Lutèce, and the moment Marianne walked in, Kate knew something was wrong.

'I'd like a double whiskey, please,' Marianne told the captain. 'Over ice.'

As a rule, Marianne drank only wine.

'What's happened, Marianne?'

'I've been to see Dr Harley.'

Kate felt a sudden stab of alarm. 'You're not ill, are you?'

'No. I'm just fine. Only . . .' The whole story came tumbling out.

It had begun a few days earlier. Marianne had not been feeling well, and she had made an appointment with John Harley . . .

'You look healthy enough,' Dr Harley smiled. 'How old are you, Mrs Blackwell?'

'Twenty-three.'

'Any history of heart disease in your family?'

'No.'

He was making notes. 'Cancer?'

'No.'

'Are your parents alive?'

'My father is. My mother died in an accident.'

'Have you ever had mumps?'

'No.'

'Measles?'

'Yes. When I was ten.'

'Whooping cough?'

'No.'

'Any surgery?'

'Tonsils. I was nine.'

'Other than that, you've never been hospitalized for anything?'

'No. Well, yes – that is, once. Briefly.'

'What was that for?'

'I was on the girls' hockey team at school and during a game I blacked out. I woke up in a hospital. I was only there two days. It was really nothing.'

'Did you suffer an injury during the game?'

'No. I – I just blacked out.'

'How old were you then?'

'Sixteen. The doctor said it was probably some kind of adolescent glandular upset.'

John Harley sat forwards in his chair. 'When you woke up, do you remember if you felt any weakness on either side of your body?'

Marianne thought a moment. 'As a matter of fact, yes. My right side. But it went away in a few days. I haven't had anything like it since.'

'Did you have headaches? Blurred vision?'

'Yes. But they went away, too.' She was beginning to be alarmed. 'Do you think there's something wrong with me, Dr Harley?'

'I'm not sure. I'd like to make a few tests – just to be on the safe side.'

'What kind of tests?'

'I'd like to do a cerebral angiogram. Nothing to be concerned about. We can have it done right away.'

Three days later, Marianne received a call from Dr Harley's nurse asking her to come in. John Harley was waiting for her in his office. 'Well, we've solved the mystery.'

'Is it something bad?'

'Not really. The angiogram showed that what you had, Mrs Blackwell, was a small stroke. Medically, it's called a berry aneurysm, and it's very common in women – particularly in teenage girls. A small blood vessel in the brain broke and leaked small amounts of blood. The pressure is what caused the headaches and blurred vision. Fortunately, those things are self-healing.'

Marianne sat there listening, her mind fighting panic. 'What – what does all this mean, exactly? Could it happen again?'

'It's very unlikely.' He smiled. 'Unless you're planning to go out for the hockey team again, you can live an absolutely normal life.'

'Tony and I like to ride and play tennis. Is that –?'

'As long as you don't overdo, everything goes. From tennis to sex. No problem.'

She smiled in relief. 'Thank God.'

As Marianne rose, John Harley said, 'There is one thing, Mrs Blackwell. If you and Tony are planning to have children, I would advise adopting them.'

Marianne froze. 'You said I was perfectly normal.'

'You are. Unfortunately, pregnancy increases the vascular volume enormously. And during the last six to eight weeks of pregnancy, there's an additional increase in the blood pressure. With the history of that aneurysm, the risk factor would be unacceptably high. It would not only be dangerous – it could be fatal. Adoptions are really quite easy these days. I can arrange –'

But Marianne was no longer listening. She was hearing Tony's voice: *I want us to have a baby. A little girl who looks exactly like you.*

'. . . I couldn't bear to hear any more,' Marianne told Kate. 'I ran out of his office and came straight here.'

Kate made a tremendous effort not to let her feelings show. It was a stunning blow. But there had to be a way. There was always a way.

She managed to smile and said, 'Well! I was afraid it was going to be something much worse.'

'But, Kate, Tony and I want so much to have a baby.'

'Marianne, Dr Harley is an alarmist. You had a minor problem years ago, and Harley's trying to turn it into something important. You know how doctors are.' She took Marianne's hand. 'You feel well, don't you, darling?'

'I felt wonderful until –'

'Well, there you are. You aren't going around having any fainting spells?'

'No.'

'Because it's all over. He said himself that those things are self-healing.'

'He said the risks –'

Kate sighed. 'Marianne, every time a woman gets pregnant, there's always a risk. Life is full of risks. The important thing in life is to decide which risks are the ones worth taking, don't you agree?'

'Yes.' Marianne sat there thinking. She made her decision. 'You're right. Let's not say anything to Tony. It would only worry him. We'll keep it our secret.'

Kate thought, *I could bloody well kill John*

Harley for scaring her to death. 'It will be our secret,' Kate agreed.

Three months later, Marianne became pregnant. Tony was thrilled. Kate was quietly triumphant. Dr John Harley was horrified.

'I'll arrange for an immediate abortion,' he told Marianne.

'No, Dr Harley. I feel fine. I'm going to have the baby.'

When Marianne told Kate about her visit, Kate stormed into John Harley's office. 'How dare you suggest my daughter-in-law have an abortion?'

'Kate, I told her that if she carried that baby to term, there's a chance it might kill her.'

'You don't *know* that. She's going to be fine. Stop alarming her.'

Eight months later, at four a.m. in early February, Marianne's labour pains began prematurely. Her moans awakened Tony.

He began hurriedly dressing. 'Don't worry, darling. I'll have you at the hospital in no time.'

The pains were agonizing. 'Please hurry.'

She wondered whether she should have told Tony about her conversations with Dr Harley. No, Kate had been right. It was her decision to make. Life was so wonderful that God would not let anything bad happen to her.

When Marianne and Tony arrived at the hospital, everything was in readiness. Tony was escorted to a waiting room. Marianne was taken into an examining room. The obstetrician, Dr Mattson took Marianne's blood pressure. He frowned and took it again. He looked up and said to his nurse, 'Get her into the operating room – fast!'

Tony was at the cigarette machine in the hospital corridor when a voice behind him said, 'Well, well, if it isn't Rembrandt.' Tony turned. He recognized the man who had been with Dominique in front of her apartment building. What had she called him? Ben. The man was staring at Tony, an antagonistic expression on his face. Jealousy? What had Dominique told him? At that moment. Dominique appeared. She said to Ben, 'The nurse said Michelline is in intensive care. We'll come –' She saw Tony and stopped.

'Tony!' What are you doing here?'

'My wife is having a baby.'

'Did your mother arrange it?' Ben asked.

'What's that supposed to mean?'

'Dominique told me your mother arranges everything for you, sonny.'

'Ben! Stop it!'

'Why? It's the truth, isn't it, baby? Isn't that what you said?'

Tony turned to Dominique. 'What is he talking about?'

'Nothing,' she said quickly. 'Ben, let's get out of here.'

But Ben was enjoying himself. 'I wish I had a

mother like yours, buddy boy. You want a beautiful model to sleep with, she buys you one. You want to have an art exhibition in Paris, she arranges it for you. You –'

'You're crazy.'

'Am I?' Ben turned to Dominique. 'Doesn't he know?'

'Don't I know what?' Tony demanded.

'Nothing, Tony.'

'He said my mother arranged the exhibition in Paris. That's a lie, isn't it?' He saw the expression on Dominique's face. *'Isn't it?'*

'No,' Dominique said reluctantly.

'You mean she had to pay Goerg to – to show my paintings?'

'Tony, he really liked your paintings.'

'Tell him about the art critic,' Ben urged.

'That's enough, Ben!' Dominique turned to go. Tony grabbed her arm. 'Wait! What about him? Did my mother arrange for him to be at the exhibition?'

'Yes.' Dominique's voice had dropped to a whisper.

'But he *hated* my paintings.'

She could hear the pain in his voice. 'No, Tony. He didn't. Andre d'Usseau told your mother you could have become a great artist.'

And he was face to face with the unbelievable. 'My mother paid d'Usseau to destroy me?'

'Not to destroy you. She believed she was doing it for your own good.'

The enormity of what his mother had done was staggering. *Everything she had told him was a lie. She had never intended to let him live his own life.* And Andre d'Usseau! How could a man like that be bought? But of course Kate would know the price of any man. Wilde could have been referring to Kate when he talked of someone who knew the price of everything, the value of nothing. Everything had always been for the company. And the company was Kate Blackwell. Tony turned and walked blindly down the corridor.

In the operating room, the doctors were fighting desperately to save Marianne's life. Her blood pressure was alarmingly low, and her heartbeat was erratic. She was given oxygen and a blood transfusion, but it was useless. Marianne was unconscious from a cerebral haemorrhage when the first baby was delivered, and dead three minutes later when the second twin was taken.

Tony heard a voice calling, 'Mr Blackwell.' He turned. Dr Mattson was at his side.

'You have two beautiful, healthy twin daughters, Mr Blackwell.'

Tony saw the look in his eyes. 'Marianne – she's all right, isn't she?'

Dr Mattson took a deep breath. 'I'm so sorry. We did everything we could. She died on the –'

'She *what*?' It was a scream. Tony grabbed Dr

Mattson's lapels and shook him. 'You're lying! She's *not* dead.'

'Mr Blackwell —'

'Where is she? I want to see her.'

'You can't go in just now. They're preparing her —'

Tony cried out, 'You killed her, you bastard! You killed her.' He began attacking the doctor. Two interns hurried in and grabbed Tony's arms.

'Now take it easy, Mr Blackwell.'

Tony fought like a madman. 'I want to see my wife!'

Dr John Harley hurried up to the group. 'Let him go,' he commanded. 'Leave us alone.'

Dr Mattson and the interns left. Tony was weeping brokenly 'John, they k-killed Marianne. They m-murdered her.'

'She's dead, Tony, and I'm sorry. But no one murdered her. I told her months ago if she went ahead with this pregnancy it could kill her.'

It took a long moment for the words to sink in. 'What are you talking about?'

'Marianne didn't tell you? Your mother didn't say anything?'

Tony was staring at him, his eyes uncomprehending. 'My mother?'

'She thought I was being an alarmist. She advised Marianne to go ahead with it. I'm so sorry, Tony. I've seen the twins. They're beautiful. Wouldn't you like to —?'

Tony was gone.

* * *

Kate's butler opened the door for Tony.

'Good morning, Mr Blackwell.'

'Good morning, Lester.'

The butler took in Tony's dishevelled appearance. 'Is everything all right, sir?'

'Everything is fine. Would you make me a cup of coffee, Lester?'

'Certainly sir.'

Tony watched the butler move towards the kitchen. *Now, Tony*, the voice in his head commanded.

Yes. Now. Tony turned and walked into the trophy room. He went to the cabinet that held the gun collection, and he stared at the gleaming array of instruments of death.

Open the cabinet, Tony.

He opened it. He selected a revolver from the gun rack and checked the barrel to make sure it was loaded.

She'll be upstairs, Tony.

Tony turned and started up the stairs. He knew now that it was not his mother's fault that she was evil. She was possessed, and he was going to cure her. The company had taken her soul, and Kate was not responsible for what she did. His mother and the company had become one, and when he killed her, the company would die.

He was outside Kate's bedroom door.

Open the door, the voice commanded.

Tony opened the door. Kate was dressing in front of a mirror when she heard the door open.

'Tony! What on earth –'

He carefully aimed the gun at her and began squeezing the trigger.

TWENTY-TWO

The right of primogeniture – the claim of the first-born to a family title or estate – is deeply rooted in history. Among royal families in Europe a high official is present at every birth of a possible heir to a queen or princess so that should twins be born, the right of succession will not be in dispute. Dr Mattson was careful to note which twin had been delivered first.

Everyone agreed that the Blackwell twins were the most beautiful babies they had ever seen. They were healthy and unusually lively, and the nurses at the hospital kept finding excuses to go in and look at them. Part of the fascination, although none of the nurses would have admitted it, was the mysterious stories that were circulating about the twins' family. Their mother had died during child-birth. The twins' father had disappeared, and there were rumours he had murdered his mother, but no one was able to substantiate the reports. There was nothing about it in the newspapers, save for a brief item that Tony Blackwell had suffered a nervous breakdown over the death of his wife and was in seclusion. When the press tried to question Dr Harley, he gave them a brusque, 'No comment.'

The past few days had been hell for John Harley. As long as he lived, he would remember the scene when he reached Kate Blackwell's bedroom after a frantic phone call from the butler. Kate was lying on the floor in a coma, bullet wounds in her neck and chest, her blood spilling onto the white rug. Tony was going through her closets, slashing his mother's clothes to shreds with a pair of scissors.

Dr Harley took one quick look at Kate and hurriedly telephoned for an ambulance. He knelt at Kate's side and felt her pulse. It was weak and thready, and her face was turning blue. She was going into shock. He swiftly gave her an injection of adrenaline and sodium bicarbonate.

'What happened?' Dr Harley asked.

The butler was soaked in perspiration. 'I – I don't know. Mr Blackwell asked me to make him some coffee. I was in the kitchen when I heard the sound of gunfire. I ran upstairs and found Mrs Blackwell on the floor, like this. Mr Blackwell was standing over her, saying. 'It can't hurt you anymore, Mother. I killed it.' And he went into the closet and started cutting her dresses.'

Dr Harley turned to Tony. 'What are you doing, Tony?'

A savage slash. 'I'm helping Mother. I'm destroying the company. It killed Marianne, you know.'

He continued slashing at the dresses in Kate's closet.

Kate was rushed to the emergency ward of a midtown private hospital owned by Kruger-Brent, Ltd. She was given four blood transfusions during the operation to remove the bullets.

It took three male nurses to force Tony into an ambulance, and it was only after Dr Harley gave him an injection that Tony was quiet. A police unit had responded to the ambulance call, and Dr Harley summoned Brad Rogers to deal with them. Through means that Dr Harley did not understand, there was no mention in the media of the shooting.

Dr Harley went to the hospital to visit Kate in intensive care. Her first words were a whispered, 'Where's my son?'

'He's being taken care of, Kate. He's all right.'

Tony had been taken to a private sanatorium in Connecticut.

'John, why did he try to kill me? Why?' The anguish in her voice was unbearable.

'He blames you for Marianne's death.'

'That's insane!'

John Harley made no comment.

He blames you for Marianne's death.

Long after Dr Harley had left, Kate lay there, refusing to accept those words. She had loved Marianne because she made Tony happy. *Everything I have done has been for you, my son. All my dreams were for you. How could you not know that?* And he hated her so much he had tried to kill her. She was filled with such a deep agony that she wanted to die. But she would not let herself die. She had done what was right. They were wrong. Tony was a weakling. They had all been weaklings. Her father had been too weak to face his son's death. Her mother had been too weak to face life alone. *But I am not weak,* Kate thought. *I can face this. I can face anything. I'm going to live. I'll survive. The company will survive.*

BOOK FIVE

Eve and Alexandra

1950–1975

TWENTY-THREE

Kate recuperated at Dark Harbor, letting the sun and the sea heal her.

Tony was in a private asylum, where he could get the best care possible. Kate had psychiatrists flown in from Paris, Vienna and Berlin, but when all the examinations and tests had been completed, the diagnosis was the same: her son was a homicidal schizophrenic and paranoiac.

'He doesn't respond to drugs or psychiatric treatment, and he's violent. We have to keep him under restraint.'

'What kind of restraint?' Kate asked.

'He's in a padded cell. Most of the time we have to keep him in a straitjacket.'

'Is that necessary?'

'Without it, Mrs Blackwell, he would kill anyone who got near him.'

She closed her eyes in pain. This was not her sweet, gentle Tony they were talking about. It was a stranger, someone possessed. She opened her eyes. 'Is there nothing that can be done?'

'Not if we can't reach his mind. We're keeping him on drugs, but the moment they wear off, he gets manic again. We can't continue this treatment indefinitely.'

Kate stood very straight. 'What do you suggest, Doctor?'

'In similar cases, we've found that removing a small portion of the brain has produced remarkable results.'

Kate swallowed. 'A lobotomy?'

'That is correct. Your son will still be able to function in every way, except that he will no longer have any strong dysfunctional emotions.'

Kate sat there, her mind and body chilled. Dr Morris, a young doctor from the Menninger Clinic, broke the silence. 'I know how difficult this must be for you, Mrs Blackwell. If you'd like to think about –'

'If that's the only thing that will stop his torment,' Kate said, 'do it.'

Frederick Hoffman wanted his granddaughters. 'I will take them back to Germany with me.'

It seemed to Kate that he had aged twenty years since Marianne's death. Kate felt sorry for him, but she had no intention of giving up Tony's children. 'They need a woman's care, Frederick. Marianne would have wanted them brought up here. You'll come and visit them often.'

And he was finally persuaded.

* * *

The twins were moved into Kate's home, and a nursery suite was set up for them. Kate interviewed governesses, and finally hired a young French woman named Solange Dunas.

Kate named the first-born Eve, and her twin, Alexandra. They were identical – impossible to tell apart. Seeing them together was like looking at an image in a mirror, and Kate marvelled at the double miracle that her son and Marianne had created. They were both bright babies, quick and responsive, but even after a few weeks, Eve seemed more mature than Alexandra. Eve was the first to crawl and talk and walk. Alexandra followed quickly, but from the beginning it was Eve who was the leader. Alexandra adored her sister and tried to imitate everything she did. Kate spent as much time with her granddaughters as possible. They made her feel young. And Kate began to dream again. *One day, when I'm old and ready to retire . . .*

On the twins' first birthday, Kate gave them a party. They each had an identical birthday cake, and there were dozens of presents from friends, company employees and the household staff. Their second birthday party seemed to follow almost immediately. Kate could not believe how rapidly the time went by and how quickly the twins were growing. She was able to discern even more clearly the differences in their personalities: Eve, the stronger, was more daring. Alexandra was softer, content to follow her sister's lead. *With no mother or father,*

Kate thought repeatedly, *it's a blessing that they have each other and love each other so much*.

The night before their fifth birthday, Eve tried to murder Alexandra.

It is written in Genesis 25:22–23:

> And the children struggled together within her . . .
> And the Lord said unto her, Two [nations] are in thy womb, and two manner of people shall be separated from thy bowels;
> and the one [people] shall be stronger than the other [people];
> and the elder shall serve the younger.

In the case of Eve and Alexandra, Eve had no intention of serving her younger sister.

Eve had hated her sister for as long as she could remember. She went into a silent rage when someone picked up Alexandra, or petted her or gave her a present. Eve felt she was being cheated. She wanted it all for herself – all the love and the beautiful things that surrounded the two of them. She could not have even a birthday of her own. She hated Alexandra for looking like her, dressing like her, stealing the part of her grandmother's love that belonged to her. Alexandra adored Eve, and Eve despised her for that. Alexandra was generous, eager to give up her toys and dolls, and that filled Eve with still more contempt. Eve shared nothing.

What was hers belonged to her; but it was not enough. She wanted everything Alexandra had. At night, under the watchful eye of Solange Dunas, both girls would say their prayers aloud, but Eve always added a silent prayer begging God to strike Alexandra dead. When the prayer went unanswered, Eve decided she would have to take care of it herself. Their fifth birthday was only a few days away, and Eve could not bear the thought of sharing another party with Alexandra. They were *her* friends, and *her* gifts that her sister was stealing from her. She had to kill Alexandra soon.

On the night before their birthday, Eve lay in her bed, wide awake. When she was sure the household was asleep, she went over to Alexandra's bed and awakened her. 'Alex,' she whispered, 'Let's go down to the kitchen and see our birthday cakes.'

Alexandra said sleepily. 'Everybody's sleeping.'

'We won't wake anyone up.'

'Mademoiselle Dunas won't like it. Why don't we look at the cakes in the morning?'

'Because I want to look at them now. Are you coming or not?'

Alexandra rubbed the sleep out of her eyes. She had no interest in seeing the birthday cakes, but she did not want to hurt her sister's feelings. 'I'm coming,' she said.

Alexandra got out of bed and put on a pair of slippers. Both girls wore pink nylon nightgowns.

'Come on,' Eve said. 'And don't make any noise.'

'I won't,' Alexandra promised.

They tiptoed out of their bedroom, into the long corridor, past the closed door of Mademoiselle Dunas's bedroom, down the steep back stairs that led to the kitchen. It was an enormous kitchen, with two large gas stoves, six ovens, three refrigerators and a walk-in freezer.

In the refrigerator Eve found the birthday cakes that the cook, Mrs Tyler, had made. One of them said Happy Birthday, Alexandra. The other said Happy Birthday, Eve.

Next year, Eve thought happily, *there will only be one.*

Eve took Alexandra's cake out of the refrigerator and placed it on the wooden chopping block in the middle of the kitchen. She opened a drawer and took out a package of brightly coloured candles.

'What are you doing?' Alexandra asked.

'I want to see how it looks with candles all lighted.' Eve began pressing the candles into the icing of the cake.

'I don't think you should do that, Eve. You'll ruin the cake. Mrs Tyler is going to be angry.'

'She won't mind.' Eve opened another drawer and took out two large boxes of kitchen matches. 'Come on, help me.'

'I want to go back to bed.'

Eve turned on her angrily. 'All right. Go back to bed, scaredy cat. I'll do it alone.'

Alexandra hesitated. 'What do you want me to do?'

Eve handed her one of the boxes of matches. 'Start lighting the candles.'

Alexandra was afraid of fire. Both girls had been warned again and again about the danger of playing with matches. They knew the horror stories about children who had disobeyed that rule. But Alexandra did not want to disappoint Eve, and so she obediently began lighting the candles.

Eve watched her a moment. 'You're leaving out the ones on the other side, silly,' she said.

Alexandra leaned over to reach the candles at the far side of the cake, her back to Eve. Quickly, Eve struck a match and touched it to the matches in the box she was holding. As they burst into flames, Eve dropped the box at Alexandra's feet, so that the bottom of Alexandra's nightgown caught fire. It was an instant before Alexandra was aware of what was happening. When she felt the first agonizing pain against her legs, she looked down and screamed, 'Help! Help me!'

Eve stared at the flaming nightgown a moment, awed by the extent of her success. Alexandra was standing there, petrified, frozen with fear.

'Don't move!' Eve said. 'I'll get a bucket of water.' She hurried off to the butler's pantry, her heart pounding with a fearful joy.

It was a horror movie that saved Alexandra's life. Mrs Tyler, the Blackwell's cook, had been escorted to the cinema by a police sergeant whose bed she shared from time to time. On this particular evening, the motion-picture screen was so filled with dead and mutilated bodies that finally Mrs Tyler could bear it no longer. In the middle of a beheading, she said, 'This may all be in a day's work for you, Richard, but I've had enough.'

Sergeant Richard Dougherty reluctantly followed her out of the theatre.

They arrived back at the Blackwell mansion an hour earlier than they had expected to, and as Mrs Tyler opened the back door, she heard Alexandra's screams coming from the kitchen. Mrs Tyler and Sergeant Dougherty rushed in, took one horrified look at the scene before them and went into action. The sergeant leaped at Alexandra and ripped off her flaming nightgown. Her legs and hips were blistered, but the flames had not reached her hair or the front of her body. Alexandra fell to the floor, unconscious. Mrs Tyler filled a large pot with water and poured it over the flames licking at the floor.

'Call an ambulance,' Sergeant Dougherty ordered. 'Is Mrs Blackwell home?'

'She should be upstairs asleep.'

'Wake her up.'

As Mrs Tyler finished phoning for an ambulance, there was a cry from the butler's pantry, and Eve ran in carrying a pan of water, sobbing hysterically.

'Is Alexandra dead?' Eve screamed. 'Is she dead?'

Mrs Tyler took Eve in her arms to soothe her. 'No, darling, she's all right. She's going to be just fine.'

'It was my fault,' Eve sobbed. 'She wanted to light the candles on her birthday cake. I shouldn't have let her do it.'

Mrs Tyler stroked Eve's back. 'It's all right. You mustn't blame yourself.'

'The m-matches fell out of my hand, and Alex caught on fire. It was t-terrible.'

Sergeant Dougherty looked at Eve and said sympathetically, 'Poor child.'

'Alexandra has second-degree burns on her legs and back,' Dr Harley told Kate, 'but she's going to be fine. We can do amazing things with burns these days. Believe me, this could have been a terrible tragedy.'

'I know,' Kate said. She had seen Alexandra's burns, and they had filled her with horror. She hesitated a moment. 'John, I think I'm even more concerned about Eve.'

'Was Eve hurt?'

'Not physically, but the poor child blames herself for the accident. She's having terrible nightmares. The last three nights I've had to go in and hold her in my arms before she could go back to sleep. I don't want this to become more traumatic. Eve is very sensitive.'

'Kids get over things pretty quickly, Kate. If

there's any problem, let me know, and I'll recommend a child therapist.'

'Thank you,' Kate said gratefully.

Eve *was* terribly upset. The birthday party had been cancelled. *Alexandra cheated me out of that*, Eve thought bitterly.

Alexandra healed perfectly, with no signs of scars. Eve got over her feelings of guilt with remarkable ease. As Kate assured her, 'Accidents can happen to anybody, darling. You mustn't blame yourself.'

Eve didn't. She blamed Mrs Tyler. Why did she have to come home and spoil everything? It had been a perfect plan.

The sanitarium where Tony was confined was in a peaceful, wooded area in Connecticut. Kate was driven out to see him once a month. The lobotomy had been successful. There was no longer the slightest sign of aggression in Tony. He recognized Kate and he always politely asked about Eve and Alexandra, but he showed no interest in seeing them. He showed very little interest in anything. He seemed happy. *No, not happy*, Kate corrected herself. *Content. But content – to do what?*

Kate asked Mr Burger, the superintendent of the asylum, 'Doesn't my son *do* anything all day?'

'Oh, yes, Mrs Blackwell. He sits by the hour and paints.'

Her son, who could have owned the world, sat

and painted all day. Kate tried not to think of the waste, that brilliant mind gone forever. 'What does he paint?'

The man was embarrassed. 'No one can quite figure it out.'

TWENTY-FOUR

During the next two years, Kate became seriously concerned about Alexandra. The child was definitely accident-prone. During Eve and Alexandra's summer vacation at the Blackwell estate in the Bahamas, Alexandra almost drowned while playing with Eve in the pool, and it was only the prompt intervention of a gardener that saved her. The following year when the two girls were on a picnic in the Palisades, Alexandra somehow slipped off the edge of a cliff and saved herself by clinging to a shrub growing out of the steep mountainside.

'I wish you would keep a closer eye on your sister,' Kate told Eve. 'She can't seem to take care of herself the way you can.'

'I know,' Eve said solemnly. 'I'll watch her, Gran.'

Kate loved both her granddaughters, but in different ways. They were seven years old now, and identically beautiful, with long, soft blonde hair, exquisite features and the McGregor eyes. They looked alike, but their personalities were quite different. Alexandra's gentleness reminded Kate of Tony, while Eve was more like her, headstrong and self-sufficient.

A chauffeur drove them to school in the family Rolls-Royce. Alexandra was embarrassed to have her classmates see her with the car and chauffeur; Eve revelled in it. Kate gave each girl a weekly allowance, and ordered them to keep a record of how they spent it. Eve invariably ran short of money before the week was out and borrowed from Alexandra. Eve learned to adjust the books so that Gran would not know. But Kate knew, and she could hardly hold back her smile. Seven years old and already a creative accountant!

In the beginning, Kate had nurtured a secret dream that one day Tony would be well again, that he would leave the asylum and return to Kruger-Brent. But as time passed, the dream slowly faded. It was tacitly understood that while Tony might leave the asylum for short visits, accompanied by a male nurse, he would never again be able to participate in the outside world.

It was 1962, and as Kruger-Brent, Ltd., prospered and expanded, the demands for new leadership grew more urgent. Kate celebrated her seventieth birthday. Her hair was white now, and she was a remarkable figure of a woman, strong and erect and vital. She was aware that the attrition of time would overtake her. She had to be prepared. The company had to be safeguarded for the family. Brad Rogers was a good manager, but he was not a Blackwell. *I have to last until the twins can take over*. She thought of Cecil Rhodes's last words: 'So little done – so much to do.'

The twins were twelve years old, on the verge of becoming young ladies. Kate had spent as much time with them as she possibly could, but now she turned even more of her attention to them. It was time to make an important decision.

During Easter week, Kate and the twins flew to Dark Harbor in a company plane. The girls had visited all the family estates except the one in Johannesburg, and of them all, Dark Harbor was their favourite. They enjoyed the wild freedom and the seclusion of the island. They loved to sail and swim and water-ski, and Dark Harbor held all these things for them. Eve asked if she could bring some schoolmates along, as she had in the past, but this time her grandmother refused. Grandmother, that powerful, imposing figure who swept in and out, dropping off a present here, a kiss on the cheek there, with occasional admonitions about how young ladies behaved, wanted to be alone with them. This time the girls sensed that something different was happening. Their grandmother was with them at every meal. She took them boating and swimming and even riding. Kate handled her horse with the sureness of an expert.

The girls still looked amazingly alike, two golden beauties, but Kate was interested less in their similarities than in their differences. Sitting on the veranda watching them as they finished a tennis game, Kate summed them up in her mind. Eve was the leader, Alexandra the follower. Eve had a stubborn streak. Alexandra was flexible. Eve was a natural athlete. Alexandra was still having accidents. Only a few days before, when the two girls were out alone in a small sailboat with Eve at the rudder, the wind had come behind the sail and the sail had luffed, swinging it crashing towards Alexandra's head. She had not gotten out of the way in time and had been swept overboard and nearly drowned. Another boat nearby had assisted Eve in rescuing her sister. Kate wondered whether all these things could have anything to do with Alexandra having been born three minutes later than Eve, but the reasons did not matter. Kate had made her decision. There was no longer any question in her mind. She was putting her money on Eve, and it was a ten-billion-dollar bet. She would find a perfect consort for Eve, and when Kate retired, Eve would run Kruger-Brent. As for Alexandra, she would have a life of wealth and comfort. She might be very good working on the charitable grants Kate had set up. Yes, that would be perfect for Alexandra. She was such a sweet and compassionate child.

The first step towards implementing Kate's plan was to see that Eve got into the proper school. Kate chose Briarcrest, an excellent school in South Carolina. 'Both my granddaughters are delightful,'

Kate informed Mrs Chandler, the headmistress. 'But you'll find that Eve is the clever one. She's an extraordinary girl, and I'm sure you'll see to it that she has every advantage here.'

'All our students have every advantage here, Mrs Blackwell. You spoke of Eve. What about her sister?'

'Alexandra? A lovely girl.' It was a pejorative. Kate stood up. 'I shall be checking their progress regularly.'

In some odd way, the headmistress felt the words were a warning.

Eve and Alexandra adored the new school, particularly Eve. She enjoyed the freedom of being away from home, of not having to account to her grandmother and Solange Dunas. The rules at Briarcrest were strict, but that did not bother Eve, for she was adept at getting around rules. The only thing that disturbed her was that Alexandra was there with her. When Eve first heard the news about Briarcrest, she begged, 'May I go alone? Please, Gran?'

And Kate said, 'No, darling. I think it's better if Alexandra goes with you.'

Eve concealed her resentment. 'Whatever you say, Gran.'

She was always very polite and affectionate around her grandmother. Eve knew where the power lay. Their father was a crazy man, locked up in an insane asylum. Their mother was dead.

It was their grandmother who controlled the money. Eve knew they were rich. She had no idea how much money there was, but it was a lot – enough to buy all the beautiful things she wanted. Eve loved beautiful things. There was only one problem: Alexandra.

One of the twins' favourite activities at Briarcrest School was the morning riding class. Most of the girls owned their own jumpers, and Kate had given each twin one for her twelfth birthday. Jerome Davis, the riding instructor, watched as his pupils went through their paces in the rings, jumping over a one-foot stile, then a two-foot stile and finally a four-foot stile. Davis was one of the best riding teachers in the country. Several of his former pupils had gone on to win gold medals, and he was adept at spotting a natural-born rider. The new girl, Eve Blackwell, was a natural. She did not have to think about what she was doing, how to hold the reins or post in the saddle. She and her horse were one, and as they sailed over the hurdles, Eve's golden hair flying in the wind, it was a beautiful sight to behold. *Nothing's going to stop that one*, Mr Davis thought.

Tommy, the young groom, favoured Alexandra. Mr Davis watched Alexandra saddle up her horse, preparing for her turn. Alexandra and Eve wore different-coloured ribbons on their sleeves so he could tell them apart. Eve was helping Alexandra saddle her horse while Tommy was busy with another student. Davis was summoned to the main building for a telephone call, and what happened after that was a matter of great confusion.

From what Jerome Davis was able to piece together later, Alexandra mounted her horse, circled the ring and started towards the first low jump. Her horse inexplicably began rearing and bucking and threw Alexandra into a wall. She was knocked unconscious, and it was only by inches that the wild horse's hooves missed her face. Tommy carried Alexandra to the infirmary, where the school doctor diagnosed a mild concussion.

'Nothing broken, nothing serious,' he said. 'By tomorrow morning, she'll be right as rain, ready to get up on her horse again.'

'But she could have been killed!' Eve screamed.

Eve refused to leave Alexandra's side. Mrs Chandler thought she had never seen such devotion in a sister. It was truly touching.

When Mr Davis was finally able to corral Alexandra's horse to unsaddle it, he found the saddle blanket stained with blood. He lifted it off and discovered a large piece of jagged metal from a beer can still protruding from the horse's back, where it had been pressed down by the saddle. When he reported this to Mrs Chandler, she started an immediate investigation. All the girls who had been in the vicinity of the stable were questioned.

'I'm sure,' Mrs Chandler said, 'that whoever put that piece of metal there thought she was playing a harmless prank, but it could have led to very serious consequences. I want the name of the girl who did it.'

When no one volunteered, Mrs Chandler talked to them in her office, one by one. Each girl denied any knowledge of what had happened. When it was Eve's turn to be questioned, she seemed oddly ill at ease.

'Do you have any idea who could have done this to your sister?' Mrs Chandler asked.

Eve looked down at the rug. 'I'd rather not say,' she mumbled.

'Then you *did* see something?'

'Please, Mrs Chandler . . .'

'Eve, Alexandra could have been seriously hurt. The girl who did this must be punished so that it does not happen again.'

'It wasn't one of the girls.'

'What do you mean?'

'It was Tommy.'

'The *groom*.'

'Yes, ma'am. I saw him. I thought he was just tightening the cinch. I'm sure he didn't mean any harm. Alexandra orders him around a lot, and I guess he wanted to teach her a lesson. Oh, Mrs Chandler, I wish you hadn't made me tell you. I don't want to get anyone in trouble.' The poor child was on the verge of hysteria.

Mrs Chandler walked around the desk and put her arm around her. 'It's all right, Eve. You did right to tell me. Now you just forget about everything. I'll take care of it.'

The following morning when the girls went out to the stables, there was a new groom.

A few months later, there was another unpleasant incident at the school. Several of the girls had been caught smoking marijuana and one of them accused Eve of supplying it and selling it. Eve angrily denied it. A search by Mrs Chandler revealed marijuana hidden in Alexandra's locker.

'I don't believe she did it,' Eve said stoutly. 'Someone put it there. I know it.'

An account of the incident was sent to Kate by the headmistress, and Kate admired Eve's loyalty in shielding her sister. She was a McGregor, all right.

On the twins' fifteenth birthday, Kate took them to the estate in South Carolina, where she gave a large party for them. It was not too early to see to it that Eve was exposed to the proper young men, and every eligible young man around was invited to the girls' party.

The boys were at the awkward age where they were not yet seriously interested in girls, but Kate made it her business to see that acquaintances were made and friendships formed. Somewhere among these young boys could be the man in Eve's future, the future of Kruger-Brent, Ltd.

Alexandra did not enjoy parties, but she always pretended she was having a good time in order not to disappoint her grandmother. Eve adored parties. She loved dressing up, being admired. Alexandra preferred reading and painting. She spent hours looking at her father's paintings at Dark Harbor, and she wished she could have known him before he became ill. He appeared at the house on holidays with his male companion, but Alexandra found it impossible to reach her father. He was a pleasant, amiable stranger who wanted to please, but had nothing to say. Their grandfather, Frederick Hoffman, lived in Germany, but was ill. The twins seldom saw him.

In her second year at school, Eve became pregnant. For several weeks she had been pale and listless and had missed some morning classes. When she began to have frequent periods of nausea, she was sent to the infirmary and examined. Mrs Chandler had been hastily summoned.

'Eve is pregnant,' the doctor told her.

'But – that's impossible! How could it have happened?'

The doctor replied mildly, 'In the usual fashion, I would presume.'

'But she's just a child.'

'Well, this child is going to be a mother.'

Eve bravely refused to talk. 'I don't want to get anyone in trouble,' she kept saying.

It was the kind of answer Mrs Chandler expected from Eve.

'Eve, dear, you must tell me what happened.'

And so at last Eve broke down. 'I was raped,' she said, and burst into tears.

Mrs Chandler was shocked. She held Eve's trembling body close to her and demanded, 'Who was it?'

'Mr Parkinson.'

Her English teacher.

If it had been anyone else but Eve, Mrs Chandler would not have believed it. Joseph Parkinson was a quiet man with a wife and three children. He had taught at Briarcrest School for eight years, and he was the last one Mrs Chandler would have ever suspected. She called him into her office, and she knew instantly that Eve had told the truth. He sat facing her, his face twitching with nervousness.

'You know why I've sent for you, Mr Parkinson?'

'I – I think so.'

'It concerns Eve.'

'Yes. I – I guessed that.'

'She says you raped her.'

Parkinson looked at her in disbelief. '*Raped* her? My God! If anyone was raped it was me.' In his excitement he lapsed into the ungrammatical.

Mrs Chandler said contemptuously, 'Do you know what you're saying? That child is –'

'She's *not* a child.' His voice was venomous. 'She's a devil.' He wiped the perspiration from his brow. 'All semester she sat in the front row of my class, with her dress hiked up. After class she would come up and ask a lot of meaningless questions while she rubbed herself against me, I didn't take her seriously. Then one afternoon about six weeks ago she came over to my house when my wife and children were away and –' His voice broke. 'Oh. Jesus! I couldn't help it.' He burst into tears.

They brought Eve into the office. Her manner was composed. She looked into Mr Parkinson's eyes, and it was he who turned away first. In the office were Mrs Chandler, the assistant principal and the chief of police of the small town where the school was located.

The chief of police said gently, 'Do you want to tell us what happened, Eve?'

'Yes, sir.' Eve's voice was calm. 'Mr Parkinson said he wanted to discuss my English work with me. He asked me to come to his house on a Sunday afternoon. He was alone in the house. He said he wanted to show me something in the bedroom, so I followed him upstairs. He forced me onto the bed, and he –'

'It's a lie!' Parkinson yelled. 'That's not the way it happened. That's not the way it happened . . .'

Kate was sent for, and the situation was explained to her. It was decided that it was in everyone's interest to keep the incident quiet. Mr Parkinson was dismissed from the school and given forty-eight hours to leave the state. An abortion was discreetly arranged for Eve.

Kate quietly bought up the school mortgage, carried by a local bank, and foreclosed.

When Eve heard the news, she sighed, 'I'm so sorry, Gran. I really liked that school.'

*　*　*

A few weeks later when Eve had recovered from her operation, she and Alexandra were registered at L'Institut Fernwood, a Swiss finishing school near Lausanne.

TWENTY-FIVE

There was a fire burning in Eve that was so fierce she could not put it out. It was not sex alone: that was only a small part of it. It was a rage to live, a need to do everything, be everything. Life was a lover, and Eve was desperate to possess it with all she had in her. She was jealous of everyone. She went to the ballet and hated the ballerina because she herself was not up there dancing and winning the cheers of the audience. She wanted to be a scientist, a singer, a surgeon, a pilot, an actress. She wanted to do everything, and do it better than anyone else had ever done it. She wanted it all, and she could not wait.

Across the valley from L'Institut Fernwood was a boys' military school. By the time Eve was seventeen, nearly every student and almost half the instructors were involved with her. She flirted outrageously and had affairs indiscriminately, but this time she took proper precautions, for she had no intention of ever getting pregnant again. She enjoyed sex, but it was not the act itself Eve loved, it was the power it gave her. She was the one in control. She gloated over the pleading looks of the boys and men who wanted to take her to bed and make love to her. She enjoyed teasing them and watching their hunger grow. She enjoyed the lying promises they made in order to possess her. But most of all, Eve enjoyed the power she had over their bodies. She could bring them to an erection with a kiss, and wither them with a word. She did not need them, they needed her. She controlled them totally, and it was a tremendous feeling. Within minutes she could measure a man's strength and weaknesses. She decided men were fools, all of them.

Eve was beautiful and intelligent and an heiress to one of the world's great fortunes, and she had had more than a dozen serious proposals of marriage. She was not interested. The only boys who attracted her were the ones Alexandra liked.

At a Saturday-night school dance, Alexandra met an attentive young French student named Rene Mallot. He was not handsome, but he was intelligent and sensitive, and Alexandra thought he was wonderful. They arranged to meet in town the following Saturday.

'Seven o'clock,' Rene said.

'I'll be waiting.'

In their room that night, Alexandra told Eve about her new friend. 'He's not like the other boys. He's rather shy and sweet. We're going to the theatre Saturday.'

'You like him a lot, don't you, little sister?' Eve teased.

Alexandra blushed. 'I just met him, but he seems – Well, you know.'

Eve lay back on her bed, hands clasped behind her head. 'No, I don't know. Tell me. Did he try to take you to bed?'

'Eve! He's not that kind of boy at all. I told you . . . he's – he's shy.'

'Well, well. My little sister's in love.'

'Of course I'm not! Now I wish I hadn't told you.'

'I'm glad you did,' Eve said sincerely.

When Alexandra arrived in front of the theatre the following Saturday, Rene was nowhere in sight. Alexandra waited on the street corner for more than an hour, ignoring the stares of passers-by, feeling like a fool. Finally she had a bad dinner alone in a small café and returned to school, miserable. Eve was not in their room. Alexandra read until curfew and then turned out the lights. It was almost two a.m. when Alexandra heard Eve sneak into the room.

'I was getting worried about you,' Alexandra whispered.

'I ran into some old friends. How was your evening – divine?'

'It was dreadful. He never even bothered to show up.'

'That's a shame,' Eve said sympathetically. 'But you must learn never to trust a man.'

'You don't think anything could have happened to him?'

'No, Alex, I think he probably found somebody he liked better.'

Of course he did, Alexandra thought. She was not really surprised. She had no idea how beautiful she was, or how admirable. She had lived all her life in the shadow of her twin sister. She adored her, and it seemed only right to Alexandra that everyone should be attracted to Eve. She felt inferior to Eve, but it never occurred to her that her sister had been carefully nourishing that feeling since they were children.

There were other broken dates. Boys Alexandra liked would seem to respond to her, and then she would never see them again. One weekend she ran into Rene unexpectedly on the streets of Lausanne. He hurried up to her and said, 'What happened? You promised you would call me.'

'Call you? What are you talking about?'

He stepped back, suddenly wary. 'Eve. . . . ?'

'No, Alexandra.'

His face flushed. 'I – I'm sorry. I have to go.' And he turned away, leaving her staring after him in confusion.

That evening when Alexandra told Eve about the incident, Eve shrugged and said, 'He's obviously *fou*. You're much better off without him, Alex.'

* * *

456

In spite of her feeling of expertise about men, there was one male weakness of which Eve was unaware, and it almost proved to be her undoing. From the beginning of time, men have boasted of their conquests, and the students at the military school were no different. They discussed Eve Blackwell with admiration and awe.

'When she was through with me, I couldn't move . . .'

'I never thought I'd have a piece of ass like that . . .'

'She's got a pussy that *talks* to you . . .'

'God, she's like a tigress in bed!'

Since at least two dozen boys and half a dozen teachers were praising Eve's libidinous talents, it soon became the school's worst-kept secret. One of the instructors at the military school mentioned the gossip to a teacher at L'Institut Fernwood, and she in turn reported it to Mrs Collins, the head-mistress. A discreet investigation was begun, and the result was a meeting between the headmistress and Eve.

'I think it would be better for the reputation of this school if you left immediately.'

Eve stared at Mrs Collins as though the lady were demented. 'What on earth are you talking about?'

'I'm talking about the fact that you have been servicing half the military academy. The other half seems to be lined up, eagerly waiting.'

'I've never heard such terrible lies in my whole

life,' Eve's voice was quivering with indignation. 'Don't think I'm not going to report this to my grandmother. When she hears –'

'I will spare you the trouble,' the headmistress interrupted. 'I would prefer to avoid embarrassment to L'Institut Fernwood, but if you do not leave quietly, I have a list of names I intend to send to your grandmother.'

'I'd like to see that list!'

Mrs Collins handed it to Eve without a word. It was a long list. Eve studied it and noted that at least seven names were missing. She sat there, quietly thinking.

Finally she looked up and said imperiously, 'This is obviously some kind of plot against my family. Someone is trying to embarrass my grandmother through me. Rather than let that happen, I will leave.'

'A very wise decision,' Mrs Collins said dryly. 'A car will drive you to the airport in the morning. I'll cable your grandmother that you're coming home. You're dismissed.'

Eve turned and started for the door, then suddenly thought of something. 'What about my sister?'

'Alexandra may remain here.'

When Alexandra returned to the dormitory after her last class, she found Eve packing. 'What are you doing?'

'I'm going home.'

'Home? In the middle of the term?'

Eve turned to face her sister. 'Alex, don't you really have any idea what a waste this school is? We're not learning anything here. We're just killing time.'

Alexandra was listening in surprise. 'I had no idea you felt that way, Eve.'

'I've felt like this every damn day for the whole bloody year. The only reason I stuck it out was because of you. You seemed to be enjoying it so much.'

'I am, but –'

'I'm sorry, Alex. I just can't take it any longer. I want to get back to New York. I want to go home where *we* belong.'

'Have you told Mrs Collins?'

'A few minutes ago.'

'How did she take it?'

'How did you expect her to take it? She was miserable – afraid it would make her school look bad. She begged me to stay.'

Alexandra sat down on the edge of the bed. 'I don't know what to say.'

'You don't have to say anything. This has nothing to do with you.'

'Of course it has. If you're that unhappy here –' She stopped. 'You're probably right. It is a bloody waste of time. Who needs to conjugate Latin verbs?'

'Right. Or who gives a fig about Hannibal or his bloody brother, Hasdrubal?'

Alexandra walked over to the closet, took out her suitcase and put it on the bed.

Eve smiled. 'I wasn't going to ask you to leave

here, Alex, but I'm really glad we're going home together.'

Alexandra pressed her sister's hand. 'So am I.'

Eve said casually, 'Tell you what. While I finish packing, call Gran and tell her we'll be on the plane home tomorrow. Tell her we can't stand this place. Will you do that?'

'Yes.' Alexandra hesitated. 'I don't think she's going to like it.'

'Don't worry about the old lady,' Eve said confidently. 'I can handle her.'

And Alexandra had no reason to doubt it. Eve was able to make Gran do pretty much what she wanted. *But then*, Alexandra thought, *how could anyone refuse Eve anything?*

She went to make the phone call.

Kate Blackwell had friends and enemies and business associates in high places, and for the last few months disturbing rumours had been coming to her ears. In the beginning she had ignored them as petty jealousies. But they persisted. Eve was seeing too much of the boys at a military school in Switzerland. Eve had an abortion. Eve was being treated for a social disease.

Thus, it was with a degree of relief that Kate learned that her granddaughters were coming home. She intended to get to the bottom of the vile rumours.

The day the girls arrived, Kate was at home waiting for them. She took Eve into the sitting room off her bedroom. 'I've been hearing some distressing

460

stories,' she said. 'I want to know why you were thrown out of school.' Her eyes bored into those of her granddaughter.

'We weren't thrown out,' Eve replied. 'Alex and I decided to leave.'

'Because of some incidents with boys?'

Eve said, 'Please, Grandmother. I'd rather not talk about it.'

'I'm afraid you're going to have to. What have you been doing?'

'I haven't been doing anything. It is Alex who –' She broke off.

'Alex who what?' Kate was relentless.

'Please don't blame her,' Eve said quickly. 'I'm sure she couldn't help it. She likes to play this childish game of pretending to be me. I had no idea what she was up to until the girls started gossiping about it. It seems she was seeing a lot of – of boys –' Eve broke off in embarrassment.

'Pretending to be you?' Kate was stunned. 'Why didn't you put a stop to it?'

'I tried,' Eve said miserably. 'She threatened to kill herself. Oh, Gran, I think Alexandra is a bit' – she forced herself to say the word – 'unstable. If you even discuss any of this with her, I'm afraid of what she might do.' There was naked agony in the child's tear-filled eyes.

Kate's heart felt heavy at Eve's deep unhappiness. 'Eve, don't. Don't cry, darling. I won't say anything to Alexandra. This will be just between the two of us.'

'I – I didn't want you to know. Oh, Gran,' she sobbed, 'I knew how much it would hurt you.'

Later, over tea, Kate studied Alexandra. *She's beautiful outside and rotten inside*, Kate thought. It was bad enough that Alexandra was involved in a series of sordid affairs, but to try to put the blame on her sister! Kate was appalled.

During the next two years, while Eve and Alexandra finished school at Miss Porter's, Eve was very discreet. She had been frightened by the close call. Nothing must jeopardize the relationship with her grandmother. The old lady could not last much longer – she was seventy-nine! – and Eve intended to make sure that she was Gran's heiress.

For the girls' twenty-first birthday, Kate took her granddaughters to Paris and bought them new wardrobes at Coco Chanel.

At a small dinner party at Le Petit Bedouin, Eve and Alexandra met Count Alfred Maurier and his wife, the Countess Vivien. The count was a distinguished-looking man in his fifties, with iron-grey hair and the disciplined body of an athlete. His wife was a pleasant-looking woman with a reputation as an international hostess.

Eve would have paid no particular attention to either of them, except for a remark she overheard someone make to the countess. 'I envy you and Alfred. You're the happiest married couple I know.

462

How many years have you been married? Twenty-five?'

'It will be twenty-six next month,' Alfred replied for her. 'And I may be the only Frenchman in history who has never been unfaithful to his wife.'

Everyone laughed except Eve. During the rest of the dinner, she studied Count Maurier and his wife. Eve could not imagine what the count saw in that flabby, middle-aged woman with her creepy neck. Count Maurier had probably never known what real love-making was. That boast of his was stupid. Count Alfred Maurier was a challenge.

The following day, Eve telephone Maurier at his office. 'This is Eve Blackwell. You probably don't remember me, but –'

'How could I forget you, child? You are one of the beautiful granddaughters of my friend Kate.'

'I'm flattered that you remember, Count. Forgive me for disturbing you, but I was told you're an expert on wines. I'm planning a surprise dinner party for Grandmother.' She gave a rueful little laugh. 'I know what I want to serve, but I don't know a thing about wines. I wondered whether you'd be kind enough to advise me.'

'I would be delighted,' he said, flattered. 'It depends on what you are serving. If you are starting with a fish, a nice, light Chablis would be –'

'Oh, I'm afraid I could never remember all this. Would it be possible for me to see you so that we could discuss it? If you're free for lunch today. . . . ?'

'For an old friend, I can arrange that.'

'Oh, good.' Eve replaced the receiver slowly. It would be a lunch the count would remember the rest of his life.

They met at Lasserre. The discussion on wines was brief. Eve listened to Maurier's boring discourse impatiently, and then interrupted. 'I'm in love with you, Alfred.'

The count stopped dead in the middle of a sentence. 'I beg your pardon?'

'I said I'm in love with you.'

He took a sip of wine. 'A vintage year.' He patted Eve's hand and smiled. 'All good friends should love one another.'

'I'm not talking about that kind of love, Alfred.'

And the count looked into Eve's eyes and knew exactly what kind of love she was talking about. It made him decidedly nervous. This girl was twenty-one years old, and he was past middle age, a happily married man. He simply could not understand what got into young girls these days. He felt uneasy sitting across from her, listening to what she was saying, and he felt even uneasier because she was probably the most beautiful, desirable young woman he had ever seen. She was wearing a beige pleated skirt and a soft green sweater that revealed the outline of a full, rich bosom. She was not wearing a brassiere, and he could see the thrust

464

of her nipples. He looked at her innocent young face, and he was at a loss for words. 'You – you don't even know me.'

'I've dreamed about you from the time I was a little girl. I imagined a man in shining armour who was tall and handsome and –'

'I'm afraid my armour's a little rusty. I –'

'Please don't make fun of me,' Eve begged. 'When I saw you at dinner last night, I couldn't take my eyes off you. I haven't been able to think of anything else. I haven't slept. I haven't been able to get you out of my mind for a moment.' Which was almost true.

'I – I don't know what to say to you, Eve. I am a happily married man. I –'

'Oh, I can't tell you how I envy your wife! She's the luckiest woman in the world. I wonder if she realizes that, Alfred.'

'Of course she does. I tell her all the time.' He smiled nervously, and wondered how to change the subject.

'Does she *really* appreciate you? Does she know how sensitive you are? Does she worry about your happiness? I would.'

The count was becoming increasingly uncomfortable. 'You're a beautiful young woman,' he said. 'And one day you're going to find your knight in shining, *unrusted* armour, and then –'

'I've found him and I want to go to bed with him.'

He looked around, afraid that someone might have overheard. 'Eve! Please!'

She leaned forwards. 'That's all I ask. The memory will last me for the rest of my life.'

The count said firmly, 'This is impossible. You are placing me in a most embarrassing position. Young women should not go around propositioning strangers.'

Slowly, Eve's eyes filled with tears. 'Is *that* what you think of me? That I go around – I've known only one man in my life. We were engaged to be married.' She did not bother to brush the tears away. 'He was kind and loving and gentle. He was killed in a mountain-climbing accident. I saw it happen. It was awful.'

Count Maurier put his hand over hers. 'I am so sorry.'

'You remind me so much of him. When I saw you, it was as though Bill had returned to me. If you would give me just one hour, I would never bother you again. You'd never even have to see me again. Please, Alfred!'

The count looked at Eve for a long time, weighing his decision.

After all, he was French.

They spent the afternoon in a small hotel on Rue Sainte-Anne. In all his experience before his marriage, Count Maurier had never bedded anyone like Eve. She was a hurricane, a nymphet, a devil. She knew too much. By the end of the afternoon, Count Maurier was completely exhausted.

As they were getting dressed, Eve said, 'When will I see you again, darling?'

'I'll telephone you,' Maurier said.

He did not plan ever to see this woman again. There was something about her that was frightening – almost evil. She was what the Americans so appropriately called *bad news*, and he had no intention of becoming involved further with her.

The matter would have ended there, had they not been seen coming out of the hotel together by Alicia Vanderlake, who had served on a charity committee with Kate Blackwell the previous year. Mrs Vanderlake was a social climber, and this was a heaven-sent ladder. She had seen newspaper photographs of Count Maurier and his wife, and she had seen photographs of the Blackwell twins. She was not sure which twin this was, but that was not important. Mrs Vanderlake knew where her duty lay. She looked in her private telephone book and found Kate Blackwell's number.

The butler answered the telephone. '*Bonjour*.'

'I would like to speak with Mrs Blackwell, please.'

'May I tell her who is calling?'

'Mrs Vanderlake. It's a personal matter.'

A minute later, Kate Blackwell was on the phone. 'Who is this?'

'This is Alicia Vanderlake, Mrs Blackwell. I'm sure you'll remember me. We served on a committee together last year and –'

'If it's for a donation, call my –'

'No, no,' Mrs Vanderlake said hastily. 'It's personal. It's about your granddaughter.'

Kate Blackwell would invite her over to tea, and they would discuss it, woman to woman. It would be the beginning of a warm friendship.

Kate Blackwell said, 'What about her?'

Mrs Vanderlake had had no intention of discussing the matter over the telephone, but Kate Blackwell's unfriendly tone left her no choice. 'Well, I thought it my duty to tell you that a few minutes ago I saw her sneaking out of a hotel with Count Alfred Maurier. It was an obvious assignation.'

Kate's voice was icy. 'I find this difficult to believe. Which one of my granddaughters?'

Mrs Vanderlake gave an uncertain laugh. 'I – I don't know. I can't tell them apart. But then, no one can, can they? It –'

'Thank you for the information.' And Kate hung up.

She stood there digesting the information she had just heard. Only the evening before they had dined together. Kate had known Alfred Maurier for fifteen years, and what she had just been told was entirely out of character for him, unthinkable. And yet, men were susceptible. If Alexandra had set out to lure Alfred into bed . . .

Kate picked up the telephone and said to the operator, 'I wish to place a call to Switzerland L'Institut Fernwood at Lausanne.'

* * *

468

When Eve returned home late that afternoon, she was flushed with satisfaction, not because she had enjoyed sex with Count Maurier, but because of her victory over him. *If I can have him so easily*, Eve thought, *I can have anyone. I can own the world.* She walked into the library and found Kate there.

'Hello, Gran. Did you have a lovely day?'

Kate stood there studying her lovely young granddaughter. 'Not a very good one, I'm afraid. What about you?'

'Oh, I did a little shopping. I didn't see anything more I really wanted. You bought me everything. You always –'

'Close the door, Eve.'

Something in Kate's voice sent out a warning signal. Eve closed the large oak door.

'Sit down.'

'Is something wrong, Gran?'

'That's what you're going to tell me. I was going to invite Alfred Maurier here, but I decided to spare us all that humiliation.'

Eve's brain began to spin. *This was impossible! There was no way anyone could have found out about her and Alfred Maurier.* She had left him only an hour earlier. 'I – I don't understand what you're talking about.'

'Then let me put it bluntly. You were in bed this afternoon with Count Maurier.'

Tears sprang to Eve's eyes. 'I – I was hoping you'd never find out what he did to me, because he's your friend.' She fought to keep her voice steady. 'It was terrible. He telephoned and invited me to lunch and got me drunk and –'

'Shut up!' Kate's voice was like a whiplash. Her eyes were filled with loathing. 'You're despicable.'

Kate had spent the most painful hour of her life, coming to a realization of the truth about her granddaughter. She could hear again the voice of the headmistress saying, *Mrs Blackwell, young women will be young women, and if one of them has a discreet affair, it is none of my business. But Eve was so blatantly promiscuous that for the good of the school . . .*

And Eve had blamed Alexandra.

Kate started to remember the accidents. The fire, when Alexandra almost burned to death. Alexandra's fall from the cliff. Alexandra being knocked out of the boat Eve was sailing, and almost drowning. Kate could hear Eve's voice recounting the details of her 'rape' by her English teacher: *Mr Parkinson said he wanted to discuss my English work with me. He asked me to come to his house on a Sunday afternoon. When I got there, he was alone in the house. He said he wanted to show me something in the bedroom. I followed him upstairs. He forced me onto the bed, and he . . .*

Kate remembered the incident at Briarcrest when Eve was accused of selling marijuana and the blame had been put on Alexandra. Eve had not *blamed* Alexandra, she had *defended* her. That was Eve's technique – to be the villain and play the heroine. Oh, she was clever.

Now Kate studied the beautiful, angel-faced monster in front of her. *I built all my future plans around you. It was you who was going to take control of Kruger-Brent one day. It was you I loved and cherished.* Kate said, 'I want you to leave this house. I never want to see you again.'

Eve had gone very pale.

'You're a whore. I think I could live with that. But you're also deceitful and cunning and a psychopathic liar. I cannot live with that.'

It was all happening too fast. Eve said desperately, 'Gran, if Alexandra has been telling you lies about me –'

'Alexandra doesn't know anything about this. I just had a long talk with Mrs Collins.'

'Is *that* all?' Eve forced a note of relief in her voice. 'Mrs Collins hates me because –'

Kate was filled with a sudden weariness. 'It won't work, Eve. Not anymore. It's over. I've sent for my lawyer. I'm disinheriting you.'

Eve felt her world crumbling around her. 'You can't. How – how will I live?'

'You will be given a small allowance. From now on, you will live your own life. Do anything you please,' Kate's voice hardened. 'But if I ever hear or read one word of scandal about you, if you ever disgrace the Blackwell name in any way, your allowance will stop forever. Is that clear?'

Eve looked into her grandmother's eyes and

knew this time there would be no reprieve. A dozen excuses sprang to her lips, but they died there.

Kate rose to her feet and said in an unsteady voice, 'I don't suppose this will mean anything to you, but this is – this is the most difficult thing I've ever had to do in my life.'

And Kate turned and walked out of the room, her back stiff and straight.

Kate sat in her darkened bedroom alone, wondering why everything had gone wrong.

If David had not been killed, and Tony could have known his father . . .

If Tony had not wanted to be an artist . . .

If Marianne had lived . . .

If. A two-letter word for futility.

The future was clay, to be moulded day by day, but the past was bedrock, immutable. *Everyone I've loved has betrayed me*, Kate thought. *Tony. Marianne. Eve. Sartre said it well: 'Hell is other people.'* She wondered when the pain would go away.

If Kate was filled with pain, Eve was filled with fury. All she had done was to enjoy herself in bed for an hour or two, and her grandmother acted as though Eve had committed some unspeakable crime. *The old-fashioned bitch!* No, not old-fashioned: *senile.* That was it. She was senile. Eve would find a good attorney and have the new will laughed out of court. Her father and grandmother were both insane. No one was going to disinherit her. Kruger-Brent was *her* company. How many times had her grandmother told her that one day it would belong to her. And Alexandra! All this time Alexandra had been undermining her, whispering God-knows-what poison into their grandmother's ears. Alexandra wanted the company for herself. The terrible part was that now she would probably get it. What had happened this afternoon was bad enough, but the thought of Alexandra gaining control was unbearable. *I can't let that happen*, Eve thought. *I'll find a way to stop her*. She closed the snaps on her suitcase and went to find her sister.

Alexandra was in the garden reading. She looked up as Eve approached.

'Alex, I've decided to go back to New York.'

Alexandra looked at her sister in surprise. '*Now*? Gran's planning a cruise to the Dalmatian coast next week. You –'

'Who cares about the Dalmatian coast? I've been thinking a lot about this. It's time I had my own apartment.' She smiled. 'I'm a big girl now. So I'm going to find the most divine little apartment, and if you're good, I'll let you spend the night once in a while.' *That's just the right note*, Eve thought. *Friendly, but not gushy. Don't let her know you're on to her*.

Alexandra was studying her sister with concern. 'Does Gran know?'

'I told her this afternoon. She hates the idea, of course, but she understands. I wanted to get a job, but she insisted on giving me an allowance.'

Alexandra asked, 'Would you like me to come with you?'

The goddamned, two-faced bitch! First she forced her out of the house, and now she was pretending she wanted to go with her. *Well, they're not going to dispose of little Eve so easily. I'll show them all.* She would have her own apartment – she would find some fabulous decorator to do it – and she would have complete freedom to come and go as she pleased. She could invite men up to her place and have them spend the night. She would be truly free for the first time in her life. It was an exhilarating thought.

Now she said, 'You're sweet, Alex, but I'd like to be on my own for a while.'

Alexandra looked at her sister and felt a deep sense of loss. It would be the first time they had ever been parted. 'We'll see each other often, won't we?'

'Of course we will,' Eve promised. 'More than you imagine.'

TWENTY-SIX

When Eve returned to New York, she checked into a midtown hotel, as she had been instructed. An hour later, Brad Rogers telephoned.

'Your grandmother called from Paris, Eve. Apparently there's some problem between you two.'

'Not really,' Eve laughed. 'It's just a little family –' She was about to launch into an elaborate defence when she suddenly realized the danger that lay in that direction. From now on, she would have to be very careful. She had never had to think about money. It had always been there. Now it loomed large in her thoughts. She had no idea how large her allowance was going to be and for the first time in her life Eve felt fear.

'She told you she's having a new will drawn up?' Brad asked.

'Yes, she mentioned something about it.' She was determined to play it cool.

'I think we had better discuss this in person. How's Monday at three?'

'That will be fine, Brad.'

'My office. All right?'

'I'll be there.'

At five minutes before three, Eve entered the Kruger-Brent, Ltd., building. She was greeted deferentially by the security guard, the elevator starter and even the elevator operator. *Everyone knows me*, Eve thought. *I'm a Blackwell.* The elevator took her to the executive floor, and a few moments later Eve was seated in Brad Roger's office.

Brad had been surprised when Kate telephoned him to say she was going to disinherit Eve, for he knew how much Kate cared about this particular granddaughter and what plans she had for her. Brad could not imagine what had happened. Well, it was none of his business. If Kate wanted to discuss it with him, she would. His job was to carry out her orders. He felt a momentary flash of pity for the lovely young woman before him. Kate had not been much older when he had first met her. Neither had he. And now he was a grey-haired old fool, still hoping that one day Kate Blackwell would realize there was someone who loved her very deeply.

He said to Eve, 'I have some papers for you to sign. If you'll just read them over and –'

'That won't be necessary.'

'Eve, it's important that you understand.' He began to explain. 'Under your grandmother's will, you're the beneficiary of an irrevocable trust fund currently in excess of five million dollars. Your grandmother is the executor. At her discretion, the money can be paid to you at any time from the age of twenty-one to thirty-five.' He cleared his throat. 'She has elected to give it to you when you reach age thirty-five.'

It was a slap in the face.

'Beginning today, you will receive a weekly allowance of two hundred fifty dollars.'

It was impossible! One decent dress cost more than that. There was no way she could live on $250 a week. This was being done to humiliate her. This bastard was probably in on it with her grandmother. He was sitting behind his big desk, enjoying himself, laughing. She wanted to pick up the large bronze paperweight in front of him and smash his head in. She could almost feel the crunch of bone under her hand.

Brad droned on. 'You are not to have any charge accounts, private or otherwise, and you are not to use the Blackwell name at any stores. Anything you purchase must be paid for in cash.'

The nightmare was getting worse and worse.

'Next. If there is any gossip connected with your name in any newspaper or magazine – local or foreign – your weekly income will be stopped. Is that clear?'

'Yes!' Her voice was a whisper.

'You and your sister Alexandra were issued insurance policies on your grandmother's life for five million dollars apiece. The policy you hold was cancelled as of this morning. At the end of one year,' Brad went on, 'if your grandmother is satisfied with your behaviour, your weekly allowance will be doubled.' He hesitated. 'There is one final stipulation.'

She wants to hang me in public by my thumbs. 'Yes?'

Brad Rogers looked uncomfortable. 'Your grandmother does not wish ever to see you again, Eve.'

Well, I want to see you one more time, old woman. I want to see you dying in agony.

Brad's voice trickled through to the cauldron of Eve's mind. 'If you have any problems, you are to telephone me. She does not want you to come to this building again, or to visit any of the family estates.'

He had tried to argue with Kate about that. 'My God, Kate, she's your granddaughter, your flesh and blood. You're treating her like a leper.'

'She *is* a leper.'

And the discussion had ended.

Now Brad said awkwardly, 'Well, I think that covers everything. Are there any questions, Eve?'

'No.' She was in shock.

'Then if you'll just sign these papers . . .'

Ten minutes later, Eve was on the street again. There was a cheque for $250 in her purse.

The following morning Eve called on a real-estate agent and began looking for an apartment. In her fantasies, she had envisioned a beautiful penthouse overlooking Central Park, the rooms done in white with modern furniture, and a terrace where she could entertain guests. Reality came as a stunning blow. It seemed there were no Park Avenue penthouses available for someone with an income of $250 a week. What *was* available was a one-room studio apartment in Little Italy with a couch that became a bed, a nook that the real-estate agent euphemistically referred to as the 'library,' a small kitchenette and a tiny bathroom with stained tile.

'Is – is this the best you have?' Eve asked.

'No,' the agent informed her. 'I've got a twenty-room townhouse on Sutton Place for a half a million dollars, plus maintenance.'

You bastard! Eve thought.

Real despair did not hit Eve until the following afternoon when she moved in. It was a prison. Her dressing room at home had been as large as this entire apartment. She thought of Alexandra enjoying herself in the huge house on Fifth Avenue. *My God, why couldn't Alexandra have burned to death? It had been so close!* If she had died and Eve had been the only heiress, things would have been different. Her grandmother would not have dared disinherit her.

But if Kate Blackwell thought that Eve intended to give up her heritage that easily, she did not know her granddaughter. Eve had no intention of trying to live on $250 a week. There was five million dollars that belonged to her, sitting in a bank, and that vicious old woman was keeping it from her. *There has to be a way to get my hands on that money. I will find it.*

The solution came the following day.

'And what can I do for you, Miss Blackwell?' Alvin Seagram asked deferentially. He was vice-president of the National Union Bank, and he was, in fact, prepared to do almost anything. What kind Fates had brought this young woman to him? If he could secure the Kruger-Brent account, or any part of it, his career would rise like a rocket.

'There's some money in trust for me,' Eve explained. 'Five million dollars. Because of the rules of the trust, it won't come to me until I'm thirty-five years old.' She smiled ingenuously. 'That seems so long from now.'

'At your age, I'm sure it does,' the banker smiled. 'You're – nineteen?'

'Twenty-one.'

'And beautiful, if you'll permit me to say so, Miss Blackwell.'

Eve smiled demurely. 'Thank you, Mr Seagram.' It was going to be simpler than she thought. *The man's an idiot.*

He could feel the rapport between them. *She likes me.* 'How exactly may we help you?'

'Well, I was wondering if it would be possible to borrow an advance on my trust fund. You see, I need the money now more than I'll need it later.

I'm engaged to be married. My fiancé is a construction engineer working in Israel, and he won't be back in this country for another three years.'

Alvin Seagram was all sympathy. 'I understand perfectly.' His heart was pounding wildly. *Of course, he could grant her request.* Money was advanced against trust funds all the time. And when he had satisfied her, she would send him other members of the Blackwell family, and he would satisfy them. Oh, how he would satisfy them! After that, there would be no stopping him. He would be made a member of the executive board of National Union. Perhaps one day its chairman. And he owed all this to the delicious little blonde seated across the desk.

'No problem at all,' Alvin Seagram assured Eve. 'It's a very simple transaction. You understand that we could not loan you the entire amount, but we could certainly let you have, say, a million immediately. Would that be satisfactory?'

'Perfectly,' Eve said, trying not to show her exhilaration.

'Fine. If you'll just give me the details of the trust . . .' He picked up a pen.

'You can get in touch with Brad Rogers at Kruger-Brent. He'll give you all the information you need.'

'I'll give him a call right away.'

Eve rose. 'How long will it take?'

'No more than a day or two. I'll rush it through personally.'

She held out a lovely, delicate hand. 'You're very kind.'

The moment Eve was out of the office, Alvin Seagram picked up the telephone. 'Get me Mr Brad Rogers at Kruger-Brent, Limited.' The very name sent a delicious shiver up his spine.

Two days later Eve returned to the bank and was ushered into Alvin Seagram's office. His first words were, 'I'm afraid I can't help you, Miss Blackwell.'

Eve could not believe what she was hearing. 'I don't understand. You said it was simple. You said –'

'I'm sorry. I was not in possession of all the facts.'

How vividly he recalled the conversation with Brad Rogers. 'Yes, there is a five-million-dollar trust fund in Eve Blackwell's name. Your bank is perfectly free to advance any amount of money you wish against it. However, I think it only fair to caution you that Kate Blackwell would consider it an unfriendly act.'

There was no need for Brad Rogers to spell out what the consequences could be. Kruger-Brent had powerful friends everywhere. And if those friends started pulling money out of National Union, Alvin Seagram did not have to guess what it would do to his career.

'I'm sorry,' he repeated to Eve. 'There's nothing I can do.'

Eve looked at him, frustrated. But she would not let this man know what a blow he had dealt her. 'Thank you for your trouble. There are other banks in New York. Good day.'

'Miss Blackwell,' Alvin Seagram told her, 'there isn't a bank in the world that will loan you one penny against that trust.'

Alexandra was puzzled. In the past, her grand-mother had made it obvious in a hundred ways that she favoured Eve. Now, overnight everything had changed. She knew something terrible had happened between Kate and Eve, but she had no idea what it could have been.

Whenever Alexandra tried to bring up the subject, her grandmother would say, 'There is noth-ing to discuss. Eve chose her own life.'

Nor could Alexandra get anything out of Eve.

Kate Blackwell began spending a great deal of time with Alexandra. Alexandra was intrigued. She was not merely in her grandmother's presence, she was becoming an actual part of her life. It was as though her grandmother were seeing her for the first time. Alexandra had an odd feeling she was being evaluated.

Kate *was* seeing her granddaughter for the first time, and because she had been bitterly deceived once, she was double careful in forming an opinion about Eve's twin. She spent every possible moment with Alexandra, and she probed and questioned and listened. And in the end she was satisfied.

It was not easy to know Alexandra. She was a private person, more reserved than Eve. Alexandra had a quick, lively intelligence, and her innocence, combined with her beauty, made her all the more endearing. She had always received countless invitations to parties and dinners and the theatre, but now it was Kate who decided which invitations Alexandra should accept and which ones she should refuse. The fact that a suitor was eligible was not enough – not nearly enough. What Kate was looking for was a man capable of helping Alexandra run Kate's dynasty. She said nothing of this to Alexandra. There would be time enough for that when Kate found the right man for her granddaughter. Sometimes, in the lonely early-morning hours when Kate had trouble sleeping, she thought about Eve.

Eve was doing beautifully. The episode with her grandmother had bruised her ego so badly that for a short time she had forgotten something very important: she had forgotten how attractive she was to men. At the first party she was invited to after she moved into her own apartment, she gave her telephone number to six men – four of them married – and within twenty-four hours she had heard from all six of them. From that day on, Eve knew she would no longer have to worry about money. She was showered with gifts: expensive jewellery, paints and, more often, cash.

'I've just ordered a new credenza, and my

allowance cheque hasn't come. Would you mind, darling?'

And they never minded.

When Eve went out in public, she made sure she was escorted by men who were single. Married men she saw afternoons at her apartment. Eve was very discreet. She was careful to see that her name was kept out of gossip columns, not because she was any longer concerned about her allowance being stopped, but because she was determined that one day her grandmother was going to come crawling to her. Kate Blackwell needed an heir to take over Kruger-Brent. *Alexandra is not equipped to be anything but a stupid housewife*, Eve gloated.

One afternoon, leafing through a new issue of *Town and Country*, Eve came across a photograph of Alexandra dancing with an attractive man. Eve was not looking at Alexandra, she was looking at the man. And realizing that if Alexandra married and had a son, it would be a disaster for Eve and her plans.

She stared at the picture a long time.

Over a period of a year, Alexandra had called Eve regularly, for lunch or dinner, and Eve had always put her off with excuses. Now Eve decided it was time to have a talk with her sister. She invited Alexandra to her apartment.

Alexandra had not seen the apartment before, and Eve braced herself for pity. But all Alexandra said was, 'It's charming, Eve. It's very cosy, isn't it?'

Eve smiled. 'It suits me. I wanted something *intime*.' She had pawned enough jewellery and paintings so that she could have moved into a beautiful apartment, but Kate would have learned of it and would have demanded to know where the money had come from. For the moment, the watchword was *discretion*.

'How is Gran?' Eve asked.

'She's fine.' Alexandra hesitated. 'Eve, I don't know what happened between you two, but you know if there's anything I can do to help, I'll –'

Eve sighed. 'She didn't tell you?'

'No. She won't discuss it.'

'I don't blame her. The poor dear probably feels as guilty as hell. I met a wonderful young doctor. We were going to be married. We went to bed together. Gran found out about it. She told me to get out of the house, that she never wanted to see me again. I'm afraid our grandmother is very old-fashioned, Alex.'

She watched the look of dismay on Alexandra's face. 'That's terrible! The two of you must go to Gran. I'm sure she would –'

'He was killed in an airplane accident.'

'Oh, Eve! Why didn't you tell me this before?'

'I was too ashamed to tell anyone, even you.' She squeezed her sister's hand. 'And you know I tell you everything.'

'Let me talk to Gran. I'll explain –'

'No! I have too much pride. Promise me you'll never discuss this with her. Ever!'

'But I'm sure she would –'

'Promise!'

Alexandra sighed. 'All right.'

'Believe me, I'm very happy here. I come and go as I please. It's great!'

Alexandra looked at her sister and thought how much she had missed Eve.

Eve put her arm around Alexandra and began to tease. 'Now, enough about me. Tell me what's going on in your life. Have you met Prince Charming yet? I'll bet you have!'

'No.'

Eve studied her sister. It was a mirror image of herself, and she was determined to destroy it. 'You will, darling.'

'I'm in no hurry. I decided it's time I started earning a living. I talked to Gran about it. Next week I'm going to meet with the head of an advertising agency about a job.'

They had lunch at a little bistro near Eve's apartment, and Eve insisted on paying. She wanted nothing from her sister.

When they were bidding each other good-bye, Alexandra said, 'Eve, if you need any money –'

'Don't be silly, darling. I have more than enough.'

Alexandra persisted. 'Still, if you run short, you can have anything I've got.'

Eve looked into Alexandra's eyes and said, 'I'm counting on that.' She smiled. 'But I really don't need a thing, Alex.' She did not need crumbs. She intended to have the whole cake. The question was: How was she going to get it?

There was a weekend party in Nassau.

'It wouldn't be the same without you, Eve. All your friends will be here.'

The caller was Nita Ludwig, a girl whom Eve had known at school in Switzerland.

She would meet some new men. The present crop was tiresome.

'It sounds like fun,' Eve said. 'I'll be there.'

That afternoon she pawned an emerald bracelet she had been given a week earlier by an infatuated insurance executive with a wife and three children, and bought some new summer outfits at Lord & Taylor and a round-trip ticket to Nassau. She was on the plane the following morning.

The Ludwig estate was a large, sprawling mansion on the beach. The main house had thirty rooms, and the smallest was larger than Eve's entire apartment. Eve was escorted to her room by a uniformed maid, who unpacked for her while Eve freshened up. Then she went down to meet her fellow guests.

There were sixteen people in the drawing room, and they had one thing in common: they were wealthy. Nita Ludwig was a firm believer in the 'birds of a feather' philosophy. These people felt the same way about the same things; they were comfortable with one another because they spoke the same language. They shared the commonality of the best boarding schools and colleges, luxurious estates, yachts, private jets and tax problems. A columnist had dubbed them the 'jet set', an appellation they derided publicly and enjoyed privately. They were the privileged, the chosen few, set apart from all others by a discriminating god. Let the rest of the world believe that money could not buy everything. These people knew better. Money bought them beauty and love and luxury and a place in heaven. And it was from all this that Eve had been excluded by the whim of a narrow-minded old lady. *But not for long*, Eve thought.

She entered the drawing room and the conversation dropped as Eve walked in. In a room full of beautiful women, she was the most beautiful of all. Nita took Eve around to greet her friends, and to introduce her to the people she did not know. Eve was charming and pleasant, and she studied each man with a knowing eye, expertly selecting her targets. Most of the older men were married, but that only made it easier.

A bald-headed man dressed in plaid slacks and Hawaiian sport shirt came up to her. 'I'll bet you get tired of people telling you you're beautiful, honey.'

Eve rewarded him with a warm smile. 'I never get tired of that, Mr –?'

'Peterson. Call me Dan. You should be a Hollywood star.'

'I'm afraid I have no talent for acting.'

'I'll bet you've got a lot of other talents, though.'

Eve smiled enigmatically. 'You never know until you try, do you, Dan?'

He wet his lips. 'You down here alone?'

'Yes.'

'I've got my yacht anchored in the bay. Maybe you and I could take a little cruise tomorrow?'

'That sounds lovely,' Eve said.

He grinned. 'I don't know why we've never met before. I've known your grandmother, Kate, for years.'

The smile stayed on Eve's face, but it took a great effort. 'Gran's a darling,' Eve said. 'I think we'd better join the others.'

'Sure, honey.' He winked. 'Remember tomorrow.'

From that moment on, he was unable to get Eve alone again. She avoided him at lunch, and after lunch she borrowed one of the automobiles kept in the garage for guests and drove into town. She drove past Blackbeard's Tower and the lovely Ardastra Gardens where the colourful flamingos were on parade. She stopped at the waterfront to watch the fishing boats unload their catch of giant turtles, enormous lobsters, tropical fish and a brilliantly coloured variety of conch shells, which would be polished and sold to the tourists.

The bay was smooth, and the sea sparkled like diamonds. Across the water Eve could see the crescent curve of Paradise Island Beach. A motorboat was leaving the dock at the beach, and as it picked up speed, the figure of a man suddenly rose into the sky, trailing behind the boat. It was a startling sight. He appeared to be hanging on to a metal bar fastened to a blue sail, his long, lean body stretched against the wind. *Para-sailing.* Eve watched, fascinated, as the motorboat roared towards the harbour, and the airborne figure swept closer. The boat approached the dock and made a sharp turn, and for an instant Eve caught a glimpse of the dark, handsome face of the man in the air, and then he was gone.

He walked into Nita Ludwig's drawing room five hours later, and Eve felt as though she had willed him there. She had known he would appear. Up close he was even more handsome. He was six foot three, with perfectly sculptured, tanned features, black eyes and a trim, athletic body. When he smiled, he revealed white, even teeth. He smiled down at Eve as Nita introduced him.

'This is George Mellis. Eve Blackwell.'

'My God, you belong in the Louvre,' George Mellis said. His voice was deep and husky, with the trace of an indefinable accent.

'Come along, darling,' Nita commanded. 'I'll introduce you to the other guests.'

He waved her away. 'Don't bother. I just met everybody.'

Nita looked at the two of them thoughtfully. 'I see. Well, if I can do anything, call me.' She walked away.

'Weren't you a little rude to her?' Eve asked.

He grinned. 'I'm not responsible for what I say or do. I'm in love.'

Eve laughed.

'I mean it. You're the most beautiful thing I've ever seen in my life.'

'I was thinking the same about you.'

Eve did not care whether this man had money or not. She was fascinated by him. It was more than his looks. There was a magnetism, a sense of power that excited her. No man had ever affected her this way before. 'Who are you?' Eve asked.

'Nita told you. George Mellis.'

'Who are you?' she repeated.

'Ah, you mean in the philosophical sense. The *real* me. Nothing colourful to tell, I'm afraid. I'm Greek. My family grows olives and other things.'

That Mellis! The Mellis food brands could be found in every corner grocery store and supermarket in America.

'Are you married?' Eve asked.

He grinned. 'Are you always this direct?'

'No.'

'I'm not married.'

The answer gave her an unexpected feeling of pleasure. Just looking at him made Eve want to possess him, to be possessed.

'Why did you miss dinner?'

'The truth?'

'Yes.'

'It's very personal.'

She waited.

'I was busy persuading a young lady not to commit suicide.' He said it matter-of-factly, as though it were a common occurrence.

'I hope you succeeded.'

'For now. I hope you're not the suicidal type.'

'No. I hope *you're* not.'

George Mellis laughed aloud. 'I love you,' he said. 'I really love you.' He took Eve's arm, and his touch made her shiver.

He stayed at Eve's side all evening, and he was totally attentive to her, oblivious to everyone else. He had long, delicate hands, and they were constantly doing things for Eve: bringing her a drink, lighting her cigarette, touching her discreetly. His nearness set her body afire, and she could not wait to be alone with him.

Just after midnight when the guests began to retire to their rooms, George Mellis asked, 'Which is your bedroom?'

'At the end of the north hall.'

He nodded, his long-lashed eyes boring into hers.

Eve undressed and bathed and put on a new sheer, black negligee that clung to her figure. At one a.m. there was a discreet tap on the door. She hurried to open it, and George Mellis stepped in.

He stood there, his eyes filled with admiration. '*Matia mou*, you make the *Venus de Milo* look like a hag.'

'I have an advantage over her,' Eve whispered. 'I have two arms.'

And she put both arms around George Mellis and drew him to her. His kiss made something explode inside her. His lips pressed hard against hers, and she felt his tonque exploring her mouth.

'Oh, my God!' Eve moaned.

He started to strip off his jacket, and she helped him. In a moment he was free of his trousers and French shorts, and he was naked before her. He had the most glorious physique Eve had ever seen. He was hard and erect.

'Quick,' Eve said. 'Make love to me.' She moved onto the bed, her body on fire.

He commanded, 'Turn over. Give me your ass.'

She looked up at him. 'I – I don't –'

And he hit her on the mouth. She stared up at him in shock.

'Turn over.'

'No.'

He hit her again, harder, and the room began to swim in front of her.

'Please, no.'

He hit her again, savagely. She felt his powerful hands turning her over, pulling her up on her knees.

'For God's sake,' she gasped, 'stop it! I'll scream.'

He smashed his arm across the back of her neck, and Eve started to lose consciousness. Dimly, she felt him raise her hips higher into the air. He pulled her cheeks apart, and his body pressed against hers.

There was a sudden, excruciating pain as he plunged deep inside her. She opened her mouth to scream, but she stopped in terror of what he might do to her.

She begged, 'Oh, please, you're hurting me . . .'

She tried to pull away from him, but he was holding her hips tightly, plunging into her again and again, tearing her apart with his enormous penis. The pain was unbearable.

'Oh, God, no!' she whispered. 'Stop it! Please stop it!'

He kept moving in, deeper and faster, and the last thing Eve remembered was a wild groan that came from deep inside him and seemed to explode in her ears.

When she regained consciousness and opened her eyes, George Mellis was sitting in a chair, fully dressed, smoking a cigarette. He moved over to the bed and stroked her forehead. She cringed from his touch.

'How do you feel, darling?'

Eve tried to sit up, but the pain was too great. She felt as though she had been ripped apart. 'You goddamned animal . . .' Her voice was a ragged whisper.

He laughed. 'I was gentle with you.'

She looked at him in disbelief.

He smiled. 'I can sometimes be very rough.' He stroked her hair again. 'But I love you, so I was kind. You'll get used to it, *Hree-se'e-moo*. I promise you.'

If she had had a weapon at that moment, Eve would have killed him. 'You're insane!'

She saw the gleam that came into his eyes, and she saw his hand clench into a fist, and in that instant she knew stark terror. He *was* insane.

She said quickly, 'I didn't mean it. It's just that I – I've never experienced anything like that before. Please, I'd like to go to sleep now. Please.'

George Mellis stared at her for a long moment, and then relaxed. He rose and walked over to the dressing table where Eve had put her jewellery. There was a platinum bracelet and an expensive diamond necklace lying there. He scooped up the necklace, examined it and slipped it into his pocket. 'I'll keep this as a little souvenir.'

She was afraid to open her mouth to protest.

'Good night, darling.' And he walked back to the bed, leaned over and gently kissed Eve's lips.

She waited until he had gone, and then crawled out of bed, her body burning with pain. Every step was an agony. It was not until she had locked the bedroom door that she felt safe again. She was not sure she would be able to make it to the bathroom, and she fell back onto the bed, waiting for the pain to recede. She couldn't believe the enormity of the rage she felt. He had sodomized her – horribly and brutally. She wondered what he had done to that other girl who had wanted to commit suicide.

When Eve finally dragged herself into the bathroom and looked in the mirror, she was aghast.

Her face was bruised and discoloured where he had hit her, and one eye was almost swollen shut. She ran a hot bath and crawled into it like a wounded animal, letting the soothing water wash away the pain. Eve lay there for a long time, and, finally, when the water was starting to cool, she got out of the tub and took a few tentative steps. The pain had lessened, but it was still agonizing. She lay awake for the rest of the night, terrified that he might return.

When Eve arose at dawn, she saw that the sheets were stained with her blood. She was going to make him pay for that. She walked into the bathroom, moving carefully, and ran another hot bath. Her face was even more swollen and the bruises were livid. She dipped a washcloth into cold water and applied it to her cheek and eye. Then she lay in the tub, thinking about George Mellis. There was something puzzling about his behaviour that had nothing to do with his sadism. And she suddenly realized what it was. The necklace. Why had he taken it?

Two hours later, Eve went downstairs to join the other guests for breakfast, even though she had no appetite. She badly needed to talk to Nita Ludwig.

'My God! What happened to your face?' Nita asked.

Eve smiled ruefully. 'The silliest thing. I got up in the middle of the night to go to the loo, and I didn't bother turning on the light. I walked right into one of your fancy doors.'

'Would you like to have a doctor look at that?'

'It's nothing,' Eve assured her. 'It's just a little bruise.' Eve looked around. 'Where's George Mellis?'

'He's out playing tennis. He's one of the top-seeded players. He said to tell you he'll see you at lunch. I think he really likes you, darling.'

'Tell me about him,' Eve said casually. 'What's his background?'

'George? He comes from a long line of wealthy Greeks. He's the oldest son, and he's filthy rich. He works at a New York brokerage firm, Hanson and Hanson.'

'He's not in the family business?'

'No. He probably hates olives. Anyway, with the Mellis fortune, he doesn't have to work. I suppose he does it just to occupy his days.' She grinned and said, 'His nights are full enough.'

'Are they?'

'Darling, George Mellis is the most eligible bachelor around. The girls can't wait to pull their little panties down for him. They all see themselves as the future Mrs Mellis. Frankly, if my husband weren't so damned jealous, I'd go for George myself. Isn't he a gorgeous hunk of animal?'

'Gorgeous,' Eve said.

George Mellis walked onto the terrace where Eve was seated alone, and in spite of herself, she felt a stab of fear.

He walked up to her and said, 'Good morning, Eve. Are you all right?' His face was filled with genuine concern. He touched her bruised cheek gently. 'My darling, you are so beautiful.' He pulled up a chair and straddled it, sitting across from her, and gestured towards the sparkling sea. 'Have you ever seen anything so lovely?'

It was as though the previous night had never happened. She listened to George Mellis as he went on talking, and she felt once again the powerful magnetism of the man. Even after the nightmare she had experienced, she could still feel that. It was incredible. *He looks like a Greek god. He belongs in a museum. He belongs in an insane asylum.*

'I have to return to New York tonight,' George Mellis was saying. 'Where can I call you?'

'I just moved,' Eve said quickly. 'I don't have a telephone yet. Let me call you.'

'All right, my darling.' He grinned. 'You really enjoyed last night, didn't you?'

Eve could not believe her ears.

'I have many things to teach you, Eve,' he whispered.

And I have something to teach you, Mr Mellis, Eve promised herself.

The moment she returned home, Eve telephoned Dorothy Hollister. In New York, where an insatiable segment of the media covered the comings and goings of the so-called beautiful people, Dorothy was the fountainhead of information. She had been married to a socialite, and when he divorced her for his twenty-one-year-old secretary, Dorothy Hollister was forced to go to work. She took a job that suited her talents well: she became a gossip columnist. Because she knew everyone in the milieu she was writing about, and because they believed she could be trusted, few people kept any secrets from her.

If anyone could tell Eve about George Mellis, it would be Dorothy Hollister. Eve invited her to lunch at La Pyramide. Hollister was a heavyset woman with a fleshy face, dyed red hair, a loud, raucous voice and a braying laugh. She was loaded down with jewellery – all fake.

When they had ordered, Eve said casually, 'I was in the Bahamas last week. It was lovely there.'

'I know you were,' Dorothy Hollister said. 'I have Nita Ludwig's guest list. Was it a fun party?'

Eve shrugged. 'I saw a lot of old friends. I met an interesting man named' – she paused, her brow wrinkled in thought – 'George somebody. Miller, I think. A Greek.'

Dorothy Hollister laughed, a loud, booming laugh that could be heard across the room. 'Mellis, dear. George Mellis.'

'That's right. Mellis. Do you know him?'

'I've seen him. I thought I was going to turn into a pillar of salt. My God, he's fantastic looking.'

'What's his background, Dorothy?'

Dorothy Hollister looked around, then leaned forwards confidentially. 'No one know this, but you'll keep it to yourself, won't you? George is the black sheep of the family. His family is in the wholesale food business, and they're too rich for words, my dear. George was supposed to take over the business, but he got in so many scrapes over there with girls and boys and goats, for all I know, that his father and his brothers finally got fed up and shipped him out of the country.'

Eve was absorbing every word.

'They cut the poor boy off without a drachma, so he had to go to work to support himself.'

So that explained the necklace!

'Of course, he doesn't have to worry. One of these days George will marry rich.' She looked over at Eve and asked, 'Are you interested, sweetie?'

'Not really.'

Eve was more than interested. George Mellis might be the key she had been looking for. The key to her fortune.

Early the next morning, she telephoned him at the brokerage firm where he worked. He recognized her voice immediately.

'I've been going mad waiting for your call, Eve. We'll have dinner tonight and –'

'No. Lunch, tomorrow.'

He hesitated, surprised. 'All right. I was supposed to have lunch with a customer, but I'll put him off.'

Eve did not believe it was a *him*. 'Come to my apartment,' Eve said. She gave him the address. 'I'll see you at twelve-thirty.'

'I'll be there.' She could hear the smug satisfaction in his voice.

George Mellis was due for a surprise.

He arrived thirty minutes late, and Eve realized it was a pattern with him. It was not a deliberate rudeness, it was an indifference, the knowledge that people would always wait for him. His pleasures would be there for him whenever he bothered to reach out and take them. With his incredible looks and charm, the world belonged to him. Except for one thing: he was poor. That was his vulnerable point.

George looked around the little apartment, expertly appraising the value of its contents. 'Very pleasant.'

He moved towards Eve, his arms outstretched. 'I've thought about you every minute.'

She evaded his embrace. 'Wait. I have something to tell you, George.'

His black eyes bored into hers. 'We'll talk later.'

'We'll talk now.' She spoke slowly and distinctly. 'If you ever touch me like that again, I'm going to kill you.'

He looked at her, his lips curved in a half smile. 'What kind of joke is that?'

'It's not a joke. I mean it. I have a business proposition for you.'

There was a puzzled expression on his face. 'You called me here to discuss business?'

'Yes. I don't know how much you make conning

silly old ladies into buying stocks and bonds, but I'm sure it's not enough.'

His face went dark with anger. 'Are you crazy? My family –'

'Your family is rich – you're not. My family is rich – *I'm* not. We're both in the same leaky rowboat, darling. I know a way we can turn it into a yacht.' She stood there, watching his curiosity get the better of his anger.

'You'd better tell me what you're talking about.'

'It's quite simple. I've been disinherited from a very large fortune. My sister Alexandra hasn't.'

'What does that have to do with me?'

'If you married Alexandra, that fortune would be yours – ours.'

'Sorry. I could never stand the idea of being tied down to anyone.'

'As it happens,' Eve assured him, 'that's no problem. My sister has always been accident-prone.'

TWENTY-SEVEN

Berkley and Matthews Advertising Agency was the diadem in Madison Avenue's roster of agencies. Its annual billings exceeded the combined billing of its two nearest competitors, chiefly because its major account was Kruger-Brent, Ltd., and its dozens of worldwide subsidiaries. More than seventy-five account executives, copywriters, creative directors, photographers, engravers, artists and media experts were employed on the Kruger-Brent account alone. It came as no surprise, therefore, that when Kate Blackwell telephoned Aaron Berkley to ask him if he could find a position in his agency for Alexandra, a place was found for her instantly. If Kate Blackwell had desired it, they would probably have made Alexandra president of the agency.

'I believe my granddaughter is interested in being a copywriter,' Kate informed Aaron Berkley.

Berkley assured Kate that there just happened

to be a copywriter vacancy, and that Alexandra could start any time she wished.

She went to work the following Monday.

Few Madison Avenue advertising agencies are actually located on Madison Avenue, but Berkley and Matthews was an exception. The agency owned a large, modern building at the corner of Madison and Fifty-seventh Street. The agency occupied eight floors of the building and leased the other floors. In order to save a salary, Aaron Berkley and his partner, Norman Matthews, decided Alexandra Blackwell would replace a young copywriter hired six months earlier. The word spread rapidly. When the staff learned the young woman who was fired was being replaced by the granddaughter of the agency's biggest client, there was general indignation. Without even having met Alexandra, the consensus was that she was a spoiled bitch who had probably been sent there to spy on them.

When Alexandra reported for work, she was escorted to the huge, modern office of Aaron Berkley, where both Berkley and Matthews waited to greet her. The two partners looked nothing alike. Berkley was tall and thin, with a full head of white hair, and Matthews was short, tubby and completely bald. They had two things in common: they were brilliant advertising men who had created some of the most famous slogans of the past decade; and they were absolute tyrants. They treated their employees like chattels, and the only reason the employees stood for such treatment was that anyone who had worked for Berkley and Matthews could work at any advertising agency in the world. It was *the* training ground.

Also present in the office when Alexandra arrived was Lucas Pinkerton, a vice-president of the firm, a smiling man with an obsequious manner and cold eyes. Pinkerton was younger than the senior partners, but what he lacked in age, he made up for in vindictiveness towards the men and women who worked under him.

Aaron Berkley ushered Alexandra to a comfortable armchair. 'What can I get you, Miss Blackwell? Would you like some coffee, tea?'

'Nothing, thank you.'

'So. You're going to work with us here as a copywriter.'

'I really appreciate your giving me this opportunity, Mr Berkley. I know I have a great deal to learn, but I'll work very hard.'

'No need for that,' Norman Matthews said quickly. He caught himself. 'I mean – you can't rush a learning experience like this. You take all the time you want.'

'I'm sure you'll be very happy here,' Aaron Berkley added. 'You'll be working with the best people in the business.'

One hour later, Alexandra was thinking. *They may be the best, but they're certainly not the friendliest.* Lucas Pinkerton had taken Alexandra around to introduce her to the staff, and the reception everywhere had been icy. They acknowledged her presence and then quickly found other things to do. Alexandra sensed their resentment, but she had no idea what had caused it. Pinkerton led her into a smoke-filled conference room. Against one wall was a cabinet filled with Clios and Art Directors' awards. Seated around a table were a woman and two men, all of them chain-smoking. The woman was short and dumpy, with rust-coloured hair. The men were in their middle thirties, pale and harassed-looking.

Pinkerton said, 'This is the creative team you'll be working with. Alice Koppel, Vince Barnes and Marty Bergheimer. This is Miss Blackwell.'

The three of them stared at Alexandra.

'Well, I'll leave you to get acquainted with one another,' Pinkerton said. He turned to Vince Barnes. 'I'll expect the new perfume copy on my desk by tomorrow morning. See that Miss Blackwell has everything she needs.' And he left.

'What do you need?' Vince Barnes asked.

The question caught Alexandra off guard. 'I – I guess I just need to learn the advertising business.'

Alice Koppel said sweetly, 'You've come to the right place, Miss Blackwell. We're dying to play teacher.'

'Lay off,' Marty Bergheimer told her.

Alexandra was puzzled. 'Have I done something to offend any of you?'

507

Marty Bergheimer replied, 'No, Miss Blackwell. We're just under a lot of pressure here. We're working on a perfume campaign, and so far Mr Berkley and Mr Matthews are underwhelmed by what we've delivered.

'I'll try not to be a bother,' Alexandra promised.

'That would be peachy,' Alice Koppel said.

The rest of the day went no better. There was not a smile in the place. One of their co-workers had been summarily fired because of this rich bitch, and they were going to make her pay.

At the end of Alexandra's first day, Aaron Berkley and Norman Mathews came into the little office Alexandra had been assigned, to make sure she was comfortable. The gesture was not lost on Alexandra's fellow workers.

Everyone in the agency was on a first-name basis – except for Alexandra. She was Miss Blackwell to everyone.

'Alexandra,' she said.

'Right.'

And the next time they addressed her, it was 'Miss Blackwell.'

Alexandra was eager to learn and to make a contribution. She attended think-tank meetings where the copywriters brainstormed ideas. She watched art editors draw up their designs. She listened to

Lucas Pinkerton tear apart the copy that was brought to him for approval. He was a nasty, mean-spirited man, and Alexandra felt sorry for the copy-writers who suffered under him. Alexandra found herself shuttling from floor to floor for meetings with department heads, meetings with clients, photographic sessions, strategy discussion meet-ings. She kept her mouth shut, listened and learned. At the end of her first week, she felt as though she had been there a month. She came home exhausted, not from the work but from the tension that her presence seemed to create.

When Kate asked how the job was going, Alexandra replied, 'Fine, Gran. It's very interest-ing.'

'I'm sure you'll do well, Alex. If you have any problems, just see Mr Berkley or Mr Matthews.'

That was the last thing Alexandra intended to do.

On the following Monday Alexandra went to work determined to find a way to solve her problem. There were daily morning and afternoon coffee breaks, and the conversation was easy and casual.

'Did you hear what happened over at National Media? Some genius there wanted to call attention to the great year they had, so he printed their finan-cial report in *The New York Times* in red ink!'

'Remember that airline promotion: *Fly Your Wife Free?* It was a smash until the airline sent letters of appreciation to the wives and got back a flood of mail demanding to know who their husbands had flown with. They –'

Alexandra walked in, and the conversation stopped dead.

'Can I get you some coffee, Miss Blackwell?'

'Thank you, I can get it.'

There was silence while Alexandra fed a quarter into the coffee machine. When she left, the conversation started again.

'Did you hear about the Pure Soap foul-up? The angelic-looking model they used turned out to be a porno star . . .'

At noon Alexandra said to Alice Koppel, 'If you're free for lunch, I thought we might –'

'Sorry. I have a date.'

Alexandra looked at Vince Barnes. 'Me, too,' he said.

She looked at Marty Bergheimer. 'I'm all booked up.'

Alexandra was too upset to eat lunch. They were making her feel as though she were a pariah, and she found herself getting angry. She did not intend to give up. She was going to find a way to reach them, to let them know that deep down under the Blackwell name she was one of *them*. She sat at meetings and listened to Aaron Berkley and Norman Matthews and Lucas Pinkerton tongue-lash the creators who were merely trying to do their jobs as well as they could. Alexandra sympathized, but they did not want her sympathy. Or her.

Alexandra waited three days before trying again. She said to Alice Koppel, 'I heard of a wonderful little Italian restaurant near here –'

'I don't eat Italian food.'

She turned to Vince Barnes. 'I'm on a diet.'

Alexandra looked at Marty Bergheimer. 'I'm going to eat Chinese.'

Alexandra's face was flushed. They did not want to be seen with her. *Well, to hell with them. To hell with all of them.* She had had enough. She had gone out of her way to try to make friends, and each time she had been slapped down. Working there was a mistake. She would find another job somewhere with a company that her grandmother had nothing to do with. She would quit at the end of the week. *But I'm going to make you all remember I was here*, Alexandra thought grimly.

At one p.m. on Thursday, everyone except the receptionist at the switchboard was out to lunch. Alexandra stayed behind. She had observed that in the executive offices there were intercoms connecting the various departments, so that if an executive wanted to talk to an underling, all he had to do was press a button on the talk box where the employee's name was written on a card. Alexandra slipped into the deserted offices of Aaron Berkley and Norman Matthews and Lucas Pinkerton and spent the next hour changing all the cards around. Thus it was that early that afternoon Lucas Pinkerton pressed down the key that connected him to his chief copywriter and said, 'Get your ass in here. Now!'

There was a moment of stunned silence, then Norman Matthews's voice bellowed, 'What did you say?'

Pinkerton stared at the machine, transfixed. 'Mr Matthews, is that you?'

'You're damned right it is. Get *your* fucking ass in *here*. Now!' A minute later, a copywriter pressed down a button on the machine on his desk and said, 'I've got some copy for you to run downstairs.'

Aaron Berkley's voice roared back him. 'You *what*?'

It was the beginning of pandemonium. It took four hours to straighten out the mess that Alexandra had created, and it was the best four hours that the employees of Berkley and Matthews had ever known. Each time a fresh incident occurred, they whooped with joy. The executives were being buzzed to run errands, fetch cigarettes and repair a broken toilet. Aaron Berkley and Norman Matthews and Lucas Pinkerton turned the place upside down trying to find out who the culprit was, but no one knew anything.

The only one who had seen Alexandra go into the various offices was Fran, the woman on the switchboard, but she hated her bosses more than she hated Alexandra, so all she would say was, 'I didn't see a soul.'

That night when Fran was in bed with Vince Barnes, she related what had happened.

He sat up in bed. 'The *Blackwell* girl did it? I'll be a sonofabitch!'

The following morning when Alexandra walked into her office, Vince Barnes, Alice Koppel and Marty Bergheimer were there, waiting. They stared at her in silence. 'Is something wrong?' Alexandra asked.

'Not a thing, Alex,' Alice Koppel said. 'The boys and I were just wondering if you'd like to join us for lunch. We know this great little Italian joint near here . . .'

TWENTY-EIGHT

From the time she was a little girl, Eve Blackwell had been aware of her ability to manipulate people. Before, it had always been a game with her, but now it was deadly serious. She had been treated shabbily, deprived of a vast fortune that was rightfully hers, by her scheming sister and her vindictive old grandmother. They were going to pay in full for what they had done to her, and the thought of it gave Eve such intense pleasure that it almost brought her to orgasm. Their lives were now in her hands.

Eve worked out her plan carefully and meticulously, orchestrating every move. In the beginning, George Mellis had been a reluctant conspirator.

'Christ, it's too dangerous. I don't need to get involved in anything like this,' he argued. 'I can get all the money I need.'

'How?' Eve asked contemptuously. 'By laying a lot of fat women with blue hair? Is that how you want to spend the rest of your life? What happens when you put on a little weight and start to get a few wrinkles around your eyes? No, George, you'll never have another opportunity like this. If you listen to me, you and I can own one of the largest conglomerates in the world. You hear me? *Own* it.'

'How do you know this plan will work?'

'Because I'm the greatest living expert on my grandmother and my sister. Believe me, it will work.'

Eve sounded confident, but she had reservations and they concerned George Mellis. Eve knew she could do her part, but she was not sure George would be able to do his. He was unstable, and there was no room for error. One mistake, and the whole plan would fall apart.

She said to him now, 'Make up your mind. Are you in or out?'

He studied her for a long time. 'I'm in.' He moved close to her and stroked her shoulders. His voice was husky. 'I want to be all the way in.'

Eve felt a sexual thrill go through her. 'All right,' she whispered, 'but we do it my way.'

They were in bed. Naked, he was the most magnificent animal Eve had ever seen. And the most dangerous, but that only added to her excitement. She had the weapon now to control him. She nibbled at his body, slowly moving down towards his groin, tiny, teasing bites that made his penis grow stiff and hard.

'Fuck me, George,' Eve said.

'Turn over.'

'No. My way.'

'I don't enjoy that.'

'I know. You'd like me to be a tight-assed little boy, wouldn't you, darling? I'm not. I'm a woman. Get on top of me.'

He mounted her and put his tumescent penis inside her. 'I can't be satisfied this way, Eve.'

She laughed. 'I don't care, sweetheart. *I* can.'

She began to move her hips, thrusting against him, feeling him going deeper and deeper inside her. She had orgasm after orgasm, and watched his frustration grow. He wanted to hurt her, to make her scream with pain, but he dared not.

'Again!' Eve commanded. And he pounded his body into her until she moaned aloud with pleasure. 'Ahh-h-h . . . that's enough for now.'

He withdrew and lay at her side. He reached for her breasts, 'Now it's my –'

And she said curtly, 'Get dressed.'

He rose from the bed, trembling with frustration and rage. Eve lay in bed watching him put on his clothes, a tight smile on her face. 'You've been a good boy, George. It's time you got your reward. I'm going to turn Alexandra over to you.'

Overnight, everything had changed for Alexandra. What was to have been her last day at Berkley and Matthews had turned into a triumph for her. She had gone from outcast to heroine. News of her caper spread all over Madison Avenue.

'You're a legend in your own time,' Vince Barnes grinned.

Now she was one of them.

Alexandra enjoyed her work, particularly the creative sessions that went on every morning. She knew this was not what she wanted to do for the rest of her life, but she was not sure what she wanted. She had had at least a dozen proposals of marriage, and she had been tempted by one or two of them, but something had been lacking. She simply had not found the right man.

On Friday morning, Eve telephoned to invite Alexandra to lunch. 'There's a new French restaurant that just opened. I hear the food is marvellous.'

Alexandra was delighted to hear from her sister. She was concerned about Eve. Alexandra telephoned her two or three times a week, but Eve was either out or too busy to see her. So now, even though Alexandra had an engagement, she said, 'I'd love to have lunch with you.'

The restaurant was chic and expensive, and the bar was filled with patrons waiting for tables. Eve had had to use her grandmother's name in order to get a reservation. It galled her, and she thought, *Just wait. One day you'll be begging me to eat at your crummy restaurant.* Eve was already seated when Alexandra arrived. She watched Alexandra as the maître d' escorted her to the table, and she had the odd sensation she was watching herself approach the table.

Eve greeted her sister with a kiss on the cheek. 'You look absolutely marvellous, Alex. Work must agree with you.'

They ordered, and then caught up with each other's lives.

'How's the job going?' Eve asked.

Alexandra told Eve everything that was happening to her, and Eve gave Alexandra a carefully edited version of her own life. In the midst of their conversation, Eve glanced up. George Mellis was standing there. He was looking at the two of them, momentarily confused. *My God*, Eve realized, *he doesn't know which one I am!*

'George!' she said.

He turned to her in relief. 'Eve!'

Eve said, 'What a pleasant surprise.' She nodded towards Alexandra. 'I don't believe you've met my sister. Alex, may I present George Mellis.'

George took Alexandra's hand and said, 'Enchanted.' Eve had mentioned that her sister was a twin, but it had not occurred to him that they would be identical twins.

Alexandra was staring at George, fascinated.

Eve said, 'Won't you join us?'

'I wish I could. I'm afraid I'm late for an appointment. Another time, perhaps.' He looked at Alexandra. 'And soon, I hope.'

They watched him leave. 'Good heavens!' Alexandra said. 'Who was *that*?'

'Oh, he's a friend of Nita Ludwig. I met him at her house party.'

'Am I crazy, or is he as stunning as I think he is?'

Eve laughed. 'He's not my type, but women seem to find him attractive.'

'I would think so! Is he married?'

'No. But it's not because they aren't out there trying, darling. George is very rich. You might say he has everything: looks, money, social background.' And Eve skillfully changed the subject.

When Eve asked for the check, the captain told her it had been taken care of by Mr Mellis.

Alexandra was unable to stop thinking about George Mellis.

On Monday afternoon, Eve called Alexandra and said, 'Well, it looks like you made a hit, darling. George Mellis called me and asked for your telephone number. Is it all right to give it to him?'

Alexandra was surprised to find that she was smiling. 'If you're sure *you're* not interested in –'

'I told you, Alex, he's not my type.'

'Then I don't mind if you give him my number.'

They chatted a few minutes more, and Eve hung up. She replaced the receiver and looked up at George, who was lying next to her on the bed, naked. 'The lady said yes.'

'How soon?'

'When I tell you.'

Alexandra tried to forget that George Mellis was
going to telephone her, but the more she tried to
put him out of her mind, the more she thought
about him. She had never been particularly
attracted to handsome men, for she had found that
most of them were self-centred. But George Mellis,
Alexandra thought, seemed different. There was
an overpowering quality about him. The mere
touch of his hand had stirred her. *You're crazy*,
she told herself. *You've only seen the man for two
minutes*.

He did not call all that week, and Alexandra's
emotions went from impatience to frustration to
anger. *To hell with him*, she thought. *He's found
someone else. Good!*

When the phone rang at the end of the following week and Alexandra heard his deep, husky
voice, her anger dissipated as if by magic.

'This is George Mellis,' he said. 'We met briefly
when you and your sister were having lunch. Eve
said you wouldn't mind if I telephoned you.'

'She did mention that you might call,' Alexandra
said casually. 'By the way, thank you for the lunch.'

'You deserve a feast. You deserve a monument.'

Alexandra laughed, enjoying his extravagance.

'I wonder if you would care to have dinner with
me one evening?'

'Why – I – yes. That would be nice.'

'Wonderful. If you had said no, I should have killed myself.'

'Please don't,' Alexandra said. 'I hate eating alone.'

'So do I. I know a little restaurant on Mulberry Street: Matoon's. It's very obscure, but the food is —'

'*Matoon's!* I love it!' Alexandra exclaimed. 'It's my favourite.'

'You know it?' There was surprise in his voice.

'Oh, yes.'

George looked over at Eve and grinned. He had to admire her ingenuity. She had briefed him on all of Alexandra's likes and dislikes. George Mellis knew everything there was to know about Eve's sister.

When George finally replaced the receiver, Eve thought, *It's started.*

It was the most enchanting evening of Alexandra's life. One hour before George Mellis was due, a dozen pink balloons arrived, with an orchid attached. Alexandra had been filled with a fear that her imagination might have led her to expect too much, but the moment she saw George Mellis again, all her doubts were swept away. She felt once again his overpowering magnetism.

They had a drink at the house and then went on to the restaurant.

'Would you like to look at the menu?' George asked. 'Or shall I order for you?'

Alexandra had her favourite dishes here, but she wanted to please George. 'Why don't you order?'

He chose every one of Alexandra's favourites, and she had the heady feeling he was reading her mind. They dined on stuffed artichokes, veal Matoon, a speciality of the house, and angel hair, a delicate pasta. They had a salad that George mixed at the table with a deft skill.

'Do you cook?' Alexandra asked.

'Ah, it's one of the passions of my life. My mother taught me. She was a brilliant cook.'

'Are you close to your family, George?'

He smiled, and Alexandra thought it was the most attractive smile she had ever seen.

'I'm Greek,' he said simply. 'I'm the oldest of three brothers and two sisters, and we are like one.' A look of sadness came into his eyes. 'Leaving them was the most difficult thing I ever had to do. My father and my brothers begged me to stay. We have a large business, and they felt I was needed there.'

'Why didn't you stay?'

'I will probably seem a fool to you, but I prefer to make my own way. It has always been difficult for me to accept gifts from anyone, and the business was a gift handed down from my grandfather to my father. No, I will take nothing from my father. Let my brothers have my share.'

How Alexandra admired him.

'Besides,' George added softly, 'if I had stayed in Greece, I never would have met you.'

Alexandra felt herself blushing. 'You've never been married?'

'No. I used to get engaged once a day,' he teased, 'but at the last moment I always felt there was something wrong.' He leaned forwards, and his voice was earnest. 'Beautiful Alexandra, you are going to think me very old-fashioned, but when I get married, it will be forever. One woman is enough for me, but it must be the right woman.'

'I think that's lovely,' she murmured.

'And you?' George Mellis asked. 'Have you ever been in love?'

'No.'

'How unlucky for someone,' he said. 'But how lucky for –'

At that moment, the waiter appeared with dessert. Alexandra was dying to ask George to finish the sentence, but she was afraid to.

Alexandra had never felt so completely at ease with anyone. George Mellis seemed so genuinely interested in her that she found herself telling him about her childhood, her life, the experiences she had stored up and treasured.

George Mellis prided himself on being an expert on women. He knew that beautiful women were usually the most insecure, for men concentrated on that beauty, leaving the women feeling like objects rather than human beings. When George was with a beautiful woman, he never mentioned her looks. He made the woman feel that he was interested in her mind, her feelings, that he was a soul mate sharing her dreams. It was an extra-ordinary experience for Alexandra. She told George about Kate, and about Eve.

'Your sister does not live with you and your grandmother?'

'No. She – Eve wanted an apartment of her own.'

Alexandra could not imagine why George Mellis had not been attracted to her sister. Whatever the reason, Alexandra was grateful. During the course of the dinner, Alexandra noted that every woman in the place was aware of George, but not once did he look around or take his eyes from her.

Over coffee, George said, 'I don't know if you like jazz, but there's a club on St Mark's Place called the Five Spot . . .'

'Where Cecil Taylor plays!'

He looked at Alexandra in astonishment. 'You've been there?'

'Often!' Alexandra laughed. 'I love him! It's incredible how we share the same tastes.'

George replied quietly, 'It's like some kind of miracle.'

They listened to Cecil Taylor's spellbinding piano playing, long solos that rocked the room with arpeggios and rippling glissandi. From there they went to a bar on Bleecker Street, where the customers drank, ate popcorn, threw darts and listened to good piano music. Alexandra watched as George got into a darts contest with one of the regular patrons. The man was good, but he never had a chance. George played with a grim intensity that was almost frightening. It was only a game, but he played it as though it meant life or death. *He's a man who has to win*, Alexandra thought.

It was two a.m. when they left the bar, and Alexandra hated for the evening to end.

George sat beside Alexandra in the chauffeur-driven Rolls-Royce he had rented. He did not speak. He just looked at her. The resemblance between the two sisters was startling. *I wonder if their bodies are alike.* He visualized Alexandra in bed with him, writhing and screaming with pain.

'What are you thinking?' Alexandra asked.

He looked away from her so she could not read his eyes. 'You'll laugh at me.'

'I won't. I promise.'

'I wouldn't blame you if you did. I suppose I'm considered something of a playboy. You know the life – yachting trips and parties, and all the rest of it.'

'Yes . . .'

He fixed his dark eyes on Alexandra. 'I think you are the one woman who could change all that. Forever.'

Alexandra felt her pulse quicken. 'I – I don't know what to say.'

'Please. Don't say anything.' His lips were very close to hers, and Alexandra was ready. But he made no move. *Don't make any advances*, Eve had warned. *Not on the first night. If you do, you become one of a long line of Romeos dying to get their hands on her and her fortune. She has to make the first move.*

And so, George Mellis merely held Alexandra's hand in his until the car glided to a smooth stop in front of the Blackwell mansion. George escorted Alexandra to her front door. She turned to him and said, 'I can't tell you how much I've enjoyed this evening.'

'It was magic for me.'

Alexandra's smile was bright enough to light up the street.

'Good night, George,' she whispered. And she disappeared inside.

Fifteen minutes later, Alexandra's phone rang. 'Do you know what I just did? I telephoned my family. I told them about the wonderful woman I was with tonight. Sleep well, lovely Alexandra.'

When he hung up, George Mellis thought, *After we're married, I will call my family. And I'll tell them all to go fuck themselves.*

TWENTY-NINE

Alexandra did not hear from George Mellis again. Not that day, or the next, or the rest of that week. Every time the phone rang, she rushed to pick it up, but she was always disappointed. She could not imagine what had gone wrong. She kept replaying the evening in her mind: *I think you are the one woman who could change all that forever*, and *I telephoned my mother and father and brothers and told them about the wonderful woman I was with tonight*. Alexandra went through a litany of reasons why he had not telephoned her.

She had offended him in some way without realizing it.

He liked her too much, was afraid of falling in love with her and had made up his mind never to see her again.

He had decided she was not his type.

He had been in a terrible accident and was lying helpless in a hospital somewhere.

He was dead.

When Alexandra could stand it no longer, she telephoned Eve. Alexandra forced herself to make small talk for a full minute before she blurted out, 'Eve, you haven't heard from George Mellis lately, by any chance, have you?'

'Why, no. I thought he was going to call you about dinner.'

'We did have dinner – last week.'

'And you haven't heard from him since?'

'No.'

'He's probably busy.'

No one is that busy, Alexandra thought. Aloud she said, 'Probably.'

'Forget about George Mellis, darling. There's a very attractive Canadian I'd like you to meet. He owns an airline and . . .'

When Eve had hung up, she sat back, smiling. She wished her grandmother could have known how beautifully she had planned everything.

'Hey, what's eating you?' Alice Koppel asked.

'I'm sorry,' Alexandra replied.

She had been snapping at everyone all morning. It had been two full weeks since she had heard from George Mellis, and Alexandra was angry – not with him, but with herself for not being able to forget him. He owed her nothing. They were strangers who had shared an evening together, and she was acting as though she expected him to marry her, for God's sake. George Mellis could have any woman in the world. Why on earth would he want her?

Even her grandmother had noticed how irritable she had become. 'What's the matter with you, child? Are they working you too hard at that agency?'

'No, Gran. It's just that I – I haven't been sleeping well lately.'

When she did sleep, she had erotic dreams about George Mellis. *Damn him!* She wished Eve had never introduced him to her.

The call came at the office the following afternoon. 'Alex? George Mellis.' As though she didn't hear that deep voice in her dreams.

'Alex?' Are you there?'

'Yes, I'm here.' She was filled with mixed emotions. She did not know whether to laugh or cry. He was a thoughless, selfish, egotist, and she did not care whether she ever saw him again.

'I wanted to call you sooner,' George apologized, 'but I just returned from Athens a few minutes ago.'

Alexandra's heart melted. 'You've been in Athens?'

'Yes. Remember the evening we had dinner together?'

Alexandra remembered.

'The next morning Steve, my brother, telephoned me – My father had a heart attack.'

'Oh, George!' She felt so guilty for having thought such terrible things about him. 'How is he?'

'He's going to be all right, thank God. But I felt as though I was being torn in pieces. He begged me to come back to Greece and take over the family business.'

'Are you going to?' She was holding her breath.

'No.'

She exhaled.

'I know now that my place is here. There isn't one day or one hour that's gone by that I haven't thought about you. When can I see you?'

Now! 'I'm free for dinner this evening.'

He was almost tempted to name another of Alexandra's favourite restaurants. Instead he said, 'Wonderful. Where would you like to dine?'

'Anywhere. I don't care. Would you like to have dinner at the house?'

'No.' He was not ready to meet Kate yet. *Whatever you do, stay away from Kate Blackwell for now. She's your biggest obstacle.* 'I'll pick you up at eight o'clock,' George told her.

Alexandra hung up, kissed Alice Koppel, Vince Barnes and Marty Bergheimer and said, 'I'm off to the hairdresser. I'll see you all tomorrow.'

They watched her race out of the office.

'It's a man,' Alice Koppel said.

They had dinner at Maxwell's Plum. A captain led them past the crowded horseshoe bar near the front door and up the stairs to the dining room. They ordered.

'Did you think about me while I was away?' George asked.

'Yes.' She felt she had to be completely honest with this man – this man who was so open, so vulnerable. 'When I didn't hear from you, I thought something terrible might have happened. I – I got panicky. I don't think I could have stood it another day.'

Full marks for Eve, George thought. *Sit tight*, Eve had said. *I'll tell you when to call her.* For the first time George had the feeling the plan really was going to work. Until now he had let it nibble at the edges of his mind, toying with the idea of controlling the incredible Blackwell fortune, but he had not really dared believe it. It had been merely a game that he and Eve had been playing. Looking at Alexandra now, seated across from him, her eyes filled with naked adoration, George Mellis knew it was no longer just a game. Alexandra was his. That was the first step in the plan. The other steps might be dangerous, but with Eve's help, he would handle them.

We're in this together all the way, George, and we'll share everything right down the middle.

George Mellis did not believe in partners. When he had what he wanted, when he had disposed of Alexandra, then he would take care of Eve. That thought gave him enormous pleasure.

'You're smiling,' Alexandra said.

He put his hand over hers, and his touch warmed her. 'I was thinking how nice it was our being here

531

together. About our being *anywhere* together.' He reached into his pocket and pulled out a jewel box. 'I brought something for you from Greece.'

'Oh, George . . .'

'Open it, Alex.'

Inside the box was an exquisite diamond necklace.

'It's beautiful.'

It was the one he had taken from Eve. *It's safe to give it to her*. Eve had told him. *She's never seen it.*

'It's too much. Really.'

'It's not nearly enough. I'll enjoy watching you wear it.'

'I –' Alexandra was trembling. 'Thank you.'

He looked at her plate. 'You haven't eaten anything.'

'I'm not hungry.'

He saw the look in her eyes again and felt the familiar soaring sense of power. He had seen that look in the eyes of so many women: beautiful women, ugly women, rich women, poor women. He had used them. In one way or another, they had all given him something. But this one was going to give him more than all of them put together.

'What would you like to do?' His husky voice was an invitation.

She accepted it, simply and openly. 'I want to be with you.'

* * *

George Mellis had every right to be proud of his apartment. It was a tasteful jewel of a place, furnished by grateful lovers – men and women – who had tried to buy his affection with expensive gifts, and had succeeded, always temporarily.

'It's a lovely apartment,' Alexandra exclaimed.

He went over to her and slowly turned her around so that the diamond necklace twinkled in the subdued lighting of the room 'It becomes you, darling.'

And he kissed her gently, and then more urgently, and Alexandra was hardly aware when he led her into the bedroom. The room was done in tones of blue, with tasteful, masculine furniture. In the centre of the room stood a large, king-size bed. George took Alexandra in his arms again and found that she was shaking. 'Are you all right, *kale' mou?*'

'I – I'm a little nervous.' She was terrified that she would disappoint this man. She took a deep breath and started to unbutton her dress.

George whispered, 'Let me.' He began to undress the exquisite blonde standing before him, and he remembered Eve's words: *Control yourself. If you hurt Alexandra, if she finds out what a pig you really are, you'll never see her again. Do you understand that? Save your fists for your whores and your pretty little boys.*

And so George tenderly undressed Alexandra and studied her nakedness. Her body was exactly the same as Eve's: beautiful and ripe and full. He

533

had an overwhelming desire to bruise the white, delicate skin; to hit her, choke her, make her scream. *If you hurt her, you'll never see her again.*

He undressed and drew Alexandra close to his body. They stood there together, looking into each other's eyes, and then George gently led Alexandra to the bed and began to kiss her, slowly and lovingly, his tongue and fingers expertly exploring every crevice of her body until she was unable to wait another moment.

'Oh, please,' she said. 'Now. Now!'

He mounted her then, and she was plunged into an ecstasy that was almost unbearable. When finally Alexandra lay still in his arms and sighed. 'Oh, my darling. I hope it was as wonderful for you,' he lied and said, 'It was.'

She held him close and wept, and she did not know why she was weeping, only that she was grateful for the glory and the joy of it.

'There, there,' George said soothingly. 'Everything is marvellous.'

And it was.

Eve would have been so proud of him.

In every love affair, there are misunderstandings, jealousies, small hurts, but not in the romance between George and Alexandra. With Eve's careful coaching, George was able to play skilfully on Alexandra's every emotion. George knew Alexandra's fears, her fantasies, her passions and aversions, and he was always there, ready to give her exactly what

534

she needed. He knew what made her laugh, and what made her cry. Alexandra was thrilled by his lovemaking, but George found it frustrating. When he was in bed with Alexandra, listening to her animal cries, her excitement aroused him to a fever pitch. He wanted to savage her, make her scream for mercy so he could have his own relief. But he knew if he did that he would destroy everything. His frustration kept growing. The more they made love, the more he grew to despise Alexandra.

There were certain places where George Mellis could find satisfaction, but he knew he had to be cautious. Late at night he haunted anonymous singles' bars and gay discos, and he picked up lonely widows looking for an evening's comfort, gay boys hungry for love, prostitutes hungry for money. George took them to a series of seedy hotels on the West Side, in the Bowery and in Greenwich Village. He never returned to the same hotel twice, nor would he have been welcomed back. His sexual partners usually were found either unconscious or semiconscious, their bodies battered and sometimes covered with cigarette burns.

George avoided masochists. They enjoyed the pain he inflicted, and that took away his pleasure. No, he had to hear them scream and beg for mercy, as his father had made him scream and beg for mercy when George was a small boy. His punishments for the smallest infractions were beatings that often left him unconscious. When George was eight years old and his father caught him and a neighbour's son naked together, George's father beat him until the blood ran from his ears and nose, and to make sure the boy never sinned again, his father pressed a lighted cigar to George's penis. The scar healed, but the deeper scar inside festered.

George Mellis had the wild, passionate nature of his Hellenic ancestors. He could not bear the thought of being controlled by anyone. He put up with the taunting humiliation Eve Blackwell inflicted upon him only because he needed her. When he had the Blackwell fortune in his hands, he intended to punish her until she begged him to kill her. Meeting Eve was the luckiest thing that had ever happened to him. *Lucky for me*, George mused. *Unlucky for her*.

Alexandra continually marvelled at how George always knew just what flowers to send her, what records to buy, what books would please her. When he took her to a museum, he was excited about the same paintings she loved. It was incredible to Alexandra how identical their tastes were. She looked for a single flaw in George Mellis, and she could find none. He was perfect. She grew more and more eager for Kate to meet him.

But George always found an excuse to avoid meeting Kate Blackwell.

'Why, darling? You'll love her. Besides, I want to show you off.'

'I'm sure she's wonderful,' George said boyishly.

'I'm terrified she'll think I'm not good enough for you.'

'That's ridiculous!' His modesty touched her. 'Gran will adore you.'

'Soon,' he told Alexandra. 'As soon as I get up my courage.'

He discussed it with Eve one night.

She thought about it. 'All right. You'll have to get it over with sooner or later. But you'll have to watch yourself every second. She's a bitch, but she's a smart bitch. Don't underestimate her for a second. If she suspects you're after anything, she'll cut your heart out and feed it to her dogs.'

'Why do we need her?' George asked.

'Because if you do anything to make Alexandra antagonize her, we'll all be out in the cold.'

Alexandra had never been so nervous. They were going to dine together for the first time, George and Kate and Alexandra, and Alexandra prayed that nothing would go wrong. She wanted more than anything in the world for her grandmother and George to like each other, for her grandmother to see what a wonderful person George was and for George to appreciate Kate Blackwell.

Kate had never seen her granddaughter so happy. Alexandra had met some of the most eligible young men in the world, and none of them had interested her, Kate intended to take a very close look at the man who had captivated her granddaughter. Kate had long years of experience with fortune hunters, and she had no intention of allowing Alexandra to be taken in by one.

She was eagerly looking forward to meeting Mr George Mellis. She had a feeling he had been reluctant to meet her, and she wondered why.

Kate heard the front doorbell ring, and a minute later Alexandra came into the drawing room leading a tall, classically handsome stranger by the hand.

'Gran, this is George Mellis.'

'At last,' Kate said. 'I was beginning to think you were avoiding me, Mr Mellis.'

'On the contrary, Mrs Blackwell, you have no idea how much I've been looking forward to this moment.' He was about to say, 'You're even more beautiful than Alex told me,' but he stopped himself.

Be careful. No flattery, George. It's like a red flag to the old lady.

A butler came in, fixed drinks and discreetly withdrew.

'Please sit down, Mr Mellis.'

'Thank you.'

Alexandra sat beside him on the couch, facing her grandmother.

'I understand you've been seeing quite a bit of my granddaughter.'

'That's been my pleasure, yes.'

Kate was studying him with her pale-grey eyes. 'Alexandra tells me you're employed by a brokerage firm.'

'Yes.'

'Frankly, I find it strange, Mr Mellis, that you should choose to work as a salaried employee when you could be heading a very profitable family business.'

'Gran, I explained that –'

'I would like to hear it from Mr Mellis, Alexandra.'

Be polite, but for Christ's sake, don't kowtow to her. If you show the slightest sign of weakness, she'll tear you apart.

'Mrs Blackwell, I'm not in the habit of discussing my personal life.' He hesitated, as though making a decision. 'However, under the circumstances, I suppose . . .' He looked Kate Blackwell in the eye and said, 'I'm a very independent man. I don't accept charity. If I had founded Mellis and Company, I would be running it today. But it was founded by my grandfather and built into a very profitable business by my father. It does not need me. I have three brothers who are perfectly capable of running it. I prefer being a salaried employee, as you call it, until I find something that I can build up myself and take pride in.'

Kate nodded slowly. This man was not what she had expected at all. She had been prepared for a playboy, a fortune hunter, the kind who had been pursuing her granddaughters ever since Kate could remember. This one appeared to be different. And yet, there was something disturbing about him that Kate could not define. He seemed almost *too* perfect.

'I understand your family is wealthy.'

All she has to believe is that you're filthy rich, and madly in love with Alex. Be charming. Keep your temper under control, and you've got it made.

'Money is a necessity, of course, Mrs Blackwell. But there are a hundred things that interest me more.'

Kate had checked on the net worth of Mellis and Company. According to the Dun & Bradstreet report, it was in excess of thirty million dollars.

'Are you close to your family, Mr Mellis?'

George's face lighted up. 'Perhaps too close.' He allowed a smile to play on his lips. 'We have a saying in our family, Mrs Blackwell. When one of us cuts his finger, the rest of us bleed. We are in touch with each other constantly.' He had not spoken to any member of his family for more than three years.

Kate nodded approvingly. 'I believe in closely knit families.'

Kate glanced at her granddaughter. There was a look of adoration on Alexandra's face. For one fleeting instant, it reminded Kate of herself and David in those long ago days when they were so much in love. The years had not dimmed the memory of how she had felt.

Lester came into the room. 'Dinner is served, madame.'

The conversation at dinner seemed more casual, but Kate's questions were pointed. George was prepared for the most important question when it came.

'Do you like children, Mr Mellis?'

She's desperate for a great-grandson . . . She wants that more than anything in the world.

George turned towards Kate in surprise. 'Like children? What is a man without sons and daughters? I am afraid that when I marry, my poor wife will be kept very busy. In Greece, a man's worth is measured by the number of children he has sired.'

He seems genuine, Kate thought. *But one can't be too careful. Tomorrow I'll have Brad Rogers run a check on his personal finances.*

Before Alexandra went to bed, she telephoned Eve. She had told Eve that George Mellis was coming to dinner.

'I can't wait to hear all about it, darling,' Eve had said. 'You must call me the moment he leaves. I want a full report.'

And now Alexandra was reporting. 'I think Gran liked him a lot.'

Eve felt a small *frisson* of satisfaction. 'What did she say?'

'She asked George a hundred personal questions. He handled himself beautifully.'

So he had behaved.

'Ah! Are you two lovebirds going to get married?'

'I – He hasn't asked me yet, Eve, but I think he's going to.'

She could hear the happiness in Alexandra's voice. 'And Gran will approve?'

'Oh, I'm sure she will. She's going to check on George's personal finances, but of course that will be no problem.'

Eve felt her heart lurch.

Alexandra was saying, 'You know how cautious Gran is.'

'Yes,' Eve said slowly. 'I know.'

They were finished. Unless she could think of something quickly.

'Keep me posted,' Eve said.

'I will. Good night.'

The moment Eve replaced the receiver, she dialled George Mellis's number. He had not reached home yet. She called him every ten minutes, and when he finally answered Eve said, 'Can you get your hands on a million dollars in a hurry?'

'What the hell are you talking about?'

'Kate is checking out your finances.'

'She knows what my family is worth. She –'

'I'm not talking about your family. I'm talking about you. I told you she's no fool.'

There was a silence. 'Where would I get hold of a million dollars?'

'I have an idea,' Eve told him.

When Kate arrived at her office the following morning, she said to her assistant, 'Ask Brad Rogers to run a personal financial check on George Mellis. He's employed by Hanson and Hanson.'

'Mr Rogers is out of town until tomorrow, Mrs Blackwell. Can it wait until then or –?'

'Tomorrow will be fine.'

At the lower end of Manhattan on Wall Street, George Mellis was seated at his desk at the brokerage firm of Hanson and Hanson. The stock exchanges were open, and the huge office was a bedlam of noise and activity. There were 225 employees working at the firm's headquarters: brokers, analysts, accountants, operators and customer representatives, and everyone was working at a feverish speed. Except for George Mellis. He was frozen at his desk, in a panic. What he was about to do would put him in prison if he failed. If he succeeded, he would own the world.

'Aren't you going to answer your phone?'

One of the partners was standing over him, and George realized that his phone had been ringing for – how long? He must act normally and not do anything that might arouse suspicion. He scooped up the phone. 'George Mellis,' and smiled reassuringly at the partner.

George spent the morning taking buy and sell orders, but his mind was on Eve's plan to steal a million dollars. *It's simple, George. All you have to do is borrow some stock certificates for one night. You can return them in the morning, and no one will be the wiser.*

Every stock brokerage firm has millions of dollars in stocks and bonds stored in its vaults as a convenience to customers. Some of the stock certificates bear the name of the owner, but the vast majority are street-name stocks with a coded CUSIP number – the Committee of Uniform Security Identification Procedures – that identifies the owner. The stock certificates are not negotiable, but George Mellis did not plan to cash them in. He had something else in mind. At Hanson and Hanson the stocks were kept in a huge vault on the seventh floor in a security area guarded by an armed policeman in front of a gate that could only be opened by a coded plastic access card. George Mellis had no such card. But he knew someone who did.

Helen Thatcher was a lonely widow in her forties. She had a pleasant face and a reasonably good figure, and she was a remarkable cook. She had been married for twenty-three years, and the death of her husband had left a void in her life. She needed a man to take care of her. Her problem was that most of the women who worked at Hanson and Hanson were younger than she, and more attractive to the brokers at the office. No one asked Helen out.

She worked in the accounting department on the floor above George Mellis. From the first time Helen had seen George, she had decided he would make a perfect husband for her. Half a dozen times she had invited him to a home-cooked evening, as she phrased it, and had hinted that he would be served more than dinner, but George had always found an excuse. On this particular morning, when her telephone rang and she said, 'Accounting, Mrs Thatcher,' George Mellis's voice came over the line. 'Helen? This is George.' His voice was warm, and she thrilled to it. 'What can I do for you, George?'

'I have a little surprise for you. Can you come down to my office?'

'Now?'

'Yes.'

'I'm afraid I'm in the middle of –'

'Oh, if you're too busy, never mind. It will keep.'

'No, no. I – I'll be right down.'

George's phone was ringing again. He ignored it. He picked up a handful of papers and walked towards the bank of elevators. Looking around to make sure no one was observing him, he walked past the elevators and took the backstairs. When he reached the floor above, he checked to make sure Helen had left her office, then casually walked in as though he had business there. If he was caught – But he could not think of that. He opened the middle drawer where he knew Helen kept her access card to the vault. There it was. He picked it up, slipped it in his pocket, left the office and hurried downstairs. When he reached his desk, Helen was there, looking around for him.

'Sorry,' George said. 'I was called away for a minute.'

'Oh, that's all right. Tell me what the surprise is.'

'Well, a little bird told me it's your birthday,'

George said, 'and I want to take you to lunch today.' He watched the expression on her face. She was torn between telling him the truth and missing the chance of a lunch date with him.

'That's – very nice of you,' she said. 'I'd love to have lunch with you.'

'All right,' he told her. 'I'll meet you at Tony's at one o'clock.' It was a date he could have made with her over the telephone, but Helen Thatcher was too thrilled to even question it. He watched as she left.

The minute she was gone, George went into action. He had a lot to accomplish before he returned the plastic card. He took the elevator to the seventh floor and walked over to the security area where the guard stood in front of the closed grilled gate. George inserted the plastic card and the gate opened. As he started inside, the guard said, 'I don't think I've seen you here before.'

George's heart began to beat faster. He smiled. 'No. This isn't my usual territory. One of my customers suddenly decided he wanted to see his stock certificates, so I've got to dig them out. I hope it doesn't take me the whole blasted afternoon.'

The guard smiled sympathetically. 'Good luck.' He watched as George walked into the vault.

The room was concrete, thirty feet by fifteen feet. George walked back to the fireproof file cabinets that contained the stocks and opened the steel drawers. Inside were hundreds of stock certificates that represented shares of every company on the New York and American stock exchanges. The number of shares represented by each certificate was printed on the face of the certificate and ranged from one share to one hundred thousand shares. George went through them swiftly and expertly. He selected certificates of various blue-chip companies, representing a value of one million dollars. He slipped the pieces of paper into his inside jacket pocket, closed the drawer and walked back to the guard.

'That was fast,' the guard said.

George shook his head. 'The computers came up with the wrong numbers. I'll have to straighten it out in the morning.'

'Those damned computers,' the guard commiserated. 'They'll be the ruination of us all yet.'

When George returned to his desk, he found he was soaked with perspiration. *But so far so good.* He picked up the telephone and called Alexandra.

'Darling,' he said, 'I want to see you and your grandmother tonight.'

'I thought you had a business engagement tonight, George.'

'I did, but I cancelled it. I have something very important to tell you.'

At exactly one p.m. George was in Helen Thatcher's office returning the access card to her desk drawer, while she waited for him at the restaurant. He desperately wanted to hang on to the card, for he would need it again, but he knew that every card that was not turned in each night was invalidated by the computer the next morning. At ten minutes past one, George was lunching with Helen Thatcher.

He took her hand in his. 'I want us to do this more often,' George said, looking at her searchingly. 'Are you free for lunch tomorrow?'

She beamed. 'Oh, yes, George.'

When George Mellis walked out of his office that afternoon, he was carrying with him one-million-dollars' worth of stock certificates.

He arrived at the Blackwell house promptly at seven o'clock and was ushered into the library, where Kate and Alexandra were waiting for him.

'Good evening,' George said. 'I hope this is not an intrusion, but I had to speak to you both.' He turned to Kate. 'I know this is very old-fashioned of me, Mrs Blackwell, but I would like your permission for your granddaughter's hand in marriage. I love Alexandra, and I believe she loves me. But it would make both of us happy if you would give us your blessing.' He reached into his jacket pocket, brought out the stock certificates and tossed them on the table in front of Kate. 'I'm giving her a million dollars as a wedding present. She won't need any of your money. But we both need your blessing.'

Kate glanced down at the stock certificates

George had carelessly scattered on the table. She recognized the names of every one of the companies. Alexandra had moved to George, her eyes shining. 'Oh, darling!' She turned to her grandmother, her eyes imploring, 'Gran?'

Kate looked at the two of them standing together, and there was no way she could deny them. For a brief instant, she envied them. 'You have my blessing,' she said.

George grinned and walked over to Kate. 'May I?' He kissed her on the cheek.

For the next two hours they talked excitedly about wedding plans. 'I don't want a large wedding, Gran,' Alexandra said. 'We don't have to do that, do we?'

'I agree,' George replied. 'Love is a private matter.'

In the end, they decided on a small ceremony, with a judge marrying them.

'Will your father be coming over for the wedding?' Kate inquired.

George laughed. 'You couldn't keep him away. My father, my three brothers and my two sisters will all be here.'

'I'll be looking forward to meeting them.'

'You'll like them, I know.' Then his eyes turned back to Alexandra.

Kate was very touched by the whole evening. She was thrilled for her granddaughter – pleased that she was getting a man who loved her so much. *I must remember*, Kate thought, *to tell*

Brad not to bother about that financial rundown on George.

Before George left, and he was alone with Alexandra, he said casually, 'I don't think it's a good idea to have a million dollars in securities lying around the house. I'll put them in my safe-deposit box for now.'

'Would you?' Alexandra asked.

George picked up the certificates and put them back into his jacket pocket.

The following morning George repeated the procedure with Helen Thatcher. While she was on her way downstairs to see him ('I have a little something for you'), he was in her office getting the access card. He gave her a Gucci scarf – 'a belated birthday present' – and confirmed his luncheon date with her. This time getting into the vault seemed easier. He replaced the stock certificates, returned the access card and met Helen Thatcher at a nearby restaurant.

She held his hand and said, 'George, why don't I fix a nice dinner for the two of us tonight?'

And George replied, 'I'm afraid that's impossible, Helen. I'm getting married.'

Three days before the wedding ceremony was to take place, George arrived at the Blackwell house, his face filled with distress. 'I've just had terrible news,' he said. 'My father suffered another heart attack.'

'Oh, I'm so sorry,' Kate said. 'Is he going to be all right?'

'I've been on the phone with the family all night. They think he'll pull through, but of course they won't be able to attend the wedding.'

'We could go to Athens on our honeymoon and see them,' Alexandra suggested.

George stroked her cheek. 'I have other plans for our honeymoon, *matia mou*. No family, just us.'

The marriage ceremony was held in the drawing room of the Blackwell mansion. There were fewer than a dozen guests in attendance, among them Vince Barnes, Alice Koppel and Marty Bergheimer. Alexandra had pleaded with her grandmother to let Eve attend the wedding, but Kate was adamant. 'Your sister will never be welcome in this house again.'

Alexandra's eyes filled with tears. 'Gran, you're being cruel. I love you both. Can't you forgive her?'

For an instant, Kate was tempted to blurt out the whole story of Eve's disloyalty, but she stopped herself. 'I'm doing what I think is best for everyone.'

A photographer took pictures of the ceremony, and Kate heard George ask him to make up some extra prints to send to his family. *What a considerate man he is*, Kate thought.

After the cake-cutting ceremony, George whispered to Alexandra, 'Darling, I'm going to have to disappear for an hour or so.'

'Is anything wrong?'

'Of course not. But the only way I could persuade the office to let me take time off for our honeymoon was to promise to finish up some business for an important client. I won't be long. Our plane doesn't leave until five o'clock.'

She smiled. 'Hurry back. I don't want to go on our honeymoon without you.'

When George arrived at Eve's apartment, she was waiting for him, wearing a filmy negligee. 'Did you enjoy your wedding, darling?'

'Yes, thank you. It was small but elegant. It went off without a hitch.'

'Do you know why, George? Because of me. Never forget that.'

He looked at her and said slowly, 'I won't.'

'We're partners all the way.'

'Of course.'

Eve smiled. 'Well, well. So you're married to my little sister.'

George looked at his watch. 'Yes. And I must get back.'

'Not yet,' Eve told him.

'Why not?'

'Because you're going to make love to me first, darling. I want to fuck my sister's husband.'

THIRTY

Eve had planned the honeymoon. It was expensive, but she told George, 'You mustn't stint on anything.'

She sold three pieces of jewellery she had acquired from an ardent admirer and gave the money to George.

'I appreciate this, Eve,' he said. 'I –'

'I'll get it back.'

The honeymoon was perfection. George and Alexandra stayed at Round Hill on Montego Bay, in the northern part of Jamaica. The lobby of the hotel was a small, white building set in the centre of approximately two dozen beautiful, privately owned bungalows that sprawled down a hill towards the clear, blue sea. The Mellises had the Noel Coward bungalow, with its own swimming pool and a maid to prepare their breakfast, which they ate in the open-air dining room. George rented a small boat and they went sailing and fishing.

They swam and read and played backgammon and made love. Alexandra did everything she could think of to please George in bed, and when she heard him moaning at the climax of their love-making, she was thrilled that she was able to bring him such pleasure.

On the fifth day, George said, 'Alex, I have to drive into Kingston on business. The firm has a branch office there and they asked me to look in on it.'

'Fine,' Alexandra said. 'I'll go with you.'

He frowned. 'I'd love you to, darling, but I'm expecting an overseas call. You'll have to stay and take the message.'

Alexandra was disappointed. 'Can't the desk take it?'

'It's too important. I can't trust them.'

'All right, then. Of course I'll stay.'

George rented a car and drove to Kingston. It was late afternoon when he arrived. The streets of the capital city were swarming with colourfully dressed tourists from the cruise ships, shopping at the straw market and in the small bazaars. Kingston is a city of commerce, with refineries, warehouses and fisheries, but with its landlocked harbour it is also a city of beautiful old buildings and museums and libraries.

George was interested in none of these things. He was filled with a desperate need that had been building up in him for weeks and had to be satisfied. He walked into the first bar he saw and spoke to the bartender. Five minutes later George was accompanying a fifteen-year-old black prostitute up the stairs of a cheap hotel. He was with her for two hours. When George left the room, he left alone, got into the car and drove back to Montego Bay, where Alexandra told him the urgent telephone call he was expecting had not come through.

The following morning the Kingston newspapers reported that a tourist had beaten up and mutilated a prostitute, and that she was near death.

At Hanson and Hanson, the senior partners were discussing George Mellis. There had been complaints from a number of clients about the way he handled their securities accounts. A decision had been reached to fire him. Now, however, there were second thoughts.

'He's married to one of Kate Blackwell's granddaughters,' a senior partner said. 'That puts things in a new light.'

A second partner added, 'It certainly does. If we could acquire the Blackwell account . . .'

The greed in the air was almost palpable. They decided George Mellis deserved another chance.

When Alexandra and George returned from their honeymoon, Kate told them, 'I'd like you to move in here with me. This is an enormous house, and we wouldn't be in one another's way. You –'

George interrupted. 'That's very kind of you,'

he said. 'But I think it would be best if Alex and I had our own place.'

He had no intention of living under the same roof with the old woman hovering over him, spying on his every move.

'I understand,' Kate replied. 'In that case, please let me buy a house for you. That will be my wedding present.'

George put his arms around Kate and hugged her. 'That's very generous of you.' His voice was hoarse with emotion. 'Alex and I accept with gratitude.'

'Thank you, Gran,' Alexandra said. 'We'll look for a place not too far away.'

'Right,' George agreed. 'We want to be close enough to keep an eye on you. You're a damned attractive woman, you know!'

Within a week they found a beautiful old brownstone near the park, a dozen blocks away from the Blackwell mansion. It was a charming three-storey house, with a master bedroom, two guest bedrooms, servants' quarters, a huge old kitchen, a panelled dining room, an elegant living room and a library.

'You're going to have to do the decorating by yourself, darling,' George told Alexandra. 'I'm all tied up with clients.'

The truth was that he spent almost no time at the office, and very little time with clients. His days were occupied with more interesting matters. The police were receiving a string of assault reports from male and female prostitutes and lonely women who visited singles' bars. The victims described their attacker as handsome and cultured, and coming from a foreign background, possibly Latin. Those who were willing to look at police mug shots were unable to come up with an identification.

Eve and George were having lunch in a small downtown restaurant where there was no chance of their being recognized.

'You've got to get Alex to make a new will without Kate knowing about it.'

'How the hell do I do that?'

'I'm going to tell you, darling . . .'

The following evening George met Alexandra for dinner at Le Plaisir, one of New York's finest French restaurants. He was almost thirty minutes late.

Pierre Jourdan, the owner, escorted him to the table where Alexandra was waiting. 'Forgive me, angel,' George said breathlessly. 'I was at my attorney's, and you know how they are. They make everything so complicated.'

Alexandra asked, 'Is anything wrong, George?'

'No. I just changed my will.' He took her hands in his. 'If anything should happen to me now, everything I have will belong to you.'

'Darling, I don't want –'

'Oh, it's not much compared to the Blackwell fortune, but it would keep you very comfortably.'

'Nothing's going to happen to you. Not ever.'

'Of course not, Alex. But sometimes life plays funny tricks. These things aren't pleasant to face, but it's better to plan ahead and be prepared, don't you think?'

She sat there thoughtfully for a moment. 'I should change my will, too, shouldn't I?'

'What for?' He sounded surprised.

'You're my husband. Everything I have is yours.'

He withdrew his hand. 'Alex, I don't give a damn about your money.'

'I know that, George, but you're right. It *is* better to look ahead and be prepared.' Her eyes filled with tears. 'I know I'm an idiot, but I'm so happy that I can't bear to think of anything happening to either of us. I want us to go on forever.'

'We will,' George murmured.

'I'll talk to Brad Rogers tomorrow about changing my will.'

He shrugged. 'If that's what you wish, darling.' Then, as an afterthought, 'Come to think of it, it might be better if my lawyer made the change. He's familiar with my estate. He can coordinate everything.'

'Whatever you like. Gran thinks –'

He caressed her cheek. 'Let's keep your grandmother out of this. I adore her, but don't you think we should keep our personal affairs personal?'

'You're right, darling. I won't say anything to

Gran. Could you make an appointment for me to see your attorney tomorrow?'

'Remind me to call him. Now, I'm starved. Why don't we start with the crab. . . . ?'

One week later George met Eve at her apartment.

'Did Alex sign the new will?' Eve asked.

'This morning. She inherits her share of the company next week on her birthday.'

The following week, 49 percent of the shares of Kruger-Brent, Ltd., were transferred to Alexandra. George called to tell Eve the news. She said, 'Wonderful! Come over tonight. We'll celebrate.'

'I can't. Kate's giving a birthday party for Alex.'

There was a silence. 'What are they serving?'

'How the hell do I know?'

'Find out.' The line went dead.

Forty-five minutes later George called Eve back. 'I don't know why you're so interested in the menu,' he said nastily, 'since you aren't invited to the party, but it's *coquille Saint-Jacques, Chateaubriand*, a bibb lettuce salad, *Brie, cappuccino* and a birthday cake with Alex's favourite ice cream, Neapolitan. Satisfied?'

'Yes, George. I'll see you tonight.'

'No, Eve. There's no way I can walk out in the middle of Alex's –'

'You'll think of something.'

God damn the bitch! George hung up the phone

and looked at his watch. *God damn everything!* He had an appointment with an important client he had stood up twice already. Now he was late. He knew the partners were keeping him on only because he had married into the Blackwell family. He could not afford to do anything to jeopardize his position. He had created an image for Alexandra and Kate, and it was imperative that nothing destroy that. Soon he would not need any of them.

He had sent his father a wedding invitation, and the old man had not even bothered to reply. Not one word of congratulations. *I never want to see you again*, his father had told him. *You're dead, you understand? Dead*. Well, his father was in for a surprise. The prodigal son was going to come to life again.

Alexandra's twenty-third birthday party was a great success. There were forty guests. She had asked George to invite some of his friends, but he had demurred. 'It's your party, Alex,' he said. 'Let's just have your friends.'

The truth was that George had no friends. He was a loner, he told himself proudly. People who were dependent on other people were weaklings. He watched as Alexandra blew out the candles on her cake and make a silent wish. He knew the wish involved him, and he thought, *You should have wished for a longer life, darling*. He had to admit that Alexandra was exquisite looking. She was wearing a long white chiffon dress with delicate silver slippers and a diamond necklace, a present from Kate. The large, pear-shaped stones were strung together on a platinum chain, and they sparkled in the candlelight.

Kate looked at them and thought, *I remember our first anniversary, when David put that necklace on me and told me how much he loved me.*

And George thought, *That necklace must be worth a hundred and fifty thousand dollars.*

George had been aware all evening that several of Alexandra's female guests were eyeing him, smiling at him invitingly, touching him as they talked to him. *Horny bitches*, he thought contemptuously. Under other circumstances, he might have been tempted to risk it, but not with Alexandra's friends. They might not dare complain to Alexandra, but there was a chance they could go to the police. No, things were moving along too smoothly to take any unnecessary chances.

At one minute before ten o'clock, George positioned himself near the telephone. When it rang a minute later, he picked it up. 'Hello.'

'Mr Mellis?'

'Yes.'

'This is your answering service. You asked me to call you at ten o'clock.'

Alexandra was standing near him. He looked over at her and frowned. 'What time did he call?'

'Is this Mr Mellis?'

'Yes.'

'You left a ten o'clock call, sir.'

Alexandra was at his side.

'Very well,' he said into the phone. 'Tell him I'm on my way. I'll meet him at the Pan Am Clipper Club.'

George slammed the phone down.

'What's the matter, darling?'

He turned to Alexandra. 'One of the idiot partners is on his way to Singapore and he left some contracts at the office that he needs to take with him. I've got to pick them up and get them to him before his plane leaves.'

'*Now?*' Alexandra's voice was filled with dismay. 'Can't someone else do it?'

'I'm the only one they trust,' George sighed. 'You'd think I was the only capable one in the whole office.' He put his arms around her. 'I'm sorry, darling. Don't let me spoil your party. You go on and I'll get back as soon as I can.'

She managed a smile. 'I'll miss you.'

Alexandra watched him go, then looked around the room to make sure all her guests were enjoying themselves.

She wondered what Eve was doing on their birthday.

Eve opened the door to let George in. 'You managed,' she said. 'You're such a clever man.'

'I can't stay, Eve. Alex is –'

She took his hand. 'Come, darling. I have a surprise for you.' She led him into the small dining room. The table was set for two, with beautiful

562

silver and white napery and lighted candles in the centre of the table.

'What's this for?'

'It's my birthday, George.'

'Of course,' he said lamely. 'I – I'm afraid I didn't bring you a present.'

She stroked his cheek. 'Yes you did, love. You'll give it to me later. Sit down.'

'Thanks,' George said. 'I couldn't eat anything. I just had a big dinner.'

'Sit down.' There was no inflection to her voice. George looked into her eyes, and sat down.

Dinner consisted of *Coquille Saint-Jacques*, *Chateaubriand*, a bibb lettuce salad, *Brie*, *cappuccino* and birthday cake with Neapolitan ice cream.

Eve sat across from him, watching George force the food down. 'Alex and I have always shared everything,' Eve told him. 'Tonight I'm sharing her birthday dinner. But next year there will be just one of us having a birthday party. The time has come, darling, for my sister to have an accident. And after that, poor old Gran is going to die of grief. It's going to be all ours, George. Now, come into the bedroom and give me my birthday present.'

He had been dreading this moment. He was a man, strong and vigorous, and Eve dominated him and made him feel impotent. She had him undress her slowly, and then she undressed him and skilfully excited him to an erection.

'There you are, darling,' She got astride him and

563

began slowly moving her hips. 'Ah, that feels so good . . . You can't have an orgasm, can you, poor baby? Do you know why? Because you're a freak. You don't like women, do you, George? You only enjoy hurting them. You'd like to hurt me, wouldn't you? Tell me you'd like to hurt me.'

'I'd like to kill you.'

Eve laughed. 'But you won't, because you want to own the company as much as I do . . . You'll never hurt me, George, because if anything ever happens to me, a friend of mine is holding a letter that will be delivered to the police.'

He did not believe her. 'You're bluffing.'

Eve raked a long, sharp nail down his naked chest. 'There's only one way you can find out, isn't there?' she taunted.

And he suddenly knew she was telling the truth. He was never going to be able to get rid of her! She was always going to be there to taunt him, to enslave him. He could not bear the idea of being at this bitch's mercy for the rest of his life. And something inside him exploded. A red film descended over his eyes, and from that moment on he had no idea what he was doing. It was as though someone outside himself was controlling him. Everything happened in slow motion. He remembered shoving Eve off him, pulling her legs apart and her cries of pain. He was battering at something over and over, and it was indescribably wonderful. The whole centre of his being was racked with a long spasm of unbearable bliss, and then another, and another, and he thought *Oh, God! I've waited so long for this*. From somewhere in the far distance, someone was screaming. The red film slowly started to clear, and he looked down. Eve was lying on the bed, covered with blood. Her nose was smashed in, her body was covered with bruises and cigarette burns and her eyes were swollen shut. Her jaw was broken, and she was whimpering out of the side of her mouth. 'Stop it, stop it, stop it . . .'

George shook his head to clear it. As the reality of the situation hit him, he was filled with sudden panic. There was no way he could ever explain what he had done. He had thrown everything away. Everything!

He leaned over her. 'Eve?'

She opened one swollen eye. 'Doctor . . . Get . . . a . . . doctor . . .' Each word was a drop of pain. 'Harley . . . John Harley.'

All George Mellis said on the phone was, 'Can you come right away? Eve Blackwell has had an accident.'

When Dr John Harley walked into the room, he took one look at Eve and the blood-spattered bed and walls and said, 'Oh, my God!' He felt Eve's fluttering pulse, and turned to George. 'Call the police. Tell them we need an ambulance.'

Through the mist of pain, Eve whispered, 'John . . .'

John Harley leaned over the bed. 'You're going to be all right. We'll get you to the hospital.'

565

She reached out and found his hand. 'No police . . .'

'I have to report this. I –'

Her grip tightened. 'No . . . police . . .'

He looked at her shattered cheekbone, her broken jaw and the cigarette burns on her body. 'Don't try to talk.'

The pain was excruciating, but Eve was fighting for her life. 'Please . . .' It took a long time to get the words out. 'Private . . . Gran would never . . . forgive me . . . No . . . police . . . Hit . . . run . . . accident . . .'

There was no time to argue. Dr Harley walked over to the telephone and dialled. 'This is Dr Harley.' He gave Eve's address. 'I want an ambulance sent here immediately. Find Dr Keith Webster and ask him to meet me at the hospital. Tell him it's an emergency. Have a room prepared for surgery.' He listened a moment, then said, 'A hit-and-run accident.' He slammed down the receiver.

'Thank you, Doctor,' George breathed.

Dr Harley turned to look at Alexandra's husband, his eyes filled with loathing. George's clothes had been hastily donned, but his knuckles were raw, and his hands and face were still spattered with blood. 'Don't thank me. I'm doing this for the Blackwells. But on one condition. That you agree to see a psychiatrist.'

'I don't need a –'

'Then I'm calling the police, you sonofabitch.

566

You're not fit to be running around loose.' Dr Harley reached for the telephone again.

'Wait a minute!' George stood there, thinking. He had almost thrown everything away, but now, miraculously, he was being given a second chance. 'All right. I'll see a psychiatrist.'

In the far distance they heard the wail of a siren.

She was being rushed down a long tunnel, and coloured lights were flashing on and off. Her body felt light and airy, and she thought, *I can fly if I want to*, and she tried to move her arms, but something was holding them down. She opened her eyes, and she was speeding down a white corridor on a gurney being wheeled by two men in green gowns and caps. *I'm starring in a play*, Eve thought. *I can't remember my lines. What are my lines?* When she opened her eyes again, she was in a large white room on an operating table.

A small, thin man in a green surgical gown was leaning over her. 'My name is Keith Webster. I'm going to operate on you.'

'I don't want to be ugly,' Eve whispered. It was difficult to talk. 'Don't let me be . . . ugly.'

'Not a chance,' Dr Webster promised. 'I'm going to put you to sleep now. Just relax.'

He gave a signal to the anaesthetist.

George managed to wash the blood off himself and clean up in Eve's bathroom, but he cursed as he glanced at his wristwatch. It was three o'clock in the morning. He hoped Alexandra was asleep, but when he walked into their living room, she was waiting for him.

'Darling! I've been frantic! Are you all right?'

'I'm fine, Alex.'

She went up to him and hugged him. 'I was getting ready to call the police. I thought something terrible had happened.'

How right you are, George thought.

'Did you bring him the contracts?'

'Contracts?' He suddenly remembered. 'Oh, those. Yes. I did.' That seemed like years ago, a lie from the distant past.

'What on earth kept you so late?'

'His plane was delayed,' George said glibly. 'He wanted me to stay with him. I kept thinking he'd take off at any minute, and then finally it got too late for me to telephone you. I'm sorry.'

'It's all right, now that you're here.'

George thought of Eve as she was being carried out on the stretcher. Out of her broken, twisted mouth, she had gasped, 'Go . . . home . . . nothing . . . happened . . .' But what if Eve died? He would be arrested for murder. If Eve lived, everything would be all right; it would be just as it was before. Eve would forgive him because she needed him.

George lay awake the rest of the night. He was thinking about Eve and the way she had screamed and begged for mercy. He felt her bones crunch again beneath his fists, and he smelled her burning flesh, and at that moment he was very close to loving her.

It was a stroke of great luck that John Harley was able to obtain the services of Keith Webster for Eve. Dr Webster was one of the foremost plastic surgeons in the world. He had a private practice on Park Avenue and his own clinic in lower Manhattan, where he specialized in taking care of those who had been born with disfigurements. The people who came to the clinic paid only what they could afford. Dr Webster was used to treating accident cases, but his first sight of Eve Blackwell's battered face had shocked him. He had seen photographs of her in magazines, and to see that much beauty deliberately disfigured filled him with a deep anger.

'Who's responsible for this, John?'

'It was a hit-and-run accident, Keith.'

Keith Webster snorted. 'And then the driver stopped to strip her and snuff out his cigarette on her behind? What's the real story?'

'I'm afraid I can't discuss it. Can you put her back together again?'

'That's what I do, John, put them back together again.'

It was almost noon when Dr Webster finally said to his assistants, 'We're finished. Get her into intensive care. Call me at the slightest sign of anything going wrong.'

The operation had taken nine hours.

Eve was moved out of intensive care forty-eight hours later. George went to the hospital. He had to see Eve, to talk to her, to make sure she was not plotting some terrible vengeance against him.

'I'm Miss Blackwell's attorney,' George told the duty nurse. 'She asked to see me. I'll only stay a moment.'

The nurse took one look at this handsome man and said, 'She's not supposed to have visitors, but I'm sure it's all right if you go in.'

Eve was in a private room, lying in bed, flat on her back, swathed in bandages, tubes connected to her body like obscene appendages. The only parts of her face visible were her eyes and her lips.

'Hello, Eve . . .'

'George . . .' Her voice was a scratchy whisper. He had to lean close to hear what she said.

'You didn't . . . tell Alex?'

'No, of course not.' He sat down on the edge of the bed. 'I came because –'

'I know why you came . . . We're . . . going ahead with it . . .'

He had a feeling of indescribably relief. 'I'm sorry about this, Eve. I really am. I –'

'Have someone call Alex . . . and tell her I've gone away . . . on a trip . . . back in a few . . . weeks . . .'

'All right.'

Two bloodshot eyes looked up at him. 'George . . . do me a favour.'

'Yes?'

'Die painfully . . .'

She slept. When she awakened, Dr Keith Webster was at her bedside.

'How are you feeling?' His voice was gentle and soothing.

'Very tired . . . What was the . . . matter with me?'

Dr Webster hesitated. The X rays had shown a fractured zygoma and a blowout fracture. There was a depressed zygomatic arch impinging on the temporal muscle, so that she was unable to open or close her mouth without pain. Her nose was broken. There were two broken ribs and deep cigarette burns on her posterior and on the soles of her feet.

'What?' Eve repeated.

Dr Webster said, as gently as possible, 'You had a fractured cheekbone. Your nose was broken. The bony floor where your eye sits had been shifted. There was pressure on the muscle that opens and closes your mouth. There were cigarette burns. Everything has been taken care of.'

'I want to see a mirror,' Eve whispered.

That was the last thing he would allow. 'I'm sorry,' he smiled. 'We're fresh out.'

She was afraid to ask the next question. 'How am I – how am I going to look when these bandages come off?'

'You're going to look terrific. Exactly the way you did before your accident.'

'I don't believe you.'

'You'll see. Now, do you want to tell me what happened? I have to write up a police report.'

There was a long silence. 'I was hit by a truck.'

Dr Keith Webster wondered again how anyone could have tried to destroy this fragile beauty, but he had long since given up pondering the vagaries of the human race and its capacity for cruelty. 'I'll need a name,' he said gently. 'Who did it?'

'Mack.'

'And the last name?'

'Truck.'

Dr Webster was puzzled by the conspiracy of silence. First John Harley, now Eve Blackwell.

'In cases of criminal assault,' Keith Webster told Eve, 'I'm required by law to file a police report.'

Eve reached out for his hand and grasped it and held it tightly. 'Please, if my grandmother or sister knew, it would kill them. If you tell the police . . . the newspapers will know. You mustn't . . . please . . .'

'I can't report it as a hit-and-run accident. Ladies don't usually run out in the street without any clothes on.'

'Please!'

He looked down at her, and was filled with pity. 'I suppose you could have tripped and fallen down the stairs of your home.'

She squeezed his hand tighter. 'That's exactly what happened . . .'

Dr Webster sighed. 'That's what I thought.'

Dr Keith Webster visited Eve every day after that, sometimes stopping by two or three times a day. He brought her flowers and small presents from the hospital gift shop. Each day Eve would ask him anxiously, 'I just lie here all day. Why isn't anyone doing anything?'

'My partner's working on you,' Dr Webster told her.

'Your partner?'

'Mother Nature. Under all those frightening-looking bandages, you're healing beautifully.'

Every few days he would remove the bandages and examine her.

'Let me have a mirror,' Eve pleaded.

But his answer was always the same: 'Not yet.'

He was the only company Eve had, and she began to look forward to his visits. He was an unprepossessing man, small and thin, with sandy, sparse hair and myopic brown eyes that constantly blinked. He was shy in Eve's presence, and it amused her.

'Have you ever been married?' she asked.

'No.'

'Why not?'

'I – I don't know. I guess I wouldn't make a very good husband. I'm on emergency call a lot.'

'But you must have a girl friend.'

He was actually blushing. 'Well, you know . . .'

'Tell me,' Eve teased him.

'I don't have a regular girl friend.'

'I'll bet all the nurses are crazy about you.'

'No. I'm afraid I'm not a very romantic kind of person.'

To say the least, Eve thought. And yet, when she discussed Keith Webster with the nurses and interns who came in to perform various indignities on her body, they spoke of him as though he were some kind of god.

'The man is a miracle worker,' one intern said. 'There's nothing he can't do with a human face.'

They told her about his work with deformed children and criminals, but when Eve asked Keith Webster about it, he dismissed the subject with, 'Unfortunately, the world judges people by their looks. I try to help those who were born with physical deficiencies. It can make a big difference in their lives.'

Eve was puzzled by him. He was not doing it for the money or the glory. He was totally selfless. She had never met anyone like him, and she wondered what motivated him. But it was an idle curiosity. She had no interest in Keith Webster, except for what he could do for her.

Fifteen days after Eve checked into the hospital, she was moved to a private clinic in upstate New York.

'You'll be more comfortable here,' Dr Webster assured her.

Eve knew it was much farther for him to travel to see her, and yet he still appeared every day.

'Don't you have any other patients?' Eve asked.

'Not like you.'

Five weeks after Eve entered the clinic, Keith Webster removed the bandages. He turned her head from side to side. 'Do you feel any pain?' he asked.

'No.'

'Any tightness?'

'No.'

Dr Webster looked up at the nurse. 'Bring Miss Blackwell a mirror.'

Eve was filled with a sudden fear. For weeks she had been longing to look at herself in a mirror. Now that the moment was here, she was terrified. She wanted her own face, not the face of some stranger.

When Dr Webster handed her the mirror, she said faintly, 'I'm afraid –'

'Look at yourself,' he said gently.

She raised the mirrow slowly. It was a miracle! There was no change at all; it was her face. She searched for the signs of scars. There were none. Her eyes filled with tears.

She looked up and said, 'Thank you,' and reached out to give Keith Webster a kiss. It was meant to be a brief thank-you kiss, but she could feel his lips hungry on hers.

He pulled away, suddenly embarrassed. 'I'm – I'm glad you're pleased,' he said.

Pleased! 'Everyone was right. You *are* a miracle worker.'

He said shyly, 'Look what I had to work with.'

THIRTY-ONE

George Mellis had been badly shaken by what had happened. He had come perilously close to destroying everything he wanted. George had not been fully aware before of how much the control of Kruger-Brent, Ltd., meant to him. He had been satisfied to live on gifts from lonely ladies, but he was married to a Blackwell now, and within his reach was a company larger than anything his father had ever conceived of. *Look at me, Papa. I'm alive again. I own a company bigger than yours.* It was no longer a game. He knew he would kill to get what he wanted.

George devoted himself to creating the image of the perfect husband. He spent every possible moment with Alexandra. They breakfasted together, he took her out to lunch and he made it a point to be home early every evening. On weekends they went to the beach house Kate Blackwell owned in East Hampton, on Long Island, or flew to Dark Harbor in the company Cessna 620. Dark

Harbor was George's favourite. He loved the rambling old house, with its beautiful antiques and priceless paintings. He wandered through the vast rooms. *Soon all this will be mine*, he thought. It was a heady feeling.

George was also the perfect grandson-in-law. He paid a great deal of attention to Kate. She was eighty-one, chairman of the board of Kruger-Brent, Ltd., and a remarkably strong, vital woman. George saw to it that he and Alexandra dined with her once a week, and he telephoned the old woman every few days to chat with her. He was carefully building up the picture of a loving husband and caring grandson-in-law.

No one would ever suspect him of murdering two people he loved so much.

George Mellis's sense of satisfaction was abruptly shattered by a telephone call from Dr John Harley.

'I've made arrangements for you to see a psychiatrist. Dr Peter Templeton.'

George made his voice warm and ingratiating. 'That's really not necessary any more, Dr Harley. I think –'

'I don't give a damn what you think. We have an agreement – I don't report you to the police, and you consult a psychiatrist. If you wish to break that agree –'

'No, no,' George said hastily. 'If that's what you want, fine.'

'Dr Templeton's telephone number is five-five-

five-three-one-six-one. He's expecting your call. Today.' And Dr Harley slammed down the receiver.

The damned busybody, George thought angrily. The last thing in the world he needed was to waste time with a shrink, but he could not risk Dr Harley's talking. He would call this Dr Templeton, see him once or twice and that would be the end of it.

Eve telephoned George at the office. 'I'm home.'

'Are you –?' He was afraid to ask. 'All right?'

'Come and see for yourself. Tonight.'

'It's difficult for me to get away just now. Alex and I –'

'Eight o'clock.'

He could hardly believe it. Eve stood in front of him, looking just as beautiful as ever. He studied her face closely and could find no sign of the terrible damage he had inflicted upon her.

'It's incredible! You – you look exactly the same.'

'Yes. I'm still beautiful, aren't I, George?' She smiled, a cat smile, thinking of what she planned to do to him. He was a sick animal, not fit to live. He would pay in full for what he had done to her, but not yet. She still needed him. They stood there, smiling at each other.

'Eve, I can't tell you how sorry I –'

She held up a hand. 'Let's not discuss it. It's over. Nothing has changed.'

But George remembered that something had

changed. 'I got a call from Harley,' he said. 'He's arranged for me to see some damned psychiatrist.'

Eve shook her head. 'No. Tell him you haven't time.'

'I tried. If I don't go, he'll turn in a report of the – the accident to the police.'

'Damn!'

She stood there, deep in thought. 'Who is he?'

'The psychiatrist? Someone named Templeton. Peter Templeton.'

'I've heard of him. He has a good reputation.'

'Don't worry. I can just lie on his couch for fifty minutes and say nothing. If –'

Eve was not listening. An idea had come to her, and she was exploring it.

She turned to George. 'This may be the best thing that could have happened.'

Peter Templeton was in his middle thirties, just over six feet, with broad shoulders, clean-cut features and inquisitive blue eyes, and he looked more like a quarterback than a doctor. At the moment, he was frowning at a notation on his schedule: *George Mellis – grandson-in-law of Kate Blackwell*.

The problems of the rich held no interest for Peter Templeton. Most of his colleagues were delighted to get socially prominent patients. When Peter Templeton had first begun his practice, he had had his share, but he had quickly found he was unable to sympathize with their problems. He had dowagers in his office literally screaming because they had not been invited to some social event, financiers threatening to commit suicide because they had lost money in the stock market, overweight matrons who alternated between feasting and fat farms. The world was full of problems, and Peter Templeton had long since decided that these were not the problems he was interested in helping to solve.

George Mellis. Peter had reluctantly agreed to see him only because of his respect for Dr John Harley. 'I wish you'd send him somewhere else, John,' Peter Templeton had said. 'I really have a full schedule.'

'Consider this a favour, Peter.'

'What's his problem?'

'That's your department. I'm just an old country doctor.'

'All right,' Peter had agreed. 'Have him call me.'

Now he was here. Dr Templeton pressed down the button on the intercom on his desk. 'Send Mr Mellis in.'

Peter Templeton had seen photographs of George Mellis in newspapers and magazines, but he was still unprepared for the overpowering vitality of the man. He gave new meaning to the word *charisma*.

They shook hands. Peter said, 'Sit down, Mr Mellis.'

George looked at the couch. 'Over there?'

'Wherever you're comfortable.'

George took the chair opposite the desk. George looked at Peter Templeton and smiled. He had thought he would dread this moment, but after his talk with Eve, he had changed his mind. Dr Templeton was going to be his ally, his witness.

Peter studied the man opposite him. When patients came to see him for the first time, they were invariably nervous. Some covered it up with bravado, others were silent or talkative or defensive. Peter could detect no signs of nervousness in this man. On the contrary, he seemed to be enjoying himself. *Curious*, Peter thought.

'Dr Harley tells me you have a problem.'

George sighed. 'I'm afraid I have two.'

'Why don't you tell me about them?'

'I feel so ashamed. That's why I – I insisted on coming to see you.' He leaned forwards in his chair and said earnestly, 'I did something I've never done before in my life, Doctor. I struck a woman.'

Peter waited.

'We were having an argument and I blacked out, and when I came to, I had . . . hit her.' He let his voice break slightly. 'It was terrible.'

Peter Templeton's inner voice told him he already knew what George Mellis's problem was. He enjoyed beating up women.

'Was it your wife you struck?'

'My sister-in-law.'

Peter had occasionally come across items about the Blackwell twins in newspapers or magazines when they appeared at charity events or society affairs. They were identical, Peter recalled, and strikingly beautiful. So this man had hit his sister-in-law. Peter found that mildly interesting. He also found it interesting that George Mellis made it sound as though he had merely slapped her once or twice. If that had been true, John Harley would not have insisted that Peter see Mellis.

'You say you hit her. Did you hurt her?'

'As a matter of fact, I hurt her pretty badly. As I told you, Doctor, I blacked out. When I came to, I – I couldn't believe it.'

When I came to. The classic defence. I didn't do it, my subconscious did it.

'Do you have any idea what caused that reaction?'

'I've been under a terrible strain lately. My father has been seriously ill. He's had several heart attacks. I've been deeply concerned about him. We're a close family.'

'Is your father here?'

'He's in Greece.'

That Mellis. 'You said you had two problems.'

'Yes. My wife, Alexandra . . .' He stopped.

'You're having marital problems?'

'Not in the sense you mean. We love each other very much. It's just that –' He hesitated. 'Alexandra hasn't been well lately.'

'Physically?'

'Emotionally. She's constantly depressed. She keeps talking about suicide.'

'Has she sought professional help?'

583

George smiled sadly. 'She refuses.'

Too bad, Peter thought. *Some Park Avenue doctor is being cheated out of a fortune.* 'Have you discussed this with Dr Harley?'

'No.'

'Since he's the family doctor, I would suggest you speak with him. If he feels it's necessary, he'll recommend a psychiatrist.'

George Mellis said nervously, 'No. I don't want Alexandra to feel I'm discussing her behind her back. I'm afraid Dr Harley would –'

'That's all right, Mr Mellis. I'll give him a call.'

'Eve, we're in trouble,' George snapped. 'Big trouble.'

'What happened?'

'I did exactly as you told me. I said I was concerned about Alexandra, that she was suicidal.'

'And?'

'The sonofabitch is going to call John Harley and discuss it with him!'

'Oh, Christ! We can't let him.'

Eve began to pace. She stopped suddenly. 'All right. I'll handle Harley. Do you have another appointment with Templeton?'

'Yes.'

'Keep it.'

The following morning Eve went to see Dr Harley at his office. John Harley liked the Blackwell family. He had watched the children grow up. He had gone through the tragedy of Marianne's death and the attack on Kate, and putting Tony away in a sanatorium. Kate had suffered so much. And then the rift between Kate and Eve. He could not imagine what had caused it, but it was none of his business. His business was to keep the family physically healthy.

When Eve walked into his office, Dr Harley looked at her and said, 'Keith Webster did a fantastic job!' The only telltale mark was a very thin, barely visible red scar across her forehead. Eve said, 'Dr Webster is going to remove the scar in a month or so.'

Dr Harley patted Eve's arm. 'It only makes you more beautiful, Eve. I'm very pleased.' He motioned her to a chair. 'What can I do for you?'

'This isn't about me, John. It's about Alex.'

Dr Harley frowned. 'Is she having a problem? Something to do with George?'

'Oh, no,' Eve said quickly. 'George is behaving perfectly. In fact, it's George who's concerned about her. Alex has been acting strangely lately. She's been very depressed. Suicidal, even.'

Dr Harley looked at Eve and said flatly, 'I don't believe it. That doesn't sound like Alexandra.'

'I know. I didn't believe it either, so I went to see her. I was shocked by the change in her. She's in a state of deep depression. I'm really worried, John. I can't go to Gran about it – that's why I came to you. You've got to do something.' Her eyes misted. 'I've lost my grandmother. I couldn't bear to lose my sister.'

'How long has this been going on?'

'I'm not sure. I pleaded with her to talk to you about it. At first she refused, but I finally persuaded her. You've got to help her.'

'Of course I will. Have her come in tomorrow morning. And try not to worry, Eve. There are new medicines that work miracles.'

Dr Harley walked her to the door of his office. He wished Kate were not so unforgiving. Eve was such a caring person.

When Eve returned to her apartment, she carefully cold-creamed away the red scar on her forehead.

The following morning at ten o'clock, Dr Harley's receptionist announced, 'Mrs George Mellis is here to see you, Doctor.'

'Send her in.'

She walked in slowly, unsure of herself. She was pale, and there were dark circles under her eyes.

John Harley took her hand and said, 'It's good to see you, Alexandra. Now what's this I hear about your having problems?'

Her voice was low. 'I feel foolish bothering you, John. I'm sure there's nothing wrong with me. If Eve hadn't insisted, I never would have come. I feel fine, physically.'

'What about emotionally?'

She hesitated. 'I don't sleep very well.'

'What else?'

'You'll think I'm a hypochondriac . . .'

'I know you better than that, Alexandra.'

She lowered her eyes. 'I feel depressed all the time. Sort of anxious and . . . tired. George goes out of his way to make me happy and to think up things for us to do together and places for us to go. The problem is that I don't feel like doing anything or going anywhere. Everything seems so – hopeless.'

He was listening to every word, studying her. 'Anything else?'

'I – I think about killing myself.' Her voice was so soft he could barely hear her. She looked up at him and said, 'Am I going crazy?'

He shook his head. 'No. I don't think you're going crazy. Have you ever heard of anhedonia?'

She shook her head.

'It's a biological disturbance that causes the symptoms you've described. It's a fairly common condition, and there are some new drugs that make it easy to treat. These drugs have no side effects, and they're effective. I'm going to examine you, but I'm sure we won't find anything really wrong.'

When the examination was completed and she had gotten dressed again, Dr Harley said, 'I'm going to give you a prescription for Wellbutrin. It's part of a new generation of anti-depressants – one of the new wonder drugs.'

She watched listlessly as he wrote out a prescription.

'I want you to come back and see me a week from today. In the meantime, if you have any problems, call me, day or. night.' He handed her the prescription.

'Thank you, John,' she said. 'I just hope these will stop the dream.'

'What dream?'

'Oh, I thought I told you. It's the same one very night. I'm on a boat and it's windy, and I hear the sea calling. I walk to the rail and look down and I see myself in the water, drowning . . .'

She walked out of Dr Harley's office and onto the street. She leaned against the building, taking deep breaths. *I did it*, Eve thought exultantly. *I got away with it*. She threw the prescription away.

THIRTY-TWO

Kate Blackwell was tired. The meeting had gone on too long. She looked around the conference table at the three men and three women on the executive board. They all seemed fresh and vital. *So it's not the meeting that has been going on too long*, Kate thought. *I've gone on too long. I'll be eighty-two. I'm getting old.* The thought depressed her, not because she had any fear of dying, but because she was not ready yet. She refused to die until Kruger-Brent, Ltd., had a member of the Blackwell family running it. After the bitter disappointment with Eve, Kate had tried to build her future plans around Alexandra.

'You know I would do anything for you, Gran, but I'm simply not interested in becoming involved with the company. George would be an excellent executive . . .'

'Do you agree, Kate?' Brad Rogers was addressing her.

The question shook Kate out of her reverie. She

looked towards Brad guiltily. 'I'm sorry. What was the question?'

'We were discussing the Deleco merger.' His voice was patient. Brad Rogers was concerned about Kate Blackwell. In recent months she had started daydreaming during board meetings, and then just when Brad Rogers decided Kate was becoming senile and should retire from the board, she would come up with some stunning insight that would make everyone wonder why *he* had not thought of it. She was an amazing woman. He thought of their brief, long-ago affair and wondered again why it had ended so abruptly.

It was George Mellis's second visit to Peter Templeton. 'Has there been much violence in your past, Mr Mellis?'

George shook his head. 'No. I abhor violence.' *Make a note of that, you smug sonofabitch. The coroner is going to ask you about that.*

'You told me your mother and father never physically punished you.'

'That is correct.'

'Would you say you were an obedient child?'

Careful. There are traps here. 'About average, I suppose.'

'The average child usually gets punished at some time or another for breaking the rules of the grown-up world.'

George gave him a deprecating smile. 'I guess I didn't break any rules.'

He's lying, Peter Templeton thought. *The question is why? What is he concealing?* He recalled the conversation he had had with Dr Harley after the first session with George Mellis.

'He said he hit his sister-in-law, John and –'

'*Hit* her!' John Harley's voice was filled with indignation. 'It was butchery, Peter. He smashed her cheekbone, broke her nose and three ribs, and burned her buttocks and the soles of her feet with cigarettes.'

Paul Templeton felt a wave of disgust wash over him. 'He didn't mention that to me.'

'I'll bet he didn't,' Dr Harley snapped. 'I told him if he didn't go to you, I was going to report him to the police.'

Peter remembered George's words: *I feel ashamed. That's why I insisted on coming to see you.* So he had lied about that, too.

'Mellis told me his wife is suffering from depression, that she's talking about suicide.'

'Yes, I can vouch for that. Alexandra came to see me a few days ago. I prescribed Wellbutrin. I'm quite concerned about her. What's your impression of George Mellis?'

Peter said slowly, 'I don't know yet. I have a feeling he's dangerous.'

Dr Keith Webster was unable to get Eve Blackwell out of his mind. She was like a beautiful goddess, unreal and untouchable. She was outgoing and vivacious and stimulating, while he was shy and dull and drab. Keith Webster had never married, because he had never found a woman he felt was unworthy enough to be his wife. Apart from his work, his self-esteem was negligible. He had grown up with a fiercely domineering mother and a weak, bullied father. Keith Webster's sexual drive was low, and what little there was of it was sublimated in his work. But now he began to dream about Eve Blackwell, and when he recalled the dreams in the morning, he was embarrassed. She was completely healed and there was no reason for him to see her anymore, yet he knew he had to see her.

He telephoned her at her apartment. 'Eve? This is Keith Webster. I hope I'm not disturbing you. I – er – I was thinking about you the other day, and I – I was just wondering how you were getting along?'

'Fine, thank you, Keith. How are *you* getting along?' There was that teasing note in her voice again.

'Jus – just fine,' he said. There was a silence. He summoned up his nerve. 'I guess you're probably too busy to have lunch with me.'

Eve smiled to herself. He was such a deliciously timid little man. It would be amusing. 'I'd love to, Keith.'

'Would you really?' She could hear the note of surprise in his voice. 'When?'

'What about tomorrow?'

'It's a date.' He spoke quickly, before she could change her mind.

*　*　*

Eve enjoyed the luncheon. Dr Keith Webster acted like a young schoolboy in love. He dropped his napkin, spilled his wine and knocked over a vase of flowers. Watching him, Eve thought with amusement, *No one would ever guess what a brilliant surgeon he is*.

When the luncheon was over, Keith Webster asked shyly, 'Could we – could we do this again sometime?'

She replied with a straight face, 'We'd better not, Keith. I'm afraid I might fall in love with you.'

He blushed wildly, not knowing what to say.

Eve patted his hand. 'I'll never forget you.'

He knocked over the vase of flowers again.

John Harley was having lunch at the hospital cafeteria when Keith Webster joined him.

Keith said, 'John, I promise to keep it confidential; but I'd feel a lot better if you told me the truth about what happened to Eve Blackwell.'

Harley hesitated, then shrugged. 'All right. It was her brother-in-law, George Mellis.'

And Keith Webster felt that now he was sharing a part of Eve's secret world.

George Mellis was impatient. 'The money is there, the will has been changed – What the hell are we waiting for?'

Eve sat on the couch, her long legs curled up under her, watching him as he paced.

'I want to get this thing over with, Eve.'

He's losing his nerve, Eve thought. He was like a deadly coiled snake. Dangerous. She had made a mistake with him once by goading him too far, and it had almost cost her her life. She would not make that mistake again.

'I agree with you,' she said slowly. 'I think it's time.'

He stopped pacing. 'When?'

'Next week.'

The session was almost over and George Mellis had not once mentioned his wife. Now, suddenly he said, 'I'm worried about Alexandra, Dr Templeton. Her depression seems to be worse. Last night she kept talking about drowning. I don't know what to do.'

'I spoke to John Harley. He's given her some medication he thinks will help her.'

'I hope so, Doctor,' George said earnestly. 'I couldn't stand it if anything happened to her.'

And Peter Templeton, his ear attuned to the unspoken words, had the uneasy feeling he was witnessing a charade. There was a deadly violence in this man. 'Mr Mellis, how would you describe your past relationships with women?'

'Normal.'

'Did you ever get angry with any of them, lose your temper?'

George Mellis saw where the questions were leading. 'Never.' *I'm too damned smart for you, Doc.* 'I told you, I don't believe in violence.'

It was butchery, Peter. He smashed her cheek-bone, broke her nose and three ribs, and burned her buttocks and the soles of her feet with cigarettes.

'Sometimes,' Peter said, 'to some people violence provides a necessary outlet, an emotional release.'

'I know what you mean. I have a friend who beats up whores.'

I have a friend. An alarm signal. 'Tell me about your friend.'

'He hates prostitutes. They're always trying to rip him off. So when he finishes with them, he roughs them up a little – just to teach them a lesson.' He looked at Peter's face, but saw no disapproval there. Emboldened, George went on. 'I remember once he and I were in Jamaica together. This little black hooker took him up to a hotel room, and after she got his pants off, she told him she wanted more money.' George smiled. 'He beat the shit out of her. I'll bet she won't try that on anyone again.'

He's psychotic, Peter Templeton decided. There was no friend, of course. He was boasting about himself, hiding behind an *alter ego*. The man was a megalomaniac, and a dangerous one.

Peter decided he had better have another talk with John Harley as quickly as possible.

The two men met for lunch at the Harvard Club. Peter Templeton was in a difficult position. He needed to get all the information he could about

George Mellis without breaching the confidentiality of the doctor-patient relationship.

'What can you tell me about George Mellis's wife?' he asked Harley.

'Alexandra? She's lovely. I've taken care of her and her sister, Eve, since they were babies.' He chuckled. 'You hear about identical twins, but you never really appreciate what that means until you see those two together.'

Peter asked slowly, 'They're identical twins?'

'Nobody could ever tell them apart. They used to play all kinds of pranks when they were little tykes. I remember once when Eve was sick and supposed to get a shot, I somehow wound up giving it to Alexandra.' He took a sip of his drink. 'It's amazing. Now they're grown up, and I still can't tell one from the other.'

Peter thought about that. 'You said Alexandra came to see you because she was feeling suicidal.'

'That's right.'

'John, how do you know it was Alexandra?'

'That's easy,' Dr Harley said. 'Eve still has a little scar on her forehead from the surgery after the beating George Mellis gave her.'

So that was a blind alley. 'I see.'

'How are you getting along with Mellis?'

Peter hesitated, wondering how much he could say. 'I haven't reached him. He's hiding behind a façade. I'm trying to break it down.'

'Be careful, Peter. If you want my opinion, the

man's insane.' He was remembering Eve lying in bed, in a pool of blood.

'Both sisters are heir to a large fortune, aren't they?' Peter asked.

Now it was John Harley's turn to hesitate. 'Well, it's private family business,' he said, 'but the answer is no. Their grandmother cut off Eve without a dime. Alexandra inherits everything.'

I'm worried about Alexandra, Dr Templeton. Her depression seems to be worse. She keeps talking about drowning. I couldn't stand it if anything happened to her.

It had sounded to Peter Templeton like a classic setup for murder – except that George Mellis was the heir to a large fortune of his own. There would be no reason for him to kill anyone for money. *You're imagining things*, Peter chided himself.

A woman was drowning in the cold sea, and he was trying to swim to her side, but the waves were too high, and she kept sinking under them and rising again. *Hold on*, he shouted. *I'm coming*. He tried to swim faster, but his arms and legs seemed leaden, and he watched as she went down again. When he reached the place where she had disappeared, he looked around and saw an enormous white shark bearing down on him. Peter Templeton woke up. He turned on the lights and sat up in bed, thinking about his dream.

Early the following morning, he telephoned Detective Lieutenant Nick Pappas.

Nick Pappas was a huge man, six feet four inches and weighing almost three hundred pounds. As any number of criminals could testify, not an ounce of it was fat. Lieutenant Pappas was with the homicide task force in the 'silk stocking' district in Manhattan. Peter had met him several years earlier while testifying as a psychiatric expert in a murder trial, and he and Pappas had become friends. Pappas's passion was chess, and the two met once a month to play.

Nick answered the phone. 'Homicide. Pappas.'

'It's Peter, Nick.'

'My friend! How go the mysteries of the mind?'

'Still trying to unravel them, Nick. How's Tina?'

'Fantastic. What can I do for you?'

'I need some information. Do you still have connections in Greece?'

'Do I!' Pappas moaned. 'I got a hundred relatives over there, and they all need money. The stupid part is I send it to them. Maybe you oughta analyse me.'

'Too late,' Peter told him. 'You're a hopeless case.'

'That's what Tina keeps telling me. What information do you need?'

'Have you ever heard of George Mellis?'

'The food family?'

'Yes.'

'He's not exactly on my beat, but I know who he is. What about him?'

'I'd like to know if he has any money.'

'You must be kiddin'. His family –'

'I mean money of his own.'

'I'll check it out, Peter, but it'll be a waste of time. The Mellises are rich-rich.'

'By the way, if you have anyone question George Mellis's father, tell him to handle it gently. The old man's had several heart attacks.'

'Okay. I'll put it out on the wire.'

Peter remembered the dream. 'Nick, would you mind making a telephone call instead? Today?'

There was a different note in Pappas's voice. 'Is there anything you'd like to tell me, Peter?'

'There's nothing to tell. I just want to satisfy my curiosity. Charge the phone call to me.'

'Damn right I will – and the dinner you're gonna buy me when you tell me what the fuck this is all about.'

'Deal.' Peter Templeton hung up. He felt a little better.

Kate Blackwell was not feeling well. She was at her desk talking on the telephone when she felt the sudden attack. The room started to spin, and she gripped her desk tightly until everything righted itself again.

Brad came into the office. He took one look at her pale face and asked, 'Are you all right, Kate?'

She let go of the desk. 'Just a little dizzy spell. Nothing important.'

'How long since you've had a medical checkup?'

'I don't have time for that nonsense, Brad.'

'Find time. I'm going to have Annette call and make an appointment for you with John Harley.'

'Bloody hell, Brad. Stop fussing, will you please?'

'Will you go see him?'

'If it will get you off my back.'

The following morning Peter Templeton's secretary said, 'Detective Pappas is calling on line one.'

Peter picked up the phone. 'Hello, Nick.'

'I think you and I better have a little talk, my friend.'

Peter felt a sudden anxiety stirring in him. 'Did you talk to someone about Mellis?'

'I talked to Old Man Mellis himself. First of all, he's never had a heart attack in his life, and second, he said as far as he's concerned, his son George is dead. He cut him off without a dime a few years ago. When I asked why, the old man hung up on me. Then I called one of my old buddies at headquarters in Athens. Your George Mellis is a real beauty. The police know him well. He gets his kicks beating up girls and boys. His last victim before he left Greece was a fifteen-year-old male prostitute. They found his body in a hotel, and tied him in with Mellis. The old man bought somebody off, and Georgie boy got his ass kicked out of Greece. For good. Does that satisfy you?'

It did more than satisfy Peter; it terrified him. 'Thanks, Nick. I owe you one.'

'Oh, no, pal. I think I'd like to collect on *this* one. If your boy's on the loose again, you'd better tell me.'

'I will as soon as I can, Nick. Give my love to Tina.' And Peter hung up. He had a lot to think about. George Mellis was coming in at noon.

Dr John Harley was in the middle of an examination when his receptionist said, 'Mrs George Mellis is here to see you, Doctor. She has no appointment, and I told her your schedule is –'

John Harley said, 'Bring her in the side door and put her in my office.'

Her face was paler than the last time, and the shadows under her eyes were darker. 'I'm sorry to barge in on you like this, John, but –'

'That's all right, Alexandra. What's the problem?'

'Everything. I – I feel awful.'

'Have you been taking the Wellbutrin regularly?'

'Yes.'

'And you still feel depressed?'

Her hands were clenched. 'It's worse than depression. It's – I feel desperate. I feel as though I have no control over anything anymore. I can't stand myself. I'm afraid I'm – I'm going to do something terrible.'

Dr Harley said reassuringly, 'There's nothing physically wrong with you. I'll stake my reputation on that. It's all emotional. I'm going to switch you to another drug, Nomifensine. It's very effective. You should notice a change within a few days.' He wrote out a prescription and handed it to her. 'If you don't feel better by Friday. I want you to call me. I may want to send you to a psychiatrist.'

Thirty minutes later, back in her apartment, Eve removed the pale foundation cream from her face and wiped away the smudges under her eyes.

The pace was quickening.

George Mellis sat opposite Peter Templeton, smiling and confident.

'How are you feeling today?'

'Much better, Doctor. These few sessions we've had have helped more than you know.'

'Have they? In what way?'

'Oh, just having someone to talk to. That's the principle the Catholic Church is built on, isn't it? Confession?'

'I'm glad you feel the sessions have been helpful. Is your wife feeling better?'

George frowned. 'I'm afraid not. She saw Dr Harley again, but she's talking about suicide more and more. I may take her away somewhere. I think she needs a change.'

It seemed to Peter that there was an ominous foreboding in those words. Could it be his imagination?

'Greece is a very relaxing place,' Peter said casually. 'Have you taken her there to meet your family?'

'Not yet. They're dying to meet Alex.' He grinned. 'The only problem is that every time Pop and I get together, he keeps trying to talk me into coming back and taking over the family business.'

And at that moment, Peter knew that Alexandra Mellis was in real danger.

Long after George Mellis had left Peter Templeton sat in his office going over his notes. Finally, he reached for the telephone and dialled a number.

'I want you to do me a favour, John. Can you find out where George Mellis took his wife on their honeymoon?'

'I can tell you right now. I gave them some shots before they left. They went to Jamaica.'

I have a friend who beats up whores . . . I remember once we were in Jamaica together. This little black whore took him up to a hotel room, and after she got his pants off, she told him she wanted more money . . . He beat the shit out of her. I'll bet she won't try that on anyone again.

Still, there was no proof that George Mellis was planning to kill his wife. John Harley had verified that Alexandra Mellis was suicidal. *It's not my problem*, Peter tried to tell himself. But he knew it *was* his problem.

Peter Templeton had had to work his way through school. His father had been the caretaker of a college in a small town in Nebraska, and even with a scholarship, Peter had not been able to afford to go to one of the Ivy League medical schools. He had been graduated from the University of Nebraska with honours and had gone on to study psychiatry. He had been successful from the start. His secret was that he genuinely liked people; he cared what happened to them. Alexandra Mellis was not a patient, yet he was involved with her. She was a missing part of the puzzle, and meeting her face-to-face might help him solve it. He took out George Mellis's file, found his home number and telephoned Alexandra Mellis. A maid summoned her to the phone.

'Mrs Mellis, my name is Peter Templeton. I'm –'

'Oh, I know who you are, Doctor. George has told me about you.'

Peter was surprised. He would have bet that George Mellis would not have mentioned him to his wife. 'I wondered if we could meet. Perhaps lunch?'

'Is it about George? Is something wrong?'

'No, nothing. I just thought we might have a talk.'

'Yes, certainly, Dr Templeton.'

They made an appointment for the following day.

They were seated at a corner table at La Grenouille. From the moment Alexandra had walked into the restaurant, Peter had been unable to take his eyes off her. She was dressed simply in a white skirt and blouse that showed off her figure, and she wore a single strand of pearls around her neck. Peter looked for signs of the tiredness and depression Dr Harley had mentioned. There were none. If Alexandra was aware of Peter's stare, she gave no sign of it.

'My husband is all right, isn't he, Dr Templeton?'

'Yes.' This was going to be much more difficult than Peter had anticipated. He was walking a very fine line. He had no right to violate the sanctity of the doctor-patient relationship, yet at the same time he felt that Alexandra Mellis must be warned.

After they had ordered, Peter said, 'Did your husband tell you why he's seeing me, Mrs Mellis?'

'Yes. He's been under a great strain lately. His partners at the brokerage firm where he works put most of the responsibility on his shoulders. George is very conscientious, as you probably know, Doctor.'

It was incredible. She was completely unaware of the attack on her sister. *Why had no one told her?*

'George told me how much better he felt having someone he could discuss his problems with.' She gave Peter a grateful smile. 'I'm very pleased that you're helping him.'

She was so innocent! She obviously idolized her husband. What Peter had to say could destroy her. How could he inform her that her husband was a psychopath who had murdered a young male prostitute, who had been banished by his family and who had brutally assaulted her sister? Yet, how could he *not?*

'It must be very satisfying being a psychiatrist,' Alexandra went on. 'You're able to help so many people.'

'Sometimes we can,' Peter said carefully. 'Sometimes we can't.'

The food arrived. They talked as they ate, and there was an easy rapport between them. Peter found himself enchanted by her. He suddenly became uncomfortably aware that he was envious of George Mellis.

'I'm enjoying this luncheon very much,' Alexandra finally said, 'but you wanted to see me for a reason, didn't you, Dr Templeton?'

The moment of truth had arrived.

'As a matter of fact, yes. I –'

Peter stopped. His next words could shatter her life. He had come to this luncheon determined to tell her of his suspicions and suggest that her husband be put in an institution. Now that he had met Alexandra, he found it was not so simple. He thought again of George Mellis's words: *She's not any better. It's the suicidal thing that worries me.* Peter thought he had never seen a happier, more normal person. Was that a result of the medication she was taking? At least he could ask her about that. He said, 'John Harley told me that you're taking –'

And George Mellis's voice boomed out. 'There

you are, darling! I called the house and they told me you'd be here.' He turned to Peter. 'Nice to see you, Dr Templeton. May I join you?'

And the opportunity vanished.

'*Why* did he want to meet Alex?' Eve demanded.

'I haven't the slightest idea,' George said. 'Thank God she left a message where she would be in case I wanted her. With Peter Templeton, for Christ's sake! I got over there fast!'

'I don't like it.'

'Believe me, there was no harm done. I questioned her afterwards, and she told me they didn't discuss anything in particular.'

'I think we'd better move up our plan.'

George Mellis felt an almost sexual thrill at her words. He had been waiting so long for this moment. 'When?'

'Now.'

THIRTY-THREE

The dizzy spells were getting worse, and things were beginning to blur in Kate's mind. She would sit at her desk considering a proposed merger and suddenly realize the merger had taken place ten years earlier. It frightened her. She finally decided to take Brad Roger's advice to see John Harley.

It had been a long time since Dr Harley had been able to persuade Kate Blackwell to have a checkup, and he took full advantage of her visit. He examined her thoroughly, and when he finished he asked her to wait for him in his office. John Harley was disturbed. Kate Blackwell was remarkably alert for her age, but there were disquieting signs. There was a definite hardening of the arteries, which would account for her occasional dizziness and weakened memory. She should have retired years ago, and yet she hung on tenaciously, unwilling to give the reins to anyone else. *Who am I to talk?* he thought. *I should have retired ages ago.*

Now, with the results of the examination in front of him, John Harley said, 'I wish I were in your condition, Kate.'

'Cut the soft-soap, John. What's my problem?'

'Age, mostly. There's a little hardening of the arteries, and –'

'Arteriosclerosis?'

'Oh. Is that the medical term for it?' Dr Harley asked. 'Whatever it is, you've got it.'

'How bad is it?'

'For your age, I'd say it was pretty normal. These things are all relative.'

'Can you give me something to stop these bloody dizzy spells? I hate fainting in front of a roomful of men. It looks bad for my sex.'

He nodded. 'I don't think that will be any problem. When are you going to retire, Kate?'

'When I have a great-grandson to take over the business.'

The two old friends who had known each other for so many years sized each other up across the desk. John Harley had not always agreed with Kate, but he had always admired her courage.

As though reading his mind, Kate sighed, 'Do you know one of the great disappointments of my life, John? Eve. I really cared for that child. I wanted to give her the world, but she never gave a damn about anyone but herself.'

'You're wrong, Kate. Eve cares a great deal about you.'

'Like bloody hell she does.'

'I'm in a position to know. Recently she' – he had to choose his words carefully – 'suffered a terrible accident. She almost died.'

Kate felt her heart lurch. 'Why – why didn't you tell me?'

'She wouldn't let me. She was so concerned you would be worried that she made me swear not to say a word.'

'Oh, my God.' It was an agonized whisper. 'Is – is she all right?' Kate's voice was hoarse.

'She's fine now.'

Kate sat, staring into space. 'Thank you for telling me, John. Thank you.'

'I'll write out a prescription for those pills.' When he finished writing the prescription, he looked up. Kate Blackwell had left.

Eve opened the door and stared unbelievingly. Her grandmother was standing there, stiff and straight as always, allowing no sign of frailty to show.

'May I come in?' Kate asked.

Eve stepped aside, unable to take in what was happening. 'Of course.'

Kate walked in and looked around the small apartment but she made no comment. 'May I sit down?'

'I'm sorry. Please do. Forgive me – this is so – Can I get you something? Tea, coffee, anything?'

'No, thank you. Are you well, Eve?'

'Yes, thank you. I'm fine.'

'I just came from Dr Harley. He told me you had been in a terrible accident.'

Eve watched her grandmother cautiously, not sure what was coming. 'Yes . . .'

'He said you were . . . near death. And that you would not allow him to tell me because you didn't want to worry me.'

So *that was it*. Eve was on surer ground now. 'Yes, Gran.'

'That would indicate to me.' Kate's voice was suddenly choked, 'that – that you cared.'

Eve started to cry from relief. 'Of course I care. I've always cared.'

And an instant later, Eve was in her grandmother's arms. Kate held Eve very close and pressed her lips to the blonde head in her lap. Then she whispered, 'I've been such a damned old fool. Can you ever forgive me?' Kate pulled out a linen handkerchief and blew her nose. 'I was too hard on you,' she declared. 'I couldn't bear it if anything happened to you.'

Eve stroked her grandmother's blue-veined hand soothingly and said, 'I'm all right, Gran. Everything's fine.'

Kate was on her feet, blinking back tears. 'We'll have a fresh start, all right?' She pulled Eve up to face her. 'I've been stubborn and unbending, like my father, I'm going to make amends for that. The first thing I'm going to do is put you back in my will, where you belong.'

What was happening was too good to be true! 'I – I don't care about the money. I only care about you.'

611

'You're my heiress – you and Alexandra. You two are all the family I have.'

'I'm getting along fine,' Eve said, 'but if it will make you happy –'

'It will make me very happy, darling. Very happy, indeed. When can you move back into the house?'

Eve hesitated for a moment. 'I think it would be better if I stayed here, but I'll see you as often as you want to see me. Oh, Gran, you don't know how lonely I've been.'

Kate took her granddaughter's hand and said, 'Can you forgive me?'

Eve looked her in the eye and said solemnly, 'Of course, I can forgive you.'

The moment Kate left, Eve mixed herself a stiff Scotch and water and sank down onto the couch to relive the incredible scene that had just occurred. She could have shouted aloud with joy. She and Alexandra were now the sole heirs to the Blackwell fortune. It would be easy enough to get rid of Alexandra. It was George Mellis Eve was concerned about. He had suddenly become a hindrance.

'There's been a change of plans,' Eve told George. 'Kate has put me back in her will.'

George paused in the middle of lighting a cigarette. 'Really? Congratulations.'

'If anything happened to Alexandra now, it

would look suspicious. So we'll take care of her later when –'

'I'm afraid later doesn't suit me.'

'What do you mean?'

'I'm not stupid, darling. If anything happens to Alexandra, *I'll* inherit her stock. You want me out of the picture, don't you?'

Eve shrugged. 'Let's say you're an unnecessary complication. I'm willing to make a deal with you. Get a divorce, and as soon as I come into the money, I'll give you –'

He laughed. 'You're funny. It's no good, baby. Nothing has changed. Alex and I have a date in Dark Harbor, Friday night. I intend to keep it.'

Alexandra was overjoyed when she heard the news about Eve and her grandmother. 'Now we're a family again,' she said.

The telephone.

'Hello. I hope I'm not disturbing you, Eve. It's Keith Webster.'

He had started telephoning her two or three times a week. At first his clumsy ardour had amused Eve, but lately he had become a nuisance.

'I can't talk to you now,' Eve said, 'I was just going out the door.'

'Oh.' His voice was apologetic. 'Then I won't keep you. I have two tickets for the horse show next week. I know you love horses, and I thought –'

'Sorry. I will probably be out of town next week.'

'I see.' She could hear the disappointment in his voice. 'Perhaps the following week, then. I'll get tickets to a play. What would you like to see?'

'I've seen them all,' Eve said curtly. 'I have to run.' She replaced the receiver. It was time to get dressed. She was meeting Rory McKenna, a young actor she had seen in an off-Broadway play. He was five years younger than she, and he was like an insatiable wild stallion. Eve visualized his making love to her, and she felt a moisture between her legs. She looked forwards to an exciting evening.

On his way home, George Mellis stopped to buy flowers for Alexandra. He was in an exuberant mood. It was a delicious irony that the old lady had put Eve back in her will, but it changed nothing. After Alexandra's accident, he would take care of Eve. The arrangements were all made. On Friday Alexandra would be waiting for him at Dark Harbor. 'Just the two of us,' he had pleaded as he kissed her. 'Get rid of all the servants, darling.'

Peter Templeton was unable to get Alexandra Mellis out of his mind. He heard the echo of George Mellis's words: *I may take her away somewhere. I think she needs a change.* Every instinct told Peter that Alexandra was in danger, yet he was powerless to act. He could not go to Nick Pappas with his suspicions. He had no proof.

* * *

Across town, in the executive offices of Kruger-Brent Ltd, Kate Blackwell was signing a new will, leaving the bulk of her estate to her two grand-daughters.

In upstate New York, Tony Blackwell was stand-ing before his easel in the garden of the sanato-rium. The painting on the easel was a jumble of colours, the kind of painting an untalented child might do. Tony stepped back to look at it and smiled with pleasure.

Friday. 10:57 a.m.

At La Guardia Airport, a taxi pulled up in front of the Eastern Airlines shuttle terminal and Eve Blackwell got out. She handed the driver a hundred-dollar bill.

'Hey, I can't change this, lady,' he said. 'Have you got anything smaller?'

'No.'

'Then you'll have to get change inside.'

'I haven't time. I have to catch the next shuttle to Washington.' She looked at the Baume & Mercier watch on her wrist and made a decision. 'Keep the hundred dollars,' she told the startled driver.

Eve hurried into the terminal. She half-walked and half-ran to the departure gate marked Washington Shuttle. 'One round trip to Washington,' Eve said breathlessly.

The man looked at the clock above his head.

'You missed this one by two minutes. It's just taking off.'

'I've got to be on that plane. I'm meeting – Isn't there anything you can do?' She was near panic.

'Take it easy, miss. There's another shuttle leaving in an hour.'

'That's too – Damn it!'

He watched her regain control of herself.

'Very well. I'll wait. Is there a coffee shop around here?'

'No ma'am. But there's a coffee machine down the corridor.'

'Thank you.'

He looked after her and thought, *What a beauty. I sure envy the guy she's in such a hurry to meet.*

Friday. 2:00 p.m.

It will be a second honeymoon, Alexandra thought. The idea excited her. *Get rid of all the servants. I want it to be just the two of us, angel. We'll have a lovely weekend.* And now Alexandra was leaving the brownstone, on her way to Dark Harbor to meet George. She was running behind schedule. She had had a luncheon engagement, and it had taken longer than Alexandra had planned. She said to the maid, 'I'm going now. I'll be back Monday morning.'

As Alexandra reached the front door, the telephone rang. *I'm late. Let it ring,* she thought, and hurried out the door.

* * *

Friday. 7:00 p.m.

George Mellis had examined Eve's plan over and over. There was not a single flaw in it. *There will be a motor launch waiting for you at Philbrook Cove. Take it to Dark Harbor and make sure you're not seen. Tie it to the stern of the* Corsair. *You'll take Alexandra for a moonlight sail. When you're out at sea, do whatever turns you on, George – just don't leave any traces of blood. Dump the body overboard, get into the launch and leave the Corsair adrift. You'll take the launch back to Philbrook Cove, then catch the Lincolnville ferry to Dark Harbor. Take a taxi to the house. Use some excuse to get the driver to go in so that you'll both notice the* Corsair *is missing from the dock. They'll never find Alexandra's body. The tide will wash it out to sea. Two eminent doctors will testify it was a probable suicide.*

He found the motorboat moored at Philbrook Cove, waiting for him, according to plan.

George crossed the bay without running lights, using the lights of the moon to steer by. He passed a number of moored boats without being detected, and arrived at the dock at the Blackwell estate. He cut the motor and made the line fast to the *Corsair*, the large motor sailer.

She was talking on the telephone, waiting for him in the living room when George walked in. She waved to him, covered the receiver with her hand and mouthed, 'It's Eve.' She listened a moment, then, 'I have to go now, Eve. My darling just arrived. I'll see you at lunch next week.' She replaced the receiver and hurried over to hug George. 'You're early. I'm so pleased.'

'I got lonely for you, so I just dropped everything and came.'

She kissed him. 'I love you.'

'I love you, *matia mou*. Did you get rid of the servants?'

She smiled. 'It's just the two of us. Guess what? I made mousaka for you.'

He traced a finger lightly across the nipples straining against her silk blouse. 'Do you know what I've been thinking about all afternoon at that dreary office? Going for a sail with you. There's a brisk wind. Why don't we go out for an hour or two?'

'If you like. But my mousaka is –'

He cupped his hand over her breast. 'Dinner can wait. I can't.'

She laughed. 'All right. I'll go change. It won't take me a minute.'

'I'll race you.'

He went upstairs to his clothes closet, changed into a pair of slacks, a sweater and boat shoes. Now that the moment was here, he was filled with a sense of wild anticipation, a feeling of excitement that was almost an explosion.

He heard her voice. 'I'm ready, darling.'

He turned. She stood in the doorway, dressed in a sweater, a pair of black slacks and canvas shoes. Her long, blonde hair was tied back with a little blue ribbon. *My God, she's beautiful!* he thought. It seemed almost a shame to waste that beauty.

'So am I,' George told her.

She noticed the motor launch secured to the stern of the yacht. 'What's that for, darling?'

'There's a little island at the end of the bay that I've always wanted to explore,' George explained. 'We'll take the launch over to it so we won't have to worry about rocks.'

He cast off the lines and powered slowly out of the slip. He nosed into the wind to raise the mainsail and jib, and the boat fell off on a starboard tack. The wind caught the large sails and the *Corsair* surged forwards. George headed out to sea. As they cleared the breakwater, they were met with a stiff force-five wind, and the boat started heeling, its lee rail running under.

'It's wild and lovely,' she called out. 'I'm so happy, darling.'

He smiled. 'So am I.'

In an odd way, it gave George Mellis pleasure that Alexandra was happy, that she was going to die happy. He scanned the horizon to make certain no other boats were close by. There were only faint lights from afar. It was time.

He put the boat on automatic pilot, took one last look around the empty horizon and walked over to the lee railing, his heart beginning to pound with excitement.

'Alex,' he called. 'Come and look at this.'

She made her way over to him and looked down at the cold, dark water racing below them.

'Come to me.' His voice was a harsh command.

She moved into his arms, and he kissed her hard on the lips. His arms closed around her, hugging her, and he felt her body relax. He flexed his muscles and began to lift her in the air towards the railing.

She was fighting him suddenly. 'George!'

He lifted her higher, and he felt her try to pull away, but he was too strong for her. She was almost on top of the railing now, her feet kicking wildly, and he braced himself to shove her over the side. At that instant, he felt a sudden white-hot pain in his chest. His first thought was, *I'm having a heart attack*. He opened his mouth to speak and blood came spurting out. He dropped his arms and looked down at his chest in disbelief. Blood was pouring from a gaping wound in it. He looked up, and she was standing there with a bloody knife in her hand, smiling at him.

George Mellis's last thought was, *Eve* . . .

THIRTY-FOUR

It was ten o'clock in the evening when Alexandra arrived at the house at Dark Harbor. She had tried telephoning George there several times, but there had been no answer. She hoped he would not be angry because she had been detained. It had been a stupid mix-up. Early that afternoon, as Alexandra was leaving for Dark Harbor, the phone had rung. She had thought, *I'm late. Let it ring*, and had gone out to the car. The maid had come hurrying after her.

'Mrs Mellis! It's your sister. She says it is urgent.'

When Alexandra picked up the telephone, Eve said, 'Darling, I'm in Washington, DC. I'm having a terrible problem. I have to see you.'

'Of course,' Alexandra said instantly. 'I'm leaving for Dark Harbor now to meet George, but I'll be back Monday morning and –'

'This can't wait.' Eve sounded desperate. 'Will you meet me at La Guardia Airport? I'll be on the five o'clock plane.'

'I'd like to, Eve, but I told George –'

'This is an emergency, Alex. But, of course, if you're too busy.'

'Wait! All right. I'll be there.'

'Thanks, darling. I knew I could count on you.'

It was so seldom that Eve asked her for a favour, she could not refuse her. She would catch a later plane to the island. She telephoned George at the office to tell him she would be detained, but he was not in. She left a message with his secretary. An hour later she took a taxi to La Guardia in time to meet the five o'clock plane from Washington. Eve was not on it. Alexandra waited for two hours, and there was still no sign of Eve. Alexandra had no idea where to reach Eve in Washington. Finally, because there was nothing else she could do, Alexandra took a plane to the island. Now as she approached Cedar Hill House, she found it dark. Surely George should have arrived by now. Alexandra went from room to room, turning on the lights.

'George?'

There was no sign of him. She telephoned her home in Manhattan. The maid answered.

'Is Mr Mellis there?' Alexandra asked.

'Why, no, Mrs Mellis. He said you would both be away for the weekend.'

'Thank you, Marie. He must have been detained somewhere.'

There had to be a logical reason for his absence. Obviously some business had come up

622

at the last minute and, as usual, the partners had asked George to handle it. He would be along at any moment. She dialled Eve's number.

'Eve!' Alexandra exclaimed. 'What on earth happened to you?'

'What happened to *you*? I waited at Kennedy, and when you didn't show up —'

'*Kennedy!* You said *La Guardia.*'

'No, darling, Kennedy.'

'But —' It did not matter any longer. 'I'm sorry,' Alexandra said. 'I must have misunderstood. Are you all right?'

Eve said, 'I am now. I've had a hellish time. I got involved with a man who's a big political figure in Washington. He's insanely jealous and —' She laughed. 'I can't go into the details over the telephone. The phone company will take out both our phones. I'll tell you all about it Monday.'

'All right,' Alexandra said. She was enormously relieved.

'Have a nice weekend,' Eve told her. 'How's George?'

'He's not here.' Alexandra tried to keep the note of concern out of her voice. 'I suppose he got tied up on business and hasn't had a chance to call me.'

'I'm sure you'll hear from him soon. Good-night, darling.'

'Good-night, Eve.'

Alexandra replaced the receiver and thought, *It would be nice if Eve found someone really wonderful. Someone as good and kind as George.* She looked at her watch. It was almost eleven o'clock. Surely he would have had a chance to call by now. She picked up the telephone and dialled the number of the brokerage firm. There was no answer. She telephoned his club. No, they had not seen Mr Mellis. By midnight, Alexandra was alarmed, and by one a.m. she was in a state of panic. She was not sure what to do. It was possible that George was out with a client and could not get to a telephone, or perhaps he had had to fly somewhere and had not been able to reach her before he left. There was some simple explanation. If she called the police and George walked in, she would feel like a fool.

At two a.m. she telephoned the police. There was no police force on the island of Isleboro itself, and the closest station was in Waldo County.

A sleepy voice said, 'Waldo County Sheriff's Department. Sergeant Lambert.'

'This is Mrs George Mellis at Cedar Hill House.'

'Yes, Mrs Mellis.' The voice was instantly alert. 'What can I do for you?'

'To tell you the truth, I'm not sure,' Alexandra said hesitantly. 'My husband was supposed to have met me at the house earlier this evening, and he – he hasn't shown up.'

'I see.' There were all kinds of implications in that phrase. The sergeant knew at least three reasons why a husband could be away from home at two a.m. in the morning: blondes, brunettes and redheads.

He said tactfully, 'Is it possible he was detained on business somewhere?'

'He – he usually calls.'

'Well, you know how it is, Mrs Mellis. Sometimes you get in a situation where you can't call. I'm sure you'll be hearing from him.'

Now she *did* feel like a fool. Of course there was nothing the police could do. She had read somewhere that a person had to be missing for twenty-four hours before the police would even start looking for him, and George was not *missing*, for heaven's sake. He was just late.

'I'm sure you're right,' Alexandra said into the telephone. 'I'm sorry to have troubled you.'

'Not at all, Mrs Mellis. I'll bet he'll be on the seven o'clock ferry first thing in the morning.'

He was not on the seven o'clock ferry, or the one after that. Alexandra telephoned the Manhattan house again. George was not there.

A feeling of disaster began to grip Alexandra. George had been in an accident; he was in a hospital somewhere, ill or dead. If only there had not been the mix-up with Eve at the airport. Perhaps George had arrived at the house, and when he found she was not there, he had gone. But that left too many things unexplained. He would have left a note. He could have surprised burglars and been attacked or kidnapped. Alexandra went through the house, room by room, looking for any possible clue. Everything was intact. She went down to the rock. The *Corsair* was there, safely moored.

She telephoned the Waldo County Sheriff's Department again. Lieutenant Philip Ingram, a twenty-year veteran of the force, was on morning duty. He was already aware that George Mellis had not been home all night. It had been the chief topic of conversation around the station all morning, most of it ribald.

Now he said to Alexandra, 'There's no trace of him at all, Mrs Mellis? All right. I'll come out there myself.' He knew it would be a waste of time. Her old man was probably tomcatting around in some alley. *But when the Blackwells call, the peasants come running*, he thought wryly. Anyway, this was a nice lady. He had met her a few times over the years.

'Back in an hour or so,' he told the desk sergeant.

Lieutenant Ingram listened to Alexandra's story, checked the house and the dock and reached the conclusion that Alexandra Mellis had a problem on her hands. George Mellis was to have met his wife the evening before at Dark Harbor, but he had not shown up. While it was not Lieutenant Ingram's problem, he knew it would do him no harm to be helpful to a member of the Blackwell family. Ingram telephoned the island airport and the ferry terminal at Lincolnville. George Mellis had used neither facility within the past twenty-four hours. 'He didn't come to Dark Harbor,' the lieutenant told Alexandra. *And where the hell did that leave things? Why would the man have dropped out of sight?* In the lieutenant's considered opinion, no man in his right mind would voluntarily leave a woman like Alexandra.

'We'll check the hospitals and mor –' He caught himself. 'And other places, and I'll put out an APB on him.'

Alexandra was trying to control her emotions, but he could see what an effort it was. 'Thank you, Lieutenant. I don't have to tell you how much I'll appreciate anything you can do.'

'That's my job,' Lieutenant Ingram replied.

When Lieutenant Ingram returned to the station, he began calling hospitals and morgues. The responses were negative. There was no accident report on George Mellis. Lieutenant Ingram's next move was to call a reporter friend on the *Maine Courier*. After that, the lieutenant sent out a missing person all-points-bulletin.

The afternoon newspapers carried the story in headlines: HUSBAND OF BLACKWELL HEIRESS MISSING.

Peter Templeton first heard the news from Detective Nick Pappas.

'Peter, remember askin' me a while ago to do some checkin' on George Mellis?'

'Yes . . .'

'He's done a vanishing act.'

'He's *what*?'

627

'Disappeared, vamoosed, gone.' He waited while Peter digested the news.

'Did he take anything with him? Money, clothes, passport?'

'Nope. According to the report we got from Maine, Mr Mellis just melted into thin air. You're his shrink. I thought you might have some idea why our boy would do a thing like that.'

Peter said truthfully, 'I haven't any idea, Nick.'

'If you think of anything, let me know. There's gonna be a lot of heat on this.'

'Yes,' Peter promised. 'I will.'

Thirty minutes later, Alexandra Mellis telephoned Peter Templeton, and he could hear the shrill edge of pain in her voice. 'I – George is missing. No one seems to know what happened to him. I was hoping he might have told you something that might have given you a clue or –' She broke off.

'I'm sorry, Mrs Mellis. He didn't. I have no idea what could have happened.'

'Oh.'

Peter wished there was some way he could comfort her. 'If I think of anything, I'll call you back. Where can I reach you?'

'I'm at Dark Harbor now, but I'm going to return to New York this evening. I'll be at my grandmother's.'

Alexandra could not bear the thought of being alone. She had talked to Kate several times that morning. 'Oh, darling, I'm sure there's nothing to worry about,' Kate said. 'He probably went off on some business deal and forgot to tell you.'

Neither of them believed it.

Eve saw the story of George's disappearance on television. There were photographs of the exterior of Cedar Hill House, and pictures of Alexandra and George after their wedding ceremony. There was a close-up of George, looking upward, with his eyes wide. Somehow it reminded Eve of the look of surprise on his face just before he died.

The television commentator was saying, 'There has been no evidence of foul play and no ransom demands have been made. The police speculate that George Mellis was possibly the victim of an accident and may be suffering from amnesia.' Eve smiled in satisfaction.

They would never find the body. It had been swept out to sea with the tide. Poor George. He had followed her plan perfectly. But she had changed it. She had flown up to Maine and rented a motor boat at Philbrook Cove, to be held for 'a friend.' She had then rented a second boat from a nearby dock and taken it to Dark Harbor, where she had waited for George. He had been totally unsuspecting. She had been careful to wipe the deck clean before she returned the yacht to the dock. After that, it had been a simple matter to tow George's rented motorboat back to its pier, return her boat and fly back to New York to await the telephone call she knew Alexandra would make.

It was a perfect crime. The police would list it as a mysterious disappearance.

The announcer was saying, 'In other news . . .' Eve switched the television set off.

She did not want to be late for her date with Rory McKenna.

At six o'clock the following morning, a fishing boat found George Mellis's body pinned against the breakwater at the mouth of Penobscot Bay. The early news reports called it a drowning and accidental death, but as more information came in, the tenor of the stories began to change. From the coroner's office came reports that what at first had been thought to have been shark bites were actually stab wounds. The evening newspaper editions screamed: MURDER SUSPECTED IN GEORGE MELLIS MYSTERY DEATH . . . MILLIONAIRE FOUND STABBED TO DEATH.

Lieutenant Ingram was studying the tide charts for the previous evening. When he was finished, he leaned back in his chair, a perplexed expression on his face. George Mellis's body would have been swept out to sea had it not been caught against the breakwater. What puzzled the lieutenant was that the body had to have been carried by the tide from the direction of Dark Harbor. Where George Mellis was not supposed to have been.

* * *

630

Detective Nick Pappas flew up to Maine to have a talk with Lieutenant Ingram.

'I think my department might be of some help to you in this case,' Nick said. 'We have some interesting background information on George Mellis. I know this is out of our jurisdiction, but if you were to ask for our cooperation, we'd be happy to give it to you, Lieutenant.'

In the twenty years Lieutenant Ingram had been with the Waldo County Sheriff's Department, the only real excitement he had seen was when a drunken tourist shot a moose head off the wall of a local curio shop. The George Mellis murder was front-page news, and Lieutenant Ingram sensed a chance to make a name for himself. With a little luck, it could lead to a job as a detective in the New York City Police Department, where the action was. And so now he looked at Nick Pappas and murmured, 'I don't know . . .'

As though reading his mind, Nick Pappas said, 'We're not looking for credit. There's gonna be a hell of a lot of pressure on this one, and it would make life easier for us if we could wrap it up fast. I could start by filling you in on George Mellis's background.'

Lieutenant Ingram decided he had nothing to lose. 'OK, you've got a deal.'

Alexandra was in bed, heavily sedated. Her mind stubbornly refused to accept the fact that George had been murdered. How could he have been?

There was no reason in the world for anyone to kill him. The police had talked of a knife wound, but they were wrong about that. It had to be some kind of accident. *No one would want to kill him . . . No one would want to kill him . . .* The opiate Dr Harley gave her finally took hold. She slept.

Eve had been stunned at the news that George's body had been found. *But perhaps it's a good thing*, Eve thought. *Alexandra will be the one under suspicion. She was there, on the island.*

Kate was seated next to Eve on the couch in the drawing room. The news had been a tremendous shock to Kate.

'Why would anyone want to murder George?' she asked.

Eve sighed. 'I don't know, Gran. I just don't know. My heart breaks for poor Alex.'

Lieutenant Philip Ingram was questioning the attendant on the Lincolnville-Isleboro ferry. 'Are you positive neither Mr not Mrs Mellis came over on the ferry Friday afternoon?'

'They didn't come over on my shift, Phil, and I checked with the morning man, and he didn't see 'em neither. They had to have come in by plane.'

'One more question, Lew. Did *any* strangers take the ferry across on Friday?'

'Hell,' the attendant said, 'you know we don't get no strangers goin' to the island this time of year. There might be a few tourists in the summer – but in *November*? She-e-e-it!'

Lieutenant Ingram went to talk to the manager of the Isleboro airport. 'George Mellis sure didn't fly in that evening, Phil. He musta come over to the island by ferry.'

'Lew said he didn't see him.'

'Well, hell, he couldn't a *swum* over, now could he?'

'What about Mrs Mellis?'

'Yep. She come in here in her Beechcraft about ten o'clock. I had my son, Charley, run her over to Cedar Hill from the airport.'

'What kind of mood did Mrs Mellis seem to be in?'

'Funny you should ask. She was as nervous as spit on a hot kettle. Even my boy noticed it. Usually she's calm, always has a pleasant word for everybody. But that night she was in a tearin' hurry.'

'One more question. Did any strangers fly in that afternoon or evening? Any unfamiliar faces?'

He shook his head. 'Nope. Just the regulars.'

An hour later, Lieutenant Ingram was on the phone talking to Nick Pappas. 'What I've got so far,' he told the New York detective, 'is damned confusing. Friday night Mrs Mellis arrived by private plane at the Isleboro airport around ten o'clock, but her husband wasn't with her, and he didn't come in by plane or ferry. In fact, there's nothin' to show he was on the island at all that night.'

'Except the tide.'

'Yeah.'

'Whoever killed him probably threw him over-board from a boat, figuring the tide would carry him out to sea. Did you check the *Corsair*?'

'I looked it over. No sign of violence, no blood-stains.'

'I'd like to bring a forensics expert up there. Would you mind?'

'Not as long as you remember our little deal.'

'I'll remember. See you tomorrow.'

Nick Pappas and a team of experts arrived the following morning. Lieutenant Ingram escorted them to the Blackwell dock, where the *Corsair* was tied up. Two hours later, the forensics expert said, 'Looks like we hit the jackpot, Nick. There are some bloodstains on the underside of the lee rail.'

That afternoon, the police laboratory verified that the stains matched George Mellis's blood type.

Manhattan's 'silk stocking' police precinct was busier than usual. A series of all-night drug busts had filled the prisoners' cage to capacity, and the holding cells were crowded with prostitutes, drunks and sex offenders. The noise and the stench competed for Peter Templeton's attention, as he was escorted through the din to Lieutenant Detective Pappas's office.

'Hey, Peter. Nice of you to drop by.'

On the phone Pappas had said, 'You're holdin'

out on me, chum. Be at my office before six o'clock, or I'll send a fuckin' SWAT team to bring you in.'

When his escort left the office, Peter asked, 'What's this all about, Nick? What's bothering you?'

'I'll tell you what's botherin' me. Someone's being clever. Do you know what we've got? A dead man who vanished from an island he never went to.'

'That doesn't make sense.'

'Tell me about it, pal. The ferryboat operator and the guy who runs the airport swear they never saw George Mellis on the night he disappeared. The only other way he could have gotten to Dark Harbor was by motorboat. We checked all the boat operators in the area. Zilch.'

'Perhaps he wasn't at Dark Harbor that night.'

'The forensic lab says different. They found evidence that Mellis was at the house and changed from a business suit into the sailing clothes he was wearin' when his body was found.'

'Was he killed at the house?'

'On the Blackwell yacht. His body was dumped overboard. Whoever did it figured the current would carry the body to China.'

'How did –?'

Nick Pappas raised a beefy hand. 'My turn. Mellis was your patient. He must have talked to you about his wife.'

'What does she have to do with this?'

'Everything. She's my first, second and third choice.'

'You're crazy.'

'Hey, I thought shrinks never used words like *crazy*.'

'Nick, what makes you think Alexandra Mellis killed her husband?'

'She was there, and she had a motive. She arrived at the island late that night with some cockamamy excuse about being delayed because she was waitin' at the wrong airport to meet her sister.'

'What does her sister say?'

'Give me a break. What the hell would you expect her to say? They're *twins*. We know George Mellis was at the house that night, but his wife swears she never saw him. It's a big house, Peter, but it's not *that* big. Next, Mrs M gave all the servants the weekend off. When I asked her why, she said it was George's idea. George's lips, of course, are sealed.'

Peter sat there, deep in thought. 'You said she had a motive. What?'

'You have a short memory span. You're the one who put me on the track. The lady was married to a psycho who got his kicks sexually abusing everything he could lay his fists on. He was probably slapping her around pretty good. Let's say she decided she didn't want to play anymore. She asked for a divorce. He wouldn't give it to her. Why should he? He had it made. She wouldn't dare take him to court – it would touch off too juicy a scandal. She had no choice. She had to kill him.' He leaned back in his chair.

'What do you want from me?' Peter asked.

'Information. You had lunch with Mellis's wife ten days ago.' He pressed the button on a tape recorder on the desk. 'We're going on the record now, Peter. Tell me about that lunch. How did Alexandra Mellis behave? Was she tense? Angry? Hysterical?'

'Nick, I've never seen a more relaxed, happily married lady.'

Nick Pappas glared at him and snapped off the tape recorder.

'Don't shaft me, my friend. I went to see Dr John Harley this morning. He's been giving Alexandra Mellis medication to stop her from committing suicide, for Christ's sake!'

Dr John Harley had been greatly disturbed by his meeting with Lieutenant Pappas. The detective had gotten right to the point. 'Has Mrs Mellis consulted you professionally recently?'

'I'm sorry,' Dr Harley said. 'I'm not at liberty to discuss my patients. I'm afraid I can't help you.'

'All right, Doc I understand. You're old friends. You'd like to keep the whole thing quiet. That's okay with me.' He rose to his feet. 'This is a homicide case. I'll be back in an hour with a warrant for your appointment records. When I find out what I want to know, I'm going to feed it to the newspapers.'

Dr Harley was studying him.

'We can handle it that way, or you can tell me

now what I want to know, and I'll do what I can to keep it quiet. Well?'

'Sit down,' Dr Harley said. Nick Pappas sat. 'Alexandra has been having some emotional problems lately.'

'What kind of emotional problems?'

'She's been in a severe depression. She was talking about committing suicide.'

'Did she mention using a knife?'

'No. She said she had a recurrent dream about drowning. I gave her Wellbutrin. She came back and told me it didn't seem to be helping, and I prescribed Nomifensine. I – I don't know whether it helped or not.'

Nick Pappas sat there, putting things together in his mind. Finally he looked up. 'Anything else?'

'That's everything, Lieutenant.'

But there was more, and John Harley's conscience was bothering him. He had deliberately refrained from mentioning the brutal attack George Mellis had made on Eve Blackwell. Part of his concern was that he should have reported it to the police at the time it happened, but mainly Dr Harley wanted to protect the Blackwell family. He had no way of knowing whether there was a connection between the attack on Eve and George Mellis's murder, but his instincts told him that it was better not to bring up the subject. He intended to do everything possible to protect Kate Blackwell.

* * *

Fifteen minutes after he had made that decision, his nurse said, 'Dr Keith Webster is on line two, Doctor.'

It was as if his conscience was prodding him.

Keith Webster said, 'John, I'd like to stop by this afternoon and see you. Are you free?'

'I'll make myself free. What time?'

'How's five o'clock?'

'Fine, Keith. I'll see you then.'

So, the matter was not going to be laid to rest so easily.

At five o'clock, Dr Harley ushered Keith Webster into his office. 'Would you like a drink?'

'No, thank you, John. Forgive me for barging in on you like this.'

It seemed to John Harley that every time he saw him, Keith Webster was apologizing about something. He was such a mild little man, so inoffensive and eager to please – a puppy waiting to be patted on the head. It was incredible to John Harley that within that pale, colourless person there lurked such a brilliant surgeon.

'What can I do for you, Keith?'

Keith Webster drew a deep breath. 'It's about that – you know – that beating George Mellis gave Eve Blackwell.'

'What about it?'

'You're aware she almost died?'

'Yes.'

'Well, it was never reported to the police. In view of what's happened – Mellis's murder and

639

everything – I was wondering if maybe I shouldn't tell the police about it.'

So there it was. There seemed no way to escape the problem.

'You have to do whatever you think best, Keith.'

Keith Webster said gloomily, 'I know. It's just that I'd hate to do anything that might hurt Eve Blackwell. She's a very special person.'

Dr Harley was watching him cautiously. 'Yes, she is.'

Keith Webster sighed. 'The only thing is, John, if I do keep quiet about it now and the police find out later, it's going to look bad for me.'

For both of us, John Harley thought. He saw a possible way out. He said casually, 'It's not very likely the police would find out, is it? Eve certainly would never mention it, and you fixed her up perfectly. Except for that little scar you'd never know she'd been disfigured.'

Keith Webster blinked. 'What little scar?'

'The red scar on her forehead. She told me you said you were going to remove it in a month or two.'

Dr Webster was blinking faster now. It was some kind of nervous tic, Dr Harley decided.

'I don't re – When did you last see Eve?'

'She came in about ten days ago to talk about a problem involving her sister. As a matter of fact, the scar was the only way I could tell it was Eve instead of Alexandra. They're identical twins, you know.'

Keith Webster nodded slowly. 'Yes. I've seen photographs of Eve's sister in the newspapers. There's an amazing likeness. And you say the only way you could tell them apart was by the scar on Eve's forehead from the operation I performed?'

'That's right.'

Dr Webster sat there, silent, chewing on his lower lip. Finally he said, 'Perhaps I shouldn't go to the police just yet. I'd like to think about this a little more.'

'Frankly, I think that's wise, Keith. They're both lovely young women. The newspapers are hinting that the police think Alexandra killed George. That's impossible. I remember when they were little girls . . .'

Dr Webster was no longer listening.

When he left Dr Harley, Keith Webster was lost in thought. He had certainly not left even the trace of a scar on that beautiful face. Yet, John Harley had seen it. It was possible that Eve could have gotten a scar afterwards in another accident, but then why had she lied? It made no sense.

He examined it from every angle, going over all the different possibilities, and when he had come to a conclusion, he thought, *If I'm right, this is going to change my whole life . . .*

Early the following morning, Keith Webster called Dr Harley. 'John,' he began, 'excuse me for disturbing you. You said that Eve Blackwell came in to talk to you about her sister, Alexandra?'

'That's right.'

'After Eve's visit, did Alexandra happen to come in to see you?'

'Yes. As a matter of fact, she came to my office the following day. Why?'

'Just curious. Can you tell me what Eve's sister came to see you about?'

'Alexandra was in a deep depression. Eve was trying to help her.'

Eve had been beaten and almost killed by Alexandra's husband. And now the man had been murdered and it was Alexandra who was being blamed.

Keith Webster had always known he was not brilliant. In school he had to work very hard in order to achieve barely passing grades. He was the perennial butt of his classmates' jokes. He was neither an athlete nor a scholar, and he was socially inept. He was as close as one could come to being a nonentity. No one was more surprised than his own family when Keith Webster was admitted to medical school. When he elected to become a surgeon, neither his peers nor his teachers expected him to become a competent one, let alone a great one. But he had surprised them all. There was a talent deep inside him that was nothing short of genius. He was like some exquisite sculptor working his magic with living flesh instead of clay, and in a short time Keith Webster's reputation spread. In spite of his success, however, he was never able to overcome the trauma of his childhood. Inside he was still the boy who bored everyone, the one at whom the girls laughed.

When he finally reached Eve, Keith's hands were slippery with sweat. She answered the phone on the first ring. 'Rory?' Her voice was low and sultry.

'No. This is Keith Webster.'

'Oh. Hello.'

He heard the change in her voice. 'How've you been?' he asked.

'Fine.'

He could sense her impatience. 'I – I'd like to see you.'

'I'm not seeing anyone. If you read the papers, you'll know my brother-in-law was murdered. I'm in mourning.'

He wiped his hands on his trousers. 'That's what I want to see you about, Eve. I have some information you should know about.'

'What kind of information?'

'I would prefer not to discuss it on the telephone.' He could almost hear Eve's mind working.

'Very well. When?'

'Now, if it's convenient.'

When he arrived at Eve's apartment thirty minutes later, Eve opened the door for him. 'I'm very busy. What did you want to see me about?'

'About this,' Keith Webster said apologetically. He opened a manila envelope he was clutching, took out a photograph and diffidently handed it to Eve. It was a photograph of herself.

She looked at it, puzzled. 'Well?'

'It's a picture of you.'

'I can see that,' she said curtly. 'What about it?'

'It was taken after your operation.'

'So?'

'There's no scar on your forehead, Eve.'

He watched the change that came over her face.

'Sit down, Keith.'

He sat opposite her, on the edge of the couch, and he could not keep from staring at her. He had seen many beautiful women in his practice, but Eve Blackwell totally bewitched him. He had never known anyone like her.

'I think you'd better tell me what this is all about.'

He started at the beginning. He told her about his visit to Dr Harley and about the mysterious scar, and as Keith Webster talked, he watched Eve's eyes. They were expressionless.

When Keith Webster finished, Eve said, 'I don't know what you're thinking, but whatever it is, you're wasting my time. As for the scar, I was playing a little joke on my sister. It's as simple as that. Now, if you've quite finished, I have a great deal to do.'

He remained seated. 'I'm sorry to have bothered you. I just thought I should talk to you before I went to the police.' He could see that he really had her attention now.

'Why on earth would you go to the police?'

'I'm obliged to report the attack George Mellis made on you. Then there's that business about you and the scar. I don't understand it, but I'm sure you can explain it to them.'

Eve felt the first stab of fear. This stupid, dreary little man in front of her had no idea what had really happened, but he knew enough to start the police asking questions.

George Mellis had been a frequent visitor to the apartment. The police could probably find witnesses who had seen him. She had lied about being in Washington the night of George's murder. She had no real alibi. She had never thought she would need one. If the police learned that George had almost killed her, it would give them a motive. The whole scheme would begin to unravel. She had to silence this man.

'What is it you want? Money?'

'No!'

She saw the indignation on his face. 'What, then?'

Dr Webster looked down at the rug, his face red with embarrassment. 'I – I like you so much, Eve. I would hate it if anything bad happened to you.'

She forced a smile. 'Nothing bad is going to happen to me, Keith. I haven't done anything wrong. Believe me, none of this has anything to do with George Mellis's murder.' She reached out and took his hand. 'I would really appreciate it very much if you would forget about this. All right?'

He covered her hand and squeezed it. 'I'd like to, Eve. I really would. But they're holding the coroner's inquest Saturday. I'm a doctor. I'm afraid it's my duty to testify at that inquest and tell them everything I know.'

He saw the alarm that appeared in her eyes.

'You don't have to do that!'

He stroked her hand. 'Yes, I do, Eve. It's my sworn obligation. There's only one thing that could prevent me from doing it.' He watched her leap to the bait of his words.

'What is that?'

His voice was very gentle. 'A husband can't be forced to testify against his wife.'

THIRTY-FIVE

The wedding took place two days before the coroner's inquest. They were married by a judge in his private chambers. The mere idea of being married to Keith Webster made Eve's skin crawl, but she had no choice. *The fool thinks I'm going to stay married to him.* As soon as the inquest was over, she would get an annulment and that would be the end of it.

Detective Lieutenant Nick Pappas had a problem. He was sure he knew who the murderer of George Mellis was, but he could not prove it. He was confronted by a conspiracy of silence around the Blackwell family that he could not break through. He discussed the problem with his superior, Captain Harold Cohn, a street-wise cop who had worked his way up from the ranks.

Cohn quietly listened to Pappas and said, 'It's all smoke, Nick. You haven't got a fucking bit of evidence. They'd laugh us out of court.'

'I know,' Lieutenant Pappas sighed. 'But I'm right.' He sat there a moment, thinking. 'Would you mind if I talked to Kate Blackwell?'

'Jesus! What for?'

'It'll be a little fishing expedition. She runs that family. She might have some information she doesn't even know she has.'

'You'll have to watch your step.'

'I will.'

'And go easy with her, Nick. Remember, she's an old lady.'

'That's what I'm counting on,' Detective Pappas said.

The meeting took place that afternoon in Kate Blackwell's office. Nick Pappas guessed that Kate was somewhere in her eighties, but she carried her age remarkably well. She showed little of the strain the detective knew she must be feeling. She was a very private person, and she had been forced to watch the Blackwell name become a source of public speculation and scandal.

'My secretary said you wished to see me about a matter of some urgency, Lieutenant.'

'Yes, ma'am. There's a coroner's inquest tomorrow on the death of George Mellis. I have reason to think your granddaughter is involved in his murder.'

Kate went absolutely rigid. 'I don't believe it.'

'Please hear me out, Mrs Blackwell. Every police investigation begins with the question of motive. George Mellis was a fortune hunter and a vicious sadist.' He saw the reaction on her face, but he pressed on. 'He married your granddaughter and suddenly found himself with his hands on a large fortune. I figured he beat up Alexandra once too often and when she asked for a divorce, he refused. Her only way to get rid of him was to kill him.'

Kate was staring at him, her face pale.

'I began looking around for evidence to back up my theory. We knew George Mellis was at Cedar Hill House before he disappeared. There are only two ways to get to Dark Harbor from the mainland – plane or ferryboat. According to the local sheriff's office, George Mellis didn't use either. I don't believe in miracles, and I figured Mellis wasn't the kind of man who could walk on water. The only possibility left was that he took a boat from somewhere else along the coast. I started checking out boat-rental places, and I struck pay dirt at Gilkey Harbour. At four p.m. on the afternoon of the day George Mellis was murdered, a woman rented a motor launch there and said a friend would be picking it up later. She paid cash, but she had to sign the rental slip. She used the name Solange Dunas. Does that ring a bell?'

'Yes. She – she was the governess who took care of the twins when they were children. She returned to France years ago.'

Pappas nodded, a look of satisfaction on his face. 'A little further up the coast, the same woman rented a second boat. She took it out and returned it three hours later. She signed her name Solange

Dunas again. I showed both attendants a photograph of Alexandra. They were pretty sure it was her, but they couldn't be positive, because the woman who rented the boats was a brunette.'

'Then what makes you think –?'

'She wore a wig.'

Kate said stiffly, 'I don't believe Alexandra killed her husband.'

'I don't either, Mrs Blackwell,' Lieutenant Pappas told her. 'It was her sister, Eve.'

Kate Blackwell was still as stone.

'Alexandra couldn't have done it. I checked on her movements the day of the murder. She spent the early part of the day in New York with a friend, then she flew directly from New York up to the island. There's no way she could have rented those two motorboats.' He leaned forwards. 'So I was left with Alexandra's look-alike, who signed the name Solange Dunas. It had to be Eve. I started looking around for her motive. I showed a photograph of George Mellis to the tenants of the apartment house Eve lives in and it turned out that Mellis was a frequent visitor there. The superintendent of the building told me that one night when Mellis was there, Eve was almost beaten to death. Did you know that?'

'No.' Kate's voice was a whisper.

'Mellis did it. It fits his pattern. And that was Eve's motive – vengeance. She lured him out to Dark Harbor and murdered him.' He looked at Kate, and felt a pang of guilt at taking advantage of this old woman. 'Eve's alibi is that she was in Washington, DC, that day. She gave the cab driver who took her to the airport a hundred-dollar bill so he would be sure to remember her, and she made a big fuss about missing the Washington shuttle. But I don't think she went to Washington. I believe she put on a dark wig and took a commercial plane to Maine, where she rented those boats. She killed Mellis, dumped his body overboard, then docked the yacht and towed the extra motorboat back to the rental dock, which was closed by then.'

Kate looked at him a long moment. Then she said, slowly, 'All the evidence you have is circumstantial, isn't it?'

'Yes.' He was ready to move in for the kill. 'I need concrete evidence for the coroner's inquest. You know your granddaughter better than anyone in the world, Mrs Blackwell. I want you to tell me anything you can that might be helpful.'

She sat there quietly, making up her mind. Finally she said, 'I think I can give you some information for the inquest.'

And Nick Pappas's heart began to beat faster. He had taken a long shot, and it had paid off. The old lady had come through. He unconsciously leaned forwards. 'Yes, Mrs Blackwell?'

Kate spoke slowly and distinctly. 'On the day George Mellis was murdered, Lieutenant, my granddaughter Eve and I were in Washington, DC, together.'

She saw the surprised expression on his face.

You fool, Kate Blackwell thought. *Did you really think I would offer up a Blackwell as a sacrifice to you? That I would let the press have a Roman holiday with the Blackwell name? No. I will punish Eve in my own way.*

The verdict from the coroner's jury was death at the hands of an unknown assailant or assailants.

To Alexandra's surprise and gratitude, Peter Templeton was at the inquest at the county courthouse.

'Just here to lend moral support,' he told her. Peter thought Alexandra was holding up remarkably well, but the strain showed in her face and in her eyes. During a recess, he took her to lunch at the Lobster Pound, a little restaurant facing the bay in Lincolnville.

'When this is over,' Peter said, 'I think it would be good for you to take a trip, get away for a while.'

'Yes. Eve has asked me to go away with her.' Alexandra's eyes were filled with pain. 'I still can't believe George is dead. I know it has happened, but it – it still seems unreal.'

'It's nature's way of cushioning the shock until the pain becomes bearable.'

'It's so senseless. He was such a fine man.' She looked up at Peter. 'You spent time with him. He talked to you. Wasn't he a wonderful person?'

'Yes,' Peter said slowly. 'Yes, he was.'

* * *

Eve said, 'I want an annulment, Keith.'

Keith Webster blinked at his wife in surprise. 'Why on earth would you want an annulment?'

'Oh, come on, Keith. You didn't really think I was going to stay married to you, did you?'

'Of course. You're my wife, Eve.'

'What are you after? The Blackwell money?'

'I don't need money, darling. I make an excellent living. I can give you anything you want.'

'I told you what I want. An annulment.'

He shook his head regretfully. 'I'm afraid I can't give you that.'

'Then I'm going to file for divorce.'

'I don't think that would be advisable. You see, nothing has really changed, Eve. The police haven't found out who killed your brother-in-law, so the case is still open. There's no statute of limitations on murder. If you divorced me, I'd be forced to . . .' He raised his hands helplessly.

'You're talking as though *I* killed him.'

'You did, Eve.'

Her voice was scornful. 'How the hell do *you* know?'

'It's the only reason you would have married me.'

She looked at him, filled with loathing. 'You bastard! How can you do this to me?'

'It's very simple. I love you.'

'I hate you. Do you understand that? I despise you!'

He smiled sadly. 'I love you so much.'

The trip with Alexandra was called off. 'I'm going to Barbados on my honeymoon,' Eve told her.

Barbados was Keith's idea.

'I won't go,' Eve told him flatly. The idea of a honeymoon with him was disgusting.

'It will look strange if we don't have a honeymoon,' he said shyly. 'And we don't want people asking a lot of awkward questions, do we, dear?'

Alexandra began to see Peter Templeton for lunch once a week. In the beginning, it was because she wanted to talk about George, and there was no one else she could discuss him with. But after several months, Alexandra admitted to herself that she enjoyed Peter Templeton's company immensely. There was a dependability about him that she desperately needed. He was sensitive to her moods, and he was intelligent and entertaining.

'When I was an intern,' he told Alexandra, 'I went out on my first house call in the dead of winter. The patient was a frail old man in bed with a terrible cough. I was going to examine his chest with my stethoscope, but I didn't want to shock him, so I decided to warm it first. I put it on the radiator while I examined his throat and his eyes. Then I got my stethoscope and put it to his chest. The old man leaped out of bed like a scalded cat. His cough went away, but it took weeks for the burn to heal.'

Alexandra laughed. It was the first time she had laughed in a long time.

'Can we do this again next week?' Peter asked.
'Yes, please.'

Eve's honeymoon turned out much better than she had anticipated. Because of Keith's pale, sensitive skin, he was afraid to go out in the sun, so Eve went down to the beach alone every day. She was never alone for long. She was surrounded by amorous lifeguards, beach bums, tycoons and playboys. It was like feasting at a wonderful smorgasbord, and Eve chose a different dish each day. She enjoyed her sexual escapades twice as much because she knew her husband was upstairs in their suite waiting for her. He could not do enough for her. He fetched and carried for her like a little lapdog, and waited on her hand and foot. If Eve expressed a wish, it was instantly gratified. She did everything she could think of to insult him, anger him, to turn him against her so that he would let her go, but his love was unshakable. The idea of letting Keith make love to her sickened Eve, and she was grateful that he had a weak libido.

The years are beginning to catch up with me, Kate Blackwell thought. There were so many of them, and they had been so full and rich.

Kruger-Brent, Ltd., needed a strong hand at the helm. It needed someone with Blackwell blood. *There's no one to carry on after I'm gone*, Kate thought. *All the working and planning and fighting for the company. And for what? For strangers to take over one day. Bloody hell! I can't let that happen.*

A week after they returned from their honeymoon, Keith said apologetically, 'I'm afraid I'm going to have to go back to work dear. I have a lot of operations scheduled. Will you be all right during the day without me?'

Eve barely managed to keep a straight face. 'I'll try.'

Keith was up and out early every morning long before Eve awakened, and when she went into the kitchen she found he had made coffee and laid out all the breakfast things for her. He opened a generous bank account in Eve's name and kept it replenished. She spent his money recklessly. As long as she was enjoying herself, Keith was happy. Eve bought expensive jewellery for Rory, with whom she spent almost every afternoon. He worked very little.

'I can't take just any part,' he complained to Eve. 'It would hurt my image.'

'I understand, darling.'

'Do you? What the fuck do you know about show business? You were born with a silver spoon up your ass.'

And Eve would buy him an extra-nice present to placate him. She paid Rory's rent and bought him clothes for interviews, and paid for his dinners at expensive restaurants so that he could be seen by important producers. She wanted to be with him twenty-four hours a day, but there was her husband. Eve would arrive home at seven o'clock at night, and Keith would be in the kitchen preparing dinner for her in his 'Kiss the Cook' apron. He never questioned her about where she had been.

During the following year, Alexandra and Peter Templeton saw each other more and more often. Each had become an important part of the other's life. Peter accompanied Alexandra when she went to visit her father at the asylum, and somehow the sharing made the pain easier to bear.

Peter met Kate one evening when he arrived to pick up Alexandra. 'So you're a doctor, eh? I've buried a dozen doctors, and I'm still around. Do you know anything about business?'

'Not a great deal, Mrs Blackwell.'

'Are you a corporation?' Kate asked.

'No.'

She snorted. 'Bloody hell. You don't know anything. You need a good tax man. I'll set up an appointment for you with mine. The first thing he'll do is incorporate you and –'

'Thank you, Mrs Blackwell. I'm getting along just fine.'

'My husband was a stubborn man, too,' Kate said. She turned to Alexandra. 'Invite him to dinner. Maybe I can talk some sense into him.'

Outside, Peter said, 'Your grandmother hates me.'

Alexandra laughed. 'She likes you. You should *hear* how Gran behaves with people she hates.'

'I wonder how she would feel if I told her that I want to marry you, Alex. . . . ?'

And she looked up at him and beamed. 'We'd both feel wonderful, Peter!'

Kate had watched the progress of Alexandra's romance with Peter Templeton with a great deal of interest. She liked the young doctor, and she decided he would be a good husband for Alexandra. But she was a trader at heart. Now she sat in front of the fireplace facing the two of them.

'I must tell you,' Kate lied, 'that this comes as a complete surprise. I always expected Alexandra to marry an executive who would take over Kruger-Brent.'

'This isn't a business proposition, Mrs Blackwell. Alexandra and I want to get married.'

'On the other hand,' Kate continued, as if there had been no interruption, 'you're a psychiatrist. You understand the way people's minds and emotions work. You would probably be a great negotiator. I would like you to become involved with the company. You can –'

'No,' Peter said firmly. 'I'm a doctor. I'm not interested in going into a business.'

'This isn't "going into a business",' Kate snapped. 'We're not talking about some corner grocery store. You'll be part of the family, and I need someone to run –'

'I'm sorry.' There was a finality in Peter's tone. 'I'll have nothing to do with Kruger-Brent. You'll have to find someone else for that . . .'

Kate turned to Alexandra. 'What do you have to say to that?'

'I want whatever makes Peter happy, Gran.'

'Damned ingratitude,' Kate glowered. 'Selfish, the both of you.' She sighed, 'Ah, well. Who knows? You might change your mind one day.' And she added innocently, 'Are you planning to have children?'

Peter laughed. 'That's a private matter. I have a feeling you're a great manipulator, Mrs Blackwell, but Alex and I are going to live our own lives, and our children – if we have children – will live *their* lives.'

Kate smiled sweetly. 'I wouldn't have it any other way, Peter. I've made it a lifelong rule never to interfere in other people's lives.'

Two months later when Alexandra and Peter returned from their honeymoon, Alexandra was pregnant. When Kate heard the news, she thought, *Good. It will be a boy.*

Eve lay in bed watching Rory walk out of the bathroom naked. He had a beautiful body, lean and trim. Eve adored the way he made love to her. She could not get enough of him. She suspected he might have other bedmates, but she was afraid to ask, afraid to say anything that might upset him. Now, as he reached the bed, he ran his finger along her skin, just below the eyes, and said, 'Hey, baby, you're gettin' a few wrinkles. They're cute.'

Each word was a stab, a reminder of the age difference between them and the fact that she was twenty-five years old. They made love again, but for the first time Eve's mind was elsewhere.

It was almost nine o'clock when Eve arrived home. Keith was basting a roast in the oven.

He kissed her on the cheek. 'Hello, dear. I've made some of your favourite dishes. We're having –'

'Keith, I want you to remove these wrinkles.'

He blinked. 'What wrinkles?'

She pointed to the area around her eyes. 'These.'

'Those are laugh lines, darling. I love them.'

'*I* don't! I hate them!' she yelled.

'Believe me, Eve, they're not –'

'For Christ's sake, just get rid of them. That *is* what you do for a living, isn't it?'

'Yes, but – All right,' he said placatingly, 'if it will make you happy, dear.'

'When?'

'In about six weeks. My schedule is full right –'

'I'm not one of your goddamned patients,' Eve snapped. 'I'm your wife. I want you to do it now – tomorrow.'

'The clinic is closed on Saturdays.'

'Then open it!' *He was so stupid*. God, she could not wait to get rid of him. And she would. One way or another. And soon.

'Come into the other room for a moment.' He took her into the dressing room

She sat in a chair under a strong light while he carefully examined her face. In an instant he was transformed from a bumbling little milquetoast to a brilliant surgeon, and Eve could sense the transformation. She remembered the miraculous job he had done on her face. This operation might seem unnecessary to Keith, but he was wrong. It was vital. Eve could not bear the thought of losing Rory.

Keith turned off the light. 'No problem,' he assured her. 'I'll do it in the morning.'

The following morning, the two of them went to the clinic. 'I usually have a nurse to assist me,' Keith told her, 'but with something as minor as this, it won't be necessary.'

'You might as well do something with this while you're at it.' Eve tugged at a bit of skin at her throat.

'If you wish, dear. I'll give you something to put you to sleep so you won't feel any discomfort. I don't want my darling to have any pain.'

Eve watched as he filled a hypodermic and skilfully gave her an injection. She would not have minded if there had been pain. She was doing this for Rory. Darling Rory. She thought of his rock-hard body and the look in his eyes when he was hungry for her. . . . She drifted off to sleep.

She woke up in a bed in the back room of the clinic. Keith was seated in a chair next to the bed.

'How did it go?' Her voice was thick with sleep.

'Beautifully,' Keith smiled.

Eve nodded, and was asleep again.

Keith was there when she woke up later. 'We'll leave the bandages on for a few days. I'll keep you here where you can be properly cared for.'

'All right.'

He checked her each day, examined her face, nodded. 'Perfect.'

'When can I look?'

'It should be all healed by Friday,' he assured her.

She ordered the head nurse to have a private telephone installed by the bedside. The first call she made was to Rory.

'Hey, baby, where the hell are you?' he asked. 'I'm horny.'

'So am I, darling. I'm still tied up with his damned medical convention in Florida, but I'll be back next week.'

'You'd better be.'

'Have you missed me?'

'Like crazy.'

Eve heard whispering in the background. 'Is there someone there with you?'

'Yeah. We're having' a little orgy.' Rory loved to make jokes. 'Gotta go.' The line went dead.

Eve telephoned Alexandra and listened, bored,

to Alexandra's excited talk about her pregnancy. 'I can't wait,' Eve told her. 'I've always wanted to be an aunt.'

Eve seldom saw her grandmother. A coolness had developed that Eve did not understand. *She'll come around*, Eve thought.

Kate never asked about Keith, and Eve did not blame her, for he was a nothing. Perhaps one day Eve would talk to Rory about helping her get rid of Keith. That would tie Rory to her forever. It was incredible to Eve that she could cuckold her husband every day and that he neither suspected nor cared. Well, thank God he had a talent for *something*. The bandages were coming off on Friday.

Eve awakened early on Friday and waited impatiently for Keith.

'It's almost noon,' she complained. 'Where the hell have you been?'

'I'm sorry, darling,' he apologized. 'I've been in surgery all morning and –'

'I don't give a damn about that. Take these bandages off. I want to see.'

'Very well.'

Eve sat up and was still, as he deftly cut the bandages away from her face. He stood back to study her, and she saw the satisfaction in his eyes. 'Perfect.'

'Give me a mirror.'

He hurried out of the room and returned a

moment later with a hand mirror. With a proud smile, he presented it to her.

Eve raised the mirror slowly and looked at her reflection.

And screamed.

EPILOGUE

Kate

1982

THIRTY-SIX

It seemed to Kate that the wheel of time was spinning faster, hurrying the days along, blending winter into spring and summer into autumn, until all the seasons and years blurred into one. She was in her late eighties now. Eighty what? Sometimes she forgot her exact age. She could face growing old, but she could not face the idea of growing old and slovenly, and she took great pains with her appearance. When she looked in the mirror, she saw a neat erect figure of a woman, proud and indomitable.

She still went to her office every day, but it was a gesture, a ruse to ward off death. She attended every board meeting, but things were no longer as clear as they once had been. Everyone around her seemed to be speaking too rapidly. The most disturbing thing to Kate was that her mind played tricks on her. The past and present were constantly intermingling. Her world was closing in, becoming smaller and smaller.

If there was a lifeline that Kate clutched, a driving force that kept her alive, it was her passionate conviction that someone in the family must one day take charge of Kruger-Brent. Kate had no intention of letting outsiders take over what Jamie McGregor and Margaret and she and David had suffered and toiled so long and so hard for. Eve, on whom Kate had twice pinned such high hopes, was a murderer. And a *grotesque*. Kate had not had to punish her. She had seen Eve once. What had been done to her was punishment enough.

On the day Eve had seen her face in the mirror, she had tried to commit suicide. She had swallowed a bottle of sleeping pills, but Keith had pumped out her stomach and brought her home, where he hovered over her constantly. When he had to be at the hospital, day and night nurses guarded her.

'Please let me die,' Eve begged her husband. 'Please, Keith! I don't want to live like this.'

'You belong to me now,' Keith told her, 'and I'll always love you.'

The image of what her face looked like was etched in Eve's brain. She persuaded Keith to dismiss the nurses. She did not want anyone around her looking at her, staring at her.

Alexandra called again and again, but Eve refused to see her. All deliveries were left outside the front door so no one could see her face. The only person who saw her was Keith. He was, finally, the only one she had left. He was her only link with the world, and she became terrified that he would leave her, that she would be left alone with nothing but her ugliness – her unbearable ugliness.

Every morning at five o'clock, Keith arose to go to the hospital or clinic, and Eve was always up before him to fix his breakfast. She cooked dinner for him every night, and when he was late, she was filled with apprehension. What if he had found some other woman? What if he did not return to her?

When she heard his key in the door, she would rush to open it and go into his arms, holding him tightly. She never suggested they make love because she was afraid he might refuse, but when he did make love to her, Eve felt as though he was bestowing upon her a wonderful kindness.

Once she asked, timidly, 'Darling, haven't you punished me enough? Won't you repair my face?'

He looked at her and said proudly, 'It can never be repaired.'

As time went on, Keith became more demanding, more peremptory, until Eve was finally and completely a slave to him, catering to his every whim. Her ugliness bound her to him more strongly than iron chains.

Alexandra and Peter had had a son, Robert, a bright, handsome boy. He reminded Kate of Tony when he was a child. Robert was almost eight now, and precocious for his age. *Very precocious indeed*, Kate thought. *A really remarkable boy.*

All the members of the family received their invitations on the same day. The invitation read: MRS KATE BLACKWELL REQUESTS THE HONOUR OF YOUR PRESENCE TO CELEBRATE HER NINETIETH BIRTHDAY AT CEDAR HILL HOUSE, DARK HARBOR, MAINE, ON SEPTEMBER 24, 1982, AT EIGHT O'CLOCK. BLACK TIE.

When Keith read the invitation, he looked at Eve and said, 'We're going.'

'Oh, no! I can't! You go. I'll –'

He said, 'We're both going.'

Tony Blackwell was in the garden of the sanatorium, painting, when his companion approached. 'A letter for you, Tony.'

Tony opened the envelope, and a vague smile lighted his face. 'That's nice,' he said. 'I like birthday parties.'

Peter Templeton studied the invitation. 'I can't believe the old girl's ninety years old. She's really amazing.'

'Yes, isn't she?' Alexandra agreed. And she added thoughtfully. 'Do you know something sweet? Robert received his own invitation, addressed to him.'

THIRTY-SEVEN

The overnight guests had long since departed by ferry and plane, and the family was gathered in the library at Cedar Hill. Kate looked at those in the room, one by one, and she saw each with remarkable clarity. Tony, the smiling, vaguely amiable vegetable who had tried to kill her, the son who had been so full of promise and hope. Eve, the murderer, who could have owned the world if she had not had the seed of evil in her. How ironic it was, Kate thought, that her terrible punishment had come from the meek little nonentity she married. And then there was Alexandra. Beautiful, affectionate and kind – the bitterest disappointment of all. She had put her own happiness before the welfare of the company. She was not interested in Kruger-Brent and had chosen a husband who refused to have anything to do with the company. Traitors, both of them. Had all the pain of the past gone for nothing? *No*, Kate thought. *I won't let it end like this. It's not all been wasted. I've built a proud dynasty. A hospital in Cape Town is named after me. I've built schools and libraries and helped Banda's people.* Her head was beginning to hurt. The room was slowly filling with ghosts. Jamie McGregor and Margaret – looking so beautiful – and Banda smiling at her. And dear, wonderful David, holding out his arms. Kate shook her head to clear it. She was not ready for any of them yet. *Soon*, she thought. *Soon.*

There was one more member of the family in the room. She turned to her handsome great-grandson and said, 'Come here, darling.'

Robert walked up to her and took her hand.

'It sure was a great birthday party, Gran.'

'Thank you, Robert. I'm glad you enjoyed it. How are you getting along in school?'

'All A's, like you told me to get. I'm at the head of my class.'

Kate looked at Peter. 'You should send Robert to the Wharton School when he's old enough. It's the best –'

Peter laughed. 'For God's sake, Kate, my darling, don't you ever give up? Robert's going to do exactly what he likes. He has a remarkable musical talent, and he wants to be a classical musician. He's going to choose his own life.'

'You're right,' Kate sighed. 'I'm an old woman, and I have no right to interfere. If he wants to be a musician, that's what he should be.' She turned to the boy, and her eyes shone with love. 'Mind you, Robert, I can't promise anything, but I'm going to try to help you. I know someone who's a dear friend of Zubin Mehta.'

The Naked Face

To the Women in my Life –
Jorja
Mary
– and –
Natalie

ONE

At ten minutes before eleven in the morning, the sky exploded into a carnival of white confetti that instantly blanketed the city. The soft snow turned the already frozen streets of Manhattan to grey slush and the icy December wind herded the Christmas shoppers towards the comfort of their apartments and homes.

On Lexington Avenue the tall, thin man in the yellow rain slicker moved along with the rushing Christmas crowd to a rhythm of his own. He was walking rapidly, but it was not with the frantic pace of the other pedestrians who were trying to escape the cold. His head was lifted and he seemed oblivious to the passers-by who bumped against him. He was free after a lifetime of purgatory, and he was on his way home to tell Mary that it was finished. The past was going to bury its dead and the future was bright and golden. He was thinking how her face would glow when he told her the news. As he reached the corner of Fifty-ninth Street, the traffic light ambered its way to red and he stopped with the impatient crowd. A few feet away, a Salvation Army Santa Claus stood over a large kettle. The man reached in his pocket for some coins, an offering to the gods of fortune. At that instant someone clapped him on the back, a sudden stinging blow that rocked his whole body. Some overhearty Christmas drunk trying to be friendly.

Or Bruce Boyd. Bruce, who had never known his own strength and had a childish habit of hurting him physically. But he had not seen Bruce in more than a year. The man started to turn his head to see who had hit him, and to his surprise, his knees began to buckle. In slow motion, watching himself from a distance, he could see his body hit the sidewalk. There was a dull pain in his back and it began to spread. It became hard to breathe. He was aware of a parade of shoes moving past his face as though animated with a life of their own. His cheek began to feel numb from the freezing sidewalk. He knew he must not lie there. He opened his mouth to ask someone to help him, and a warm, red river began to gush out and flow into the melting snow. He watched in dazed fascination as it moved across the sidewalk and ran down into the gutter. The pain was worse now, but he didn't mind it so much because he suddenly remembered his good news. He was free.

He was going to tell Mary that he was free. He closed his eyes to rest them from the blinding whiteness of the sky. The snow began to turn to icy sleet, but he no longer felt anything.

TWO

Carol Roberts heard the sounds of the reception door opening and closing and the men walking in, and before she even looked up, she could smell what they were. There were two of them. One was in his middle forties. He was a big mother, about six foot three, and all muscle. He had a massive head with deep-set steely blue eyes and a weary, humourless mouth. The second man was younger. His features were clean-cut, sensitive. His eyes were brown and alert. The two men looked completely different and yet, as far as Carol was concerned, they could have been identical twins.

They were fuzz. That was what she had smelled. As they moved towards her desk she could feel the drops of perspiration begin to trickle down her armpits through the shield of anti-perspirant. Frantically her mind darted over all the treacherous areas of vulnerability. Chick?

4

Christ, he had kept out of trouble for over six months. Since that night in his apartment when he had asked her to marry him and had promised to quit the gang.

Sammy? He was overseas in the Air Force, and if anything had happened to her brother, they would not have sent these two mothers to break the news. No, they were here to bust her. She was carrying grass in her purse, and some loud-mouthed prick had rapped about it. But why two of them? Carol tried to tell herself that they could not touch her. She was no longer some dumb black hooker from Harlem that they could push around. Not any more. She was the receptionist for one of the biggest psychoanalysts in the country. But as the two men moved towards her, Carol's panic increased. There was the feral memory of too many years of hiding in stinking, overcrowded tenement apartments while the white Law broke down doors and hauled away a father, or a sister, or a cousin.

But nothing of the turmoil in her mind showed on her face. At first glance the two detectives saw only a young and nubile, tawny-skinned Negress in a smartly tailored beige dress. Her voice was cool and impersonal. 'May I help you?' she asked.

Then Lt Andrew McGreavy, the older detective, spotted the spreading perspiration stain under the armpit of her dress. He automatically filed it away as an interesting piece of information for future use.

The doctor's receptionist was up-tight. McGreavy pulled out a wallet with a worn badge pinned onto the cracked imitation leather. 'Lieutenant McGreavy, Nineteenth Precinct.' He indicated his partner. 'Detective Angeli. We're from the Homicide Division.'

Homicide? A muscle in Carol's arm twitched involuntarily. *Chick! He had killed someone. He had broken his promise to her and gone back to the gang. He had pulled a robbery and had shot someone, or – was he shot? Dead? Is that what they had come to tell her?* She felt the perspiration stain begin to widen. Carol suddenly became conscious of it. McGreavy was looking at her face, but she knew that he had noticed it. She and the McGreavys of the world needed no words. They recognized each other on sight. They had known each other for hundreds of years.

'We'd like to see Dr Judd Stevens,' said the younger detective. His voice was gentle and polite, and went with his appearance. She noticed for the first time that he carried a small parcel wrapped in brown paper and held together with string.

It took an instant for his words to sink in. So it wasn't Chick. Or Sammy. Or the grass.

'I'm sorry,' she said, barely hiding her relief. 'Dr Stevens is with a patient.'

'This will only take a few minutes,' McGreavy said. 'We want to ask him some questions.' He

6

paused. 'We can either do it here, or at Police Headquarters.'

She looked at the two of them a moment, puzzled. What the hell could two Homicide detectives want with Dr Stevens? Whatever the police might think, the doctor had not done anything wrong. She knew him too well. How long had it been? Four years. It had started in night court . . .

It was three a.m. and the overhead lights in the courtroom bathed everyone in an unhealthy pallor. The room was old and tired and uncaring, saturated with the stale smell of fear that had accumulated over the years like layers of flaked paint.

It was Carol's lousy luck that Judge Murphy was sitting on the bench again. She had been up before him only two weeks before and had got off with probation. First offence. Meaning it was the first time the bastards had caught her. This time she knew the judge was going to throw the book at her.

The case on the docket ahead of hers was almost over. A tall, quiet-looking man standing before the judge was saying something about his client, a fat man in handcuffs who trembled all over. She figured the quiet-looking man must be a mouthpiece. There was a look about him, an air of easy confidence, that made her feel the fat man was lucky to have him. She didn't have anyone.

The men moved away from the bench and Carol heard her name called. She stood up, pressing her knees together to keep them from trembling. The bailiff gave her a gentle push towards the bench. The court clerk handed the charge sheet to the judge.

Judge Murphy looked at Carol, then at the sheet of paper in front of him.

'"Carol Roberts. Soliciting on the streets, vagrancy, possession of marijuana, and resisting arrest."'

The last was a lot of shit. The policeman had shoved her and she had kicked him in the balls. After all, she was an American citizen.

'You were in here a few weeks ago, weren't you, Carol?'

She made her voice sound uncertain. 'I believe I was, Your Honour.'

'And I gave you probation.'

'Yes, sir.'

'How old are you?'

She should have known they would ask. 'Sixteen. Today's my sixteenth birthday. Happy birthday to me,' she said. And she burst into tears, huge sobs that wracked her body.

The tall, quiet man had been standing at a table at the side gathering up some papers and putting them in a leather attache case. As Carol stood there sobbing, he looked up and watched her for a moment. Then he spoke to Judge Murphy.

The judge called a recess and the two men disappeared into the judge's chambers. Fifteen minutes later, the bailiff escorted Carol into the judge's chambers, where the quiet man was earnestly talking to the judge.

'You're a lucky girl, Carol,' Judge Murphy said. 'You're going to get another chance. The Court is remanding you to the personal custody of Dr Stevens.'

So the tall mother wasn't a mouthpiece – he was a quack. She wouldn't have cared if he was Jack the Ripper. All she wanted was to get out of that stinking courtroom before they found out it wasn't her birthday.

The doctor drove her to his apartment, making small talk that did not require any answers, giving Carol a chance to pull herself together and think things out. He stopped the car in front of a modern apartment building on Seventy-first Street overlooking the East River. The building had a doorman and an elevator operator, and from the calm way they greeted him, you would think he came home every morning at three a.m. with a sixteen-year-old black hooker.

Carol had never seen an apartment like the doctor's. The living-room was done in white with two long, low couches covered in oatmeal tweed. Between the couches was an enormous square coffee table with a thick glass top. On it was a large chessboard with carved Venetian figures. Modern paintings hung on the wall. In the foyer was a closed-circuit television monitor that showed the entrance to the lobby. In one corner of the living-room was a smoked glass bar with shelves of crystal glasses and decanters. Looking out the window, Carol could see tiny boats, far below, tossing their way along the East River.

'Courts always make me hungry,' Judd said. 'Why don't I whip up a little birthday supper?' And he took her into the kitchen where she watched him skilfully put together a Mexican omelette, French-fried potatoes, toasted English muffins, a salad, and coffee. 'That's one of the advantages of being a bachelor,' he said. 'I can cook when I feel like it.'

So he was a bachelor without any home pussy. If she played her cards right, this could turn out to be a bonanza. When she had finished devouring the meal, he had taken her into the guest bedroom. The bedroom was done in blue, dominated by a large double bed with a blue checked bedspread. There was a low Spanish dresser of dark wood with brass fittings.

'You can spend the night here,' he said. 'I'll rustle up a pair of pyjamas for you.'

As Carol looked around the tastefully decorated room she thought, *Carol, baby! You've hit the jackpot! This mother's looking for a piece of jailbait black ass. And you're the baby who is gonna give it to him.*

She undressed and spent the next half hour in the shower. When she came out, a towel wrapped around her shining, voluptuous body, she saw that the motherfucking ofay had placed a pair of his pyjamas on the bed. She laughed knowingly and left them there. She threw the towel down and strolled into the living-room. He was not there. She looked through the door leading into a den. He was sitting at a large, comfortable desk with an old-fashioned desk lamp hanging over it. The den was crammed with books from floor to ceiling. She walked up behind him and kissed him on the neck. 'Let's get started, baby,' she whispered. 'You got me so horny I can't stand it.' She pressed closer to him.

'What are we waitin' for, big daddy? If you don't ball me quick, I'll go out of my cotton-pickin' mind.'

He regarded her for a second with thoughtful dark grey eyes. 'Haven't you got enough trouble?' he asked mildly. 'You can't help being born a Negro, but who told you you had to be a black dropout pot-smoking sixteen-year-old whore?'

She stared at him, baffled, wondering what she had said wrong. Maybe he had to get himself worked up and whip her first to get his kicks. Or maybe it was the Reverend Davidson bit. He was going to pray over her black ass, reform her, and

11

then lay her. She tried again. She reached between his legs and stroked him, whispering, 'Go, baby. Sock it to me.'

He gently disengaged himself and sat her in an armchair. She had never been so puzzled. He didn't look like a fag, but these days you never knew. 'What's your bag, baby? Tell me how you like to freak out and I'll give it to you.'

'All right,' he said. 'Let's rap.'

'You mean – *talk*?'

'That's right.'

And they talked. All night long. It was the strangest night that Carol had ever spent. Dr Stevens kept leaping from one subject to another, exploring, testing her. He asked her opinion about Vietnam, ghettos, and college riots. Every time Carol thought she had figured out what he was really after, he switched to another subject. They talked of things she had never heard of, and about subjects in which she considered herself the world's greatest living expert. Months afterwards she used to lie awake, trying to recall the word, the idea, the magic phrase that had changed her. She had never been able to because she finally realized that there had been no magic word. What Dr Stevens had done was simple. He had talked to her. Really talked to her. No one had ever done that before. He had treated her like a human being, an equal, whose opinions and feelings he cared about.

12

Somewhere during the course of the night she suddenly became aware of her nakedness and went in and put on his pyjamas. He came in and sat on the edge of the bed and they talked some more. They talked about Mao Tse-tung and hula hoops and the Pill. And having a mother and father who had never been married. Carol told him things she had never told anybody in her life. Things that had been long buried deep in her subconscious. And when she had finally fallen asleep, she had felt totally empty. It was as though she had had a major operation, and a river of poison had been drained out of her.

In the morning, after breakfast, he handed her a hundred dollars.

She hesitated, then finally said, 'I lied. It's not my birthday.'

'I know.' He grinned. 'But we won't tell the judge.' His tone changed. 'You can take the money and walk out of here and no one will bother you until the next time you get caught by the police.' He paused. 'I need a receptionist. I think you'd be marvellous at the job.'

She looked at him unbelievingly. 'You're putting me on. I can't take shorthand or type.'

'You could if you went back to school.'

Carol looked at him a moment and then said enthusiastically, 'I never thought of that. That sounds groovy.' She couldn't wait to get the hell out of the apartment with his hundred dollars and flash it at the boys and girls at Fishman's Drug Store in Harlem, where the gang hung out. She could buy enough kicks with this money to last a week.

When she walked into Fishman's Drug Store, it was as though she had never been away. She saw the same bitter faces and heard the same hip, defeated chatter. She was home. She kept thinking of the doctor's apartment. It wasn't the furniture that made the big difference. It was so – clean. And quiet. It was like a little island somewhere in another world. And he had offered her a passport to it. What was there to lose? She could try it for laughs, to show the doctor that he was wrong, that she couldn't make it.

To her own great surprise, Carol enrolled in night school. She left her furnished room with the rust-stained washbasin and broken toilet and the torn green window shade and the lumpy iron cot where she would turn tricks and act out plays. She was a beautiful heiress in Paris or London or Rome, and the man pumping away on top of her was a wealthy, handsome prince, dying to marry her. And as each man had his orgasm and crawled off her, her dream died. Until the next time.

She left the room and all her princes without a backward glance and moved back in with her parents. Dr Stevens gave her an allowance while she was studying. She finished high school with top grades. The doctor was there on graduation day,

14

his grey eyes bright with pride. Someone believed in her. She was somebody. She took a day job at Nedick's and took a secretarial course at night. The day after she finished, she went to work for Dr Stevens and could afford her own apartment.

In the four years that had passed Dr Stevens had always treated her with the same grave courtesy he had shown her the first night. At first she had waited for him to make some reference to what she had been, and what she had become. But she had finally come to the realization that he had always seen her as what she was *now*. All he had done was to help her fulfil herself. Whenever she had a problem, he always found time to discuss it with her. Recently she had been meaning to tell him about what had happened with her and Chick and ask him whether she should tell Chick, but she kept putting it off. She wanted her Dr Stevens to be proud of her. She would have done anything for him. She would have slept with him, killed for him . . .

And now here were these two mothers from the Homicide Squad wanting to see him.

McGreavy was getting impatient. 'How about it, miss?' he asked.

'I have orders never to disturb him when he's with a patient,' said Carol. She saw the expression that came into McGreavy's eyes. 'I'll ring him.' She picked up the phone and pressed the intercom buzzer. After thirty seconds of silence, Dr Stevens' voice came over the phone. 'Yes?'

'There are two detectives here to see you, Doctor. They're from the Homicide Division.'

She listened for a change in his voice . . . nervousness . . . fear. There was nothing. 'They'll have to wait,' he said. He went off the line.

A surge of pride flared through her. Maybe they could panic her, but they could never get her doctor to lose his cool. She looked up defiantly. 'You heard him,' she said.

'How long will his patient be in there?' asked Angeli, the younger man.

She glanced at the clock on the desk. 'Another twenty-five minutes. It's his last patient for the day.'

The two men exchanged a look.

'We'll wait,' sighed McGreavy.

They took chairs. McGreavy was studying her. 'You look familiar,' he said.

She wasn't deceived. The mother was on a fishing expedition. 'You know what they say,' replied Carol. 'We all look alike.'

Exactly twenty-five minutes later, Carol heard the click of the side door that led from the doctor's private office directly to the corridor. A few minutes later, the door of the doctor's office opened and Dr Judd Stevens stepped out. He hesitated as

16

he saw McGreavy. 'We've met before,' he said. He could not remember where.

McGreavy nodded impassively. 'Yeah . . . Lieutenant McGreavy.' He indicated Angeli. 'Detective Frank Angeli.'

Judd and Angeli shook hands. 'Come in.'

The men walked into Judd's private office and the door closed. Carol looked after them, trying to piece it together. The big detective had seemed antagonistic towards Dr Stevens. But maybe that was just his natural charm. Carol was sure of only one thing. Her dress would have to go to the cleaner's.

Judd's office was furnished like a French country living-room. There was no working desk. Instead, comfortable easy chairs and end tables with authentic antique lamps were scattered about the room. At the far end of the office a private door led out to the corridor. On the floor was an exquisitely patterned Edward Fields area rug, and in a corner was a comfortable damask-covered contour couch. McGreavy noted that there were no diplomas on the walls. But he had checked before coming here. If Dr Stevens had wanted to, he could have covered his walls with diplomas and certificates.

'This is the first psychiatrist's office I've ever been in,' Angeli said, openly impressed. 'I wish my house looked like this.'

'It relaxes my patients,' Judd said easily. 'And by the way, I'm a psychoanalyst.'

'Sorry,' Angeli said. 'What's the difference?'

'About fifty dollars an hour,' McGreavy said. 'My partner doesn't get around much.'

Partner. And Judd suddenly remembered. McGreavy's partner had been shot and killed and McGreavy had been wounded during the holdup of a liquor store four – or was it five? – years ago. A petty hoodlum named Amos Ziffren had been arrested for the crime. Ziffren's attorney had pleaded his client not guilty by reason of insanity. Judd had been called in as an expert for the defence and asked to examine Ziffren. He had found that he was hopelessly insane with advanced paresis. On Judd's testimony, Ziffren had escaped the death penalty and had been sent to a mental institution.

'I remember you now,' Judd said. 'The Ziffren case. You had three bullets in you; your partner was killed.'

'And I remember you,' McGreavy said. 'You got the killer off.'

'What can I do for you?'

'We need some information, Doctor,' McGreavy said. He nodded to Angeli. Angeli began fumbling at the string on the package he carried.

'We'd like you to identify something for us,' McGreavy said. His voice was careful, giving nothing away.

18

Angeli had the package open. He held up a yellow oilskin rain slicker. 'Have you ever seen this before?'

'It looks like mine,' Judd said in surprise.

'It is yours. At least your name is stencilled inside.'

'Where did you find it?'

'Where do you think we found it?' The two men were no longer casual. A subtle change had taken place in their faces.

Judd studied McGreavy a moment, then picked up a pipe from a rack on a long, low table and began to fill it with tobacco from a jar. 'I think you'd better tell me what this is all about,' he said quietly.

'It's about this raincoat, Dr Stevens,' said McGreavy. 'If it's yours, we want to know how it got out of your possession.'

'There's no mystery about it. It was drizzling when I came in this morning. My raincoat was at the cleaner's, so I wore the yellow slicker. I keep it for fishing trips. One of my patients hadn't brought a raincoat. It was beginning to snow pretty heavily, so I let him borrow the slicker.' He stopped, suddenly worried. 'What's happened to him?'

'Happened to who?' McGreavy asked.

'My patient – John Hanson.'

'Check,' Angeli said gently. 'You hit the bull's-eye.

19

The reason Mr Hanson couldn't return the coat himself is that he's dead.'

Judd felt a small shock go through him. 'Dead?'

'Someone stuck a knife in his back,' McGreavy said.

Judd stared at him incredulously. McGreavy took the coat from Angeli and turned it around so that Judd could see the large, ugly slash in the material. The back of the coat was covered with dull, henna-coloured stains. A feeling of nausea swept over Judd.

'Who would want to kill him?'

'We were hoping that you could tell us, Dr Stevens,' said Angeli. 'Who'd know better than his psychoanalyst?'

Judd shook his head helplessly. 'When did it happen?'

McGreavy answered. 'Eleven o'clock this morning. On Lexington Avenue, about a block from your office. A few dozen people must have seen him fall, but they were busy going home to get ready to celebrate the birth of Christ, so they let him lie there bleeding to death in the snow.'

Judd squeezed the edge of the table, his knuckles white.

'What time was Hanson here this morning?' asked Angeli.

'Ten o'clock.'

'How long do your sessions last, Doctor?'

'Fifty minutes.'

'Did he leave as soon as it was over?'

'Yes. I had another patient waiting.'

'Did Hanson go out through the reception office?'

'No. My patients come in through the reception office and leave by that door.' He indicated the private door leading to the outside corridor. 'In that way they don't meet each other.'

McGreavy nodded. 'So Hanson was killed within a few minutes of the time he left here. Why was he coming to see you?'

Judd hesitated. 'I'm sorry. I can't discuss a doctor-patient relationship.'

'Someone murdered him,' McGreavy said. 'You might be able to help us find his killer.'

Judd's pipe had gone out. He took his time lighting it again.

'How long had he been coming to you?' This time it was Angeli. Police teamwork.

'Three years,' Judd said.

'What was his problem?'

Judd hesitated. He saw John Hanson as he had looked that morning; excited, smiling, eager to enjoy his new freedom. 'He was a homosexual.'

'This is going to be another one of those beauties,' McGreavy said bitterly.

'*Was* a homosexual,' Judd said. 'Hanson was cured. I told him this morning that he didn't have

21

to see me any more. He was ready to move back in with his family. He has – had – a wife and two children.'

'A fag with a family?' asked McGreavy.

'It happens often.'

'Maybe one of his homo playmates didn't want to cut him loose. They got in a fight. He lost his temper and slipped a knife in his boyfriend's back.'

Judd considered. 'It's possible,' he said thoughtfully, 'but I don't believe it.'

'Why not, Dr Stevens?' asked Angeli.

'Because Hanson hadn't had any homosexual contacts in more than a year. I think it's much more likely that someone tried to mug him. Hanson was the kind of man who would have put up a fight.'

'A brave married fag,' McGreavy said heavily. He took out a cigar and lit it. 'There's only one thing wrong with the mugger theory. His wallet hadn't been touched. There was over a hundred dollars in it.' He watched Judd's reaction.

Angeli said, 'If we're looking for a nut, it might make it easier.'

'Not necessarily,' Judd objected. He walked over to the window. 'Take a look at that crowd down there. One out of twenty is, has been, or will be in a mental hospital.'

'But if a man's crazy . . . ?'

'He doesn't have to necessarily appear crazy,'

22

Judd explained. 'For every obvious case of insanity there are at least ten cases undiagnosed.'

McGreavy was studying Judd with open interest. 'You know a lot about human nature, don't you, Doctor?'

'There's no such thing as human nature,' Judd said. 'Any more than there's such a thing as animal nature. Try to average out a rabbit and a tiger. Or a squirrel and an elephant.'

'How long you been practising psychoanalysis?' asked McGreavy.

'Twelve years. Why?'

McGreavy shrugged. 'You're a good-looking guy. I'll bet a lot of your patients fall in love with you, huh?'

Judd's eyes chilled. 'I don't understand the point of the question.'

'Oh, come on, Doc. Sure you do. We're both men of the world. A fag walks in here and finds himself a handsome young doctor to tell his troubles to.' His tone grew confidential. 'Now do you mean to say that in three years on your couch Hanson didn't get a little hard-on for you?'

Judd looked at him without expression. 'Is that your idea of being a man of the world, Lieutenant?'

McGreavy was unperturbed. 'It could have happened. And I'll tell you what else could have happened. You said you told Hanson you didn't want to see him again. Maybe he didn't like that. He'd grown dependent on you in three years. The two of you had a fight.'

Judd's face darkened with anger.

Angeli broke the tension. 'Can you think of anyone who had reason to hate him, Doctor? Or someone *he* might have hated?'

'If there were such a person,' Judd said, 'I would tell you. I think I knew everything there was to know about John Hanson. He was a happy man. He didn't hate anyone and I don't know of anyone who hated him.'

'Good for him. You must be one helluva doctor,' McGreavy said. 'We'll take his file along with us.'

'No.'

'We can get a court order.'

'Get it. There's nothing in that file that can help you.'

'Then what harm could it do if you gave it to us?' asked Angeli.

'It could hurt Hanson's wife and children. You're on the wrong track. You'll find that Hanson was killed by a stranger.'

'I don't believe it,' McGreavy snapped.

Angeli rewrapped the raincoat and tied the string around the bundle. 'We'll get this back to you when we've run some more tests on it.'

'Keep it,' Judd said.

McGreavy opened the private door leading to the corridor. 'We'll be in touch with you, Doctor.'

He walked out. Angeli nodded to Judd and followed McGreavy out.

Judd was still standing there, his mind churning, when Carol walked in. 'Is everything all right?' she asked hesitantly.

'Someone killed John Hanson.'

'*Killed* him?'

'He was stabbed,' Judd said.

'Oh my God! But why?'

'The police don't know.'

'How terrible!' She saw his eyes and the pain in them. 'Is there anything I can do, Doctor?'

'Would you close up the office, Carol? I'm going over to see Mrs Hanson. I'd like to break the news to her myself.'

'Don't worry. I'll take care of everything,' said Carol.

'Thanks.'

And Judd left.

Thirty minutes later Carol had finished putting the files away and was locking her desk when the corridor door opened. It was after six o'clock and the building was closed. Carol looked up as the man smiled and moved towards her.

THREE

Mary Hanson was a doll of a woman; small, beautiful, exquisitely made. On the outside, she was soft, Southern-helpless-feminine, and on the inside, granite bitch. Judd had met her a week after beginning her husband's therapy. She had fought hysterically against it and Judd had asked her to have a talk with him. 'Why are you so opposed to your husband going through analysis?'

'I won't have my friends saying I married a crazy man,' she had told Judd. 'Tell him to give me a divorce; then he can do any damn thing he pleases.'

Judd had explained that a divorce at that point could destroy John completely.

'There's nothing left to destroy,' Mary had screamed. 'If I'd known he was a fairy, do you think I would have married him? He's a woman.'

'There's some woman in every man,' Judd had said. 'Just as there's some man in every woman.

And in your husband's case, there are some difficult psychological problems to overcome. But he's trying, Mrs Hanson. I think you owe it to him and his children to help him.'

He had reasoned with her for more than three hours, and in the end she had reluctantly agreed to hold off on the divorce. In the months that followed, she had become interested and then involved in the battle that John was waging. Judd made it a rule never to treat married couples, but Mary had asked him to let her become a patient, and he had found it helpful. As she had begun to understand herself and where she had failed as a wife, John's progress had become dramatically rapid.

And now Judd was here to tell her that her husband had been senselessly murdered. She looked up at him, unable to believe what he had just said, sure that it was some kind of macabre joke. And then realization set in. 'He's never coming back to me!' she screamed. 'He's never coming back to me!' She started tearing at her clothes in anguish, like a wounded animal. The six-year-old twins walked in. And from that moment on, there was bedlam. Judd managed to calm the children down and take them to a neighbour's house. He gave Mrs Hanson a sedative and called the family doctor. When he was sure there was nothing more he could do, he left. He got into his car and drove aimlessly, lost in thought. Hanson had fought his way through a hell, and at the moment of his victory . . . It was such a pointless death. *Could* it have been some homosexual who had attacked him? Some former lover who was frustrated because Hanson had left him? It was possible, of course, but Judd did not believe it. Lieutenant McGreavy had said that Hanson was killed a block away from the office. If the murderer had been a homosexual, full of hatred, he would have made a rendezvous with Hanson at some private place, either to try to persuade Hanson to come back to him or to pour out his recriminations before he killed him. He would not have plunged a knife into him on a crowded street and then fled.

On the corner ahead he saw a phone booth and suddenly remembered that he had promised to have dinner with Dr Peter Hadley and his wife, Norah. They were his closest friends, but he was in no mood to see anyone. He stopped the car at the kerb, went into the phone booth and dialled the Hadleys' number. Norah answered the phone. 'You're late! Where are you?'

'Norah,' Judd said, 'I'm afraid I'm going to have to beg off tonight.'

'You can't,' she wailed. 'I have a sexy blonde sitting here dying to meet you.'

'We'll do it another night,' Judd said. 'I'm really not up to it. Please apologize for me.'

'Doctors!' snorted Norah. 'Just a minute and I'll put your chum on.'

Peter got on the phone. 'Anything wrong, Judd?'

Judd hesitated. 'Just a hard day, Pete. I'll tell you about it tomorrow.'

'You're missing some delicious Scandinavian smorgasbord. I mean *beautiful*.'

'I'll meet her another time,' promised Judd. He heard a hurried whisper, and then Norah got on the phone again.

'She'll be here for Christmas dinner, Judd. Will you come?'

He hesitated. 'We'll talk about it later, Norah. I'm sorry about tonight.' He hung up. He wished he knew of some tactful way to stop Norah's matchmaking.

Judd had got married in his senior years in college. Elizabeth had been a social science major, warm and bright and gay, and they had both been young and very much in love and full of wonderful plans to remake the world for all the children they were going to have. And on the first Christmas of their marriage, Elizabeth and their unborn child had been killed in a head-on automobile collision. Judd had plunged himself totally into his work, and in time had become one of the outstanding psychoanalysts in the country. But he was still not able to bear being with other people celebrating Christmas Day. Somehow, even though he told himself he was wrong, that belonged to Elizabeth and their child.

He pushed open the door of the phone booth. He was aware of a girl standing outside the booth waiting to use the phone. She was young and pretty, dressed in a tight-fitting sweater and a miniskirt, with a bright-coloured raincoat. He stepped out of the booth. 'Sorry,' he apologized.

She gave him a warm smile. 'That's all right.' There was a wistful look on her face. He had seen that look before. Loneliness seeking to break through the barrier that he had unconsciously set up.

If Judd knew that he had a quality that was attractive to women, it was deep in his subconscious. He had never analysed why. It was more of a handicap than an asset to have his female patients falling in love with him. It sometimes made life very difficult.

He moved past the girl with a friendly nod. He sensed her standing there in the rain, watching as he got into his car and drove away.

He turned the car onto the East River Drive and headed for the Merritt Parkway. An hour and a half later he was on the Connecticut Turnpike. The snow in New York was dirty and slushy, but the same storm had magically transformed the Connecticut landscape into a Currier and Ives picture postcard.

He drove past Westport and Danbury, deliberately forcing his mind to concentrate on the ribbon of road that flashed beneath his wheels and the wintry wonderland that surrounded him. Each time his thought reached out to John Hanson, he made himself think of other things. He drove on through the darkness of the Connecticut countryside and hours later, emotionally worn out, finally turned the car around and headed for home.

Mike, the red-faced doorman who usually greeted him with a smile, was preoccupied and distant. Family difficulties, Judd supposed. Usually Judd would chat with him about Mike's teenage son and married daughters, but Judd did not feel like talking this evening. He asked Mike to have the car sent down to the garage.

'Right, Dr Stevens.' Mike seemed about to add something, then thought better of it.

Judd walked into the building. Ben Katz, the manager, was crossing the lobby. He saw Judd, gave a nervous wave, and hurriedly disappeared into his apartment.

What's the matter with everyone tonight? thought Judd. *Or is it just my nerves?* He stepped into the elevator.

Eddie, the elevator operator, nodded. 'Evening, Dr Stevens.'

'Good evening, Eddie.'

Eddie swallowed and looked away self-consciously. 'Is anything wrong?' Judd asked.

Eddie quickly shook his head and kept his eyes averted.

My God, thought Judd. *Another candidate for my couch*. The building was suddenly full of them.

Eddie opened the elevator door and Judd got out. He started towards his apartment. He didn't hear the elevator door close, so he turned around. Eddie was staring at him. As Judd started to speak, Eddie quickly closed the elevator door. Judd went to his apartment, unlocked the door, and entered.

Every light in the apartment was on. Lieutenant McGreavy was opening a drawer in the living-room. Angeli was coming out of the bedroom. Judd felt anger flare in him. 'What are you doing in my apartment?'

'Waitin' for you, Dr Stevens,' McGreavy said.

Judd walked over and slammed the drawer shut, narrowly missing McGreavy's fingers. 'How did you get in here?'

'We have a search warrant,' said Angeli.

Judd stared at him incredulously. 'A search warrant? For my apartment?'

'Suppose we ask the questions, Doctor,' McGreavy said.

'You don't have to answer them,' interjected

Angeli, 'without benefit of legal counsel. Also, you should know that anything you say can be used as evidence against you.'

'Do you want to call a lawyer?' McGreavy asked.

'I don't need a lawyer. I told you that I loaned the raincoat to John Hanson this morning and I didn't see it again until you brought it to my office this afternoon. I couldn't have killed him. I was with patients all day. Miss Roberts can verify that.'

McGreavy and Angeli exchanged a silent signal.

'Where did you go after you left your office this afternoon?' Angeli said.

'To see Mrs Hanson.'

'We know that,' McGreavy said. 'Afterwards.'

Judd hesitated. 'I drove around.'

'Where?'

'I drove up to Connecticut.'

'Where did you stop for dinner?' McGreavy asked.

'I didn't. I wasn't hungry.'

'So no one saw you?'

Judd thought for a moment. 'I suppose not.'

'Perhaps you stopped for gas somewhere,' suggested Angeli.

'No,' Judd said. 'I didn't. What difference does it make where I went tonight? Hanson was killed this morning.'

'Did you go back to your office any time after you left it this afternoon?' McGreavy's voice was casual.

'No,' Judd said. 'Why?'

'It was broken into.'

'What? By whom?'

'We don't know,' said McGreavy. 'I want you to come down and take a look around. You can tell us if anything is missing.'

'Of course,' Judd replied. 'Who reported it?'

'The night watchman,' said Angeli. 'Do you keep anything of value in the office, Doctor? Cash? Drugs? Anything like that?'

'Petty cash,' Judd said. 'No addictive drugs. There was nothing there to steal. It doesn't make any sense.'

'Right,' McGreavy said. 'Let's go.'

In the elevator Eddie gave Judd an apologetic look. Judd met his eyes and nodded that he understood.

Surely, Judd thought, the police couldn't suspect him of breaking into his own office. It was as though McGreavy was determined to pin something on him because of his dead partner. But that had been five years ago. Could McGreavy have been brooding all these years, blaming it on the doctor? Waiting for a chance to get him?

There was an unmarked police car a few feet

from the entrance. They got in and rode to the office in silence.

When they reached the office building, Judd signed the lobby register. Bigelow, the guard, looked at him strangely. Or did he imagine it?

They took the elevator to the fifteenth floor and walked down the corridor to Judd's office. A uniformed policeman was standing in front of the door. He nodded to McGreavy and stepped aside. Judd reached for his key.

'The door's unlocked,' Angeli said. He pushed the door open and they went in, Judd leading the way.

The reception office was in chaos. All the drawers had been pulled out of the desk and papers were strewn about the floor. Judd stared unbelievingly, feeling a shock of personal violation.

'What do you suppose they were looking for, Doctor?' asked McGreavy.

'I have no idea,' Judd said. He walked to the inner door and opened it, McGreavy close behind him.

In his office two end tables had been overturned, a smashed lamp lay on the floor, and blood soaked the Fields rug.

In the far corner of the room, grotesquely spread out, was the body of Carol Roberts. She was nude. Her hands were tied behind her back with piano wire, and acid had been splashed on her face and breasts and between her thighs. The fingers of her right hand were broken. Her face was battered and swollen. A wadded handkerchief was stuffed in her mouth.

The two detectives watched Judd as he stared at the body.

'You look pale,' Angeli said. 'Sit down.'

Judd shook his head and took several deep breaths. When he spoke, his voice was shaking with rage. 'Who – who could have done this?'

'That's what you're going to tell us, Dr Stevens,' said McGreavy.

Judd looked up at him. 'No one could have wanted to do this to Carol. She never hurt anyone in her life.'

'I think it's about time you started singing another tune,' McGreavy said. 'No one wanted to hurt Hanson, but they stuck a knife in his back. No one wanted to hurt Carol, but they poured acid all over her and tortured her to death.' His voice became hard. 'And you stand there and tell me no one would want to hurt them. What the hell are you – deaf, dumb, and blind? The girl worked for you for four years. You're a psychoanalyst. Are you trying to tell me you didn't know or care about her personal life?'

'Of course I cared,' Judd said tightly. 'She had a boyfriend she was going to marry –'

'Chick. We've talked to him.'

'But he could never have done this. He's a decent boy and he loved Carol.'

'When was the last time you saw Carol alive?' asked Angeli.

'I told you. When I left here to go to see Mrs Hanson. I asked Carol to close up the office.' His voice broke and he swallowed and took a deep breath.

'Were you scheduled to see any more patients today?'

'No.'

'Do you think this could have been done by a maniac?' Angeli asked.

'It must have been a maniac, but – even a maniac has to have some motivation.'

'That's what I think,' McGreavy said.

Judd looked over to where Carol's body lay. It had the sad appearance of a disfigured rag doll, useless and discarded. 'How long are you going to leave her like this?' Judd asked angrily.

'They'll take her away now,' said Angeli. 'The coroner and the Homicide boys have already finished.'

Judd turned to McGreavy. 'You left her like this for me?'

'Yeah,' McGreavy said. 'I'm going to ask you again. Is there anything in this office that someone could want badly enough to' – he indicated Carol – 'do that?'

'No.'

'What about the records of your patients?'

Judd shook his head. 'Nothing.'

'You're not being very cooperative, Doctor, are you?' asked McGreavy.

'Don't you think I want to see you find whoever did this?' Judd snapped. 'If there was anything in my files that would help, I would tell you. I know my patients. There isn't any one among them who could have killed her. This was done by an outsider.'

'How do you know it wasn't someone after your files?'

'My files weren't touched.'

McGreavy looked at him with quickened interest. 'How do you know that?' he asked. 'You haven't even looked.'

Judd walked over to the far wall. As the two men watched, he pressed the lower section of the panelling and the wall slid open, revealing racks of built-in shelves. They were filled with tapes. 'I record every session with my patients,' Judd said. 'I keep the tapes here.'

'Couldn't they have tortured Carol to try to force her to tell where those tapes were?'

'There is nothing in any of these tapes worth anything to anyone. There was some other motive for her murder.'

Judd looked at Carol's scarred body again, and

he was filled with helpless, blind rage. 'You've got to find whoever did this!'

'I intend to,' McGreavy said. He was looking at Judd.

On the windy, deserted street in front of Judd's office building, McGreavy told Angeli to drive Judd home. 'I've got an errand to do,' McGreavy said. He turned to Judd. 'Goodnight, Doctor.'

Judd watched the huge, lumbering figure move down the street.

'Let's go,' Angeli said. 'I'm freezing.'

Judd slid into the front seat beside Angeli, and the car pulled away from the kerb.

'I've got to go tell Carol's family,' Judd said.

'We've already been over there.'

Judd nodded wearily. He still wanted to see them himself, but it could wait.

There was a silence. Judd wondered what errand Lieutenant McGreavy could have at this hour of the morning.

As though reading his thoughts, Angeli said, 'McGreavy's a good cop. He thought Ziffren should have got the electric chair for killing his partner.'

'Ziffren was insane.'

Angeli shrugged. 'I'll take your word for it, Doctor.'

But McGreavy hadn't, Judd thought. He turned

his mind to Carol and remembered her brightness and her affection and her deep pride in what she was doing, and Angeli was speaking to him and he saw that they had arrived at his apartment building.

Five minutes later Judd was in his apartment. There was no question of sleep. He fixed himself a brandy and carried it into his den. He remembered the night Carol had strolled in here, naked and beautiful, rubbing her warm, lithe body against his. He had acted cool and aloof because he had known that that was the only chance he had of helping her. But she had never known what willpower it had taken for him to keep from making love to her. Or had she? He raised his brandy glass and drained it.

The city morgue looked like all city morgues at three o'clock in the morning, except that someone had placed a wreath of mistletoe over the door. Someone, thought McGreavy, who had either an overabundance of holiday spirit or a macabre sense of humour.

McGreavy had waited impatiently in the corridor until the autopsy was completed. When the coroner waved to him, he walked into the sickly-white autopsy room. The coroner was scrubbing his hands at the large white sink. He was a small, birdlike man with a high, chirping voice and quick, nervous movements. He answered all of McGreavy's questions in a rapid, staccato manner, then fled. McGreavy remained there a few minutes, absorbed in what he had just learned. Then he walked out into the freezing night air to find a taxi. There was no sign of one. The sons of bitches were all vacationing in Bermuda. He could stand out here until his ass froze off. He spotted a police cruiser, flagged it down, showed his identification to the young rookie behind the wheel, and ordered him to drive him to the Nineteenth Precinct. It was against regulations, but what the hell. It was going to be a long night.

When McGreavy walked into the precinct, Angeli was waiting for him. 'They just finished the autopsy on Carol Roberts,' McGreavy said.

'And?'

'She was pregnant.'

Angeli looked at him in surprise.

'She was three months gone. A little late to have a safe abortion, and a little early to show.'

'Do you think that had anything to do with her murder?'

'That's a good question,' McGreavy said. 'If Carol's boyfriend knocked her up and they were going to get married anyway – what's the big deal? So they get married and have the kid a few months later. It happens every day of the week. On the other hand, if he knocked her up and he *didn't* want to marry her – that's no big deal, either. So she has the baby and no husband. That happens *twice* every day of the week.'

'We talked to Chick. He wanted to marry her.'

'I know,' replied McGreavy. 'So we have to ask ourselves where that leaves us. It leaves us with a coloured girl who's pregnant. She goes to the father and tells him about it, and he murders her.'

'He'd have to be insane.'

'Or very foxy. Look at it this way: supposing Carol went to the father and broke the bad news and told him she wasn't going to have an abortion; she was going to have his baby. Maybe she used it to try to blackmail him into marrying her. But supposing he couldn't marry her because he was married already. Or maybe he was a white man. Let's say a well-known doctor with a fancy practice. If a thing like this ever got out, it would ruin him. Who the hell would go to a head-shrinker who knocked up his coloured receptionist and had to marry her?'

'Stevens is a doctor,' said Angeli. 'There are a dozen ways he could have killed her without arousing suspicion.'

'Maybe,' McGreavy said. 'Maybe not. If there was any suspicion and it could be traced back to him, he'd have a hard time getting out of it. He buys poison – someone has a record of it. He buys a rope or a knife – they can all be traced. But look at this cute little setup. Some maniac comes in for no reason and murders his receptionist and he's the grief-stricken employer demanding that the police find the killer.'

'It sounds like a pretty flimsy case.'

'I'm not finished. Let's take his patient, John Hanson. Another senseless killing by this unknown maniac. I'll tell you something, Angeli. I don't believe in coincidences. And two coincidences like that in one day make me nervous. So I asked myself what connection there could be between the death of John Hanson and Carol Roberts, and suddenly it didn't seem so coincidental, after all. Suppose Carol walked into his office and broke the bad news that he was going to be a daddy. They had a big fight and she tried to blackmail him. She said he had to marry her, give her money – whatever. John Hanson was waiting in the outer office, listening. Maybe Stevens wasn't sure he had heard anything until he got on the couch. Then Hanson threatened him with exposure. Or tried to get him to sleep with him.'

'That's a lot of guesswork.'

'But it fits. When Hanson left, the doctor slipped out and fixed him so he couldn't talk. Then he had to come back and get rid of Carol. He made it look like some maniac did the job, then he stopped by to see Mrs Hanson, and took a ride to Connecticut. Now his problems are solved. He's sitting pretty and the police are running their asses off searching for some unknown nut.'

'I can't buy it,' Angeli said. 'You're trying to build a murder case without a shred of concrete evidence.'

'What do you call "concrete"?' McGreavy asked. 'We've got two corpses. One of them is a pregnant lady who worked for Stevens. The other is one of his patients, murdered a block from his office. He's coming to him for treatment because he's a homosexual. When I asked to listen to his tapes, he wouldn't let me. Why? Who is Dr Stevens protecting? I asked him if anyone could have broken into his office looking for something. Then maybe we could have cooked up a nice theory that Carol caught them and they tortured her to try to find out where this mysterious something was. But guess what? There is no mysterious something. His tapes aren't worth a tinker's damn to anybody. He had no drugs in the office. No money. So we're looking for some goddamn maniac. Right? Except that I won't buy it. I think we're looking for Dr Judd Stevens.'

'I think you're out to nail him,' said Angeli quietly.

McGreavy's face flushed with anger. 'Because he's as guilty as hell.'

'Are you going to arrest him?'

'I'm going to give Dr Stevens some rope,' McGreavy said. 'And while he's hanging himself, I'm going to be digging into every little skeleton in his closet. When I nail him, he's going to stay nailed.' McGreavy turned and walked out.

Angeli looked after him thoughtfully. If he did nothing, there was a good chance that McGreavy would try to railroad Dr Stevens. He could not let that happen. He made a mental note to speak to Captain Bertelli in the morning.

FOUR

The morning newspapers headlined the sensational torture murder of Carol Roberts. Judd was tempted to have his telephone exchange call his patients and cancel his appointments for the day. He had not gone to bed, and his eyes felt heavy and gritty. But when he reviewed the list of patients, he decided that two of them would be desperate if he cancelled; three of them would be badly upset; the others could be handled. He decided it was better to continue with his normal routine, partly for his patients' sake, and partly because it was good therapy for him to try to keep his mind off what had happened.

Judd arrived at his office early, but already the corridor was crowded with newspaper and television reporters and photographers. He refused to let them in or to make a statement, and finally managed to get rid of them. He opened the door to his inner office slowly, filled with trepidation. But the blood-stained rug had been removed and everything else had been put back in place. The office looked normal. Except that Carol would never walk in here again, smiling and full of life.

Judd heard the outer door open. His first patient had arrived.

Harrison Burke was a distinguished-looking silver-haired man who looked like the prototype of a big business executive, which he was: a vice-president of the International Steel Corporation. When Judd had first seen Burke, he had wondered whether the executive had created his stereotyped image, or whether the image had created the executive. Some day he would write a book on face values; a doctor's bedside manner, a lawyer's flamboyance in a courtroom, an actress's face and figure – these were the universal currencies of acceptance: the surface image rather than the basic values.

Burke lay down on the couch, and Judd turned his attention to him. Burke had been sent to Judd by Dr Peter Hadley two months ago. It had taken Judd ten minutes to ascertain that Harrison Burke was a paranoiac with tendencies towards homicide. The morning headlines had been full of a murder that had taken place in this office the night before, but Burke never mentioned it. That was typical of his condition. He was totally immersed in himself.

'You didn't believe me before,' Burke said, 'but now I've got proof that they're after me.'

'I thought we had decided to keep an open mind about that, Harrison,' Judd replied carefully. 'Remember yesterday we agreed that the imagination could play –'

'It isn't my imagination,' shouted Burke. He sat up, his fists clenched. 'They're trying to kill me!'

'Why don't you lie down and try to relax?' Judd suggested soothingly.

Burke got to his feet. 'Is that all you've got to say? You don't even want to hear my proof!' His eyes narrowed. 'How do I know you're not one of them?'

'You know I'm not one of them,' Judd said. 'I'm your friend. I'm trying to help you.' He felt a stab of disappointment. The progress he had thought they were making over the past month had completely eroded away. He was looking now at the same terrified paranoiac who had first walked into his office two months ago.

Burke had started with International Steel as a mail boy. In twenty-five years his distinguished good looks and his affable personality had taken him almost to the top of the corporate ladder. He had been next in line for the presidency. Then, four years ago, his wife and three children had perished in a fire at their summer home in

Southampton. Burke had been in the Bahamas with his mistress. He had taken the tragedy harder than anyone realized. Reared as a devout Catholic, he was unable to shake off his burden of guilt. He began to brood, and he saw less of his friends. He stayed home evenings, reliving the agonies of his wife and children burning to death while, in another part of his mind, he lay in bed with his mistress. It was like a motion picture that he ran over and over in his mind. He blamed himself completely for the death of his family. If only he had been there, he could have saved them. The thought became an obsession. He was a monster. He knew it and God knew it. Surely others could see it! They must hate him as he hated himself. People smiled at him and pretended sympathy, but all the while they were waiting for him to expose himself, waiting to trap him. But he was too cunning for them. He stopped going to the executive dining-room and began to have lunch in the privacy of his office. He avoided everyone as much as possible.

Two years ago, when the company had needed a new president, they had passed over Harrison Burke and had hired an outsider. A year later the post of executive vice-president had opened up, and a man was given the job over Burke's head. Now he had all the proof he needed that there was a conspiracy against him. He began to spy on the people around him. At night he hid tape recorders in the offices of other executives. Six months ago he had been caught. It was only because of his long seniority and position that he was not fired.

Trying to help him and relieve some of the pressure on him, the president of the company began to cut down on Burke's responsibilities. Instead of helping, it convinced Burke more than ever that *they* were out to get him. *They* were afraid of him because he was smarter than they were. If he became president, *they* would all lose their jobs because *they* were stupid fools. He began to make more and more mistakes. When these errors were called to his attention, he indignantly denied having made them. Someone was deliberately changing his reports, altering the figures and statistics, trying to discredit him. Soon he realized that it was not only the people in the company who were after him. There were spies outside. He was constantly followed in the streets. They tapped his telephone line, read his mail. He was afraid to eat, lest they poison his food. His weight began to drop alarmingly. The worried president of the company arranged an appointment for him with Dr Peter Hadley and insisted that Burke keep it. After spending half an hour with him, Dr Hadley had phoned Judd. Judd's appointment book was full, but when Peter had told him how urgent it was, Judd reluctantly agreed to take him on.

Now Harrison Burke stood by the damask-covered contour couch, his fists clenched tightly at his sides.

'Tell me about your proof.'

'They broke into my house last night. They came to kill me. But I was too clever for them. I sleep in my den now, and I have extra locks on all the doors so they can't get to me.'

'Did you report the break-in to the police?' Judd asked.

'Of course not! The police are in it with them. They have orders to shoot me. But they wouldn't dare do it while there are other people around, so I stay in crowds.'

'I'm glad you gave me this information,' Judd said.

'What are you going to do with it?' Burke asked eagerly.

'I'm listening very carefully to everything you say,' Judd said. He indicated the tape recorder. 'I've got it all down on tape so if they do kill you, we'll have a record of the conspiracy.'

Burke's face lit up. 'By God, that's good! Tape! That'll really fix them!'

'Why don't you lie down again?' Judd suggested.

Burke nodded and slid onto the couch. He closed his eyes. 'I'm tired. I haven't slept in months. I don't dare close my eyes. You don't know what it's like, having everybody after you.'

Don't I? He thought of McGreavy.

'Didn't your houseboy hear anyone break in?' Judd asked.

'Didn't I tell you?' Burke replied. 'I fired him two weeks ago.'

Judd quickly went over in his mind his recent sessions with Harrison Burke. Only three days ago Burke had described a fight he had had that day with his houseboy. So his sense of time had become disoriented. 'I don't believe you mentioned it,' Judd said casually. 'Are you sure it was two weeks ago that you let him go?'

'I don't make mistakes,' snapped Burke. 'How the hell do you think I got to be vice-president of one of the biggest corporations in the world? Because I've got a brilliant mind, Doctor, and don't forget it.'

'Why did you fire him?'

'He tried to poison me.'

'How?'

'With a plate of ham and eggs. Loaded with arsenic.'

'Did you taste it?' Judd asked.

'Of course not,' Burke snorted.

'How did you know it was poisoned?'

'I could smell the poison.'

'What did you say to him?'

A look of satisfaction came over Burke's face. 'I didn't say anything. I beat the shit out of him.'

A feeling of frustration swept over Judd. Given time, he was sure he could have helped Harrison Burke. But time had run out. There was always the danger in psychoanalysis that under the venting of free-flow association, the thin veneer of the id could blow wide open, letting escape all the primitive passions and emotions that huddled together in the mind like terrified wild beasts in the night. The free verbalizing was the first step in treatment. In Burke's case, it had boomeranged. These sessions had released all the latent hostilities that had been locked in his mind. Burke had seemed to improve with each session, agreeing with Judd that there was no conspiracy, that he was only overworked and emotionally exhausted. Judd had felt that he was guiding Burke to a point where they could begin deep analysis and start to attack the root of the problem. But Burke had been cunningly lying all along. He had been testing Judd, leading him on to try to trap him and find out whether he was one of *them*. Harrison Burke was a walking time bomb that could explode at any second. There was no next of kin to notify. Should Judd call the president of the company and tell him what he felt? If he did, it would instantly destroy Burke's future. He would have to be put away in an institution. Was he right in his diagnosis that Burke was a potential homicidal paranoiac? He would like to get another opinion before he called, but Burke would never consent. Judd knew he would have to make the decision alone.

'Harrison, I want you to make me a promise,' Judd said.

'What kind of promise?' Burke asked warily.

'If they are trying to trick you, then they want you to do something violent so they can have you locked up . . . But you're too smart for that. No matter how they provoke you, I want you to promise me that you won't do anything to them. That way, they can't touch you.'

Burke's eyes lit up. 'By God, you're right,' he said. 'So that's their plan! Well, we're too clever for them, aren't we?'

Outside, Judd heard the sound of the reception door open and close. He looked at his watch. His next patient was here.

Judd quietly snapped off the tape recorder. 'I think that's enough for today,' he said.

'You got all this down on the tape recorder?' Burke asked eagerly.

'Every word,' Judd said. 'No one's going to hurt you.' He hesitated. 'I don't think you should go to the office today. Why don't you go home and get some rest?'

'I can't,' Burke whispered, his voice filled with despair. 'If I'm not in my office, they'll take my name off the door and put someone else's name on it.' He leaned towards Judd. 'Be careful. If they know you're my friend, they'll try to get you, too.' Burke walked over to the door leading to the corridor. He opened it a crack and peered up and down the corridor. Then he swiftly sidled out.

Judd looked after him, his mind filled with the pain of what he would have to do to Harrison Burke's life. Perhaps if Burke had come to him six months earlier . . . And then a sudden thought sent a chill through him. Was Harrison Burke *already* a murderer? Was it possible that he had been involved in the deaths of John Hanson and Carol Roberts? Both Burke and Hanson were patients. And they could have easily met. Several times in the past few months Burke's appointments had followed Hanson's. And Burke had been late more than once. He could have run into Hanson in the corridor. And seeing him several times could easily have triggered his paranoia, made him feel that Hanson was following him, threatening him. As for Carol, Burke had seen her every time he came to the office. Had his sick mind conceived some menace from her that could only be removed by her death? How long had Burke really been mentally ill? His wife and three children had died in an accidental fire. Accidental? Somehow, he had to find out.

He went to the door leading to the reception office and opened it. 'Come in,' he said.

Anne Blake rose gracefully to her feet and moved towards him, a warm smile lighting her face. Judd felt again the same heart-turning feeling that had hit him when he had first seen her. It was the first time that he had felt any deep emotional response towards any woman since Elizabeth.

In no way did they look alike. Elizabeth had been blonde and small and blue-eyed. Anne Blake had black hair and unbelievable violet eyes framed by long, dark lashes. She was tall, with a lovely, full-curved figure. She had an air of lively intelligence and a classical patrician beauty that would have made her seem inaccessible, except for the warmth in her eyes. Her voice was low and soft, with a faint, husky quality.

Anne was in her middle twenties. She was, without question, the most beautiful woman Judd had ever seen. But it was something beyond her beauty that caught at Judd. There was an almost palpable force that pulled him to her, some unexplainable reaction that made him feel as though emotions long since dead had suddenly surfaced again, surprising him by their intensity.

She had appeared in Judd's office three weeks earlier, without an appointment. Carol had explained that his schedule was full and he could not possibly take on any new patients. But Anne had quietly asked if she could wait. She had sat in the outer office for two hours, and Carol had finally taken pity on her and brought her in to Judd.

He had felt such an instant powerful emotional reaction to Anne that he had no idea what she said during the first few minutes. He remembered he had asked her to sit down and she had told him her name, Anne Blake. She was a housewife. Judd had asked her what her problem was. She had hesitated and said that she was not certain. She was not even sure she had a problem. A doctor friend of hers had mentioned that Judd was one of the most brilliant analysts in the country, but when Judd had asked who the doctor was, Anne had demurred. For all Judd knew, she could have got his name out of the telephone directory.

He had tried to explain to her how impossible his schedule was, that he simply was unable to take on any new patients. He offered to recommend half a dozen good analysts. But Anne had quietly insisted that she wanted him to treat her. In the end Judd had agreed. Outwardly, except for the fact that she appeared to be under some stress, she seemed perfectly normal, and he was certain that her problem would be a relatively simple one, easily solved. He broke his rule about not taking any patient without another doctor's recommendation, and he gave up his lunch hour in order to treat Anne. She had appeared twice a week for the past three weeks, and Judd knew very little more about her than he had known when she first came in. He knew something more about himself. He was in love – for the first time since Elizabeth.

At their first session, Judd had asked her if she loved her husband, and hated himself for wanting to hear her say that she did not. But she had said, 'Yes. He's a kind man, and very strong.'

'Do you think he represents a father figure?' Judd had asked.

Anne had turned her incredible violet eyes on him. 'No. I wasn't looking for a father figure. I had a very happy home life as a child.'

'Where were you born?'

'In Revere, a small town near Boston.'

'Are both your parents still alive?'

'Father is alive. Mother died of a stroke when I was twelve.'

'Did your father and mother have a good relationship?'

'Yes. They were very much in love.'

It shows in you, thought Judd happily. With all the sickness and aberration and misery that he had seen, having Anne here was like a breath of April freshness.

'Any brothers or sisters?'

'No. I was an only child. A spoiled brat.' She

smiled up at him. It was an open, friendly smile without guile or affectation.

She told him that she had lived abroad with her father, who was serving in the State Department, and when he had remarried and moved to California, she had gone to work at the UN as an interpreter. She spoke fluent French, Italian, and Spanish. She had met her future husband in the Bahamas when she was on vacation. He owned a construction firm. Anne had not been attracted to him at first, but he had been a persistent and persuasive suitor. Two months after they met, Anne had married him. She had now been married for six months. They lived on an estate in New Jersey.

And that was all Judd had been able to find out about her in half a dozen visits. He still had not the slightest clue as to what her problem was. She had an emotional block about discussing it. He remembered some of the questions he had asked her during their first session.

'Does your problem involve your husband, Mrs Blake?'

No answer.

'Are you and your husband compatible, physically?'

'Yes.' Embarrassed.

'Do you suspect him of having an affair with another woman?'

'No.' Amused.

'Are you having an affair with another man?'

'No.' Angry.

He hesitated, trying to figure out the best approach to take to break down the barrier. He decided on a buckshot technique: he would touch on every major category until he struck a nerve.

'Do you quarrel about money?'

'No. He's very generous.'

'Any in-law problems?'

'He's an orphan. My father lives in California.'

'Were you or your husband ever addicted to drugs?'

'No.'

'Do you suspect your husband of being homosexual?'

A low, warm laugh. 'No.'

He pressed on, because he had to. 'Have you ever had a sexual relationship with a woman?'

'No.' Reproachful.

He had touched on alcoholism, frigidity, a pregnancy she was afraid to face – everything he could think of. And each time she had looked at him with her thoughtful, intelligent eyes and had merely shaken her head. Whenever he tried to pin her down, she would head him off with, 'Please be patient with me. Let me do it my own way.'

With anyone else, he might have given up. But

he knew that he had to help her. And he had to keep seeing her.

He had let her talk about any subject she chose. She had travelled to a dozen countries with her father and had met fascinating people. She had a quick mind and an unexpected humour. He found that they liked the same books, the same music, the same playwrights. She was warm and friendly, but Judd could never detect the slightest sign that she reacted to him as anything other than a doctor. It was bitter irony. He had been subconsciously searching for someone like Anne for years, and now that she had walked into his life, his job was to help her solve whatever her problem was and send her back to her husband.

Now, as Anne walked into the office, Judd moved to the chair next to the couch and waited for her to lie down.

'Not today,' she said quietly. 'I just came to see if I could help.'

He stared at her, speechless for a moment. His emotions had been stretched so tight in the past two days that her unexpected sympathy unnerved him. As he looked at her, he had a wild impulse to pour out everything that was happening to him. To tell her about the nightmare that was engulfing him, about McGreavy and his idiotic suspicions. But he knew he could not. He was the doctor and she was his patient. Worse than that. He was in love with her, and she was the untouchable wife of a man he did not even know.

She was standing there, watching him. He nodded, not trusting himself to speak.

'I liked Carol so much,' said Anne. 'Why would anyone kill her?'

'I don't know,' said Judd.

'Don't the police have any idea who did it?'

Do they? Judd thought bitterly. *If she only knew.*

Anne was looking at him curiously.

'The police have some theories,' Judd said.

'I know how terrible you must feel. I just wanted to come and tell you how very sorry I am. I wasn't even sure you'd be in the office today.'

'I wasn't going to come in,' Judd said. 'But – well, here I am. As long as we're both here, why don't we talk a little about you?'

Anne hesitated. 'I'm not sure that there's anything to talk about any more.'

Judd felt his heart jump. *Please, God, don't let her say that I'm not going to see her any more.*

'I'm going to Europe with my husband next week.'

'That's wonderful,' he made himself say.

'I'm afraid I've wasted your time, Dr Stevens, and I apologize.'

'Please don't,' Judd said. He found that his voice was husky. She was walking out on him. But of course she couldn't know that. He was being infantile. His mind told him this clinically while his stomach ached with the physical hurt of her going away. For ever.

She opened her purse and took out some money. She was in the habit of paying cash after each visit, unlike his other patients, who sent him cheques.

'No,' said Judd quickly. 'You came here as a friend. I'm grateful.'

Judd did something he had never done before with a patient. 'I would like you to come back once more,' he said.

She looked up at him quietly. 'Why?'

Because I can't bear to let you go so soon, he thought. *Because I'll never meet anyone like you again. Because I wish I had met you first. Because I love you*. Aloud he said, 'I thought we might – round things out. Talk a little to make sure that you really are over your problem.'

She smiled mischievously. 'You mean you want me to come back for my graduation?'

'Something like that,' he said. 'Will you do it?'

'If you want me to – of course.' She rose. 'I haven't given you a chance with me. But I know you're a wonderful doctor. If I should ever need help, I'd come to you.'

She held out her hand and he took it. She had a warm firm handclasp. He felt again that compelling current that ran between them and marvelled that she felt nothing.

'I'll see you Friday,' she said.

'Friday.'

He watched her walk out the private door leading to the corridor, then sank into a chair. He had never felt so completely alone in his life. But he couldn't sit here and do nothing. There had to be an answer, and if McGreavy wasn't going to find it, *he* had to discover it before McGreavy destroyed him. On the dark side, Lieutenant McGreavy suspected him of two murders that he couldn't prove he did not commit. He might be arrested at any moment, which would mean that his professional life would be destroyed. He was in love with a married woman he would only see once more. He forced himself to turn to the bright side. He couldn't think of a single bloody thing.

FIVE

The rest of the day went by as though he were under water. A few of the patients made reference to Carol's murder, but the more disturbed ones were so self-absorbed that they could only think of themselves and their problems. Judd tried to concentrate, but his thoughts kept drifting away, trying to find answers to what had happened. He would go over the tapes later to pick up what he had missed.

At seven o'clock, when Judd had ushered out the last patient, he went over to the recessed liquor cabinet and poured himself a stiff scotch. It hit him with a jolt, and he suddenly remembered that he had not had any breakfast or lunch. The thought of food made him ill. He sank into a chair and thought about the two murders. There was nothing in the case histories of any of his patients that would cause someone to commit murder. A blackmailer might have tried to steal them. But blackmailers were cowards, preying on the weaknesses of others, and if Carol had caught one breaking in and he had killed her, it would have been done quickly, with a single blow. He would not have tortured her. There had to be some other explanation.

Judd sat there a long time, his mind slowly sifting the events of the past two days. Finally, he sighed and gave it up. He looked at the clock and was startled to see how late it was.

By the time he left his office, it was after nine o'clock. As he stepped out of the lobby into the street, a blast of icy wind hit him. It had started to snow again. The snow swirled through the sky, gently blurring everything so that it looked as though the city had been painted on a canvas that had not dried and the paints were running, melting down skyscrapers and streets into watery greys and whites. A large red-and-white sign in a store window across the street on Lexington Avenue warned: Christmas. He resolutely turned his thoughts away from it and started to walk.

The street was deserted except for a lone pedestrian in the distance, hurrying home to his wife or sweetheart. Judd found himself wondering what Anne was doing. She was probably at home with her husband, discussing his day at the office, interested, caring. Or they had gone to bed, and . . . *Stop it!* he told himself.

There were no cars on the windswept street, so just before he reached the corner, Judd began to cross at an angle, heading towards the garage where he parked his car during the day. As he reached the middle of the street, he heard a noise behind him, and turned. A large black limousine without lights was coming towards him, its tyres fighting for traction in the light powder of snow. It was less than ten feet away. *The drunken fool*, thought Judd. *He's in a skid and he's going to kill himself.* Judd turned and leaped back towards the kerb and safety. The nose of the car swerved towards him, the car accelerating. Too late Judd realized the car was deliberately trying to run him down.

The last thing he remembered was something hard smashing against his chest, and a loud crash that sounded like thunder. The dark street suddenly lit up with bright Roman candles that seemed to explode in his head. In that split second of illumination, Judd suddenly knew the answer to everything. He knew why John Hanson and Carol Roberts had been murdered. He felt a sense of wild elation. He had to tell McGreavy. Then the light faded, and there was only the silence of the wet darkness.

From the outside, the Nineteenth Police Precinct looked like an ancient weatherbeaten four-storey school building: brown brick, plaster façade, and cornices white with the droppings of generations of pigeons. The Nineteenth Precinct was responsible for the area of Manhattan from Fifty-ninth Street to Eighty-sixth Street, from Fifth Avenue to the East River.

The call from the hospital reporting the hit-and-run accident came through the police switchboard a few minutes after ten and was transferred to the Detective Bureau. The Nineteenth Precinct was having a busy night. Because of the weather, there had been a heavy increase in rapes and muggings. The deserted streets had become a frozen wasteland where marauders preyed on the hapless stragglers who wandered into their territory.

Most of the detectives were out on squeals, and the Detective Bureau was deserted except for Detective Frank Angeli and a sergeant, who was interrogating an arson suspect.

When the phone rang, Angeli answered it. It was a nurse who had a hit-and-run patient at the city hospital. The patient was asking for Lieutenant McGreavy. McGreavy had gone to the Hall of Records. When she gave Angeli the name of the patient, he told the nurse that he would be right over.

Angeli was hanging up the receiver as McGreavy walked in. Angeli quickly told him about the call. 'We'd better get right over to the hospital,' Angeli said.

'He'll keep. First I want to talk to the captain of the precinct where that accident occurred.'

Angeli watched as McGreavy dialled the number. He wondered whether Captain Bertelli had told McGreavy about his conversation with Angeli. It had been short and to the point.

'Lieutenant McGreavy is a good cop,' Angeli had said, 'but I think he's influenced by what happened five years ago.'

Captain Bertelli had given him a long, cold stare. 'Are you accusing him of framing Dr Stevens?'

'I'm not accusing him of anything, Captain. I just thought you should be aware of the situation.'

'Okay, I'm aware of it.' And the meeting was over.

McGreavy's phone conversation took three minutes while McGreavy grunted and made notes and Angeli impatiently paced back and forth. Ten minutes later the two detectives were in a squad car on the way to the hospital.

Judd's room was on the sixth floor at the end of a long, dreary corridor that had the sickly-sweet smell of all hospitals. The nurse who had phoned was escorting them to Judd's room.

'What shape is he in, Nurse?' asked McGreavy.

'The doctor will have to tell you that,' she said primly. And then continued, compulsively, 'It's a miracle the man wasn't killed. He has a possible concussion, some bruised ribs, and an injured left arm.'

'Is he conscious?' asked Angeli.

'Yes. We're having a terrible time keeping him in bed.' She turned to McGreavy. 'He keeps saying he has to see you.'

They walked into the room. There were six beds in the room, all occupied. The nurse indicated a bed at the far corner that was curtained off, and McGreavy and Angeli walked over to it and stepped behind the curtain.

Judd was in bed, propped up. His face was pale and there was a large adhesive plaster on his forehead. His left arm was in a sling.

McGreavy spoke. 'I hear you had an accident.'

'It wasn't an accident,' said Judd. 'Someone tried to kill me.' His voice was weak and shaky.

'Who?' asked Angeli.

'I don't know, but it all fits in.' He turned to McGreavy. 'The killers weren't after John Hanson or Carol. They were after me.'

McGreavy looked at him in surprise. 'What makes you think so?'

'Hanson was killed because he was wearing my yellow slicker. They must have seen me go into my building wearing that coat. When Hanson came out of my office wearing it, they mistook him for me.'

'That's possible,' said Angeli.

'Sure,' said McGreavy. He turned to Judd. 'And when they learned that they had killed the wrong man, they came into your office and tore your clothes off and found out you were really a coloured girl, and they got so mad they beat you to death.'

'Carol was killed because they found her there when they came to get me,' Judd said.

McGreavy reached in his overcoat pocket and took out some notes. 'I just talked to the captain of the precinct where the accident happened.'

'It was no accident.'

'According to the police report, you were jay-walking.'

Judd stared at him. 'Jaywalking?' he repeated weakly.

'You crossed in the middle of the street, Doctor.'

'There were no cars so I –'

'There *was* a car,' McGreavy corrected. 'Only you didn't see it. It was snowing and the visibility was lousy. You stepped out of nowhere. The driver put on his brakes, went into a skid, and hit you. Then he panicked and drove away.'

'That's not the way it happened and his head-lights were off.'

'And you think *that's* evidence that he killed Hanson and Carol Roberts?'

'Someone tried to kill me,' repeated Judd insis-tently.

McGreavy shook his head. 'It won't work, Doctor.'

'What won't work?' asked Judd.

'Did you really expect me to start beating the bushes for some mythical killer while you take the heat off yourself?' His voice was suddenly hard. 'Did you know your receptionist was pregnant?'

Judd closed his eyes and let his head sink back on the pillow. So that was what Carol had wanted to speak to him about. He had half-guessed. And now McGreavy would think . . . He opened his eyes. 'No,' he said wearily. 'I didn't.'

Judd's head began pounding again. The pain was returning. He swallowed to fight off the nausea that engulfed him. He wanted to ring for the nurse, but he was damned if he would give McGreavy the satisfaction.

'I went through the records at City Hall,' said McGreavy. 'What would you say if I told you that your cute little pregnant receptionist had been a hooker before she went to work for you?' The pounding in Judd's head was becoming steadily worse. 'Were you aware of that, Dr Stevens? You don't have to answer. I'll answer for you. You knew it because you picked her up in night court four years ago, when she was arrested on a charge of soliciting. Now isn't it a little far-out for a respectable doctor to hire a hooker as a receptionist in a high-class office?'

72

'No one is born a hooker,' said Judd. 'I was trying to help a sixteen-year-old child have a chance in life.'

'And get yourself a little free black tail on the side?'

'You dirty-minded bastard!'

McGreavy smiled without mirth. 'Where did you take Carol after you found her in night court?'

'To my apartment.'

'And she slept there?'

'Yes.'

McGreavy grinned. 'You're a beauty! You picked up a good-looking young whore in night court and took her to your apartment to spend the night. What were you looking for – a chess partner? If you really didn't sleep with her, there's a damn good chance you're a homosexual. And guess who that ties you in with? Right. John Hanson. If you *did* sleep with Carol, then the chances are pretty good that you continued sleeping with her until you finally got her knocked up. And you have the gall to lie there and tell me some cock-and-bull story about a hit-and-run maniac who's going around murdering people?' McGreavy turned and strode out of the room, his face red with anger.

The pounding in Judd's head had turned to a throbbing agony.

Angeli was watching him, worried. 'You all right?'

73

'You've got to help me,' Judd said. 'Someone is trying to kill me.' It sounded like a threnody in his ears.

'Who'd have a motive for killing you, Doctor?'

'I don't know.'

'Do you have any enemies?'

'No.'

'Have you been sleeping with anyone's wife or girlfriend?'

Judd shook his head and instantly regretted the motion.

'Is there any money in your family – relatives who might want to get you out of the way?'

'No.'

Angeli sighed. 'Okay. So there's no motive for anyone wanting to murder you. What about your patients? I think you'd better give us a list so we can check them out.'

'I can't do that.'

'All I'm asking for is their names.'

'I'm sorry.' It was an effort to speak. 'If I were a dentist or a chiropodist I'd give it to you. But don't you see? These people have problems. Most of them serious problems. If you started questioning them, you'd not only shatter them; you'd destroy their confidence in me. I wouldn't be able to treat them any more. I can't give you that list.' He lay back on the pillow, exhausted.

Angeli looked at him quietly, then asked, 'What

do you call a man who thinks that everyone's out to kill him?'

'A paranoiac,' said Judd. He saw the look on Angeli's face. 'You don't think I'm . . . ?'

'Put yourself in my place,' Angeli said. 'If I were in that bed right now, talking like you, and you were my doctor, what would you think?'

Judd closed his eyes against the stabs of pain in his head. He heard Angeli's voice continue. 'McGreavy's waiting for me.'

Judd opened his eyes. 'Wait . . . Give me a chance to prove that I'm telling the truth.'

'How?'

'Whoever's trying to kill me is going to try again. I want someone with me. Next time they try, he can catch them.'

Angeli looked at Judd. 'Dr Stevens, if someone really wants to kill you, all the policemen in the world can't stop them. If they don't get you today, they'll get you tomorrow. If they don't get you here, they'll get you somewhere else. It doesn't matter whether you're a king or a president, or just plain John Doe. Life is a very thin thread. It only takes a second to snap it.'

'There's nothing – nothing at all you can do?'

'I can give you some advice. Have new locks put on the doors of your apartment, and check the windows to make sure they're securely bolted. Don't let anyone in the apartment unless you know

75

them. No delivery boys unless you've ordered the delivery yourself.'

Judd nodded, his throat dry and aching.

'Your building has a doorman and an elevator man,' continued Angeli. 'Can you trust them?'

'The doorman has worked there for ten years. The elevator operator has been there eight years. I'd trust them with my life.'

Angeli nodded approvingly. 'Good. Ask them to keep their eyes open. If they're on the alert, it's going to be hard for anyone to sneak up to your apartment. What about the office? Are you going to hire a new receptionist?'

Judd thought of a stranger sitting at Carol's desk, in her chair. A spasm of helpless anger wracked him. 'Not right away.'

'You might think about hiring a man,' said Angeli.

'I'll think about it.'

Angeli turned to go, then stopped. 'I have an idea,' he said hesitantly, 'but it's a long shot.'

'Yes?' He hated the eagerness in his voice.

'This man who killed McGreavy's old partner . . .'

'Ziffren.'

'Was he really insane?'

'Yes. They sent him to the Matteawan State Hospital for mentally ill criminals.'

'Maybe he blames you for having him put away. I'll check him out. Just to make sure he hasn't escaped or been released. Give me a call in the morning.'

'Thanks,' Judd said gratefully.

'It's my job. If you're involved in any of this, I'm going to help McGreavy nail you.' Angeli turned to go. He stopped again. 'You don't have to mention to McGreavy that I'm checking on Ziffren for you.'

'I won't.'

The two men smiled at each other. Angeli left. Judd was alone again.

If the situation was bleak that morning it was even bleaker now. Judd knew that he would already have been arrested for murder except for one thing – McGreavy's character. McGreavy wanted vengeance and he wanted it so badly that he would make sure that every last bit of evidence was in place. *Could* the hit-and-run have been an accident? There had been snow on the street, and the limousine could have accidentally skidded into him. But then, why had the headlights been off? And where had the car come from so suddenly?

He was convinced now that an assassin had struck – and would strike again. With that thought, he fell asleep.

Early the next morning Peter and Norah Hadley came to the hospital to see Judd. They had heard about the accident on the morning news.

Peter was Judd's age, smaller than Judd and painfully thin. They had come from the same town in Nebraska and had gone through medical school together.

Norah was English. She was blonde and chubby with a large, soft bosom a bit too large for her five feet three inches. She was vivacious and comfortable, and after five minutes' conversation with her, people felt they had known her for ever.

'You look lousy,' Peter said, studying Judd critically.

'That's what I like, Doctor. A bedside manner.' Judd's headache was almost gone and the pain in his body had been reduced to a dull, aching soreness.

Norah handed him a bouquet of carnations. 'We brought you some flowers, love,' she said. 'You poor old darling.' She leaned over and kissed him on the cheek.

'How did it happen?' asked Peter.

Judd hesitated. 'It was a hit-and-run accident.'

'Everything hit the fan at once, didn't it? I read about poor Carol.'

'It's dreadful,' said Norah. 'I liked her so much.'

Judd felt a tightness in his throat. 'So did I.'

'Any chance of catching the bastard who did it?' Peter asked.

'They're working on it.'

'In this morning's paper it said that a Lieutenant McGreavy is close to making an arrest. Do you know anything about it?'

'A little,' Judd said dryly. 'McGreavy likes to keep me up to date.'

'You never know how wonderful the police are until you really need them,' Norah said.

'Dr Harris let me take a look at your X-rays. Some nasty bruises – no concussion. You'll be out of here in a few days.'

But Judd knew he had no time to spare.

They spent the next half hour in small talk, carefully avoiding the subject of Carol Roberts. Peter and Norah were unaware that John Hanson had been a patient of Judd's. For some reason of his own, McGreavy had kept that part of the story out of the newspapers.

When they got up to leave, Judd asked to speak to Peter alone. While Norah waited outside, Judd told Peter about Harrison Burke.

'I'm sorry,' said Peter. 'When I sent him to you, I knew he was in a bad way, but I was hoping there was still time for you to help him. Of course you have to put him away. When are you going to do it?'

'As soon as I get out of here,' Judd said. And he knew he was lying. He didn't want Harrison Burke sent away. Not just yet. He wanted to find out first whether Burke could have committed the two murders.

'If there's anything I can do for you, old buddy – call.' And Peter was gone.

Judd lay there, planning his next move. Since there was no rational motive for anyone wanting to kill him, it stood to reason that the murders had been committed by someone who was mentally unbalanced, someone with an imagined grievance against him. The only two people he could think of who might fit into that category were Harrison Burke and Amos Ziffren, the man who had killed McGreavy's partner. If Burke had no alibi for the morning Hanson was killed, then Judd would ask Detective Angeli to check him out further. If Burke had an alibi, then he would concentrate on Ziffren. The feeling of depression that had enveloped him began to lift. He felt that at last he was doing something. He was suddenly desperately impatient to get out of the hospital.

He rang for the nurse and told her he wanted to see Dr Harris. Ten minutes later Seymour Harris walked into the room. He was a little gnome of a man with bright blue eyes and tufts of black hair sticking out of his cheeks. Judd had known him a long time and had a great respect for him.

'Well! Sleeping Beauty's awake. You look terrible.'

Judd was getting tired of hearing it. 'I feel fine,' he lied. 'I want to get out of here.'

'When?'

'Now.'

Dr Harris looked at him reprovingly. 'You just

got here. Why don't you stick around a few days? I'll send you in a few nymphomaniac nurses to keep you company.'

'Thanks, Seymour. I really do have to leave.'

Dr Harris sighed. 'Okay. You're the doctor, Doctor. Personally, I wouldn't let my cat walk around in your condition.' He looked at Judd keenly. 'Anything I can do to help?'

Judd shook his head.

'I'll have Miss Bedpan get your clothes.'

Thirty minutes later the girl at the reception desk called a taxi for him. He was at his office at ten-fifteen.

SIX

His first patient, Teri Washburn, was waiting in the
corridor. Twenty years earlier Teri had been one of
the biggest stars in the Hollywood firmament. Her
career had fizzled overnight, and she had married
a lumberman from Oregon and dropped out of
sight. Teri had been married five or six times since
then and was now living in New York with her
latest husband, an importer. She looked up angrily
as Judd came down the corridor.

'Well . . .' she said. The speech of reproval she
had rehearsed died away as she saw his face. 'What
happened to you?' she asked. 'You look like you
got caught between two horny mix-masters.'

'Just a little accident. Sorry I'm late.' He unlocked
the door and ushered Teri into the reception office.
Carol's empty desk and chair loomed in front of him.

'I read about Carol,' Teri said. There was an
excited edge to her voice. 'Was it a sex murder?'

'No,' Judd said shortly. He opened the door to his inner office. 'Give me ten minutes.'

He went into the office, consulted his calendar pad, and began dialling the numbers of his patients, cancelling the rest of his appointments for the day. He was able to reach all but three patients. His chest and arm hurt every time he moved, and his head was beginning to pound again. He took two Darvan from a drawer and washed them down with a glass of water. He walked over to the reception door and opened it for Teri. He steeled himself to put everything out of his mind for the next fifty minutes except the problems of his patient. Teri lay down on the couch, her skirt hiked up, and began talking.

Twenty years ago Teri Washburn had been a raving beauty, and traces of it were still there. She had the largest, softest, most innocent eyes that Judd had ever seen. The sultry mouth had a few hard lines around it, but it was still voluptuous, and her breasts were rounded and firm beneath a close-fitting Pucci print. Judd suspected that she had had a silicone injection, but he was waiting for her to mention it. The rest of her body was still good, and her legs were great.

At one time or another, most of Judd's female patients thought they were in love with him, the natural transference from patient-doctor to patient-protector-lover. But Teri's case was different. She had been trying to have an affair with Judd from the first minute she had walked into his office. She had tried to arouse him in every way she could think of – and Teri was an expert. Judd had finally warned her that unless she behaved herself, he would send her to another doctor. Since then she had behaved reasonably well with him: studying him, trying to find his Achilles heel. An eminent English physician had sent Teri to him after a nasty international scandal at Antibes. A French gossip columnist had accused Teri of spending a weekend on the yacht of a famous Greek shipping magnate to whom she was engaged, and sleeping with his three brothers while the ship's owner flew to Rome for a day on business. The story was quickly hushed up and the columnist printed a retraction and was then quietly fired. In her first session with Judd, Teri had boasted that the story was true.

'It's wild,' she had said. 'I need sex all the time. I can't get enough of it.' She had rubbed her hands against her hips, sliding her skirt up, and looked at Judd innocently. 'Do you know what I mean, honey?' she had asked.

Since that first visit, Judd had found out a great deal about Teri. She had come from a small coal-mining town in Pennsylvania.

'My father was a dumb Polack. He got his kicks getting drunk on boilermakers every Saturday night and beating the shit out of my old lady.'

When she was thirteen, Teri had the body of a woman and the face of an angel. She learned that she could earn nickels by going to the back of the coal tips with the miners. The day her father had found out, he had come into their small cabin screaming incoherently in Polish, and had thrown Teri's mother out. He had locked the door, taken off his heavy belt, and begun beating Teri. When he was through, he had raped her.

Judd had watched Teri as she lay there describing the scene, her face empty of any emotion.

'That was the last time I saw my father or mother.'

'You ran away,' Judd said.

Teri twisted around on the couch in surprise. 'What?'

'After your father raped you –'

'Ran away?' Teri said. She threw back her head and let out a whoop of laughter. 'I *liked* it. It was my bitch of a mother who threw me out!'

Now Judd switched on the tape recorder. 'What would you like to talk about?' he asked.

'Fucking,' she said. 'Why don't we psychoanalyse you and find out why you're so straight?'

He ignored it. 'Why did you think Carol's death might have something to do with a sexual attack?'

'Because everything reminds me of sex, honey.' She squirmed and her skirt rode a little higher.

'Pull your skirt down, Teri.'

She gave him an innocent look. 'Sorry . . . You missed a great birthday party Saturday night, Doc.'

'Tell me about it.'

She hesitated, an unaccustomed note of concern in her voice. 'You won't hate me?'

'I've told you that you don't need my approval. The only one whose approval you need is you. Right and wrong are the rules we make up ourselves so that we can play in the game with other people. Without rules, there can't be a game. But never forget – the rules are artificial.'

There was a silence. Then she spoke. 'It was a swinging party. My husband hired a six-piece band.'

He waited.

She twisted around to look at him. 'Are you sure you won't lose respect for me?'

'I want to help you. We've all done things we're ashamed of, but that does not signify that we have to continue doing them.'

She studied him a moment, then lay back on the couch. 'Did I ever tell you I suspected my husband, Harry, is impotent?'

'Yes.' She talked of it constantly.

'He hasn't really done it to me since we've been married. He always has some goddamn excuse . . . Well . . .' Her mouth twisted bitterly. 'Well . . . Saturday night I fucked the band while Harry watched.' She began to cry.

Judd handed her some Kleenex and sat there, watching her.

No one had ever given Teri Washburn anything in her life that she had not been overcharged for. When she had first gone to Hollywood, she had landed a job as a waitress in a drive-in and used most of her wages to go to a third-rate dramatic coach. Within a week the coach had her move in with him, doing all his household chores and confining her coaching to the bedroom. A few weeks later, when she realized that he could not have got her an acting job even if he had wanted to, she had walked out on him and taken a job as a cashier in a Beverly Hills hotel drugstore. A movie executive had appeared on Christmas Eve to buy a last-minute gift for his wife. He had given Teri his card and told her to call him. Teri had made a screen test a week later. She was awkward and untrained, but she had three things going for her. She had a sensational face and figure, the camera loved her, and the studio executive was keeping her.

Teri Washburn appeared in bit parts in a dozen pictures the first year. She began to get fan mail. Her parts grew larger. At the end of a year her benefactor died of a heart attack, and Teri was afraid the studio would fire her. Instead, the new executive called her in and told her that he had big plans for her. She got a new contract, a raise, and a larger apartment with a mirrored bedroom.

Teri's roles gradually grew to leads in B pictures, and finally, as the public showed their adoration by putting down their money at the box office to see each new Teri Washburn picture, she began to star in A pictures.

All that had been a long time ago, and Judd felt sorry for her as she lay on his couch, trying to control her sobs.

'Would you like some water?' he asked.

'N-no,' she said, 'I'm f-fine.' She took a handkerchief out of her purse and blew her nose. 'I'm sorry,' she said, 'for behaving like a goddamn idiot.' She sat up.

Judd sat there quietly, waiting for her to get control of herself.

'Why do I marry men like Harry?'

'That's an important question. Do you have any idea why?'

'How the hell should I know!' screamed Teri. 'You're the psychiatrist. If I knew they were like that, you don't think I'd marry those creeps, do you?'

'What do you think?'

She stared at him, shocked. 'You mean you think I *would*?' She got to her feet angrily. 'Why, you dirty sonofabitch! You think I *liked* fucking the band?'

'Did you?'

In a fury she picked up a vase and flung it at him. It shattered against a table. 'Does that answer you?'

'No. That vase was two hundred dollars. I'll put it on your bill.'

She stared at him helplessly. 'Did I really like it?' she whispered.

'You tell me.'

Her voice dropped even lower. 'I must be sick,' she said. 'Oh, God, I'm sick. Please help me, Judd. Help me!'

Judd walked over to her. 'You've got to help me help you.'

She nodded her head, dumbly.

'I want you to go home and think about how you feel, Teri. Not while you're doing these things, but before you do them. Think about why you want to do them. When you know that, you'll know a great deal about yourself.'

She looked at him a moment, then her face relaxed. She took out her handkerchief and blew her nose again. 'You're a helluva man, Charlie Brown,' she said. She picked up her purse and gloves. 'See you next week?'

'Yes,' he said. 'See you next week.' He opened the door to the corridor, and Teri exited.

He knew the answer to Teri's problem, but she would have to work it through for herself. She would have to learn that she could not buy love, that it had to be given freely. And she could not accept the fact that it could be given to her freely until she learned to believe that she was worthy of receiving love. Until that time, Teri would go on trying to buy it, using the only currency she had: her body. He knew the agony she was going through, the bottomless despair of self-loathing, and his heart went out to her. But the only way in which he could help her was to give the appearance of being impersonal and detached. He knew that to his patients he seemed remote and aloof from their problems, dispensing wisdom from some Olympian height. But that was a vital part of the façade of therapy. In reality he cared deeply about the problems of his patients. They would have been amazed if they had known how often the unspeakable demons that tried to batter down the ramparts of their emotions appeared in Judd's own nightmares.

During the first six months of his practice as a psychiatrist, when he was undergoing the required two years of analysis necessary to become a psychoanalyst, Judd had developed blinding headaches. He was empathetically taking on the symptoms of all his patients, and it had taken him almost a year to learn to channel and control his emotional involvement.

Now, as Judd locked Teri Washburn's tape away, his mind came forcibly back to his own dilemma. He walked over to the phone and dialled information for the number of the Nineteenth Precinct.

The switchboard operator connected him with the Detective Bureau. He heard McGreavy's deep bass voice over the phone, 'Lieutenant McGreavy.'

'Detective Angeli, please.'

'Hold on.'

Judd heard the clatter of the phone as McGreavy put the receiver down. A moment later Angeli's voice came over the wire. 'Detective Angeli.'

'Judd Stevens. I wondered whether you'd got that information yet?'

There was an instant's hesitation. 'I checked into it,' said Angeli carefully.

'All you have to do is say "yes" or "no".' Judd's heart was pounding. It was an effort for him to ask the next question. 'Is Ziffren still at Matteawan?'

It seemed an eternity before Angeli answered. 'Yes. He's still there.'

A wave of disappointment surged through Judd. 'Oh. I see.'

'I'm sorry.'

'Thanks,' Judd said. Slowly he hung up.

So that left Harrison Burke. Harrison Burke, a hopeless paranoiac who was convinced that everyone was out to kill him. Had Burke decided to strike first? John Hanson had left Judd's office at ten-fifty on Monday and had been killed a few minutes later. Judd had to find out whether Harrison Burke was in his office at that time. He looked up Burke's office number and dialled it.

'International Steel.' The voice had the remote, impersonal timbre of an automaton.

'Mr Harrison Burke, please.'

'Mr Harrison Burke . . . Thank you . . . One moment, please . . .'

Judd was gambling on Burke's secretary answering the phone. If she had stepped out for a moment and Burke answered it himself . . . 'Mr Burke's office.' It was a girl's voice.

'This is Dr Judd Stevens. I wonder if you could give me some information?'

'Oh, yes, Dr Stevens!' There was a note of relief in her voice, mixed with apprehension. She must have known that Judd was Burke's analyst. Was she counting on him for help? What had Burke been doing to upset her?

'It's about Mr Burke's bill . . .' Judd began.

'His *bill*?' She made no effort to conceal her disappointment.

Judd went on quickly. 'My receptionist is – is no longer with me, and I'm trying to straighten out the books. I see that she charged Mr Burke for a nine-thirty appointment this past Monday, and I wonder if you'd mind checking his calendar for that morning?'

'Just a moment,' she said. There was disapproval in her voice now. He could read her mind. Her employer was cracking up and his analyst was only concerned about getting his money. She came back

92

on the phone a few minutes later. 'I'm afraid your receptionist made a mistake, Dr Stevens,' she said tartly. 'Mr Burke couldn't have been at your office Monday morning.'

'Are you sure?' persisted Judd. 'It's down in her book – nine-thirty to –'

'I don't care what's down in her book, Doctor.' She was angry now, upset by his callousness. 'Mr Burke was in a staff meeting all morning on Monday. It began at eight o'clock.'

'Couldn't he have slipped out for an hour?'

'No, Doctor,' she said. 'Mr Burke never leaves his office during the day.' There was an accusation in her voice. *Can't you see that he's ill? What are you doing to help him?*

'Shall I tell him you called?'

'That won't be necessary,' Judd said. 'Thank you.' He wanted to add a word of reassurance, of comfort, but there was nothing he could say. He hung up.

So that was that. He had struck out. If neither Ziffren nor Harrison Burke had tried to kill him – then there could be no one else with any motive. He was back where he had started. Some person – or persons – had murdered his receptionist and one of his patients. The hit-and-run incident could have been deliberate or accidental. At the time it happened, it seemed to be deliberate. But looking at it dispassionately, Judd admitted to himself that he had been wrought up by the events of the last few days. In his highly emotional state he could easily have turned an accident into something sinister. The simple truth was that there was no one who could have any possible motive for killing him. He had an excellent relationship with all his patients, warm relationships with his friends. He had never, to his knowledge, harmed anyone. The phone rang. He recognized Anne's low, throaty voice instantly.

'Are you busy?'

'No. I can talk.'

There was concern in her voice. 'I read that you were hit by a car. I wanted to call you sooner, but I didn't know where to reach you.'

He made his voice light. 'It was nothing serious. It will teach me not to jaywalk.'

'The papers said it was a hit-and-run accident.'

'Yes.'

'Did they find the person who did it?'

'No. It was probably some kid out for a lark.' *In a black limousine without lights.*

'Are you sure?' asked Anne.

The question caught him by surprise. 'What do you mean?'

'I don't really know.' Her voice was uncertain. 'It's just that – Carol was murdered. And now – this.'

So she had put it together, too.

'It – it almost sounds as if there's a maniac running around loose.'

'If there is,' Judd assured her, 'the police will catch him.'

'Are you in any danger?'

His heart warmed. 'Of course not.' There was an awkward silence. There was so much he wanted to say, but he couldn't. He must not mistake a friendly phone call for anything more than the natural concern that a patient would have for her doctor. Anne was the type who would have called anyone who was in trouble. It meant no more than that.

'I'll still see you on Friday?' he asked.

'Yes.' There was an odd note in her voice. Was she going to change her mind?

'It's a date,' he said quickly. But of course it was not a date. It was a business appointment.

'Yes. Goodbye, Dr Stevens.'

'Goodbye, Mrs Blake. Thanks for calling. Thanks very much.' He hung up. And thought about Anne. And wondered if her husband had any idea what an incredibly lucky man he was.

What was her husband like? In the little Anne had said about him, Judd had formed the image of an attractive and thoughtful man. He was a sportsman, bright, was a successful businessman, donated money to the arts. He sounded like the kind of person Judd would have liked for a friend. Under different circumstances.

What could Anne's problem have been that she was afraid to discuss with her husband? Or her analyst? With a person of Anne's character, it was probably an overwhelming feeling of guilt because of an affair she had had either before she was married or after her marriage. He could not imagine her having casual affairs. Perhaps she would tell him on Friday. When he saw her for the last time.

The rest of the afternoon went by swiftly. Judd saw the few patients he had not been able to cancel. When the last one had departed, he took out the tape of Harrison Burke's last session and played it, making occasional notes as he listened.

When he had finished, he switched the tape recorder off. There was no choice. He had to call Burke's employer in the morning and inform him of Burke's condition. He glanced out of the window and was surprised to see that night had fallen. It was almost eight o'clock. Now that he had finished concentrating on his work, he suddenly felt stiff and tired. His ribs were sore and his arm had begun to throb. He would go home and soak in a nice hot bath.

He put away all the tapes except Burke's, which he locked in a drawer of a side table. He would turn it over to a court-appointed psychiatrist. He put on his overcoat and was halfway out the door when the phone rang. He went to the phone and picked it up. 'Dr Stevens.'

There was no answer on the other end. He heard breathing, heavy and nasal.

'Hello?'

There was no response. Judd hung up. He stood there a moment, frowning. Wrong number, he decided. He turned out the office lights, locked the doors, and moved towards the bank of elevators. All the tenants were long since gone. It was too early for the night shift of maintenance workers, and except for Bigelow, the watchman, the building was deserted.

Judd walked over to the elevator and pressed the call button. The signal indicator did not move. He pressed the button again. Nothing happened.

And at that moment all the lights in the corridor blacked out.

SEVEN

Judd stood in front of the elevator, the wave of darkness lapping at him like a physical force. He could feel his heart slow and then begin to beat faster. A sudden, atavistic fear flooded his body, and he reached in his pockets for a book of matches. He had left them in the office. Perhaps the lights were working on the floors below. Moving slowly and cautiously, he groped his way towards the door that led to the stairwell. He pushed the door open. The stairwell was in darkness. Carefully holding onto the railing, he started down into the blackness. In the distance below, he saw the wavering beam of a flashlight moving up the stairs. He was filled with a sudden relief. Bigelow, the watchman. 'Bigelow!' he yelled. 'Bigelow! It's Dr Stevens!' His voice bounced against the stone walls, echoing eerily through the stairwell. The figure holding the flashlight kept climbing silently, inexorably upward.

'Who's there?' Judd demanded. The only answer was the echo of his words.

And Judd suddenly knew who was there. His assassins. There had to be at least two of them. One had cut off the power in the basement while the other blocked the stairs to prevent his escape.

The beam of the flashlight was coming closer, only two or three floors below now, climbing rapidly. Judd's body went cold with fear. His heart began to pound like a trip-hammer, and his legs felt weak. He turned quickly and went back up the stairs to his floor. He opened the door and stood, listening. What if someone were waiting up here in the dark corridor for him?

The sounds of footsteps advancing up the stairs were louder now. His mouth dry, Judd turned and made his way along the inky corridor. When he reached the elevators, he began counting office doors. As he reached his office, he heard the stairwell door open. The keys slipped from his nervous fingers and dropped to the floor. He fumbled for them frantically, found them, opened the door to his reception room, and went in, double-locking the door behind him. No one could open it now without a special key.

From the corridor outside, he could hear the sound of approaching footsteps. He went into his private office and flicked the light switch. Nothing happened. There was no power at all in the building. He locked the inner door, then moved to the phone. He fumbled for the dial and dialled the operator. There were three long, steady rings, and then the operator's voice, Judd's only link to the outside world.

He spoke softly. 'Operator, this is an emergency. This is Dr Judd Stevens. I want to speak to Detective Frank Angeli at the Nineteenth Precinct. Please hurry!'

'Thank you. Your number, please?'

Judd gave it to her.

'One moment, please.'

He heard the sound of someone testing the corridor entrance to his private office. They could not get in that way because there was no outside knob on the door.

'Hurry, Operator!'

'One moment, please,' replied the cool, unhurried voice.

There was a buzz on the line and then the police switchboard operator spoke. 'Nineteenth Precinct.'

Judd's heart leaped. 'Detective Angeli,' he said. 'It's urgent!'

'Detective Angeli . . . just a moment, please.'

Outside in the corridor, something was happening. He could hear the sound of muted voices. Someone had joined the first man. What were they planning?

A familiar voice came on the phone. 'Detective Angeli's not here. This is his partner, Lieutenant McGreavy. Can –'

'This is Judd Stevens. I'm in my office. The lights are all out and someone's trying to break in and kill me!'

There was a heavy silence on the other end. 'Look, Doctor,' said McGreavy. 'Why don't you come down here and we'll talk a –'

'I can't come down there.' Judd almost shouted. 'Someone's trying to murder me!'

There was another silence at the other end of the line. McGreavy did not believe him and was not going to help him. Outside, Judd heard a door open, and then the sound of voices in the reception office. They were in the reception office! It was impossible for them to have got in without a key. But he could hear them moving, coming towards the door to his private office.

McGreavy's voice was coming over the phone, but Judd did not even listen. It was too late. He replaced the receiver. It would not have mattered even if McGreavy had agreed to come. The assassins were here! *Life is a very thin thread and it only takes a second to snap it.* The fear that gripped him turned to a blind rage. He refused to be slaughtered like Hanson and Carol. He was going to put up a fight. He felt around in the dark for a possible weapon. An ashtray . . . a letter opener . . . useless. The assassins would have guns. It was a Kafka nightmare. He was being condemned for no reason by faceless executioners.

He heard them moving closer to the inner door and knew that he only had a minute or two left to live. With a strange, dispassionate calm, as though he were his own patient, he examined his final thoughts. He thought of Anne, and a sense of aching loss filled him. He thought of his patients, and of how much they needed him. Harrison Burke. With a pang he remembered that he had not yet told Burke's employer that Burke had to be committed. He would put the tapes where they could be . . . His heart lurched. Perhaps he *did* have a weapon to fight with!

He heard the doorknob turning. The door was locked, but it was flimsy. It would be simple for them to break in. He quickly groped his way in the dark to the table where he had locked away Burke's tape. He heard a creak as pressure was applied against the reception-room door. Then he heard someone fumbling at the lock. *Why don't they just break it down?* he thought. Somewhere, far back in his mind, he felt the answer was important, but he had no time to think about it now. With trembling fingers he unlocked the drawer with the tape in it. He ripped it out of its cardboard container, then moved over to the tape player and started to thread it. It was an outside chance, but it was the only one he had.

He stood there, concentrating, trying to recall his exact conversation with Burke. The pressure on the door increased. Judd gave a quick, silent prayer. 'I'm sorry about the power going out,' he said aloud. 'But I'm sure they'll have it fixed in a few minutes, Harrison. Why don't you lie down and relax?'

The noise at the door suddenly ceased. Judd had finished threading the tape into the player. He pressed the 'on' button. Nothing happened. Of course! All the power in the building was off. He could hear them begin to work on the lock again. A feeling of desperation seized him. 'That's better,' he said loudly. 'Just make yourself comfortable.' He fumbled for the packet of matches on the table, found it, tore out a match and lit it. He held the flame close to the tape player. There was a switch marked 'battery'. He turned the knob, then pressed the 'on' button again. At that moment, there was a sudden click as the lock on the door sprung open. His last defence was gone!

And then Burke's voice rang through the room. 'Is that all you've got to say? You don't even want to hear my proof! How do I know you're not one of them?'

Judd froze, not daring to move, his heart roaring like thunder.

'You know I'm not one of them,' said Judd's voice from the tape. 'I'm your friend. I'm trying to help you . . . Tell me about your proof.'

'They broke into my house last night,' Burke's voice said. 'They came to kill me. But I was too clever for them. I sleep in my den now, and I have extra locks on all the doors so they can't get to me.'

The sounds in the outer office had ceased.

Judd's voice again. 'Did you report the break-in to the police?'

'Of course not! The police are in it with them. They have orders to shoot me. But they wouldn't dare do it while there are other people around, so I stay in crowds.'

'I'm glad you gave me this information.'

'What are you going to do with it?'

'I'm listening very carefully to everything you say,' said Judd's voice. 'I've got it all down' – at that moment a warning screamed in Judd's brain; the next words were – 'on tape.'

He made a dive for the switch and pressed it. '– in my mind,' Judd said loudly. 'And we'll work out the best way to handle it.' He stopped. He could not play the tape again because he had no way of telling where to pick it up. His only hope was that the men outside were convinced that Judd had a patient in the office with him. Even if they believed it, would it stop them?

'Cases like this,' Judd said, raising his voice, 'are really more common than you'd believe, Harrison.' He gave an impatient exclamation. 'I wish they'd get these lights back on. I know your chauffeur's waiting out in front for you. He'll probably wonder what's wrong and come up.'

Judd stopped and listened. He could hear whispering from the other side of the door. What were they deciding? From the distant street below, he suddenly heard the insistent wail of an approaching siren. The whispering stopped. He listened for the sound of the outer door closing, but he could hear nothing. Were they still out there, waiting? The scream of the siren grew louder. It stopped in front of the building.

And suddenly all the lights went on.

EIGHT

'Drink?'

McGreavy shook his head moodily, studying Judd. Judd poured himself his second stiff scotch while McGreavy watched without comment. Judd's hands were still trembling. As the warmth of the whisky floated through him, he felt himself beginning to relax.

McGreavy had arrived at the office two minutes after the lights had come on. With him was a stolid police sergeant who now sat making notes in a shorthand notebook.

McGreavy was talking. 'Let's go over it once more, Dr Stevens.'

Judd took a deep breath and began again, deliberately keeping his voice calm and low. 'I locked the office and went to the elevator. The corridor lights blacked out. I thought that the lights on the lower floors might be working, and I started to walk down.' Judd hesitated, reliving the fear. 'I saw someone coming up the stairs with a flashlight. I called out. I thought it was Bigelow, the guard. It wasn't.'

'Who was it?'

'I've told you,' said Judd. 'I don't know. They didn't answer.'

'What made you think they were coming to kill you?'

An angry retort came to Judd's lips, and he checked it. It was essential to make McGreavy believe him. 'They followed me back to my office.'

'You think there were two men trying to kill you?'

'At least two,' Judd said. 'I heard them whispering.'

'You said that when you entered your reception office, you locked the outside door leading to the corridor. Is that right?'

'Yes.'

'And that when you came into your inner office, you locked the door leading to the reception office.'

'Yes.'

McGreavy walked over to the door leading from the reception office to Judd's inner office. 'Did they try to force this door?'

'No,' admitted Judd. He remembered how puzzled he had been by that.

'Right,' said McGreavy. 'When you lock the

reception-office door that opens onto the corridor, it takes a special key to open it from the outside.'

Judd hesitated. He knew what McGreavy was leading up to. 'Yes.'

'Who had the keys to that lock?'

Judd felt his face reddening. 'Carol and I.'

McGreavy's voice was bland. 'What about the cleaning people? How did they get in?'

'We had a special arrangement with them. Carol came in early three mornings a week and let them in. They were finished before my first patient arrived.'

'That seems inconvenient. Why couldn't they get into these offices when they cleaned all the other offices?'

'Because the files I keep in here are of a highly confidential nature. I prefer the inconvenience to having strangers in here when no one is around.'

McGreavy looked over at the sergeant to make sure he was getting it all down. Satisfied, he turned back to Judd. 'When we walked into the reception office, the door was unlocked. Not forced – unlocked.'

Judd said nothing.

McGreavy went on. 'You just told us that the only ones who had a key to that lock were you and Carol. And we have Carol's key. Think again, Dr Stevens. Who else had a key to that door?'

'No one.'

'Then how do you suppose those men got in?'

And Judd suddenly knew. 'They made a copy of Carol's key when they killed her.'

'It's possible,' conceded McGreavy. A bleak smile touched his lips. 'If they made a copy, we'll find paraffin traces on her key. I'll have the lab run a test.'

Judd nodded. He felt as though he had scored a victory, but his feeling of satisfaction was short-lived.

'So the way you see it,' McGreavy said, 'two men – we'll assume for the moment there's no woman involved – had a key copied so they could get into your office and kill you. Right?'

'Right,' said Judd.

'Now you said that when you went into your office, you locked the inner door. True?'

'Yes,' Judd said.

McGreavy's voice was almost mild. 'But we found that door unlocked, too.'

'They must have had a key to it.'

'Then after they got it open, why didn't they kill you?'

'I told you. They heard the voices on the tape and –'

'These two desperate killers went to all the trouble to knock out the lights, trap you up here, break into your office – and then just vanished into thin air without harming a hair of your head?' His voice was filled with contempt.

Judd felt cold anger rising in him. 'What are you implying?'

'I'll spell it out for you, Doctor. I don't think anyone was here and I don't believe anyone tried to kill you.'

'You don't have to take my word for it,' Judd said angrily. 'What about the lights? What about the night watchman, Bigelow?'

'He's in the lobby.'

Judd's heart missed a beat. 'Dead?'

'He wasn't when he let us in. There was a faulty wire in the main power switch. Bigelow was down in the basement trying to fix it. He got it working just as I arrived.'

Judd looked at him numbly. 'Oh,' he said finally.

'I don't know what you're playing at, Dr Stevens,' McGreavy said, 'but from now on, count me out.' He moved towards the door. 'And do me a favour. Don't call me again – I'll call you.'

The sergeant snapped his notebook shut and followed McGreavy out.

The effects of the whisky had evaporated. The euphoria had gone, and he was left with a deep depression. He had no idea what his next move should be. He was on the inside of a puzzle that had no key. He felt like the boy who cried 'wolf', except that the wolves were deadly, unseen phantoms, and every time McGreavy came, they seemed to vanish. Phantoms or . . . There was one other possibility. It was so horrifying that he couldn't bring himself to even acknowledge it. But he had to.

He had to face the possibility that he was a paranoiac.

A mind that was overstressed could give birth to delusions that seemed totally real. He had been working too hard. He had not had a vacation in years. It was conceivable that the deaths of Hanson and Carol could have been the catalyst that had sent his mind over some emotional precipice so that events became enormously magnified and out of joint. People suffering from paranoia lived in a land where everyday, commonplace things represented nameless terrors. Take the car accident. If it had been a deliberate attempt to kill him, surely the driver would have got out and made sure that the job was finished. And the two men who had come here tonight. He did not *know* that they had guns. Would a paranoiac not assume that they were there to kill him? It was more logical to believe that they were sneak thieves. When they had heard the voices in his inner office, they had fled. Surely, if they were assassins, they would have opened the unlocked door and killed him. How could he find out the truth? He knew it would be useless to appeal to the police again. There was no one to whom he could turn.

An idea began to form. It was born of desperation, but the more he examined it, the more sense it made. He picked up the telephone directory and began to riffle through the yellow pages.

NINE

At four o'clock the following afternoon Judd left his office and drove to an address on the lower West Side. It was an ancient, run-down brownstone apartment house. As he pulled up in front of the dilapidated building, Judd began to have misgivings. Perhaps he had the wrong address. Then a sign in a window of a first-floor apartment caught his eye:

NORMAN Z. MOODY
Private Investigator
SATISFACTION GUARANTEED

Judd alighted from the car. It was a raw, windy day with a forecast of late snow. He moved gingerly across the icy sidewalk and walked into the vestibule of the building.

The vestibule smelled of mingled odours of stale

cooking and urine. He pressed the button marked
'Norman Z. Moody – 1', and a moment later a
buzzer sounded. He stepped inside and found
Apartment 1. A sign on the door read:

NORMAN Z. MOODY
Private Investigator
RING BELL AND ENTER

He rang the bell and entered.

Moody was obviously not a man given to
throwing his money away on luxuries. The office
looked as though it had been furnished by a blind,
hyperthyroid pack rat. Odds and ends crammed
every spare inch of the room. In one corner stood
a tattered Japanese screen. Next to it was an East
Indian lamp, and in front of the lamp a scarred
Danish-modern table. Newspapers and old magazines were piled everywhere.

A door to an inner room burst open and Norman
Z. Moody emerged. He was about five foot five
and must have weighed three hundred pounds. He
rolled as he walked, reminding Judd of an animated
Buddha. He had a round, jovial face with wide,
guileless, pale blue eyes. He was totally bald and
his head was egg-shaped. It was impossible to guess
his age.

'Mr Stevenson?' Moody greeted him.

'Dr Stevens,' Judd said.

'Sit down, sit down.' Buddha with a Southern drawl.

Judd looked around for a seat. He removed a pile of old body-building and nudist magazines from a scrofulous-looking leather armchair with strips torn out of it, and gingerly sat down.

Moody was lowering his bulk into an over-sized rocking chair. 'Well, now! What can I do for you?'

Judd knew that he had made a mistake. Over the phone he had carefully given Moody his full name. A name that had been on the front page of every New York newspaper in the last few days. And he had managed to pick the only private detective in the whole city who had never even heard of him. He cast about for some excuse to walk out.

'Who recommended me?' Moody prodded.

Judd hesitated, not wanting to offend him. 'I got your name out of the yellow pages.'

Moody laughed. 'I don't know what I'd do without the yellow pages,' he said. 'Greatest invention since corn liquor.' He gave another little laugh.

Judd got to his feet. He was dealing with a total idiot. 'I'm sorry to have taken up your time, Mr Moody,' he said, 'I'd like to think about this some more before I . . .'

'Sure, sure. I understand,' Moody said. 'You'll have to pay me for the appointment, though.'

'Of course,' Judd said. He reached in his pocket and pulled out some bills. 'How much is it?'

'Fifty dollars.'

'Fifty –?' Judd swallowed angrily, peeled off some bills and thrust them in Moody's hand. Moody counted the money carefully.

'Thanks a lot,' Moody said. Judd started towards the door, feeling like a fool. 'Doctor . . .'

Judd turned. Moody was smiling at him benevolently, tucking the money into the pocket of his waistcoat. 'As long as you're stuck for the fifty dollars,' he said mildly, 'you might as well sit down and tell me what your problem is. I always say that nothin' takes more weight off than gettin' things off your chest.'

The irony of it, coming from this silly fat man, almost made Judd laugh. Judd's whole life was devoted to listening to people get things off their chests. He studied Moody a moment. What could he lose? Perhaps talking it out with a stranger would help. Slowly he went back to his chair and sat down.

'You look like you're carryin' the weight of the world, Doc. I always say that four shoulders are better than two.'

Judd was not certain how many of Moody's aphorisms he was going to be able to stand.

Moody was watching him. 'What brought you here? Women, or money? I always say if you took away women and money, you'd solve most of the world's problems right there.' Moody was eyeing him, waiting for an answer.

'I – I think someone is trying to kill me.'

Blue eyes blinked. 'You think?'

Judd brushed the question aside. 'Perhaps you could give me the name of someone who specializes in investigating that kind of thing.'

'I certainly can,' Moody said. 'Norman Z. Moody. Best in the country.'

Judd sighed in despair.

'Why don't you tell me about it, Doc?' Moody suggested. 'Let's see if the two of us can't sort it out a little.'

Judd had to smile in spite of himself. It sounded so much like himself. *Just lie down and say anything that comes into your mind.* Why not? He took a deep breath and, as concisely as possible, told Moody the events of the past few days. As he spoke, he forgot that Moody was there. He was really speaking to himself, putting into words the baffling things that had occurred. He carefully said nothing to Moody about his fears for his own sanity. When Judd had finished, Moody regarded him happily.

'You got yourself a dilly of a problem there. Either somebody's out to murder you, or you're afraid that you're becoming a schizophrenic paranoiac.'

Judd looked up in surprise. Score one for Norman Z. Moody.

Moody went on. 'You said there are two detectives on the case. Do you remember their names?'

Judd hesitated. He was reluctant to get too deeply committed to this man. All he really wanted to do was to get out of there. 'Frank Angeli,' he answered, 'and Lieutenant McGreavy.'

There was an almost imperceptible change in Moody's expression.

'What reason would anyone have to kill you, Doc?'

'I have no idea. As far as I know, I haven't any enemies.'

'Oh, come on. Everybody's got a few enemies layin' around. I always say enemies give a little salt to the bread of life.'

Judd tried not to wince.

'Married?'

'No,' Judd said.

'Are you a fairy?'

Judd sighed. 'Look, I've been through all this with the police and –'

'Yeah. Only you're payin' me to help you,' Moody said, unperturbed. 'Owe anybody any money?'

'Just the normal monthly bills.'

'What about your patients?'

'What about them?'

'Well, I always say if you're lookin' for seashells,

118

go down to the seashore. Your patients are a lot of loonies. Right?'

'Wrong,' Judd said curtly. 'They're people with problems.'

'Emotional problems that they can't solve themselves. Could one of them have it in for you? Oh, not for any real reason, but maybe somebody with an imaginary grievance against you.'

'It's possible. Except for one thing. Most of my patients have been under my care for a year or more. In that length of time I've got to know them as well as one human being can know another.'

'Don't they never get mad at you?' Moody asked innocently.

'Sometimes. But we're not looking for someone who's angry. We're looking for a homicidal paranoiac who has murdered at least two people and has made several attempts to murder me.' He hesitated, then made himself go on. 'If I have a patient like that and don't know it, then you're looking at the most incompetent psychoanalyst who ever lived.'

He looked up and saw Moody studying him.

'I always say first things first,' Moody said cheerfully. 'The first thing we've gotta do is find out whether someone's trying to knock you off, or whether you're nuts. Right, Doc?' He broke into a broad smile, taking the offence out of his words.

'How?' Judd asked.

'Simple,' Moody said. 'Your problem is, you're standin' at home plate strikin' at curve balls, an' you don't know if anyone's pitchin'. First we gonna find out if there's a ball-game goin' on; then we're gonna find out who the players are. You got a car?'

'Yes.'

Judd had forgotten about walking out and finding another private detective. He sensed now behind Moody's bland, innocent face and his homespun maxims a quiet, intelligent capability.

'I think your nerves are shot,' Moody said. 'I want you to take a little vacation.'

'When?'

'Tomorrow morning.'

'That's impossible,' Judd protested. 'I have patients scheduled . . .'

Moody brushed it aside. 'Cancel them.'

'But what good –'

'Do I tell you how to run your business?' Moody asked. 'When you leave here, I want you to go straight to a travel agency. Have them get you a reservation at' – he thought a moment – 'Grossinger's. That's a pretty drive up through the Catskills . . . Is there a garage in the apartment building where you live?'

'Yes.'

'Okay. Tell them to service your car for the trip.

120

You don't want to have any breakdown on the road.'

'Couldn't I do this next week? Tomorrow is a full –'

'After you make your reservation, you're going back to your office and call all your patients. Tell them you've had an emergency and you'll be back in a week.'

'I really can't,' Judd said. 'It's out of the –'

'You'd better call Angeli, too,' Moody continued. 'I don't want the police hunting for you while you're gone.'

'Why am I doing this?' Judd asked.

'To protect your fifty dollars. That reminds me. I'm gonna need another two hundred for a retainer. Plus fifty a day for expenses.'

Moody hauled his large bulk up out of the big rocker. 'I want you to get a nice early start tomorrow,' he said, 'so you can get up there before dark. Can you leave about seven in the morning?'

'I . . . I suppose so. What will I find when I get up there?'

'With a little luck, a scorecard.'

Five minutes later Judd was thoughtfully getting into his car. He had told Moody that he could not go away and leave his patients on such short notice. But he knew that he was going to. He was literally putting his life into the hands of the Falstaff of the private detective world. As he started to drive away, his eye caught Moody's sign in the window.

SATISFACTION GUARANTEED

He'd better be right, Judd thought grimly.

The plan for the trip went smoothly. Judd stopped at a travel agency on Madison Avenue. They reserved a room for him at Grossinger's and provided him with a road map and a variety of colour brochures on the Catskills. Next he telephoned his answering service and arranged for them to call his patients and cancel all his appointments until further notice. He phoned the Nineteenth Precinct and asked for Detective Angeli.

'Angeli's home sick,' said an impersonal voice. 'Do you want his home number?'

'Yes.'

A few moments later he was talking to Angeli. From the sound of Angeli's voice, he had a heavy cold.

'I've decided I need to get out of town for a few days,' Judd said. 'I'm leaving in the morning. I wanted to check it with you.'

There was a silence while Angeli thought it over. 'It might not be a bad idea. Where will you go?'

'I thought I'd drive up to Grossinger's.'

'All right,' Angeli said. 'Don't worry. I'll clear

it with McGreavy.' He hesitated. 'I heard what happened at your office last night.'

'You mean you heard McGreavy's version,' Judd said.

'Did you get a look at the men who tried to kill you?'

'No.'

'Nothing at all that could help us find them? Colour, age, height?'

'I'm sorry,' Judd said. 'It was dark.'

Angeli sniffed. 'Okay. I'll keep looking. Maybe I'll have some good news for you when you get back. Be careful, Doctor.'

'I will,' Judd said gratefully. And he hung up.

Next he phoned Harrison Burke's employer and briefly explained Burke's situation. There was no choice but to have him committed as soon as possible. Judd then called Peter, explained that he had to go out of town for a week, and asked him to make the necessary arrangements for Burke. Peter agreed.

The decks were clear.

The thing that disturbed Judd the most was that he would be unable to see Anne on Friday. Perhaps he would never see her again.

As he drove back towards his apartment, he thought about Norman Z. Moody. He had an idea what Moody was up to. By having Judd notify all his patients that he was going away, Moody was

123

making sure that if one of Judd's patients was the killer – if there was a killer – a trap, using Judd as the bait, would be set for him.

Moody had instructed him to leave his forwarding address with his telephone exchange and with the doorman at the apartment building. He was making certain that everyone would know where Judd was going.

When Judd pulled up in front of the apartment house, Mike was there to greet him.

'I'm leaving on a trip in the morning, Mike,' Judd informed him. 'Will you make sure the garage services my car and fills the tank?'

'I'll have it taken care of, Dr Stevens. What time will you be needing the car?'

'I'll be leaving at seven.' Judd sensed Mike watching him as he walked into the apartment building.

When he entered his apartment, he locked the doors and carefully checked the windows. Everything seemed to be in order.

He took two codeine pills, got undressed, and ran a hot bath, gingerly easing his aching body into it, feeling the tensions soaking out of his back and neck. He lay in the blessedly relaxing tub, thinking. Why had Moody warned him not to let the car break down on the road? Because that was the most likely place for him to be attacked, somewhere on a lonely road in the Catskills? And what could

Moody do about it if Judd were attacked? Moody had refused to tell him what his plan was – if there was a plan. The more Judd examined it, the more convinced he became that he was walking into a trap. Moody had said he was setting it up for Judd's pursuers. But no matter how many times he went over it, the answer always came out the same: the trap seemed designed to catch Judd. But why? What interest could Moody have in getting him killed? *My God*, thought Judd. *I've picked a name at random out of the yellow pages of the Manhattan Telephone Directory and I believe he wants to have me murdered! I am paranoiac!*

He felt his eyes beginning to close. The pills and the hot bath had done their work well. Wearily he pulled himself out of the tub, carefully patted his bruised body dry with a fluffy towel, and put on a pair of pyjamas. He got into bed and set the electric alarm clock for six. The Catskills, he thought. It was an appropriate name. And he fell into a deep, exhausted sleep.

At six a.m., when the alarm went off, Judd was instantly awake. As though there had been no time lapse at all, his first thought was, *I don't believe in a series of coincidences and I don't believe that one of my patients is a mass murderer*. Ergo, *I am either a paranoiac, or am becoming one*. What he needed was to consult another psychoanalyst without delay. He would phone Dr Robbie. He knew that it would mean the end of his professional career, but there was no help for it. If he were suffering from paranoia, they would have to commit him. Did Moody suspect that he was dealing with a mental case? Was that why he suggested a vacation? Not because he believed anyone was after Judd's life, but because he could see the signs of a nervous breakdown? Perhaps the wisest course would be to follow Moody's advice and go to the Catskills for a few days. Alone, with all the pressures removed, he would calmly try to evaluate himself, try to reason out when his mind had started to trick him, when he had begun to lose touch with reality. Then, when he returned, he would make an appointment with Dr Robbie and put himself under his care.

It was a painful decision to make, but having made it, Judd felt better. He dressed, packed a small suitcase with enough clothes for five days, and carried it out to the elevator.

Eddie was not on duty yet, and the elevator was on self-service. Judd rode down to the basement garage. He looked round for Wilt, the attendant, but he was nowhere around. The garage was deserted.

Judd spotted his car parked in a corner against the cement wall. He walked over to it, put his suitcase in the back seat, opened the front door, and eased in behind the wheel. As he reached for the ignition key, a man loomed up at his side from nowhere. Judd's heart skipped a beat.

'You're right on schedule.' It was Moody.

'I didn't know you were going to see me off,' Judd said.

Moody beamed at him, his cherubic face breaking into a huge smile. 'I had nothing better to do and I couldn't sleep.'

Judd was suddenly grateful for the tactful way Moody had handled the situation. No reference to the fact that Judd was a mental case, just an ingenuous suggestion that he drive up to the country and take a rest. Well, the least Judd could do was to keep up the pretence that everything was normal.

'I decided you were right. I'm going to drive up and see if I can find a scorecard to the ball-game.'

'Oh, you don't have to go anywhere for that,' Moody said. 'That's all taken care of.'

Judd looked at him blankly. 'I don't understand.'

'It's simple. I always say when you want to get to the bottom of anything, you gotta start diggin'.'

'Mr Moody . . .'

Moody leaned against the door of the car. 'You know what I found intriguin' about your little problem, Doc? Seemed like every five minutes somebody was tryin' to kill you – maybe. Now that "maybe" fascinated me. There was nothin' for us to bite into till we found out whether you were crackin' up, or whether someone was really tryin' to turn you into a corpse.'

Judd looked at him. 'But the Catskills . . .' he said weakly.

'Oh, you wasn't never goin' to the Catskills, Doc.' He opened the door of the car. 'Step out here.'

Bewildered, Judd stepped out of the car.

'You see, that was just advertising. I always say if you wanta catch a shark, you've gotta bloody up the water first.'

Judd was watching his face.

'I'm afraid you never would have got to the Catskills,' Moody said gently. He walked around to the hood of the car, fumbled with the catch, and raised the hood. Judd walked over to his side. Taped to the distributor lead were three sticks of dynamite. Two thin wires were dangling loose from the ignition.

'Booby-trapped,' Moody said.

Judd looked at him, baffled. 'But how did you . . .'

Moody grinned at him. 'I told you, I'm a bad sleeper. I got here around midnight. I paid the nightman to go out and have some fun, an' I just kinda waited in the shadows. The nightman'll cost another twenty dollars,' he added. 'I didn't want you to look cheap.'

Judd felt a sudden wave of affection towards the little fat man. 'Did you see who did it?'

'Nope. It was done before I got here. At six o'clock this mornin' I figured no one was gonna show up any more, so I took a look.' He pointed to the dangling wires. 'Your friends are real cute. They rigged a second booby-trap so if you lifted the hood all the way, this wire would detonate the dynamite. The same thing would happen if you turned on your ignition. There's enough stuff here to wipe out half the garage.'

Judd felt suddenly sick to his stomach. Moody looked at him sympathetically. 'Cheer up,' he said. 'Look at the progress we've made. We know two things. First of all, we know you're not nuts. And secondly' – the smile left his face – 'we know that somebody is God Almighty anxious to murder you, Dr Stevens.'

TEN

They were sitting in the living-room of Judd's apartment, talking, Moody's enormous body spilling over the large couch. Moody had carefully put the pieces of the already defused bomb in the trunk of his own car.

'Shouldn't you have left it there so the police could have examined it?' Judd asked.

'I always say that the most confusin' thing in the world is too much information.'

'But it would prove to Lieutenant McGreavy that I've been telling the truth.'

'Would it?'

Judd saw his point. As far as McGreavy was concerned, Judd could have placed it there himself. Still, it seemed odd to him that a private detective would withhold evidence from the police. He had a feeling that Moody was like an enormous iceberg. Most of the man was concealed under the surface, under that façade of gentle, small-town bumbler. But now, as he listened to Moody talking, he was filled with elation. He was not insane and the world had not suddenly become filled with wild coincidences. There was an assassin on the loose. A flesh-and-blood assassin. And for some reason he had chosen Judd as his target. *My God*, thought Judd, *how easily our egos are destroyed*. A few minutes ago he had been ready to believe that he was paranoiac. He owed Moody an incalculable debt.

'. . . You're the doctor,' Moody was saying. 'I'm just an old gumshoe. I always say when you want honey, go to a beehive.'

Judd was beginning to understand Moody's jargon. 'You want my opinion about the kind of man, or men, we're looking for.'

'That's it,' beamed Moody. 'Are we dealin' with some homicidal maniac who broke out of a loony bin' –

Mental institution, Judd thought automatically.

– 'or have we got somethin' deeper goin' here?'

'Something deeper,' said Judd instantly.

'What makes you think so, Doc?'

'First of all, *two* men broke into my office last night. I might swallow the theory of one lunatic, but two lunatics working together is too much.'

Moody nodded approvingly. 'Gotcha. Go on.'

'Secondly, a deranged mind may have an

obsession, but it works in a definite pattern. I don't know why John Hanson and Carol Roberts were killed, but unless I'm wrong, I'm scheduled to be the third and last victim.'

'What makes you think you're the last?' asked Moody curiously.

'Because,' replied Judd, 'if there were going to be other murders, then the first time they failed to kill me, they would have gone on to get whoever else was on their list. But instead of that, they've been concentrating on trying to kill me.'

'You know,' said Moody approvingly, 'you have the natural born makin's of a detective.'

Judd was frowning. 'There are several things that make no sense.'

'Such as?'

'First, the motive,' said Judd. 'I don't know anyone who –'

'We'll come back to that. What else?'

'If somebody really was that anxious to kill me, when the car knocked me down, all the driver had to do was to back up and run over me. I was unconscious.'

'Ah! That's where Mr Benson comes in.'

Judd looked at him blankly.

'Mr Benson is the witness to your accident,' explained Moody benevolently. 'I got his name from the police report and went to see him after you left my office. That'll be three-fifty for taxicabs. Okay?'

Judd nodded, speechless.

'Mr Benson – he's a furrier, by the way. Beautiful stuff. If you ever want to buy anything for your sweetheart, I can get you a discount. Anyway, Tuesday, the night of the accident, he was comin' out of an office building where his sister-in-law works. He dropped some pills off because his brother Matthew, who's a Bible salesman, had the flu an' she was goin' to take the pills home to him.'

Judd controlled his impatience. If Norman Z. Moody had felt like sitting there and reciting the entire Bill of Rights, he was going to listen.

'So Mr Benson dropped off these pills an' was comin' out of the building when he saw this limousine headin' towards you. Of course, he didn't know it was you at the time.'

Judd nodded.

'The car was kinda crabbin' sideways, an' from Benson's angle, it looked like it was in a skid. When he saw it hit you, he started runnin' over to see if he could help. The limousine backed up to make another run at you. He saw Mr Benson an' got out of there like a bat outta hell.'

Judd swallowed. 'So if Mr Benson hadn't happened along . . .'

'Yeah,' said Moody mildly. 'You might say you an' me wouldn't have met. These boys ain't playin' games. They're out to get you, Doc.'

'What about the attack in my office? Why didn't they break the door down?'

Moody was silent for a moment, thinking. 'That's a puzzler. They coulda broken in an' killed you an' whoever was with you an' got away without anybody seein' them. But when they thought you weren't alone, they left. It don't fit in with the rest.' He sat there worrying his lower lip. 'Unless . . .' he said.

'Unless what?'

A speculative look came over Moody's face. 'I wonder . . .' he breathed.

'What?'

'It'll keep for the time bein'. I got me a little idea, but it don't make sense until we find a motive.'

Judd shrugged helplessly. 'I don't know of anyone who has a motive for killing me.'

Moody thought about this a moment. 'Doc, could you have any secret that you shared with this patient of yours, Hanson, an' Carol Roberts? Somethin' maybe only the three of you knew about?'

Judd shook his head. 'The only secrets I have are professional secrets about my patients. And there's not one single thing in any of their case histories that would justify murder. None of my patients is a secret agent, or a foreign spy, or an escaped convict. They're just ordinary people –

housewives, professional men, bank clerks – who have problems they can't cope with.'

Moody looked at him guilelessly. 'An' you're sure that you're not harbouring a homicidal maniac in your little group?'

Judd's voice was firm. 'Positive. Yesterday I might not have been sure. To tell you the truth, I was beginning to think that I was suffering from paranoia and that you were humouring me.'

Moody smiled at him. 'The thought had crossed my mind,' he said. 'After you phoned me for an appointment, I did some checking up on you. I called a couple of pretty good doctor friends of mine. You got quite a reputation.'

So the 'Mr Stevenson' had been part of Moody's country bumpkin façade.

'If we go to the police now,' Judd said, 'with what we know, we can at least get them to start looking for whoever's behind all this.'

Moody looked at him in mild surprise. 'You think so? We don't really have much to go on yet, do we, Doc?'

It was true.

'I wouldn't be discouraged,' Moody said. 'I think we're makin' real progress. We've narrowed it down nicely.'

A note of frustration crept into Judd's voice. 'Sure. It could be anyone in the Continental United States.'

Moody sat there a moment, contemplating the ceiling. Finally he shook his head. 'Families,' he sighed.

'Families?'

'Doc – I believe you when you say you know your patients inside out. If you tell me they couldn't do anything like this, I have to go along with you. It's your beehive an' you're th' keeper of the honey.' He leaned forward on the couch. 'But tell me somethin'. When you take on a patient, do you interview his family?'

'No. Sometimes the family isn't even aware that the patient is undergoing psychoanalysis.'

Moody leaned back, satisfied. 'There you are,' he said.

Judd looked at him. 'You think that some member of a patient's family is trying to kill me?'

'Could be.'

'They'd have no more motive than the patient. Less, probably.'

Moody painfully pushed himself to his feet. 'You never know, do you, Doc? Tell you what I'd like you to do. Get me a list of all the patients you've seen in the last four or five weeks. Can you do that?'

Judd hesitated. 'No,' he said, finally.

'That confidential patient-doctor business? I think maybe it's time to bend that a little. Your life's at stake.'

'I think you're on the wrong track. What's been happening has nothing to do with my patients or their families. If there had been any insanity in their families, it would have come out in the psychoanalysis.' He shook his head. 'I'm sorry, Mr Moody. I have to protect my patients.'

'You said there was nothing in the files that was important.'

'Nothing that's important to us.' He thought of some of the material in the files. John Hanson picking up sailors in gay bars on Third Avenue. Teri Washburn making love to the boys in the band. Fourteen-year-old Evelyn Warshak, the resident prostitute in the ninth grade . . . 'I'm sorry,' he said again. 'I can't show you the files.'

Moody shrugged. 'Okay,' he said. 'Okay. Then you're gonna have to do part of my job for me.'

'What do you want me to do?'

'Take out the tapes on everybody you've had on your couch for the last month. Listen real careful to each one. Only this time don't listen like a doctor – listen like a detective – look for anything the least bit offbeat.'

'I do that anyway. That's my job.'

'Do it again. An' keep your eyes open. I don't want to lose you till we solve this case.' He picked up his overcoat and struggled into it, making it look like an elephant ballet. Fat men were supposed to be graceful, thought Judd, but that did not include Mr Moody. 'Do you know the most peculiar thing about this whole megillah?' queried Moody thoughtfully.

'What?'

'You put your finger on it before, when you said there were *two* men. Maybe one man might have a burning itch to knock you off – but why *two*?'

'I don't know.'

Moody studied him a moment, speculatively. 'By God!' he finally said.

'What is it?'

'I just might have a brainstorm. If I'm right, there could be *more* than two men out to kill you.'

Judd stared at him incredulously. 'You mean there's a whole group of maniacs after me? That doesn't make sense.'

There was a look of growing excitement on Moody's face. 'Doctor, I've got an idea who the umpire in this ball-game might be.' He looked at Judd, his eyes bright. 'I don't know how yet, or why – but it could be I know *who*.'

'Who?'

Moody shook his head. 'You'd have me sent to a cracker factory if I told you. I always say if you're gonna shoot off your mouth, make sure it's loaded first. Let me do a little target practice. If I'm on the right track, I'll tell you.'

'I hope you are,' Judd said earnestly.

Moody looked at him a moment. 'No, Doc. If you value your life worth a damn – pray I'm wrong.'

And Moody was gone.

He took a taxi to the office.

It was Friday noon, and with only three more shopping days until Christmas, the streets were crowded with late shoppers, bundled up against the raw wind sweeping in from the Hudson River. The store windows were festive and bright, filled with lighted Christmas trees and carved figures of the Nativity. Peace on Earth. Christmas. And Elizabeth, and their unborn baby. One day soon – if he survived – he would have to make his own peace, free himself from the dead past and let go. He knew that with Anne he could have . . . He firmly stopped himself. What was the point in fantasizing about a married woman about to go away with her husband, whom she loved?

The taxi pulled up in front of his office building and Judd got out, nervously looking around. But what could he look for? He had no idea what the murder weapon would be, or who would wield it.

When he reached his office, he locked the outer door, went to the panelling that concealed the tapes, and opened it. The tapes were filed chronologically, under the name of each patient. He selected the most recent ones and carried them over to the tape recorder. With all his appointments cancelled for the day, he would be able to concentrate on trying to find some clue that might involve the friends or families of his patients. He felt that Moody's suggestion was far-fetched, but he had too much respect for him to ignore it.

As he put on the first tape, he remembered the last time he had used the machine. Was it only the night before last? The memory filled him again with the sharp sense of nightmare. Someone had planned to murder him here in this room, where they had murdered Carol.

He suddenly realized that he had given no thought to his patients at the free hospital clinic where he worked one morning a week. It was probably because the murders had revolved around this office rather than the hospital. Still . . . He walked over to the section of the cabinets labelled 'CLINIC', looked through some of the tapes, and finally selected half a dozen. He put the first one on the tape recorder.

Rose Graham.

'. . . an accident, Doctor. Nancy cries a lot. She's always been a whiny baby, so when I hit her, it's for her own good y'know?'

'Did you ever try to find out why Nancy cries a lot?' Judd's voice asked.

''Cause she's spoiled. Her daddy spoiled her rotten and then run off and left us. Nancy always thought she was daddy's girl, but how much could Harry really have loved her if he run off like that?'

'You and Harry were never married, were you?'

'Well . . . Common law, I guess you'd call it. We was goin' to get married.'

'How long did you live together?'

'Four years.'

'How long was it after Harry left you that you broke Nancy's arm?'

''Bout a week, I guess. I didn't mean to break it. It's just that she wouldn't stop whining, so I finally picked up this curtain rod an' started beating on her.'

'Do you think Harry loved Nancy more than he loved you?'

'No. Harry was crazy about me.'

'Then why do you think he left you?'

'Because he was a man. An' y'know what men are? Animals! All of you! You should all be slaughtered like pigs!' Sobbing.

Judd switched off the tape and thought about Rose Graham. She was a psychotic misanthrope, and she had nearly beaten her six-year-old child to death on two separate occasions. But the pattern of the murders did not fit Rose Graham's psychosis.

He put on the next tape from the clinic.

Alexander Fallon.

'The police say that you attacked Mr Champion with a knife, Mr Fallon.'

'I only did what I was told.'

'Someone told you to kill Mr Champion?'

'He told me to do it.'

'He?'

'God.'

'Why did God tell you to kill him?'

'Because Champion's an evil man. He's an actor. I saw him on the stage. He kissed this woman. This actress. In front of the whole audience. He kissed her and . . .'

Silence.

'Go on.'

'He touched her – her titty.'

'Did that upset you?'

'Of course! It upset me terribly. Don't you understand what that meant? He had carnal knowledge of her. When I came out of that theatre, I felt like I had just come from Sodom and Gomorrah. They had to be punished.'

'So you decided to kill him.'

'I didn't decide it. God decided. I just carried out His orders.'

'Does God often talk to you?'

'Only when there's His work to be done. He's chosen me as His instrument, because I'm pure. Do you know what makes me pure? Do you know what the most cleansing thing in the world is? Slaying the wicked!'

Alexander Fallon. Thirty-five, a part-time baker's assistant. He had been sent to a mental home for six months and then released. Could God have told him to destroy Hanson, a homosexual, and Carol, a former prostitute, and Judd, their benefactor? Judd decided that it was unlikely. Fallon's thought processes took place in brief, painful spasms. Whoever had planned the murders was highly organized.

He played several more of the tapes from the clinic, but none of them fitted into the pattern he was searching for. No. It wasn't any patient at the clinic.

He looked over the office files again and a name caught his eye.

Skeet Gibson.

He put on the tape.

''Mornin', Dockie. How do you like this bee-u-ti-ful day I cooked up for you?'

'You're feeling good today.'

'If I was feelin' any better, they'd have me locked up. Did you catch my show last night?'

'No. I'm sorry, I wasn't able to.'

'I was only a smash. Jack Gould called me "the most lovable comedian in the world". An' who am I to argue with a genius like Jack Gould? You shoulda heard that audience! They were applauding like it was going out of style. Do ya know what that proves?'

'That they can read "Applause" cards?'

'You're sharp, you devil you. That's what I like – a

head-shrinker with a sense of humour. The last one I had was a drag. Had a great big beard that really bugged me.'

'Why?'

'Because it was a lady!'

Loud laughter.

'Gotcha that time, didn't I, old cock? Seriously, folks, one of the reasons I'm feelin' so good is because I just pledged a million dollars – count 'em: one million bucks – to help the kids in Biafra.'

'No wonder you feel good.'

'You bet your sweet ass. That story hit the front pages all over the world.'

'Is that important?'

'What do you mean, "Is that important?" How many guys pledge that kind of loot? You've gotta blow your own horn, Peter Pan. I'm glad I can afford to pledge the money.'

'You keep saying "pledge". Do you mean "give"?'

'Pledge – give – what's the difference? You pledge a million – give a few grand – an' they kiss your ass . . . Did I tell you it's my anniversary today?'

'No. Congratulations.'

'Thanks. Fifteen great years. You never met Sally. There's the sweetest broad that ever walked God's earth. I really got lucky with my marriage. You know what a pain in the keester in-laws can be? Well, Sally's got these two brothers, Ben an' Charley. I told you about them. Ben's head writer on my TV show an' Charley's my producer. They're geniuses. I've been on the air seven years now. An' we're never outta the top ten in the Nielsen's. I was smart to marry into a family like that, huh? Most women get fat an' sloppy once they've hooked their husband. But Sally, bless her, is slimmer now than the day we were married. What a dame! . . . Got a cigarette?'

'Here. I thought you quit smoking.'

'I just wanted to show myself I had the old willpower, so I quit. Now I'm smoking because I want to . . . I made a new deal with the network yesterday. I really shafted 'em. Is my time up yet?'

'No. Are you restless, Skeet?'

'To tell you the truth, sweetie, I'm in such great shape I don't know what the hell I'm coming in here any more for.'

'No more problems?'

'Me? The world's my oyster an' I'm Diamond Jim Brady. I've gotta hand it to you. You've really helped me. You're my man. With the kind of money you make, maybe I should go into business and set up my own shingle, huh? . . . That reminds me of the great story of the guy who goes to a wig-picker, but he's so nervous he just lays on the couch and doesn't say anything. At the end of the hour, the shrink says, "That'll be fifty dollars." Well, that goes on for two whole years without the schmuck saying one word. Finally the little guy opens his mouth one day and says, "Doctor – could I ask you a question?" "Sure," says the Doc. And the little guy says, "Would you like a partner?"'

Loud laughter.

'You got a shot of aspirin or somethin'?'

'Certainly. Is it one of your bad headaches?'

'Nothin' I can't handle, old buddy . . . Thanks. That'll do the trick.'

'What do you think brings these headaches on?'

'Just normal show-biz tension . . . We have our script reading this afternoon.'

'Does that make you nervous?'

'Me? Hell, no! What have I got to be nervous about? If the jokes are lousy, I make a face, wink at the audience, an' they eat it up. No matter how bad the show is, little old Skeet comes out smelling like a rose.'

'Why do you think you have these headaches every week?'

'How the fuck do I know? You're supposed to be a doctor. *You* tell *me*. I don't pay you to sit on your fat ass for an hour asking stupid questions. Jesus Christ, if an idiot like you can't cure a simple headache, they shouldn't let you be running around loose, messing up people's lives. Where'd you get your medical certificate? From a veterinarian school? I wouldn't trust my fuckin' cats with you. You're a goddamn quack! The only reason I came to you in the first place was because Sally shitted me into it. It was the only way I could get her off my back. Do ya know my definition of Hell? Bein' married to an ugly, skinny nag for fifteen years. If you're lookin' for some more suckers to cheat, take on her two idiot brothers, Ben an' Charley. Ben, my head writer, doesn't know which end of the pencil has the lead in it, an' his brother's even stupider. I wish they'd all drop dead. They're out to get me. You think I like you? You stink! You're so goddamn smug, sitting there looking down on everybody. You haven't got any problems, have you? Do you know why? Because you're not for real. You're out of it. All you do is sit on your fat keester all day long an' steal money from sick people. Well, I'm gonna get you, you sonofabitch. I'm gonna report you to the AMA . . .'

Sobbing.

'I wish I didn't have to go to that goddamn reading.'

Silence.

'Well – keep your pecker up. See ya next week, sweetie.'

Judd switched off the recorder. Skeet Gibson, America's most beloved comedian, should have been institutionalized ten years ago. His hobbies were beating up young, blonde showgirls and getting into bar-room brawls. Skeet was a small man, but he had started out as a prizefighter, and he knew how to hurt. One of his favourite sports was going into a gay bar, coaxing an unsuspecting homosexual into the men's room, and beating him unconscious. Skeet had been picked up by the police several times, but the incidents had always been hushed up. After all, he was America's most lovable comic. Skeet was paranoid enough to want to kill, and he was capable of killing in a fit of rage. But Judd did not think he was cold-blooded enough to carry out this kind of planned vendetta. And in that, Judd felt certain, lay the key to the solution. Whoever was trying to murder him was doing it not in the heat of any passion, but methodically and cold-bloodedly. A madman.

Who was not mad.

ELEVEN

The phone rang. It was his answering service. They had been able to reach all his patients except Anne Blake. Judd thanked the operator and hung up.

So Anne was coming here today. He was disturbed at how unreasonably happy he was at the thought of seeing her. He must remember that she was only coming by because he had asked her to, as her doctor. He sat there thinking about Anne. How much he knew her . . . and how little.

He put Anne's tape on the tape recorder and listened to it. It was one of her first visits.

'Comfortable, Mrs Blake?'

'Yes, thank you.'

'Relaxed?'

'Yes.'

'You're clenching your fists.'

'Perhaps I am a little tense.'

'About what?'

A long silence.

'Tell me about your home life. You've been married six months.'

'Yes.'

'Go on.'

'I'm married to a wonderful man. We live in a beautiful house.'

'What kind of house is it?'

'Country French . . . It's a lovely old place. There's a long, winding driveway leading to it. High up on the roof there's a funny old bronze rooster with its tail missing. I think some hunter shot it off a long time ago. We have about five acres, mostly wooded. I go for long walks. It's like living in the country.'

'Do you like the country?'

'Very much.'

'Does your husband?'

'I think so.'

'A man doesn't usually buy five acres in the country unless he loves it.'

'He loves me. He would have bought it for me. He's very generous.'

'Let's talk about him.'

Silence.

'Is he good-looking?'

'Anthony's very handsome.'

Judd felt a pang of unreasonable, unprofessional jealousy.

'You're compatible physically?' It was like a tongue probing at a sore tooth.

'Yes.'

He knew what she could be like in bed: exciting and feminine and giving. *Christ*, he thought, *get off the subject.*

'Do you want children?'

'Oh, yes.'

'Does your husband?'

'Yes, of course.'

A long silence except for the silky rustling of the tape. Then:

'Mrs Blake, you came to me because you said you had a desperate problem. It concerns your husband, doesn't it?'

Silence.

'Well, I'm assuming it does. From what you told me earlier, you love each other, you're both faithful, you both want children, you live in a beautiful home, your husband is successful, handsome, and he spoils you. And you've only been married six months. I'm afraid it's a little like the old joke: "What's my problem, Doctor?"'

There was silence again except for the impersonal whirring of the tape. Finally she spoke. 'It's . . . it's difficult for me to talk about. I thought

I could discuss it with a stranger, but' – he remembered vividly how she had twisted around on the couch to look up at him with those large, enigmatic eyes – 'it's harder. You see' – and she was speaking more rapidly now, trying to overcome the barriers that had kept her silent – 'I overheard something and I – I could easily have jumped to the wrong conclusion.'

'Something to do with your husband's personal life? Some woman?'

'No.'

'His business?'

'Yes . . .'

'You thought he lied about something? Tried to get the better of someone in a deal?'

'Something like that.'

Judd was on surer ground now. 'And it upset your confidence in him. It showed you a side of him that you had never seen before.'

'I – I can't discuss it. I feel disloyal to him even being here. Please don't ask me anything more today, Dr Stevens.'

And that had ended that session. Judd switched off the tape.

So Anne's husband had pulled a sharp business deal. He could have cheated on his taxes. Or forced someone into bankruptcy. Anne, naturally, would be upset. She was a sensitive woman. Her faith in her husband would be shaken.

He thought about Anne's husband as a possible suspect. He was in the construction business. Judd had never met him, but whatever business problem he was involved in could not, by any stretch of the imagination, have included John Hanson, Carol Roberts, or Judd.

But what about Anne herself? Could she be a psychopath? A homicidal maniac? Judd leaned back in his chair and tried to think about her objectively.

He knew nothing about her except what she had told him. Her background could have been fictitious, she could have made it all up, but what would she have to gain? If this was some elaborate charade as a cover to murder, there had to be a motivation. The memory of her face and her voice flooded his mind, and he knew that she could have nothing to do with any of this. He would stake his life on it. The irony of the phrase made him grin.

He went over to get the tapes of Teri Washburn. Perhaps there was something there that he might have missed.

Teri had been having extra sessions lately at her own request. Was she under some new pressure that she had not yet confided to him? Because of her incessant preoccupation with sex, it was difficult to determine accurately her current progress. Still – why had she suddenly, urgently asked for more time with him?

Judd picked up one of her tapes at random and put it on.

'Let's talk about your marriages, Teri. You've been married five times.'

'Six, but who's counting?'

'Were you faithful to your husbands?'

Laughter.

'You're putting me on. There isn't a man in the world who can satisfy me. It's a physical thing.'

'What do you mean by "a physical thing"?'

'I mean that's the way I'm built. I just got a hot hole and it's gotta be kept filled all the time.'

'Do you believe that?'

'That it's gotta be kept filled?'

'That you're different, physically, from any other woman.'

'Certainly. The studio doctor told me. It's a glandular thing or something.' A pause. 'He was a lousy lay.'

'I've seen all your charts. Physiologically your body is normal in every respect.'

'Fuck the charts, Charley. Why don't you find out for yourself?'

'Have you ever been in love, Teri?'

'I could be in love with you.'

Silence.

'Get that look off your face. I can't help it. I

told you. It's the way I'm built. I'm always hungry.'

'I believe you. But it's not your body that's hungry. It's your emotions.'

'I've never been fucked in my emotions. Do you want to give it a whirl?'

'No.'

'What do you want?'

'To help you.'

'Why don't you come over here and sit down next to me?'

'That will be all for today.'

Judd switched off the tape. He remembered a dialogue they had had when Teri was talking about her career as a big star and he had asked her why she had left Hollywood.

'I slapped some obnoxious jerk at a drunken party,' she had said. 'And he turned out to be Mr Big. He had me thrown out of Hollywood on my Polack ass.'

Judd had not probed any farther because at that time he was more interested in her home background, and the subject had never come up again. Now he felt a small nagging doubt. He should have explored it farther. He had never had any interest in Hollywood except in the way Dr Louis Leakey or Margaret Mead might be interested in the natives of Patagonia. Who would know about Teri Washburn, the glamour star?

Norah Hadley was a movie buff. Judd had seen a collection of movie magazines at their house and had kidded Peter about them. Norah had spent the entire evening defending Hollywood. He picked up the receiver and dialled.

Norah answered the phone.

'Hello,' said Judd.

'Judd!' Her voice was warm and friendly. 'You called to tell me when you're coming to dinner.'

'We'll do it soon.'

'You'd better,' she said. 'I promised Ingrid. She's beautiful.'

Judd was sure she was. But not in the way Anne was beautiful.

'You break another date with her and we'll be at war with Sweden.'

'It won't happen again.'

'Are you all over your accident?'

'Oh, yes.'

'What a horrible thing that was.'

There was a hesitant note in Norah's voice. 'Judd . . . about Christmas Day. Peter and I would like you to share it with us. Please.'

He felt the old familiar tightening in his chest. They went through this every year. Peter and Norah were his dearest friends, and they hated it that he spent every Christmas alone, walking among strangers, losing himself in alien crowds, driving his body to keep moving until he was too exhausted to think. It was as though he were celebrating some terrible black mass for the dead, letting his grief take possession of him and tear him apart, lacerating and shriving him in some ancient ritual over which he had no control. *You're dramatizing it*, he told himself wearily.

'Judd . . .'

He cleared his throat. 'I'm sorry, Norah.' He knew how much she cared. 'Perhaps next Christmas.'

She tried to keep the disappointment out of her voice. 'Sure. I'll tell Pete.'

'Thanks.' He suddenly remembered why he had called. 'Norah – do you know who Teri Washburn is?'

'*The* Teri Washburn? The star? Why do you ask?'

'I – I saw her on Madison Avenue this morning.'

'In person? Honestly?' She was like an eager child. 'How did she look? Old? Young? Thin? Fat?'

'She looked fine. She used to be a pretty big star, didn't she?'

'*Pretty* big? Teri Washburn was the *biggest* – and in every way, if you know what I mean.'

'Whatever made a girl like that leave Hollywood?'

'She didn't exactly leave. She was booted out.'

So Teri had told him the truth. Judd felt better. 'You doctors keep your heads buried in the sand, don't you? Teri Washburn was involved in one of the hottest scandals Hollywood ever had.'

'Really?' said Judd. 'What happened?'

'She murdered her boyfriend.'

TWELVE

It had started to snow again. From the street fifteen floors below, the sounds of traffic floated up, muted by the white, cottony flakes in the arctic wind. In a lighted office across the street he saw the blurred face of a secretary streaming down the window.

'Norah – are you certain?'

'When it comes to Hollywood, you're talking to a walking encyclopaedia, love. Teri was living with the head of Continental Studios but she was keeping an assistant director on the side. She caught him cheating on her one night and she stabbed him to death. The head of the studio pulled a lot of strings and paid off a lot of people and it was hushed up and called an accident. Part of the arrangement was that she get out of Hollywood and never come back. And she never has.'

Judd stared at the phone numbly.

'Judd, are you there?'

'I'm here.'

'You sound funny.'

'Where did you hear all this?'

'Hear it? It was in all the newspapers and fan magazines. Everybody knew about it.'

Except him. 'Thanks, Norah,' he said. 'Say hello to Peter.' He hung up.

So that was the 'casual incident'. Teri Washburn had murdered a man and had never mentioned it to him. And if she had murdered once . . .

Thoughtfully he picked up a pad and wrote down 'Teri Washburn.'

The phone rang. Judd picked it up. 'Dr Stevens . . .'

'Just checking to see if you're all right.' It was Detective Angeli. His voice was still hoarse with a cold.

A feeling of gratitude filled Judd. Someone was on his side.

'Anything new?'

Judd hesitated. He could see no point in keeping quiet about the bomb.

'They tried again.' Judd told Angeli about Moody and the bomb that had been planted in his car. 'That should convince McGreavy,' he concluded.

'Where's the bomb?' Angeli's voice was excited.

Judd hesitated. 'It's been dismantled.'

'It's been *what*?' Angeli asked incredulously. 'Who did that?'

'Moody. He didn't think it mattered.'

'*Didn't matter!* What does he think the Police Department is for? We might have been able to tell who planted that bomb just by looking at it. We keep a file of MOs.'

'MO?'

'*Modus operandi*. People fall into habit patterns. If they do something one way the first time, chances are they'll keep doing it the same – I don't have to tell *you*.'

'No,' said Judd thoughtfully. Surely Moody had known that. Had he some reason for not wanting to show the bomb to McGreavy?

'Dr Stevens – how did you hire Moody?'

'I found him in the yellow pages.' It sounded ridiculous even as he said it.

He could hear Angeli swallow. 'Oh. Then you really don't know a damn thing about him.'

'I know I trust him. Why?'

'Right now,' Angeli said, 'I don't think you should trust anybody.'

'But Moody couldn't possibly be connected with any of this. My God! I picked him out of the phone book at random.'

'I don't care where you got him. Something smells fishy. Moody says he set a trap to catch whoever's after you, but he doesn't close the trap until the bait's already been taken, so we can't pin it on anyone. Then he shows you a bomb in your car that he could have put there himself. And wins your confidence. Right?'

'I suppose you could look at it that way,' Judd said. 'But –'

'Maybe your friend Moody is on the level, and maybe he's setting you up. I want you to play it nice and cool until we find out.'

Moody *against* him? It was difficult to believe. And yet, he remembered his earlier doubts when he had thought Moody was sending him into an ambush.

'What do you want me to do?' asked Judd.

'How would you feel about leaving town? I mean *really* leaving town.'

'I can't leave my patients.'

'Dr Stevens –'

'Besides,' Judd added, 'it really wouldn't solve anything, would it? I wouldn't even know what I'm running away from. When I came back, it would just start all over again.'

There was a moment's silence. 'You have a point.' Angeli gave a sigh, and it turned into a wheeze. He sounded terrible. 'When do you expect to hear from Moody again?'

'I don't know. He thinks he has some idea of who's behind all this.'

'Has it occurred to you that whoever's behind this can pay Moody a lot more than you can?' There was an urgency in Angeli's voice. 'If he asks you to meet him, call me. I'll be home in bed for the next day or two. Whatever you do, Doctor, don't meet him alone!'

'You're building up a case out of nothing,' countered Judd. 'Just because Moody removed the bomb from my car –'

'There's more to it than that,' said Angeli. 'I have a hunch you picked the wrong man.'

'I'll call you if I hear from him,' promised Judd. He hung up, shaken. Was Angeli being overly suspicious? It was true that Moody could have been lying about the bomb in order to win Judd's confidence. Then the next step would be easy. All he would have to do would be to call Judd and ask him to meet him in some deserted place on the pretext of having some evidence for him. Then . . . Judd shuddered. Could he have been wrong about Moody's character? He remembered his reaction when he had first met Moody. He had thought that the man was ineffectual and not very bright. Then he realized that his homespun cover was a façade that concealed a quick, sharp brain. But that didn't mean that Moody could be trusted. And yet . . . He heard someone at the outer reception door and looked at his watch. *Anne!* He quickly locked the tapes away, walked over to the private corridor door, and opened it.

Anne was standing in the corridor. She was wearing a smartly tailored navy blue suit and a small hat that framed her face. She was dreamily lost in thought, unaware that Judd was watching her. He studied her, filling himself with her beauty, trying to find some imperfection, some reason for him to tell himself that she would be wrong for him, that he would one day find someone else better suited to him. The fox and the grapes. Freud was not the father of psychiatry. Aesop was.

'Hello,' he said.

She looked up, startled for an instant. Then she smiled. 'Hello.'

'Come in, Mrs Blake.'

She moved past him into the office, her firm body brushing his. She turned and looked at him with those incredible violet eyes. 'Did they find the hit-and-run driver?' There was concern on her face, a worried, genuine interest.

He felt again the insane urge to tell her everything. But he knew he could not. At best, it would be a cheap trick to win her sympathy. At worst, it might involve her in some unknown danger.

'Not yet.' He indicated a chair.

Anne was watching his face. 'You look tired. Should you be back at work so soon?'

Oh, God. He didn't think he could stand any sympathy. Not just now. And not from her. He said, 'I'm fine. I cancelled my appointments for today. My exchange wasn't able to reach you.'

An anxious expression crossed her face. She was afraid she was intruding. Anne – intruding. 'I'm so sorry. If you'd rather I left . . .'

'Please, no,' he said quickly. 'I'm glad they couldn't reach you.' This would be the last time he saw her. 'How are you feeling?' he asked.

She hesitated, started to say something, then changed her mind. 'A little confused.'

She was looking at him oddly, and there was something in her look that touched a faint, long-lost chord that he could almost, but not quite, remember. He felt a warmth, flowing from her, an overpowering physical longing – and he suddenly realized what he was doing. He was attributing his own emotions to her. And for an instant he had been fooled, like any first-year psychiatry student.

'When do you leave for Europe?' he asked.

'On Christmas morning.'

'Just you and your husband?' He felt like a gibbering idiot, reduced to banalities. Babbitt, on an off day.

'Where will you go?'

'Stockholm – Paris – London – Rome.'

I'd love to show you Rome, thought Judd. He had spent a year there interning at the American hospital. There was a fantastic old restaurant called Cybèle near the Tivoli Gardens, high on a mountaintop by an ancient pagan shrine, where you could sit in the sun and watch the hundreds of wild pigeons darken the sky over the dappled cliffs.

And Anne was on her way to Rome with her husband.

'It will be a second honeymoon,' she said. There was strain in her voice, so faint that he might almost have imagined it. An untrained ear would not have caught it.

Judd looked at her more closely. On the surface she seemed calm, normal, but underneath he sensed a tension. If this was the picture of a young girl in love going to Europe on a second honeymoon, then a piece of the picture was missing.

And he suddenly realized what it was.

There was no excitement in Anne. Or if there was, it was overshadowed by a patina of some stronger emotion. Sadness? Regret?

He realized that he was staring at her. 'How – how long will you be away?' Babbitt strikes again.

A small smile crossed her lips, as though she knew what he was doing. 'I'm not certain,' she answered gravely. 'Anthony's plans are indefinite.'

'I see.' He looked down at the rug, miserable. He had to put an end to this. He couldn't let Anne leave, feeling that he was a complete fool. Send her away now. 'Mrs Blake . . .' he began.

'Yes?'

He tried to keep his voice light. 'I really got you

166

back here under false pretences. It wasn't necessary for you to see me again. I just wanted to – to say goodbye.'

Oddly, puzzlingly, some of the tension seemed to drain out of her. 'I know,' she said quietly. 'I wanted to say goodbye, too.' There was something in her voice that caught at him again.

She was getting to her feet. 'Judd . . .' She looked up at him, holding his eyes with hers, and he saw in her eyes what she must have seen in his. It was a mirrored reflection of a current so strong that it was almost physical. He started to move towards her, then stopped. He could not let her become involved in the danger that surrounded him.

When he finally spoke, his voice was almost under control. 'Drop me a card from Rome.'

She looked at him for a long moment. 'Please take care of yourself, Judd.'

He nodded, not trusting himself to speak.

And she was gone.

The phone rang three times before Judd heard it. He picked it up.

'That you, Doc?' It was Moody. His voice practically leaped out of the telephone, crackling with excitement. 'You alone?'

'Yes.'

There was an odd quality in Moody's excitement that Judd could not quite identify. Caution? Fear?

'Doc – remember I told you I had a hunch who might be behind this?'

'Yes . . .'

'I was right.'

Judd felt a quick chill go through him. 'You know who killed Hanson and Carol?'

'Yeah. I know who. And I know why. You're next, Doctor.'

'Tell me –'

'Not over the phone,' said Moody. 'We'd better meet somewhere and talk about it. Come alone.'

Judd stared at the phone in his hand.

COME ALONE!

'Are you listening?' asked Moody's voice.

'Yes,' said Judd quickly. What had Angeli said? *Whatever you do, Doctor, don't meet him alone.* 'Why can't we meet here?' he asked, stalling for time.

'I think I'm being followed. I managed to shake them off. I'm calling from the Five Star Meat Packing Company. It's on Twenty-third Street, west of Tenth Avenue, near the docks.'

Judd still found it impossible to believe that Moody was setting a trap for him. He decided to test him. 'I'll bring Angeli.'

Moody's voice was sharp. 'Don't bring anyone. Come by yourself.'

And there it was.

Judd thought of the fat little Buddha at the other end of the phone. His guileless friend who was charging him fifty dollars a day and expenses to set him up for his own murder.

Judd kept his voice controlled. 'Very well,' he said. 'I'll be right over.' He tried one parting shot. 'Are you sure you really know who's behind this, Moody?'

'Dead sure, Doc. Have you ever heard of Don Vinton?' And Moody hung up.

Judd stood there, trying to sort out the storm of emotions that raced through him. He looked up Angeli's home number and dialled it. It rang five times, and Judd was filled with a sudden panicky fear that Angeli might not be at home. Dare he go meet Moody alone?

Then he heard Angeli's nasal voice. 'Hello.'

'Judd Stevens. Moody just called.'

There was a quickening in Angeli's voice. 'What did he say?'

Judd hesitated, feeling a last vestige of unreasonable loyalty and – yes, affection – towards the bumbling little fat man who was plotting to cold-bloodedly murder him. 'He asked me to meet him at the Five Star Meat Packing Company. It's on Twenty-third Street near Tenth Avenue. He told me to come alone.'

Angeli laughed mirthlessly. 'I'll bet he did. Don't budge out of that office, Doctor. I'm going to call Lieutenant McGreavy. We'll both pick you up.'

'Right,' said Judd. He hung up slowly. Norman

Z. Moody. The jolly Buddha from the yellow pages. Judd felt a sudden, inexplicable sadness. He had liked Moody. And trusted him.

And Moody was waiting to kill him.

THIRTEEN

Twenty minutes later Judd unlocked his office door to admit Angeli and Lieutenant McGreavy. Angeli's eyes were red and teary. His voice was hoarse. Judd had a momentary pang at having dragged him out of a sick-bed. McGreavy's greeting was a curt, unfriendly nod.

'I told Lieutenant McGreavy about the phone call from Norman Moody,' Angeli said.

'Yeah. Let's find out what the hell this is all about,' McGreavy said sourly.

Five minutes later they were in an unmarked police car speeding downtown on the West Side. Angeli was at the wheel. The light snowfall had stopped and the gruel-thin rays of the late afternoon sun had surrendered to the oppressive cover of storm clouds sweeping across the Manhattan sky. There was a loud clap of thunder in the distance and then a bright, jagged sword of lightning. Drops of rain began to spatter the windscreen. As the car continued downtown, tall, soaring skyscrapers gave way to small, grimy tenements huddled together as if for comfort against the biting cold.

The car turned into Twenty-third Street, going west towards the Hudson River. They moved into a land of junk-yards and fix-it shops and dingy bars, then past that to blocks of garages, trucking yards and freight companies. As the car neared the corner of Tenth Avenue, McGreavy directed Angeli to pull over to the kerb.

'We'll get out here.' McGreavy turned to Judd. 'Did Moody say whether anyone would be with him?'

'No.'

McGreavy unbuttoned his overcoat and transferred his service revolver from his holster to his overcoat pocket. Angeli followed suit. 'Stay in back of us,' McGreavy ordered Judd.

The three men started walking, ducking their heads against the wind-lashed rain. Halfway down the block, they came to a dilapidated-looking building with a faded sign above the door that read:

FIVE STAR MEAT PACKING COMPANY

There were no cars or trucks or lights, no sign of life.

The two detectives walked up to the door, one on either side. McGreavy tested the door. It was locked. He looked around, but could see no bell. They listened. Silence, except for the sound of the rain.

'It looks closed,' Angeli said.

'It probably is,' McGreavy replied. 'The Friday before Christmas – most companies are knocking off at noon.'

'There must be a loading entrance.'

Judd followed the two detectives as they moved cautiously towards the end of the building, trying to avoid the puddles in their path. They came to a service alley, and looking down it, they could discern a loading platform with deserted trucks pulled up in front of it. There was no activity. They moved forward until they reached the platform.

'Okay,' McGreavy said to Judd. 'Sing out.'

Judd hesitated, feeling unreasonably sad that he was betraying Moody. Then he lifted his voice. 'Moody!' The only response was the yowling of an angry tomcat disturbed in his search for dry shelter. 'Mr Moody!'

There was a large wooden sliding door on top of the platform, used to move the deliveries from inside the warehouse to the area where the trucks were loaded. There were no steps leading onto the platform. McGreavy hoisted himself up, moving with surprising agility for such a large man. Angeli followed, then Judd. Angeli walked over to the sliding door and pushed against it. It was unlocked. The great door rolled open with a loud, high-pitched scream of protest. The tomcat answered hopefully, forgetting about shelter. Inside the warehouse it was pitch black.

'Did you bring a flashlight?' McGreavy asked Angeli.

'No.'

'Shit!'

Cautiously they inched their way into the gloom. Judd called out again. 'Mr Moody! It's Judd Stevens.'

There was no sound except for the creaking of the boards as the men moved across the room. McGreavy rummaged in his pockets and pulled out a book of matches. He lit one and held it up. Its feeble, sputtering light cast a wavering yellow glow in what seemed to be an enormous empty cavern. The match guttered out. 'Find the goddamn light switch,' McGreavy said. 'That was my last match.'

Judd could hear Angeli groping along the walls looking for the light switch. Judd kept moving forward. He could not see the other two men. 'Moody!' he called.

He heard Angeli's voice from across the room. 'Here's a switch.' There was a click. Nothing happened.

'The master switch must be off,' McGreavy said.

Judd bumped against a wall. As he put his hands out to brace himself, his fingers closed over a doorlatch. He shoved the latch up and pulled. A massive door swung open and a blast of frigid air hit him. 'I've found a door,' he called out. He stepped over a sill and cautiously moved forward. He heard the door close behind him and his heart began to hammer. Impossibly, it was darker here than in the other room, as though he had stepped into a deeper blackness.

'Moody! Moody . . .'

A thick, heavy silence. Moody *had* to be here somewhere. If he weren't, Judd knew what McGreavy would think. It would be the boy who cried wolf again.

Judd took another step forward and suddenly felt cold flesh lick against his face. He jerked away in panic, feeling the short hairs on his neck rise. He became aware of the strong smell of blood and death surrounding him. There was an evil in the darkness around him, waiting to close in on him. His scalp tingled with fear and his heart was beating so rapidly that it was difficult to breathe. With trembling fingers he fumbled for a book of matches in his overcoat, found one, and scraped a match against the cover. In its light he saw a huge dead eye loom up in front of his face, and it took a shocked second before he realized that he was looking at a slaughtered cow dangling from a meat hook. He had one brief glimpse of other animal carcasses hanging from hooks and the outline of a door in the far corner, before the match went out. The door probably led to an office. Moody could be in there, waiting for him.

Judd moved farther into the interior of the inky black cavern towards the door. He felt the cold brush of dead animal flesh again. He quickly stepped away and kept walking cautiously towards the office door. 'Moody!'

He wondered what was detaining Angeli and McGreavy. He moved past the slaughtered animals, feeling as though someone with a macabre sense of humour was playing a horrible maniacal joke. But who and why were beyond his imagining. As he neared the door, he collided with another hanging carcass.

Judd stopped to get his bearings. He lit his last remaining match. In front of him, impaled on a meat hook and grinning obscenely, was the body of Norman Z. Moody. The match went out.

FOURTEEN

The coroner's men had finished their work and gone. Moody's body had been taken away and everyone had departed except Judd, McGreavy, and Angeli. They were sitting in the manager's small office, decorated with several impressive calendar nudes, an old desk, a swivel chair, and two filing cabinets. The lights were on and an electric heater was going.

The manager of the plant, a Mr Paul Moretti, had been tracked down and pulled away from a pre-Christmas party to answer some questions. He had explained that since it was a holiday weekend, he had let his employees off at noon. He had locked up at twelve-thirty, and to the best of his knowledge, there had been no one on the premises at that time. Mr Moretti was belligerently drunk, and when McGreavy saw that he was going to be no further help, he had him driven home. Judd was barely conscious of what was happening in the room. His thoughts were on Moody, how cheerful and how full of life he had been, and how cruelly he had died. And Judd blamed himself. If he had not involved Moody, the little detective would be alive today.

It was almost midnight. Judd had wearily reiterated the story of Moody's phone call for the tenth time. McGreavy, hunched up in his overcoat, sat there watching him, chewing savagely on a cigar. Finally he spoke. 'Do you read detective stories?'

Judd looked at him, surprised. 'No, why?'

'I'll tell you why. I think you're just too goddamn good to be true, Dr Stevens. From the very beginning I've thought that you were in this thing up to your neck. And I told you so. So what happens? Suddenly you turn into the target instead of the killer. First you claim a car ran you down and –'

'A car *did* run him down,' Angeli reminded him.

'A rookie could answer that one,' McGreavy snapped. 'It could have been arranged by someone who's in this with the doctor.' He turned back to Judd. 'Next, you call Detective Angeli with a wild-eyed yarn about two men breaking into your office and trying to kill you.'

'They *did* break in,' said Judd.

'No, they didn't,' snapped McGreavy. 'They

used a special key.' His voice hardened. 'You said there were only two of those keys to that office – yours and Carol Roberts's.'

'That's right. I told you – they copied Carol's key.'

'I know what you told me. I had a paraffin test run. Carol's key was never copied, Doctor.' He paused to let it sink in. 'And since I have her key – that leaves yours, doesn't it?'

Judd looked at him, speechless.

'When I didn't buy the loose maniac theory, you hire a detective out of the yellow pages and he conveniently finds a bomb planted in your car. Only I can't see it because it's not there any more. Then you decide it's time to throw me another body, so you go through that rigmarole with Angeli about a phone call to meet Moody, who knows this mysterious nut who's out to kill you. But guess what? We get here and find him hanging on a meat hook.'

Judd flushed angrily. 'I'm not responsible for what happened.'

McGreavy gave him a long, hard look. 'Do you know the only reason you're not under arrest? Because I haven't found any motive to this Chinese puzzle yet. But I will, Doctor. That's a promise.' He got to his feet.

Judd suddenly remembered. 'Wait a minute!' he said. 'What about Don Vinton?'

'What about him?'

'Moody said he was the man behind all this.'

'Do you know anyone named Don Vinton?'

'No,' Judd said. '– I assumed he'd be known by the police.'

'I never heard of him.' McGreavy turned to Angeli. Angeli shook his head.

'Okay. Send out a make on Don Vinton. FBI. Interpol. Police chiefs in all major American cities.' He looked at Judd. 'Satisfied?'

Judd nodded. Whoever was behind all this must have some kind of criminal record. It should not be difficult to identify him.

He thought again of Moody, with his homely aphorisms and his quick mind. He must have been followed here. It was unlikely that he would have told anyone else about the rendezvous, because he had stressed the need for secrecy. At least they now knew the name of the man they were looking for.

Praemonitus, praemunitas.

Forewarned, forearmed.

The murder of Norman Z. Moody was splashed all over the front pages of the newspapers the next morning. Judd picked up a paper on his way to the office. He was briefly mentioned as being a witness who had come across the body with the police, but McGreavy had managed to keep the full story out of the papers. McGreavy was playing his cards close to his chest. Judd wondered what Anne would think.

This was Saturday, when Judd made his morning rounds at the clinic. He had arranged for someone else to fill in for him there. He went to his office, travelling alone in the elevator and making sure that no one was lurking in the corridor. He wondered, even as he did so, how long anyone could live like this, expecting an assassin to strike at any moment.

Half a dozen times during the morning he started to pick up the phone and call Detective Angeli to ask about Don Vinton, but each time he controlled his impatience. Angeli would surely call him as soon as he knew something. Judd puzzled over what Don Vinton's motivation could be. He could have been a patient whom Judd had treated years ago, perhaps when he was an intern. Someone who felt that Judd had slighted him or injured him in some way. But he could remember no patient named Vinton.

At noon he heard someone try to open the corridor door to the reception room. It was Angeli. Judd could tell nothing from his expression except that he looked even more drawn and haggard. His nose was red, and he was sniffling. He walked into the inner office and wearily flopped into a chair.

'Have you got any answers yet on Don Vinton?' Judd asked eagerly.

Angeli nodded. 'We got back teletypes from the FBI, the police chiefs and every big city in the United

States, and Interpol.' Judd waited, afraid to breathe. 'None of them ever heard of Don Vinton.'

Judd looked at Angeli incredulously, a sudden sinking sensation in his stomach. 'But that's impossible! I mean – *someone* must know him. A man who could do all this just didn't come out of nowhere!'

'That's what McGreavy said,' replied Angeli wearily. 'Doctor, my men and I spent the night checking out every Don Vinton in Manhattan and all the other boroughs. We even covered New Jersey and Connecticut.' He took a ruled sheet of paper out of his pocket and showed it to Judd. 'We found eleven Don Vintons in the phone book who spell their name "ton" – four who spell it "ten" – and two who spell it "tin". We even tried it as one name. We narrowed it down to five possibles and checked out every one of them. One is a paralytic. One of them is a priest. One is first vice-president of a bank. One of them is a fireman who was on duty when two of the murders occurred. It just left the last one. He runs a pet shop and he must be damn near eighty years old.'

Judd's throat was dry. He was suddenly aware of how much he had counted on this. Surely Moody wouldn't have given him the name unless he was certain. And he hadn't said that Don Vinton was an accomplice; he had said he was behind the whole thing. It was inconceivable that the police would have no record of a man like that. Moody had been murdered because he had got onto the truth. And now that Moody was out of the way, Judd was completely alone. The web was drawing tighter.

'I'm sorry,' Angeli said.

Judd looked at the detective and suddenly remembered that Angeli had not been home all night. 'I appreciate your trying,' he said gratefully.

Angeli leaned forward. 'Are you positive you heard Moody right?'

'Yes.' Judd closed his eyes in concentration. He had asked Moody if he was sure who was really behind this. He heard Moody's voice again. *Dead sure. Have you ever heard of Don Vinton? Don Vinton.* He opened his eyes. 'Yes,' he repeated.

Angeli sighed. 'Then we're at a dead end.' He laughed mirthlessly. 'No pun intended.' He sneezed.

'You'd better get to bed.'

Angeli stood up. 'Yeah. I guess so.'

Judd hesitated. 'How long have you been McGreavy's partner?'

'This is our first case together. Why?'

'Do you think he's capable of framing me for murder?'

Angeli sneezed again. 'I think maybe you're right, Doctor. I'd better get to bed.' He walked over to the door.

'I may have a lead,' Judd said.

Angeli stopped and turned. 'Go on.'

Judd told him about Teri. He added that he was also going to check out some of John Hanson's former boyfriends.

'It doesn't sound like much,' Angeli said frankly. 'But I guess it's better than nothing.'

'I'm sick and tired of being a target. I'm going to start fighting back. I'm going after them.'

Angeli looked at him. 'With what? We're fighting shadows.'

'When witnesses describe a suspect, the police have an artist draw up a composite picture of all the descriptions. Right?'

Angeli nodded. 'An identikit.'

Judd began to pace in restless excitement. 'I'm going to give you an identikit of the personality of the man who's behind this.'

'How can you? You've never seen him. It could be anyone.'

'No it couldn't,' Judd corrected. 'We're looking for someone very, very special.'

'Someone who's insane.'

'Insanity is a catchall phrase. It has no medical meaning. Sanity is simply the ability of the mind to adjust to reality. If we can't adjust, we either hide from reality, or we put ourselves above life, where we're super-beings who don't have to follow the rules.'

'Our man thinks he's a super-being.'

'Exactly. In a dangerous situation we have three choices, Angeli. Flight, constructive compromise, or attack. Our man attacks.'

'So he's a lunatic.'

'No. Lunatics rarely kill. Their concentration span is extremely short. We're dealing with someone more complicated. He could be somatic, hypophrenic, schizoid, cycloid – or any combination of these. We could be dealing with a fugue – temporary amnesia preceded by irrational acts. But the point is, his appearance and behaviour will seem perfectly normal to everyone.'

'So we have nothing to go on.'

'You're wrong. We have a good deal to go on. I can give you a physical description of him,' said Judd. He narrowed his eyes, concentrating. 'Don Vinton is above average height, well proportioned, and has the build of an athlete. He's neat in his appearance and meticulous about everything he does. He has no artistic talent. He doesn't paint or write or play the piano.'

Angeli was staring at him, open-mouthed.

Judd continued, speaking more quickly now, warming up. 'He doesn't belong to any social clubs or organizations. Not unless he runs them. He's a man who has to be in charge. He's ruthless, and he's impatient. He thinks big. For example, he'd never get involved in petty thefts. If he had a record, it would be for bank robbery, kidnapping, or murder.' Judd's excitement was growing. The picture was growing sharper in his mind. 'When you catch him, you'll find that he was probably rejected by one of his parents when he was a boy.'

Angeli interrupted. 'Doctor, I don't want to shoot down your balloon, but it could be some crazy, hopped-up junkie who –'

'No. The man we're looking for doesn't take drugs.' Judd's voice was positive. 'I'll tell you something else about him. He played contact sports in school. Football or hockey. He has no interest in chess, word games, or puzzles.'

Angeli was watching him sceptically. 'There was more than one man,' he objected. 'You said so yourself.'

'I'm giving you a description of Don Vinton,' said Judd. 'The man who's masterminding this. I'll tell you something more about him. He's a Latin type.'

'What makes you think so?'

'Because of the methods used in the murders. A knife – acid – a bomb. He's South American, Italian, or Spanish.' He took a breath. 'There's your identikit. That's the man who's committed three murders and is trying to kill me.'

Angeli swallowed. 'How the hell do you know all this?'

186

Judd sat down and leaned towards Angeli. 'It's my profession.'

'The mental side, sure. But how can you give a physical description of a man you've never seen?'

'I'm playing the odds. A doctor named Kretschmer found that eighty-five per cent of people suffering from paranoia have well-built, athletic bodies. Our man is an obvious paranoiac. He has delusions of grandeur. He's a megalomaniac who thinks he's above the law.'

'Then why wasn't he locked up a long time ago?'

'Because he's wearing a mask.'

'He's what?'

'We all wear masks, Angeli. From the time we're past infancy, we're taught to conceal our real feelings, to cover up our hatreds and fears.' There was authority in his voice. 'But under stress, Don Vinton is going to drop his mask and show his naked face.'

'I see.'

'His ego is his vulnerable point. If it's threatened – really threatened – he'll crack. He's on the thin edge now. It won't take much to send him completely over.' He hesitated, then went on, speaking almost to himself. 'He's a man with – mana.'

'With what?'

'Mana. It's a term that the primitives use for a man who exerts influence on others because of the demons in him, a man with an overpowering personality.'

'You said he doesn't paint, write, or play the piano. How do you know that?'

'The world is full of artists who are schizoids. Most of them manage to get through life without any violence because their work gives them an outlet in which to express themselves. Our man doesn't have that outlet. So he's like a volcano. The only way he can get rid of the pressure inside him is to erupt: Hanson – Carol – Moody.'

'You mean these were just senseless crimes that he committed to –'

'Not senseless to him. On the contrary . . .' His mind raced ahead swiftly. Several more pieces of the puzzle were beginning to fall into place. He cursed himself for having been too blind, or frightened, to see them. 'I'm the only one Don Vinton has been after – the prime target. John Hanson was killed because he was mistaken for me. When the killer found out his mistake, he came to the office for another try. I had gone, but he found Carol there.' His voice was angry.

'He killed her so she couldn't identify him?'

'No. The man we're looking for isn't a sadist. Carol was tortured because he wanted something.

Say, a piece of incriminating evidence. And she wouldn't – or couldn't – give it to him.'

'What kind of evidence?' probed Angeli.

'I have no idea,' Judd said. 'But it's the key to this whole thing. Moody found out the answer, and that's why they killed him.'

'There's one thing that still doesn't make sense. If they had killed you on the street, then they couldn't have got the evidence. It doesn't fit with the rest of your theory,' Angeli persisted.

'It could. Let's assume that the evidence is on one of my tapes. It might be perfectly harmless by itself, but if I put it together with other facts, it could threaten them. So they have two choices. Either take it away from me, or eliminate me so I can't reveal it to anyone. First they tried to eliminate me. But they made a mistake and killed Hanson. Then they went to the second alternative. They tried to get it from Carol. When that failed, they decided to concentrate on killing me. That was the car accident. I was probably followed when I went to hire Moody, and he, in turn, was followed. When he got onto the truth, they murdered him.'

Angeli looked at Judd, a thoughtful frown on his face.

'That's why the killer is not going to stop until I'm dead,' Judd concluded quietly. 'It's become a deadly game, and the man I've described can't stand losing.'

Angeli was studying him, weighing what Judd had said. 'If you're right,' he said finally, 'you're going to need protection.' He took his service revolver out, flipped the chamber open to make sure it was fully loaded.

'Thanks, Angeli, but I don't need a gun. I'm going to fight them with my own weapons.'

There was a sharp click of the outer door opening. 'Were you expecting anyone?'

Judd shook his head. 'No. I have no patients this afternoon.'

Gun still in hand, Angeli moved quietly to the door leading to the reception room. He stepped to one side and yanked the door open. Peter Hadley stood there, a bewildered expression on his face. 'Who are you?' Angeli snapped.

Judd moved over to the door. 'It's all right,' Judd said quickly. 'He's a friend of mine.'

'Hey! What the hell goes?' asked Peter.

'Sorry,' Angeli apologized. He put his gun away.

'This is Dr Peter Hadley – Detective Angeli.'

'What kind of nutty psychiatric clinic are you running here?' Peter asked.

'There's been a little trouble,' Angeli explained. 'Dr Stevens' office has been . . . burgled, and we thought whoever did it might be returning.'

Judd picked up the cue. 'Yes. They didn't find what they were looking for.'

'Does this have anything to do with Carol's murder?' Peter asked.

Angeli spoke before Judd could answer. 'We're not sure, Dr Hadley. For the moment, the Department has asked Dr Stevens not to discuss the case.'

'I understand,' Peter said. He looked at Judd. 'Is our luncheon date still on?'

Judd realized he had forgotten about it. 'Of course,' he said quickly. He turned to Angeli. 'I think we've covered everything.'

'And then some,' Angeli agreed. 'You're sure you don't want . . .' He indicated his revolver.

Judd shook his head. 'Thanks.'

'Okay. Be careful,' Angeli said.

'I will,' Judd promised. 'I will.'

Judd was preoccupied during luncheon, and Peter did not press him. They talked of mutual friends, patients that they had in common. Peter told Judd he had spoken to Harrison Burke's employer and it had been quietly arranged for Burke to have a mental examination. He was being sent to a private institution.

Over coffee Peter said, 'I don't know what kind of trouble you're having, Judd, but if I can be of any help . . .'

Judd shook his head. 'Thanks, Peter. This is something I have to take care of myself. I'll tell you all about it when it's over.'

'I hope that's soon,' Peter said lightly. He hesitated. 'Judd – are you in any danger?'

'Of course not,' replied Judd.

Unless you counted a homicidal maniac who had committed three murders and was determined to make Judd his fourth victim.

FIFTEEN

After lunch Judd returned to his office. He went through the same careful routine, checking to make sure that he exposed himself to minimum vulnerability.

For whatever that was worth.

He began going through the tapes again, listening for anything that might provide some clue. It was like turning on a torrent of verbal graffiti. The gusher of sounds that spewed forth was filled with hatred . . . perversion . . . fear . . . self-pity . . . megalomania . . . loneliness . . . emptiness . . . pain . . .

At the end of three hours he had found only one new name to add to his list: Bruce Boyd, the man with whom John Hanson had last lived. He put the Hanson tape on the recorder again.

'. . . I suppose I fell in love with Bruce the first time I saw him. He was the most beautiful man I had ever seen.'

'Was he the passive or dominant partner, John?'

'Dominant. That's one of the things that attracted me to him. He's very strong. In fact, later, when we became lovers, we used to quarrel about that.'

'Why?'

'Bruce didn't realize how strong he really was. He used to walk up behind me and hit me on the back. He meant it as a loving gesture, but one day he almost broke my spine. I wanted to kill him. When he shook hands, he would crush your fingers. He always pretended to be sorry, but Bruce enjoys hurting people. He didn't need whips. He's very strong . . .'

Judd stopped the tape and sat there, thinking. The homosexual pattern did not fit into his concept of the killer, but on the other hand, Boyd had been involved with Hanson and was a sadist and an egotist.

He looked at the two names on his list: Teri Washburn, who had killed a man in Hollywood and had never mentioned it; and Bruce Boyd, John Hanson's last lover. If it were one of them – which one?

Teri Washburn lived in a penthouse suite on Sutton Place. The entire apartment was decorated in shocking pink: walls, furniture, drapes. There were expensive pieces scattered around the room, and the wall was covered with French impressionists.

Judd recognized two Manets, two Degas, a Monet, and a Renoir before Teri walked into the room. He had phoned her to tell her that he wanted to come by. She had got ready for him. She was wearing a wispy pink negligee with nothing on underneath it.

'You really came,' she exclaimed happily.

'I wanted to talk to you.'

'Sure. A little drinkie?'

'No, thanks.'

'Then I think I'll fix myself one to celebrate,' Teri said. She moved towards the coral-shell bar in the corner of the large living-room.

Judd watched her thoughtfully.

She returned with her drink and sat next to him on the pink couch. 'So your cock finally got you up here, honey,' she said. 'I knew you couldn't hold out on little Teri. I'm nuts about you, Judd. I'd do anything for you. You name it. You make all the crummy pricks I've known in my life look like dirt.' She put her drink down and put her hand on his trousers.

Judd took her hands in his. 'Teri,' he said. 'I need your help.'

Her mind was travelling in its own groove. 'I know, baby,' she moaned. 'I'm going to fuck you like you've never been fucked in your life.'

'Teri – listen to me! Someone is trying to murder me!'

Her eyes registered slow surprise. Acting – or

real? He remembered a performance he had seen her give on one of the late late shows. Real. She was good, but not that good an actress.

'For Christ sake! Who – Who'd want to murder *you*?'

'It could be someone connected with one of my patients.'

'But – Jesus – why?'

'That's what I'm trying to find out, Teri. Have any of your friends ever talked about killing . . . or murder? Maybe as a party game, for laughs?'

Teri shook her head. 'No.'

'Do you know anyone named Don Vinton?' He watched her closely.

'Don Vinton? Uhn-uhn. Should I?'

'Teri – how do you feel about murder?' A small shiver went through her body. He was holding her wrists and he could feel her pulse racing. 'Does murder excite you?'

'I don't know.'

'Think about it,' Judd insisted. 'Does the thought of it excite you?'

Her pulse was beginning to skip irregularly. 'No! Of course not.'

'Why didn't you tell me about the man you killed in Hollywood?'

Without warning she reached out to rake his face with her long fingernails. He grabbed her wrists.

'You rotten sonofabitch! That was twenty years ago . . . So that's why you came. Get out of here. Get out!' She collapsed in sobbing hysteria.

Judd watched her a moment. Teri was capable of being involved in a thrill murder. Her insecurity, her total lack of self-esteem, would make her easy prey to anyone who wanted to use her. She was like a piece of soft clay lying in the gutter. The person who picked her up could mould her into a beautiful statue – or into a deadly weapon. The question was, who had picked her up last? Don Vinton?

Judd got to his feet. 'I'm sorry,' he said.

He walked out of the pink apartment.

Bruce Boyd occupied a house in a converted mews off the park in Greenwich Village. The door was opened by a white-jacketed Filipino butler. Judd gave his name and was invited to wait in the foyer. The butler disappeared. Ten minutes went by, then fifteen. Judd checked his irritation. Perhaps he should have told Detective Angeli he was coming here. If Judd's theory was right, the next attempt on his life would take place very soon. And his attacker would try to make certain of his success.

The butler reappeared. 'Mr Boyd will see you now,' he said. He led Judd upstairs to a tastefully decorated study, then discreetly withdrew.

Boyd was at a desk, writing. He was a beautiful man with sharp, delicate features, an aquiline nose, and a sensuous, full mouth. He had blond hair curled into ringlets. He got to his feet as Judd entered. He was about six foot three with the chest and shoulders of a football player. Judd thought about his physical identikit of the killer. Boyd matched it. Judd wished more than ever that he had left some word with Angeli.

Boyd's voice was soft and cultured. 'Forgive me for keeping you waiting, Dr Stevens,' he said pleasantly. 'I'm Bruce Boyd.' He held out his hand.

Judd reached out to take it and Boyd hit him in the mouth with a granite fist. The blow was totally unexpected, and the impact of it sent Judd crashing against a standing lamp, knocking it over as his body fell to the floor.

'I'm sorry, Doctor,' said Boyd, looking down at him. 'You had that coming. You've been a naughty boy, haven't you? Get up and I'll fix you a drink.'

Judd shook his head groggily. He started to push himself up from the floor. When he got halfway up, Boyd kicked him in the groin with the tip of his shoe and Judd fell writhing to the floor in agony. 'I've been waiting for you to call,' Boyd said.

Judd looked up through the blinding waves of pain at the figure that towered over him. He tried to speak, but he couldn't get the words out.

'Don't try to talk,' Boyd said sympathetically.

'It must hurt. I know why you're here. You want to ask me about Johnny.'

Judd started to nod and Boyd kicked him in the head. Through a red blur he heard Boyd's voice coming from some distant place through a cottony filter, fading in and out. 'We loved each other until he went to you. You made him feel like a freak. You made him feel our love was dirty. Do you know who made it dirty, Dr Stevens? You.'

Judd felt something hard smash into his ribs, sending an exquisite river of pain through his veins. He was seeing everything in beautiful colours now, as though his head were filled with shimmering rainbows.

'Who gave you the right to tell people how to love, Doctor? You sit there in your office like some kind of god, condemning everyone who doesn't think like you.'

That's not true, Judd was answering somewhere in his mind. *Hanson had never had choices before. I gave him choices. And he didn't choose you.*

'Now Johnny's dead,' said the blond giant towering over him. 'You killed my Johnny. And now I'm going to kill you.'

He felt another kick behind his ear, and he began to slip into unconsciousness. Some remote part of his mind watched with a detached interest as the rest of him began to die. That small isolated piece of intelligence in his cerebellum continued to function, its impulses flashing out weakening patterns of thought. He reproached himself for not having come closer to the truth. He had expected the killer to be a dark, Latin type, and he was blond. He had been sure that the killer was not a homosexual, and he had been wrong. He had found his homicidal maniac, and now he was going to die for it.

He lost consciousness.

SIXTEEN

Some distant, remote part of his mind was trying to send him a message, trying to communicate something of cosmic importance, but the hammering deep inside his skull was so agonizing that he was unable to concentrate on anything else. Somewhere nearby, he could hear a high-pitched keening, like a wounded wild animal. Slowly, painfully, Judd opened his eyes. He was lying in a bed in a strange room. In a corner of the room, Bruce Boyd was weeping uncontrollably.

Judd started to sit up. The wracking pain in his body flooded his memory with recollection of what had happened to him, and he was suddenly filled with a wild, savage fury.

Boyd turned as he heard Judd stir. He walked over to the bed. 'It's your fault,' he whimpered. 'If it hadn't been for you, Johnny would still be safe with me.'

Without volition, propelled by some long-forgotten, deeply buried instinct for vengeance, Judd reached for Boyd's throat, his fingers closing around his windpipe, squeezing with all their strength. Boyd made no move to protect himself. He stood there, tears streaming down his face. Judd looked into his eyes, and it was like looking into a pool of hell. Slowly his hands dropped away. *My God*, he thought, *I'm a doctor. A sick man attacks me and I want to kill him.* He looked at Boyd, and he was looking at a destroyed, bewildered child.

And suddenly he realized what his subconscious had been trying to tell him: Bruce Boyd was not Don Vinton. If he had been, Judd would not be alive now. Boyd was incapable of committing murder. So he had been right about him not fitting the identikit of the killer. There was a certain ironic consolation in that.

'If it weren't for you, Johnny would be alive,' Boyd sobbed. 'He'd be here with me and I could have protected him.'

'I didn't ask John Hanson to leave you,' Judd said wearily. 'It was his idea.'

'You're a liar!'

'Things had been going wrong between you and John *before* he came to see me.'

There was a long silence. Then Boyd nodded. 'Yes. We – we were quarrelling all the time.'

'He was trying to find himself, and his instincts kept telling him that he wanted to go back to his wife and children. Deep down inside, John wanted to be heterosexual.'

'Yes,' whispered Boyd. 'He used to talk about it all the time, and I thought it was just to punish me.' He looked up at Judd. 'But one day he left me. He just – moved out. He stopped loving me.' There was despair in his voice.

'He didn't stop loving you,' Judd said. 'Not as a friend.'

Boyd was looking at him now, his eyes riveted on Judd's face. 'Will you help me?' His eyes were filled with desperation. 'H-help me. You've got to help me!'

It was a cry of anguish. Judd looked at him a long moment. 'Yes,' Judd said. 'I'll help you.'

'Will I be normal?'

'There's no such thing as normal. Each person carries his own normality within him, and no two people are alike.'

'Can you make me heterosexual?'

'That depends on how much you really want to be. We can give you psychoanalysis.'

'And if it fails?'

'If we find that you're meant to be homosexual, at least you'll be better adjusted to it.'

'When can we start?' Boyd asked.

And Judd was jolted back to reality. He was

sitting here talking about treating a patient when, for all he knew, he was going to be murdered within the next twenty-four hours. And he was still no closer to finding out who Don Vinton was. He had eliminated Teri and Boyd, the last suspects on his list. He knew no more now than when he had started. If his analysis of the killer was correct, by now he would have worked himself up to a murderous rage. The next attack would come very, very soon.

'Call me Monday,' he said.

As the taxi took him towards his apartment building, Judd tried to weigh his chances of survival. They looked bleak. What could he have that Don Vinton wanted so desperately? And who was Don Vinton? How could he have had no police record? Could he be using some other name? No. Moody had clearly said 'Don Vinton'.

It was difficult to concentrate. Every movement of the taxi sent spasms of excruciating pain through his bruised body. Judd thought about the murders and attempted murders that had been committed so far, looking for some kind of pattern that made sense. A knifing, murder by torture, a hit-and-run 'accident', a bomb in his car, strangulation. There was no pattern that he could discern. Only a ruthless, maniacal violence.

He had no way of knowing how the next attempt would be made. Or by whom. His greatest vulnerability would be the office and his apartment. He remembered Angeli's advice. He must have stronger locks put on the doors of the apartment. He would tell Mike, the doorman, and Eddie, the elevator operator, to keep their eyes open. He could trust them.

The taxi pulled up in front of his apartment house. The doorman opened the taxi door.

He was a total stranger.

SEVENTEEN

He was a large, swarthy man with a pockmarked face and deep-set black eyes. An old scar ran across his throat. He was wearing Mike's uniform coat and it was too tight for him.

The taxi pulled away and Judd was alone with the man. He was struck by a sudden wave of pain. My God, not now! He gritted his teeth. 'Where's Mike?' he asked.

'On vacation, Doctor.'

Doctor. So the man knew who he was. And Mike on vacation? In December?

There was a small smile of satisfaction on the man's face. Judd looked up and down the windswept street, but it was completely deserted. He could try to make a run for it, but in his condition he wouldn't stand a chance. His body was beaten and sore, and it hurt every time he took a breath.

'You look like you been in an accident.' The man's voice was almost genial.

Judd turned without answering and walked into the lobby of the apartment building. He could count on Eddie to get help.

The doorman followed Judd into the lobby. Eddie was in the elevator, his back turned. Judd started walking towards the elevator, every step a separate agony. He knew he dared not falter now. The important thing was not to let the man catch him alone. He would be afraid of witnesses. 'Eddie!' Judd called.

The man in the elevator turned.

Judd had never seen him before. He was a smaller version of the doorman, except that there was no scar. It was obvious that the two men were brothers.

Judd stopped, trapped between the two of them. There was no one else in the lobby.

'Goin' up,' said the man in the elevator. He had the same satisfied smile as his brother.

So these, finally, were the faces of death. Judd was sure that neither of them was the brain behind what was happening. They were hired professional killers. Would they kill him in the lobby, or would they prefer to do it in his apartment? His apartment, he reasoned. That would give them more time to make their escape before his body was found.

Judd took a step towards the manager's office. 'I have to see Mr Katz about –'

The larger man blocked his way. 'Mr Katz is busy, Doc,' he said softly.

The man in the elevator spoke. 'I'll take you upstairs.'

'No,' Judd said. 'I –'

'Do like he says.' There was no emotion in his voice.

There was a sudden blast of cold air as the lobby door opened. Two men and two women hurried in, laughing and chattering, huddled in their coats.

'It's worse than Siberia,' said one of the women.

The man holding her arm was pudgy-faced, with a Mid-western accent. 'Tain't a fit night for man nor beast.'

The group was moving towards the elevator. The doorman and elevator operator looked at each other silently.

The second woman spoke. She was a tiny, platinum blonde with a heavy Southern accent. 'It's been a perfectly dreamy evening. Thank you all so much.' She was sending the men away.

The second man gave a howl of protest. 'You're not going to let us go without a little night cap, are you?'

'It's awfully late, George,' simpered the first woman.

'But it's below zero outside. You've gotta give us a little anti-freeze.'

The other man added his plea. 'Just one drink and then we go.'

'Well . . .'

Judd was holding his breath. *Please!*

The platinum blonde relented. 'All right. But just one, you-all hear?'

Laughing, the group stepped into the elevator. Judd quickly moved in with them. The doorman stood there uncertainly, looking at his brother. The one in the elevator shrugged, closed the door, and started the elevator up. Judd's apartment was on the fifth floor. If the group got out before him, he was in trouble. If they got out after him, he had a chance to get into his apartment, barricade himself, and call for help.

'Floor?'

The little blonde giggled. 'I don't know what my husband would say if he saw me inviting two strange men up to my apartment.' She turned to the elevator operator. 'Ten.'

Judd exhaled and realized that he had been holding his breath. He spoke quickly. 'Five.'

The elevator operator gave him a patient, knowing look and opened the door at Five. Judd got out. The elevator door closed.

Judd moved towards his apartment, stumbling with pain. He took out his key, opened the door, and went in, his heart pounding. He had five minutes at the most before they came to kill him. He closed the door and started to put the chain lock in the bolt. It came off in his hand. He looked at it and saw that it had been cut through. He flung it down and moved towards the phone. A wave of dizziness swept over him. He stood there, fighting the pain, his eyes closed, while precious time passed. With an effort, he started towards the phone again, moving slowly. The only person he could think of to call was Angeli, but Angeli was at home, ill. Besides – what could he say? *We have a new doorman and elevator operator and I think they're going to kill me?* He slowly became aware that he was holding the receiver in his hand, standing there numbly, too dazed to do anything. Concussion, he thought. Boyd may have killed me, after all. They would walk in and find him like this – helpless. He remembered the look in the eyes of the big man. He had to outwit them, keep them off balance. But good God – how?

He turned on the small TV set that monitored the lobby. The lobby was deserted. The pain returned, washing over him in waves, making him feel faint. He forced his tired mind to focus on the problem. He was in an emergency . . . Yes . . . Emergency. He had to take emergency measures. Yes . . . His vision was blurring again. His eyes focused on the phone. Emergency . . . He moved the dial close to his eyes so that he could read the numbers. Slowly, painfully, he dialled. A voice answered on the fifth ring. Judd spoke, his words slurred and indistinct. His eye was caught by a flurry of motion in the TV monitor. The two men, in street clothes, were crossing the lobby and moving towards the elevator.

His time had run out.

The two men moved soundlessly towards Judd's apartment and took positions on either side of the door. The larger of the men, Rocky, softly tried the door. It was locked. He took out a celluloid card and carefully inserted it over the lock. He nodded to his brother, and both men took out revolvers with silencers on them. Rocky slid the celluloid card inside the lock and pushed the unresisting door open, slowly. They walked into the living-room, guns held out in front of them. They were confronted by three closed doors. There was no sign of Judd. The smaller brother, Nick, tried the first door. It was locked. He smiled at his brother, put the muzzle of his gun against the lock, and pulled the trigger. The door noiselessly swung open into a bedroom. The two men moved inside, guns sweeping the room.

There was no one inside. Nick checked the closets while Rocky returned to the living-room. They moved without haste, knowing that Judd was in the apartment hiding, helpless. There was almost deliberate enjoyment in their unhurried movements, as though they were savouring the moments before the kill.

Nick tried the second closed door. It was locked. He shot the bolt out and moved into the room. It was the den. Empty. They grinned at each other and walked towards the last closed door. As they passed the TV monitor, Rocky caught his brother's arm. On the set they could see three men hurrying into the lobby. Two of them, wearing the white jackets of interns, were pushing a wheeled stretcher. The third carried a medical bag.

'What the hell!'

'Keep your cool, Rocky. So someone's sick. There must be a hundred apartments in this building.'

They watched the TV set in fascination as the two interns wheeled the stretcher into the elevator. The group disappeared inside it, and the elevator door closed.

'Give them a couple of minutes.' It was Nick. 'It could be some kind of accident. That means there might be cops.'

'Of all the fuckin' luck!'

'Don't worry. Stevens ain't goin' nowhere.'

The door to the apartment burst open and the doctor and the two interns entered, pushing the stretcher ahead of them. Swiftly the two killers shoved their guns into their overcoat pockets.

The doctor walked up to the brothers. 'Is he dead?'

'Who?'

'The suicide victim. Is he dead or alive?'

The two killers looked at each other, bewildered. 'You guys got the wrong apartment.'

The doctor pushed past the two killers and tried the bedroom door. 'It's locked. Help me break it down.'

The two brothers watched helplessly as the doctor and the interns smashed the door open with their shoulders. The doctor stepped into the bedroom. 'Bring the stretcher.' He moved to the bedside where Judd lay on the bed. 'Are you all right?'

Judd looked up, trying to make his eyes focus. 'Hospital,' mumbled Judd.

'You're on your way.'

As the two killers watched in frustration, the interns wheeled the stretcher into the bedroom, skilfully slid Judd onto it, and wrapped him in blankets.

'Let's blow,' said Rocky.

The doctor watched the two men leave. Then he turned to Judd, who lay on the stretcher, his face white and haggard. 'Are you all right, Judd?' His voice was filled with deep concern.

Judd tried a smile that didn't come off. 'Great,'

he said. He could scarcely hear his own voice. 'Thanks, Pete.'

Peter looked down at his friend, then nodded to the two interns. 'Let's go!'

EIGHTEEN

The hospital room was different, but the nurse was the same. A glaring bundle of disapproval. Seated at his bedside, she was the first thing that Judd saw when he opened his eyes.

'Well. We're up,' she said primly. 'Dr Harris wants to see you. I'll tell him we're awake.' She walked stiffly out of the room.

Judd sat up, moving carefully. Arm and leg reflexes a bit slow, but unimpaired. He tried focusing on a chair across the room, one eye at a time. His vision was a little blurred.

'Want a consultation?'

He looked up. Dr Seymour Harris had come into the room.

'Well,' Dr Harris said cheerfully, 'you're turning out to be one of our best customers. Do you know how much your stitching bill alone is? We're going to have to give you discount rates . . . How did you sleep, Judd?' He sat down on the edge of the bed.

'Like a baby. What did you give me?'

'A shot of sodium luminol.'

'What time is it?'

'Noon.'

'My God,' Judd said. 'I've got to get out of here.'

Dr Harris removed the chart from the clipboard he carried. 'What would you like to talk about first? Your concussion? Lacerations? Contusions?'

'I feel fine.'

The doctor put the chart aside. His voice grew serious. 'Judd, your body's taken a lot of punishment. More than you realize. If you're smart, you'll stay right in this bed for a few days and rest. Then you'll take a vacation for a month.'

'Thanks, Seymour,' Judd said.

'You mean thanks, but – no, thanks.'

'There's something I have to take care of.'

Dr Harris sighed. 'Do you know who make the worst patients in the world? Doctors.' He changed the subject, conceding defeat. 'Peter was here all night. He's been calling every hour. He's worried about you. He thinks someone tried to kill you last night.'

'You know how doctors are – over-imaginative.'

Harris eyed him a moment, shrugged, then said, 'You're the analyst. I'm only Ben Casey. Maybe you know what you're doing – but I wouldn't bet a nickel on it. Are you sure you won't stay in bed a few days?'

'I can't.'

'Okay, Tiger. I'll let you leave tomorrow.'

Judd started to protest, but Harris cut him off.

'Don't argue. Today's Sunday. The guys who beat you up need a rest.'

'Seymour . . .'

'Another thing. I hate to sound like a Jewish mother, but have you been eating lately?'

'Not much,' Judd said.

'Okay. I'm giving Miss Bedpan twenty-four hours to fatten you up. And Judd . . .'

'Yes?'

'Be careful. I'd hate to lose such a good customer.' And Dr Harris was gone.

Judd closed his eyes to rest a moment. He heard the rattle of dishes, and when he looked up, a beautiful Irish nurse was wheeling in a dining tray.

'You're awake, Dr Stevens.' She smiled.

'What time is it?'

'Six o'clock.'

He had slept the day away.

She was placing the food on his bed tray. 'You're having a treat tonight – turkey. Tomorrow's Christmas Eve.'

'I know.' He had no appetite for dinner until he took the first bite and suddenly discovered that he was ravenous. Dr Harris had shut off all phone calls, so he lay in bed, undisturbed, gathering his strength, marshalling the forces within him. Tomorrow he would need all the energy he could muster.

At ten o'clock the next morning Dr Seymour Harris bustled into Judd's room. 'How's my favourite patient?' he beamed. 'You look almost human.'

'I feel almost human,' smiled Judd.

'Good. You're going to have a visitor. I wouldn't want you to scare him.'

Peter. And probably Norah. They seemed to be spending most of their time lately visiting him in hospitals.

Dr Harris went on. 'It's a Lieutenant McGreavy.'

Judd's heart sank.

'He's very anxious to talk to you. He's on his way over here. He wanted to be sure you were awake.'

So he could arrest him. With Angeli home sick, McGreavy had been free to manufacture evidence that would convict Judd. Once McGreavy got his hands on him, there was no hope. He had to escape before McGreavy arrived.

'Would you ask the nurse to get the barber?' Judd said. 'I'd like a shave.' His voice must have sounded odd, because Dr Harris was looking at him strangely. Or was that because of something McGreavy had told Dr Harris about him?

'Certainly, Judd.' He left.

The moment the door closed, Judd got out of bed and stood up. The two nights of sleep had done miracles for him. He was a little unsteady on his feet, but that would pass. Now he had to move quickly. It took him three minutes to dress.

He opened the door a crack, made sure that no one was around who would try to stop him, and headed for the service stairs. As he started down the stairs, the elevator door opened and he saw McGreavy get off and start towards the room he had just left. He was moving swiftly, and behind him were a uniformed policeman and two detectives. Quickly, Judd went down the stairs and headed for the ambulance entrance. A block away from the hospital he hailed a taxi.

McGreavy walked into the hospital room and took one look at the unoccupied bed and the empty closet. 'Fan out,' he said to the others. 'You might still catch him.' He scooped up the phone. The operator connected him with the police switchboard. 'This is McGreavy,' he said rapidly. 'I want an all-points bulletin put out. Urgent . . . Dr Stevens, Judd. Male. Caucasian. Age . . .'

The taxi pulled up in front of Judd's office building. From now on, there was no safety for him anywhere. He could not go back to his apartment. He would have to check into some hotel. Returning to his office was dangerous, but it had to be done this once.

He needed a phone number.

He paid the driver and walked into the lobby. Every muscle in his body ached. He moved quickly. He knew he had very little time. It was unlikely that they would be expecting him to return to his office, but he must take no chances. It was now a question of who got him first. The police or his assassins.

When he reached his office, he opened the door and went inside, locking the door after him. The inner office seemed strange and hostile, and Judd knew that he could not treat his patients here any longer. He would be subjecting them to too much danger. He was filled with anger at what Don Vinton was doing to his life. He could visualize the scene that must have occurred when the two brothers went back and reported that they had failed to kill him. If he had read Don Vinton's character correctly, he would have been in a towering rage. The next attack would come at any moment.

Judd went across the room to get Anne's phone number. For he had remembered two things in the hospital.

Some of Anne's appointments were scheduled just ahead of John Hanson's.

And Anne and Carol had had several chats

together; Carol might have innocently confided some deadly information to Anne. If so, she could be in danger.

He took his address book out of a locked drawer, looked up Anne's phone number, and dialled. There were three rings, and then a neutral voice came on.

'This is a special operator. What number are you calling, please?'

Judd gave her the number. A few moments later the operator was back on the line. 'I am sorry. You are calling a wrong number. Please check your directory or consult Information.'

'Thank you,' Judd said. He hung up. He sat there a moment, remembering what his answering service had said a few days ago. *They had been able to reach all his patients except Anne.* The numbers could have been transposed when they were put in the book. He looked in the telephone directory, but there was no listing under her husband's name or her name. He suddenly felt that it was very important that he talk to Anne. He copied down her address: 617 Woodside Avenue, Bayonne, New Jersey.

Fifteen minutes later, he was at an Avis counter, renting a car. There was a sign behind the counter that read: 'We're second, so we try harder.' *We're in the same boat*, thought Judd.

A few minutes later, he drove out of the garage. He rode around the block, satisfied himself that

221

he was not being followed, and headed over the George Washington Bridge for New Jersey.

When he reached Bayonne, he stopped at a filling station to ask directions. 'Next corner and make a left – third street.'

'Thanks.' Judd drove off. At the thought of seeing Anne again, his heart began to quicken. What was he going to say to her without alarming her? Would her husband be there?

Judd made a left turn onto Woodside Avenue. He looked at the numbers. He was in the nine hundred block. The houses on both sides of the street were small, old, and weatherbeaten. He drove to the seven hundred block. The houses seemed to become progressively older and smaller.

Anne lived on a beautiful wooded estate. There were virtually no trees here. When Judd reached the address Anne had given him, he was almost prepared for what he saw.

617 was a weed-covered vacant lot.

NINETEEN

He sat in the car across from the vacant lot, trying to put it all together. The wrong phone number could have been a mistake. Or the address could have been a mistake. But not both. Anne had deliberately lied to him. And if she had lied about who she was and where she lived, what else had she lied about? He forced himself to objectively examine everything he really knew about her. It came to almost nothing. She had walked into his office unannounced and insisted on becoming a patient. In the four weeks that she had been coming to him, she had carefully managed not to reveal what her problem was, and then had suddenly announced that it was solved and she was going away. After each visit she had paid him in cash so that there would be no way of tracing her. But what reason could she have had for posing as a patient and then vanishing? There was only one answer. And as it hit Judd, he became physically sick.

If someone wanted to set him up for murder – wanted to know his routine at the office – wanted to know what the inside of the office looked like – what better way than to gain access as a patient? That was what she was doing there. Don Vinton had sent her. She had learned what she needed to know and then had disappeared without a trace.

It had all been pretence, and how eager he had been to be taken in by it. How she must have laughed when she went back to report to Don Vinton about the amorous idiot who called himself an analyst and pretended to be an expert about people. He was head over heels in love with a girl whose sole interest in him was setting him up to be murdered. How was *that* for a judge of character? What an amusing paper that would make for the American Psychiatric Association.

But what if it were not true? Supposing Anne had come to him with a legitimate problem, had used a fictitious name because she was afraid of embarrassing someone? In time the problem had solved itself and she had decided that she no longer needed the help of an analyst. But Judd knew that it was too easy. There was an 'x' quantity about Anne that needed to be discovered. He had a strong feeling that in that unknown quantity could lie the answer to what was happening. It was possible that she was being forced to act against her will. But even as he thought it, he knew he was being foolish. He was trying to cast her as a damsel in distress with himself as a knight in shining armour. Had she set him up for murder? Somehow, he had to find out.

An elderly woman in a torn housecoat had come out of a house across the street and was staring at him. He turned the car around and headed back for the George Washington Bridge.

There was a line of cars behind him. Any one of them could be following him. But why would they have to follow him? His enemies knew where to find him. He couldn't sit and passively wait for them to attack. He had to do the attacking himself, keep them off guard, enrage Don Vinton into making a blunder so that he could be checkmated. And he had to do it before McGreavy caught him and locked him up.

Judd drove towards Manhattan. The only possible key to all this was Anne – and she had disappeared without a trace. The day after tomorrow she would be out of the country.

And Judd suddenly realized that he had one chance of finding her.

It was Christmas Eve and the Pan-Am office was crowded with travellers and would-be travellers on standby, fighting to get space on planes flying all over the world.

Judd made his way to the counter through the waiting lines and asked to see the manager. The uniformed girl behind the counter gave him a professionally coded smile and asked him to wait; the manager was on the phone.

Judd stood there hearing a babel of phrases.

'I want to leave India on the fifth.'

'Will Paris be cold?'

'I want a car to meet me in Lisbon.'

He felt a desperate desire to get on a plane and run away. He suddenly realized how exhausted he was, physically and emotionally. Don Vinton seemed to have an army at his disposal, but Judd was alone. What chance did he have against him?

'Can I help you?'

Judd turned. A tall, cadaverous-looking man stood behind the counter. 'I'm Friendly,' he said. He waited for Judd to appreciate the joke. Judd smiled dutifully. 'Charles Friendly. What can I do for you?'

'I'm Dr Stevens. I'm trying to locate a patient of mine. She's booked on a flight leaving for Europe tomorrow.'

'The name?'

'Blake. Anne Blake.' He hesitated. 'Possibly it's under Mr and Mrs Anthony Blake.'

'What city is she flying to?'

'I – I'm not sure.'

'Are they booked on one of our morning or afternoon flights?'

'I'm not even certain if it's with your airline,' Judd said.

The friendliness dropped out of Mr Friendly's eyes. 'Then I'm afraid I can't help you.'

Judd felt a sudden feeling of panic. 'It's really urgent. I must find her before she goes.'

'Doctor, Pan-American has one or more flights leaving every day for Amsterdam, Barcelona, Berlin, Brussels, Copenhagen, Dublin, Düsseldorf, Frankfurt, Hamburg, Lisbon, London, Munich, Paris, Rome, Shannon, Stuttgart, and Vienna. So have most of the other international airlines. You'll have to contact each one individually. And I doubt if they can help you unless you can give them the destination and time of departure.' The expression on Mr Friendly's face was one of impatience. 'If you'll excuse me . . .' He turned to walk away.

'Wait!' said Judd. How could he explain that this might be his last chance to stay alive? His last link to finding out who was attempting to kill him.

Friendly was regarding him with barely concealed annoyance. 'Yes?'

Judd forced a smile on his face, hating himself for it. 'Don't you have some kind of central

227

computing system,' he asked, 'where you can get passengers' names by . . . ?'

'Only if you know the flight number,' Mr Friendly said. He turned and was gone.

Judd stood there at the counter, feeling sick. Check and checkmate. He was defeated. There was nowhere else to move.

A group of Italian priests bustled in, dressed in long, flapping black robes and wide black hats, looking like something out of the Middle Ages. They were weighed down with cheap cardboard suitcases, boxes and gift baskets of fruit. They were speaking loudly in Italian and obviously teasing the youngest member of their group, a boy who looked no more than eighteen or nineteen. They were probably returning home to Rome after a vacation, thought Judd, as he listened to their babbling. Rome . . . where Anne would be . . . Anne again.

The priests were moving towards the counter.

'E molto bene di ritornare a casa.'

'Si, d'accordo.'

'Signore, per piacere, guardatemi.'

'Tutto va bene?'

'Si, ma –'

'Dio mio, dove sono i miei biglietti?'

'Cretino, hai perduto i biglietti.'

'Ah, eccoli.'

The priests handed their airline tickets to the youngest priest, who moved bashfully towards the girl at the counter. Judd looked towards the exit. A large man in a grey overcoat was lounging in the doorway.

The young priest was talking to the girl behind the counter. '*Dieci. Dieci.*'

The girl stared at him blankly. The priest summoned up his knowledge of English and said very carefully, 'Ten. Billetta. Teeket.' He pushed the tickets towards her.

The girl smiled happily and began to process the tickets. The priests burst into delighted cries of approval at their companion's linguistic abilities and clapped him on the back.

There was no point in staying here any longer. Sooner or later he would have to face whatever was out there. Judd slowly turned and started to move past the group of priests.

'*Guardate che ha fatto il Don Vinton.*'

Judd stopped, the blood suddenly rushing to his face. He turned to the tubby little priest who had spoken and took his arm. 'Excuse me,' he said. His voice was hoarse and unsteady. 'Did you say "Don Vinton"?'

The priest looked up at him blankly, then patted him on the arm and started to move away.

Judd tightened his grip. 'Wait!' he said.

The priest was looking at him nervously. Judd forced himself to speak calmly. 'Don Vinton. Which one is he? Show him to me.'

All the priests were now staring at Judd. The little priest looked at his companions. '*E un americano matto.*'

A babble of excited Italian rose from the group. Out of the corner of his eye, Judd saw Friendly watching him from behind the counter. Friendly opened the counter gate and started to move towards him. Judd fought to control a rising panic. He let go of the priest's arm, leaned close to him, and said slowly and distinctly, 'Don Vinton.'

The little priest looked into Judd's face for a moment and then his own face splintered into merriment. '*Don Vinton!*'

The manager was approaching rapidly, his manner hostile. Judd nodded to the priest encouragingly. The little priest pointed to the boy. '*Don Vinton* – "big man".'

And suddenly the puzzle fell into place.

TWENTY

'Slow down, slow down,' Angeli said hoarsely. 'I can't understand a word you're saying.'

'Sorry,' Judd said. He took a deep breath. 'I've got the answer!' He was so relieved to hear Angeli's voice over the phone that he was almost babbling. 'I know who's trying to kill me. I know who Don Vinton is.'

There was a sceptical note in Angeli's voice. 'We couldn't find any Don Vinton.'

'Do you know why? Because it isn't a him – it's a *who*.'

'Will you speak more slowly?'

Judd's voice was trembling with excitement. 'Don Vinton isn't a name. It's an Italian expression. It means "the big man". That's what Moody was trying to tell me. That The Big Man was after me.'

'You lost me, Doctor.'

'It doesn't mean anything in English,' said Judd,

'but when you say it in Italian – doesn't it suggest anything to you? An organization of killers run by The Big Man?'

There was a long silence over the phone. 'La Cosa Nostra?'

'Who else could assemble a group of killers and weapons like that? Acid, bombs – guns! Remember I told you the man we're looking for would be a Southern European? He's Italian.'

'It doesn't make sense. Why would La Cosa Nostra want to kill you?'

'I have absolutely no idea. But I'm right. I know I'm right. And it fits in with something Moody said. He said there was a group of men out to kill me.'

'It's the craziest theory I've ever heard,' Angeli said. There was a pause, then he added, 'But I suppose it could be possible.'

Judd was flooded with sudden relief. If Angeli had not been willing to listen to him, he would have had no one to turn to.

'Have you discussed this with anyone?'

'No,' Judd said.

'Don't!' Angeli's voice was urgent. 'If you're right, your life depends on it. Don't go near your office or apartment.'

'I won't,' Judd promised. He suddenly remembered. 'Did you know McGreavy has a warrant out for my arrest?'

'Yes.' Angeli hesitated. 'If McGreavy picks you

up, you'll never get to the station alive.'

My God! So he had been right about McGreavy. But he could not believe that McGreavy was the brain behind this. There was someone directing him . . . Don Vinton, The Big Man.

'Can you hear me?'

Judd's mouth was suddenly dry. 'Yes.'

A man in a grey overcoat stood outside the phone booth looking in at Judd. Was it the same man he had seen before? 'Angeli . . .'

'Yes?'

'I don't know who the others are. I don't know what they look like. How do I stay alive until they're caught?'

The man outside the booth was staring at him.

Angeli's voice came over the line. 'We're going straight to the FBI. I have a friend who has connections. He'll see that you're protected until you're safe. Okay?' There was a note of assurance in Angeli's voice.

'Okay,' Judd said gratefully. His knees felt like jelly.

'Where are you?'

'In a phone booth in the lower lobby of the Pan-Am Building.'

'Don't move. Keep plenty of people around you. I'm on my way.' There was a click at the other end of the line as Angeli hung up.

*　　　*　　　*

233

He put the phone back on the squad-room desk, a sick feeling deep inside him. Over the years he had become accustomed to dealing with murderers, rapists, perverts of every description, and somehow, in time, a protective shell had formed, allowing him to go on believing in the basic dignity and humanity of man.

But a rogue cop was something different.

A rogue cop was a corruption that touched everyone on the force, that violated everything that decent cops fought and died for.

The squad room was filled with the passage of feet and the murmur of voices, but he heard none of it. Two uniformed patrolmen passed through the room with a giant drunk in handcuffs. One of the officers had a black eye and the other had a handkerchief to a bloody nose. The sleeve of his uniform had been ripped half off. The patrolman would have to pay for that himself. These men were ready to risk their lives every day and night of the year. But that wasn't what made headlines. A crooked cop made headlines. One crooked cop tainted them all. His own partner.

Wearily he got up and walked down the ancient corridor to the Captain's office. He knocked once and went in.

Behind a battered desk pocked with the lighted cigar butts of countless years sat Captain Bertelli.

Two FBI men were in the room, dressed in business suits. Captain Bertelli looked up as the door opened. 'Well?'

The detective nodded. 'It checks out. The property custodian said he came in and borrowed Carol Roberts's key from the evidence locker Wednesday afternoon and returned it late Wednesday night. That's why the paraffin test was negative – he got into Dr Stevens's office by using an original key. The custodian never questioned it because he knew he was assigned to the case.'

'Do you know where he is now?' asked the younger of the FBI men.

'No. We had a tail on him, but he lost him. He could be anywhere.'

'He'll be hunting for Dr Stevens,' said the second FBI agent.

Captain Bertelli turned to the FBI men. 'What are the chances of Dr Stevens staying alive?'

The man shook his head. 'If they find him before we do – none.'

Captain Bertelli nodded. 'We've got to find him first.' His voice grew savage. 'I want Angeli brought back, too. I don't care how you get him.' He turned to the detective. 'Just get him, McGreavy.'

The police radio began to crackle out a staccato message: 'Code Ten . . . Code Ten . . . All cars . . . pick up five . . .'

Angeli switched the radio off. 'Anyone know I picked you up?' he asked.

'No one,' Judd assured him.

'You haven't discussed La Cosa Nostra with anybody?'

'Only you.'

Angeli nodded, satisfied.

They had crossed the George Washington Bridge and were headed for New Jersey. But everything had changed. Before, he had been filled with apprehension. Now, with Angeli at his side, he no longer felt like the hunted. He was the hunter. And the thought filled him with deep satisfaction.

At Angeli's suggestion, Judd had left his rented car in Manhattan and he was riding in Angeli's unmarked police car. Angeli had headed north on the Palisades Interstate Parkway and exited at Orangeburg. They were approaching Old Tappan.

'It was smart of you to spot what was going on, Doctor,' Angeli said.

Judd shook his head. 'I should have figured it out as soon as I knew there was more than one man involved. It had to be an organization using professional killers. I think Moody suspected the truth when he saw the bomb in my car. They had access to every kind of weapon.'

And Anne. She was part of the operation, setting him up so that they could murder him. And yet – he couldn't hate her. No matter what she had done, he could never hate her.

Angeli had turned off the main highway. He deftly tooled the car onto a secondary road that led towards a wooded area.

'Does your friend know we're coming?' Judd asked.

'I phoned him. He's all ready for you.'

A side road appeared abruptly, and Angeli turned the car into it. He drove for a mile, then braked to a stop in front of an electric gate. Judd noticed a small television camera mounted above the gate. There was a click and the gate swung open, then closed solidly behind them. They began driving up a long, curving driveway. Through the trees ahead, Judd caught a glimpse of the sprawling roof of an enormous house. High on top, flashing in the sun, was a bronze rooster.

Its tail was missing.

TWENTY-ONE

In the soundproofed, neon-lit communications centre at Police Headquarters, a dozen shirtsleeved police officers manned the giant switchboard. Six operators sat on each side of the board. In the middle of the board was a pneumatic chute. As the calls came in, the operators wrote a message, put it in the chute, and sent it upstairs to the dispatcher, for immediate relay to a sub-station or patrol car. The calls never ceased. They poured in day and night, like a river of tragedy flooding in from the citizens of the huge metropolis. Men and women who were terrified . . . lonely . . . desperate . . . drunk . . . injured . . . homicidal . . . It was a scene from Hogarth, painted with vivid, anguished words instead of colours.

On this Monday afternoon there was a feeling of added tension in the air. Each telephone operator handled his job with full concentration, and yet each was aware of the number of detectives and FBI agents who kept moving in and out of the room, receiving and giving orders, working efficiently and quietly as they spread a vast electronic net for Dr Judd Stevens and Detective Frank Angeli. The atmosphere was quickened, strangely staccato, as though the action were being staged by some grim, nervous puppeteer.

Captain Bertelli was talking to Allen Sullivan, a member of the Mayor's Crime Commission, when McGreavy walked in. McGreavy had met Sullivan before. He was tough and honest. Bertelli broke off his conversation and turned to the detective, his face a question mark.

'Things are moving,' McGreavy said. 'We found an eye-witness, a night watchman who works in the building across the street from Dr Stevens's office building. On Wednesday night, when someone broke into Dr Stevens's office, the watchman was just going on duty. He saw two men go into the building. The street door was locked and they opened it with a key. He figured they worked there.'

'Did you get an ID?'

'He identified a picture of Angeli.'

'Wednesday night Angeli was supposed to have been home in bed with the flu.'

'Right.'

'What about the second man?'

'The watchman didn't get a good look at him.'

An operator plugged in one of the innumerable red lights blinking across the switchboard and turned to Captain Bertelli. 'For you, Captain. New Jersey Highway Patrol.'

Bertelli snatched up an extension phone. 'Captain Bertelli.' He listened a moment. 'Are you sure? . . . Good! Will you get every unit you can in there? Set up roadblocks. I want that area covered like a blanket. Keep in close touch . . . Thanks.' He hung up and turned to the two men. 'It looks like we got a break. A rookie patrolman in New Jersey spotted Angeli's car on a secondary road near Orangeburg. The Highway Patrol's combing the area now.'

'Dr Stevens?'

'He was in the car with Angeli. Don't worry. They'll find them.'

McGreavy pulled out two cigars. He offered one to Sullivan, who refused it, handed one to Bertelli, and put the other one between his teeth. 'We've got one thing going for us. Dr Stevens leads a charmed life.' He struck a match and lit the two cigars. 'I just talked to a friend of his – Dr Peter Hadley. Dr Hadley told me he went to pick up Stevens in his office a few days ago and found Angeli there with a gun in his hand. Angeli told some cock-and-bull story about expecting a burglar. My guess is that Dr Hadley's arrival saved Stevens's life.'

'How did you first get onto Angeli?' Sullivan asked.

'It started with a couple of tips that he was shaking down some merchants,' McGreavy said. 'When I went to check them out, the victims wouldn't talk. They were scared, but I couldn't figure out why. I didn't say anything to Angeli. I just started keeping a close watch on him. When the Hanson murder broke, Angeli came and asked if he could work on the case with me. He gave me some bullshit about how much he admired me and how he had always wanted to be my partner. I knew he had to have an angle, so with Captain Bertelli's permission, I played along with him. No wonder he wanted to work on the case – he was in it up to his ass! At that time I wasn't sure whether Dr Stevens was involved in the murders of Hanson and Carol Roberts, but I decided to use him to set up Angeli. I built up a phoney case against Stevens and told Angeli I was going to nail the doctor for the murders. I figured that if Angeli thought he was off the hook, he'd relax and get careless.'

'Did it work?'

'No. Angeli surprised the hell out of me by putting up a fight to keep Stevens out of jail.'

Sullivan looked up, puzzled. 'But why?'

'Because he was trying to knock him off and he couldn't get to him if he were locked up.'

'When McGreavy began to put the pressure

on,' Captain Bertelli said, 'Angeli came to me hinting that McGreavy was trying to frame Dr Stevens.'

'We were sure then that we were on the right track,' McGreavy said. 'Stevens hired a private detective named Norman Moody. I checked Moody out and learned that he had tangled with Angeli before when a client of Moody's was picked up by Angeli on a drugs rap. Moody said his client was framed. Knowing what I know now, I'd say Moody was telling the truth.'

'So Moody lucked into the answer from the beginning.'

'It wasn't all luck. Moody was bright. He knew Angeli was probably involved. When he found the bomb in Dr Stevens's car, he turned it over to the FBI and asked them to check it out.'

'He was afraid if Angeli got hold of it, he'd find a way to get rid of it?'

'That's my guess. But someone slipped up and a copy of the report was sent to Angeli. He knew then that Moody was onto him. The real break we got was when Moody came up with the name "Don Vinton".'

'Cosa Nostra for "The Big Man".'

'Yeah. For some reason, someone in La Cosa Nostra was out to get Dr Stevens.'

'How did you tie up Angeli with La Cosa Nostra?'

'I went back to the merchants Angeli had been putting the squeeze on. When I mentioned La Cosa Nostra, they panicked. Angeli was working for one of the Cosa Nostra families, but he got greedy and was doing a little shake-down business of his own on the side.'

'Why would La Cosa Nostra want to kill Dr Stevens?' Sullivan asked.

'I don't know. We're working on several angles.' He sighed wearily. 'We got two lousy breaks. Angeli slipped the men we had tailing him, and Dr Stevens ran away from the hospital before I could warn him about Angeli and give him protection.'

The switchboard flashed. An operator plugged in the call and listened a moment. 'Captain Bertelli.'

Bertelli grabbed the extension phone. 'Captain Bertelli.' He listened, saying nothing, then slowly replaced the receiver and turned to McGreavy. 'They lost them.'

TWENTY-TWO

Anthony DeMarco had mana.

Judd could feel the burning power of his personality across the room, coming in waves that struck like a tangible force. When Anne had said her husband was handsome, she had not exaggerated.

DeMarco had a classic Roman face with a perfectly sculptured profile, coal-black eyes, and attractive streaks of grey in his dark hair. He was in his middle forties, tall and athletic, and moved with a restless animal grace. His voice was deep and magnetic. 'Would you care for a drink, Doctor?'

Judd shook his head, fascinated by the man before him. Anyone would have sworn that DeMarco was a perfectly normal, charming man, a perfect host welcoming an honoured guest.

There were five of them in the richly panelled library. Judd, DeMarco, Detective Angeli, and the two men who had tried to kill Judd at his apartment building, Rocky and Nick Vaccaro. They had formed a circle around Judd. He was looking into the faces of the enemy, and there was a grim satisfaction in it. Finally he knew who he was fighting. If 'fighting' was the right word. He had walked into Angeli's trap. Worse. He had phoned Angeli and invited him to come and get him! Angeli, the Judas goat who had led him here to the slaughter.

DeMarco was studying him with deep interest, his black eyes probing. 'I've heard a great deal about you,' he said.

Judd said nothing.

'Forgive me for having you brought here in this fashion, but it is necessary to ask you a few questions.' He smiled apologetically, radiating warmth.

Judd knew what was coming, and his mind moved swiftly ahead.

'What did you and my wife talk about, Dr Stevens?'

Judd put surprise into his voice. 'Your wife? I don't know your wife.'

DeMarco shook his head reproachfully. 'She's been going to your office twice a week for the last three weeks.'

Judd frowned thoughtfully. 'I have no patient named DeMarco . . .'

De Marco nodded understandingly. 'Perhaps she used another name. Maybe her maiden name. Blake – Anne Blake.'

Judd carefully registered surprise. 'Anne Blake?' The two Vaccaro brothers moved in closer.

'No,' DeMarco said sharply. He turned to Judd. His affable manner was gone. 'Doctor, if you try to play games with me, I'm going to do things to you that you wouldn't believe.'

Judd looked into his eyes and believed him. He knew that his life was hanging by a thread. He forced indignation into his voice. 'You can do what you please. Until this moment I had no idea that Anne Blake was your wife.'

'That could be true,' Angeli said. 'He –'

DeMarco ignored Angeli. 'What did you and my wife talk about for three weeks?'

They had arrived at the moment of truth. From the instant Judd had seen the bronze rooster on the roof, the final pieces of the puzzle had fallen into place. Anne had not set him up for murder. She had been a victim, like himself. She had married Anthony DeMarco, successful owner of a large construction firm, without any idea of who he really was. Then something must have happened to make her suspect that her husband was not what he had seemed to be, that he was involved in something dark and terrible. With no one to talk to, she had turned for help to an analyst, a stranger, in whom she could confide. But in Judd's office her basic loyalty to her husband had kept her from discussing her fears.

'We didn't talk about much of anything,' said Judd evenly. 'Your wife refused to tell me what her problem was.'

DeMarco's black eyes were fixed on him, probing, weighing. 'You'll have to come up with something better than that.'

How DeMarco must have panicked when he learned that his wife was going to a psychoanalyst – the wife of a leader in La Cosa Nostra. No wonder DeMarco had killed, trying to get hold of Anne's file.

'All she told me,' Judd said, 'was that she was unhappy about something, but couldn't discuss it.'

'That took ten seconds,' DeMarco said. 'I've got a record of every minute she spent in your office. What did she talk about for the rest of the three weeks? She must have told you who I am.'

'She said you owned a construction company.'

DeMarco was studying him coldly. Judd could feel beads of perspiration forming on his forehead.

'I've been reading up on analysis, Doctor. The patient talks about everything that's on his mind.'

'That's part of the therapy,' Judd said matter-of-factly. 'That's why I wasn't getting anywhere with Mrs Blake – with Mrs DeMarco. I intended to dismiss her as a patient.'

'But you didn't.'

'I didn't have to. When she came to see me Friday, she told me that she was leaving for Europe.'

'Annie's changed her mind. She doesn't want to go to Europe with me. Do you know why?'

Judd looked at him, genuinely puzzled. 'No.'

'Because of you, Doctor.'

Judd's heart gave a little leap. He carefully kept his feelings out of his voice. 'I don't understand.'

'Sure you do. Annie and I had a long talk last night. She thinks she made a mistake about our marriage. She's not happy with me anymore, because she thinks she goes for you.' When DeMarco spoke, it was almost in a hypnotic whisper. 'I want you to tell me all about what happened when you two were alone in your office and she was on your couch.'

Judd steeled himself against the mixed emotions that were coursing through him. She *did* care! But what good was it going to do either of them? DeMarco was looking at him, waiting for an answer. 'Nothing happened. If you read up on analysis, you'll know that every female patient goes through an emotional transference. At one time or another, they all think they're in love with their doctor. It's just a passing phase.'

DeMarco was watching him intently, his black eyes probing into Judd's.

'How did you know she was coming to see me?' Judd asked, making the question casual.

DeMarco looked at Judd a moment, then walked over to a large desk and picked up a razor-sharp letter opener in the shape of a dagger. 'One of my men saw her go into your building. There are a lot of baby doctors there and they figured maybe Annie was keeping back a little surprise from me. They followed her up to your office.' He turned to Judd.

'It was a surprise, all right. They found out she was going to a psychiatrist. The wife of Anthony DeMarco spilling my personal business to a head-shrinker.'

'I told you she didn't –'

DeMarco's voice was soft. 'The *Commissione* held a meeting. They voted for me to kill her, like we'd kill any traitor.' He was pacing now, reminding Judd of a dangerous, caged animal. 'But they can't give me orders like a peasant soldier. I am Anthony DeMarco, a Capo. I promised them that if she had discussed any of our business, I would kill the man she talked to. With these two hands.' He held up his fists, one of them holding the razor-edged dagger. 'That's you, Doctor.'

DeMarco was circling him now as he talked,

and each time that DeMarco walked in back of him, Judd unconsciously braced himself.

'You're making a mistake if –' Judd started.

'No. You know who made the mistake? Annie.' He looked Judd up and down. He sounded genuinely puzzled. 'How could she think you're a better man than I am?'

The Vaccaro brothers snickered.

'You're nothing. A patsy who goes to an office every day and makes – what? Thirty grand a year? Fifty? A hundred? I make more than that in a week.' DeMarco's mask was slipping away more quickly now, eroding under the pressure of his emotions. He was beginning to speak in short, excited bursts, a patina of ugliness warping his handsome features. Anne had only seen him behind his façade. Judd was looking into the naked face of a homicidal paranoiac. 'You and that little *putana* pick each other!'

'We haven't picked each other,' Judd said.

DeMarco was watching him, his eyes blazing. 'She doesn't mean anything to you?'

'I told you. She's just another patient.'

'Okay,' DeMarco said at last. 'You tell her.'

'Tell her what?'

'That you don't give a damn about her. I'm going to send her down here. I want you to talk to her, alone.'

Judd's pulse began to race. He was going to be given a chance to save himself and Anne.

DeMarco flicked his hand and the men moved out into the hallway. DeMarco turned to Judd. His deep black eyes were hooded. He smiled gently, the mask in place again. 'As long as Annie doesn't know anything, she will live. You're going to convince her that she should go to Europe with me.'

Judd felt his mouth go suddenly dry. There was a triumphant glint in DeMarco's eyes. Judd knew why. He had underestimated his opponent.

Fatally.

DeMarco was not a chess player, and yet he had been clever enough to know that he held a pawn that made Judd helpless. Anne. Whatever move Judd made, she was in danger. If he sent her away to Europe with DeMarco, he was certain that her life would be in jeopardy. He did not believe that DeMarco was going to let her live. La Cosa Nostra would not allow it. In Europe DeMarco would arrange an 'accident'. But if Judd told Anne not to go, if she found out what was happening to him, she would try to interfere, and that would mean instant death for her. There was no escape: only a choice of two traps.

From the window of her bedroom on the second floor, Anne had watched the arrival of Judd and Angeli. For one exhilarating moment, she had believed that Judd was coming to take her away, to rescue her from the terrifying situation she was in. But then she had seen Angeli take out a gun and force Judd into the house.

She had known the truth about her husband for the last forty-eight hours. Before that, it had only been a dim, glimmering suspicion, so incredible that she had tried to brush it aside. It had begun a few months ago, when she had gone to a play in Manhattan and had come home unexpectedly early because the star was drunk and the curtain had been rung down in the middle of the second act. Anthony had told her that he was having a business meeting at the house, but that it would be over before she returned. When she had arrived, the meeting was still going on. And before her surprised husband had been able to close the library door, she had heard someone angrily shouting, 'I vote that we hit the factory tonight and take care of the bastards once and for all!' The phrase, the ruthless appearance of the strangers in the room, and Anthony's agitation at seeing her combined to unnerve Anne. She had let his glib explanations convince her because she had wanted desperately to be convinced. In the six months of their marriage, he had been a tender, considerate husband. She had seen occasional flashes of a violent temper, but he had always quickly managed to gain control of himself.

A few weeks after the theatre incident, she had picked up a telephone and had overheard Anthony's voice on an extension phone. 'We're taking over a shipment from Toronto tonight. You'll have to have someone handle the guard. He's not with us.'

She had hung up, shaken. 'Take over a shipment' . . . 'handle the guard' . . . They sounded ominous, but they could have been innocent business phrases. Carefully, casually, she tried to question Anthony about his business activities. It was as though a steel wall went up. She was confronted by an angry stranger who told her to take care of his home and keep out of his business. They had quarrelled bitterly, and the next evening he had given her an outrageously expensive necklace and tenderly apologized.

A month later, the third incident had occurred. Anne had been awakened at four o'clock in the morning by the slamming of a door. She had slipped into a negligee and gone downstairs to investigate. She heard voices coming from the library, raised in argument. She went towards the door, but stopped as she saw Anthony in the room talking to half a dozen strangers. Afraid that he would be angry if she interrupted, she quietly went back upstairs and returned to bed. At breakfast the next morning, she asked him how he had slept.

'Great. I fell off at ten o'clock and never opened my eyes once.'

And Anne knew that she was in trouble. She had no idea what kind of trouble or how serious it was. All she knew was that her husband had lied to her for reasons that she could not fathom. What kind of business could he be involved in that had to be conducted secretly in the middle of the night with men who looked like hoodlums? She was afraid to broach the subject again with Anthony. A panic began to build in her. There was no one with whom she could talk.

A few nights later, at a dinner party at the country club to which they belonged, someone had mentioned a psychoanalyst named Judd Stevens, and talked about how brilliant he was.

'He's a kind of analyst's analyst, if you know what I mean. He's terribly attractive, but it's wasted – he's one of those dedicated types.'

Anne had carefully noted the name and the following week had gone to see him.

The first meeting with Judd had turned her life topsy-turvy. She had felt herself drawn into an emotional vortex that had left her shaken. In her confusion, she had been scarcely able to talk to him, and she had left feeling like a schoolgirl, promising herself that she would not go back. But she had gone back to prove to herself that what had happened was a fluke, an accident. Her reaction the second time was even stronger. She had always prided herself on being sensible and realistic, and now she was acting like a seventeen-year-old girl in love for the first time. She found herself unable to discuss her husband with Judd, and so they had talked about other things, and after each session Anne found herself more in love with this warm, sensitive stranger.

She knew it was hopeless because she would never divorce Anthony. She felt there must be some terrible flaw in her that would allow her to marry a man and six months later fall in love with another man. She decided that it would be better if she never saw Judd again.

And then a series of strange things had begun to happen. Carol Roberts was killed, and Judd was knocked down by a hit-and-run driver. She read in the newspapers that Judd was there when Moody's body was found in the Five Star warehouse. She had seen the name of the warehouse before.

On the letterhead of an invoice on Anthony's desk.

And a terrible suspicion began to form in her mind.

It seemed incredible that Anthony could be involved in any of the awful things that had been happening, and yet . . . She felt as though she was trapped in a terrifying nightmare, and there was no way out. She could not discuss her fears with Judd, and she was afraid to discuss them with Anthony. She told herself that her suspicions were groundless: Anthony did not even know of Judd's existence.

And then, forty-eight hours ago, Anthony had come into her bedroom and started questioning her about her visits to Judd. Her first reaction had been anger that he had been spying on her, but that had quickly given way to all the fears that had been preying upon her. As she looked into his twisted, enraged face, she knew that her husband was capable of anything.

Even murder.

During the questioning, she had made one terrible mistake. She had let him know how she felt about Judd. Anthony's eyes had turned deep black, and he had shaken his head as though warding off a physical blow.

It was not until she was alone again that she realized how much danger Judd was in, and that she could not leave him. She told Anthony that she would not go to Europe with him.

And now Judd was here, in this house. His life in peril, because of her.

The bedroom door opened and Anthony walked in. He stood watching her for a moment.

'You have a visitor,' he said.

She walked into the library wearing a yellow skirt and blouse, her hair back loosely over her shoulders.

Her face was drawn and pale, but there was an air of quiet composure about her. Judd was in the room, alone.

'Hello, Dr Stevens. Anthony told me that you were here.'

Judd had the sensation that they were acting out a charade for the benefit of an unseen, deadly audience. He intuitively knew that Anne was aware of the situation and was placing herself in his hands, waiting to follow whatever lead he offered.

And there was nothing he could do except try to keep her alive a little longer. If Anne refused to go to Europe, DeMarco would certainly have her killed here.

He hesitated, choosing his words carefully. Each word could be as dangerous as the bomb planted in his car. 'Mrs DeMarco, your husband is upset because you changed your mind about going to Europe with him.'

Anne waited, listening, weighing.

'I'm sorry,' she said.

'So am I. I think you should go,' Judd said, raising his voice.

Anne was studying his face, reading his eyes. 'What if I refuse? What if I just walk out?'

Judd was filled with sudden alarm. 'You mustn't do that.' She would never leave this house alive.

'Mrs DeMarco,' he said deliberately, 'your husband is under the mistaken impression that you're in love with me.'

She opened her lips to speak and he quickly went on, 'I explained to him that that's a normal part of analysis – an emotional transference that all patients go through.'

She picked up his lead. 'I know. I'm afraid it was foolish of me to go to you in the first place. I should have tried to solve my problem myself.' Her eyes told him how much she meant it, how much she regretted the danger she had placed him in. 'I've been thinking it over. Perhaps a holiday in Europe would be good for me.'

He breathed a quick sigh of relief. She had understood.

But there was no way he could warn her of the real danger. Or did she know? And even if she knew, was there anything she could do about it? He looked past Anne towards the library window framing the tall trees that bordered the woods. She had told him that she took long walks in them. It was possible she might be familiar with a way out. If they could get to the woods . . . He lowered his voice, urgently. 'Anne –'

'Finished your little chat?'

Judd spun around. DeMarco had quietly walked into the room. Behind him came Angeli and the Vaccaro brothers.

Anne turned to her husband. 'Yes,' she said. 'Dr Stevens thinks I should go to Europe with you. I'm going to take his advice.'

DeMarco smiled and looked at Judd. 'I knew I could count on you, Doctor.' He was radiating charm, beaming with the expansive satisfaction of a man who has achieved total victory. It was as though the incredible energy that flowed through DeMarco could be converted at will, switched from a dark evil to an overpowering, attractive warmth. No wonder Anne had been taken in by him. Even Judd found it hard to believe at this instant that this gracious, friendly Adonis was a cold-blooded, psychopathic murderer.

DeMarco turned to Anne. 'We'll be leaving early in the morning, darling. Why don't you go upstairs and start packing?'

Anne hesitated. She did not want to leave Judd alone with these men. 'I . . .' She looked at Judd helplessly. He nodded imperceptibly.

'All right.' Anne held out her hand. 'Goodbye, Dr Stevens.'

Judd took her hand. 'Goodbye.'

And this time it *was* goodbye. There was no way out. Judd watched as she turned, nodded at the others, and walked out of the room.

DeMarco looked after her. 'Isn't she beautiful?' There was a strange expression on his face. Love, possessiveness – and something else. Regret? For what he was about to do to Anne?

'She doesn't know anything about all this,' Judd said. 'Why don't you keep her out of it? Let her go away.'

He watched the switch turn in DeMarco, and it was almost physical. The charm vanished, and hate began to fill the room, a current flowing from DeMarco to Judd, not touching anyone else. There was an ecstatic, almost orgiastic expression on DeMarco's face. 'Let's go, Doctor.'

Judd looked around the room, measuring his chances of escape. Surely DeMarco would prefer not to kill him in his home. It had to be now or never. The Vaccaro brothers were watching him hungrily, hoping he would make a move. Angeli was standing near the window, his hand near his gun holster. 'I wouldn't try it,' DeMarco said softly. 'You're a dead man – but we're going to do it my way.'

He gave Judd a push towards the door. The others closed in on him, and they headed towards the entrance hall.

When Anne reached the upstairs hallway, she waited near the landing, watching the hall below. She drew back out of sight as she saw Judd and the others move towards the front door. She hurried into her bedroom and looked out the window. The men were pushing Judd into Angeli's car.

Quickly Anne reached for the telephone and dialled operator. It seemed an eternity before there was an answer.

'Operator, I want the police! Hurry – it's an emergency!'

And a man's hand reached in front of her and pressed down the receiver. Anne gave a little scream and whirled around. Nick Vaccaro was standing over her, grinning.

TWENTY-THREE

Angeli switched on the headlights. It was four o'clock in the afternoon, but the sun was buried somewhere behind the mass of cumulus clouds that scudded overhead, pushed by the icy winds. They had been driving for over an hour.

Angeli was at the wheel. Rocky Vaccaro was seated next to him. Judd was in the back seat with Anthony DeMarco.

In the beginning Judd had kept an eye out for a passing police car, hoping that he might somehow make a desperate bid to attract attention, but Angeli was driving through little-used side roads where there was almost no traffic. They skirted the edges of Morristown, picked up Route 206 and headed south towards the sparsely populated, bleak plains of central New Jersey. The grey sky opened up and it began to pour: a cold, icy sleet that beat against the windscreen like tiny drums gone mad.

'Slow down,' DeMarco commanded. 'We don't want to have an accident.'

Angeli obediently lightened his foot on the accelerator.

DeMarco turned to Judd. 'That's where most people make their mistake. They don't plan things out like me.'

Judd looked at DeMarco, studying him clinically. The man was suffering from megalomania, beyond the reach of reason or logic. There was no way to appeal to him. There was some moral sense missing in him that allowed him to kill without compunction. Judd knew most of the answers now.

DeMarco had committed the murders with his own hand out of a sense of honour – a Sicilian's revenge, to erase the stain that he thought his wife had placed on him and his Cosa Nostra family. He had killed John Hanson by mistake. When Angeli had reported back to him and told him what had happened, DeMarco had gone back to the office and found Carol. Poor Carol. She could not give him the tapes of Mrs DeMarco because she did not know Anne by that name. If DeMarco had kept his temper, he could have helped Carol figure out whom he was talking about; but it was part of his sickness that he had no tolerance for frustration and he had gone into an insane rage, and Carol had died. Horribly. It was DeMarco who had run Judd down, and later had come to kill him at his office with Angeli. Judd had been puzzled by the fact that they had not broken in and shot him. But he realized now that since McGreavy was sure Judd was guilty, they had decided to make his death look like a suicide, committed in remorse. That would stop any further police investigation.

And Moody . . . poor Moody. When Judd had told him the names of the detectives on the case, he had thought he was reacting to McGreavy – when it was really Angeli. Moody had learned that Angeli was involved with the Cosa Nostra, and when he followed up on it . . .

He looked over at DeMarco. 'What's going to happen to Anne?'

'Don't worry. I'll take care of her,' DeMarco said.

Angeli smiled. 'Yeah.'

Judd felt a helpless rage sweep over him.

'I was wrong to marry someone outside the family,' brooded DeMarco. 'Outsiders can never understand it like it is. Never.'

They were travelling in an almost barren section of flatlands. An occasional factory dotted the sleet-blurred skyline in the distance.

'We're almost there,' Angeli announced.

'You've done a good job,' DeMarco said. 'We're going to hide you away somewhere until the heat cools down. Where would you like to go?'

'I like Florida.'

DeMarco nodded approvingly. 'No problem. You'll stay with one of the *family*.'

'I know some great broads down there.' Angeli smiled.

DeMarco smiled back at him in the mirror. 'You'll come back with a tanned ass.'

'I hope that's all I come back with.'

Rocky Vaccaro laughed.

In the distance, on the right, Judd saw the sprawled buildings of a factory spuming smoke into the air. They reached a small side road leading to the factory. Angeli turned into it and drove until they came to a high wall. The gate was closed. Angeli leaned on the horn and a man in a raincoat and rain hat appeared behind the gate. When he saw DeMarco, he nodded, unlocked the gate, and swung it open. Angeli drove the car inside, and the gate closed behind them. They had arrived.

At the Nineteenth Precinct, Lieutenant McGreavy was in his office, going over a list of names with three detectives, Captain Bertelli, and the two FBI men.

'This is a list of the Cosa Nostra families in the East. All the Sub-Capos and Capo Regimes. Our problem is, we don't know which one Angeli is hooked up with.'

'How long would it take to get a rundown on them?' asked Bertelli.

One of the FBI men spoke. 'There are over sixty names here. It would take at least twenty-four hours, but . . .' He stopped.

McGreavy finished the sentence for him. 'But Dr Stevens won't be alive in twenty-four hours from now.'

A young uniformed policeman hurried up to the open door. He hesitated as he saw the group of men.

'What is it?' McGreavy asked.

'New Jersey didn't know if it's important, Lieutenant, but you asked them to report anything unusual. An operator got a call from an adult female asking for Police Headquarters. She said it was an emergency, and then the line went dead. The operator waited, but there was no call back.'

'Where did the call come from?'

'A town called Old Tappan.'

'Did she get the number?'

'No. The caller hung up too quickly.'

'Great,' McGreavy said bitterly.

'Forget it,' Bertelli said. 'It was probably some old lady reporting a lost cat.'

McGreavy's phone rang, a long, insistent peal. He picked up the phone. 'Lieutenant McGreavy.' The others in the room watched his face draw tight with tension. 'Right! Tell them not to make a move until I get there. I'm on my way!' He slammed the receiver down. 'The Highway Patrol just spotted

Angeli's car going south on Route 206, just outside Millstone.'

'Are they tailing it?' It was one of the FBI men.

'The patrol car was going in the opposite direction. By the time they got turned around, it had disappeared. I know that area. There's nothing out there but a few factories.' He turned to one of the FBI men. 'Can you get me a fast rundown on the names of the factories there and who owns them?'

'Will do.' The FBI man reached for the phone.

'I'm heading out there,' McGreavy said. 'Call me when you get it.' He turned to the men. 'Let's move!' He started out the door, the three detectives and the second FBI man on his heels.

Angeli drove past the watchman's shack near the gate and continued towards a group of odd-looking structures that reached into the sky. There were high brick chimneys and giant flumes, their curved shapes rearing up out of the grey drizzle like prehistoric monsters in an ancient, timeless landscape.

The car rolled up to a complex of large pipes and conveyor belts and braked to a stop. Angeli and Vaccaro got out of the car and Vaccaro opened the rear door on Judd's side. He had a gun in his hand. 'Out, Doctor.'

Slowly, Judd got out of the car, followed by DeMarco. A tremendous din and wind hurtled at them. In front of them, about twenty-five feet away, was an enormous pipeline filled with roaring, compressed air, sucking in everything that came near its open, greedy lip.

'This is one of the biggest pipelines in the country,' DeMarco boasted, raising his voice to make himself heard. 'Do you want to see how it works?'

Judd looked at him incredulously. DeMarco was acting the part of the perfect host again, entertaining a guest. No – not acting. He *meant* it. That was what was terrifying. DeMarco was about to murder Judd, and it would be a routine business transaction, something that had to be taken care of, like disposing of a piece of useless equipment, but he wanted to impress him first.

'Come on, Doctor. It's interesting.'

They moved towards the pipeline, Angeli leading the way. DeMarco at Judd's side and Rocky Vaccaro bringing up the rear.

'This plant grosses over five million dollars a year,' DeMarco said proudly. 'The whole operation is automatic.'

As they got closer to the pipeline, the roar increased, the noise became almost intolerable. A hundred yards from the entrance to the vacuum chamber, a large conveyor belt carried giant logs to a planing machine twenty feet long and five feet high, with half a dozen razor-sharp cutter heads. The planed logs were then carried upwards to a hog, a fierce porcupine-looking rotor bristling with knives. The air was filled with flying sawdust mixed with rain, being sucked into the pipeline.

'It doesn't matter how big the logs are,' DeMarco said proudly. 'The machines cut them down to fit that thirty-six-inch pipe.'

DeMarco took a snub-nosed .38 Colt out of his pocket and called out, 'Angeli.'

Angeli turned.

'Have a good trip to Florida.' DeMarco squeezed the trigger, and a red hole exploded in Angeli's shirt front. Angeli stared at DeMarco with a puzzled half-smile on his face, as though waiting for the answer to a riddle he had just heard. DeMarco pulled the trigger again. Angeli crumpled to the ground. DeMarco nodded to Rocky Vaccaro, and the big man picked up Angeli's body, slung it over his shoulder, and moved towards the pipeline.

DeMarco turned to Judd. 'Angeli was stupid. Every cop in the country's looking for him. If they found him, he'd lead them to me.'

The cold-blooded murder of Angeli was shock enough, but what followed was even worse. Judd watched, horrified, as Vaccaro carried Angeli's body towards the lip of the giant pipeline. The tremendous pressure caught at Angeli's body, greedily sucking it in. Vaccaro had to grab a large metal handle on the lip of the pipe to keep himself from being pulled in by the deadly cyclone of air. Judd had one last glimpse of Angeli's body whirling into the pipe through the vortex of sawdust and logs, and it was gone. Vaccaro reached for the valve next to the lip of the pipe and turned it. A cover slid over the mouth of the pipe, shutting off the cyclone of air. Then the sudden silence was deafening.

DeMarco turned to Judd and raised his gun. There was an exalted, mystic expression on his face, and Judd realized that murder was almost a religious experience for him. It was a crucible that purified. Judd knew that his moment of death had come. He felt no fear for himself, but he was consumed by rage that this man would be allowed to live, to murder Anne, to destroy other innocent, decent people. He heard a growling, a moan of rage and frustration, and realized it was coming from his own lips. He was like a trapped animal obsessed with the desire to kill his captor.

DeMarco was smiling at him, reading his thoughts. 'I'm going to give it to you in the gut, Doctor. It'll take a little longer, but you'll have more time to worry about what's going to happen to Annie.'

There was one hope. One slim hope.

'Someone should worry about her,' Judd said. 'She's never had a man.'

DeMarco stared at him blankly.

Judd was yelling now, fighting to make

DeMarco listen. 'Do you know what your cock is? That gun in your hand. Without a gun or a knife, you're a woman.'

He saw DeMarco's face fill with slow rage.

'You have no balls, DeMarco. Without that gun, you're a joke.'

A red film was filling DeMarco's eyes, like a warning flag of death. Vaccaro took a step forward. DeMarco waved him back.

'I'll kill you with these bare hands,' DeMarco said as he threw the gun to the ground. 'With these bare hands!' Slowly, like a powerful animal, he started towards Judd.

Judd backed away, out of reach. He knew he stood no chance against DeMarco physically. His only hope was to work on DeMarco's sick mind, making it unable to function. He had to keep striking at DeMarco's most vulnerable area – his pride in his manhood. 'You're a homosexual, DeMarco!'

DeMarco laughed and lunged at him. Judd moved out of reach.

Vaccaro picked up the gun from the ground. 'Chief! Let me finish him!'

'Keep out of this!' DeMarco roared.

The two men circled, feinting for position. Judd's foot slipped on a pile of soggy sawdust, and DeMarco rushed at him like a charging bull. His huge fist hit Judd on the side of the mouth, knocking him back. Judd recovered and lashed out at DeMarco, hitting him in the face. DeMarco rocked back, then lunged forward and drove his fists into Judd's stomach. Three smashing blows that knocked the breath out of Judd. He tried to speak to taunt DeMarco, but he was gasping for air. DeMarco was hovering over him like a savage bird of prey.

'Getting winded, Doctor?' he laughed. 'I was a boxer. I'm going to give you lessons. I'm going to work on your kidneys and then your head and your eyes. I'm gonna put your eyes out, Doctor. Before I'm through with you, you're going to beg me to shoot you.'

Judd believed him. In the eerie light that spilled from the clouded sky, DeMarco looked like an enraged animal. He rushed at Judd again and caught him with his fist, splitting his cheek open with a heavy cameo ring. Judd lashed out at DeMarco, pounding at his face with both fists. DeMarco did not even flinch.

DeMarco began hitting Judd's kidneys, his hands working like pistons. Judd pulled away, his body a sea of pain.

'You're not getting tired, are you, Doctor?' He started to close in again. Judd knew that his body could not take much more punishment. He had to keep talking. It was his only chance.

'DeMarco . . .' He gasped.

DeMarco feinted and Judd swung at him.

DeMarco ducked, laughed, and slammed his fist squarely between Judd's legs. Judd doubled over, filled with an unbelievable agony, and fell to the ground. DeMarco was on top of him, his hands at his throat.

'My bare hands,' DeMarco screamed. 'I'm going to tear your eyes out with my bare hands.' He dug his huge fists into Judd's eyes.

They were speeding past Bedminster heading south on Route 206, when the call cracked in over the radio. 'Code Three . . . Code Three . . . All cars stand by . . . New York Unit Twenty-seven . . . New York Unit Twenty-seven . . .'

McGreavy grabbed the radio microphone. 'New York Twenty-seven . . . Come in!'

Captain Bertelli's excited voice came over the radio. 'We've got it pinned down, Mac. There's a New Jersey pipeline company two miles south of Millstone. It's owned by the Five Star Corporation – the same company that owns the meat-packing plant. It's one of the fronts Tony DeMarco uses.'

'Sounds right,' McGreavy said. 'We're on our way.'

'How far are you from there?'

'Ten miles.'

'Good luck.'

'Yeah.'

McGreavy switched off the radio, hit the siren, and slammed the accelerator to the floorboard.

The sky was spinning in wet circles overhead and something was pounding at him, tearing his body apart. He tried to see, but his eyes were swollen shut. A fist smashed into his ribs, and he felt the agonizing splinter of bones breaking. He could feel DeMarco's hot breath on his face, coming in quick excited gasps. He tried to see him, but he was locked in darkness. He opened his mouth and forced words past his thick, swollen tongue. 'You s-see,' he gasped. 'I was r-right . . . You can – you can only hit a man – when he's down . . .'

The breathing in his face stopped. He felt two hands grab him and pull him to his feet.

'You're a dead man, Doctor. And I did it with my bare hands.'

Judd backed away from the voice. 'You're an – an a-animal,' he said, gasping for breath. 'Psychopath . . . You should be locked up . . . in an . . . insane asylum.'

DeMarco's voice was thick with rage. 'You're a liar!'

'It's the t-truth,' Judd said, moving back. 'Your . . . your brain is diseased . . . Your mind is going to . . . snap and you'll be . . . like an idiot baby.' Judd backed away, unable to see where he was going. Behind him he heard the faint hum of the closed pipeline, waiting like a sleeping giant.

DeMarco lunged at Judd, his huge hands clutching his throat. 'I'm going to break your neck!' His enormous fingers closed on Judd's windpipe, squeezing.

Judd felt his head begin to swim. This was his last chance. Every instinct in him screamed out to grab DeMarco's hands and pull them away from his throat so that he could breathe. Instead, with a final tremendous effort of will, he put his hands in back of him, fumbling for the pipe valve. He felt himself beginning to slide into unconsciousness, and in that instant his hands closed on the valve. With a final, desperate burst of energy, he turned the handle and swerved his body around so that DeMarco was nearest the opening. A tremendous vacuum of air suddenly blasted at them, trying to pull them into the vortex of the pipe. Judd clung frantically to the valve with both hands, fighting the cyclonic fury of the wind. He felt DeMarco's fingers digging into his throat as DeMarco was pulled towards the pipe. DeMarco could have saved himself, but in his mindless insane fury, he refused to let go. Judd could not see DeMarco's face, but the voice was a demented animal cry, the words lost in the roar of the wind.

Judd's fingers started to slip off the valve. He was going to be pulled into the pipeline with

DeMarco. He gave a quick, last prayer, and in that instant he felt DeMarco's hands slip away from his throat. There was a loud, reverberating scream, and then only the roar from the pipeline. DeMarco had vanished.

Judd stood there, bone weary, unable to move, waiting for the shot from Vaccaro.

A moment later it rang out.

He stood there, wondering why Vaccaro had missed. Through the dull haze of pain, he heard more shots, and the sound of feet running, and then his name being called. And then someone had an arm around him and McGreavy's voice was saying, 'Mother of God! Look at his face!'

Strong hands gripped his arm and pulled him away from the awful roaring tug of the pipeline. Something wet was running down his cheeks and he did not know whether it was blood or tears, and he did not care.

It was over.

He forced one puffed eye open and through a narrow, blood-red slit, he could dimly see McGreavy. 'Anne's at the house,' Judd said. 'DeMarco's wife. We've got to go to her.'

McGreavy was looking at him strangely, not moving, and Judd realized that no words had come out. He lifted his mouth up to McGreavy's ear and spoke slowly, in a hoarse, broken croak. 'Anne DeMarco . . . She's at the . . . house . . . help.'

McGreavy walked over to the police car, picked up the radio transmitter, and issued instructions. Judd stood there, unsteady, still rocking back and forth from DeMarco's blows, letting the cold, biting wind wash over him. In front of him he could see a body lying on the ground, and knew it was Rocky Vaccaro.

We've won, he thought. *We've won*. He kept saying the phrase over and over in his mind. And even as he said it, he knew it was meaningless. What kind of victory was it? He had thought of himself as a decent, civilized human being – a doctor, a healer – and he had turned into a savage animal filled with the lust to kill. He had sent a sick man over the brink of insanity and then murdered him. It was a terrible burden he would have to live with always. Because even though he could tell himself it was in self-defence, he knew – God help him – that he had enjoyed doing it. And for that he could never forgive himself. He was no better than DeMarco, or the Vaccaro brothers, or any of the others. Civilization was a thin, dangerously fragile veneer, and when that veneer cracked, man became one of the beasts again, falling back into the slime of the primeval abyss he prided himself on having climbed up from.

Judd was too weary to think about it any longer. Now he wanted only to see that Anne was safe.

McGreavy was standing there, his manner strangely gentle.

'There's a police car on the way to her house, Dr Stevens. Okay?'

Judd nodded gratefully.

McGreavy took his arm and guided him towards a car. As he moved slowly, painfully, across the courtyard, he realized that it had stopped raining. On the far horizon the thunderheads had been swept away by the raw December wind, and the sky was clearing. In the west a small ray of light appeared as the sun began to fight its way through, growing brighter and brighter.

It was going to be a beautiful Christmas.

Are You Afraid of the Dark?

Sidney Sheldon

In New York, Denver, Paris and Berlin, four people have died in what appear to be random accidents.

When two women – widows of the dead – find themselves under merciless attack, their fear and confusion help them to form an unlikely alliance. But why are they being targeted? Is there a connection to their husbands' mysterious deaths?

Meanwhile, the Chief Executive of an international Think Tank is on the cusp of a discovery which could change the world – and deliver unbelievable power into the company's hands. Could the mysterious deaths be connected to this volatile secret?

Taut with suspense and vivid characterization, and with an unnervingly realistic premise, *Are You Afraid of the Dark?* is a *tour de force* from a master storyteller.

ISBN 0 00 716516 1

A Stranger in the Mirror

Sidney Sheldon

Toby Temple, the world's funniest man. A superstar who gets any woman he wants. But underneath the callous super-stud image is a lonely man, desperate for attention, greedy for love.

Jill Castle, beautiful, sensuous starlet. She has a dark and mysterious past and an ambition even greater than Toby's.

Together they rule the glittering kingdom of Hollywood until lust, jealousy and revenge turn triumph into tragedy in a nightmare scenario that rolls relentlessly on to a stunning, sensational climax . . .

'Utterly compelling tale of steamy entertainment industry emotions, ambitions and machinations'

Hollywood Reporter

ISBN 13: 978 0 00 722826 0
ISBN 10: 0 00 722826 0